P9-DDS-065

NEW YORK TIMES
#1 BESTSELLING AUTHOR

OVER 15 MILLION COPIES
OF
MARY HIGGINS CLARK BOOKS IN PRINT

CRITICS RAVE ABOUT
MARY HIGGINS CLARK

"Buying a Mary Higgins Clark book is like buying a ticket to ride the roller coaster. We strap ourselves in and, once on the track, we're there until the ride is over. . . . Clark is a master manipulator."

—*The Washington Post*

"Truly a mistress of high tension."

—*The New Yorker*

"Mary Higgins Clark is a master plotter."

—*The New York Times Book Review*

"Clark can prickle scalps with shivery skill."

—*Cosmopolitan*

WEEP NO MORE, MY LADY

"Well-done and very scary, not to be read alone at night unless you have an unnatural tolerance for vulnerable women and stalking killers."

—*Cosmopolitan*

"A murder mystery decorated with glamorous people, set in a California health spa. . . . the ideal book for the beach, picnic hamper, or carry-on luggage."

—*The New York Times Book Review*

"Taut, suspenseful . . . thrilling . . . a page-turner!"

—*UPI*

STILLWATCH

"Clark skillfully draws the reader into the mounting tensions of life gone awry."

—*Chicago Tribune*

"Designed to be read at breathtaking speed!"

—*Chicago Tribune*

"Mary Higgins Clark is a master plotter, seeding the book with crimes, clues, and psychopathic quirks that pay off."

—*The New York Times Book Review*

A CRY IN THE NIGHT

"A harrowing tale by a master of horror."

—*The New York Times Book Review*

"A stunning achievement . . . Could become a suspense classic."

—*Associated Press*

"Gripping . . . A story to be devoured in a single sitting."

—*Daily New (New York)*

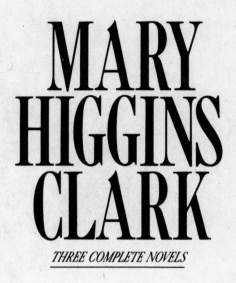

MARY HIGGINS CLARK

THREE COMPLETE NOVELS

MARY HIGGINS CLARK

THREE COMPLETE NOVELS

WEEP NO MORE, MY LADY

STILLWATCH

A CRY IN THE NIGHT

WINGS BOOKS
NEW YORK • AVENEL, NEW JERSEY

This edition contains the complete and unabridged texts of the original editions. They have been completely reset for this volume.

This omnibus was originally published in separate volumes under the titles:

This 1991 edition is published by Wings Books, a division of Random House Value Publishing, Inc., 40 Engelhard Avenue, Avenel, New Jersey 07001, by arrangement with Simon & Schuster.

Random House
New York • Toronto • London • Sydney • Auckland
http://www.randomhouse.com/

Book design by Jamila Miller

Printed and bound in the United States of America

Library of Congress Cataloging–in–Publication Data
Clark, Mary Higgins.
[Novels. Selections]
Mary Higgins Clark—three complete novels.
p. cm.
Contents: Weep no more, my lady—Stillwatch—A cry in the night.
ISBN 0-517-06462-6
1. Detective and mystery stories. American. I. Clark, Mary Higgins. Weep no more, my lady. 1992. II. Clark, Mary Higgins. Stillwatch. 1992. III. Clark, Mary Higgins. Cry in the night. 1992. IV. Title.
[PS3553.L287A6 1992]
813'.54—dc20 91-29394
CIP

25 24 23 22 21 20 19 18

CONTENTS

WEEP NO MORE, MY LADY

For my grandchildren . . .
Elizabeth Higgins Clark
and
Andrew Warren Clark
the two ''Dirdrews''
With love, amusement and delight

Acknowledgments

Stillwatch, my last novel, was set in Washington, D.C. Special thanks are in order for the good friends who assisted me in my attempt to give that book an authentic Washington flavor.

Mrs. Frances Humphrey Howard, sister of the late Vice-President Hubert H. Humphrey, generously shared her vast knowledge of life in the nation's capital with me. She and her network of friends were always readily available to answer my questions about everything from protocol to the inner workings of Congress.

John and Catherine Keeley assisted me in creating the Cable Network background and planning the crucial travel times and routes. William Jackman, vice-president of the Air Transport Association of America, lent his expertise to guide me in the technical aspects of a vital airline investigation.

Abiding thanks to my editor, Michael V. Korda, whose perception and understanding make it a challenge and a pleasure to embark on the long road between story concept and completed novel.

Finally, my love and gratitude to my agent, Pat Myrer, who before her retirement helped me to plan this new book and christened it with the title *Weep No More, My Lady.*

Prologue
July, 1969

The Kentucky sun was blazing hot. Eight-year-old Elizabeth huddled in a corner of the narrow porch, trying to tuck herself into the thin band of shade from the overhang. Her hair was heavy on her neck even though she had tied it back with a ribbon. The street was deserted; almost everyone was taking a Sunday-afternoon nap or had gone to the local pool. She wanted to go swimming too, but she knew better than to ask. Her mother and Matt had been drinking all day, and they'd begun to quarrel. She hated it when they fought, especially in summer, when the windows were open. All the kids would stop playing and listen. Today's fight had been really loud. Her mother had screamed bad words at Matt until he hit her again. Now they were both asleep, sprawled on the bed with no cover on them, the empty glasses on the floor beside them.

She wished her sister, Leila, didn't work every Saturday and Sunday. Before she took the Sunday job, Leila used to call it their *day, and she'd taken Elizabeth around with her. Most of the nineteen-year-old girls like Leila were hanging around with boys, but Leila never did. She was going to go to New York to be an actress, not get stuck in Lumber Creek, Kentucky. "The trouble with these hick towns, Sparrow, is that everybody marries right out of high school and ends up with whiny little kids and Pablum all over their cheerleader sweaters. That won't be me."*

Elizabeth liked to hear Leila talk about how it would be when she was a star, but it was scary too. She couldn't imagine living in this house with Mama and Matt without Leila.

It was too hot to play. Quietly she stood up and smoothed her T-shirt under the waistband of her shorts. She was a thin child with long legs and a spray of freckles across her nose. Her eyes were wide-set and mature—"Queen Solemn Face" Leila called her. Leila was always making up names for people—sometimes funny names; sometimes, if she didn't like the people, pretty mean ones.

If anything, the inside of the house was hotter than the porch. The glaring four-o'clock sun shone through the dingy windows, onto the couch with its sagging springs and the stuffing that was beginning to come out at the seams, and the linoleum floor, so old that you couldn't even tell what color it had been, cracked and buckled under the sink. They'd lived here for four years now. Elizabeth could vaguely remember the other house, in Milwaukee. It was a little bit bigger, with a real kitchen and two bathrooms and a big yard. Elizabeth was tempted to straighten up the living room, but she knew that as soon as Matt got up the room would be a mess again, with beer bottles and cigar ashes and his clothes dropped where he shed them. But maybe it would be worth a try.

Snores, unpleasant and gruff, came from behind the open door of Mama's bedroom. She peeked in. Mama and Matt must have made up their fight. They were all wrapped up in each other, his right leg thrown over her left, his face buried in her hair. She hoped they'd wake up before Leila got home. Leila hated to see them like that. "You must bring your friends to visit Mama and her fiancé," she'd whisper to Elizabeth in her actressy voice. "Show off your elegant background."

Leila must be working overtime. The drive-in was near the beach, and sometimes on hot days a couple of the waitresses didn't show up. "I've got my period," they'd whine to the manager on the phone. "Real bad cramps."

Leila had told her about that and explained what it meant. "You're only eight and that's young, but Mama never got around to telling me, and when it happened I could hardly walk home, my back hurt so much, and I thought I was dying. I won't let that happen to you, and I don't want other kids hinting around like it's something crazy."

Elizabeth did the best she could to make the living room look better. She pulled down the shades three-quarters of the way, so that the sun didn't glare so much. She emptied the ashtrays and washed the tops of the tables and threw away the beer bottles that Matt and Mama had emptied before their fight. Then she went into her room. It was just big enough to hold a cot, a bureau and a chair with a broken cane seat. Leila had given her a white chenille bedspread for her birthday and bought a secondhand bookcase which she'd painted red and hung on the wall.

At least half the books in the bookcase were plays. Elizabeth selected one of her favorites, Our Town. *Leila had played Emily last year in high school, and she'd rehearsed her part with Elizabeth so often that Elizabeth knew the part too. Sometimes in arithmetic class she'd read a favorite play in her mind. She liked it a lot more than chanting times tables.*

She must have dozed off, because when she opened her eyes, Matt was bending over her. His breath smelled of tobacco and beer, and when he smiled he breathed heavier and that made it worse. Elizabeth pulled back, but there was no way to escape him. He patted her leg. "Must be a pretty dull book, Liz."

He knew that she liked to be called by her whole name.

"Is Mama awake? I can start to fix supper."

“Your mama is going to be sleeping for a while. Why don’t I just have me a little lie-down and maybe you and I can read together?” In an instant, Elizabeth was pushed against the wall and Matt was taking up all the room on the cot. She began to squirm. “I guess I’ll get up and start to make hamburgers,” she said, trying not to sound scared.

His grip was tight on her arms. “Give Daddy a nice big squeeze first, honey.”

“You’re not my daddy.” Suddenly she felt trapped. She wanted to call Mama, to try to wake her up, but now Matt was kissing her.

“You’re a pretty little girl,” he said. “You’re going to be a real beauty when you grow up.” His hand was moving up her leg now.

“I don’t like that,” she said.

“Like what, baby?”

And then over Matt’s shoulder she could see Leila in the doorway. Her green eyes were dark with anger. In a second, she was across the room, pulling Matt’s hair so hard his head yanked back, shouting words at him that Elizabeth didn’t understand. And then she screamed, “Bad enough what those other bastards did to me, but I’ll *kill* you before you start on her!”

Matt’s feet hit the floor with a thud. He pulled to one side, trying to get away from Leila. But she kept twisting his long hair, so that every move he made hurt. He began to yell back at Leila and try to hit her.

Mama must have heard the noise, because her snoring stopped. She came into the room, a sheet wrapped around her, her eyes circled and bleary, her pretty red hair disheveled. “What’s going on here?” she mumbled in a sleepy, angry voice, and Elizabeth saw the bruise on her forehead.

“You better tell this crazy kid of yours that when I’m just being nice and reading to her sister, she better not act like there’s something wrong with it.” Matt sounded mad, but Elizabeth could tell he was scared.

“And you’d better tell this filthy child molester to get out of here or I’ll call the police.” With a final tug, Leila released Matt’s hair, stepped around him and sat on the cot with Elizabeth, hugging her tight.

Mama started to yell at Matt; then Leila started to yell at Mama, and in the end, Mama and Matt went to their room and kept on fighting; then there were long silences. When they came out of the room, they were dressed and said everything was a misunderstanding and as long as the girls were together, they’d just go out for a while.

After they left, Leila said, “Want to open a can of soup and maybe fix us a hamburger? I’ve got to do some thinking.” Obediently Elizabeth went into the kitchen and prepared the meal. They ate in silence, and Elizabeth realized how glad she was that Mama and Matt were gone. When they were home, they were either drinking and kissing or fighting and kissing. Either way it was awful.

Finally, Leila said, “She’ll never change.”

''Who?''

''Mama. She's a boozer, and if it isn't one guy it will be another, until she just runs out of all the men left alive. But I can't leave you with Matt.''

Leave! Leila couldn't be leaving. . . .

''So get packed,'' Leila said. ''If that creep is starting to paw you, you're not safe here. We're going to take the late bus to New York.'' Then she reached over and tousled Elizabeth's hair. ''God alone knows how I'll manage when we get there, Sparrow, but I promise I'll take care of you.''

Later, Elizabeth was to remember that moment so clearly. Leila's eyes, emerald green again, the anger gone, but with a steely look in them; Leila's slim, taut body and catlike grace; Leila's brilliant red hair brightened even more by the light from the overhead fixture; Leila's rich, throaty voice saying, ''Don't be scared, Sparrow. It's time to shake the dust of our old Kentucky home off our feet!''

Then with a defiant laugh, Leila began to sing, ''Weep no more, my lady. . . .''

Saturday,
August 29, 1987

CHAPTER 1

Pan American flight 111 from Rome began to circle on its final approach to Kennedy Airport. Elizabeth pressed her forehead against the glass, drinking in the brilliance of the sun gleaming on the ocean, the distant outline of the Manhattan skyscrapers. This was the moment she had once loved at the end of a trip, the sense of coming home. But today she passionately wanted to be able to stay on the plane, to go wherever its next destination might be.

"It's a lovely sight, isn't it?" When she'd boarded the plane, the grandmotherly-looking woman next to her had smiled pleasantly and opened her book. Elizabeth had been relieved; the last thing she'd wanted was a seven-hour conversation with a stranger. But now it was all right. They'd be landing in a few minutes. She agreed that it was a lovely sight.

"This was my third trip to Italy," her seatmate continued. "But it's the last time I'll go in August. Tourists all over the place. And so terribly hot. What countries did you visit?"

The plane banked and began its descent. Elizabeth decided it was just as easy to give a direct answer as to be noncommittal. "I'm an actress. I was working on a film in Venice."

"How exciting. My first impression was that you reminded me a little of Candy Bergen. You're just about as tall as she is and have the same lovely blond hair and blue-gray eyes. Should I know your name?"

"Not at all."

There was a faint bump as the plane landed on the runway and began taxiing. To deter any more questions, Elizabeth made a business of pulling her carry-on bag from under the seat and checking its contents. If Leila were here, she thought, there wouldn't be any question about identifying *her.* Everyone recognized Leila LaSalle. But Leila would have been in first class, not coach.

Would have been. After all these months, it was time the reality of her death set in.

A newsstand just beyond the Customs enclosure had stacks of the early-afternoon edition of the *Globe.* She couldn't help seeing the headline: TRIAL BEGINS SEPTEMBER 8. The lead read: "A visibly angry Judge Michael Harris scathingly denied further postponements in the murder trial of multimillionaire Ted Winters.'' The rest of the front page was filled with a blowup of Ted's face. There was a stunned bitterness in his eyes, a rigid set to his mouth. It was a picture snapped after he'd learned that the grand jury had indicted him for the murder of his fiancée, Leila LaSalle.

As the cab sped toward the city, Elizabeth read the story—a rehash of the details of Leila's death and the evidence against Ted. Pictures of Leila were splashed over the next three pages of the paper: Leila at a premiere, with her first husband; Leila on safari, with her second husband; Leila with Ted; Leila accepting her Oscar—stock publicity shots. One of them caught Elizabeth's eye. In it, Leila had a hint of softness in her smile, a suggestion of vulnerability that contrasted with the arrogant tilt of her chin, the mocking expression in her eyes. Half the young girls in America had imitated that expression, copied Leila's way of tossing her hair back, of smiling over her shoulder. . . .

''Here we are, lady.''

Startled, Elizabeth looked up. The cab had stopped in front of the Hamilton Arms, at Fifty-seventh Street and Park Avenue. The paper slid off her lap. She forced herself to try to sound calm. ''I'm so sorry. I gave you the wrong address. I want to go to Eleventh and Fifth.''

''I already turned off the meter.''

''Then start a new fare.'' Her hands shook as she fumbled for her wallet. She sensed the doorman was approaching and did not raise her eyes. She did not want to be recognized. Unthinkingly she had given Leila's address. This was the building where Ted had murdered Leila. Here, in a drunken rage, he had pushed her off the terrace of her apartment.

Elizabeth began to shiver uncontrollably at the image she could not banish from her mind: Leila's beautiful body, wrapped in the white satin pajamas, her long red hair cascading behind her, plummeting forty stories to the concrete courtyard.

And always the questions. . . . Was she conscious? How much did she realize?

How awful those last seconds must have been for her!

If I had stayed with her, Elizabeth thought, it never would have happened. . . .

CHAPTER 2

After a two-month absence, the apartment felt close and stuffy. But as soon as she opened the windows, a breeze blew in, carrying the peculiarly satisfying combination of scents that was so specially New York: the pungent aura of the small Indian restaurant around the corner, a hint of the flowers from the terrace across the street, the acrid smell of fumes from the Fifth Avenue buses, a suggestion of sea air from the Hudson River. For a few minutes Elizabeth breathed deeply and felt herself begin to unwind. Now that she was here, it was good to be home. The job in Italy had been another escape, another temporary respite. But never out of her mind was the realization that eventually she would have to go to court, as a prosecution witness against Ted.

She unpacked quickly and placed her plants in the sink. It was clear that the superintendent's wife had not honored her promise to water them regularly. After plucking away the dead leaves, she turned to the mail that was stacked on the dining-room table. Rapidly she skimmed through it, tossing out ads and coupons, separating personal letters from bills. She smiled eagerly at the beautiful handwriting on one envelope and the precise return address in the upper corner: *Miss Dora Samuels, Cypress Point Spa, Pebble Beach, California.* Sammy. But before she read that one, Elizabeth reluctantly opened the business-size envelope with the return address OFFICE OF THE DISTRICT ATTORNEY.

The letter was brief. It was a confirmation that she would phone Assistant District Attorney William Murphy upon her return on August 29 and make an appointment to review her testimony.

Even reading the newspaper and giving Leila's address to the cabbie had not prepared her for the shock of this official notice. Her mouth went dry. The walls seemed to close in around her. The hours she had testified at the grand jury hearings flashed through her mind. The time she had fainted on the sand after being shown the pictures of Leila's body. Oh, God, she thought, it was starting all over again. . . .

The phone rang. Her ''Hello'' was barely audible.

''Elizabeth,'' a voice boomed. ''How are you? You're on my mind.''

It was Min von Schreiber! Of all people! Elizabeth instantly felt wearier. Min had given Leila her first modeling job, and now she was married to an Austrian baron and owned the glamorous Cypress Point Spa in Pebble Beach, California. She was an old and dear friend; but Elizabeth didn't feel up to her today. Still, Min was one of the people Elizabeth could never say no to.

Elizabeth tried to sound cheerful. ''I'm fine, Min. A little tired, maybe. I just got home a few minutes ago.''

''Don't unpack. You're coming to the Spa tomorrow morning. There's a ticket waiting at the American Airlines counter. The usual flight. Jason will pick you up at the airport in San Francisco.''

"Min, I can't."

"As my guest."

Elizabeth almost laughed. Leila had always said those were the three hardest words for Min to utter. "But, Min—"

"No 'buts.' When I saw you in Venice you looked too thin. That damn trial will be hell. So come. You need rest. You need pampering."

Elizabeth could see Min, her raven-black hair coiled around her head, always assuming in her imperious way that what she wanted was automatically granted. After more futile protests in which she listed all the reasons why she should not come, could not, she heard herself agreeing to Min's plans. "Tomorrow, then. It will be good to see you, Min." She was smiling when she put the receiver down.

Three thousand miles away, Minna von Schreiber waited for the connection to break, then immediately began to dial another number. When she reached her party, she whispered, "You were right. It was easy. She agreed to come. *Don't forget to act surprised when you see her.*"

Her husband entered the room as she was talking. He waited until the call was completed, then burst out, "You did invite her, then?"

Min looked up, defiantly. "Yes, I did."

Helmut von Schreiber frowned. His china-blue eyes darkened. "After all my warnings? Minna, Elizabeth could pull this house of cards down around our ears. By the end of the week, you will regret that invitation as you have never regretted anything in your life."

Elizabeth decided to get her call to the district attorney over with immediately. William Murphy was obviously glad to hear from her. "Miss Lange, I just started to sweat you out."

"I told you I'd be back today. I wouldn't have expected to find you in on Saturday."

"There's a lot of work. We definitely go to trial on September eighth."

"I read that."

"I'll need to review your testimony with you so it will be fresh in your mind."

"It's never *not* been in my mind," Elizabeth said.

"I understand. But I have to discuss the kind of questions the defense attorney will ask you. I suggest you come in on Monday for several hours and then let's plan to have long sessions next weekend. You *will* be around?"

"I'm leaving tomorrow morning," she told him. "Can't we talk about everything on Friday?"

She was dismayed at the answer. "I'd rather have one preliminary meeting. It's only three o'clock. You could be down here in a cab in fifteen minutes."

Reluctantly she agreed. Glancing at Sammy's letter, she decided to wait until she came back to read it. At least it would be something to look forward to. Showering quickly, she twisted her hair into a topknot and put on a blue cotton jumpsuit and sandals.

Half an hour later, she was sitting across from the assistant district attorney in his crowded office. The furniture consisted of his desk, three chairs and a row of battleship-gray steel files. There were expandable cardboard files piled on his desk, on the floor and on top of the metal cabinets. William Murphy seemed unaware of the messiness of his work space—or else, Elizabeth thought, he had finally come to terms with what could not be changed.

A balding, chubby-faced man in his late thirties with a strong New York accent, Murphy conveyed an impression of keen intelligence and driving energy. After the grand jury hearings, he had told her that her testimony was the main reason Ted had been indicted. She knew he considered that high praise.

Now he opened a thick file: *The People of the State of New York* v. *Andrew Edward Winters III.* "I know how hard this is for you," he said. "You're going to be forced to relive your sister's death, and with that all the pain you experienced. And you're going to testify against a man you liked and trusted."

"Ted killed Leila; the man I knew doesn't exist."

"There are no 'ifs' in this case. He deprived your sister of her life; it's my job—with your help—to see that he's deprived of his freedom. The trial will be a terrible ordeal for you, but I promise that once it's over it will be easier to get on with your own life. After you are sworn, you will be asked to state your name. I know 'Lange' is your stage name. Be sure to tell the jury your legal name is LaSalle. Let's review your testimony again.

"You will be asked if you lived with your sister."

"No, when I left college I got my own apartment."

"Are your parents living?"

"No, my mother died three years after Leila and I came to New York, and I never knew my father."

"Now let's review again your testimony, starting with the day before the murder."

"I had been out of town for three months with a stock company. . . . I got in on Friday night, March twenty-eighth, just in time to catch the last preview of Leila's play."

"How did you find your sister?"

"She was obviously under a terrible strain; she kept forgetting her lines. Her performance was a shambles. Between acts I went to her dressing room. She never drank anything but a little wine, and yet she was drinking straight Scotch. I took it from her and poured it down the sink."

"How did she respond?"

"She was furious. She was a totally different person. She had never been a big drinker, but she was suddenly drinking a lot. . . . Ted came into the dressing room. She shouted at both of us to get out.''

''Were you surprised by her behavior?''

''I think it would be more accurate to say that I was shocked.''

''Did you discuss it with Winters?''

''He seemed bewildered. He'd been away a lot too.''

''On business?''

''Yes. I suppose so. . . .''

''The play went badly?''

''It was a disaster. Leila refused to come out for a curtain call. When it was over we went on to Elaine's.''

''Who do you mean by 'we'?''

''Leila . . . Ted and Craig . . . myself . . . Syd and Cheryl . . . Baron and Baroness von Schreiber. We were all close friends.''

''You will be asked to identify these people for the jury.''

''Syd Melnick was Leila's agent. Cheryl Manning is a well-known actress. Baron and Baroness von Schreiber own Cypress Point Spa in California. Min—the Baroness—used to have a model agency in New York. She gave Leila her first job. Ted Winters—everyone knows who he is, and he was Leila's fiancé. Craig Babcock is Ted's assistant. He's executive vice-president of Winters Enterprises.''

''What happened at Elaine's?''

''There was a dreadful scene. Someone yelled to Leila that he'd heard her play was a turkey. She went wild. She shouted, 'You bet it's a turkey, but I'm wringing its neck. You hear that, everybody? I *quit*!'' Then she fired Syd Melnick. She told him he had only stuck her in the play because he wanted his percentage—that for the last couple of years he'd been putting her in anything he could because he needed the money.'' Elizabeth bit her lip. ''You have to understand this wasn't the real Leila. Oh, sure, she could get uptight when she was in a new play. She was a star. A perfectionist. But she never behaved like that.''

''What did you do?''

''We all tried to calm her down. But it only made her worse. When Ted tried to reason with her, she took off her engagement ring and threw it across the room.''

''How did he respond?''

''He was furious, but he tried not to show it. A waiter brought the ring back and Ted slipped it into his pocket. He tried to make a joke of it. He said something like 'I'll hold it till tomorrow when she's in better shape.' Then we got her to the car and brought her home. Ted helped me to put her to bed. I told him I'd have her call him in the morning, when she woke up.''

''Now on the stand I'll ask you what their living arrangements were.''

''He had his own apartment on the second floor in the same building. I spent the night with Leila. She slept past noon. When she woke up, she felt rotten. I gave her aspirin and she went back to bed. I phoned Ted for her. He was in his office. He asked me to tell her he'd come up about seven o'clock that evening."

Elizabeth felt her voice quaver.

"I'm sorry to have to keep going, but try to think of this as a rehearsal. The more prepared you are, the easier it will be for you when you are actually on the stand."

"It's all right."

"Did you and your sister discuss the previous night?"

"No. It was obvious she didn't want to talk about it. She was very quiet. She told me to go to my place and get settled. I had literally dropped my bags home and rushed to her play. She asked me to call her around eight and we'd have dinner together. I assumed she meant she and Ted and I would have dinner together. But then she said she wasn't going to take his ring back. She was through with him."

"Miss Lange, this is very important. Your sister told you she was planning to break her engagement to Ted Winters?"

"Yes." Elizabeth stared down at her hands. She remembered how she had put those hands on Leila's shoulders, then run them across Leila's forehead. *Oh, stop it, Leila. You don't mean that.*

But I do, Sparrow.

No, you don't.

Have it your way, Sparrow. But call me around eight, okay?

The last moment of being with Leila, of putting the cold compress on her forehead, of tucking the blankets around her and thinking that in a few hours she'd be herself again, laughing and amused and ready to tell the story. "So I fired Syd and threw Ted's ring, and quit the play. How's that for a fast two minutes in Elaine's?" And then she'd throw back her head and laugh, and in retrospect it would suddenly become funny—a star having a public tantrum.

"I let myself believe it, because I wanted to believe it," Elizabeth heard herself telling William Murphy.

In a rush she began the rest of her testimony. "I phoned at eight. . . . Leila and Ted were arguing. She sounded as if she'd been drinking again. She asked me to call back in an hour. I did. She was crying. They were still quarreling. She had told Ted to get out. She kept saying she couldn't trust any man; she didn't want any man; she wanted me to go away with her."

"How did you respond?"

"I tried everything. I tried to calm her. I reminded her that she always got uptight when she was in a new show. I told her the play was really a good vehicle for her. I told her Ted was crazy about her and she knew it. Then I tried acting angry. I told her . . ." Elizabeth's voice faltered. Her face paled. "I told her she sounded just like Mama in one of her drunks."

"What did she say?"

''It was as if she hadn't heard me. She just kept saying, 'I'm finished with Ted. You're the only one I can ever trust. Sparrow, promise you'll go away with me.' ''

Elizabeth no longer tried to check the tears that welled in her eyes. ''She was crying and sobbing. . . .''

''And then . . .''

''Ted came back. He began shouting at her.''

William Murphy leaned forward. The warmth disappeared from his voice. ''Now, Miss Lange, this will be a crucial point in your testimony. On the stand, before you can say whose voice you heard, I have to lay a foundation so that the judge is satisfied that you truly recognized that voice. So this is how we'll do it. . . .'' He paused dramatically.

''Question: You heard a voice?''

''Yes,'' Elizabeth said tonelessly.

''How loud was that voice?''

''Shouting.''

''What was the tone of that voice?''

''Angry.''

''How many words did you hear that voice say?''

In her mind, Elizabeth counted them. ''Eleven words. Two sentences.''

''Now, Miss Lange, had you ever heard that voice before?''

''Hundreds of times.'' Ted's voice was filling her ears. Ted, laughing, calling to Leila: *''Hey, Star, hurry up, I'm hungry''*; Ted deftly protecting Leila from an overly enthusiastic admirer: *''Get in the car, honey, quick''*; Ted coming to her own opening performance last year Off Broadway: *''I'm to memorize every detail to tell Leila. I can wrap it all up in three words: You were sensational. . . .''*

What was Mr. Murphy asking her? . . . ''Miss Lange, did you *recognize* whose voice shouted at your sister?''

''Absolutely!''

''Miss Lange. *Whose* voice was that shouting in the background?''

''It was Ted's . . . Ted Winters'.''

''What did he shout?''

Unconsciously she raised her own voice. '' 'Put that phone down! I *told* you, put that phone down.' ''

''Did your sister respond?''

''Yes.'' Elizabeth stirred restlessly. ''Do we have to go through this?''

''It will be easier for you if you get used to talking about it before the trial. Now, what did Leila say?''

''She was still sobbing . . . she said, 'Get out of here. You're *not* a falcon. . . .' And then the phone slammed down.''

''She slammed the phone down?''

''I don't know which one of them did it.''

''Miss Lange, does the word 'falcon' mean anything to you?''

''Yes.'' Leila's face filled Elizabeth's mind: the tenderness in Leila's eyes when she looked at Ted, the way she would go up and kiss him. "God, Falcon, I love you."

"Why?"

"It was Ted's nickname . . . my sister's pet name for him. She did that, you see. The people close to her—she gave them special names."

"Did she ever call anyone else by that name—the name *Falcon?*"

"No . . . never." Abruptly, Elizabeth got up and walked to the window. It was grimy with dust. The faint breeze was hot and muggy. She thought longingly of getting away from here.

"Only a few minutes more, I promise. Miss Lange, do you know what time the phone was slammed down?"

"Precisely nine thirty."

"Are you absolutely sure?"

"Yes. There must have been a power failure when I was away. I reset my clock that afternoon. I'm sure it was right."

"What did you do then?"

"I was terribly upset. I had to see Leila. I ran out. It took me at least fifteen minutes to get a cab. It was after ten when I got to Leila's apartment."

"And there was no one there."

"No. I tried to phone Ted. There was no answer at his place. I just waited." Waited all night, not knowing what to think, half-worried, half-relieved; hoping that Leila and Ted had made up and were out somewhere, not knowing that Leila's broken body was lying in the courtyard.

"The next morning, when the body was discovered, you thought she must have *fallen* from the terrace? It was a rainy March night. Why would she have gone out there?"

"She loved to go out and stand and just look at the city. In any weather. I used to tell her to be careful . . . that railing wasn't very high. I thought she must have leaned over; she had been drinking; she fell. . . ."

She remembered: Together she and Ted had grieved. Hands entwined, they had wept at the memorial service. Later, he had held her when she could no longer control her racking sobs. "I know, Sparrow. I know," he said, comforting her. On Ted's yacht they had sailed ten miles out to sea to scatter Leila's ashes.

And then, two weeks later, an eyewitness had come forth and sworn she had seen Ted push Leila off the terrace at nine thirty-one.

"Without your testimony, that witness, Sally Ross, could be destroyed by the defense," she heard William Murphy saying. "As you know, she has a history of severe psychiatric problems. It's not good that she waited that length of time before coming forward with her story. The fact that her psychiatrist was out of town and she wanted to tell him first at least explains it somewhat."

"Without my testimony it's her word against Ted's, and he denies going back up to Leila's apartment." When she had heard about the eyewitness, she had been outraged. She had totally trusted Ted until this man, William Murphy, told her that Ted denied going back to Leila's apartment.

''You can swear that he was there, that they were quarreling, that the phone was slammed down at nine thirty. Sally Ross saw Leila pushed off the terrace at nine thirty-one. Ted's story that he left Leila's apartment at about ten after nine, went to his own apartment, made a phone call, then took a cab to Connecticut doesn't hold up. In addition to what you and that other woman testify, we also have a strong circumstantial case. The scratches on his face. His skin tissue under Leila's fingernails. The testimony of the cabbie that he was white as a sheet and trembling—he could hardly give directions to his place. And why the hell didn't he send for his own chauffeur to take him to Connecticut? Because he was in a panic, that's why! He can't come forward with proof of anyone he reached on the phone. He has a motive—Leila rejected him. But one thing you have to realize: the defense will harp on the fact that you and Ted Winters were so close after her death.''

''We were the two people who loved her best,'' Elizabeth said quietly. ''Or at least, I thought we were. Please, can I go now?''

''We'll leave it at that. You do look pretty beat. This is going to be a long trial, and it won't be pleasant. Try to relax next week. Have you decided where you'll be staying these next few days?''

''Yes. Baroness von Schreiber has invited me to be her guest at Cypress Point Spa.''

''I hope you're joking.''

Elizabeth stared at him. ''Why would I joke about that?''

Murphy's eyes narrowed. His face flushed and his cheekbones suddenly became prominent. He seemed to be struggling not to raise his voice. ''Miss Lange, I don't think you appreciate the seriousness of your position. Without you, the other witness would be annihilated by the defense. That means that your testimony is about to put one of the richest and most influential men in this country in prison for at least twenty years, and thirty if I can make Murder Two stick. If this were a Mafia case I'd have you hidden away in a hotel under an assumed name and with a police guard until this trial is over. Baron and Baroness von Schreiber may be friends of yours, but they're also friends of Ted Winters' and are coming to New York to testify for him. *And you seriously propose to stay with them at this time?*''

''I know that Min and the Baron are testifying as character witnesses for Ted,'' Elizabeth said. ''They don't think he's capable of murder. If I hadn't heard him with my own ears I wouldn't have believed it either. They're following their conscience. I'm following mine. We all do what we have to do.''

She was not prepared for the tirade Murphy let loose at her. His urgent, sometimes sarcastic words pounded in her ears. ''There's something fishy about that invitation. You should see that for yourself. You claim the Von Schreibers loved your sister? Then ask yourself why the hell they're going to bat for her murderer. I insist you keep away from them, if not for my sake or your own neck then because you want justice for Leila."

In the end, embarrassed at his obvious contempt for her naïveté, Elizabeth agreed to call off the trip, promised that instead she'd go to East Hampton and there either visit friends or stay in a hotel.

"Whether you're alone or with someone, *be careful,*" Murphy told her. Now that he had gotten his way, he attempted a smile; but it froze on his face, and the expression in his eyes was both grim and worried. "Never forget that without you as a witness, Ted Winters walks."

Even with the oppressive mugginess, Elizabeth decided to walk home. She felt like one of those punching bags that were weighted with sand and flopped from side to side, unable to avoid the blows rained on them. She knew the district attorney was right. She should have refused Min's invitation. She decided she wouldn't contact anyone in the Hamptons. She'd check into a hotel and just lie on the beach quietly for the next few days.

Leila had always joked, "Sparrow, you'll never need a shrink. Put you in a bikini, dunk you in the briny and you're in heaven." It was true. She remembered her delight in showing Leila her blue ribbons for swimming. Eight years ago, she'd been a runner-up for the Olympic team. For four summers she'd taught water aerobics at Cypress Point Spa.

Along the way she stopped to pick up groceries—just enough to have a salad for dinner and a quick breakfast. As she walked the last two blocks home she thought of how remote everything seemed—as if she were seeing her whole life before Leila's death through the far lens of a telescope.

Sammy's letter was on top of the mail on the dinette table. Elizabeth reached for the envelope and smiled at the exquisite handwriting. It so vividly brought Sammy to mind—the frail, birdlike figure; the wise eyes, owlish behind rimless glasses; the lace-edged blouses and sensible cardigans. Sammy had answered Leila's ad for a part-time secretary ten years ago and within a week had become indispensable. After Leila's death, Min had hired her as a receptionist-secretary at the Spa.

Elizabeth decided to read the letter over dinner. It took only a few minutes to change into a light caftan, fix a salad and pour a glass of chilled chablis. Okay, Sammy, time for our visit, she thought as she slit the envelope.

The first page of the letter was predictable:

Dear Elizabeth,

I hope this finds you well and as content as possible. Each day

I seem to miss Leila more and can only imagine how you feel. I do think that after the trial is behind you, it will get better.

Working for Min has been good for me, although I think I will be giving it up soon. I really have never recovered from that operation.

Elizabeth turned the page, read a few lines; then, as her throat closed, pushed aside the salad.

As you know, I've continued to answer the letters from Leila's fans. There are still three large bags to finish. The reason I am writing is I have just found a very troubling anonymous letter. It is vicious and apparently was one in a series. Leila had not opened this one, but she must have seen its predecessors. Perhaps they would explain why she was so distraught those last weeks.

What is so terrible is that the letter I found was clearly written by someone who knew her well.

I had thought to enclose it in this envelope, but am not sure who is collecting your mail while you are away and would not want this seen by a stranger's eyes. Will you call me as soon as you return to New York?

My love to you.

Sammy

With a growing sense of horror, Elizabeth read and reread Sammy's letter. Leila had been receiving unsigned *very troubling, vicious* letters from someone who knew her well. Sammy, who never exaggerated, thought they might explain Leila's emotional collapse. For all these months, Elizabeth had lain awake trying to understand what had driven Leila into hysteria. Poison-pen letters from someone who knew her well. *Who? Why?* Did Sammy have any inkling?

She grabbed the phone and dialed the office at the Spa. Let Sammy answer, she prayed. But it was Min who picked up the receiver. Sammy was away, she told Elizabeth. She was visiting her cousin somewhere near San Francisco and would be back Monday night. ''You'll see her then.'' Min's tone became curious. ''You sound upset, Elizabeth. Is it something about Sammy that can't wait?''

It was the moment to tell Min that she was not coming. Elizabeth started to say, ''Min, the district attorney . . .'' Then she glanced down at Sammy's letter. The overwhelming need to see Sammy swept over her. It was the same kind of compulsion that had sent her rushing to Leila that last fateful night. She changed the sentence. ''No hurry at all, Min. I'll see you tomorrow.''

Before she went to bed, she wrote a note to William Murphy with the address and phone number of the Spa. Then she tore it up. To hell with his warning. She wasn't a Mafia witness; she was going to visit old friends—people she loved and trusted, people who loved and cared about her. Let him think she was in East Hampton.

He had known for months that it would be necessary to kill Elizabeth. He had lived with the everpresent knowledge of the danger that she represented, and had planned to eliminate her in New York.

With the trial coming, her mind must be constantly reliving every moment of those last days. Inevitably, she would realize what she already knew—*the fact that would seal his fate.*

There were ways to get rid of her at the Spa and make it seem to be an accident. Her death would cause less official suspicion in California than in New York. He thought about her and her habits, looking for a way.

He consulted his watch. It was midnight in New York. Sweet dreams, Elizabeth, he thought.

Your time is running out.

Sunday, August 30

QUOTE FOR THE DAY:
Where is the love, beauty and truth we seek?

—Shelley

Good morning, dear guest!

Welcome to another day of luxury at Cypress Point Spa.

Besides your personalized program, we are happy to tell you that there will be special makeup classes in the women's spa between 10 A.M. and 4 P.M. Why not fill in one of your free hours learning the enchanting secrets of the world's most beautiful women, as taught by Madame Renford of Beverly Hills?

Today's guest expert in the men's spa is famous bodybuilder Jack Richard, who will share his personal workout schedule at 4 P.M.

The musical program after dinner is a very special one. Cellist Fione Navaralla, one of the most acclaimed new artists in England, will play selections by Ludwig van Beethoven.

We hope all our guests will have a pleasant and pampered day. Remember, to be really beautiful we must keep our minds tranquil and free of distressing or troubling thoughts.

Baron and Baroness Helmut von Schreiber

CHAPTER 1

Min's longtime chauffeur, Jason, was waiting at the passenger gate, his silver-gray uniform gleaming in the sunny terminal. He was a small man with a trim, neat build, who had been a jockey in his youth. An accident had ended his racing career, and he had been working as a stable hand when Min hired him. Elizabeth knew that, like all of Min's people, he was intensely loyal to her. Now his leathery face broke into welcoming furrows as he saw her approach. "Miss Lange, it's good to have you back," he said. She wondered if, like her, he was remembering that the last time she came to the Spa she had been with Leila.

She bent over to kiss him on the cheek. "Jason, will you cut that 'Miss Lange' number? You'd think I was a paying guest or something." She noticed the discreet card in his hand with the name Alvirah Meehan on it. "You're picking up someone else?"

"Just one. I thought she'd be out by now. First-class passengers usually are."

Elizabeth reflected that few people economized on air fare when they could afford to pay a minimum of three thousand dollars a week at Cypress Point Spa. With Jason she studied the disembarking passengers. Jason held the card up prominently as several elegantly dressed women passed, but they ignored it. "Hope she didn't miss the flight," he was murmuring as one final straggler came from the passageway. She was a bulky woman of about fifty-five with a large, sharp-featured face and thinning reddish-brown hair. The purple-and-pink print she was wearing was obviously expensive, but absolutely wrong for her. It bulged at the waist and thighs and hiked unevenly over her knees. Intuitively Elizabeth sensed that this lady was Mrs. Alvirah Meehan.

She spotted her name on the card and approached them eagerly, her smile delighted and relieved. Reaching out, she pumped Jason's hand vigorously. "Well, here I am," she announced. "And boy, am I glad to see you! I was so afraid there'd be a foul-up and no one would meet me."

"Oh, we never fail a guest."

Elizabeth felt her lips twitch at Jason's bewildered expression. Clearly Mrs. Meehan was not the usual Cypress Point guest. "Ma'am, may I have your claim checks?"

"Oh, that's nice. I hate to wait for luggage. Sort of a pain in the neck at the end of a trip. Course, Willy and I usually go Greyhound, and the bags are right there, but even so . . . I don't have too much stuff. I was going to buy a lot, but my friend, May, said, 'Alvirah, wait and see what other people are wearing. All these fancy places have shops. . . . You'll pay through the nose,' she said, 'but at least you'll get the right thing, you know what I mean.' '' She thrust her ticket envelope with the baggage stubs at Jason and turned to Elizabeth. ''I'm Alvirah Meehan. Are you going to the Spa too? You sure don't look like you need to, honey!''

Fifteen minutes later, they were settled in the sleek silver limousine. Alvirah settled back against the brocaded upholstery with a gusty sigh. ''Now, *that* feels good,'' she announced.

Elizabeth studied the other woman's hands. They were the hands of a working person, thick-knuckled and callused. The brightly colored fingernails were short and stubby, even though the manicure looked expensive. Her curiosity about Alvirah Meehan was a welcome respite from thinking about Leila. Instinctively she liked the woman—there was something remarkably candid and appealing about her—but who *was* she? What was bringing her to the Spa?

''I still can't get used to it,'' Alvirah continued happily. ''I mean, one minute, I'm sitting in my living room soaking my feet. Let me tell you, cleaning five different houses a week is no joke, and the Friday one was the killer—six kids and they're all slobs and the mother's worse. Then we hit the lottery. We had all the winning numbers. Willy and I couldn't believe it. 'Willy,' I said, 'we're rich.' And he yelled, 'You bet we are!' You must have read about it last month? Forty million dollars, and a minute before, we didn't have two quarters to rub together.''

''You won *forty million* dollars in the lottery?''

''I'm surprised you didn't see it. We're the biggest single winners in the history of the New York State lottery. How about that?''

''I think it's wonderful,'' Elizabeth said sincerely.

''Well, I knew what I wanted to do right away, and that was to get to Cypress Point Spa. I've been reading about it for ten years now. I used to dream about how it would be to spend time there and hobnob with the celebrities. Usually you have to wait months for a reservation, but I got one just like that!'' She snapped her fingers.

Because Min undoubtedly recognized the publicity value of Alvirah Meehan's telling the world about her lifelong ambition to go to the Spa, Elizabeth thought. Min never missed a trick.

They were on the Coastal Highway. ''I thought this was supposed to be a beautiful drive,'' Alvirah said. ''It don't look so hot to me.''

''A little farther on it becomes breathtaking,'' Elizabeth murmured.

Alvirah Meehan straightened up in the seat and turned to Elizabeth, studying her intently.''By the way, I've been talking so much I missed your name.''

''Elizabeth Lange.''

Large brown eyes, already magnified by thick-rimmed glasses, widened perceptibly. "I know who you are. You're Leila LaSalle's sister. She was my favorite actress in the whole world. I know all about Leila and you. I think the story of the two of you coming to New York when you were just a little girl is so beautiful. Two nights before she died, I saw a preview of her last play. Oh, I'm sorry—I didn't mean to upset you. . . ."

"It's all right. I just have a terrible headache. Maybe if I just rest a bit . . ."

Elizabeth turned her head toward the window and dabbed at her eyes. To understand Leila, you had to have lived that childhood, that trip to New York, the fear and the disappointments. . . . And you had to know that however good it sounded in *People* magazine, it wasn't a beautiful story at all. . . .

It was a fourteen-hour bus ride from Lexington to New York. Elizabeth slept curled up in her seat, her head on Leila's lap. She was a little scared, and it made her sad to think of Mama coming home to find them gone, but she knew Matt would say, "Have a drink, honey" and pull Mama into the bedroom, and in a little while they'd be laughing and squealing and the springs of the bed would creak and groan. . . .

Leila told her which states they were going through: Maryland, Delaware, New Jersey. Then the fields were replaced with ugly tanks and the road got more and more crowded. At the Lincoln Tunnel, the bus kept stopping and starting. Elizabeth's stomach began to feel kind of funny. Leila noticed. "Good God, Sparrow, don't get sick now. It's just another few minutes."

She couldn't wait to get off the bus. She just wanted to smell cool, clean air. But the air was heavy, and it was so hot—hotter even than at home. Elizabeth felt fretful and tired. She was about to complain, but then she saw how tired Leila looked.

They had just left the platform when a man came over to Leila. He was thin, and his dark hair was curly but started pretty far back. He had long sideburns and small brown eyes that got squinty when he smiled. "I'm Lon Pedsell," he said. "Are you the model the Arbitron Agency from Maryland sent?"

Of course Leila wasn't the model, but Elizabeth could tell she didn't want to just say no. "There wasn't anyone else my age on this bus" was the way she answered him.

"And obviously you are a model."

"I'm an actress."

The man brightened up as though Leila had given him a present. "This is a break for me, and I hope for you. If you can use a modeling job, you'd be perfect. The pay is one hundred dollars for the sitting."

Leila put down her bags and squeezed Elizabeth's shoulder. It was her way of saying, "Let me do the talking."

''I can tell that you're agreeable,'' Lon Pedsell said. ''Come on. I've got my car outside.''

Elizabeth was surprised at his studio. When Leila talked about New York, she'd thought that every place Leila worked would be beautiful. But Lon Pedsell took them to a dirty street about six blocks from the bus terminal. Lots of people were sitting on stoops, and garbage was spilled all over the sidewalk. ''I have to apologize for my temporary situation,'' he said. ''I lost the lease on my place across town, and the new one is still being equipped.''

The apartment he brought them to was on the fourth floor and as messy as Mama's house. Lon was breathing hard because he insisted on carrying the two big suitcases. ''Why don't I get a Coke for your sister, and she can watch television while you pose?'' he said to Leila.

Elizabeth could tell that Leila just wasn't sure what to do. ''What kind of model am I supposed to be?'' she asked.

It's for a new swimsuit line. Actually, I'm doing the test shots for the agency. The girl they choose will do a whole series of ads. You're pretty lucky you ran into me today. I have a hunch you're just the type they have in mind.''

He brought them into the kitchen. It was a tiny, dingy room with a small television set on a ledge over the sink. He poured a Coke for Elizabeth and wine for Leila and himself. ''I'll have a Coke,'' Leila said.

''Suit yourself.'' He turned on the television set. ''Now, Elizabeth, I'm going to close the door so I can concentrate. You just stay here and keep yourself amused.''

Elizabeth watched three programs. Sometimes she could hear Leila saying in a loud voice, ''I don't like that idea,'' but she didn't sound scared, just kind of worried. After a while she came out. ''I'm finished, Sparrow. Let's get our bags.'' Then she turned to Lon. ''Do you know where we can get a furnished room?''

''Would you like to stay here?''

''No. Just give me my hundred dollars.''

''If you'll sign this release . . .''

When Leila signed, he smiled over at Elizabeth. ''You must be proud of your big sister. She's on her way to becoming a famous model.''

Leila handed him the paper. ''Give me the hundred dollars.''

''Oh, the agency will pay you. Here's their card. Just go over in the morning and they'll issue a check.''

''But you said—''

''Leila, you really are going to have to learn the business. Photographers don't pay models. The agency pays when it gets the release.''

He didn't offer to help them carry down their bags.

* * *

A hamburger and milk shake at a restaurant called Chock Full o' Nuts made both of them feel better. Leila had bought a street map of New York City and a newspaper. She began to read the real estate section. "Here's an apartment that sounds about right: 'Penthouse; fourteen rooms, spectacular view, wraparound terrace.' Someday, Sparrow. I promise."

They found an ad for an apartment to share. Leila looked at the street map. "It doesn't look too bad," she said. "Ninety-fifth Street and West End Avenue isn't that far, and we can get a bus."

The apartment turned out to be okay, but the woman's nice smile disappeared when she learned that Elizabeth was part of the deal. "No kids," she said flatly.

It was the same everywhere they went. Finally, at seven o'clock, Leila asked a cabdriver if he knew of any cheap but decent place to stay where she could bring Elizabeth. He suggested a rooming house in Greenwich Village.

The next morning they went to the model agency on Madison Avenue to collect Leila's money. The door of the agency was locked, and a sign read, "PUT YOUR COMPOSITE IN THE MAILBOX." *The mailbox had a half-dozen manila envelopes in it already. Leila pressed her finger on the bell. A voice came over the intercom. "Do you have an appointment?"*

"We're here to pick up my money," Leila said.

She and the woman began to argue. Finally the woman shouted, "Get lost." Leila pressed the bell again and didn't stop until someone yanked the door open. Elizabeth shrank back. The woman had heavy dark hair all done up in braids on her head. Her eyes were coal black, and her whole face was terribly angry. The woman wasn't young, but she was beautiful. Her white silk suit made Elizabeth realize that the blue shorts she was wearing were faded and the dye on her polo shirt had run around the pocket. She had thought Leila looked so pretty when they started out, but next to this woman Leila seemed overdressed and shabby.

"Listen," the woman said, "if you want to leave your picture you can. You try barging in here again and I'll have you arrested."

Leila thrust out the paper in her hand. "You owe me one hundred dollars and I'm not leaving without it."

The woman took the paper, read it and began to laugh so hard she had to lean against the door. "You really are *dumb! Those jokers pull that stuff on all you hicks. Where'd he pick you up? In the bus terminal? Did you end up in the sack with him?"*

"No, I did not." Leila grabbed the paper, tore it up and ground the pieces under her heel. "Come on, Sparrow. That guy made a fool of me, but we don't have to give this bitch a good laugh about it."

Elizabeth could see that Leila was so upset she was about to cry and didn't want the woman to see it. She shook Leila's arm off her shoulder and stood in front of the woman. "I think you're mean," she said. "That man acted nice, and if he made my sister work for nothing you should feel sorry about it, not make fun of us.'' She spun around and tugged Leila's hands. ''Let's go.''

They started for the elevator, and the woman called after them, ''Come on back, you two.'' They ignored her. Then she yelled, ''I said come back!''

Two minutes later they were in her private office.

''You've got possibilities,'' the woman told Leila. ''But those clothes . . . You don't know a thing about makeup; you'll need a good haircut; you'll need composites. Did you pose in the raw for that creep?''

''Yes.''

''Terrific. If you're any good, I'll submit you for an Ivory Soap commercial, and right then is when your picture will show up in a girlie magazine. He didn't take any movies of you, did he?''

''No. At least, I don't think so.''

''That's something. From now on, I do the booking for you.''

They left in a daze. Leila had a list of appointments at a beauty salon for the next day. Then she would meet the woman from the model agency at the photographer's. ''Call me Min,'' the woman had said. ''And don't worry about clothes. I'll bring everything you need.''

Elizabeth was so happy her feet could hardly touch the ground, but Leila was very quiet. They walked down Madison Avenue. Well-dressed people hurried by; the sun was shining brightly; hot dog carts and pretzel stands seemed to be on every corner; buses and cars honked at each other; nearly everyone ignored the red lights and sauntered through the heavy traffic. Elizabeth had a wonderful sense of being home. ''I like it here,'' she said.

''So do I, Sparrow. And you saved the day for me. I swear, I don't know who's taking care of who. And Min is good people. But, Sparrow, there's something I've found out from that stinking father of mine, and from Mama's lousy boyfriends, and now from that bastard yesterday.

''Sparrow—I'm never going to trust a man again.''

CHAPTER 2

Elizabeth opened her eyes. The car was sliding noiselessly past Pebble Beach Lodge, along the tree-lined road where glimpses of estate homes could be seen through hedges of bougainvillea and azaleas. It slowed down as it rounded a bend and the tree that gave Cypress Point Spa its name came into view.

Disoriented for a moment, she brushed the hair back from her forehead and looked around. Alvirah Meehan was beside her, a blissful smile on her face. ''You must be worn out, poor thing,'' Alvirah said. ''You've been asleep practically since we left the airport.'' She shook her head as she gazed out the window. ''Now, this is really something!'' The car passed through the ornate iron gates and wound its way up toward the main house, a rambling three-story ivory stucco mansion with pale blue shutters. Several swimming pools were dotted through the grounds near the clusters of bungalows. At the north end of the property there was a patio, with umbrella tables scattered around both sides of the Olympic-size pool. Identical adobe buildings were on either side of the pool. ''These are the men's and women's spas,'' Elizabeth explained.

The clinic, a smaller edition of the main house, was at its right. A series of paths lined by high flowering hedges led to individual doorways. The treatment rooms were entered through these doors, and treatments were spaced far enough apart so that guests avoided encountering each other.

Then, as the limousine followed the curve of the driveway, Elizabeth gasped and leaned forward. Between the main house and the clinic, but placed well behind them, a huge new structure had come into view, its black marble exterior, accentuated by massive columns, making it loom like an ominous volcano about to erupt. Or like a mausoleum, Elizabeth thought.

''What's *that?*'' Alvirah Meehan asked.

''It's a replica of a Roman bath. They had just broken ground for it when I was here two years ago. Jason, is it open yet?''

''Not finished, Miss Lange. The construction just goes on and on.''

Leila had openly mocked the plans for the bathhouse. ''Another of Helmut's grand schemes for separating Min from her money,'' she said. ''He won't be happy until Min is officially declared a shopping-bag lady.''

The car stopped at the steps of the main house. Jason leaped out and rushed to open the door. Alvirah Meehan struggled back into her shoes and, stooping awkwardly, hoisted herself from the seat. ''It's like sitting on the floor,'' she commented. ''Oh, look, here comes Mrs. von Schreiber. I know her from her pictures. Or should I call her Baroness?''

Elizabeth did not answer. She stretched out her arms as Min descended the steps from the veranda, her gait rapid but stately. Leila had always compared Min in motion to the *Q.E. 2* steaming into harbor. Min was wearing a deceptively simple Adolfo print. Her luxurious dark hair was piled on her head in a swirling French knot. She pounced on Elizabeth and hugged her fiercely. ''You're much too thin,'' she hissed. ''In a swimsuit I bet you look scrawny.'' Another bear hug and Min turned her attention to Alvirah. ''Mrs. Meehan. 'The world's luckiest woman.' We are *enchanted* to have you!'' She eyed Alvirah up and down. ''In two weeks, the world will think you were born with a forty-million-dollar spoon in your mouth.''

Alvirah Meehan beamed. ''That's the way I feel right now.''

''Elizabeth, you go up to the office. Helmut is waiting to see you. I'll escort Mrs. Meehan to her bungalow, then join you.''

Obediently Elizabeth went into the main house and walked through the cool marble-floored foyer, past the salon, the music room, the formal dining rooms and up the sweeping staircase that led to the private rooms. Min and her husband shared a suite of offices that overlooked the front and both sides of the property. From there Min could observe the movements of guests and staff as they went back and forth between the areas of activity. At dinner she was frequently known to admonish a guest. ''You should have been in aerobics when I saw you reading in the garden!'' She also had an uncanny knack of noticing when an employee kept a guest waiting.

Elizabeth knocked softly on the door of the private office suite. When there was no answer she opened it. Like every room in Cypress Point Spa, the offices were furnished exquisitely. An abstract watercolor by Will Moses hung on the wall over the oyster-colored couch. An Aubusson rug shimmered on the dark tile. The reception desk was authentic Louis XV, but there was no one seated there. She felt an immediate sense of sharp disappointment, but reminded herself that Sammy would be back tomorrow night.

Tentatively, she walked to the partially open door of the office Min and the Baron shared, then gasped in surprise. Baron Helmut von Schreiber was standing at the far wall, where pictures of Min's most famous clients were hung. Elizabeth's eyes followed him and she bit her lip to keep from crying out.

It was Leila's portrait Helmut was studying, the one Leila had posed for the last time she was here. The vivid green of Leila's dress was unmistakable, the brilliant red hair that floated around her face, the way she was holding up a champagne glass as though offering a toast.

Helmut's hands were clasped tightly behind his back. Everything about his stance suggested tension.

Elizabeth did not want him to know that he had been observed. Swiftly she retraced her steps to the reception room, opened and closed the door with a loud thud, then called, ''Anyone home?''

An instant later he rushed from the inner office. The change in his demeanor was dramatic. This was the gracious, urbane European she had always known, with the warm smile, the kiss on both cheeks, the murmured compliment. ''Elizabeth, you grow more beautiful every day. So young, so fair, so divinely tall.''

''Tall, anyhow.'' Elizabeth stepped back. ''Let me look at you, Helmut.'' She studied him carefully, observing that no trace of tension showed in his baby-blue eyes. His smile was relaxed and natural. His parted lips showed perfect white teeth. How had Leila described him? *"I swear, Sparrow, that guy makes me think of a toy soldier. Do you suppose Min winds him up in the morning? He may have decent ancestry, but I bet he never had more than a nickel behind him till he latched on to Min."*

Elizabeth had protested, "He's a plastic surgeon, and certainly he's knowledgeable about spas. The place is famous."

"It may be famous," Leila had retorted, "but it costs a bundle to run, and I'd bet my last dollar even those prices can't carry that overhead. Listen, Sparrow, I should know. I've married two freeloaders so far, right? Sure he treats Min like a queen, but he's putting that tinted head on two-hundred-dollar pillowcases every night, and besides what she's spent on the Spa, Min's dumped a pile of dough into that broken-down castle of his in Austria."

Like everyone else, Helmut had seemed griefstricken at Leila's death, but now Elizabeth wondered if that had only been an act.

"Well, tell me. Am I all right? You look so troubled. Perhaps you have found some wrinkles?" His laugh was low, well bred, amused.

She made herself smile up at him. "I think you look splendid," she said. "Perhaps I'm just shocked to realize how long it's been since I've seen you."

"Come." He took her hand and led her to the grouping of Art Deco wicker furniture near the front windows. He grimaced as he sat down. "I keep trying to convince Minna that these objects were meant to be seen, not used. So tell me, how has it been for you?"

"Busy. Of course, that's the way I want it to be."

"Why haven't you come to see us before this?"

Because in this place I knew I'd be seeing Leila everywhere I turned. "I did see Min in Venice three months ago."

"And also, the Spa holds too many memories for you, yes?"

"It holds memories. But I've missed you two. And I'm looking forward to seeing Sammy. How do you think she's feeling?"

"You know Sammy. She never complains. But my guess would be—not well. I don't think she's ever recovered, either from the surgery or from the shock of Leila's death. And she is past seventy now. No great age physiologically, but still . . ."

The outer door closed with a decided thump, and Min's voice preceded her entrance. "Helmut, wait until you see the lottery winner. You have your work cut out for you. We'll need to arrange interviews for her. She'll make this place sound like seventh heaven."

She rushed across the room and embraced Elizabeth fiercely. "If you knew the nights I've lain awake worrying about you! How long can you stay?"

"Not very long. Just until Friday."

"That's only five days!"

''I know, but the district attorney's office has to review my testimony.'' Elizabeth realized how good it felt to have loving arms around her.

''What do they have to review?''

''The questions they'll be asking me at the trial. The questions Ted's lawyers will be asking me. I thought telling the simple truth would be enough, but apparently the defense will try to prove I'm mistaken about the time of the phone call.''

''Do *you* think you might be mistaken?'' Min's lips were grazing her ear, her voice a suggested stage whisper. Startled, Elizabeth pulled back from the embrace in time to see the warning frown on Helmut's face.

''Min, do you think if I had the slightest doubt—''

''All right,'' Min said hastily. ''We shouldn't talk about that now. So you have five days. You're going to be pampered; you're going to rest. I made out your schedule myself. You start with a facial and massage this afternoon.''

Elizabeth left them a few minutes later. The slanting rays of the sun danced on the beds of wildflowers along the path to the bungalow Min had assigned her. Somewhere in her subconscious she experienced a sense of calm observing the brilliant checkerblooms, the wood roses, the flowering currant hedges. But the momentary tranquillity could not mask the fact that behind the warm welcome and seeming concern, Min and Helmut were different.

They were angry and worried and hostile. And that hostility was directed at *her*.

CHAPTER 3

Syd Melnick did not find the drive from Beverly Hills to Pebble Beach enjoyable. For the entire four hours, Cheryl Manning sat like a stone, rigid and uncommunicative, in the seat beside him. For the first three hours she had not allowed him to put the top down on the convertible. She wasn't going to risk drying out her face and hair. It was only when they approached Carmel and she wanted to be recognized going through town that she'd permitted the change.

Occasionally during the long ride, Syd glanced over at her. There was no question she looked good. The blue-black hair exploding in a mass of tendrils around her face was sexy and exciting. She was thirty-six now, and what had once been a *gamin* quality had evolved into a sultry sophistication that became her well. *Dynasty* and *Dallas* were getting long in the tooth. Audiences eventually got restless. There was a definite move to say "Enough" to the steamy love affairs of women in their fifties. And in Amanda, Cheryl had finally found the role that could make her a superstar.

When that happened, Syd in turn would be a bigtime agent again. An author was as good as his last book. An actor as bankable as his last picture. An agent needed megabucks deals to be considered topflight. It was again within his grasp to become a legend, the next Swifty Lazar. And *this* time, he told himself, he wouldn't screw it up at the casinos, or blow it on the horses.

He would know in a few days if Cheryl had the part. Just before they left, at Cheryl's insistence, he had phoned Bob Koenig at home. Twenty-five years ago, Bob, fresh out of college, and Syd, a studio gofer, had met on a Hollywood set and become friends. Now Bob was president of World Motion Pictures. He even *looked* the part of the new breed of studio head, with his rugged features and broad shoulders. Syd knew that he himself could be typecast for the stereotypical Brooklynite, with his long, slightly mournful face, receding curly hair and slight paunch that even rigorous exercise didn't help. It was another thing he envied Bob Koenig for.

Today Bob had let his irritation show. "Look, Syd, don't call me at home on a Sunday to talk business again! Cheryl did a damn good test. We're still seeing other people. You'll hear one way or another in the next few days. And let me give you a tip. Sticking her in that play last year when Leila LaSalle died was a lousy judgment call, and it's a big part of the problem with choosing her. Calling me at home on Sunday is a lousy judgment call too."

Syd's palms began to sweat at the memory of the conversation. Oblivious of the scenery, he pondered the fact that he had made the mistake of abusing a friendship. If he wasn't more careful, everyone he knew would be "in conference" when he phoned.

And Bob was right. He *had* made a terrible mistake, talking Cheryl into going into the play with only a few days' rehearsal. The critics had slaughtered her.

Cheryl had been standing next to him when he called Bob. She'd heard what Bob said about the play's being the reason she might not get the part. And of course, *that* triggered an explosion. Not the first one, nor the last.

That goddamn play! He'd believed in it enough to beg and borrow until he had a million dollars to invest in it! It could have been a smash hit. And then Leila had started boozing and trying to act as if the play were the problem. . .

Anger parched Syd's throat. All he had done for that bitch, and she'd fired him in Elaine's in front of a roomful of show-business people, cursing him out at the top of her voice! And she knew how much he'd sunk into the play! He only hoped she'd been conscious enough to know what was happening before she hit the concrete!

They were driving through Carmel: crowds of tourists on the streets;

the sun bright; everybody looking relaxed and happy. He took the long way and threaded along the busiest streets. He could hear people comment when they started to recognize Cheryl. Now, of course, she was smiling, little Miss Gracious! She needed an audience the way other people needed air and water.

They reached the gate to Pebble Beach. He paid the toll. They drove past Pebble Beach Lodge, the Crocker Woodland, to the gates of the Spa.

"Drop me off at my bungalow," Cheryl snapped. "I don't want to bump into anybody until I get myself together."

She turned to him and pulled off her sunglasses. Her extraordinary eyes blazed. "Syd, what are my chances of becoming Amanda?"

He answered the question as he had answered it a dozen times in the last week. "The best, baby," he said sincerely. "The best."

They'd better be, he told himself, or it was all over.

CHAPTER 4

The *Westwind* banked, turned and began its descent into Monterey airport. With methodical care, Ted checked the instrument panel. It had been a good flight from Hawaii—smooth air every foot of the way, the cloud banks lazy and floating like cotton candy at a circus. Funny; he liked the clouds, liked to fly over them and through them, but even as a kid he had despised cotton candy. One more contradiction in his life . . .

In the copilot's seat John Moore stirred, a quiet reminder that he was there if Ted elected to turn over the controls to him. Moore had been the chief pilot for Winters Enterprises for ten years. But Ted wanted to make this landing, to see how smoothly he could bring the plane in. Set the wheels down. Land on his feet. It was all one, wasn't it?

Craig had come forward an hour ago and urged him to let John take over.

"Cocktails are ready at your fahvoreet tahbl' in the cornaire, Monsieur Wintairs."

He'd done his flawless imitation of the captain at the Four Seasons.

"For Christ's sake," Ted had snapped, "no more of your impersonations today. I don't need that now."

Craig had known enough not to argue when Ted decided to stay at the controls.

The runway was rushing toward them. Ted eased the nose of the plane up slightly. How much longer would he be free to fly planes, to travel, to have a drink or not have a drink, to function as a human being? The trial would begin next week. He didn't like his new lawyer. Henry Bartlett was too pompous, too conscious of his own image. Ted could imagine Bartlett in a *New Yorker* ad, holding up a bottle of Scotch, the caption reading, "This is the only brand I ever serve my guests."

The main wheels touched the ground. The impact inside the plane was almost unnoticeable. Ted threw the engines into reverse. "Nice landing, sir," John said quietly.

Wearily, Ted brushed his hand over his forehead. He wished he could get John over the habit of calling him "sir." He also wished he could get Henry Bartlett over the habit of calling him "Teddy." Did all criminal lawyers think that because you need their services, they have the right to be condescending? An interesting question. Had circumstances been different, he wouldn't have had anything to do with a man like Bartlett. But firing the man who was supposed to be the best defense lawyer in the country at a time when you're facing a long prison sentence wouldn't be smart. He had always thought of himself as smart. He wasn't so sure anymore.

A few minutes later, they were in a limousine heading for the Spa. "I've heard a lot about the Monterey Peninsula," Bartlett commented as they turned onto Highway 68. "I still don't see why we couldn't have worked on the case at your place in Connecticut or your New York apartment; but you're paying the bills."

"We're here because Ted needs the kind of relaxation he gets at Cypress Point," Craig said. He did not bother to hide the edge in his voice.

Ted was sitting on the right side of the roomy back seat, Henry beside him. Craig had taken the seat facing them, next to the bar. Craig raised the lid of the bar and mixed a martini. With a half-smile he handed it to Ted. "You know Min's rules about booze. You'd better drink up fast."

Ted shook his head. "I seem to remember another time when I drank up fast. Have you got a cold beer in there?"

"Teddy, I absolutely have to insist that you stop referring to that night in a way that suggests you don't have complete recall."

Ted turned to look directly at Henry Bartlett, absorbing the man's silver hair, his urbane manner, the faint hint of an English accent in his voice. "Let's get something straight," he said. "You are not, I repeat *not* to call me Teddy again. My name, in case you don't remember it from that very sizable retainer, is Andrew Edward Winters. I have always been called Ted. If you find that too difficult to remember, you may call me Andrew. My grandmother always did. Nod if you understand what I just said."

"Take it easy, Ted," Craig said quietly.

"I'll take it a lot easier if Henry and I establish a few ground rules."

He felt his hand grip the glass. He was unraveling. He could feel it. These months since the indictment, he'd managed to keep his sanity by staying at his place in Maui, doing his own analysis of urban expansion and population trends, designing hotels and stadiums and shopping centers he would build when all this was over. Somehow he'd managed to make himself believe that something would happen, that Elizabeth would realize she was wrong about the time of the phone call, that the so-called eyewitness would be declared mentally incompetent . . .

But Elizabeth was sticking to her story, the eyewitness was adamant about her testimony and the trial was looming. Ted had been shocked when he realized his first lawyer was virtually conceding a guilty verdict. That was when he had hired Henry Bartlett.

''All right, let's put this aside until later,'' Henry Bartlett said stiffly. He turned to Craig. ''If Ted doesn't want a drink, I do.''

Ted accepted the beer Craig held out to him and stared out the window. Was Bartlett right? Was it crazy to come here instead of just working from Connecticut or New York? But somehow whenever he was at the Spa, he had a sense of calm, of well-being. It came from all the summers he'd spent on the Monterey Peninsula when he was a kid.

The car stopped at the gate to Pebble Beach onto the Seventeenth Mile Drive, and the chauffeur paid the toll. The estate homes overlooking the ocean came into view. Once he had planned to buy a house here. He and Kathy had agreed it would be a good vacation place for Teddy. And then Teddy and Kathy were gone.

On the left side, the Pacific sparkled, clear and beautiful in the bright afternoon sun. It wasn't safe for swimming here—the undertow was too strong—but how good it would feel to dive in and let the salty water wash over him! He wondered if he would ever feel clean again, ever stop seeing those pictures of Leila's broken body. In his thoughts they were always there, gigantically enlarged, like billboards on a highway. And in these last few months, the doubts had begun.

''Quit thinking whatever you're thinking, Ted,'' Craig said mildly.

''And stop trying to read my thoughts,'' Ted snapped. Then he managed a weak smile. ''Sorry.''

''No problem.'' Craig's tone was hearty and genial.

Craig had always had a knack for defusing situations, Ted thought. They'd met at Dartmouth as freshmen. Craig had been chunky then. At seventeen, he'd looked like a big blond Swede. At thirty-four he was trim, the chunkiness hardened into solid muscle. The strong, heavy features were more becoming to a mature man than to a kid. Craig had had a partial scholarship to college but had worked his backside off at every job he could get—as a dishwasher in the kitchen, as a room clerk in the Hanover Inn, as an orderly in the local hospital.

And still he's always been around for me, Ted reminded himself. After college, he'd been surprised to bump into Craig in the washroom at the executive office of Winters Enterprises. ''Why didn't you ask *me* if you wanted a job here?'' He hadn't been sure he was pleased.

''Because if I'm any good, I'll make it on my own.''

You couldn't argue with that. And he'd made it, clear up to executive vice-president. If I go to prison, Ted thought, he gets to run the show. I wonder how often he thinks about that. A sense of disgust at his own mental processes washed over him. I think like a cornered rat. I *am* a cornered rat!

They drove past the Pebble Beach Lodge, the golf course, the Crocker Woodland, and the grounds of Cypress Point Spa came into view. "Pretty soon you'll understand why we wanted to come here," Craig told Henry. He looked directly at Ted. "We're going to put together an airtight defense. You know this place has always been lucky for you." Then, as he glanced out the side window, he stiffened. "Oh, my God, I don't believe it. The convertible—Cheryl and Syd are here!"

Grimly he turned to Henry Bartlett. "I'm beginning to think you're right. We should have gone to Connecticut."

CHAPTER 5

Min had assigned Elizabeth the bungalow where Leila had always stayed. It was one of the most expensive units, but Elizabeth was not sure that she was flattered. Everything in these rooms shouted Leila's name: the slipcovers in the shade of emerald green Leila loved, the deep armchair with the matching ottoman. Leila used to sprawl on that after a strenuous exercise class—"My God, Sparrow, if I keep this up they can measure me for a thin shroud"; the exquisite inlaid writing desk—"Sparrow, remember the furniture in poor Mama's place? Early Garage Sale."

In the short time Elizabeth had been with Min and Helmut, a maid had unpacked her bags. A blue tank suit and ivory terry-cloth robe were lying on the bed. Pinned to the robe was the schedule of her afternoon appointments: four o'clock, massage; five o'clock, facial.

The building housing the women's spa facilities was at one end of the Olympic pool—a rambling, self-contained one-story structure built to resemble a Spanish adobe. Placid from the outside, it was usually a whirlwind of activity within as women of all ages and shapes hurried along the tiled floors in terry-cloth robes, rushing to their next appointments.

Elizabeth braced herself to see familiar faces—some of the regulars who came to the Spa every three months or so and whom she had gotten to know well during her summers working here. She knew that inevitably condolences would be offered, heads shaken: "I never would have believed Ted Winters capable . . ."

But she did not see one single familiar face in the array of women padding from exercise classes to beauty treatments. Nor did the spa seem as busy as usual. At peak it accommodated about sixty women; the men's spa held about the same number. There were nothing like that many.

She reminded herself of the color coding of the doors: pink for facial rooms; yellow for massage; orchid for herbal wraps; white for steam cabinets; blue for sloofing. The exercise rooms were beyond the indoor pool and seemed to have been enlarged. There were more individual Jacuzzis in the central solarium. With a touch of disappointment, Elizabeth realized it was too late to soak in one of them for even a few minutes.

Tonight, she promised herself, she'd go for a long swim.

The masseuse who had been assigned to her was one of the old-timers. Small of frame but with powerful arms and hands, Gina was clearly delighted to see her. ''You're coming back to work here, I hope? Of course not. No such luck.''

The massage rooms had obviously been done over. Did Min ever stop spending money on this place? But the new tables were luxuriously padded, and under the expert hands of Gina she could feel herself begin to relax.

Gina was kneading her shoulder muscles. ''You're in knots.''

''I guess I am.''

''You have plenty of reason.''

Elizabeth knew that that was Gina's way of expressing her sympathy. She knew too that unless she began a conversation, Gina would be silent. One of Min's firm rules to her help was that if guests wanted to talk, it was all right to converse with them. ''But don't you be yakking about your own problems,'' Min would say at the weekly staff meetings. ''Nobody wants to hear them.''

It would be helpful to get Gina's impressions of how the Spa was doing. ''It doesn't seem to be too busy today,'' she suggested. ''Is everybody on the golf course?''

''I wish. Listen, this place hasn't been busy in nearly two years. Relax, Elizabeth, your arm feels like a board.''

''Two years! What's happened?''

''What can I say? It started with that stupid mausoleum. People don't pay these prices to look at mounds of dirt or listen to hammering. And that place still isn't finished. Will you tell me why they needed a Roman bath here?''

Elizabeth thought of Leila's remarks about the Roman bath. ''That's what Leila used to say.''

''She was right. I'll need to have you turn over now.'' Expertly the masseuse re-draped the sheet. ''And listen, you brought up her name. Do you realize how much glamour Leila gave this place? People wanted to be around her. They'd come here hoping to see her. She was a one-woman ad for the Spa. And she always talked about meeting Ted Winters here.

Now—I don't know. There's something so different. The Baron spends money like a maniac—you saw the new Jacuzzis. The interior work on that bathhouse goes on and on. And Min is trying to cut corners. It's a joke. He puts in a Roman bath, and she tells us not to waste towels!''

The facialist was new, a Japanese woman. The unwinding that had begun with the massage was completed by the warm mask she applied after the cleansing and steaming. Elizabeth drifted off to sleep. She was awakened by the woman's soft voice. ''Have you had a nice nap? I left you an extra forty minutes. You looked so peaceful, and I had plenty of time.''

CHAPTER 6

While the maid unpacked her bags, Alvirah Meehan investigated her new quarters. She went from room to room, her eyes darting about, missing nothing. In her mind she was composing what she would dictate into her brand-new recording machine.

''Will that be all, madame?''

The maid was at the door of the sitting room. ''Yes, thank you.'' Alvirah tried to imitate the tone of her Tuesday job, Mrs. Stevens. A little hoity-toity, but still friendly.

The minute the door closed behind the maid, she raced to get her recorder out of her voluminous pocketbook. The reporter from the *New York Globe* had taught her how to use it. She settled herself on the couch in the living room and began:

''Well, here I am at Cypress Point Spa and buh-lieve me it's the cat's meow. This is my first recording and I want to start by thanking Mr. Evans for his confidence in me. When he interviewed me and Willy about winning the lottery and I told him about my lifelong ambition to come to Cypress Point Spa, he said that I clearly have a sense of the dramatic and the *Globe* readers would love to know all about the goings-on in a classy spa from my point of view.

''He said that the kind of people I'll be meeting would never think of me as a writer and so I might hear a lot of interesting stuff. Then when I explained I'd been a real fan of movie stars all my life, and know lots about the private lives of the stars, he said he had a hunch I could write a good series of articles and who knows, maybe even a book.''

Alvirah smiled blissfully and smoothed the skirt of her purple-and-pink traveling dress. The skirt tended to hike up.

''A book,'' she continued, being careful to speak directly into the microphone. ''Me, Alvirah Meehan. But when you think of all the celebrities who write books and how many of them really stink, I believe I just might be able to do that.

''To get to what's happened so far, I rode in a limousine to the Spa with Elizabeth Lange. She is a lovely young woman and I feel so sorry for her. Her eyes are very sad, and you can tell she's under a big strain. She slept practically the whole way from San Francisco. Elizabeth is Leila LaSalle's sister, but very different in looks. Leila was a redhead with green eyes. She could look sexy and queenly at the same time—kind of like a cross between Dolly Parton and Greer Garson. I think a good way to describe Elizabeth is 'wholesome.'

''She's a little too thin; her shoulders are broad; she has wide blue eyes with dark lashes, and honey-colored hair that falls around her shoulders. She has strong, beautiful teeth, and the one time she smiled she gave off just the warmest glow. She's pretty tall—about five foot nine, I guess. I bet she sings. Her speaking voice is so pleasant, but not that exaggerated actressy voice you hear from so many of these young starlets. I guess you don't call them starlets anymore. Maybe if I get friendly with her, she'll tell me some interesting things about her sister and Ted Winters. I wonder if the *Globe* will want me to cover the trial.''

Alvirah paused, pushed the rewind button and then the replay. It was all right. The machine was working. She thought she ought to say something about her surroundings.

''Mrs. von Schreiber escorted me to my bungalow. I almost laughed out loud when she called it a bungalow. We used to rent a bungalow in Rockaway Beach on Ninety-ninth Street right near the amusement park. The place used to shake every time the roller coaster went down the last steep drop, which was every five minutes during the summer.

''This bungalow has a sitting room all done in light blue chintz and Oriental scatter rugs . . . they're handmade—I checked . . . a bedroom with a canopy bed, a small desk, a slipper chair, a bureau, a vanity table filled with cosmetics and lotions, and two huge bathrooms, each with its own Jacuzzi. There's also a room with built-in bookshelves, a real leather couch and chairs and an oval table. Upstairs there are two more bedrooms and baths, which of course I really don't need. Luxury! I keep pinching myself.

''Baroness von Schreiber told me that the day starts at seven A.M. with a brisk walk, which everyone in the Spa is requested to take. After that I will be served a low-calorie breakfast in my own dining room. The maid will also bring my personal daily schedule, which will include things like a facial, a massage, a herbal wrap, a sloofing treatment—whatever that is—the steam cabinet, a pedicure and a manicure and a hair treatment. Imagine! After I have been checked out by the doctor, they will add my exercise classes.

''Now I'm going to take a little rest, and then it will be time to dress for dinner. I'm going to wear my rainbow caftan, which I bought at

Martha's on Park Avenue. I showed it to the Baroness and she said it would be perfect, but not to wear the crystal beads I won at the shooting gallery in Coney Island.''

Alvirah turned off the recorder and beamed in satisfaction. Who ever said writing was hard? With a recorder it was a cinch. Recorder! Quickly, she got up and reached for her pocketbook. From inside a zippered compartment she took out a small box containing a sunburst pin.

But not just *any* sunburst pin, she thought proudly. This one had a microphone, and the editor had told her to wear it to record conversations. ''That way,'' he had explained, ''no one can claim you misquoted them later on.''

CHAPTER 7

''Sorry to do this to you, Ted, but we simply don't have the luxury of time.'' Henry Bartlett leaned back in the upholstered armchair at the end of the library table.

Ted was aware that his left temple was throbbing, and shafts of pain were finding a target behind and above his left eye. Deliberately he moved his head to avoid the streams of late-afternoon sun that were coming through the window opposite him.

They were in the study of Ted's bungalow in the Meadowcluster area, one of the two most expensive accommodations at Cypress Point Spa. Craig was sitting diagonally across from him, his face grave, his hazel eyes cloudy with worry.

Henry had wanted a conference before dinner. ''Time is running out,'' he had said, ''and until we decide on our final strategy, we can't make any progress.''

Twenty years in prison, Ted thought incredulously. That was the sentence he was facing. He'd be fifty-four years old when he got out. Incongruously, all the old gangster movies he'd used to watch late at night sprang into his mind. Steel bars, tough prison guards, Jimmy Cagney starring as a mad-dog killer. He used to revel in them.

''We have two ways we can go,'' Henry Bartlett said. ''We can stick to your original story—''

''My *original* story,'' Ted snapped.

''Hear me out! You left Leila's apartment at about ten after nine. You went to your own apartment. You tried to phone Craig.'' He turned to Craig. ''It's a damn shame you didn't pick up the phone.''

''I was watching a program I wanted to see. The telephone recorder was on. I figured I'd call back anyone who left a message. And I can swear the phone rang at nine twenty, just as Ted says.''

''Why *didn't* you leave a message, Ted?''

''Because I hate talking to machines, and especially that one.'' His lips tightened. Craig's habit of talking like a Japanese houseboy on his recorder irritated Ted wildly.

''What were you calling Craig about, anyhow?''

''It's blurry. I was drunk. My impression is that I wanted to tell him I was taking off for a while.''

''That doesn't help us. Probably if you had reached him it wouldn't help us. Not unless he can back you up that you were talking to him at precisely nine thirty-one P.M.''

Craig slammed his hand on the table. ''Then I'll say it. I'm not in favor of lying under oath, but neither am I in favor of Ted getting railroaded for something he didn't do.''

''It's too late for that. You've already made a statement. You change it now and the situation gets worse.'' Bartlett skimmed the papers he had pulled from his briefcase. Ted got up and walked to the window. He had planned to go to the men's spa and work out for a while. But Bartlett had been insistent about this meeting. Already his freedom was being infringed.

How many times had he come to Cypress Point with Leila in their three-year relationship? Eight or ten probably. Leila had loved it here. She'd been amused by Min's bossiness, by the Baron's pretentiousness. She'd enjoyed long hikes along the cliffs. ''All right, Falcon, if you won't come with me, play your darn golf and I'll meet you at my pad later.'' That mischievous wink, the deliberate leer, her long, slender fingers running along his shoulders. ''God, Falcon, you do turn me on.'' Lying with her in his arms on the couch watching late-night movies. Her murmured ''Min knows better than to give us any of those damn narrow antiques of hers. She knows I like to cuddle with my fellow.'' It was here that he had found the Leila he loved; the Leila she herself wanted to be.

What was Bartlett saying? ''Either we attempt to flatly contradict Elizabeth Lange and the so-called eyewitness or we try to turn that testimony to our benefit.''

''How does one do that?'' God, I hate this man, Ted thought. Look at him sitting there, cool and comfortable. You'd think he was discussing a chess game, not the rest of my life. Irrational fury almost choked him. He had to get out of this spot. Even being in a room with someone he disliked gave him claustrophobia. How could he share a cell with another man for two or three decades? He couldn't. At any price, he couldn't do it.

''You have no memory of hailing the cab, of the ride to Connecticut.''

''Absolutely none.''

''Your last conscious memory of that evening. Tell me again: what was it?''

''I had been with Leila for several hours. She was hysterical. Kept accusing me of cheating on her.''

''Did you?''

''No.''

''Then why did she accuse you?''

''Leila was—terribly insecure. She'd had bad experiences with men. She had convinced herself she could never trust one. I thought I'd gotten her over that as far as our relationship was concerned, but every once in a while she'd throw a jealous fit.'' That scene in the apartment. Leila lunging at him, scratching his face; her wild accusations. His hands on her wrists, restraining her. What had he felt? Anger. Fury. And disgust.

''You tried to give her back the engagement ring?''

''Yes, and she refused it.''

''Then what happened?''

''Elizabeth phoned. Leila began sobbing into the phone and shouting at me to get out. I told her to put the phone down. I wanted to get to the bottom of what had brought all this on.

''I saw it was hopeless and left. I went to my own apartment. I think I changed my shirt. I tried to call Craig. I remember leaving the apartment. I don't remember anything else until the next day when I woke up in Connecticut.''

''Teddy, do you realize what the prosecutor will do to that story? Do you know how many cases are on record of people who kill in a fit of rage and then have a psychotic episode where they block it out? As your lawyer I have to tell you something: *That story stinks!* It's no defense. Sure, if it weren't for Elizabeth Lange there wouldn't be a problem. . . . Hell, there wouldn't even be a case. I could make mincemeat of that so-called eyewitness. She's a nut, a real off-the-wall nut. But with Elizabeth swearing you were in the apartment fighting with Leila at nine thirty, the nut becomes believable when she says you shoved Leila off the terrace at nine thirty-one.''

''Then what do we do about it?'' Craig asked.

''We gamble,'' Bartlett said. ''Ted agrees with Elizabeth's story. He now remembers going back upstairs. Leila was still hysterical. She slammed the phone down and ran to the terrace. Everybody who was in Elaine's the night before can testify to her emotional state. Her sister admits she had been drinking. She was despondent about her career. She had decided to break off her relationship with you. She felt washed up. She wouldn't be the first one to take a dive in that situation.''

Ted winced. A *dive.* Christ, were all lawyers so insensitive? And then the image came of Leila's broken body; the garish police pictures. He felt perspiration break out over his entire body.

But Craig looked hopeful. ''It might work. What that eyewitness saw was Ted struggling to *save* Leila, and when Leila fell, he blacked out. That's when he had the psychotic episode. *That* explains why he was almost incoherent in the cab.''

Ted stared through the window at the ocean. It was unusually calm now, but he knew the tide would soon be roaring in. The calm before the storm, he thought. Right now we're having a clinical discussion. In nine days I'll be in the courtroom. *The People of the State of New York* v. *Andrew Edward Winters III.* "There's one big hole in your theory," he said flatly. "If I admit I went back to that apartment and was on the terrace with Leila, I'm putting my head in a noose. If the jury decides I was in the process of killing her, I'll be found guilty of Murder Two."

"It's a chance you may have to take."

Ted came back to the table and began to stuff the open files into Bartlett's briefcase. His smile was not pleasant. "I'm not sure I can take that chance. There has to be a better solution, and at any cost I intend to find it. *I will not go to prison!*"

CHAPTER 8

Min sighed gustily. "That feels good. I swear, you've got better hands than any masseuse in this place."

Helmut leaned down and kissed her cheek. "*Liebchen,* I love touching you, even if it's only to ease your shoulders."

They were in their apartment, which covered the entire third floor of the main house. Min was seated at her dressing table wearing a loose kimono. She had unpinned her heavy raven-colored hair, and it fell below her shoulders. She looked at her reflection in the mirror. Today she was no ad for this place. Shadows under her eyes—how long since she'd had her eyes done? Five years? Something hard to accept was happening. She was fifty-nine years old. Until this last year she could have passed for ten years younger. No more.

Helmut was smiling at her in the mirror. Deliberately, he rested his chin on her head. His eyes were a shade of blue that always reminded her of the waters in the Adriatic Sea around Dubrovnik, where she had been born. The long, distinguished face with its picture-perfect tan was unlined, the dark brown sideburns untouched by gray. Helmut was fifteen years her junior. For the first years of their marriage it hadn't mattered. But now?

She had met him at the spa in Baden-Baden, after Samuel died. Five years of catering to that fussy old man had paid off. He'd left her twelve million dollars and this property.

She hadn't been stupid about Helmut's sudden attentiveness to her. No man becomes enamored of a woman fifteen years his senior unless there's something he wants. At first she had accepted his attentions cynically, but by the end of two weeks she had realized that she was becoming deeply

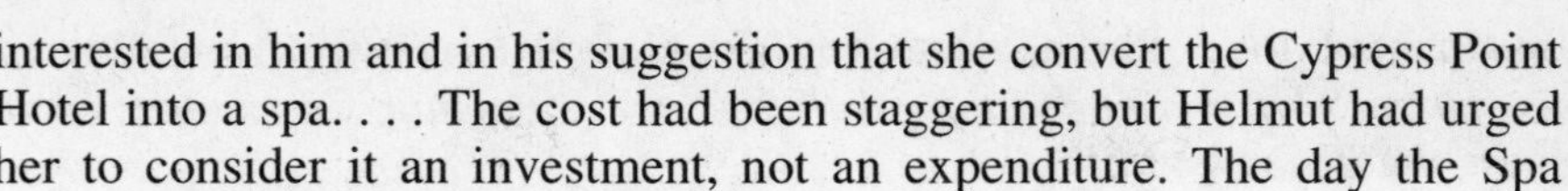

interested in him and in his suggestion that she convert the Cypress Point Hotel into a spa. . . . The cost had been staggering, but Helmut had urged her to consider it an investment, not an expenditure. The day the Spa opened, he had asked her to marry him.

She sighed heavily.

"Minna, what is it?"

How long had they been staring at each other in the mirror? "You know."

He bent down and kissed her cheek.

Incredibly, they'd been happy together. She had never dared tell him how much she loved him, instinctively afraid to hand him that weapon, always watching for signs of restlessness. But he ignored the young women who flirted with him. It was only Leila who had seemed to dazzle him, only Leila who had made her churn in an agony of fear. . . .

Perhaps she had been wrong. If one could believe him, Helmut had actually disliked Leila, even hated her. Leila had been openly contemptuous of him—but then, Leila had been contemptuous of every man she knew well. . . .

The shadows had become long in the room. The breeze from the sea was sharply cooler. Helmut reached his hands under her elbows. "Rest a little. You'll have to put up with the lot of them in less than an hour."

Min clutched his hand. "Helmut, how do you think she'll react?"

"Very badly."

"Don't tell me that," she wailed. "Helmut, you know why I have to try. It's our only chance."

CHAPTER 9

At seven o'clock, chimes from the main house announced the arrival of the "cocktail" hour, and immediately the paths to the main house became filled with people—singles, couples, groups of three or four. All were well dressed, in semiformal wear, the women in elegant caftans or flowing tunics, the men in blazers, slacks and sport shirts. Blazing gemstones were mixed with amusing costume pieces. Famous faces greeted each other warmly, or nodded distantly. Soft lights glowed on the veranda, where waiters in ivory-and-blue uniforms served delicate canapés and alcohol-free "cocktails."

Elizabeth decided to wear the dusty-pink silk jumpsuit with a magenta sash that had been Leila's last birthday present to her. Leila always wrote a note on her personal stationery. The note that had accompanied this outfit was tucked in the back of Elizabeth's wallet, a talisman of love. She'd written: *''It's a long, long way from May to December. Love and Happy Birthday to my darling Capricorn sister from the Taurus kid.''*

Somehow, wearing that outfit, rereading that note made it easier for Elizabeth to leave the bungalow and start up the path to the main house. She kept a half-smile on her face as she finally saw some of the regulars. Mrs. Lowell from Boston, who had been coming here since Min opened the place; Countess d'Aronne, the brittle, aging beauty, who was at last showing most of her seventy years. The Countess had been an eighteen-year-old bride when her much older husband was murdered. She'd married four times since then, but after every divorce petitioned the French courts to restore her former title.

''You look gorgeous. I helped Leila pick out that jumpsuit on Rodeo Drive.'' Min's voice boomed in her ear; Min's arm was solidly linked in hers. Elizabeth felt herself being propelled forward. A scent of the ocean mingled with the perfume of roses. The well-bred voices and laughter of the people on the veranda hummed around her. The background music was Serber playing Mendelssohn's *Concerto for Violin in E minor.* Leila would drop everything to attend a Serber concert.

A waiter offered her a choice of beverages—non-alcoholic wine or a soft drink. She chose the nonalcoholic wine. Leila had been cynical about Min's firm no-alcohol rule. *''Listen, Sparrow, half the people who go to that joint are boozers. They all bring some stuff with them, but even so they have to cut down a lot. So they lose some weight, and Min claims credit for the Spa. Don't you think the Baron keeps a supply in that study of his? You* bet *he does!''*

I should have gone to East Hampton, Elizabeth thought. Anywhere—anywhere but here. It was as if she were filled with a sense of Leila's presence, as if Leila were trying to reach her. . . .

''Elizabeth.'' Min's voice was sharp. Sharp, but also nervous, she realized. ''The Countess is talking to you.''

''I'm terribly sorry.'' Affectionately she reached out to grasp the aristocratic hand that was extended to her.

The Countess smiled warmly. ''I saw your last film. You're developing into a very fine actress, *chérie.*''

How like Countess d'Aronne to sense she would not want to discuss Leila. ''It was a good role. I was lucky.'' And then Elizabeth felt her eyes widen. ''Min, coming down the path. Isn't that Syd and Cheryl?''

''Yes. They just called this morning. I forgot to tell you. You don't mind that they're here?''

''Of course not. It's only . . .'' Her voice trailed off. She was still embarrassed over the way Leila had humiliated Syd that night in Elaine's. Syd had made Leila a star. No matter what mistakes he'd talked her into those last few years, they didn't stack up against the times he'd nailed down the parts she wanted. . . .

And Cheryl? Under the veneer of friendship, she and Leila had shared an intense professional and personal rivalry. Leila had taken Ted from Cheryl. Cheryl had almost wrecked her career by stepping into Leila's play. . . .

Unconsciously, Elizabeth straightened her back. On the other hand, Syd had made a fortune off Leila's earnings. Cheryl had tried every trick in the book to get Ted back. If only she'd succeeded, Elizabeth thought, Leila might still be alive. . . .

They had spotted her. They both looked as surprised as she felt. The Countess murmured, "Not that dreadful tart, Cheryl Manning . . ."

They were coming up the steps toward her. Elizabeth studied Cheryl objectively. Her hair was a tangled web around her face. It was much darker than it had been the last time she had seen her, and very becoming. The last time? That had been at Leila's memorial service.

Reluctantly Elizabeth conceded to herself that Cheryl had never looked better. Her smile was dazzling; the famous amber-colored eyes assumed a tender expression. Her greeting would have fooled anyone who didn't know her. "Elizabeth, my darling, I never dreamed I'd see you here, but how wonderful! Has it gone fairly well?"

Then it was Syd's turn. Syd, with his cynical eyes and mournful face. She knew he'd put a million dollars of his own money into Leila's play—money he had probably borrowed. Leila had called him "the Dealer." *"Sure, he works hard for me, Sparrow, but that's because I make a lot of money for him. The day I quit being an asset to him, he'll walk over my dead body."*

Elizabeth felt a chill as Syd gave her a perfunctory show-business kiss. "You look good; I may have to steal you from your agent. I didn't expect to see you till next week."

Next week. Of course. The defense was probably going to use Cheryl and Syd to testify to Leila's emotional state that night in Elaine's.

"Are you filling in for one of the instructors?" Cheryl asked.

"Elizabeth is here because I invited her," Min snapped.

Elizabeth wondered why Min seemed so terribly nervous. Min's eyes were darting around, and her hand was still gripping Elizabeth's elbow as though she were afraid of losing her.

"Cocktails" were offered to the newcomers. Friends of the Countess drifted over to join them. The host of a famous talk show greeted Syd genially. "Next time you want us to book one of your clients, make sure he's sober."

"That one's never sober."

Then she heard a familiar voice coming from behind her, an astonished voice: "Elizabeth, what are you doing here?"

She turned and felt Craig's arms around her—the solid, dependable arms of the man who had rushed to her when he heard the news flash, who had stayed with her in Leila's apartment, listening as she babbled out her grief, who had helped her to answer the questions of the police, who had finally located Ted. . . .

She'd seen Craig three or four times in the last year. He'd look her up when she was filming. "I can't be in the same city without at least saying hello," he'd say. By tacit agreement they avoided discussing the impending trial, but they never got through a dinner without some reference to it. It was through Craig that she'd learned that Ted was staying in Maui, that he was jumpy and irritable, that he was practically ignoring business and out of touch with his friends. It was from Craig, inevitably, that she'd heard the question "Are you *sure?*"

The last time she'd seen him, she'd burst out, "How can anyone be sure of anything or anybody?" and asked him not to contact her again until after the trial. "I know where your loyalty has to be."

But what was he doing here now? She'd have thought he'd be with Ted preparing for the trial. And then as she stepped back from his embrace, she saw Ted coming up the steps of the veranda.

She felt her mouth go dry. Her arms and legs trembled; her heart beat so wildly she could hear its pounding in her ears. Somehow in these months she had managed to bar his image from her conscious mind, and in her nightmares, he was always shadowy—she'd seen only the murderous hands, pushing Leila over the railing, the merciless eyes watching her fall. . . .

Now he was walking up these stairs with his usual commanding presence. Andrew Edward Winters III, his dark hair contrasting with the white dinner jacket, his strong, even features deeply tanned, looking all the better for his self-imposed exile in Maui.

Outrage and hatred made Elizabeth want to lunge at him; to push him down those steps as he had pushed Leila, to scratch that composed, handsome face as Leila had scratched it, trying to save herself. The brackish taste of bile filled her mouth and she gulped, trying to fight back nausea.

"There he is!" Cheryl cried. In an instant she was sliding through the clusters of people on the veranda, her heels clattering, the scarf of her red silk evening pajamas trailed behind her. Conversation stopped, heads turned as she threw herself into Ted's arms.

Like a robot, Elizabeth stared down at them. It was as though she were looking through a kaleidoscope. Loose fragments of colors and impressions rotated before her. The white of Ted's jacket; the red of Cheryl's outfit; Ted's dark brown hair; his long, well-shaped hands holding Cheryl's shoulders as he tried to free himself.

At the grand jury hearing, Elizabeth remembered, she had brushed past him, filled with self-loathing that she had been so deceived, so taken in by his performance as Leila's grief-stricken fiancé. Now he glanced up, and she knew he had seen her. He looked shocked and dismayed—or was that just another act? Pulling his arm away from

Cheryl's clinging fingers, he came up the steps. Unable to move, she was dimly aware of the hushed silence of the people around them, the murmurs and laughter of those farther away who did not realize what was happening, of the last strains of the concerto, of the bouquet of fragrances from the flowers and ocean.

He looked older. The lines around his eyes and mouth that had appeared at the time of Leila's death had deepened and were now permanently etched on his face. Leila had loved him so, and he had killed her. A fresh passion of hatred surged through Elizabeth. All the intolerable pain, the awful sense of loss, the guilt that permeated her soul like a cancer because at the end she had failed Leila. This man was the cause of all of it.

''Elizabeth . . .''

How dare he speak to her? Shocked out of her immobility, she spun around, stumbled across the veranda and into the foyer. She heard the click of heels behind her. Min had followed her in. Elizabeth turned to her fiercely. ''Damn you, Min. What in hell do you think you're pulling?''

''In here.'' Min's head jerked toward the music room. She did not speak until she had closed the door behind them. ''Elizabeth, I know what I'm doing.''

''I don't.'' With an acute sense of betrayal, Elizabeth stared at Min. No *wonder* she had seemed nervous. And she was even more nervous now—she, who always seemed impervious to stress, who always gave off the commanding air of one who could change and resolve any problem, was actually trembling.

''Elizabeth, when I saw you in Venice, you told me yourself that something in you still couldn't believe Ted would hurt Leila. I don't care how it looks. I've known him longer than you—years longer. . . . You're making a mistake. Don't forget, I was in Elaine's that night too. Listen, Leila had gone crazy. There's no other way of saying it. And *you* knew it! You say you set your clock the next day. You were distraught about her. Are you so infallible that maybe you didn't set it wrong? When Leila was on the phone with you just before she died, were you watching the clock? Look at Ted these next few days as if he's a human being, not a monster. Think about how good he was to Leila.''

Min's face was impassioned. Her low, intense voice was more piercing than a scream. She grasped Elizabeth's arm. ''You're one of the most honest people I know. From the time you were a little girl you always told the truth. Can't you face the fact that your mistake means that Ted will rot in prison for the rest of his life?''

The melodious sound of chimes echoed through the room. Dinner was about to be served. Elizabeth put her hand on Min's wrist, forcing Min to release her. Incongruously, she remembered how a few minutes ago Ted had pulled away from Cheryl.

''Min, next week a jury will begin to decide who is telling the truth.

You think you can run everything, but you're out of your element this time. . . . Get someone to call me a taxi."

"Elizabeth, you can't leave!"

"Can't I? Do you have a number where I can reach Sammy?"

"No."

"Exactly when is she expected back?"

"Tomorrow night after dinner." Min clasped her hands beseechingly. "Elizabeth, I beg you."

From behind her, Elizabeth heard the door open. She whirled around. Helmut was in the doorway. He put his hands on her arms in a gesture that both embraced and restrained her. "Elizabeth." His voice was soft and urgent. "I tried to warn Minna. She had the crazy idea that if you saw Ted you would think of all the happy times, would remember how much he loved Leila. I implored her not to do this. Ted is as shocked and upset as you are."

"He should be. Will you please let go of me!"

Helmut's voice became soothing, pleading. "Elizabeth, next week is Labor Day. The Peninsula is alive with tourists. There are hundreds of college kids having one last fling before school opens. You could drive around half the night and not find a room. Stay here. Be comfortable. See Sammy tomorrow night, then go if you must."

It was true, Elizabeth thought. Carmel and Monterey were meccas for tourists in late August.

"Elizabeth, please." Min was weeping. "I was so foolish. I thought, I believed that if you just saw Ted . . . not in court, but here . . . I'm sorry."

Elizabeth felt her anger drain away, to be replaced by bone-weary emptiness. Min was Min. Incongruously, she remembered the time Min had sent a reluctant Leila to a casting for a cosmetics commercial. Min had stormed, "Listen, Leila, I don't need you to tell me they didn't ask to see you. Get over there. Force your way in. You're just what they're looking for. You make your breaks in this world."

Leila got the job and became the model the cosmetic company used in all its commercials for the next three years.

Elizabeth shrugged. "Which dining room will Ted be in?"

"The Cypress Room," Helmut answered hopefully.

"Syd? Cheryl?"

"The same."

"Where did you plan to put me?"

"With us as well. But the Countess sends her love and asks you to join her table in the Ocean Room."

"All right. I'll stay over till I see Sammy." Elizabeth looked sternly at Min, who seemed almost to cringe. "Min, I'm the one who's warning *you* now," she said. "Ted is the man who killed my sister. Don't dare try to arrange any more 'accidental' meetings between him and me."

CHAPTER 10

Five years before, in an attempt to resolve the vociferous differences between smokers and nonsmokers, Min had divided the spacious dining room into two areas, separating them by a glass wall. The Cypress Room was for nonsmokers only; the Ocean Room accommodated both. The seating was open, except for the guests who were invited to share Min and Helmut's table. When Elizabeth stood at the door of the Ocean Room, she was waved to a table by Countess d'Aronne. The problem, she soon realized, was that from her seat she had an unbroken view of Min's table in the other room. It was with a sense of *déjà vu* that she saw them all sitting together: Min, Helmut, Syd, Cheryl, Ted, Craig.

The two other people at Min's table were Mrs. Meehan, the lottery winner, and a distinguished-looking older man. Several times she caught him glancing over at her.

Somehow she got through the dinner, managing to nibble at the chop and salad, to make some attempts at conversation with the Countess and her friends. But as though drawn to a magnet, she found herself again and again watching Ted.

The Countess noticed it, naturally. ''Despite everything he looks quite wonderful, doesn't he? Oh, I'm sorry, my dear. I made a pact with myself not to mention him at all. It's just that you do realize I've known Ted since he was a little boy. His grandparents used to bring him here, when this place was a hotel.''

As always, even among celebrities, Ted was the center of attention. Everything he did was effortless, Elizabeth thought—the attentive bend of his head toward Mrs. Meehan, the easy smile for the people who came to his table to greet him, the way he allowed Cheryl to slip her hand into his, then managed to disengage it casually. It was a relief to see him and Craig and the older man leave the table early.

She did not linger for the coffee that was served in the music room. Instead, she slipped out onto the veranda and down the path to her bungalow. The mist had blown off, and stars were brilliant in the dark night sky. The crashing and pounding of the surf blended with the faint sounds of the cello. There was always a musical program after dinner.

An intense sense of isolation came over Elizabeth, an indefinable sadness that was beyond Leila's death, beyond the incongruity of the company of these people who had been so much a part of her life. Syd, Cheryl, Min. She'd known them since she was the eight-year-old Miss Tag Along. The Baron. Craig. Ted.

They went back a long way, these people whom she had considered close friends and who had now closed ranks on her, who sympathized with Leila's murderer, who would come to New York to testify for him. . . .

When she reached her bungalow, Elizabeth hesitated and then decided to sit outside for a while. The veranda furniture was comfortable—a padded sofa swing and matching deck chairs. She settled on a corner of the sofa and, with one foot against the floor, set it moving. Here in the almost-dark, she could see the lights of the big house and quietly think about the people who had incongruously been gathered here tonight.

Gathered at whose request?

And why?

CHAPTER 11

"For a nine-hundred-calorie dinner, it wasn't bad." Henry Bartlett came from his bungalow carrying a handsome leather case. He placed it on the table in Ted's sitting room and opened it, revealing a portable mini-bar. He reached for the Courvoisier and brandy snifters. "Gentlemen?"

Craig nodded assent. Ted shook his head. "I think you should know that one of the firm rules of this spa is no liquor."

"When I—or should I say *you?*—pay over seven hundred dollars a day for me to be at this place, I decide what I drink."

He poured a generous amount into the two glasses, handed one to Craig and walked over to the sliding glass doors. A full, creamy moon and a galaxy of brilliant silver stars lighted the inky darkness of the ocean; the crescendo of the waves attested to the awesome power of the surf. "I'll never know why Balboa called this the *Pacific* Ocean," Bartlett commented. "Not when you hear that sound coming from it." He turned to Ted. "Having Elizabeth Lange here could be the break of the century for you. She's an interesting girl."

Ted waited. Craig turned the stem of the glass in his hand. Bartlett looked reflective. "Interesting in a lot of ways, and most particularly for something neither one of you could have seen. Every expression in the gamut marched across her face when she saw you, Teddy. Sadness. Uncertainty. Hatred. She's been doing a lot of thinking, and my guess is that something in her is saying two plus two doesn't equal five."

"You don't know what you're talking about," Craig said flatly.

Henry pushed open the sliding glass door. Now the crescendo of the ocean became a roar. "Hear that?" he asked. "Makes it kind of hard to concentrate, doesn't it? You're paying me a lot of money to get Ted out of this mess. One of the best ways to do it is to know what I'm up against and what I have going for me."

A sharply cool gust of air interrupted him. Quickly he pulled the door shut and walked back to the table. "We were very fortunate the way the seating worked out. I spent a good part of the dinner studying Elizabeth

Lange. Facial expressions and body language tell a lot. She never took her eyes off you, Teddy. If ever a woman was caught in a love-hate situation, she's it. Now my job is to figure out how we can make it work for you.''

CHAPTER 12

Syd walked an unnaturally silent Cheryl back to her bungalow. He knew that dinner had been an ordeal for her. She'd never gotten over losing Ted Winters to Leila. Now it must absolutely gall her that even with Leila out of the way, Ted wouldn't respond to her. In a crazy way, that lottery winner had been a good diversion for Cheryl. Alvirah Meehan knew all about the series, told her she was perfect for the role of Amanda. ''You know how sometimes you can just see a star in a role,'' Alvirah had said. ''I read *Till Tomorrow* when it was in paperback, and I said, 'Willy, that would make a great television series, and only one person in the world should play Amanda, and that's Cheryl Manning.' '' Of course, it was unfortunate she had also told Cheryl that Leila was her favorite actress in the whole world.

They were walking along the highest point of the property back to Cheryl's bungalow. The paths were lighted with ground-level Japanese lanterns which threw shadows on the cypress trees. The night was sparkling with stars, but the weather was supposed to change, and already the air was carrying the touch of dampness that preceded a typical Monterey Peninsula fog. Unlike the people who considered Pebble Beach the nearest spot to heaven, Syd had always felt somewhat uncomfortable around cypress trees, with their crazy twisted shapes. No wonder some poet had compared them to ghosts. He shivered.

Matter-of-factly, he took Cheryl's arm as they turned from the main path to her bungalow. Still he waited for her to begin to talk, but she remained silent. He consoled himself with the thought that he'd had enough of her moods anyway for one day; but when he started to say good night, she interrupted him: ''Come inside.''

Groaning to himself, he followed her in. She wasn't ready to quit on him yet. ''Where's the vodka?'' he asked.

''Locked in my jewelry case. It's the only place these damn maids don't check for booze.'' She tossed him the key and settled herself on the striped satin couch. He poured vodka on ice for the two of them, handed her a glass and sat down opposite her, sipping his drink, watching her make a production out of tasting hers. Finally she looked squarely at him. ''What did you think about tonight?''

''I'm not sure I get your meaning.''

She looked scornful. "Of course you do. When Ted drops his guard, he looks haunted. It's obvious Craig is worried sick. Min and the Baron make me think of a pair of high-wire acrobats on a slippery rope. That lawyer never took his eyes off Elizabeth, and *she* was spying on our table all night. I've always suspected she had a case on Ted. As for that crazy lottery winner—if Min puts me next to her tomorrow night, I'll *strangle* her!"

"The hell you will! Listen, Cheryl, you may get the part. Great. There's still always the chance the series will die in the ratings. A slight chance, I grant you, but a chance. If that happens, you're going to need a movie role. There are plenty of them around, but movies need backing. That lady's gonna have a lot of bucks for investment capital. Keep smiling at her."

Cheryl's eyes narrowed. "Ted could be talked into financing a movie for me. I know he could. He told me it wasn't fair that I was stuck with the play last year."

"Get this straight: Craig is a lot more cautious than Ted. If Ted goes to prison, he'll run the show. And another thing. You're crazy if you think Elizabeth has the hots for Ted. If she did, why the hell would she be putting a noose around his neck? All she has to do is say she was wrong about the time and how wonderful Ted was to Leila. Period. Case dismissed."

Cheryl finished her drink and imperiously held out her empty glass. Silently, Syd got up, refilled it and added a generous splash of vodka to his own. "Men are too dumb to see," Cheryl told him as he placed the drink in front of her. "You remember the kind of kid Elizabeth was. Polite, but if you asked her a direct question, you got a direct answer. And she never made excuses. She just doesn't know *how* to lie. She'd never lie for herself, and unfortunately she won't lie for Ted. But before this is over she's going to look under stones to try to find some sort of positive proof of what happened that night. That can make her very dangerous.

"Something else, Syd. You heard that nutty Alvirah Meehan say she read in a fan magazine that Leila LaSalle's apartment was like a motel? That Leila gave out keys to all her friends in case they wanted to stay over?"

Cheryl got up from the couch, walked over to Syd, sat beside him and put her hands on his knees. "*You* had a key to the apartment, didn't you, Syd?"

"So did you."

"I know it. Leila got a kick out of patronizing me, knowing I couldn't afford one room in that building, never mind a duplex. But when she died, the bartender in the Jockey Club can testify I was lingering over a drink. My dinner date was late. *You* were my dinner date, Syd, dear. How much did you put up for that goddamn play?"

Syd felt his knuckles harden and hoped that Cheryl could not feel the instant rigidity of his body. ''What are you driving at?''

''The afternoon before Leila died, you told me you were going to see Leila, to beg her to reconsider. You had at least a million tied up in that play. Your million or borrowed money, Syd? You shoved me into that disaster as a replacement, just the way you'd send a lamb to slaughter. Why? Because you were willing to risk *my* career on the faint chance that maybe the play could still work. And my memory has improved a lot. You're *always* on time. That night, you were fifteen minutes late. You came into the Jockey Club at nine forty-five. You were dead white. Your hands kept trembling. You spilled a drink on the table. Leila had died at nine thirty-one. Her apartment was less than a ten-minute walk from the Jockey Club.''

Cheryl put her hands on the sides of his face. ''Syd, I want that part. See that I get it. If I do, I promise you, drunk or sober, I'll never remember that you were late that night, that you looked terrible, that you had a key to Leila's apartment and that Leila had virtually driven you into bankruptcy. Now get the hell out of here. I need my beauty sleep.''

CHAPTER 13

Min and Helmut kept their smiles fixed and warm until they were safely in their own apartment. Then, wordlessly, they turned to each other. Helmut put his arms around Min. His lips brushed her cheeks. With practiced skill, his hands massaged her neck. ''*Liebchen.*''

''Helmut, was it as bad as I think?''

His voice was soft. ''Minna, I tried to warn you it would be a mistake to bring Elizabeth here, yes? You understand her. Now she's furious at you, but beyond that, something else has happened. Your back was to her at dinner, but I could see the way she was observing us from her table. It was as if she were seeing us for the first time.''

''I thought if she just *saw* Ted . . . You know how much she cared about him . . . I've always suspected that she was in love with him herself.''

''I know what you thought. But it hasn't worked. So, no more about it tonight, Minna. Get into bed. I'm going to make a cup of hot milk for you, and give you a sleeping pill. Tomorrow you'll be your usual overbearing self.''

Min smiled wanly and allowed him to lead her toward the bedroom. His arm was still around her; she was half-leaning against him. Her head fitted into the crook of his shoulder. After ten years she still loved the scent of him, the hint of expensive cologne, the feel of his superbly tailored jacket. In his arms, she could forget about his predecessor, with his cold hands and his petulance.

When Helmut returned with the hot milk, she was propped up in bed, silken pillows framing her loosened hair. She knew the rose-tinted shade on the night table threw a flattering glow on her high cheekbones and dark eyes. The appreciation she saw in her husband's eyes when he handed her the delicate Limoges cup was gratifying. *''Liebchen,''* he whispered, ''I wish you knew how I feel about you. After all this time, you still don't trust that feeling, do you?''

Seize the moment. She had to do it. ''Helmut, something is terribly wrong, something you haven't told me. What is it?''

He shrugged. ''You know what's wrong. Spas are springing up all over the country. The rich are restless people, fickle. . . . The cost of the Roman bath has exceeded my expectation—I admit it. . . . Nevertheless, I am sure that when we finally open it—''

''Helmut, promise me one thing. No matter what, we won't touch the Swiss account. I'd rather let this place go. At my age, I can't be broke again.'' Min tried to keep her voice from rising.

''We won't touch it, Minna. I promise.'' He handed her the sleeping pill. ''So. As your husband . . . as a doctor . . . I *order* you to swallow this, immediately.''

''I'll take it, gladly.''

He sat on the edge of the bed as she sipped the milk. ''Aren't you coming to bed?'' Her voice was drowsy.

''Not yet. I'll read for a bit. That's my sleeping pill.''

After he turned out the light and left the room, Min felt herself drifting off to sleep. Her last conscious thought became an inaudible whisper. ''Helmut,'' she pleaded, ''what are you hiding from me?''

CHAPTER 14

At quarter of ten Elizabeth saw the guests begin to stream from the main house. She knew that in a few minutes the whole place would be silent, curtains drawn, lights extinguished. The day began early at the Spa. After the strenuous exercise classes and the relaxing beauty treatments, most people were more than ready to retire by ten o'clock.

She sighed when she saw one figure leave the main path and turn in her direction. Instinctively she knew it was Mrs. Meehan.

''I thought you might be a little lonesome,'' Alvirah said as, uninvited, she settled herself on one of the deck chairs. ''Wasn't dinner good? You'd never guess you were counting calories, would you? Buh-lieve me, I wouldn't weigh one hundred and sixty-five pounds if I'd eaten like this all my life.''

She rearranged the shawl on her shoulders. ''This thing keeps slipping.'' She looked around. ''It's a beautiful night, isn't it? All those stars. I guess they don't have as much pollution here as in Queens. And the ocean. I love that sound. What was I saying? Oh, yes—dinner. You could have knocked me over when the waiter—or was he a butler?—put that tray in front of me, with the spoon and fork. You know, at home we just kind of dig *in.* I mean who needs a spoon *and* fork to get at string beans, or an itsy-bitsy lamb chop? But then I remembered the way Greer Garson helped herself from the fancy silver platter in *Valley of Decision,* and I was okay. You can always count on the movies.''

Unwillingly, Elizabeth smiled. There was something so genuinely honest about Alvirah Meehan. Honesty was a rare commodity at the Spa. ''I'm sure you did fine.''

Alvirah fiddled with her sunburst pin. ''To tell the truth, I couldn't take my eyes off Ted Winters. I was all set to hate him, but he was so *nice* to me. Boy, was I surprised at how snippy that Cheryl Manning is. She certainly hated Leila, didn't she?''

Elizabeth moistened her lips. ''What makes you think that?''

''I just happened to say at dinner that I thought Leila would become a legend like Marilyn Monroe, and *she* said that if it's still fashionable to consider a washed-up drunk a legend, Leila just might make it.'' Alvirah felt a pang of regret at having to tell this to Leila's sister. But as she'd always read, a good reporter gets the story.

''How did the others respond to that?'' Elizabeth asked quietly.

''They all laughed, except Ted Winters. He said that was a sickening thing to say.''

''You can't mean Min and Craig thought it was funny?''

''It's hard to be sure,'' Alvirah said hastily. ''Sometimes people laugh when they're embarrassed. But even that lawyer who's with Ted Winters said something like it's pretty clear Leila wouldn't win any popularity contests around here.''

Elizabeth stood up. ''It was nice of you to drop by, Mrs. Meehan. I'm afraid I have to change now. I always like to take a swim before I go to bed.''

''I know. They talked about that at the table. Craig—is that his name, Mr. Winters' assistant—?''

''Yes.''

''He asked the Baroness how long you were going to stay. She told him probably until day after tomorrow because you were waiting to see someone named Sammy.''

''That's right.''

"And Syd Melnick said that he has a hunch you're going to avoid all of them. Then the Baroness said that the one place you can always find Elizabeth is swimming in the Olympic pool around ten o'clock at night. I guess she was right."

"She knows I like to swim. Do you know your way to your cottage, Mrs. Meehan? If not, I'll walk with you. It can be confusing in the dark."

"No, I'm fine. I enjoyed talking to you." Alvirah pulled herself up from the chair and, ignoring the path, began to cut across the lawn to her bungalow. She was disappointed that Elizabeth hadn't said anything that would be helpful for her articles. But on the other hand, she had gotten a lot of material at dinner. She certainly could do a meaty article on jealousy!

Wouldn't the reading public be interested to hear that Leila LaSalle's very best friends all acted as if they were glad she was dead!

CHAPTER 15

Carefully, he drew the shades and extinguished the lights. He was frantic to hurry. It might already be too late, but there was no way he could have ventured out before now. When he opened the outside door, he shivered for a moment. The air had become chilly, and he was wearing only swim trunks and a dark T-shirt.

The grounds were quiet, lighted only by the now-dimmed lanterns along the footpaths and in the trees. It was easy to stay hidden in the shadows as he hurried toward the Olympic pool. Would she still be there?

The change in wind had caused a mist to blow in from the sea. In minutes, the stars had been covered by clouds, the moon had disappeared. Even if anyone happened to stand at a window and look out, he would not be seen.

Elizabeth planned to stay at the Spa until she saw Sammy tomorrow night. That gave him only a day and a half—until Tuesday morning—to arrange her death.

He stopped at the shrubbery that edged the patio around the Olympic pool. In the darkness he could barely see Elizabeth's moving form as she swam with swift, sure strokes from one end of the pool to the other. Carefully, he calculated his chance of success. The idea had come to him when Min said Elizabeth was always in this pool around ten o'clock. Even strong swimmers have accidents. A sudden cramp, no one within hearing distance if she cried out, no marks, no signs of struggle . . . His plan was to slip into the pool when she was almost at the opposite end, wait and pounce on her as she passed him, hold her down until she stopped struggling. Now, he edged his way from behind the shrubbery. It was dark enough to risk a closer look.

He had forgotten how fast she swam. Though she was so slender, the muscles in her arms were like steel. Suppose she was able to fight long enough to attract attention? And she was probably wearing one of those damn whistles Min insisted lone swimmers put on.

His eyes narrowed in anger and frustration as he crouched nearer and nearer the edge of the pool, ready to spring, not sure if this was the precisely right moment. She was a faster swimmer than he was. In the water she might have the advantage over him. . . .

He could not afford to make a second mistake.

In Aqua santinas. The Romans had chiseled the motto into the walls of their bathhouses. If I believed in reincarnation, I would think I had lived in those times, Elizabeth thought as she glided across the dark recess of the pool. When she had begun to swim, it had been possible to see not only the perimeter of the pool, but the surrounding area with its lounge chairs and umbrella tables and flowering hedges. Now they were only dark silhouettes.

The persistent headache she'd had all evening began to ebb, the sense of enclosure faded; once again she began to experience the release she had always found in water. "Do you think it started in the womb?" she'd once joked to Leila. "I mean this absolute sensation of being free when I'm immersed."

Leila's answer had shocked her: "Maybe Mama was happy when she was carrying you, Sparrow. I've always thought that your father was Senator Lange. He and Mama had a big thing going after my daddy-dear split the scene. When *I* was in the womb, I gather they called me 'the mistake.' "

It was Leila who had suggested that Elizabeth use the stage name *Lange*. "It probably should be your real name, Sparrow," she had said. "Why not?"

As soon as Leila began making money, she had sent a check to Mama every month. One day the check was returned uncashed by Mama's last boyfriend. Mama had died of acute alcoholism.

Elizabeth touched the far wall, brought her knees to her chest and flipped her body over, changing from a backstroke to a breaststroke in one fluid movement. Was it possible that Leila's fear of personal relationships had begun at the moment of conception? Can a speck of protoplasm sense that the climate is hostile, and can that realization color a whole life? Wasn't it because of Leila that she'd never experienced that terrible sense of parental rejection? She remembered her mother's description of bringing her home from the hospital: "Leila took her out of my arms. She moved the crib into her room. She was only eleven, but she became that child's mother. I wanted to call her Laverne, but Leila put her foot down.

She said, *'Her name is Elizabeth!'* " One more reason to be grateful to Leila, Elizabeth thought.

The soft ripple that her body made as she moved through the water masked the faint sound of footsteps at the other end of the pool. She had reached the north end and was starting back. For some reason she began to swim furiously, as though sensing danger.

The shadowy figure edged its way along the wall. He coldly calculated the speed of her swift, graceful progress. Timing was essential. Grab her from behind as she passed, lie over her body, hold her face in the water until she stopped struggling. How long would it take? A minute? Two? But suppose she wasn't that easy to subdue? This had to appear to be an accidental drowning.

Then an idea came to him, and in the darkness his lips stretched in the semblance of a smile. Why hadn't he thought of the scuba equipment earlier? Wearing the oxygen tank would make it possible for him to hold her at the bottom of the pool until he was certain she was dead. The wet suit, the gloves, the mask, the goggles were a perfect disguise, if anyone happened to see him cutting across the grounds.

He watched as she began to swim toward the steps. The impulse to get rid of her now *was almost overwhelming. Tomorrow night, he promised himself. Carefully he moved closer as she placed her foot on the bottom step of the ladder and straightened up. His narrowed eyes strained to watch as she slipped on her robe and began to walk along the path to her bungalow.*

Tomorrow night he would be waiting here for her. The next morning someone would spot her body at the bottom of the pool, as the workman had spotted Leila's body in the courtyard.

And he would have nothing left to fear.

Monday, August 31

QUOTE FOR THE DAY:
A witty woman is a treasure; a witty beauty is a power.
—George Meredith

Good morning, dear guests,

We hope you have slept blissfully. The weatherman promises us yet another beautiful Cypress Point Spa day.

A little reminder. Some of us are forgetting to fill out our luncheon menu. We don't want you to have to wait for service after all that vigorous exercise and delicious pampering of the morning. So do please take a tiny moment to circle your choices before you leave your room now.

In just a moment, we'll be greeting you on our morning walk. Hurry and join us.

And remember, another day at Cypress Point Spa means another set of dazzling hours dedicated to making you a more beautiful person, the kind of person people long to be with, to touch, to love.

Baron and Baroness Helmut von Schreiber

CHAPTER 1

Elizabeth woke long before dawn on Monday morning. Even the swim had not performed its usual magic. For what seemed most of the night, she had been troubled with broken dreams, fragments that came and went intermittently. They were all in the dreams: Mama, Leila, Ted, Craig, Syd, Cheryl, Sammy, Min, Helmut—even Leila's two husbands, those transitory charlatans who had used her success to get themselves into the spotlight: the first an actor, the second a would-be producer and socialite. . . .

At six o'clock she got out of bed, pulled up the shade, then huddled back under the light covers. It was chilly, but she loved to watch the sun come up. It seemed to her that the early morning had a dreamy quality of its own, the human quiet was so absolute. The only sounds came from the seabirds along the shore.

At six thirty there was a tap on the door. Vicky, the maid who brought in the wake-up glass of juice, had been with the Spa for years. She was a sturdy sixty-year-old woman who supplemented her husband's pension by what she sardonically called ''carrying breakfast roses to fading blossoms.'' They greeted each other with the warmth of old friends.

''It feels strange to be on the guest end of the place,'' Elizabeth commented.

''You earned your right to be here. I saw you in *Hilltop.* You're a damn good actress.''

''I feel surer of myself teaching water aerobics.''

''And Princess Di can always get a job teaching kindergarten. Come off it.''

She deliberately waited until she was sure that the daily procession called The Cypress Hike was in progress. By the time she went out, the marchers, led by Min and the Baron, were already nearing the path that led to the coast. The hike took in the Spa property, the Crocker wooded preserve and Cypress Point, wound past the Pebble Beach golf course, circled the Lodge and backtracked to the Spa. In all, it was a brisk fifty-minute exercise, followed by breakfast.

Elizabeth waited until the hikers were out of sight before she began jogging in the opposite direction from them. It was still early, and traffic was light. She would have preferred to run along the coast, where she could have an unbroken view of the ocean, but that would have meant risking being noticed by the others.

If only Sammy were back, she thought as she began to quicken her pace. I could talk to her and be on a plane this afternoon. She wanted to get away from here. If Alvirah Meehan was to be believed, Cheryl had called Leila a ''washed-up drunk'' last night. And except for Ted, her murderer, everyone else had laughed.

Min, Helmut, Syd, Cheryl, Craig, Ted. The people who had been closest to Leila; the weeping mourners at her memorial service. Oh, Leila! Elizabeth thought. Incongruously, lines from a song she had learned as a child came back to her.

Though all the world betray thee,
One sword at least thy rights shall guard,
One faithful heart shall praise thee.

I'll sing your praises, Leila! Tears stung her eyes, and she dabbed at them impatiently. She began to jog faster, as if to outrun her thoughts. The early-morning mist was being burned away by the sun; the thick shrubbery that bordered the homes along the road was bathed in morning dew; the sea gulls arced overhead and swooped back to the shore. How accurate a witness was Alvirah Meehan? There was something oddly intense about the woman, something that went beyond her excitement at being here.

She was passing the Pebble Beach golf links. Early golfers were already on the course. She had taken up golf in college. Leila had never played. She used to tell Ted that someday she'd make time to learn. She never would have, Elizabeth thought, and a smile touched her lips; Leila was too impatient to traipse after a ball for four or five hours. . . .

Her breath was coming in gulps, and she slowed her pace. I'm out of shape, she thought. Today she would go to the women's spa and take a full schedule of exercises and treatments. It would be a useful way to pass the time. She turned down the road that led back to the Spa—and collided with Ted.

He grasped her arms to keep her from falling. Gasping at the force of the impact, she struggled to push him away from her. ''Let go of me.'' Her voice rose. *''I said, let go of me.''* She was aware that there was no one else on the road. He was perspiring, his T-shirt clinging to his body. The expensive watch Leila had given him glistened in the sun.

He released her. Stunned and frightened, she watched as he stared down at her, his expression inscrutable. ''Elizabeth, I've got to talk to you.''

He wasn't even going to pretend he hadn't planned this.

"Say what you have to say in court." She tried to pass him, but he blocked her way. Inadvertently she stepped back. Was this what Leila had felt at the end: this sense of being trapped?

"I said listen to me." It seemed that he had sensed her fear and was infuriated by it.

"Elizabeth, you haven't given me a chance. I know how it looks. Maybe—and this is something I just don't know—*maybe* you're right, and I went back upstairs. I *was* drunk and angry, but I was also terribly worried about Leila. Elizabeth, think about this: if you are right, if I did go back up, if that woman is right who says she saw me struggling with Leila, won't you at least grant that I might have been trying to *save* her? You know how depressed Leila was that day. She was almost out of her mind."

"*If* you went back upstairs. Are you telling me now that you're willing to concede you went back upstairs?" Elizabeth felt as though her lungs were closing. The air seemed suddenly humid and heavy with the scent of still-damp cypress leaves and moist earth. Ted was just over six feet tall, but the three-inch difference in their heights seemed to disappear as they stared at each other. She was aware again of the intensity of the lines that seared the skin around his eyes and mouth.

"Elizabeth, I know how you must feel about me, but there is something you *have* to understand. I don't remember what happened that night. I was so damn drunk; so damn upset. Over these months I've begun to have some vague impression of being at the door of Leila's apartment, of pushing it open. So maybe you're right, maybe you *did* hear me call something to her. *But I have absolutely no memory beyond that!* That is the truth as I know it. The next question: do you think, drunk or sober, that I'm capable of murder?"

His dark blue eyes were clouded with pain. He bit his lip and held his hands out imploringly. "Well, Elizabeth?"

In a quick move she darted around him and ran for the gates of the Spa. The district attorney had predicted this. If Ted didn't think he could lie his way out of being on the terrace with Leila, he would say he was trying to save her.

She didn't look back until she was at the gates. Ted had not attempted to follow her. He was standing where she had left him, staring after her, his hands on his hips.

Her arms were still burning from the force with which his hands had grabbed her. She remembered something else the district attorney had told her.

Without her as a witness, Ted would go free.

CHAPTER 2

At eight A.M., Dora ''Sammy'' Samuels backed her car out of her cousin Elsie's driveway and with a sigh of relief began the drive from the Napa Valley to the Monterey Peninsula. With any luck, she'd be there about two o'clock. Originally she'd planned to leave in the late afternoon, and Elsie had been openly annoyed that she'd changed her mind, but she was eager to get back to the Spa and go through the rest of the mailbags.

She was a wiry seventy-one-year-old woman with steel-gray hair pulled back in a neat bun. Old-fashioned rimless glasses sat on the bridge of her small, straight nose. It had been a year and a half since an aneurism had nearly killed her, and the massive surgery had left her with a permanent air of fragility, but until now she had always impatiently shaken off any talk of retirement.

It had been a disquieting weekend. Her cousin had always disapproved of Dora's job with Leila. ''Answering fan mail from vapid women'' was the way she put it. ''I should think with your brains, you'd find a better way to spend your time. Why don't you do volunteer teaching?''

Long ago, Dora had given up trying to explain to Elsie that after thirty-five years of teaching, she never wanted to see a textbook again, that the eight years she'd worked for Leila had been the most exciting of her own uneventful life.

This weekend had been particularly trying, because when Elsie saw her going through the sack of fan mail, she'd been astonished. ''You mean to tell me that seventeen months after that woman died, you're *still* writing to her fans? Are you crazy?''

No, she wasn't, Dora told herself as she drove well within the speed limit through the wine country. It was a hot, lazy day, but even so, busloads of sightseers were already passing her, heading for vineyard tours and wine-tasting parties.

She had not tried to explain to Elsie that sending personal notes to the people who had loved Leila was a way of assuaging her own sense of loss. She had also *not* told her cousin the reason why she had brought up the heavy sack of mail. She was searching to see if Leila had received other poison-pen letters than the one she had already found.

That one had been mailed three days before Leila died. The address on the envelope and the enclosed note were put together with words and phrases snipped from magazines and newspapers. It read:

Leila,

How many Times Do I Have to write? Can't YOU get it straight THAT Ted is sick OF You? His new girl is beautiful and much younger THaN you. I told you ThAT the emerald necklace HE gave Her matcHes the bracelet he gave you. It cost Twice as much And looks ten Times better. I hear your play is Lousy. You really should Learn your lines. I'll write again soon.

Your friend.

Thinking of that note, of the others that must have preceded it, brought a fresh burst of outrage. Leila, Leila, she whispered. Who would *do* that to you?

She of all people had understood Leila's terrible vulnerability, understood that her outward confidence, her flamboyant public image was the facade of a deeply insecure woman.

She remembered how Elizabeth had gone off to school just at the time she'd started working for Leila. She'd seen Leila come back from the airport, lonely, devastated, in tears. ''God, Sammy,'' she said. ''I can't believe I may not see Sparrow for months. But a Swiss boarding school! Won't that be a great experience for her? A big difference from Lumber Creek High, my alma mater.'' Then she said hesitantly, ''Sammy, I'm not doing anything tonight. Will you stay, and let's get something to eat?''

The years went by so quickly, Dora thought as another bus honked impatiently and passed her. Today, for some reason, the memory of Leila seemed particularly vivid to her: Leila with her wild extravagances, spending money as fast as she made it; Leila's two marriages. . . . Dora had begged her not to marry the second one. *''Haven't you learned your lesson yet?'' she pleaded. ''You can't afford another leech.''*

Leila with her arms hugging her knees. ''Sammy, he's not that bad. He makes me laugh, and that's a plus.''

If you want to laugh, hire a clown.''

Leila's fierce hug. ''Oh, Sammy, promise you'll always say it straight. You're probably right, but I guess I'll go through with it.''

Getting rid of the funnyman had cost her two million dollars.

Leila with Ted. ''Sammy, it can't last. Nobody's that wonderful. What does he see in me?''

''Are you crazy? Have you stopped looking in the mirror?''

Leila, always so apprehensive when she started a new film. ''Sammy, I stink in this part. I shouldn't have taken it. It's not me.''

''Come off it. I saw the dailies too. You're wonderful.''

She'd won the Oscar for that performance.

But in those last few years she had been miscast in three films. Her worry about her career became an obsession. Her love for Ted was equaled only by her fear of losing him. And then Syd had brought her the play. ''Sammy, I swear I don't have to act in this one. I just have to be me. I love it.''

Then it was over, Dora thought. In the end, each of us left her alone. I was sick, she told herself; Elizabeth was touring with her own play; Ted was constantly away on business. And someone who knew Leila well attacked her with those poison-pen letters, shattered that fragile ego, precipitated the drinking. . . .

Dora realized that her hands were trembling. She scanned the road for signs of a restaurant. Perhaps she would feel better if she stopped for a cup of tea. When she got to the Spa, she would begin going through the rest of the unopened mail.

She knew that Elizabeth would somehow find a way to trace the poison-pen mail back to its sender.

CHAPTER 3

When Elizabeth reached her bungalow, she found a note from Min pinned with her schedule to the terry-cloth robe folded on the bed. It read:

My dear Elizabeth,

I do hope that while you are here you will enjoy a day of treatment and exercise at the Spa. As you know, it is necessary that all new guests consult briefly with Helmut before beginning any activities. I have scheduled you for his first appointment.

Please know that your ultimate happiness and well-being are very important to me.

The letter had been written in Min's florid, sweeping penmanship. Quickly, Elizabeth scanned her schedule. Interview with Dr. Helmut von Schreiber at 8:45; aerobic dance class at 9; massage at 9:30; trampoline at 10; advanced water aerobics at 10:30—that had been the class she taught when she worked here; facial at 11; cypress curves 11:30; herbal wrap at noon. The afternoon schedule included a loofah, a manicure, a yoga class, a pedicure, two more water exercises . . .

She would have preferred to avoid seeing Helmut, but she didn't want to make an issue of it. Her interview with him was brief. He checked her pulse and blood pressure, then examined her skin under a strong light. "Your face is like a fine carving," he told her. "You are one of those fortunate women who will become more beautiful as you age. It's all in the bone structure."

Then, as if he were thinking aloud, he murmured, "Wildly lovely as Leila was, her beauty was the kind that peaks and begins to slip away. The last time she was here I suggested that she begin collagen treatments, and we had planned to do her eyes as well. Did you know that?"

"No." Elizabeth realized with a pang of regret that her reaction to the Baron's remark was to be hurt that Leila had not confided her plans to her. Or was he lying?

"I am sorry," Helmut said softly. "I should not have brought up her name. And if you wonder why she did not confide in you, I think you must realize that Leila had become very conscious of the three-year age difference between her and Ted. I was able to assure her honestly that it made no difference between people who love each other—after all, I should know—but even so, she had begun to worry. And to see you growing lovelier, as she began to find those small signs of age in herself, was a problem for her."

Elizabeth got up. Like all the other offices at the Spa, this one had the look of a well-appointed living room. The blue-and-green prints on the couches and chairs were cool and restful, the draperies tied back to allow the sunshine to stream in. The view included the putting green and the ocean.

She knew Helmut was studying her intently. His extravagant compliments were the sugar coating on a bitter pill. He was trying to make her believe that Leila had begun to consider her a competitor. But why? Remembering the hostility with which he had studied Leila's picture when he thought he was unobserved, she wondered if Helmut was viciously trying to get even for Leila's barbs by suggesting she had been beginning to lose her beauty.

Leila's face flashed in her mind: the lovely mouth; the dazzling smile; the emerald-green eyes; the glorious red hair, like a blazing fire around her shoulders. To steady herself, she pretended to be reading one of the framed ads about the Spa. One phrase caught her eye: *a butterfly floating on a cloud.* Why did it seem familiar?

The belt of her terry-cloth robe had loosened. As she tightened it, she turned to Helmut. "If one tenth of the women who spend a fortune in this place had even a fragment of Leila's looks, you'd be out of business, Baron."

He did not reply.

The women's spa was busier than it had been the previous afternoon, but certainly not at the level she remembered. Elizabeth went from exercise class to treatment, glad to really work out again, then equally glad to relax under the skillful hands of the masseuse or facialist. She encountered Cheryl several times in the ten-minute breaks between appointments. *A washed-up drunk.* She was barely civil to Cheryl, who didn't seem to notice. Cheryl acted preoccupied.

Why not? Ted was on the premises, and Cheryl was obviously still dazzled by him.

Alvirah Meehan was in the same aerobic dance class—a surprisingly agile Alvirah, with a good sense of rhythm. Why in the name of heaven did she wear that sunburst pin on her robe? Elizabeth noticed that Alvirah fiddled with the pin whenever she got into a conversation. She also noticed, with some amusement, Cheryl's unsuccessful efforts not to be cornered by Mrs. Meehan.

She went back to her own bungalow for lunch; she did not want to risk running into Ted again by lunching at one of the poolside tables. As she ate the fresh fruit salad and sipped the iced tea, she phoned the airline and changed her reservation. She could get a ten o'clock flight to New York from San Francisco the next morning.

She had been frantic to get out of New York. Now, with equal fervor, she wanted to be out of here.

She put on her robe and prepared to go back to the spa for the afternoon session. All morning she had tried to push Ted's face from her mind. Now it filled her vision again. Pain-racked. Angry. Imploring. Vengeful. What expression had she seen in it? And would she spend the rest of her life trying to escape it, after the trial—and the verdict?

CHAPTER 4

Alvirah collapsed on her bed with a grateful sigh. She was dying for a nap, but knew it was important to record her impressions while they were fresh in her mind. She propped herself on her pillows, reached for the recorder and began to speak.

"It is four o'clock and I am resting in my bungalow. I have finished my first full day of activities at the Spa and I must report I am absolutely exhausted. Go, go, go. We started with a hike; then I came back here and the maid brought in my schedule for the day on my breakfast tray. Breakfast was a poached egg on a couple of crumbs of whole-wheat toast and coffee. My schedule, which is on a tag that you tie to your robe, showed me as having two water aerobics classes, a yoga class, a facial, a massage, two dance classes, a warm hose treatment, fifteen minutes in the steam box and a whirlpool dip. . . .

"The water aerobics classes are very interesting. I push a beach ball around in the water, which sounds very easy, but now my shoulders hurt and I've got muscles in my thighs I didn't know existed. The yoga class wasn't bad except that I can't get my knees in the Lotus position. The dance exercise was fun. If I do say so myself I was always a good dancer, and even though this is just hopping from one foot to the other and doing a lot of kicking, I put some of the younger women to shame. Maybe I should have been a Rockette.

"The warm hose treatment is another word for crowd control. I mean they turn these powerful hoses on you while you're standing in the buff, and you hang on to a metal bar hoping you won't get washed away. But supposedly it breaks down fatty cells, and if so, I'm ready for two treatments a day.

"The clinic is a very interesting building. From the outside it looks just like the main house, but inside it's totally different. All the treatment rooms have private entrances, with high hedges leading to them. The idea is that people don't bump into each other coming and going for appointments. I mean, I really don't care that the whole world knows I'm going to have some collagen injections to fill out the lines around my mouth, but I can well understand why someone like Cheryl Manning would be very upset if that was general knowledge.

"I had my interview with Baron von Schreiber about my collagen injections this morning. The Baron is a charming man. So handsome, and the way he bowed over my hand made me very fluttery. If I were his wife, I think I'd be pretty nervous about holding him, especially if I had fifteen years on him. I think it *is* fifteen years, but I'll check that when I write my article.

"The Baron examined my face under a strong light and said that I had remarkably tight skin and the only treatment he would suggest besides the regular facials and a peeling mask would be the collagen injections. I explained to him that when I made my reservations, his receptionist, Dora

Samuels, suggested that I have a test to see if I'd be allergic to collagen, and I did. I'm not allergic, but I told the Baron how scared I am of needles, and how many would he have to use?

''He was so nice. He said that a lot of people feel that way about needles, and when I go for my treatment the nurse will give me a double-strength Valium, and by the time he's ready to start the injections, I'll think I'm just getting a couple of mosquito bites.

''Oh, one more thing. The Baron's office has lovely paintings in it, but I was really fascinated by the ad for the Spa that has appeared in magazines like *Architectural Digest* and *Town and Country* and *Vogue.* He told me there's a copy of it on the wall in all the bungalows. It's so cleverly worded.

''The Baron seemed pleased that I noticed. He said he'd had a hand in creating it.''

CHAPTER 5

Ted spent the morning working out in the gym in the men's spa. With Craig at his side, he rowed stationary boats, pedaled stationary bicycles and methodically made his way through the aerobics machines. They decided to finish with a swim and found Syd pacing laps in the indoor pool. Impulsively, Ted challenged him and Craig to a race. He had been swimming daily in Hawaii, but finished barely ahead of Craig. To his surprise, even Syd was only a few feet behind him. ''You're keeping in shape,'' he told him. He had always thought of Syd as sedentary, but the man was surprisingly strong.

''I've had time to keep in shape. Sitting in an office waiting for the phone to ring gets boring.'' With unspoken consent, they walked to deck chairs far enough away from the pool to avoid being overheard.

''I was surprised to find you here, Syd. When we talked last week, you didn't tell me you were coming.'' Craig's eyes were cold.

Syd shrugged. ''You didn't tell me you people were coming either. This place isn't my idea. Cheryl made the decision.'' He glanced at Ted. ''She must have found out you'd be around.''

''Min would know better than to blab—''

Syd interrupted Craig. With one finger, he beckoned to the waiter who was going from table to table offering soft drinks. ''Perrier.''

''Make it three,'' Craig said.

''Do you want to swallow it for me too?'' Ted snapped. ''I'll have a Coke,'' he told the waiter.

''You never drink colas,'' Craig commented mildly. His light hazel eyes were tolerant. He amended the order. "Bring two Perriers and an orange juice."

Syd chose to ignore the byplay. "Min wouldn't blab, but don't you think there are people on the staff who get paid to tip the columnists? Bettina Scuda called Cheryl yesterday morning. She probably put the bug in her ear that you were on the way. What's the difference? So she makes a play for you again. Is that new? Use it. She's dying to be a witness for you at the trial. If anyone can convince a jury how nutty Leila acted in Elaine's, Cheryl can. And I'll back her up."

He put a friendly hand on Ted's shoulder. "This whole thing stinks. We're going to help you beat it. You can count on us."

"Translated, that means you owe him one," Craig commented as they walked back to Ted's bungalow. "Don't fall for it. So what if he lost a million bucks in that goddamn play? You lost *four* million, and he talked you into investing."

"I invested because I read the play and felt that someone had managed to capture the essence of Leila; created a character who was funny and vulnerable and willful and impossible and sympathetic all at the same time. It ought to have been a triumph for her."

"It was a four-million-dollar mistake," Craig said. "Sorry, Ted, but you do pay me to give you good advice."

Henry Bartlett spent the morning in Ted's bungalow reviewing the transcript of the grand jury hearing and on the phone to his Park Avenue office. "In case we go for a temporary-insanity defense, we'll need plenty of documentation of similar successful pleas," he told them. He was wearing an open-necked cotton shirt and baggy khaki walking shorts. The Sahib! Ted thought. He wondered if Bartlett wore knickers on the golf course.

The library table was covered with annotated piles of paper. "Remember how Leila and Elizabeth and you and I used to play Scrabble at this table?" he asked Craig.

"And you and Leila always won. Elizabeth was stuck with me. As Leila put it, 'Bulldogs can't spell.' "

"What's that supposed to mean?" Henry asked.

"Oh, Leila had nicknames for all her close friends," Craig explained. "Mine was Bulldog."

"I'm not sure I'd have been flattered."

"Yes, you would have. When Leila gave you a nickname, it meant you were part of her inner circle."

Was that true? Ted wondered. When you looked up the definitions of the nicknames Leila bestowed, there was always a double edge to them. Falcon: a hawk trained to hunt and kill. Bulldog: a short-haired, square-jawed, heavily built dog with a tenacious grip.

''Let's order lunch,'' Henry said. ''We've got a long afternoon of work ahead of us.''

Over a club sandwich, Ted described his encounter with Elizabeth. ''So you can forget yesterday's suggestion,'' he told Henry. ''It's just as I thought. If I admit the possibility that I went back to Leila's apartment, when Elizabeth gets through testifying I'll be on my way to Attica.''

It *was* a long afternoon. Ted listened as Henry Bartlett explained the theory of temporary insanity. ''Leila had publicly rejected you; she had quit a play in which you invested four million dollars. The next day you pleaded with her for a reconciliation. She continued to insult you, to demand that you match her drink for drink.''

''I could afford the tax write-off,'' Ted interrupted.

''You know that. I know it. But the guy on the jury who's behind in his car payments won't believe it.''

''I refuse to concede that I might have killed Leila. I won't even consider it.''

Bartlett's face was becoming flushed. ''Ted, you'd better understand I'm trying to help you. All right, you were smart to get a reading on Elizabeth Lange's reaction today. So we can't admit you might have gone back upstairs. If we don't claim a total blackout on your part, we have to destroy both Elizabeth Lange's testimony and the eyewitness'. One or the other: maybe. I've told you this before. Both: no.''

''There's one possibility I'd like to explore,'' Craig suggested. ''We've got psychiatric information on that so-called eyewitness. I'd suggested to Ted's first lawyer that we put a detective on her trail and get a more rounded picture of her. I still think that's a good idea.''

''It is.'' Bartlett's eyes disappeared beneath a heavy-lidded frown. ''I wish it had been done a long time ago.''

They are talking about me, Ted thought. They are discussing what can and cannot be done to win my eventual freedom as though I weren't here. A slow, hard anger that now seemed to be part of his persona made him want to lash out at them. Lash out at them? The lawyer who supposedly would win his case? The friend who had been his eyes and ears and voice these last months? But I don't want them to take my life out of my hands, Ted thought, and tasted the acid that suddenly washed his mouth. I can't blame them, but I can't trust them either. No matter what, it's as I've known right along: I have to take care of this myself.

Bartlett was still talking to Craig. ''Have you an agency in mind?''

''Two or three. We've used them when there's been an internal problem we had to solve without publicity.'' He named the investigative agencies.

Bartlett nodded. ''They're all fine. See which one can get right on the case. I want to know if Sally Ross is a drinker; if she has friends she confides in; if she's ever discussed the case with them; if any of them were with her the night Leila LaSalle died. Don't forget, everyone's taking her word that she was in her apartment and happened to be looking at Leila's terrace at the precise moment Leila plunged off it.''

He glanced at Ted. ''With or without *Teddy's* help.''

When Craig and Henry finally left him at quarter of five, Ted felt drained. Restlessly he switched on the television set and in a reflex gesture switched it off. He certainly wouldn't clear his mind by watching soap operas. A walk would feel good, a long, long walk where he could breathe in the salty spray of the ocean and maybe wander past his grandparents' house where he'd spent so much time as a kid.

Instead, he elected to shower. He went into the bathroom and for a moment stared at his reflection in the paneled mirror that covered half the wall around the oversize marble sink. Flecks of gray around his temples. Signs of strain around his eyes. A tautness around his mouth. *Stress manifests itself both mentally and physically.* He'd heard a pop psychologist deliver that line on a morning news program. No kidding, he thought.

Craig had suggested that they might share a two-bedroom unit. Ted hadn't answered, and obviously Craig got the message; he hadn't pursued the idea.

Wouldn't it be nice if everybody understood without being told that you needed a certain amount of space? He stripped and tossed his discarded clothes into the bathroom hamper. With a half-smile he remembered how Kathy, his wife, had gotten him out of the habit of dropping clothes as he stepped out of them. ''I don't care how rich your family is,'' she would chide. ''I think it's disgusting to expect another human being to pick your laundry off the floor.''

''But it's distinguished laundry.''

His face in her hair. The scent she always used, a twenty-dollar cologne. ''Save your money. I can't wear expensive perfume. It overwhelms me.''

The icy shower helped to relieve the dull, throbbing headache. Feeling somewhat better, Ted wrapped the terry-cloth robe around him, rang for the maid and requested iced tea. It would have been enjoyable to sit on the deck, but too much of a risk. He didn't want to get into a conversation with someone walking by. Cheryl. It would be just like her to ''accidentally'' pass. Good God, would she never get over their casual affair? She was beautiful, she had been amusing and she did have a certain hardheaded ability to cut through the bull—but even if he didn't have the trial hanging over his head, there was no way he would get involved with her again.

He settled on the couch, where he could look out on the ocean and watch the sea gulls arcing over the foaming surf, beyond the threat of the undertow, beyond the power of the waves to crash them against the rocks.

He felt himself begin to perspire as the prospect of the trial loomed in his mind. Impatiently, he got up and pushed open the door to the side deck. Late August usually carried this welcome tang of chill. He put his hands on the railing.

When had he begun to realize that he and Leila wouldn't make it, in the long run? The mistrust for men so ingrained in her head had become intolerable. Was that the reason he'd overruled Craig's advice and put the millions in her play? Subconsciously had he hoped that she would get so caught up in a smash hit that she would decide she didn't want to accept the social demands of his life, or his desire for a family? Leila was an actress—first, last, always. She *talked* about wanting a child, but it wasn't true. She had satisfied her maternal instincts by raising Elizabeth.

The sun was beginning to lower over the Pacific. The air was filled with the humming of the crickets and the katydids. Evening. Dinner. He could already see the expressions on the faces around the table. Min and Helmut, phony smiles, worried eyes. Craig trying to read his mind. Syd, a certain defiant nervousness about him. How much did Syd owe the wrong people for the money he'd put into the play? How much was Syd hoping to borrow? How much was his testimony worth? Cheryl, all seductive enticement. Alvirah Meehan, fiddling with that damn sunburst pin, her eyes snapping with curiosity. Henry watching Elizabeth through the glass partition. Elizabeth, her face cold and scornful, studying them all.

Ted glanced down. The bungalow was set on sloping ground, and the side veranda jutted out over a ten-foot drop. He stared at the red-flowered bushes below. Images formed in his mind, and he rushed back inside.

He was still trembling when the maid came with the iced tea. Heedless of the delicate satin puff, he threw himself down on the massive king-size bed. He wished that dinner were over; that the night, with all it entailed, were over.

His mouth curved in a grim attempt at a smile. Why was he wishing the evening away? What kind of dinners do they serve in prison? he wondered.

He would have plenty of evenings to find out.

CHAPTER 6

Dora arrived back at the Spa at two o'clock, dropped her bag in her room and went directly to her desk in the reception office.

Min had allowed her to keep the sacks of unanswered fan mail in a closet in the file room. Dora usually took out a handful at a time and kept them in the bottom drawer of her desk. She knew the sight of Leila's mail was an irritant to Min. Now she didn't care if Min was annoyed. She had the rest of the day off, and she intended to search for any further letters.

For the tenth time since she had found it, Dora re-examined the poison-pen letter. With each reading, her conviction grew that there might have been at least an element of truth in it. Happy as Leila had been with Ted, her distress over the last three or four films had often made her temperamental and moody. Dora had noticed Ted's increasing impatience with the outbursts. Had he become involved with another woman?

That was exactly the way Leila would have been thinking if she opened this kind of letter or a series of these letters. It would explain the anxiety, the drinking, the despondency of those last months. Leila often said, "There are just two people I know I can trust in this world: Sparrow and Falcon. Now you, Sammy, are getting there." Dora had felt honored. "And the *Q.E. Two*"—Leila's name for Min—"is a do-or-die friend, provided there's a buck in it for her and it doesn't conflict with anything the Toy Soldier wants."

Dora reached the office and was glad to see that Min and Helmut weren't there. Outside, the day was sunny, the breeze from the Pacific gentle. Far down on the rocky embankments over the ocean, she could see the traces of ice plants, the henna-and-green-and-rust-shaded leaves that lived on water and air. Elizabeth and Ted had been water and air to Leila.

Quickly she went into the file room. With Min's passion for beautiful surroundings, even this small storage area was extravagantly designed. The custom-made files were a sunny yellow, the ceramic-tile floor was in shades of gold and umber, a Jacobean sideboard had been converted into a supply cupboard.

There were still two full sacks of letters to Leila. They ranged from lined paper torn from a child's notebook to expensive, perfumed stationery. Dora scooped a batch of them into her arms and brought them to her desk.

It was a slow process. She could not assume that another anonymous letter would necessarily come addressed with snipped and pasted words and numbers like the one she had found. She began with the letters already opened, the ones Leila had seen. But after forty minutes she'd gotten nowhere. Most of the mail was the usual. *You're my favorite actress . . . I named my daughter after you . . . I saw you on Johnny Carson. You looked beautiful, and you were so funny* . . . But there were also several surprisingly harsh critical notes. *That's the last time I spend five dollars to see you. What a lousy movie . . . Do you read your scripts, Leila, or just take what roles you can get?*

Her rapt concentration caused her to be unaware of Min and Helmut's four-o'clock arrival. One minute she was alone; the next they were approaching her desk. She looked up, tried to summon a natural smile and with a casual movement of her hand slid the anonymous letter into the pile.

It was clear that Min was upset. She did not seem to notice that Dora was early. "Sammy, get me the file on the bathhouse."

Min waited while she went for it. When she returned, Helmut reached out his hand to take the manila folder, but Min literally grabbed it first. Min was ghastly pale. Helmut patted her arm. ''Minna, please, you are hyperventilating.''

Min ignored him. ''Come inside,'' she ordered Dora.

''I'll just tidy up first.'' Dora indicated her desk.

''Forget it. It's not going to make any difference.''

There was nothing she could do. If she made any attempt to put the anonymous letter into her drawer, Min would demand to see it. Dora patted her hair and followed Min and Helmut into their private office. Something was dreadfully wrong, and it had to do with that blasted Roman bath.

Min went to her own desk, opened the file and began to race through the papers in it. Most of the correspondence was in the form of bills from the contractor. ''Five hundred thousand down, three hundred thousand, twenty-five thousand . . .'' She kept reading, her voice going higher and higher. *''And now another four hundred thousand dollars before he can continue working on the interior rooms.''* She slapped the papers down and slammed her fist on them.

Dora hurried to get a glass of ice water from the office refrigerator. Helmut rushed around the desk, put his hands on Min's temples and made soft, shushing sounds. ''Minna, Minna, you must relax. Think about something pleasant. You'll bring on high blood pressure.''

Dora handed the glass to Min and looked contemptuously at Helmut. That spendthrift, she thought, would put Min in her grave with his crazy projects! Min had been absolutely right when she'd suggested that they add a self-contained budget-price spa on the back half of the property. *That* would have worked. Secretaries as well as socialites were going to spas these days. Instead, this pompous fool had persuaded Min to build the bathhouse. ''It will make a statement about us to the world'' was his favorite phrase when he talked Min into plunging into debt. Dora knew the finances of this place as well as they did. It couldn't go on. She cut through Helmut's soothing ''Minna, Minna—''

''Stop work on the bathhouse immediately,'' she suggested crisply. ''The outside is finished, so the place looks all right. Say the special marble you ordered for the interior has been held up. No one will know the difference. The contractor's pretty much paid to date, isn't he?''

''Very nearly,'' Helmut agreed. He smiled brightly at Dora as though she had just solved an intricate puzzle. ''Dora is right, Minna. We'll put off finishing the bathhouse.''

Min ignored him. ''I want to go over those figures again.'' For the next half-hour they had their heads together comparing the contracts, the estimates and the actual figures. At one point Min and then Helmut left the room. Don't let them go to my desk, Dora prayed. She knew the minute Min calmed down, she would be annoyed to see clutter in the reception area.

Finally Min tossed the original sketches across her desk. "I want to talk to that damn lawyer. It looks to me as if the contractor is entitled to price over-runs on every phase of the job."

"This contractor has soul," Helmut said. "He understands the concept of what we are doing. Minna, we stop building for the moment. Dora is right. We turn the problem into a virtue. We are awaiting shipment of Carrara marble. We still settle for nothing less, yes? So. We shall be admired as purists. *Liebchen,* don't you know that to *create* a desire for something is every bit as important as *fulfilling* it?"

Dora was suddenly aware of another presence in the room. She looked up quickly. Cheryl was standing there, her shapely body curved against the doorframe, her eyes amused. "Have I come at a bad time?" she asked brightly. Without waiting for an answer, she strolled over and leaned past Dora. "Oh, I see you're going over the sketches of the Roman bath." She bent over to examine them.

"Four pools, steam rooms, saunas, more massage rooms, *sleeping* rooms? I love the idea of nap time after a strenuous romp through the mineral baths! Incidentally, won't it cost a fortune to provide real mineral water for the baths? Do you intend to fake it or pipe it in from Baden-Baden?" She straightened up gracefully. "It looks as though you two could use a little investment capital. Ted respects my opinion, you know. In fact, he used to listen to me quite a bit before Leila got her fangs into him. See you people at dinner."

At the door she turned back and looked over her shoulder. "Oh, by the way, Min, dear. I left my bill on Dora's desk. I'm sure it was just an oversight that one was left in my bungalow. I *know* you planned to have me as your guest, dear."

Cheryl had left the bill on her desk. Dora knew that meant she had gone through the mail. Cheryl was what she was. She had probably seen the letter to Leila.

Min looked at Helmut. Frustrated tears welled in her eyes. "She knows we're in a bad financial bind, and it would be just like her to tip the columnists off! Now we have another freebie—and don't think she won't use this place as a second home!" Despairingly, Min jammed the scattered bills and sketches back into the file.

Dora took it from her and replaced it in the file room. Her heart fluttering rapidly, she went back to the reception room. The letters to Leila were scattered on her desk; the poison-pen one was missing.

Dismayed, Dora tried to assess what harm that letter might do. Could it be used to blackmail Ted? *Or was whoever sent it anxious to have it back, just in case someone tried to trace it?*

If only she hadn't been reading it when Min and Helmut came in! Dora sat down at her desk; only then did she notice that propped against her calendar was Cheryl's bill for her week at the Spa.

Scrawled across it Cheryl had written *Paid in full.*

CHAPTER 7

At six thirty the phone in Elizabeth's bungalow rang. It was Min. "Elizabeth, I want you to have dinner with Helmut and me tonight. Ted, his lawyer, Craig, Cheryl, Syd—they're all going out." For a moment she sounded like the familiar Min, imperious, brooking no refusal. Then, before Elizabeth could answer, her tone softened. "Please, Elizabeth. You're going home in the morning. We have missed you."

"Is this another one of your games, Min?"

"I was absolutely wrong to have forced that meeting last night. I can only ask you to forgive me."

Min sounded weary, and Elizabeth felt reluctant sympathy. If Min chose to believe in Ted's innocence, so be it. Her scheme to throw them together had been outrageous, but that was Min's way.

"You're *certain* none of them will be in the dining room . . . ?"

"I am certain. Do join us, Elizabeth. You're leaving tomorrow. I've hardly seen you."

It was totally out of character for Min to plead. This would be her only chance to visit with Min, and besides, Elizabeth was not sure she welcomed the prospect of a solitary dinner.

She had had a full afternoon at the Spa, including a loofah treatment, two stretch-exercise classes, a pedicure and manicure, and finally a yoga class. In the yoga class, she'd tried to free her mind, but no matter how much she concentrated, she could not obey the soothing suggestions of the instructor. Over and over, against her will, she kept hearing Ted's question: *If I did go back upstairs . . . Was I trying to save her?*

"Elizabeth . . . ?"

Elizabeth gripped the phone and glanced around, drinking in the restful monochromatic color scheme of this expensive bungalow. "Leila green," Min called it. Min had been sickeningly high-handed last night, but she had certainly loved Leila. Elizabeth heard herself accepting the invitation.

The large bathroom included a step-in tub, whirlpool, stall shower and personal steam-room facility. She chose Leila's favorite way to wind down. Lying in the tub, she took advantage of both steam and whirlpool. Eyes closed, her head cushioned by a terry-cloth neck rest, she felt tension slip away under the soothing mist and churning water.

Again she marveled at the cost of this place. Min must be racing through the millions she'd inherited. She had noticed that that worry was shared by all the old-timers on the staff. Rita, the manicurist, had told her virtually the same story that she'd heard from the masseuse. "I tell you, Elizabeth," she had complained, "Cypress Point just doesn't have the same excitement since Leila died. The celebrity followers are going to La Costa now. Sure you see some pretty big names, but the word is half of them aren't paying."

After twenty minutes the steam automatically turned off. Reluctantly Elizabeth stood under a cold shower, then draped herself in a thick terry robe and twisted a towel around her hair. There was something else she had overlooked in her anger at finding Ted here. Min had genuinely loved Leila. Her anguish after Leila's death had not been faked. But Helmut? The hostile way he had looked at Leila's picture, his sly suggestion that Leila was losing her looks . . . What had *provoked* that venom? Surely not just the cracks about his being a "toy soldier" that Leila made at his expense? When he overheard them, he was always amused. She remembered the time he'd arrived for dinner at Leila's apartment wearing the tall, old-fashioned cap of a toy soldier.

"I was passing a costume shop, saw it in the window and couldn't resist," he explained as they all applauded. Leila had laughed uproariously and kissed him. "You're a good sport, Your Lordship," she said. . . .

Then what had triggered his anger? Elizabeth toweled her hair dry, brushed it back and caught it in a Psyche knot. As she applied makeup and touched her lips and cheeks with gloss, she could hear Leila's voice: "My God, Sparrow, you get better-looking all the time. I swear you were lucky Mama was having an affair with Senator Lange when you were conceived. You remember some of her other men. How would you like to have been Matt's kid?"

Last year she'd been in summer stock. When the show got to Kentucky, she'd gone to the leading newspaper in Louisville and searched for references to Everett Lange. His obituary notice was four years old at that time. It gave details of his family background, his education, his marriage to a socialite, his achievements in Congress. In his photograph, she had seen a masculine version of her own features. . . . Would her life have been different if she had known her father? She suppressed the thought.

It was a fact of life that everyone at Cypress Point Spa dressed for dinner. She decided to wear a white silk jersey tunic with a knotted cord belt and silver sandals. She wondered if Ted and the others had gone to the Cannery in Monterey. That used to be his favorite spot.

One night, three years ago, when Leila had to leave unexpectedly to shoot extra scenes, Ted had taken her to the Cannery. They had sat for hours talking, and he had told her about spending summers with his grandparents in Monterey, about his mother's suicide when he was twelve, about how much he had despised his father. And he told her about the automobile accident that took the lives of his wife and child. "I couldn't function," he said. "For nearly two years I was a zombie. If it hadn't been for Craig, I'd have had to turn over executive control of my business to someone else. He functioned for me. He became my voice. He practically *was* me."

The next day he told her, "You're too good a listener."

She had known that he was uncomfortable about having revealed so much of himself to her.

She deliberately waited until the ''cocktail'' hour was nearly over before she left her bungalow. As she followed the path that led to the main house, she stopped to observe the scene on the veranda. The lighted main house, the well-dressed people standing in twos and threes, sipping their make-believe cocktails, talking, laughing, separating, forming into new social units.

She was acutely aware of the breathtaking clarity of the stars against the backdrop of the sky, the artfully placed lanterns that illuminated the path and accentuated the blossoms on the hedges, the placid slap of the Pacific as it washed against the shoreline; and behind the main house, the looming shadow of the bathhouse, its black marble exterior glistening in the reflected light.

Where *did* she belong? Elizabeth wondered. When she was in Europe working, it had been easier to forget the sense of isolation, the alienation from every other human being that had become a fact of her existence. As soon as the movie was in the can, she rushed home, so sure that her apartment would be a haven, the familiarity of New York a welcoming comfort, but in ten minutes, she had been frantic to flee, had grasped at Min's invitation like a drowning woman. Now she was marking the hours until she could go back to New York, and the apartment. She felt as if she had no home.

Would the trial be a purge for her emotions? Would knowing that she had helped to bring about the punishment of Leila's murderer in some way release her, let her reach out to other people, start a new life for herself? ''Excuse me.'' A young couple were behind her. She recognized him as a top-seeded tennis player. How long had she been blocking their path?

''I'm sorry. I guess I'm woolgathering.'' She stepped aside, and he and the young woman, whose hand was entwined in his, smiled indifferently and passed her. She followed them slowly to the end of the path, up the steps of the veranda. A waiter offered her a drink. She accepted it and quickly moved to the far railing. She had no small talk in her.

Min and Helmut were circulating among their guests with the practiced skill of veteran party givers. Min was triumphantly visible in a flowing yellow satin caftan and cascading diamond earrings. With a measure of surprise, Elizabeth realized that Min was really quite slim. It was her full breasts and overbearing manner that created the imposing illusion.

As always, Helmut was impeccable, in a navy silk jacket and light gray flannel slacks. He exuded charm as he bowed over hands, smiled, raised one perfectly arched eyebrow—the perfect gentleman.

But why did he hate Leila?

* * *

Tonight the dining rooms were decorated in peach: peach tablecloths and napkins, centerpieces of peach roses, Lenox china in a delicate peach-and-gold design. Min's table was set for four. As Elizabeth approached it, she saw the *maître d'* touch Min's arm and direct her to the phone on his desk.

When Min came back to the table, she was visibly annoyed. Nevertheless, her greeting seemed genuine. "Elizabeth, at last a little time to be with you. I had hoped to give both you and Sammy a happy surprise. Sammy returned early. She must have missed my note and didn't realize you were here. I invited her to join us at our table, but she's just phoned to say she doesn't feel very well. I told her you were with us and she'll see you in your bungalow after dinner."

"Is she ill?" Elizabeth asked anxiously.

"She had a long drive. Still, she ought to eat. I wish she had made the effort." Min clearly wanted to dismiss any more discussion.

Elizabeth watched as, with a practiced eye, Min surveyed the surroundings. Woe to a waiter who did not have the proper demeanor, who rattled, or spilled, or brushed against the chair of a guest. The thought struck her that it was not like Min to invite Sammy to join her table. Was it possible that Min had guessed there was a special reason she had waited to see Sammy, and wanted to know what it was?

And was it possible that Sammy had shrewdly avoided that trap?

"I'm sorry I'm late," Alvirah Meehan yanked out the chair before the waiter could help her. "The cosmetician did a special makeup after I got dressed," she said, beaming. "How do you like it?"

Alvirah was wearing a scoop-necked beige caftan with intricate brown beading. It looked very expensive. "I bought this in the boutique," she explained. "You have lovely things there. And I bought every single product the makeup woman suggested. She was so helpful."

As Helmut came to the table, Elizabeth studied Min's face with amusement. One was *invited* to join Min and Helmut—something which Mrs. Meehan did not understand. Min could explain that and place her at another table. On the other hand, Mrs. Meehan was in the most expensive bungalow in the Spa; she was clearly buying everything in sight, and offending her could be very foolish. A strained smile tugged at the corners of Min's lips. "You look charming," she told Alvirah. "Tomorrow I shall personally help you select other outfits."

"That's very nice of you." Alvirah fiddled with her sunburst pin and turned to Helmut. "Baron, I have to tell you I was re-reading your ad—you know, the one you have framed in the bungalows."

"Yes?"

Elizabeth wondered if it was just her imagination that made Helmut suddenly seem wary.

"Well, let me tell you that everything you say about the place is true. Remember how the ad says, 'At the end of a week here, you will feel as free and untroubled as a butterfly floating on a cloud'?"

"The ad reads something like that, yes."

"But you wrote it—didn't you tell me that?"

"I had some input, I said. We have an agency."

"Nonsense, Helmut. Mrs. Meehan obviously agrees with the text of the ad. Yes, Mrs. Meehan, my husband is very creative. He personally writes the daily greeting, and ten years ago when we converted the hotel into the Spa, he simply would not accept the advertising copy we were given, and rewrote it himself. That ad won many awards, which is why we have a framed copy in every bungalow."

"It certainly made important people want to come here," Alvirah told them. "How I wish I'd been a fly on the wall to listen to all of them. . . ." She beamed at Helmut. "Or a butterfly floating on a cloud."

They were eating the low-calorie mousse when it dawned on Elizabeth how skillfully Mrs. Meehan had drawn out Helmut and Min. They had told her stories Elizabeth had never heard before: about an eccentric millionaire who had arrived on opening day on his bicycle, with his Rolls-Royce majestically trailing him, or about how a chartered plane had been sent from Arabia to pick up a fortune in jewels that one of a sheikh's four wives had left behind on a table near the pool. . . .

As they were about to leave the table, Alvirah posed her final question: "Who was the most exciting guest you've ever had?"

Without hesitation, without even looking at each other, they answered "Leila LaSalle."

For some reason, Elizabeth shivered.

Elizabeth did not linger for coffee or the musical program. As soon as she reached her bungalow, she phoned Sammy. There was no answer in her apartment. Puzzled, she dialed Sammy's office.

Sammy's voice had an excited urgency to it when she answered. "Elizabeth, I nearly fainted when Min told me you were here. No, I'm perfectly all right. I'll be right over."

Ten minutes later, Elizabeth flung open the door of her bungalow and threw her arms around the frail, fiercely loyal woman who had shared with her the last years of Leila's life.

Sitting opposite each other on the matching sofas, they took each other's measure. Elizabeth was shocked to see how much Dora had changed. "I know," Dora said with a wry smile. "I don't look that hot."

"You don't look *well,* Sammy," Elizabeth said. "How's it really going?"

Dora shrugged. "I still feel so guilty. You were away, and couldn't see the day-to-day change in Leila. When she came to visit me in the hospital, *I* could see it. Something was destroying her, but she wouldn't talk about it. I ought to have contacted you. I feel I let her down so terribly. And now it's as if I have to find out what happened. I can't let it rest until I do."

Elizabeth felt tears begin to spill from her eyes. "Now don't you dare get *me* started," she said. "For the entire first year I had to carry dark glasses with me. I just never knew when I'd start crying. I used to call the glasses my grief equipment."

She clasped her hands together. "Sammy, tell me. Is there *any* chance I'm wrong about Ted? I was *not* mistaken about the time, and if he pushed Leila off that terrace he has to pay for it. But is it possible he *was* trying to hold her? Why was she so upset? Why was she drinking? You heard her talk about how disgusted she was with people who drank too much. That night, a few minutes before she died, I was nasty to her. I tried to do what she used to do to Mama—shock her, make her see what she was doing to herself. Maybe if I'd been more sympathetic. Sammy, if I'd only asked her *why*!"

In a spontaneous gesture they moved together. Dora's thin arms encircled Elizabeth, felt the trembling in the slender young body and remembered the teenager who had so worshiped her big sister. "Oh, Sparrow," she said, unthinkingly using Leila's name for Elizabeth, "what would Leila think about the two of us going on like this?"

"She'd say, 'Quit moaning and do something about it.' " Elizabeth dabbed at her eyes and managed a smile.

"Exactly." With quick, nervous movements, Dora smoothed the thin strands of hair that always wanted to slip out from her bun. "Let's backtrack. Had Leila started to act upset before you left on the tour?"

Elizabeth frowned as she tried to focus, to weed out extraneous memories. "It was just before I left that Leila's divorce had come through. She'd been with her accountant. It was the first time in years I'd seen her worried about money. She said something like 'Sparrow, I've made an awful lot of loot, and honest to God, now I'm on thin ice.'

"I told her that two deadbeat husbands had put her in that bind, but I didn't consider being about to marry a multimillionaire like Ted being on thin ice. And she said something like 'Ted really *does* love me, doesn't he?' And I told her to, for God's sake, get off that line. I said, 'You keep doubting him and you'll drive him away. He's *nuts* about you. Now go earn the four million bucks he just invested in you!' "

"What did she say?" Dora asked.

"She started to laugh—you know that big, gorgeous laugh of hers—and she said, 'As usual, you're right, Sparrow.' She was terribly excited about the play."

"And then when you were gone, and I was sick, and Ted was traveling, someone began a campaign to destroy her." Dora reached into the pocket of her cardigan. "Today the letter I wrote you about was stolen from my desk. But just before you phoned I found *another* one in Leila's mail. She never got to read it either—it was still sealed—but it speaks for itself."

Horrified, Elizabeth read and reread the uneven, carelessly pasted words:

Leila,

Why won't you admit Ted is trying to Dump you? His new girl is getting tired of waiting. That four million Dollars was his Kiss-off to you. And more than you're worth. Don't blow it, honey. The word's Out it's A Lousy play-And you're Ten years too old for the part Too.

Your friend.

Dora watched as Elizabeth's face turned stony pale.

"Leila hadn't seen this?" Elizabeth asked quietly.

"No, but she must have been receiving a series of them."

"Who could have taken the other one today?"

Briefly Dora filled her in on the explosion over the expenses for the bathhouse and about Cheryl's unexpected arrival. "I know Cheryl was at my desk. She left her bill there. But so could anyone else have taken it."

"This smacks of Cheryl's touch." Elizabeth held the letter by the corner, loath to handle it. "I wonder if this can be traced."

"Fingerprints?"

"That, and typeface has a code. Even knowing what magazines and newspapers these words were snipped from could be helpful. Wait a minute." Elizabeth went into the bedroom and returned with a plastic bag. Carefully she slipped the anonymous note into it. "I'll find out where to send this to be analyzed." She sat down again and folded her arms on her knees. "Sammy, do you remember exactly what the other letter said?"

"I think so."

"Then write it down. Just a minute. There's paper in the desk."

Dora wrote, crossed out, rewrote, finally handed the paper to Elizabeth. ''That's pretty close.''

> Leila,
> How many times do I have to write? Can't you get it straight that Ted is sick of you? His new girl is beautiful and *much* younger than you. I told you that the emerald necklace he gave her matches the bracelet he gave you. It cost twice as much and looks ten times better. I hear your play is lousy. You really should learn your lines. I'll write again soon.
>
> Your friend.

This letter Elizabeth read and reread. ''That bracelet, Sammy. When did Ted give it to Leila?''

''Sometime after Christmas. The anniversary of their first date, wasn't it? She had me put it in the safety-deposit box because she was starting rehearsals and knew she wouldn't be wearing it.''

''That's what I mean. How many people could have known about that bracelet? Ted gave it to her at a dinner party. Who was there?''

''The usual people. Min. Helmut. Craig. Cheryl. Syd. Ted. You and I.''

''And the same group of people knew how much Ted put into the play. Remember, he didn't want it publicized. Sammy, have you finished going through the mail?''

''Besides the one I started this afternoon, there's one more large sack. It may have six or seven hundred letters in it.''

''Tomorrow morning I'm going to help you go through them. Sammy, think about who might have written these letters. Min and the Baron had nothing to do with the play; they had everything to gain by having Ted and Leila together here, with all the people they attracted. Syd had a million dollars in the play. Craig acted as though the four million Ted invested was out of his own pocket. He certainly wouldn't do anything to wreck the play's chances. But Cheryl never forgave Leila for taking Ted from her. She never forgave Leila for becoming a superstar. She knew Leila's vulnerabilities. And she would be the very one who'd want the letters back now.''

''What good are they to her?''

Elizabeth stood up slowly. She walked to the window and pushed back the curtain. The night was still brilliantly clear. ''Because if some way they can be traced to her, they can ruin her career? How would the public feel if it learned that Leila had been driven to suicide by a woman she considered a friend?''

''Elizabeth, did you hear what you just said?''

Elizabeth turned. ''Don't you think I'm right?''

''You have just conceded the fact that Leila might have committed suicide.''

Elizabeth gasped. She stumbled across the room, fell to her knees, and put her head on Sammy's lap. "Sammy, help me," she pleaded. "I don't know what to believe anymore. I don't know what to do."

CHAPTER 8

It was at Henry Bartlett's suggestion that they went out for dinner and invited Cheryl and Syd to join them. When Ted protested that he did not want to get involved with Cheryl, Henry cut him off sharply. "Teddy, like it or not, you *are* involved with Cheryl. She and Syd Melnick can be very important witnesses for you."

"I fail to see how."

"If we don't admit that you may have gone back upstairs, we've got to prove that Elizabeth Lange was confused about the exact time of that phone conversation and we've got to make the jury believe that Leila may have committed suicide."

"What about the eyewitness?"

"She saw a tree on the terrace moving. Her lively imagination decided it was you struggling with Leila. She's a nut case."

They went to the Cannery. A chattering, happy end-of-summer crowd filled the popular restaurant; but Craig had phoned ahead, and there was a window table with a sweeping view of Monterey Harbor awaiting them. Cheryl slipped in beside Ted. Her hand rested on his knee. "This is like old times," she whispered. She was wearing a lamé halter and matching skin-tight pants. A buzz of excitement had followed her as she walked across the room.

In the months since he'd seen her, Cheryl had phoned him repeatedly but he'd never returned the calls. Now as her warm, restless fingers caressed his knee, Ted wondered if he was being a fool for not taking what was being offered to him. Cheryl would say anything he wanted that might help his defense. But at what price?

Syd, Bartlett and Craig were visibly relieved to be here instead of at the Spa. "Wait till you start eating," Syd told Henry. "You'll know what seafood is all about."

The waiter came. Bartlett ordered a Johnnie Walker Black Label. His champagne-toned linen jacket was an impeccable fit; his sport shirt in the exact champagne shade and cinnamon-colored trousers were obviously custom-made. His thick but meticulously barbered white hair contrasted handsomely with his unlined, tanned face. Ted imagined him by turn informing, wooing, scolding a jury. A grandstander. Obviously, it worked for him. But what percentage of the time? He started to order a vodka martini and changed it to a beer. This was no time to dull any of his faculties.

It was early for dinner, only seven o'clock. But he had insisted on that. Craig and Syd were having an animated conversation. Syd seemed almost cheerful. Testimony for sale, Ted thought. Make Leila sound like a maniacal drunk. *It could all backfire, kids, and if it does, I'm the one who pays.*

Craig was asking Syd about his agency; was sympathizing with him over the money he'd lost in Leila's play. ''We took a bath too,'' he said. He looked over at Cheryl and smiled warmly. ''And we think you were a hell of a good sport to try to save the ship, Cheryl.''

For God's sake, don't shovel it on! Ted bit his lip to keep from shouting at Craig. But everyone else was smiling broadly. He was the alien in the group, the Unidentified Flying Object. He could sense the eyes of the other diners on this table, on him. He might as well have been able to overhear the *sotto voce* conversations. ''His trial starts next week.'' . . . ''Do you think he did it?'' . . . ''With his money, he'll probably get off. They always do.''

Not necessarily.

Impatiently, Ted looked out at the bay. The harbor was filled with boats—large, small, sailing vessels, yachts. Whenever she could, his mother had brought him to visit here. It was the only place where she'd been happy.

''Ted's mother's family came from Monterey,'' Craig was telling Henry Bartlett.

Again Ted experienced the wild irritation that Craig had begun to trigger in him. When had it started? In Hawaii? Before that? *Don't read my thoughts. Don't speak for me. I'm sick of it.* Leila used to ask him if he didn't get sick of having the Bulldog at his heels all the time. . . .

The drinks came. Bartlett took over the conversation. ''As you know, you are all listed as potential defense witnesses for Teddy. Obviously you can testify to the scene at Elaine's. So can about two hundred other people. But on the stand, I'd like you to help me paint for the jurors a more complete picture of Leila. You all know her public image. But you also know that she was a deeply insecure woman who had no faith in herself, who was haunted by a fear of failure.''

''A Marilyn Monroe defense,'' Syd suggested. ''With all the wild stories about Monroe's death, everyone has pretty well conceded that she committed suicide.''

''Exactly.'' Bartlett favored Syd with a friendly smile. ''Now the question is motive. Syd, tell me about the play.''

Syd shrugged. ''It was perfect for her. It could have been written about her. She loved the script. The rehearsals started like a cakewalk. I used to tell her we could open in a week. And then something happened. She came into the theater smashed at nine in the morning. After that it was all downhill.''

''Stage fright?''

''Lots of people get stage fright. Helen Hayes threw up before every performance. When Jimmy Stewart finished a movie, he was sure no one would ever ask him to be in another one. Leila threw up *and* worried. That's show biz.''

''That's just what I don't want to hear on the stand,'' Henry said sharply. ''I intend to paint the picture of a woman with a drinking problem who was experiencing severe depression.''

A teenager was standing over Cheryl. ''Could I please have your autograph?'' He plunked a menu in front of her.

''Of course.'' Cheryl beamed and scrawled her signature.

''Is it true you're going to be Amanda in that new series?''

''Keep your fingers crossed. I think so.'' Cheryl's eyes drank in the adolescent's homage.

''You'll be great. Thank you.''

''Now, if we just had a tape of this to send to Bob Koenig,'' Syd said drily.

''When will you know?'' Craig asked.

''Maybe in the next few days.''

Craig held up his glass. ''To Amanda.''

Cheryl ignored him and turned to Ted. ''Aren't you going to drink to that?''

He raised his glass. ''Of course.'' He meant it. The naked hope in her eyes was in an odd way touching. Leila had always overshadowed Cheryl. Why had they kept up the farce of friendship? Was it because Cheryl's endless quest to become bigger than Leila had been a challenge for Leila, a constant prod that she welcomed, that kept her on her mettle?

Cheryl must have seen something in his face, because her lips brushed his cheek. He did not pull away.

It was over coffee that Cheryl leaned her elbows on the table and cupped her chin in her hands. The champagne she had drunk had clouded her eyes so that they now seemed to smolder with secret promises. Her voice was slightly blurred as she half-whispered to Bartlett, ''Suppose Leila believed that Ted wanted to dump her for another woman? What would that do to help the suicide theory?''

''I was not involved with another woman,'' Ted said flatly.

''Darling, this isn't True Confessions. You don't have to say a word,'' Cheryl chided. ''Henry, answer my question.''

''If we had *proof* that Ted was interested in someone else, and that Leila knew it, we give Leila a reason to be despondent. We damage the prosecutor's claim that Ted killed Leila because she rejected him. Are you telling me there was something going on between you and Ted before Leila died?'' Bartlett asked hopefully.

''I'll answer that,'' Ted snapped. ''No!''

"You didn't listen," Cheryl protested. "I said I may have proof that Leila *thought* Ted was ready to dump her for someone else."

"Cheryl, I suggest you shut up. You don't know what you're talking about," Syd told her. "Now let's get out of here. You've had too much to drink.

"You're right," Cheryl said amiably. "You're not often right, Syd, dear, but this time you are."

"Just a minute," Bartlett interrupted. "Cheryl, unless this is some sort of game, you'd better put your cards on the table. Anything that clarifies Leila's state of mind is vital to Ted's defense. What do you call 'proof'?"

"Maybe something that wouldn't even interest you," Cheryl said. "Let me sleep on it."

Craig signaled for a check. "I have a feeling this conversation is a waste of time."

It was nine thirty when the limousine dropped them at the Spa. "I want Ted to walk me to my place." Now Cheryl's voice had an edge to it.

"I'll walk you," Syd snapped.

"Ted will walk me," Cheryl insisted.

She leaned against him as they went down the path toward her bungalow. Other guests were just beginning to leave the main house. "Wasn't it fun to be out together?" Cheryl murmured.

"Cheryl, is this 'proof' talk one of your games?" Ted pushed the cloud of black hair away from her face.

"I like it when you touch my hair." They were at her bungalow. "Come in, darling."

"No. I'll say good night."

She pulled his head down until their lips were barely apart. In the starlight her eyes blazed up at him. Had she faked the business of acting tight? he wondered. "Darling," she whispered feverishly, "don't you understand that I'm the one who can help you walk out of that courtroom a free man?"

Craig and Bartlett said good night to Syd and made their way to their bungalows. Henry Bartlett was visibly satisfied. "Teddy looks as if he's finally getting the message. Having that little lady in his corner at the trial will be important. What do you think she meant by that mumbo jumbo about Ted being involved with another woman?"

"Wishful thinking. She probably wants to volunteer for the part."

"I see. If he's smart, he'll accept."

They reached Craig's bungalow. "I'd like to come in for a minute," Bartlett told him. "It's a good chance to talk alone." Inside the bungalow, he glanced around. "This is a different look."

"It's Min's masculine, rustic effect," Craig explained. "She didn't miss a trick—pine tables, wide-planked floors. The bed even has a cord spring. She automatically puts me in one of these units. I think she subconsciously views me as the simple type.''

''Are you?''

''I don't think so. And even though I lean to king-size beds with box springs, this *is* a hell of a step up from Avenue B and Eighth Street, where my old man had a deli.''

Bartlett studied Craig carefully. ''Bulldog'' was an apt description for him, he decided. Sandy hair, neutral complexion, cheeks that would fold into jowls if he let himself put weight on. A solid citizen. A good person to have in your corner. ''Ted is lucky to have you,'' he said. ''I don't think he appreciates it.''

''That's where you're wrong. Ted has to rely on me now to front for him in the business, and he resents it. To clarify that, he only *thinks* he resents me. The problem is, my very presence in his place is a symbol of the jam he's in.''

Craig went to the closet and pulled out a suitcase. ''Like you, I carry my private supply.'' He poured Courvoisier into two glasses, handed one of them to Bartlett and settled on the couch, leaning forward, turning his glass in his hand. ''I'll give you the best example I can. My cousin was in an accident and flat on her back in the hospital for nearly a year. Her mother knocked herself out taking care of the kids. You want to know something? My cousin was jealous of her mother. She said her mother was enjoying her children and *she* should be the one with them. It's like that with Ted and me. The minute my cousin got out of the hospital, she was singing her mother's praises for the good job she did. When Ted is acquitted, things will be back to normal between us. And let me tell you, I'd a lot rather put up with his outbursts than be in his boots.''

Bartlett realized that he had been too quick to dismiss Craig Babcock as a glorified lackey. The problem, he told himself sourly, of being too cocky. He chose his response carefully. ''I see your point, and I think you're quite perceptive.''

''Unexpectedly perceptive?'' Craig asked with a half-smile.

Bartlett chose to ignore the bait. ''I also am starting to feel somewhat better about this case. We might be able to put together a defense that will at least create reasonable doubt in a jury's mind. Did you take care of the investigative agency?''

''Yes. We've got two detectives finding out everything they can about the Ross woman. We've got another detective trailing her. Maybe that's overkill, but you never know.''

''Nothing that helps is overkill.'' Bartlett moved to the door. ''As you can certainly see, Ted Winters resents the hell out of me for probably the same reason he's jumping at *you.* We both want him to walk out of that courtroom a free man. One line of defense that I hadn't considered before tonight is to convince the jury that shortly before Leila LaSalle died, he and Cheryl had gotten back together, and the money he put in the play was a kiss-off for Leila.''

Bartlett opened the door and glanced back over his shoulder. ''Sleep on it, and come back to me in the morning with a game plan.''

He paused. ''But we've got to prevail on *Teddy* to go along with us.''

When Syd reached his bungalow the message light on the phone was flashing. He sensed immediately that it was Bob Koenig. The president of World Motion Pictures was famed for his habit of placing after-hour calls. It could only mean that a decision had been made about Cheryl and the role of Amanda. He broke into a cold sweat.

With one hand he reached for a cigarette, with the other for the phone. As he barked ''Syd Melnick,'' he cradled the receiver against his shoulder and lit the cigarette.

''Glad you reached me tonight, Syd. I had a six-o'clock call in to you in the morning.''

''I'd have been awake. Who can sleep in this business?''

''I sleep like a top, myself. Syd, I've got a couple of questions.''

He had been sure that Cheryl had lost the part. Something about the flashing light had signaled doom. *But Bob had questions. No decision had been made.*

He could visualize Bob at the other end of the line, leaning back in the leather swivel chair in his library at home. Bob hadn't gotten to be head of the studio by making sentimental decisions. Cheryl's test was great, Syd told himself hopefully. But then what? ''Shoot,'' he said, trying to sound relaxed.

''We're still battling it out between Cheryl and Margo Dresher. You know how tough it is to launch a series. Margo's a bigger name. Cheryl was good, damn good—probably better than Margo, even though I'll deny having said that. But Cheryl hasn't done anything big in years, and that fiasco on Broadway kept coming up at the meeting.''

The play. Once again the play. Leila's face drifted across Syd's mind. The way she'd screamed at him in Elaine's. He had wanted to bludgeon her then, to drown out that cynical, mocking voice forever. . . .

''That play was a vehicle for Leila. I take full blame for rushing Cheryl into it.''

''Syd, we've been through all that. I'm going to be absolutely candid with you. Last year, as all the columnists reported, Margo had a little drug problem. The public is getting damn sick of stars who spend half their lives in drug-rehab centers. I want it straight. Is there anything about Cheryl that could embarrass us, if we choose her?''

Syd gripped the phone. Cheryl had the inside track. A burst of hope made his pulse fluctuate wildly. Sweat poured from his palms. ''Bob, I swear to you—''

''Everybody swears to me. Try telling me the truth instead. If I put myself on the line and decide on Cheryl, will it backfire on me? If it ever does, Syd, you're finished."

"I swear. I swear on my mother's grave. . . ."

Syd hung up the phone, hunched over and put his face in his hands. Clammy perspiration broke over his entire body. Once again the golden ring was within his grasp.

Only this time it was Cheryl, not Leila, who could screw it up for him. . . .

CHAPTER 9

When she left Elizabeth, Dora carried the plastic-wrapped anonymous letter in the pocket of her cardigan. They had decided that she would make a copy of the letter on the office machine, and in the morning Elizabeth would take the original to the sheriff's office in Salinas.

Scott Alshorne, the county sheriff, was a regular dinner guest at the Spa. He'd been friendly with Min's first husband and was always discreetly helpful when a problem, like missing jewelry, arose. Leila had adored him.

"Poison-pen letters aren't the same as missing jewelry," Dora warned Elizabeth.

"I know, but Scott can tell us where to send the letter for analysis, or if I should just give it to the district attorney's office in New York. Anyway, I want a copy myself."

"Then let me make it tonight. Tomorrow, when Min is around, we can't risk having her reading it."

As Dora was leaving, Elizabeth wrapped her in her arms. "You don't believe Ted is guilty, do you, Sammy?"

"Of calculated murder? No, I simply can't believe that. And if he was interested in another woman, there was no motive for him to kill Leila."

Dora had to go back to the office anyhow. She'd left mail scattered on the desk and the unsearched plastic bags on the floor of the reception room. Min would have a fit if she saw them.

Her dinner tray was still on a table near her desk, almost untouched. Funny how little appetite she had these days. Seventy-one really wasn't that old. It was just that between the operation and losing Leila, there was a spark gone, the old zest that Leila had always teased her about.

The copy machine was camouflaged by a walnut cabinet. She opened the top of the cabinet and turned on the machine, took the letter from her pocket and slipped it free of the plastic bag, carefully touching it only by the edges. Her movements were quick. There was always the worry that Min might take it into her head to come down to the office. Helmut was undoubtedly locked in his study. He was an insomniac and read late into the night.

She happened to glance out the half-open window. Just the sound of the Pacific—its truculent roar—and the smell of the salty breeze were invigorating. She did not mind the rush of cool air that caused her to shiver. But what had caught her attention?

All the guests were settled by now. Lights were visible from behind the curtained windows of the bungalows. Just against the horizon she could see the outlines of the umbrella tables around the Olympic pool. To the left, the silhouette of the Roman bathhouse loomed against the sky. The night was starting to turn misty. It was getting harder to see. Then Dora leaned forward. Someone was walking not on the path, but in the shadows of the cypress trees, as though afraid of being seen. She adjusted her glasses and was astonished to realize that whoever was there was wearing a scuba-diving outfit. What ever was he doing on the grounds? He seemed to be heading toward the Olympic pool.

Elizabeth had told her she was going swimming. An unreasoning fear gripped Dora. Shoving the letter into the pocket of her cardigan, she hurried out of the office and as swiftly as she could move her arthritic body rushed down the stairs, across the darkened foyer and out the seldom-used side door. Now the interloper was passing the Roman bathhouse. She hurried to cut him off. It was probably one of the college kids who were staying at Pebble Beach Lodge, she told herself. Every once in a while they'd sneak onto the grounds and go for a swim in the Olympic pool. But she didn't like the idea of this one coming upon Elizabeth if she was alone there.

She turned and realized that he had seen her. The lights of the security guard's golf cart were coming up the hill from near the gates. The figure in the scuba outfit ran toward the Roman bathhouse. Dora could see that the door was ajar. That fool Helmut probably hadn't bothered to close it this afternoon.

Her knees were trembling as she hurried behind him. The guard would drive by in a moment, and she didn't want the intruder to get away. Tentatively she stepped inside the doorway of the bathhouse.

The entrance foyer was a giant open expanse of marbled walls with twin staircases at the far end. There was enough light from the Japanese lanterns in the trees outside for Dora to see that this area was empty. They actually had done quite a bit more work since she'd looked in a few weeks ago.

Through the open doorway to the left, she saw the beam of a flashlight. The archway led to the lockers, and beyond was the first of the saltwater pools.

For an instant, her indignation was replaced by fear. She decided to go out and wait for the guard.

''Dora, in here!''

The familiar voice made her weak with relief. Carefully making her way across the darkened foyer, she went through the locker room and into the area of the indoor pool.

He was waiting for her, flashlight in hand. The blackness of the wet suit, the thick underwater goggles, the bend of the head, the sudden convulsive movement of the flashlight made her step back uncertainly. ''For goodness' sake, don't shine that thing at me. I can't see,'' she said.

One hand, thick and menacing in the heavy black glove, stretched out toward her, reaching for her throat. The other flashed the light directly in her eyes, blinding her.

Horrified, Dora began to back up. She raised her hands to protect herself and was unaware that she had brushed the letter from her pocket. She barely felt the empty space under her feet before her body toppled backward.

Her last thought as her head smashed against the piles of jagged concrete at the bottom of the pool was that at last she knew who had killed Leila.

CHAPTER 10

Elizabeth swam from one end of the pool to the other at a demanding, furious pace. The fog was just beginning to roll in—uneven bits of mist that at one moment blew like a dark vapor over the surrounding area, the next were gone. She preferred it when it was dark. She could work every inch of her body knowing that the punishing physical effort somehow would diffuse the built-up emotional anxiety.

She reached the north end of the pool, touched the wall, inhaled, turned, pivoted and with a furious breaststroke began racing toward the opposite end. Now her heart was pounding with the strain of the pace she had set herself. It was crazy. She wasn't in condition for this kind of swimming. But still she raced, trying with the expenditure of physical energy to outrun her thoughts.

At last she felt herself begin to calm down, and flipping onto her back, she began to tread water, her arms rotating in even, sweeping motions.

The letters. The one they had; the one someone had taken; the others they might find in the unopened mail. The ones Leila had probably seen and destroyed. *Why didn't Leila tell me about them? Why did she shut me out? She always used me as a sounding board. She always said I could snap her out of taking criticism too seriously.*

Leila hadn't told her because she had believed that Ted was involved with someone else, that there was nothing she could do about it. But Sammy was right: *If Ted was involved with someone else, he had no motive to kill Leila.*

But I wasn't mistaken about the time of the call.

Suppose Leila had fallen—had slipped from his grasp—and he'd blacked out? Suppose those letters had driven her to suicide? I've got to find out who sent them, Elizabeth thought.

It was time to go in. She was dead tired, and at last somewhat calmer. In the morning, she'd go through the rest of the mail with Sammy. She'd take the letter they'd found to Scott Alshorne. He might want her to take it directly to the district attorney in New York. Was she handing Ted an alibi? And whom had he been involved with?

As she climbed the ladder from the pool, she shivered. The night air was chilly now, and she'd stayed longer than she'd realized. She slipped on her robe and reached into the pocket for her wristwatch. The luminous dial showed that it was half-past ten.

She thought she heard a rustling sound from behind the cypress trees that bordered the patio. "Who's there?" She knew her voice sounded nervous. There was no answer, and she walked to the edge of the patio and strained her eyes to see past the hedges and between the scattered trees. The silhouettes of the cypress trees seemed grotesque and ominous in the dark, but there was no movement other than the faint rustling of the leaves. The cool sea breeze was becoming more forceful. That was it, of course.

With a gesture of dismissal, she wrapped the robe around her and pulled the hood over her hair.

But somehow the feeling of uneasiness persisted, and her footsteps quickened along the path to her bungalow.

He hadn't touched Sammy. But there would be questions. What was she doing in the bathhouse? He cursed the fact that the door had been open, that he had run in there. If he had simply gone around it, she'd never have caught him.

Something so simple could betray him.

But the fact that she had the letter with her, that it had fallen from her pocket—that had been simple good luck. Should he destroy it? He wasn't sure. It was a double-edged sword.

Now the letter was buried against his skin inside the wet suit. The door of the bathhouse was snap-locked. The guard had made his desultory rounds and wouldn't be back tonight. Slowly, with infinite caution, he made his way toward the pool. Would she be there? Probably. Should he take the chance tonight? Two accidents. Was that more risky than letting her live? Elizabeth would demand answers when Sammy's body was found. Had Elizabeth seen that letter?

* * *

He heard the lapping of the water in the pool. Cautiously he stepped from behind the tree and watched the swiftly moving body. He would have to wait until she slowed down. By then she would be tired. It might be the time to go ahead. Two unrelated accidents in one night. Would the ensuing confusion keep people off the track? He took a step forward toward the pool.

And saw him. Standing behind the shrubbery. Watching Elizabeth. What was he doing there? Did he suspect she was in danger? Or had he too decided she was an unacceptable risk?

The wet suit glistened with mist as its wearer slipped behind the sheltering branches of cypress and vanished into the night.

Tuesday,
September 1

QUOTE FOR THE DAY:
To the best, to the most beautiful who is my joy and well-being.
—Charles Baudelaire

Good morning. *Bonjour,* to our dear guests.

It is to be a bit brisker this morning, so brace yourselves for the exciting tingle of the fresh sunlit air.

For the nature lovers, we offer a 30-minute after-luncheon walk along our beautiful Pacific coast, to explore the native flowers of our beloved Monterey Peninsula. So if you are of a mind, do join our expert guide at the main gate at 12:30.

A fleeting thought. Our menu tonight is especially exquisite. Wear your prettiest or handsomest outfit, and feast on our gourmet offerings knowing that the delicate taste treats are balanced by the delicate amount of calories you are consuming.

A fascinating thought: Beauty is in the eye of the beholder, but when you look in the mirror, *you* are the beholder.

—Baron and Baroness Helmut von Schreiber

CHAPTER 1

The first hint of dawn found Min lying wide awake in the canopied king-size bed she shared with Helmut. Moving carefully to keep from disturbing him, she turned her head and pulled herself up on one elbow. Even in sleep he was a handsome man. He was lying on his side, facing her, his one hand outstretched as though reaching for her, his breath now quiet and soft.

He had not slept like that all night. She didn't know what time he'd come to bed, but at two she'd awakened to the awareness of agitated movement, his head shaking, his voice angry and muffled. There had been no more sleep for her when she heard what he was saying: ''Damn you, Leila, damn you.''

Instinctively, she had laid her hand on his shoulder, murmured a soft shushing sound, and he had settled back. Would he remember the dream, remember that he had cried out? She had given no indication of having heard him. It would be useless to expect him to tell her the truth. Incredible as it seemed, had something been going on between him and Leila after all? Or had it been a one-sided attraction on Helmut's part toward Leila?

That didn't make it any easier.

The light, more golden than rosy now, began to brighten the room. Carefully Min eased out of bed. Even in her heartsick distress, she felt a moment of appreciation for the beauty of this room. Helmut had chosen the furnishings and color scheme. Who else would have visualized the exquisite balance of the peach satin draperies and bedding against the deep blue-violet tone of the carpet?

How much longer would she be living here? This could be their last season. The million dollars in the Swiss account, she reminded herself. Just the interest on that will be enough. . . .

Enough for whom? Herself? Maybe. Helmut? Never! She'd always known that a large part of her attraction for him was this place, the ability to strut around with this background, to mingle with celebrities. Did she really think he'd be content to follow a relatively simple lifestyle with an aging wife?

Noiselessly, Min glided across the room, slipped on a robe and went down the stairs. Helmut would sleep for another half-hour. She always had to awaken him at six thirty. In this half-hour it would be safe to go through some of the records, particularly the American Express bills. In those weeks before Leila died, Helmut had been away from the Spa frequently. He'd been asked to speak at several medical seminars and conventions; he'd lent his name to some charity balls and flown in to attend them. That was good for business. But what else had he been doing when he was on the East Coast? That was the time Ted had been traveling a great deal. She understood Helmut. Leila's obvious scorn for him would be a challenge. Had he been seeing her?

The night before Leila died, they'd attended the last preview of her show; they'd been at Elaine's. They'd stayed at the Plaza and in the morning flown to Boston to attend a charity luncheon. He'd put her on a plane to San Francisco at six thirty in the evening. Had he gone to the dinner he was supposed to attend in Boston, or had he taken the seven-o'clock shuttle to New York?

The possibility haunted her.

At midnight California time, three A.M. Eastern time, Helmut had phoned to make sure she was home safely. She had assumed he was calling from the hotel in Boston.

That was something she could check.

At the bottom of the staircase, Min turned left and, key in hand, went to the office. The door was unlocked. Her senses were assaulted by the condition of the room. The lights were still on; a dinner tray was on a table at one side of Dora's desk; the desk itself was piled with letters. Plastic bags, their contents spilling on the floor, bordered the desk. The window was partly open, and a cold breeze was rustling the letters. Even the copy machine was on.

Min stalked over to the desk and flipped through the mail. Angrily she realized that everything was fan mail to Leila. Her lips tightened ominously. She was sick to death of that mournful look Dora got whenever she answered those letters. At least till now she'd had the brains not to mess up the office with that silly drivel. From now on, if she wants to do that mail, she'll do it in her apartment. Period. Or maybe it was time to get rid of anyone who insisted on canonizing Leila. What a field day Cheryl would have had if she'd come in here and started going through the personal files. Dora had probably gotten tired and decided to wait to clear up the office this morning. But to leave the copy machine and the lights on was unforgivable. In the morning she'd tell Dora to start making plans for her retirement.

But now she had to get about the reason she had come here. In the storage room, Min went to the file marked "TRAVEL EXPENSES, BARON VON SCHREIBER."

It took less than two minutes to find what she wanted. The phone call from the East Coast to the Spa the night Leila died was listed on his telephone credit-card bill.

It had been made from New York.

CHAPTER 2

Sheer fatigue made Elizabeth fall into sleep; but it was a restless sleep, filled with dreams. Leila was standing in front of stacks of fan mail; Leila was reading the letters to her; Leila was crying. "I can't trust anyone . . . I can't trust anyone."

In the morning, there was no question in her mind of going on the walk. She showered, pulled her hair into a topknot, slipped on her jogging suit and after waiting just long enough for the hikers to be on their way, headed for the main house. She knew Sammy was always at her desk by a few minutes after seven.

It was a shock to find the usually impeccable receptionist's office cluttered with stacks of mail on and around Dora's desk. A large sheet of paper with the ominous words *See me* and signed by Min clearly revealed that Min had seen the mess.

How unlike Sammy! Never once in all the years she'd known her had Sammy left her desk cluttered. It was unthinkable she'd have chanced leaving it this way in the reception area. It was a surefire way of bringing on one of Min's famous rages.

But suppose she was ill? Quickly Elizabeth hurried down the stairs to the foyer of the main house and rushed to the stairway leading to the staff wing. Dora had an apartment on the second floor. She knocked briskly at the door, but there was no answer. The sound of a vacuum came from around the corner. The maid, Nelly, was a longtime employee who had been here when Elizabeth was working as an instructor. It was easy to get her to open Sammy's door. With a growing sense of panic, Elizabeth walked through the pleasant rooms: the sitting room in shades of lime green and white, with Sammy's carefully tended plants on the windowsills and tabletops; the single bed primly neat, with Sammy's Bible on the night table.

Nelly pointed to the bed. "She didn't sleep here last night, Miss Lange. And look!" Nelly walked to the window. "Her car's in the parking lot. Do you suppose she felt sick and sent for a cab or something to go to the hospital? That would be just like Miss Samuels. You know how independent she is."

But there was no record of a Dora Samuels' having signed herself into the community hospital. With growing apprehension, Elizabeth waited for Min to come back from the morning walk. In an effort to keep her mind from the fearful worry that something had happened to Sammy, she began to scan the fan mail. Where was the unsigned letter Dora had planned to copy?

Was she still carrying it?

CHAPTER 3

At five of seven, Syd walked up the path to join the others for the morning hike. Cheryl could read him like a book. He'd have to be careful. Bob wasn't making his final decision until this afternoon. If it weren't for that damn play, it would be in the bag now.

''You hear that, everybody? I quit!''

And you wiped me out, you bitch, he thought. He managed to twist his face into the contortion of a smile. The Greenwich, Connecticut, set were there, all turned out for the morning hike, every hair in place, flawless skin, manicured hands. Pretty clear none of *them* had ever hung by their fingernails waiting for a call, ever clawed their way up in a cutthroat business, ever had someone throw them into the financial gutter with the toss of a head.

It would be a perfect Pebble Beach day. The sun was already warming the cool morning air; the faint smell of salt from the Pacific mingled with the fragrance of the flowering trees that surrounded the main house. Syd remembered the tenement in Brooklyn where he'd been raised. The Dodgers had been in Brooklyn then. Maybe they should have stayed there. Maybe *he* should have stayed there too.

Min and the Baron came out onto the veranda. Syd was immediately aware of how drawn Min looked. Her expression was frozen on her face, the way people get when they've witnessed an accident and cannot believe what they've seen. *How much had she guessed?* He did not glance at Helmut but instead turned his head to watch Cheryl and Ted coming up the path. Syd could read Ted's mind. He'd always felt guilty about dumping Cheryl for Leila, but it was obvious he didn't want to pick up with her again. Obvious to everyone except Cheryl.

What in hell had she meant with that dumb remark about ''proof'' that Ted was innocent? What was she up to now?

''Good morning, Mr. Melnick.'' He turned to see Alvirah Meehan beaming up at him. ''Why don't we just walk together?'' she asked. ''I know how disappointed you must be that Margo Dresher is probably going to be Amanda in the series. I'm telling you, they're making a terrible mistake.''

Syd did not realize how hard he had grasped her arm until he saw her flinch. ''Sorry, Mrs. Meehan, but you don't know what you're talking about.''

Too late, Alvirah realized that only the insiders had that tip—the reporter from the *Globe* who was her contact for her article had told her to study Cheryl Manning's reaction when she got the news. She'd made a bad slip. ''Oh, am I wrong?'' she asked. ''Maybe it's just that my husband was saying that he read it's neck and neck between Cheryl and Margo Dresher.''

Syd made his voice confidential. ''Mrs. Meehan, do me a favor, won't you? Don't talk about that to anyone. It isn't true, and you can imagine how it would upset Miss Manning.''

Cheryl had her hand on Ted's arm. Whatever she had been saying, she had him laughing. She was a hell of a good actress—but not good enough to keep her cool if she lost the Amanda role. And she'd turn on him like an alley cat. Then, as Syd watched, Ted raised his hand in a careless salute and started jogging toward the front gate.

"Good morning, everyone," Min boomed in a hollow attempt at her usual vigor. "Let us be on our way. Remember, a brisk pace and deep breathing, please."

Alvirah stepped back as Cheryl caught up with them. They fell into line on the walkway that led to the woods. Scanning the clusters of people ahead, Syd picked out Craig walking with the lawyer, Henry Bartlett. The Countess and her entourage were directly behind them. The tennis pro and his girlfriend were holding hands. The talk-show host was with his date for the week, a twenty-year-old model. The various other guests in twos and threes were unfamiliar.

When Leila made this place her hangout, she put it on the map, Syd thought. You never knew when you'd find her here. Min needs a new superstar. He had noticed the way all eyes drank in Ted as he jogged away. Ted was a superstar.

Cheryl was clearly in a buoyant mood. Her dark hair exploded around her face. Her coal-black brows arced above the huge amber eyes. Her petulant mouth was carved into a seductive smile. She began to hum "That Old Feeling." Her breasts were high and pointed under her jogging suit. No one else could make a jogging suit look like a second coat of skin.

"We've got to talk," Syd told her quietly.

"Go ahead."

"Not here."

Cheryl shrugged. "Then later. Don't look so sour, Syd. Breathe deeply. Get rid of poisonous thoughts."

"Don't bother being cute with me. When we get back, I'll come to your place."

"What is this about?" Cheryl clearly did not want to have the euphoric mood spoiled.

Syd glanced over his shoulder. Alvirah was directly behind them. Syd could almost feel her breath on his neck.

He gave Cheryl's arm a warning pinch.

When they reached the road, Min continued to lead in the direction of the lone cypress tree, and Helmut began dropping back to chat with the hikers. "Good morning . . . Wonderful day . . . Try to pick up the pace . . . You're doing marvelously." His artificial cheerfulness grated on Syd. Leila had been right. The Baron was a toy soldier. Wind him up and he marches forward.

Helmut stopped abreast of Cheryl. "I hope you two enjoyed your dinner last night." His smile was dazzling and mechanical. Syd could not remember what he had eaten. "It was okay."

"Good." Helmut dropped back to ask Alvirah Meehan how she was feeling.

"Absolutely fine." Her voice was hard and strident. "You might say I'm as bright as a butterfly floating on a cloud." Her noisy laugh sent a chill through Syd.

Had even Alvirah Meehan caught on?

Henry Bartlett was not feeling good about the world or his particular situation. When he was asked to take on the case of Ted Winters, he'd rearranged his calendar immediately. Few criminal lawyers would be too busy to represent a prominent multimillionaire. But there was an ongoing problem between him and Ted Winters. The definitive word was "chemistry," and it was bad between them.

As he grudgingly plodded on the forced march behind Min and the Baron, Henry admitted to himself that this place was luxurious, that the setting was beautiful, that under different circumstances he could come to appreciate the charms of the Monterey Peninsula and Cypress Point Spa. But now he was on a countdown. The trial of *The People of the State of New York* v. *Andrew Edward Winters III* would begin in exactly one week. Publicity was eminently desirable when you won a headline case; but unless Ted Winters started cooperating, this case would not be won.

Min was picking up the pace. Henry quickened his footsteps. He hadn't missed the appreciative glances of the fiftyish ash-blonde who was with the Countess. Under different circumstances, he'd check that out. But not now.

Craig was marching at a solid, steady pace behind him. Henry still couldn't put his finger on what made Craig Babcock tick. On the one hand he'd talked about Pop's deli on the Lower East Side. On the other, he was clearly the hatchet man for Ted Winters. It was a pity that it was too late for him to testify that he and Ted had been on the phone when that so-called eyewitness claimed she saw Ted. That thought reminded Henry of what he wanted to ask Craig.

"What's with the investigator on Sally Ross?"

"I put *three* investigators on her—two for background, one to shadow her."

"It should have been done months ago."

"I agree. Ted's first lawyer didn't think it was necessary."

They were leaving the path that exited the Spa grounds and proceeding onto the road that led to the Lone Cypress.

"How did you arrange to get reports?"

"The head guy will call me every morning, nine thirty New York time, six thirty here. I just spoke to him. Nothing too important to report yet. Pretty much what we know already. She's been divorced a couple of times; she fights with her neighbors; she's always accusing people of staring at her. She treats 911 like it's her own personal hot line, always calling to report suspicious-looking characters.''

''I could chew her up and spit her out on the stand,'' Bartlett said. ''Without Elizabeth Lange's testimony, the prosecution would be flying on one wing. Incidentally, I want to know how good her eyesight is, if she needs glasses, what strength glasses, when they were changed last, and so on . . . everything about her vision.''

''Good. I'll phone it in.''

For a few minutes they walked in silence. The morning was silvery bright; the sun was absorbing the dew from the leaves and bushes; the road was quiet, with only an occasional car passing; the narrow bridge that led to the Lone Cypress was empty.

Bartlett glanced over his shoulder. ''I'd hoped to see Ted holding hands with Cheryl.''

''He always jogs in the morning. Maybe he was holding hands with her all night.''

''I hope so. Your friend Syd doesn't look happy.''

''The rumor is Syd's broke. He was riding high with Leila as a client. He'd sign her up for a picture and part of the deal was they'd use a couple of his other clients somewhere else. That's how he kept Cheryl working. Without Leila and with all the money he lost in that play, he's got problems. He'd love to put the arm on Ted right now. I won't let him.''

''He and Cheryl are the most important defense witnesses we have,'' Henry snapped. ''Maybe you'd better be more generous. In fact, I'm going to make that suggestion to Ted.''

They had passed the Pebble Beach Lodge and were on the way back to the Spa. ''We'll get to work after breakfast,'' Bartlett announced. ''I've got to decide the strategy of this case and whether to put Ted on the stand. My guess is that he'll make a lousy witness for himself; but no matter how much the judge instructs the jury, it makes a big psychological difference when a defendant won't subject himself to questioning.''

Syd walked back to Cheryl's bungalow with her. ''Let's make this short,'' she said when the door closed behind them. ''I want to shower, and I invited Ted for breakfast.'' She pulled the sweat shirt over her head, stepped out of the sweat pants and reached for her robe. ''What *is* it?''

''Always practicing, aren't you?'' Syd snapped. ''Save it for the dopes, honey. I'd rather wrestle with a tiger.'' For a long minute he studied her. She had darkened her hair for the Amanda audition, and the effect was startling. The softer color had obliterated the brassy, cheap-at-the-core look she'd never quite conquered and had accentuated those marvelous eyes. Even in a terry-cloth robe she looked like someone with class. Inside, Syd knew, she was the same scheming little hooker he'd been dealing with for nearly two decades.

Now she smiled dazzlingly at him. "Oh, Syd, let's not fight. What do you want?"

"I'll be happy to make it brief. Why did you suggest that Leila might have committed suicide? Why would she have believed that Ted was involved with another woman?"

"Proof."

"What kind of proof?"

"A letter." Quickly she explained. "I went up to see Min yesterday. They had the nerve to leave a bill here, when they know perfectly well I'm a draw for this place. They were inside, and I just happened to notice all that fan mail on Sammy's desk, and when I looked around I saw this crazy letter. And I took it."

"You took it!"

"Of course. Let me show it to you." She hurried into her bedroom, brought it back, and leaning over his shoulder, read it with him.

Leila,

How many Times Do I Have to write? Can't YOU get it straight THAT Ted is sick OF You? His new girl is beautiful and much younger THaN you. I told you ThAT the emerald necklace HE gave Her matcHes the bracelet he gave you. It cost Twice as much And looks ten Times better. I hear your play is Lousy. You really should Learn your lines. I'll write again soon.

Your friend.

"Don't you see? Ted must have been having a fling with someone else. But wouldn't that make him glad to break up with Leila? And if he wants to say it was with me, that's fine. I'll back him up."

"You stupid bitch."

Cheryl straightened up and walked over to the other couch. She sat down, leaned forward and spoke precisely, as though she were addressing a not-very-bright child. "You don't seem to realize that this letter is my chance to make Ted understand that I have his best interests at heart."

Syd walked over, grabbed the letter from Cheryl's hand and shredded it. "Last night Bob Koenig phoned me to make sure there was nothing unfavorable that might come out about you. You know why, as of this minute, you have the inside track for Amanda? Because Margo Dresher's had more than her share of lousy publicity. What kind of publicity do you think *you'd* get if Leila's fans find out you drove her to suicide with poison-pen letters?"

"I didn't write that letter."

"The hell you didn't! How many people knew about that bracelet? I saw your eyes when Ted gave it to Leila. You were ready to stab her right then. Those rehearsals were closed. How many people knew Leila was having trouble with her lines? You knew. Why? Because I told you myself. You wrote that letter and others like it. How much time did it take you to cut and paste? I'm surprised you had the patience. How many more are there, and are they likely to show up?"

Cheryl looked alarmed. "Syd, I swear to you I did not write that letter or any others. Syd, tell me about Bob Koenig."

Now it was Syd who, enunciating slowly, repeated the conversation. When he finished, Cheryl reached out her hand. "Got a match? You know I gave up smoking."

Syd watched as the shredded paper with its bizarre, uneven scraps of print curled and disappeared in the ashtray.

Cheryl came over to him and put her arms around his neck. "I knew you were going to get that part for me, Syd. You're right about getting rid of the letter. I think I should still testify at the trial. The publicity will be wonderful. But don't you think my attitude should be shock that my very dearest friend was so distraught and depressed? Then I could explain how even those of us at the top have terrible periods of anxiety."

Her eyes opened wide; two tears ran down her cheeks. "I think Bob Koenig would like that approach, don't you?"

CHAPTER 4

"Elizabeth!" Min's startled voice made her jump. "Is something wrong? Where is Sammy?"

Min and Helmut were in matching jogging outfits; Min's black hair was pulled regally into a chignon, but her makeup only partially masked the unfamiliar wrinkles around her eyes, the puffiness of her lids. The Baron seemed, as always, to be striking a pose, his legs slightly parted, his hands clasped behind his back, his head bent forward, his eyes puzzled and guileless.

Briefly, Elizabeth told them what had happened. Sammy was missing; her bed had not been slept in.

Min looked alarmed. "I came down at about six o'clock. The lights were on; the window was open; the copy machine was on. I was annoyed. I thought Sammy was getting careless."

"*The copy machine was on!* Then she *did* come back to the office last night." Elizabeth darted across the room. "Did you look to see if the letter she wanted to copy is in the machine?"

It was not there. But next to the copier Elizabeth found the plastic bag the letter had been wrapped in.

Within fifteen minutes a search party had been quietly organized. Reluctantly, Elizabeth acceded to Min's pleadings not to call the police immediately. "Sammy was very ill last year," Min reminded her. "She had a slight stroke and was disoriented. It may have happened again. You know how she hates fuss. Let us try to find her first."

"I'll give it until lunchtime," Elizabeth said flatly, "and then I'm going to report her missing. For all we know, if she did have some kind of attack, she's wandering on the beach somewhere."

"Minna gave Sammy a job out of pity," Helmut snapped. "The essence of this place is privacy, seclusion. We have deputies swarming about and half the guests will pack up and go home."

Elizabeth felt red-hot anger, but it was Min who answered. "Too much has been concealed around here," she said quietly. "We will delay calling the sheriff's office for Sammy's sake, not for ours."

Together they scooped the piled-up letters back into the bags. "This is Leila's mail," Elizabeth told them. She twisted the tops of the bags into intricate knots. "I'll take these to my bungalow later." She studied the knots and was satisfied no one could undo them without tearing the bags.

"Then you're planning to stay?" Helmut's attempt to sound pleased did not come off.

"At least until Sammy is found," Elizabeth told him. "Now let's get some help."

The search party consisted of the oldest and most trusted employees: Nelly, the maid who had let her into Dora's apartment; Jason, the chauffeur; the head gardener. They stood huddled at a respectful distance from Min's desk waiting for instructions.

It was Elizabeth who addressed them. "To protect Miss Samuel's privacy, we don't want anyone to suspect that there is a problem." Crisply she divided their responsibilities. "Nelly, check the empty bungalows. Ask the other maids if they've seen Dora. Be casual. Jason, you contact the cab companies. Find out if anyone made a pickup here between nine o'clock last night and seven this morning." She nodded to the gardener. "I want every inch of the grounds searched." She turned to Min and the Baron. "Min, you go through the house and the women's spa. Helmut, see if she's anywhere in the clinic. I'm going around the neighborhood."

She looked at the clock. "Remember, noon is the deadline for finding her."

As she headed for the gates, Elizabeth realized it had not been for Min and Helmut that she had made the concession, but because she knew that for Sammy it was already too late.

CHAPTER 5

Ted flatly refused to begin working on his defense until he'd spent an hour in the gym. When Bartlett and Craig arrived at his bungalow, he had just finished breakfast and was wearing a blue sport shirt and white shorts. Looking at him, Henry Bartlett could understand why women like Cheryl threw themselves at him, why a superstar like Leila LaSalle had been head over heels in love with him. Ted had that indefinable combination of looks and brains and charm which attracted men and women alike.

Over the years Bartlett had defended the rich and the powerful. The experience had left him cynical. No man is a hero to his valet. Or to his lawyer. It gave Bartlett a certain sense of power of his own to get guilty defendants acquitted, to shape a defense on loopholes in the law. His clients were grateful to him and paid his huge fees with alacrity.

Ted Winters was one of a kind. He treated Bartlett with contempt. He was the devil's advocate of his own defense strategy. He did not pick up the hints Bartlett threw to him, the hints which ethically Bartlett could not bluntly state. Now he said, "You start planning my defense, Henry. I'm going to the gym for an hour. And then I might just take a swim. And possibly jog again. By the time I get back, I'd like to see exactly what your line of defense is and see if I can live with it. I assume you understand that I have no intention of saying, Yes, perhaps, maybe I *did* stumble back upstairs?"

''Teddy, I . . .''

Ted stood up. He pushed the breakfast tray aside. His posture was menacing as he stared at the older man. ''Let me explain something. Teddy is the name of a two-year-old boy. I'll describe him for you. He was what my grandmother used to call a towhead . . . very, very blond. He was a tough little guy who walked at nine months and spoke sentences at fifteen months. He was my son. His mother was a very sweet young woman who unfortunately could not get used to the idea she had married a very rich man. She refused to hire a housekeeper. She did her own marketing. She refused to have a chauffeur. She wouldn't hear of driving an expensive automobile. Kathy lived in fear that folks from Iowa City would think she was getting uppity. One rainy night she was driving back from grocery shopping and—we think—a goddamn can of tomato soup rolled out of the bag and under her foot. And so she couldn't stop at the stop sign, and a trailer truck plowed into that goddamn piece of tin she called a car. And she and that little boy, Teddy, *died.* That was eight years ago. Now have you got it straight that when you call me Teddy, I see a little blond kid who walked early and talked early and would be ten years old next month?''

Ted's eyes glistened. ''Now *you* plan my defense. You're being paid for it. I'm going to the gym. Craig, take your pick.''

''I'll work out with you.''

They left the bungalow and started toward the men's spa. ''Where did you *find* him?'' Ted asked. ''For Christ's *sake!*''

''Have a heart, Ted. He's the best criminal lawyer in the country.''

''No, he isn't. And I'll tell you why. Because he came in with a preconceived notion and he's trying to mold me into the ideal defendant. And it's phony.''

The tennis player and his girlfriend were coming out of their bungalow. They greeted Ted warmly. ''Missed you at Forest Hills last time,'' the pro told Ted.

''Next year for sure.''

''We're all rooting for you.'' This time it was the pro's girlfriend with her model's smile flashing.

Ted returned the smile. ''Now, if I can just get you on the jury . . .'' He raised his hand in a gesture of acknowledgment and walked on. The smile disappeared. ''I wonder if they have celebrity tennis in Attica.''

''You won't have to give a damn one way or the other. It will have nothing to do with you.'' Craig stopped. ''Look, isn't that Elizabeth?''

They were almost directly in front of the main house. From across the vast lawn they watched as the slender figure ran down the steps of the veranda and turned toward the outer gates. There was no mistaking the honey-colored loop of hair twirled on the top of her head, the thrust of the chin, the innate grace of her movements. She was dabbing at her eyes, and as they watched, she pulled sunglasses from her pocket and put them on.

"I thought she was going home this morning." Ted's voice was impersonal. "Something's wrong."

"Do you want to see what it is?"

"Obviously my presence would only upset her more. Why don't *you* follow her? She doesn't think *you* killed Leila."

"Ted, for God's sake, knock it off! I'd put my hand in the fire for you and you know it, but being a punching bag isn't going to make me function any better. And I fail to see how it helps you."

Ted shrugged. "My apologies. You're quite right. Now see if you can help Elizabeth. I'll meet you back at my place in about an hour."

Craig caught up with her at the gate. Quickly she explained what had happened. His reaction was comforting. "You mean to say that Sammy may have been missing for hours and the police haven't been called?"

"They're going to be as soon as the grounds are searched, and I thought I'd just see if maybe . . ." Elizabeth could not finish. She swallowed and went on: "You remember when she had that first attack. She was so disoriented and then so embarrassed."

Craig's arm was around her. "Okay—steady. Let's walk a bit." They crossed the road toward the path that led to the Lone Cypress. The sun had dispersed the last of the morning mist, and the day was bright and warm. Sandpipers flurried over their heads, circled and returned to their perches on the rocky shore-line. Waves broke like foaming geysers against the rocks and retreated to the sea. The Lone Cypress, always a tourist attraction, was already the center of attention of the camera buffs.

Elizabeth began to question them. "We're looking for an older lady. . . . She may be ill. . . . She's quite small. . . ."

Craig took over. He gave an accurate description of Dora. "What was she wearing, Elizabeth?"

"A beige cardigan, a beige cotton blouse, a tan skirt."

"Sounds like my mother," commented a tourist in a red sport shirt with a camera slung over his shoulder.

"She's kind of everybody's mother," Elizabeth said.

They rang doorbells of the secluded homes hidden by shrubbery from the road. Maids, some sympathetic, some annoyed, promised to "keep an eye out."

They went to the Pebble Beach Lodge. "Sammy has breakfast here sometimes on her days off," Elizabeth said. With a clutch of hope, she searched the dining rooms, praying that her eyes would find the small straight figure, that Sammy would be surprised at all the fuss. But there were only the vacationers, dressed in casually expensive sport clothes, most of them awaiting their tee-off time.

Elizabeth turned to leave, but Craig held her arm. "I'll bet you didn't have any breakfast." He signaled to the headwaiter.

Over coffee they surveyed each other. ''If there's no sign of her when we get back, we'll insist on calling the police,'' he told her.

''Something's happened to her.''

''You can't be sure of that. Tell me exactly when you saw her, whether she said anything about going out.''

Elizabeth hesitated. She was not sure if she wanted to tell Craig about the letter Sammy was going to copy or about the letter that had been stolen. She did know that the deep concern on his face was a tremendous comfort, that if it became necessary, he would put the awesome power of Winters Enterprises into the search for Sammy. Her response was careful. ''When Sammy left me, she said she was going back to the office for a while.''

''I can't believe that she's so overworked she has to burn midnight oil.''

Elizabeth half-smiled. ''Not quite midnight. Nine thirty.'' To avoid further questions, she gulped the rest of the coffee. ''Craig, do you mind if we go back now? Maybe there's been some word.''

But there was not. And if the maids, the gardener and the chauffeur could be believed, every inch of the grounds had been searched. Now even Helmut agreed not to wait until noon, that it was time to phone in a missing-person report.

''That not good enough,'' Elizabeth told them. ''I want you to ask for Scott Alshorne.''

She waited for Scott at Sammy's desk. ''Do you want me to hang around?'' Craig asked.

''No.''

He glanced at the trash bags. ''What's all that?''

''Leila's fan mail. Sammy was answering it.''

''Don't start going through it. It will only upset you.'' Craig glanced into Min and Helmut's office. They were sitting side by side on the Art Deco wicker couch, speaking in low tones. He leaned over the desk. ''Elizabeth, you have to know I'm between a rock and a hard place. But when this is over, no matter how it ends, we've got to talk. I've missed you terribly.'' In a surprisingly agile move, he was around the desk; his hand was on her hair, his lips on her cheek. ''I'm always here for you,'' he whispered. ''If anything has happened to Sammy and you need a shoulder or an ear . . . You know where to find me.''

Elizabeth clutched at his hand and for an instant held it against her cheek. She felt its solid strength, its warmth, the width of his blunt fingers. And incongruously thought of Ted's long-fingered graceful hands. She dropped his hand and pulled away. ''Watch out or you'll get me crying.'' She tried to make her voice light, to dispel the intensity of the moment.

Craig seemed to understand. He straightened up and said matter-of-factly, ''I'll be in Ted's bungalow if you need me.''

Waiting was the hardest. It was like the night when she'd sat in Leila's apartment hoping, praying that Leila and Ted had made up, had gone off together and knowing with every nerve in her body that something was wrong. Sitting at Sammy's desk was agony. She wanted to run in a dozen different directions; to walk along the road and ask people if they'd seen her; to search the Crocker Woodland in case she'd wandered in there in a daze.

Instead, Elizabeth opened one of the bags of fan mail and brought out a handful of envelopes. At least she could accomplish something.

She could search for more anonymous letters.

CHAPTER 6

Sheriff Scott Alshorne had been a lifelong friend of Samuel Edgers, Min's first husband, the man who had built the Cypress Point Hotel. He and Min had liked each other from the start, and it had pleased him to see that Min kept her part of her bargain. She gave the ailing and cantankerous octogenarian a new lease on life for the five years she was married to him.

Scott had watched with mingled curiosity and awe as Min and that titled jerk she married next had taken a comfortable, profitable hotel and turned it into a self-consuming monster. Min now invited him at least once a month to dinner at the Spa, and in the last year and a half he'd come to know Dora Samuels well. That was why when Min called with the news of her disappearance, he instinctively feared the worst.

If Sammy had had some kind of stroke and started wandering around, she'd have been noticed. Old sick people didn't get overlooked on the Monterey Peninsula. Scott was proud of his jurisdiction.

His office was in Salinas, the seat of Monterey County and twenty-two miles from Pebble Beach. Crisply he issued instructions for the posting of a missing-person notice and directed that deputies from the Pebble Beach area meet him at the Spa.

He was silent on the drive. The deputy who chauffeured him noticed there were unusually deep creases in his boss's forehead, that the craggy, tanned face under the wealth of unmanageable white hair was furrowed in thought. When the chief looked like this, it meant he anticipated a big problem.

It was ten thirty when they drove through the gates. The houses and grounds had an air of tranquillity. There were few people walking around. Scott knew that most of the guests were in the spas, working out, being pummeled and patted and scrubbed and plucked so that when they went home at the end of their stay, their families and friends would gush over how marvelous they looked. Or they were in the clinic having one of Helmut's sophisticated and ultra-expensive treatments.

He had heard that Ted Winters' private jet had landed at the airport on Sunday afternoon and that Ted was here. He'd debated with himself as to whether or not to call him. Ted was under indictment for second-degree murder. He was also the kid who used to delight in sailing with his grandfather and Scott.

Knowing that Ted was booked at the Spa caused Scott to register openmouthed astonishment when he saw Elizabeth sitting at Sammy's desk. She had not heard him come up the stairs, and he took a moment to study her unobserved. She was deathly pale, and her eyes were red-rimmed. Strands of hair had slipped from the knot on top of her head and curled around her face. She was pulling letters from envelopes, glancing at them and tossing them aside impatiently. Clearly she was searching for something. He noticed that her hands were trembling.

He knocked loudly on the open door and watched her jump up. Relief and apprehension mingled in her expression. Spontaneously she ran around the desk and with outstretched arms hurried toward him. Just before she reached him, she stopped abruptly. "I'm sorry . . . I mean, how are you, Scott? It's good to see you."

He knew what she was thinking. Because of his longtime friendship with Ted, he might regard her as the enemy. Poor kid. He gathered her in a quick bear hug. To disguise his own emotion, he said gruffly, "You're too skinny. I hope you're not on one of Min's celebrity diets."

"I'm on a get-fat-fast. Banana splits and brownies."

"Good."

Together they went into Min's office. Scott raised his eyebrows when he saw the haggard expression on Min's face, the wary, veiled eyes of the Baron. They were both worried, and somehow he felt it went beyond concern for Sammy. His direct questions garnered the information he needed. "I'd like to take a look at Sammy's apartment."

Min led the way. Elizabeth and Helmut trailed behind. Somehow Scott's presence gave Elizabeth a faint touch of hope. At least something would be done. She had seen the disapproval in his face at the realization they had waited so long to phone him.

Scott glanced around the sitting room and walked into the bedroom. He pointed to the suitcase on the floor near the closet. "Was she planning to go somewhere?"

"She just got back," Min explained, then looked puzzled. "It's not like Sammy not to unpack immediately."

Scott opened the bag. There was a cosmetic case on top filled with pill bottles. He read the directions: "One every four hours; twice a day; two at bedtime." He frowned. "Sammy was careful about her medication.

She didn't want another siege. Min, show me the condition of the office as you found it.''

It was the copy machine that seemed to intrigue him most. ''The window was open. The machine was on.'' He stood in front of it. ''She was about to copy something. She looked out the window, and then what? She felt dizzy? She wandered outside? But where was she trying to go?'' He stared out the window. This view took in the expanse of the north lawn, the scattered bungalows along the way to the Olympic pool and the Roman bath—that god-awful monstrosity!

''You say every inch of the grounds, every building was searched?''

''Yes.'' Helmut answered first. ''I personally saw to it.''

Scott cut him off. ''We'll start all over.''

Elizabeth spent the next hours at Sammy's desk. Her fingers were dry from handling the dozens of letters she examined. They read alike—requests for Leila's autograph, requests for her picture. There was so far no sign of any more anonymous letters.

At two o'clock Elizabeth heard a shout. She raced to the window in time to see one of the policemen gesturing from the door of the bathhouse. Her feet flew on the stairs. At the next-to-last step, she tripped and fell, smashing her arms and legs against the polished tiles. Heedless of the sharp sting in her palms and knees, she ran across the lawn to the bathhouse, arriving as Scott disappeared inside. She followed him through the locker room into the pool area.

A policeman was standing at the side of the pool pointing down at Sammy's crumpled body.

Later, she vaguely remembered kneeling beside Sammy, reaching her hand to brush back the matted, bloody hair from her forehead, feeling Scott's iron grasp, hearing his sharp command: ''Don't touch her!'' Sammy's eyes were open, her features frozen in terror, her glasses still caught on her ears but dropped down on her nose, her palms outstretched as though pushing something back. Her beige cardigan was still buttoned, the wide patch pockets suddenly prominent. ''See if she has the letter to Leila,'' Elizabeth heard herself say. ''Look in the pockets.'' Then her own eyes widened. The beige wool cardigan became Leila's white satin pajamas, and she was kneeling over Leila's body again. . . .

Mercifully, she fainted.

When she regained consciousness, she was lying on the bed in her bungalow. Helmut was bending over her, holding something that smelled harsh and pungent under her nostrils. Min was chafing her hands. Uncontrollable sobs racked her body, and she heard herself wailing, ''Not Sammy, too, not Sammy too.''

Min held her tightly. ''Elizabeth, don't . . . Don't.''

Helmut muttered, ''This will help you.'' The prick of a needle in her arm.

When she awoke, the shadows were long in the room. Nelly, the maid who had helped in the search, was touching her shoulder. ''I'm so sorry to disturb you, miss,'' she said, ''but I did bring tea and something for you to eat. The sheriff can't wait any longer. He has to talk with you.''

CHAPTER 7

The news of Dora's death rippled through the Spa like an unwelcome rainstorm at a family picnic. There was mild curiosity: ''What ever was she doing wandering in that place?'' A sense of mortality: ''How old was she, did you say?'' An attempt to place her—''Oh, you mean that prim little woman in the office?''—then a quick return to the pleasant activities of the Spa. This was, after all, an extremely expensive retreat. One came here to escape problems, not find them.

In midafternoon Ted had gone for a massage, hoping to obtain some relief from tension in the pounding hands of the Swedish masseur. He'd just returned to his bungalow when Craig told him the news. ''They found her body in the bathhouse. She must have gotten dizzy and fallen.''

Ted thought of the afternoon in New York when Sammy had had that first stroke. They were all in Leila's apartment, and in the middle of a sentence Sammy's voice had trailed off. It was he who had realized there was something seriously wrong.

''How is Elizabeth taking it?'' he asked Craig.

''Pretty badly. I gather she fainted.''

''She was close to Sammy. She . . .'' Ted bit his lip and changed the subject. ''Where's Bartlett?''

''On the golf course.''

''I wasn't aware I brought him out here to play golf.''

''Ted, come off it! He's been on the job since early this morning. Henry claims he can think better if he gets some exercise.''

''Remind him that I go on trial next week. He'd better curtail his exercise.'' Ted shrugged. ''It was crazy to come here. I don't know why I thought it would help me calm down; it's not working.''

''Give it a chance. It wouldn't be any better in New York or Connecticut. Oh, I just bumped into your old friend Sheriff Alshorne.''

''Scott's here? Then they must think there's something peculiar about Sammy's death.''

''I don't know about that. It's probably just routine for him to show up.''

"Does he know I'm here?"

"Yes. As a matter of fact, he asked about you."

"Did he suggest that I call him?"

Craig hesitation was barely perceptible. "Well, not exactly—but look, it wasn't a social conversation."

Another person avoiding me, Ted thought. Another person waiting to see the full evidence laid out in court. Restlessly he wandered around the living room of his bungalow. Suddenly it had become a cage to him. But all rooms had seemed like that since the indictment. It must be a psychological reaction. "I'm going for a walk," he said abruptly. Then, to forestall Craig's offer of company, he added, "I'll be back in time for dinner."

As he passed the Pebble Beach Lodge, he wondered at the sense of isolation that made him feel so totally apart from the people who wandered along the paths, heading for the restaurants, the tourist shops, the golf courses. His grandfather had started bringing him to these courses when he was eight. His father had detested California, and so when they came it was just his mother and himself, and he'd seen her shed her nervous mannerisms and become younger, lighthearted.

Why hadn't she left his father? he wondered. Her family didn't have the Winters millions, but she would certainly have had enough money. Wasn't it because she was afraid of losing custody of him that she'd stayed in that cursed marriage? His father had never let her forget that first suicide attempt. And so she had stayed and endured his periodic drunken rages, his verbal abuse, his mimicking of her mannerisms, his scorn of her private fears until one night she had decided she couldn't endure any more.

Unseeingly, Ted walked along the Seventeen Mile Drive, unaware of the Pacific, glimmering and gleaming below the houses that rose above Stillwater Cove and Carmel Bay, unaware of the luxuriant bougainvillea, heedless of the expensive cars that sped past him.

Carmel was still crowded with summer tourists, college students getting in one last fling before the fall semester. When he and Leila walked through town, she'd stopped traffic. The thought made him pull his sunglasses from his pocket. In those days, men used to look at him with envy. Now he was aware of hostility on the faces of strangers who recognized him.

Hostility. Isolation. Fear.

These last seventeen months had disrupted his entire life, had forced him to do things he would not have believed possible. Now he accepted the fact that there was one more monumental hurdle he had to overcome before the trial.

Drenching perspiration soaked his body at the image of what that would be.

CHAPTER 8

Alvirah sat at the dressing table in her bungalow, happily surveying the shiny rows of creams and cosmetics that had been presented to her in the makeup class that afternoon. As the instructor had told her, she had flat cheekbones that could be beautifully enhanced with a soft blush rather than the crimson rouge she favored. She also had been persuaded to try wearing a brown mascara instead of the jet black which she believed drew attention to her eyes. ''Less is better,'' the makeup expert had assured her, and truth to tell, there was a difference. In fact, Alvirah decided, the new makeup, combined with the way they'd toned down her hair to a rich brown, made her look just like the way she remembered Aunt Agnes, and Agnes always was the beauty in the family. It also felt good that her hands were starting to lose their calluses. No more heavy cleaning for her. Ever. Period.

''And if you think you look good now, wait till you see how glamorous you are when Baron von Schreiber is finished with you,'' the makeup lady had said. ''His collagen injections will make those little lines around your mouth, nose and forehead disappear. It's almost miraculous.''

Alvirah sighed. She was bursting with happiness. Willy had always claimed that she was the finest-looking woman in Queens and that he liked being able to put his arms around her and feel that he had something to hold on to. But these last years, she'd put on weight. Wouldn't it be good to really look classy when they were hunting for a new house? Not that she had any intention of trying to get in with the Rockefellers—just middle-class people like themselves who'd made good. And if she and Willy made out a lot better than most others, were luckier than just about anybody else, it was nice to know that they could do some good for other people.

After she finished the articles for the *Globe,* she really would write that book. Her mother had always said, ''Alvirah, you've got such a lively imagination, you're going to be a writer someday.'' Maybe *someday* was here.

Alvirah pursed her lips and carefully applied coral lip gloss with her newly acquired brush. Years ago, in the belief that her lips were too narrow, she'd gotten into the habit of making a kind of Kewpie doll curve to accentuate them, but now she'd been persuaded that that wasn't necessary. She put down the brush and surveyed the results.

Somehow she really did feel a little guilty about being so happy and interested in everything when that nice little lady was stretched out somewhere in the morgue. But she was seventy-one, Alvirah comforted herself, and it must have been real quick. That's the way I want to go when it's my turn. Not that she expected it to be her turn for a long time to come. As her mother said, ''Our women make old bones.'' Her mother was eighty-four and still went bowling every Wednesday night.

Her makeup adjusted to her satisfaction, Alvirah took her tape recorder from her suitcase and inserted the cassette from Sunday night's dinner. As she listened, a puzzled frown creased her forehead. Funny—when you're just listening to people, you get a different perspective than when you're sitting with them. Like Syd Melnick was supposed to be a big agent. But he sure let Cheryl Manning push him around. And *she* could turn on a dime, one minute hassling Syd Melnick about the water she'd spilled herself and then all sweetness and light, asking Ted Winters if she could go with him sometime to see the Winters Gym at Dartmouth College. *Dartmuth,* Alvirah thought, not *Dart-mouth.* Craig Babcock had corrected her on that. He had such a nice calm voice. She'd told him that. ''You sound so educated.''

He'd laughed. ''You should have heard me in my teens.''

Ted Winters' voice was so well-bred. Alvirah knew *he* hadn't had to work on it. The three of them had a nice talk on that subject.

Alvirah checked her microphone to see that it was securely in place in the center flower of her sunburst pin and delivered an observation. ''Voices,'' she declared, ''tell a lot about people.''

She was surprised to hear the phone ring. It was only nine o'clock New York time, and Willy was supposed to be at a union meeting. She wished that he'd quit his job, but he said to give him time. He wasn't used to being a millionaire.

It was Charley Evans, the special features editor of the *New York Globe.* ''How's my star reporter?'' he asked. ''Any problems with the recorder?''

''It works like a charm,'' Alvirah assured him. ''I'm having a wonderful time and meeting some very interesting people.''

''Any celebrities?''

''Oh, yes.'' Alvirah couldn't help bragging. ''I came from the airport in a limousine with Elizabeth Lange, and I'm at the same dinner table as Cheryl Manning and Ted Winters.'' She was rewarded by an audible gasp on the other end of the phone.

''Are you telling me that Elizabeth Lange and Ted Winters are together?''

''Oh, not exactly together,'' Alvirah said hastily. ''In fact, she wouldn't go near him at all. She was going to leave right away, but she wanted to see her sister's secretary. The only trouble is Leila's secretary was found dead this afternoon in the Roman bathhouse.''

''Mrs. Meehan, hold on a minute. I want you to repeat everything you just said, very slowly. Someone will be taking it down.''

CHAPTER 9

At Scott Alshorne's request, the coroner of Monterey County performed an immediate autopsy on the remains of Dora Samuels. Death had been caused by a severe head injury, pressure on the brain from skull fragments, contributing cause a moderately severe stroke.

In his office, Scott studied the autopsy report in reflective silence and tried to pinpoint the reasons he felt there was something sinister about Dora Samuels' death.

That bathhouse. It looked like a mausoleum; it had turned out to be Sammy's sepulcher. Who the hell did Min's husband think he was to have foisted that on her? Incongruously, Scott thought of the contest Leila had run: Should the Baron be called the *tin* soldier or the *toy* soldier? Twenty-five words or less. Leila bought dinner for the winner.

Why had Sammy been in the bathhouse? Had she just wandered in there? Was she planning to meet someone? That didn't make sense. The electricity wasn't turned on. It would have been pitch black.

Min and Helmut had both stated that the bathhouse should have been locked. But they'd also admitted they had left it in a hurry yesterday afternoon. ''Minna was upset by the overrun costs,'' Helmut had explained. ''I was worried about her emotional state. It is a heavy door. Possibly I did not pull it shut.''

Sammy's death had been caused by the injuries to the back of her head. She had toppled backward into the pool. But had she fallen or been pushed? Scott got up and began backing across his office. A practical, if not a scientific test, he decided. No matter how dazed or confused you are, most people don't start walking backward unless they're backing *away* from someone, or something. . . .

He settled at his desk again. He was supposed to attend a civic dinner with the mayor of Carmel. He'd have to pass. He was going back to the Spa and he was going to talk to Elizabeth Lange. It was his hunch that she knew what urgent business had made Sammy go back to the office at nine thirty at night and what document had been so important to copy.

On the drive back to the Spa, two words flashed in his mind.

Fallen?

Pushed?

Then as the car passed the Pebble Beach Lodge, he realized what had been bothering him. That was the same question that was bringing Ted Winters to trial on a murder indictment!

CHAPTER 10

Craig spent the rest of the afternoon in Ted's bungalow going through the bulky package of mail that had been expressed from the New York office. With a practiced eye he skimmed memos, reviewed printouts, studied projection charts. His frown deepened as he read. That group of Harvard and Wharton Business M.B.A.'s Ted had hired a couple of years ago were a constant irritant to him. If they had their way, Ted would be building hotels on space platforms.

At least they had had the brains to recognize that they couldn't try to go around Craig anymore. The memos and letters were all addressed to him and Ted jointly.

Ted got back at five o'clock. Obviously the walk hadn't relaxed him any. He was in a foul mood. "Is there any reason you can't work in your place?" was his first question.

"None except that it seemed simpler to be here for you." Craig indicated the business files. "There are some things I'd like to go over."

"I'm not interested. Do what you think best."

"I think 'best' would be for you to have a Scotch and unwind a little. And I think 'best' for Winters Enterprises is to get rid of those two assholes from Harvard. Their expense accounts amount to armed robbery."

"I don't want to go into that now."

Bartlett came in pink-faced from his afternoon in the sun. Craig noticed the way Ted's mouth tightened at Bartlett's genial greeting. There was no question Ted was starting to unravel. He drank the first Scotch quickly and didn't protest when Craig refilled it.

Bartlett wanted to discuss the list of defense witnesses Craig had prepared for him. He read it off to Ted—a glittering array of famous names.

"You don't have the President on it," Ted said sarcastically.

Bartlett fell into the trap. "Which president?"

"Of the United States, of course. I used to be one of his golf partners."

Bartlett shrugged and closed the file. "Obviously this isn't going to be a good working session. Are you planning to eat out tonight?"

"No, I'm planning to stay right here. And right now I'm planning to nap."

Craig and Bartlett left together. "You do realize this is getting hopeless," Bartlett told him.

At six thirty Craig received a call from the agency he'd hired to investigate the eyewitness, Sally Ross. "There was some excitement in Ross's apartment building," he was told. "The woman who lived directly above her walked in on an attempted burglary. They caught the guy—a petty thief with a long record. Ross didn't go out at all."

At seven o'clock, Craig met Bartlett at Ted's bungalow. Ted wasn't there. They started toward the main house together. ''You're about as popular as I am with Teddy these days,'' Bartlett commented.

Craig shrugged. ''Listen, if he wants to take it out on me, it's all right. In a way, I brought this on him.''

''How do you figure that one?''

''I introduced him to Leila. She was my date first.''

They reached the veranda in time to hear the newest witticism. *At Cypress Point, for four thousand dollars a week you get to use some of the pools. For five thousand you get to use the ones with water in them.*

There was no sign of Elizabeth during the ''cocktail'' hour. Craig watched for her to come up the path, but she did not appear. Bartlett drifted over to the tennis pro and his girlfriend. Ted was talking to the Countess and her group; Cheryl was hanging on his arm. A morose-looking Syd was standing off by himself. Craig went over to him. ''That business about 'proof.' Was Cheryl drunk last night or just talking her usual drivel?'' he asked.

He knew Syd wouldn't have minded taking a swing at him. Syd considered him to be, like all the parasites in Ted's world, the bottleneck to Ted's largesse. Craig considered himself more of a goalie—you had to pass him to score.

''I would say,'' Syd told him, ''that Cheryl was giving her usual splendid dramatic performance.''

Min and Helmut did not appear in the dining rooms until after the guests had settled. Craig noticed how gaunt they looked, how fixed their smiles were as they visited from table to table. Why not? They were in the business of staving off old age, illness and death. This afternoon Sammy had proved it was a pointless game.

As she sat down, Min murmured an apology for being late. Ted ignored Cheryl, whose hand clung persistently to his. ''How *is* Elizabeth?''

Helmut answered him: ''She's taking it very hard. I gave her a sedative.''

Would Alvirah Meehan never stop fooling with that damn pin? Craig wondered. She had parked herself between him and Ted. He glanced around. Min. Helmut. Syd. Bartlett. Cheryl. Ted. The Meehan woman. Himself. There was one more place setting next to him. He asked Min who would be joining them.

''Sheriff Alshorne. He just came back. He's talking to Elizabeth now.'' Min bit her lip. ''Please. We all know how sad we feel about losing Sammy, but I think it would be better if we do not discuss it during dinner.''

''Why does the sheriff want to talk to Elizabeth Lange?'' Alvirah Meehan asked. ''He doesn't think there's anything funny about Miss Samuels dying in that bathhouse, does he?''

Seven stony pairs of eyes discouraged further questions.

The soup was chilled peach and strawberry, a specialty of the Spa. Alvirah sipped hers contentedly. The *Globe* would be interested to learn that Ted Winters was very clearly concerned about Elizabeth.

She could hardly wait to meet the sheriff.

CHAPTER 11

Elizabeth stood at the window of her bungalow and glanced at the main house just in time to see the guests drifting inside for dinner. She had insisted that Nelly leave: "You've had a long day, and I'm perfectly all right now." She'd propped herself up in bed for the tea and toast, then showered quickly, hoping that the splashing cold water would clear her head. The sedative had left her groggy.

An off-white cable-knit sweater and tan stretch pants were her favorite comfortable clothes. Somehow, wearing them, her feet bare, her hair twisted up casually, she felt like herself.

The last of the guests had disappeared. But as she watched, she saw Scott cut across the lawn in her direction.

They sat across from each other, leaning slightly forward, anxious to communicate, wary of how to begin. Looking at Scott with his kind, questioning eyes made Elizabeth remember how Leila had once said, "He's the kind of guy I would have liked for a father." Last night Sammy had suggested that they take the anonymous letter to him.

"I'm sorry I couldn't wait until the morning to see you," Scott told her. "But there are too many things about Sammy's death that trouble me. From what I've learned so far, Sammy drove six hours from Napa Valley yesterday, arriving at about two o'clock. She wasn't due till late evening. She must have been pretty tired, but she didn't even stop to unpack. She went directly to the office. She claimed she wasn't feeling well and wouldn't come down to the dining room for dinner, but the maid tells me she had a tray in the office and was busily going through bags of mail. Then she came to visit you and left around nine thirty. Sammy should have been pretty beat by then, but she apparently went back to the office and turned on the copy machine. Why?"

Elizabeth got up and walked into the bedroom. From her suitcase she took the letter from Sammy that had been waiting for her in New York. She showed it to Scott. "When I realized Ted was here I would have left immediately, but I had to wait and see Sammy about this." She told him about the letter that had been taken from Sammy's office and showed him the transcript Sammy had made from memory. "This is pretty much the text of it."

Her eyes filled as she looked at Sammy's graceful penmanship. "She found another poison-pen letter in one of those sacks last evening. She was going to make a copy for me, and we were planning to give the original to you. I've written it down as I remembered. We had hoped the original could be traced. The typeface for magazines is coded, isn't it?"

"Yes." Scott read and re-read the transcripts of the letters. "Stinking business."

"Somebody was systematically trying to destroy Leila," Elizabeth said. "Somebody doesn't want those letters found. Somebody took one from Sammy's desk yesterday afternoon and perhaps the other one from Sammy's body last night."

"Are you saying that you think Sammy may have been murdered?"

Elizabeth flinched, then looked directly at him. "I simply can't answer that. I do know that someone was worried enough about those letters to want them back. I do know that a series of those letters would have explained Leila's behavior. Those letters precipitated that quarrel with Ted, and those letters have something to do with Sammy's death. I swear this to you, Scott. I'm going to find out who wrote them. Maybe there's no criminal prosecution possible, but there has to be a way of making that person pay. It's someone who was very close to Leila, and I have my suspicions."

Fifteen minutes later Scott left Elizabeth, the transcripts of both anonymous letters in his pocket. Elizabeth believed Cheryl had written those letters. It made sense. It was Cheryl's kind of trick. Before he went into the dining room, he walked around to the right side of the main house. Up there was the window where Sammy had stood when she turned on the copy machine. If someone had been on the steps of the bathhouse and signaled to her to come down . . .

It was possible. But, of course, he told himself sadly, Sammy wouldn't have come down except for someone she knew. And trusted.

The others were halfway through the main course when he joined them. The empty seat was between Craig and a woman who was introduced as Alvirah Meehan. Scott took the initiative in greeting Ted. *Presumption of innocence.* Ted had always had outstanding looks. It was no wonder that a woman would go to any extreme to separate him from another woman. Scott did not miss the way Cheryl constantly managed to touch Ted's hand, to brush her shoulder against his.

He helped himself to lamb chops from the silver tray the waiter was offering him.

"They're delicious," Alvirah Meehan confided, her voice barely a whisper. "They'll never go broke in this place from the size of the portions, but I'm telling you when you're finished you feel as though you've had a big meal.''

Alvirah Meehan. Of course. He'd read in the *Monterey Review* about the forty-million-dollar lottery winner who was going to realize her fondest dream by coming to Cypress Point Spa. ''Are you enjoying yourself, Mrs. Meehan?''

Alvirah beamed. ''I sure am. Everyone has been just wonderful, and so friendly.'' Her smile encompassed the entire table. Min and Helmut attempted to return it. ''The treatments make you feel like a princess. The nutritionist said that in two weeks I should be able to lose five pounds and a couple of inches. Tomorrow I'm having collagen to get rid of the lines around my mouth. I'm scared of injections, but Baron von Schreiber will give me something for my nerves. I'll leave here a new woman feeling . . . like . . . like a butterfly floating on a cloud.'' She pointed to Helmut. ''The Baron wrote that. Isn't he a real author?''

Alvirah realized she was talking too much. It was just that she felt kind of guilty being an undercover reporter and wanted to say nice things about these people. But now she'd better be quiet and listen to see if the sheriff had anything to say about Dora Samuels' death. But, disappointingly, no one brought it up at all. It was only when they had just about finished the vanilla mousse that the sheriff asked, not quite casually, ''You people will all be around here for the next few days? No one has plans to leave?''

''Our plans are undetermined,'' Syd told him. ''Cheryl may have to go back to Beverly Hills on short notice.''

''I think it would be better if she checks with me before she goes to Beverly Hills, or anywhere else,'' Scott said pleasantly. ''And by the way, Baron—those bags of Leila's fan mail. I'll be taking them with me.''

He put down the spoon he was holding and began to push back his chair. ''It's funny,'' he said, ''but it's my guess that one of the people at this table, with the exception of Mrs. Meehan, may have been writing some pretty rotten letters to Leila LaSalle. I'm real anxious to find out who that might be.''

To Syd's dismay, Scott's now steely glance rested squarely on Cheryl.

CHAPTER 12

It was nearly ten o'clock before they were alone in their apartment. Min had agonized all day about whether or not to confront Helmut with the proof that he had been in New York the night Leila died. To confront him was to force the admission that he had been involved with Leila. Not to confront him was to allow him to remain vulnerable. How stupid he had been not to destroy the record of the telephone call!

He went directly into his dressing room, and a few minutes later she heard the whirling of the Jacuzzi in his bathroom. When he came back, she was waiting in one of the deep armchairs near the bedroom fireplace. Impersonally, she studied him. His hair was combed as precisely as though he were leaving for a formal ball; his silk dressing gown was knotted by a silk cord; his military posture made him seem taller than his true height. Five feet ten inches was barely above the average for men these days.

He prepared a Scotch and soda for himself and, without asking, poured a sherry for her. "It's been a difficult day, Minna. You handled it well," he said. Still she did not speak, and at last he seemed to sense that her silence was unusual. "This room is so restful," he said. "Aren't you glad you let me have my head with this color scheme? And it suits you. Strong, beautiful colors for a strong and beautiful woman."

"I would not consider peach a strong color."

"It *becomes* strong when it is wedded with deep blue. Like me, Minna. I become strong because I am with you."

"Then why this?" From the pocket of her robe she pulled out the telephone-credit-card bill and watched as his expression changed from bewilderment to fear. "Why did you lie to me? You were in New York that night. Were you with Leila? Had you gone to her?"

He sighed. "Minna, I'm glad you have found this. I wanted so much to tell you."

"Tell me now. You were in love with Leila. You were having an affair with her."

"No. I swear not."

"You're lying."

"Minna, I am telling the truth. I did go to her—as a friend—as a doctor. I got there at nine thirty. The door to her apartment was just barely open. I could hear Leila crying hysterically. Ted was shouting at her to put the phone down. She screamed back at him. The elevator was coming. I didn't want to be seen. You know the right angle the foyer takes. I went around that corner . . ."

Helmut sank to the floor at Min's feet. "Minna, it has been killing me not to tell you. Minna, Ted did push her. I heard her scream, *'Don't. Don't.'* And then her shriek as she fell."

Min paled. "Who got off the elevator? Did anyone see you?"

"I don't know. I ran down the fire stairs."

Then, as if his composure, his sense of order, had abandoned him, he leaned forward, his head in his hands, and began to cry.

Wednesday, September 2

QUOTE FOR THE DAY:

Beauty is bought by judgment of the eye.

—Shakespeare

Good morning, treasured guests.

Are you feeling a bit lazy this morning? Never mind. After a few days we all begin to unwind into delicious and refreshing slumber and think that maybe, just maybe this morning we shall lie abed.

No. No. We beckon to you. Join us in that wonderful and invigorating morning walk through our beautiful grounds and along the coast. You will be glad. Perhaps by now you have already learned the pleasure of meeting new friends, of revisiting old ones on our sun-bright journey.

A gentle reminder. All guests who swim in any of the pools alone *must* wear the regulation Spa whistle. It has never been needed, but it is a safety factor that we deem essential.

Look in the mirror. Isn't all the exercise and pampering starting to show? Aren't your eyes brighter? Isn't your skin firmer? Won't it be fun showing off the new you to your family and friends?

And a final thought. Whatever troubles you brought with you to the Spa should by now be completely forgotten. *Think* happy.

Baron and Baroness Helmut von Schreiber

CHAPTER 1

Elizabeth's phone rang at six o'clock. Sleepily she groped for it. Her eyelids were heavy and drooping. The aftereffects of the sedative made it impossible to think clearly.

It was William Murphy, the New York assistant district attorney. His opening words snapped her awake. "Miss Lange, I thought you wanted your sister's killer convicted." Without waiting for her to answer, he rushed on: "Can you please explain to me why you are in the same spa with Ted Winters?"

Elizabeth pulled herself up and swung her feet onto the floor. "I didn't know he was going to be here. I haven't been near him."

"That may be true, but the minute you saw him you should have been on the next plane home. Take a look at this morning's *Globe*. They've got a picture of you two in a clinch."

"I was never—"

"It was at the memorial service, but the way you're looking at each other is open to interpretation. Get out of there *now!* And what's this about your sister's secretary?"

"She's the reason I can't leave here." She told him about the letters, about Sammy's death. "I won't go near Ted," she promised, "but I am staying here until Friday. That gives me two days to find the letter Dora was carrying or to figure out who took it from her."

She would not change her mind, and finally Murphy hung up with a parting shot: "If your sister's killer walks, look to yourself for the reason." He paused. "And I told you before: *Be careful!*"

She jogged into Carmel. The New York papers would be on the stands there. Once again it was a glorious late-summer day. Sleek limousines and Mercedes convertibles followed each other on the road to the golf course. Other joggers waved at her amiably. Privacy hedges protected the estate homes from the curious eyes of the tourists, but in between, glimpses of the Pacific could be seen. A glorious day to be alive, Elizabeth thought, and she shuddered at the mental image of Sammy's body in the morgue.

Over coffee in a breakfast shop on Ocean Avenue, she read the *Globe*. Someone had snapped that picture at the end of the memorial service. She had started to weep. Ted was beside her. His arm had come around her and he'd turned her to him. She tried not to remember how it had felt to be in his arms.

With a surge of heartsick contempt for herself, she laid money on the table and left the restaurant. On the way out she tossed the paper into a wastebasket. She wondered who at the Spa had tipped off the *Globe*. It could have been one of the staff. Min and Helmut were plagued with leaks. It could have been one of the guests who in exchange for personal publicity fed items to the columnists. It also could have been Cheryl.

When she got back to her bungalow, Scott was sitting on the porch waiting for her. ''You're an early bird,'' she told him.

There were circles under his eyes. ''I didn't do much sleeping last night. Something about Sammy falling backward into that pool just doesn't sit right with me.''

Elizabeth winced as she thought of Sammy's bloodstained head.

''I'm sorry,'' Scott told her.

''It's all right. I feel exactly the same way. Did you find any more of those letters in the mailbags?''

''No. I've got to ask you to go through Sammy's personal effects with me. I don't know what I'm looking for, but you might spot something I'd miss.''

''Give me ten minutes to shower and change.''

''You're sure it won't upset you too much?''

Elizabeth leaned against the porch railing and ran her hand through her hair. ''If that letter had been found, I could believe Sammy might have had some sort of attack and wandered into the bathhouse. But with the letter gone . . . Scott, if someone pushed her or frightened her so that she backed away, that person is a murderer.''

The doors of the bungalows around them were opening. Men and women in identical ivory terrycloth robes headed for the spa buildings. ''Treatments start in fifteen minutes,'' Elizabeth said. ''Massages and facials and steam baths and God knows what-all. Isn't it incredible to think that one of the people being pampered here today left Sammy to die in that god-awful mausoleum?''

Craig's early-morning call was from the private investigator, and it was obvious he was troubled. ''Nothing more on Sally Ross,'' he said, ''but the word is that the burglar who was picked up in her building claims he has information about Leila LaSalle's death. He's trying to make a deal with the district attorney.''

''What *kind* of information? This might be the break we're looking for.''

''My contact doesn't get that feeling.''

''What's *that* supposed to mean?''

"The district attorney is happy. You have to conclude his case is stronger, not weaker."

Craig phoned Bartlett and reported the conversation. "I'll put my office on it," Bartlett said. "My people may be able to find out something. We'll have to sit tight until we find out what's up. In the meantime I intend to see Sheriff Alshorne. I want a full explanation of those 'poison-pen' letters he talked about. You're *sure* Teddy wasn't involved with another woman, somebody he may be protecting? He doesn't seem to realize how much that could help his case. Maybe you might mention that to him."

Syd was about to leave for the hike when his telephone rang. Something told him it would be Bob Koenig. He was wrong. For three endless minutes he pleaded with a loan shark for a little more time to pay the rest of his debts. "If Cheryl gets this part, I can borrow against my commissions," he argued. "I swear she has the edge over Margo Dresher. . . . Koenig told me himself . . . I swear. . . ."

When he hung up the receiver, he sat on the edge of the bed trembling. He had no choice. He had to go to Ted and use what he knew to get the money he needed.

Time had run out.

There was something indefinably different about Sammy's apartment. Elizabeth felt it was as though her aura as well as her physical being had departed. Her plants had not been watered. Dead leaves rimmed the planters. "Min was in touch with Sammy's cousin about the funeral arrangements," Scott explained.

"Where is her body now?"

"It will be picked up from the morgue tomorrow and shipped to Ohio for burial in the family plot."

Elizabeth thought of the concrete dust that had smudged Sammy's skirt and cardigan. "Can I give you clothes for Sammy?" she asked. "Is it too late?"

"It's not too late."

The last time she'd performed this service had been for Leila. Sammy had helped her select the dress in which Leila would be buried. "Remember, the casket won't be open," Sammy had reminded her.

"It isn't that," Elizabeth had said. "You know Leila. If she ever wore anything that didn't feel right, she was uncomfortable all evening even if everyone else thought she looked great. If there's such a thing as knowing . . ."

Sammy had understood. And together they had decided on the green chiffon-and-velvet gown Leila had worn the night she won the Oscar. They were the only two who had seen her in the casket. The undertaker had skillfully covered the bruises, had reconstructed the beautiful face, now curiously peaceful at last. For a time they had sat together reminiscing. Sammy holding Elizabeth's hand, finally reminding her that it was time to allow the fans to file past the bier, that the funeral director needed time to close the casket and drape it in the floral blanket that Elizabeth and Ted had ordered.

Now, with Scott watching her, Elizabeth examined the closet. ''The blue tie silk,'' she murmured, ''the one Leila gave her for her birthday two years ago. Sammy used to say that if she'd had clothes like this when she was young, her whole life might have been different.''

She packed a small overnight case containing underthings, stockings, shoes and the inexpensive pearl necklace Sammy always wore with her ''good dresses.'' ''At least that's one thing I know I can do for her,'' she told Scott. ''Now let's get about the business of finding what happened to her.''

Sammy's dresser drawers revealed only personal items. Her desk held her checkbook, daily memo pad, personal stationery. On a shelf of the closet, pushed back behind a stack of sweaters, they found a year-old appointment book and a bound copy of *Merry-Go-Round* by Clayton Anderson.

''Leila's play,'' Elizabeth said.''I never did get to read it.'' She opened the folder and flipped through the pages. ''Look, it's her working script. She always made so many notes and changed lines so that they sounded right for her.''

Scott watched as Elizabeth ran her fingers over the ornate penmanship that dotted the margins of the pages. ''Why don't you take that?'' he asked.

''I'd like to.''

He opened the appointment book. The entries were in the same curlicued handwriting. ''This was Leila's too.'' There were no entries after March 31. On that page Leila had printed OPENING NIGHT! Scott flipped through the earlier pages. Most of them had the daily entry marked *Rehearsal* with a line drawn through.

There were appointments indicated for the hairdresser, for costume fittings, visit Sammy at Mount Sinai, send flowers, Sammy, publicity appearances. In the last six weeks, more and more of the extraneous appointments had been crossed out. There were also notations: *Sparrow, L.A.; Ted, Budapest; Sparrow, Montreal; Ted, Bonn.* . . . ''She seems to have kept both your schedules right in front of her.''

''She did. So she'd know where to reach us.''

Scott stopped at one page. ''You two were in the same city that night.'' He turned the pages more slowly. ''Actually, Ted seems to have shown up fairly regularly in the same cities where your play was booked.''

''Yes. We'd go out for supper after the performance and call Leila together.''

Scott scrutinized Elizabeth's face. For just an instant something else had come over it. Was it possible that Elizabeth had fallen in love with Ted and refused to face that fact? And if so, was it possible that a sense of guilt was subconsciously demanding that Ted be punished for Leila's death, knowing that she would be punishing herself at the same time? It was a disquieting thought. He tried to dismiss it. "This appointment book probably doesn't have any bearing on the case, but I still think the district attorney in New York should have it," he said.

"Why?"

"No particular reason. But it could be considered an exhibit."

There was nothing more to be found in Sammy's apartment. "I've got a suggestion," Scott told her. "Go over to the spa and follow whatever schedule you had planned. As I told you, there are no more anonymous letters in that fan mail. My boys went through everything in those bags last night. Our chance of finding out who sent them is remote. I'll talk to Cheryl, but she's pretty cagey. I don't think she'll give herself away."

Together they walked down the long hall that led to the main house. "You haven't gone through Sammy's desk in the office, have you?" Scott asked.

"No." Elizabeth realized how tightly she was gripping the script. Something was compelling her to read it. She'd only seen that one terrible performance. She'd heard it was a good vehicle for Leila. Now she wanted to judge for herself. Reluctantly she accompanied Scott to the office. That had become another place she wanted to avoid.

Helmut and Min were in their private office. The door was open. Henry Bartlett and Craig were with them. Bartlett lost no time in demanding an explanation for the anonymous letters. "They may very well contribute to my client's defense," he told Scott. "We have a right to be fully briefed on them."

Elizabeth watched Henry Bartlett as he absorbed Scott's explanation of the anonymous letters. His look grew intense. His face was all sharp planes; his eyes were hard. This was the man who would be cross-examining her in court. He looked like a predator watching for prey.

"Let me get this straight," Bartlett said. "Miss Lange and Miss Samuels agreed that Leila LaSalle may have been profoundly upset by poison-pen letters suggesting that Ted Winters was involved with someone else? Those letters have now disappeared? On Monday night Miss Samuels wrote her impressions of the first letter? Miss Lange has transcribed the second one? I want copies."

"I see no reason why you can't have them," Scott told him. He placed Leila's appointment book on Min's desk. "Oh, for the record, this is something else I'm sending on to New York," he said. "It was Leila's calendar for the last three months of her life."

Without asking for permission, Henry Bartlett reached for it. Elizabeth waited for Scott to protest, but he did not. Watching Bartlett thumb through Leila's personal daily diary, she felt an enormous sense of intrusion. What business had he? She threw an angry glance at Scott. He was looking at her impassively.

He's trying to prepare me for next week, she thought bleakly, and realized that maybe she should be grateful. Next week, all that Leila was would be laid out for twelve people to analyze; her own relationship with Leila, with Ted—nothing would be hidden, no privacy beyond violation. "I'll look through Sammy's desk," she said abruptly.

She was still holding the script of the play. She laid it on Sammy's desk and quickly went through the drawers. There was absolutely nothing personal in them. Spa letterheads; Spa publicity folders; Spa follow-up memos; the usual office paraphernalia.

Min and the Baron had followed her out. She glanced up to see them standing in front of Sammy's desk. Both of them were staring at the leather-bound folder with the bold title *Merry-Go-Round* on the cover.

"Leila's play?" Min asked.

"Yes. Sammy kept Leila's copy. I'll take it now."

Craig, Bartlett and the sheriff came out of the private office. Henry Bartlett was smiling—a self-satisfied, smug, chilly smile. "Miss Lange, you've been a great help to us today. But I think I should warn you that the jury won't take kindly to the fact that as a woman scorned, you put Ted Winters through this hellish nightmare."

Elizabeth stood up, her lips white. "What are you talking about?"

"I'm talking about the fact that in her own handwriting, your sister made the connection between you and Ted 'happening' to be in the same city so often. I'm talking about the fact that someone else also made that connection and tried to warn her with those letters. I'm talking about the look on your face when Ted put his arms around you at the memorial service. Surely you've seen this morning's paper? Apparently what may have been a mild flirtation for Ted was serious to you, and so when he dropped you, you discovered a way to take your revenge."

"You filthy liar!" Elizabeth did not know she had thrown the copy of the play at Henry Bartlett until it struck him in the chest.

His expression was impassive, even pleased. Bending, he picked up the script and handed it back to her. "Do me a favor, young lady, and stage that kind of outburst in front of the jury next week," he said. "They'll *exonerate* Ted."

CHAPTER 2

While Craig and Bartlett went to confront the sheriff, Ted worked out with the Nautilus equipment in the men's spa. Each piece of equipment he used seemed to emphasize his own situation. The rowboat that went nowhere; the bicycle that no matter how furiously pedaled, stayed in place. On the surface he managed to exchange pleasantries with some of the other men in the gym—the head of the Chicago stock exchange, the president of Atlantic banks, a retired admiral.

He sensed in all of them a wariness: they didn't know what to say to him, didn't want to say "Good luck." It was easier for them—and for him—when they got busy with the machines and concentrated on building muscles.

Men in prison tended to get pretty soft. Not enough exercise. Boredom. Pallid skin. Ted studied his own tan. It wouldn't last long behind bars.

He was supposed to meet Bartlett and Craig in his bungalow at ten o'clock. Instead, he went for a swim in the indoor pool. He'd have preferred the Olympic pool, but there was always the chance Elizabeth might be there. He didn't want to run into her.

He had swum about ten laps when he saw Syd dive in at the opposite end of the pool. They were six lanes apart, and after a brief wave, he ignored Syd. But after twenty minutes, when the three swimmers between them had left, he was surprised to see that Syd was keeping pace with him. He had a powerful backstroke and moved with swift precision from one end of the pool to the other. Ted deliberately set out to beat him. Syd obviously caught on. After six laps they were in a dead heat.

They left the water at the same time. Syd slung a towel over his shoulders and came around the pool. "Nice workout. You're in good shape."

"I've been swimming every day in Hawaii for nearly a year and a half. I should be."

"The pool at my health club isn't like Hawaii, but it keeps me fit." Syd looked around. There were Jacuzzis in two corners of the glass-enclosed room. "Ted, I have to talk to you privately."

They went to the opposite end. There were three new swimmers in the pool, but they were well out of earshot. Ted watched as Syd rubbed the towel through his dark brown hair. He noticed that the hair on Syd's chest was completely gray. That'll be the next thing, he decided. He would grow old and gray in prison.

Syd did not hedge. "Ted, I'm in trouble. Big trouble. With guys who play rough. It all began with that damn play. I borrowed too much. I thought I could sweat it out. If Cheryl gets this part, I'm on my way up again. But I can't stall them anymore. I need a loan. Ted, I mean a *loan.* But I need it now."

"How much?"

"Six hundred thousand dollars. Ted, it's small change for you, and it's a loan. But you owe it to me."

"I owe it to you?"

Syd looked around and then stepped closer. His mouth was within inches of Ted's ear. "I'd never have said this . . . never even told you I knew . . . But Ted, I *saw* you that night. You ran past me, a block from Leila's apartment. Your face was bleeding. Your hands were scratched. You were in shock. You don't remember, do you? You didn't even hear me when I called you. You just kept running." Syd's voice dropped to a whisper. "Ted, I caught up with you. I asked what had happened and you told me Leila was dead, that she had fallen off the terrace. Ted, then you said to me . . . I swear to God . . . you said to me, 'My father pushed her, my father pushed her.' You were like a little kid, trying to blame what you did on someone else. You even *sounded* like a little kid."

Ted felt waves of nausea. "I don't believe you."

"Why should I lie? Ted, you ran into the street. A cab came along. You nearly got run over stopping it. Ask that cabbie who took you to Connecticut. He's going to be a witness, isn't he? Ask him if he didn't almost sideswipe you. Ted, I'm your *friend.* I know how you felt when Leila went nuts in Elaine's. I know how *I* felt. When I saw you, I was on my way to try to talk sense to Leila. I was mad enough to kill her myself. Have I mentioned this once to you, to anyone? I wouldn't do it now, except I'm desperate. You've got to help me! If I don't come up with that money in forty-eight hours—I'm finished."

"You'll have the money."

"Oh, Christ, Ted, I *knew* I could count on you. God, thanks, Ted." Syd put his hands on Ted's shoulders.

"Get away from me." Ted's voice was almost a shout. The swimmers looked at them curiously. Ted shook himself free, grabbed his towel and ran blindly out of the pool area.

CHAPTER 3

Scott questioned Cheryl in her bungalow. This one was furnished in a splashy yellow-and-green-and-white print, with white carpeting and white walls. Scott felt the thickness of the carpet under his feet. All wool. Top quality. Sixty . . . seventy dollars a yard? No wonder Min had that haunted look! Scott knew exactly how much old Samuel had left her. There couldn't be much left, after what she'd poured into this place. . . .

Cheryl was not happy about having been paged in the spa to meet him. She was wearing her own version of the standard tank suit, a skimpy scrap of material which did not quite cover her breasts and arched up on either side of her hipbones. The terrycloth robe was slung on her shoulders. She did not attempt to conceal her impatience. "I'm due in a calisthenics class in ten minutes," she told him.

"Well, let's hope you make it," he said. His throat muscles tightened as the active dislike he felt for Cheryl swelled within him. "Your chances will improve a lot if you give me some straight answers. Like did you write some pretty nasty letters to Leila before she died?"

As he had anticipated, the interrogation was, at first, fruitless. Cheryl cleverly dodged his questions. Anonymous letters? Why would she be interested in sending them? Break up Ted and Leila? What difference would it have made if they *had* ended up married? It wouldn't have lasted. Leila didn't have it in her to stick with one man. She had to hurt men before they hurt her. The play? She had no idea of how the rehearsals for Leila's play had gone. Frankly, she hadn't been that interested.

Finally Scott had had enough. "Listen, Cheryl, I think there's something you'd better realize. I'm not satisfied that Sammy's death was from natural causes. The second anonymous letter she was carrying is missing.

"You went to Sammy's desk. You left a bill marked *Paid in full.* An anonymous letter was on top of the desk with other fan mail. And then the letter disappeared. Granted someone else *may* have entered the reception area so quietly that even though the door was open, neither Min nor the Baron nor Sammy heard anyone come in. But that's a bit unlikely, isn't it?" He did not share with Cheryl the fact that Min and the Baron both had had access to the desk, out of Sammy's presence. He was rewarded by a faint glow of alarm in Cheryl's eyes. She licked her lips nervously.

"You're not suggesting I had anything to do with Sammy's death?"

"I'm suggesting that you took that first letter from Sammy's desk, and I want it now. That is state's evidence in a murder trial."

She looked away, and as Scott studied her, he saw an expression of naked panic come over her face. He followed her gaze and saw a sliver of charred paper wedged under the baseboard. Cheryl lunged from the couch to pick it up, but he was too quick for her.

On the ragged piece of cheap paper were pasted three words:

Learn your lines.

Scott took out his wallet and carefully inserted the tiny scrap in it. "So you did steal that letter," he said. "Destroying evidence is a felony, punishable by imprisonment. What about the second letter? The one Sammy was carrying? Did you destroy that one too? And how did you get it from her? You'd better get yourself a lawyer, lady."

Cheryl clutched his arm. "Scott, my God, please. I swear I didn't write those letters. I swear the only time I saw Sammy was in Min's office. All right. I took this letter from Sammy's desk. I thought it might help Ted.

I showed it to Syd. He said people would think I wrote it. He tore it up; I didn't. I swear that's as much as I know.'' Tears were spilling down her cheeks. ''Scott, any publicity, *any publicity about this at all* could kill my chances of being Amanda. Scott, please.''

Scott heard the contempt in his voice. ''I really don't give a damn how publicity affects your career, Cheryl. Why don't we make a bargain? I'll hold off bringing you in for formal questioning and you do some hard thinking. Maybe your memory will suddenly get better. For your sake, I hope so.''

CHAPTER 4

In a state of dazed relief, Syd headed back to his bungalow. *Ted was going to lend him the money.* It had been so tempting to make the story stronger, to say that Ted had outright admitted killing Leila. But at the last instant, he'd changed his mind and quoted Ted exactly. God, Ted had sounded creepy when he'd rambled about his father that night. Syd still felt a violent wrench in his gut whenever he thought of running after Ted. It had been immediately obvious that Ted had been in some sort of psychotic state. After Leila's death, he'd waited to see whether Ted would ever sound him out about that meeting. His reaction today proved he had no memory of it.

He cut across the lawn, deliberately avoiding the path. He didn't want to make small talk with anyone. There'd been some new arrivals yesterday. One of them he recognized as a young actor who'd been leaving his photos at the agency and phoning constantly. He wondered what old broad was paying his way. Today of all days, Syd didn't want to spend his time dodging eager would-be clients.

His first move when he reached the privacy of his own place was to make a drink. He needed one. He *deserved* one. His second was to phone his early-morning caller. ''I'll have the money to you by the weekend,'' he said, with newfound confidence.

Now if he could just hear from Bob Koenig. The phone rang before he could complete the thought. The operator asked him to hold on for Mr. Koenig. Syd felt his hands begin to tremble. He caught a look at his reflection in the mirror. The expression wasn't of the kind that inspired confidence in Los Angeles.

Bob's first words were ''Congratulations, Syd.''

Cheryl had the part! Syd's mind began clicking percentages. With two words, Bob had put him in the big time again.

''I don't know what to say.'' His voice became stronger, more confident. ''Bob, I'm telling you, you've made the right choice. Cheryl's going to be fantastic.''

''I know all that, Syd. The bottom line is that rather than risk any bad press with Margo, we're going with Cheryl. I talked her up. So what if she's box-office poison now? That's what they said about Joan Collins and look what she's done.''

''Bob, that's what I've been telling you all along.''

''We'd better both be right. I'll arrange a press reception for Cheryl at the Beverly Hilton for Friday afternoon about five o'clock.''

''We'll be there!''

''Syd, this is very important. From now on, we treat Cheryl as a superstar. And by the way, tell Cheryl to plaster a smile on her face. Amanda is a strong, but *likable* character. I don't want to read about any more outbursts at waiters or limo drivers. And I mean it.''

Five minutes later, Syd was confronting a hysterical Cheryl Manning. ''You mean you *admitted* to Scott that you took that letter, you dumb bitch?'' He grabbed her shoulders. ''Shut up and listen to me. *Are there any more letters?''*

''Let go. You're hurting me. I don't know.'' Cheryl tried to shrink away from him. ''I can't lose that part. I can't. I *am* Amanda.''

''You bet you can't lose that part!'' Syd shoved her backward, and she toppled against the couch.

Fury replaced fear. Cheryl brushed back her hair and clenched her teeth. Her mouth became a thin, menacing slash. ''Do you always push when you're angry, Syd? You'd better get something straight. *You* tore up that letter. *I* didn't. And I didn't *write* that letter, or any others. Scott doesn't believe me. So you march yourself over to him and tell him the truth: that I planned to give that letter to Ted to help his defense. You convince Scott, do you hear me, Syd? Because on Friday I'm not going to be here. I'm going to be at my press reception, and there isn't going to be a whisper to connect me to any poison-pen letters or destroyed evidence.''

They glared at each other. In a frenzy of frustration, Syd realized that she might be telling the truth and that by destroying the letter he might have thrown away the series. If one hint of unfavorable publicity hit the papers before Friday . . . If Scott refused to let Cheryl leave the Spa . . .

''I've got to think,'' he said. ''I'll figure something out.''

He had one last card to play.

The question was how to play it.

CHAPTER 5

When Ted returned to his bungalow, he found Henry Bartlett and Craig waiting for him. A jubilant Bartlett did not seem to notice his silence. ''I think we've had a break,'' he announced. As Ted took his place at the table, Bartlett told him about the discovery of Leila's diary. ''In her own hand, she'd checked off when you and Elizabeth Lange were in the same cities. Did you see her every time you were there?''

Ted leaned back and folded his arms behind his head and closed his eyes. It seemed so long ago.

''Ted, at least here I can *help* you.'' Craig's enthusiasm was a quality that had for a long time been missing from his voice and demeanor. ''You kept Elizabeth's schedule on your desk. I can swear that you adjusted your travel plans so that you'd be able to see her.''

Ted did not open his eyes. ''Will you kindly explain that?''

Henry Bartlett had been driven past irritation. ''Listen, Mr. Winters. I wasn't hired to take on this case so that you could wipe your feet on me. It's the rest of your life; but it's also my professional reputation. If you can't or won't cooperate in your own defense, maybe it's not too late for you to get another attorney.'' He shoved his files across the table and watched as papers spilled from them. ''You insisted on coming here when it would have been much better to have ready access to my staff. You disappeared for a long walk yesterday when we were supposed to work. You were supposed to be here an hour ago and we're twiddling our thumbs waiting for you. You've blackballed one line of defense that might work. Now we have a decent shot at destroying Elizabeth Lange's credibility as a witness and you're not interested.''

Ted opened his eyes. Slowly he lowered his arms until they rested on the table. ''Oh, but I *am* interested. Tell me about it.''

Bartlett chose to ignore the sarcasm. ''Listen, we're going to be able to produce a facsimile of two letters Leila received that suggest you were involved with someone else. Cheryl is one possibility as that someone else. We know she'd say anything. But there's a better way. You did try to coordinate your schedule with Elizabeth's—''

Ted interrupted him. ''Elizabeth and I were very good friends. We liked each other. We enjoyed each other's company. If I had my choice of being in Chicago on Wednesday and Dallas on Friday or the other way around, and found that a good friend with whom I could enjoy a late supper and relax was in those same cities, yes, I would arrange my schedule to do that. So what?''

''Come off it, Ted. You did it half a dozen times in the same weeks that Leila started to fall apart—*when she was receiving those letters.*''

Ted shrugged.

''Ted, Henry is trying to plan your defense,'' Craig snapped. ''At least pay attention to him.''

Bartlett continued. ''What we are trying to show you is this: Step One. Leila was receiving letters saying that you were involved with someone else. Step Two. Craig is witness to the fact that you synchronized your schedule with Elizabeth's. Step Three. In her own handwriting, Leila made the obvious connection between you two in her diary. Step Four. You had no reason to kill Leila if you were no longer interested in her. Step Five. What to you was a mild flirtation was very, very different to Elizabeth. She was head over heels in love with you.'' Triumphantly Henry threw the copy of the *Globe* at Ted. ''Look at that picture.''

Ted studied it. He remembered the moment at the end of the service when some fool had asked the organist to play ''My Old Kentucky Home.'' Leila had told him about singing that to Elizabeth when they took off for New York. Beside him, Elizabeth had gasped; then the tears that she'd held back flooded her face. He'd put his arms around her, turned her to him and whispered, ''Don't, Sparrow.''

''She was in love with you,'' Henry continued. ''When she realized that for you it was simply a flirtation, she turned on you. She took advantage of that wacko's crazy accusation to destroy you. I'm telling you, Teddy, we may be able to make this stick.''

Ted tore the paper in half. ''Apparently, my job is to be the devil's advocate. Let's suppose your scenario is true. Elizabeth was in love with me. But let's carry it one step further. Suppose I had come to realize that life with Leila would be a succession of constant ups and downs, of tantrums, of an insecurity that resulted in jealous accusations every time I spoke pleasantly to another woman. Suppose I'd come to realize that Leila was an actress first, last and always, that she didn't want a child. Suppose I'd realized that in Elizabeth I had found something I'd been looking for all my life.''

Ted slammed his fist on the table. ''Don't you know that you have just given me the very best reason in the world for killing Leila? Because do you think that Elizabeth would have looked at me twice while her sister was alive?'' He pushed back his chair with a vehemence that caused it to topple over. ''Why don't you two play golf or go for a swim or do anything that makes you feel good? Don't waste your time here. *I* don't plan to.''

Bartlett's face turned crimson. ''I've had enough,'' he snapped. ''Listen, *Mr.* Winters, you may know how to run hotels, but you don't know a damn thing about what goes on in a criminal courtroom. You hired me to keep you out of prison, but I can't do it alone. What's more, I don't intend to. Either you start cooperating with me or get yourself another lawyer.''

''Calm down, Henry,'' Craig said.

''No, I won't calm down. I don't need this case. I can *possibly* win it, but not the way it's going now.'' He pointed at Ted. ''If you are so sure that any defense I raise won't work, why don't you plea-bargain right now? I might get you a maximum of seven to ten years. Is that what you want? Say so. Or else sit down at that table.''

Ted picked up the chair he had knocked over. ''Let's get to work,'' he said tonelessly. ''I probably owe you an apology. I realize you're the best in your field, but I guess you can understand how trapped I feel. Do you really think there *is* a chance for an acquittal?''

''I've gotten acquittals in cases as rough as this,'' Bartlett told him. ''What you don't seem to fathom,'' he added, ''is that being guilty has nothing to do with the verdict.''

CHAPTER 6

Somehow Min managed to get through the rest of the morning. She was too busy fielding phone calls from the media to even think of the scene in the office between Elizabeth and Ted's lawyer. They had all left immediately after the blowup: Bartlett and Elizabeth furious, Craig distressed, Scott grim-faced. Helmut had escaped to the clinic. He had known she wanted to talk to him. He had avoided her this morning as he'd avoided her last night, when after telling her that he'd heard Ted attacking Leila, he'd locked himself in his study.

Who in hell had tipped off the press that Elizabeth and Ted were here? She answered the persistent inquiries with her standard reply: ''We never release the names of our guests.'' She was told that both Elizabeth and Ted had been spotted in Carmel. ''No comment.''

Any other time she'd have loved the publicity. But now? She was asked if there was anything unusual about her secretary's death. ''Certainly not.''

At noon she told the operator to hold all calls and went to the women's spa. She was relieved to see that the atmosphere there was normal. There seemed to be no more talk about Sammy's death. She made it a point to chat with the guests lunching around the pool. Alvirah Meehan was there. She had spotted Scott's car and tried to pepper Min with questions about his presence.

When Min got back to the main house she went directly up to the apartment. Helmut was sitting on the couch, sipping a cup of tea. His face was a sickly gray. ''Ah, Minna.'' He attempted a smile.

She did not return it. ''We have got to talk,'' she told him abruptly. ''What is the real reason you went to Leila's apartment that night? Were you having an affair with her? Tell me the truth!''

The cup rattled in the saucer as he put it down. ''An affair! Minna, I hated that woman!''

Min watched as his face blotched and his hands clenched. "Do you think I was amused at the way she ridiculed me? An affair with her?" He slammed his fist on the cocktail table. "Minna, you are the only woman in my life. There has never been another woman since I met you. I swear that to you."

"Liar!" Min rushed over to him, bent down and grabbed his lapels. "Look at me. I tell you, look at me. Stop the phony aristocratic crap and the dramatics. You were dazzled by Leila. What man wasn't? Every time you looked at her, you raped her with your eyes. You were all like that, the pack of you. Ted. Syd. Even that clod, Craig. But you were the worst. Love. Hate. It's all one. And in your entire life, you've never put yourself out for anyone. I want the truth. *Why did you go to her that night?*" She released him, suddenly drained and exhausted.

He jumped to his feet. His hand brushed the teacup and it tipped over, sending splatters of tea onto the table and carpet. "Minna, this is impossible. I will not have you treating me like a germ under a microscope." Disdainfully he glanced at the mess. "Send for someone to clean this up," he ordered. "*I* have to get to the clinic. Mrs. Meehan is due for her collagen injections this afternoon." His tone became sarcastic. "Take heart, my dear. As you know, that's another outrageous fee in the till."

"I saw that dreary woman an hour ago," Min said. "You've made yet another conquest. She was gushing about how talented you are and how you are going to make her feel like a butterfly floating on a cloud. If I hear that idiotic expression from her once more . . ."

She broke off. Helmut's knees had begun to sag. She grabbed him before he could fall. "Tell me what is wrong!" she shrieked. "Tell me what you've done!"

CHAPTER 7

When she left Min's office, Elizabeth rushed back to her bungalow, furious at herself for allowing Bartlett to goad her. He would say anything, do anything to discredit her testimony, and she was playing into his hands.

To distract herself, she opened the script of Leila's play. But the words were a jumble. She could not focus on them.

Was there the ring of truth to Bartlett's accusations? Had Ted deliberately sought her out?

She thumbed through the script restlessly, deciding to read it later. Then her glance fell on one of Leila's marginal notes. Shocked, she sank down on the couch and turned back to the first page.

Merry-Go-Round. A comedy by Clayton Anderson.

She read the play through rapidly, then sat for a long time totally absorbed in her thoughts. Finally she reached for a pen and pad and began rereading slowly, making her own notations.

At two thirty she laid the pen down. Pages of the pad were filled with her jottings. She became aware that she had skipped lunch, that her head ached dully. Some of Leila's markings in the margin had been almost indecipherable, but eventually she'd made them all out.

Clayton Anderson. The playwright of *Merry-Go-Round.* The wealthy college professor who had invested one million dollars of his own money in the play, but whose true identity was known to no one. Who was he? He had known Leila intimately.

She phoned the main house. The operator told her that Baroness von Schreiber was in her apartment but was not to be disturbed. "I'll be right there," Elizabeth told her crisply. "Tell the Baroness I have to see her."

Min was in bed. She did look ill. There was no bravado, no bossiness in her demeanor or voice. "Well, Elizabeth?"

She's afraid of me, Elizabeth thought. With a rush of her old affection she sat by the bed. "Min, why did you bring me here?"

Min shrugged. "Because believe it or not, I was worried about you, because I love you."

"I believe that. And the other reason?"

"Because I am appalled at the idea that Ted may spend the rest of his life in prison. Sometimes people do terrible things in anger, because they are out of control, things they might never do if they were not goaded beyond their ability to stop themselves. I believe that happened. I *know* that happened to Ted."

"What do you mean you *know* that happened?"

"Nothing . . . nothing." Min closed her eyes. "Elizabeth, you do what you must. But I warn you. You will have to live with destroying Ted for the rest of your life. Someday you will again face Leila. I think she will not thank you. You know how she was after she had been utterly outrageous. Contrite. Loving. Generous. All of it."

"Min, isn't there another reason why you want Ted to be acquitted? It has to do with this place, doesn't it?"

"What do you mean?"

"I mean that just before Leila died, Ted was considering putting a Cypress Point Spa in all his new hotels. What happened to that plan?"

"Ted has not gone ahead with plans for new hotels since his indictment."

"Exactly. So there are a couple of reasons why you want Ted acquitted. Min, who is Clayton Anderson?"

"I have no idea. Elizabeth, I am very tired. Perhaps we can talk later."

"Min, come on. You're not that tired." The sharper tone in her voice made Min open her eyes and pull herself up on the pillows. I was right, Elizabeth thought. She's not so much sick as *afraid.* "Min, I just read and re-read that play Leila was in. I saw it with all of you that last preview, but I didn't pay attention to it. I was too worried about Leila. Min, someone who knew Leila inside and out wrote that play. That's why it was so perfect for her. Someone even used Helmut's expressions in it—'a butterfly floating on a cloud.' Leila noticed it too. She had a notation in the margin: *'Tell the Baron someone is stealing his thunder.'* Min . . ."

They stared at each other as the same thought struck them. "Helmut wrote the ads for this place," Elizabeth whispered. "He writes the daily bulletins. Maybe there *is* no wealthy college professor. Min, did Helmut write the play?"

"I . . . don't . . . know." Min struggled out of bed. She was wearing a loose caftan that suddenly seemed too large, as if she were shriveling inside it. "Elizabeth, will you excuse me? I have to make a call to Switzerland."

CHAPTER 8

With an unfamiliar sense of worry, Alvirah walked reluctantly down the hedged path that led to treatment room C. The instructions the nurse had given her were re-confirmed by the note that had been on her breakfast tray this morning. The note was friendly and reassuring, but even so, now that the time had come, Alvirah still felt squeamish.

To ensure absolute privacy, the note said, patients entered the treatment rooms by the individual outside doors. Alvirah was to go to treatment room C at three P.M. and settle herself on the table. In view of the fact that Mrs. Meehan has an aversion to needles, she would be given a special-strength Valium and allowed to rest until three thirty, at which time Dr. von Schreiber would perform the treatment. She would continue to rest for an additional half-hour to allow the Valium to wear off.

The flowering hedges were over six feet high, and walking between them made her feel like a young girl in a bower. The day had become really warm, but in here the hedges held moisture, and the azaleas made her think of her own azalea plants in front of the house. They'd been really pretty last spring.

She was at the treatment-room door. It was painted a pale blue, and a tiny gold *C* confirmed that she was in the right place. Hesitantly, she turned the handle and went in.

The room looked like a lady's boudoir. It had flowered wallpaper and a pale green carpet, a little dressing table and a love seat. The treatment table was made up like a bed, with sheets that matched the wallpaper, a pale pink comforter and a lace-edged pillow. On the closet door was a gilt-framed mirror with beveled edges. Only the presence of a cabinet with medical supplies suggested the real purpose of the room, and even that was finished in white wood with leaded glass doors.

Alvirah removed her sandals and placed them, neatly, side by side under the table. She had a size nine foot and didn't want the doctor tripping when he was giving the collagen injections. She lay down on the table, pulled up the comforter and closed her eyes.

They sprang open a moment later when the nurse came in. She was Regina Owens, the chief assistant, the one who had taken her medical history. "Don't look so worried," Miss Owens said. Alvirah liked her. She reminded her of one of the women whose houses she cleaned. She was about forty, with dark short hair, nice wide eyes and a pleasant smile.

She brought a glass of water and a couple of pills to Alvirah. "These will make you feel nice and drowsy, and you won't even know you're getting made gorgeous."

Obediently Alvirah put them into her mouth and swallowed the water. "I feel like a baby," she apologized.

"Not at all. You'd be amazed how many people are terrified of needles." Miss Owens came behind her and began massaging her temples. "You *are* tense. Now, I'm going to put a nice, cool cloth over your eyes and you just let yourself drift off to sleep. The doctor and I will be back in about a half-hour. By then you probably won't even know we're here."

Alvirah felt the strong fingers press against her temples. "That feels good," she murmured.

"I'll bet it does." For a few minutes Miss Owens continued to knead Alvirah's forehead, the back of her neck. Alvirah felt herself drifting into a pleasant dreamy state. Then a cool cloth was placed over her eyes. She barely heard the click of the door when Miss Owens tiptoed out.

There were so many thoughts running through her head, like loose threads that she couldn't quite pull together.

A butterfly floating on a cloud . . .

She was beginning to remember why that seemed familiar. It was almost there.

"Can you hear me, Mrs. Meehan?"

She hadn't realized that Baron von Schreiber had come in. His voice sounded low and a little hoarse. She hoped the microphone would pick it up. She wanted everything on record.

"Yes." Her own voice sounded far away.

"Don't be afraid. You'll barely feel a pinprick."

He was right. She felt hardly anything, just a tiny sensation like a mosquito bite. And to think, she'd been worried! She waited. The doctor had told her he'd be injecting the collagen in ten or twelve spots on each side of her mouth. What was he waiting for?

It was getting hard to breathe. She *couldn't* breathe. "Help!" she cried, but the word wouldn't come out. She opened her mouth, gasping desperately. She was slipping away. Her arms, her chest, nothing moved. Oh, God, help me, help me, she thought.

Then darkness overcame her as the door opened and Nurse Owens said briskly. "Well, here we are, Mrs. Meehan. All set for your beauty treatment?"

CHAPTER 9

What does it prove? Elizabeth asked herself as she walked from the main house along the path to the clinic. If Helmut wrote that play, he must be going through hell. The author had put one million dollars into the production. That was why Min was calling Switzerland. Her nest egg in a numbered account was a standing joke. "I'll never be broke," she had always bragged.

Min had wanted Ted acquitted so that she could license Cypress Point Spas in all his new hotels. Helmut had a much more compelling reason. If he was "Clayton Anderson," he knew that even the nest egg was gone.

She would force him to tell her the truth, Elizabeth decided.

The foyer of the clinic was hushed and quiet, but the receptionist was not at her desk. From down the hall, Elizabeth heard running feet, raised voices. She hurried toward the sounds. Doors were open on the corridor as guests in the process of treatment peeked out. The room at the end of the hall was open. It was from there that the sounds were coming.

Room C. Dear God, that was where Mrs. Meehan was going to have the collagen treatment. There wasn't anyone in the Spa who hadn't heard about it. Had something gone wrong? Elizabeth almost collided with a nurse coming out of the room.

"You can't go in there!" The nurse was trembling.

Elizabeth pushed her aside.

Helmut was bent over the treatment table. He was compressing Alvirah Meehan's chest. An oxygen mask was on Alvirah's face. The noise of a respirator dominated the room. The coverlet had been pulled back; her robe was crumpled under her, the incongruous sunburst pin gleaming upward. As Elizabeth watched, too horrified to speak, a nurse handed Helmut a needle. He attached it to tubing and started an intravenous in Alvirah's arm. A male nurse took over compressing her chest.

From the distance Elizabeth could hear the wail of an ambulance siren screeching through the gates of the Spa.

* * *

It was four fifteen when Scott was notified that Alvirah Meehan, the forty-million-dollar lottery winner, was in the Monterey Peninsula hospital, a possible victim of an attempted homicide. The deputy who phoned had responded to the emergency call and accompanied the ambulance to the Spa. The attendants suspected foul play, and the emergency-room doctor agreed with them. Dr. von Schreiber claimed that she had not yet received a collagen treatment; but a drop of blood on her face seemed to indicate a very recent injection.

Alvirah Meehan! Scott rubbed his hands over suddenly weary eyes. That woman was bright. He thought of her comments at dinner. She was like the child in the fable *The Emperor's New Clothes* who says, ''But he has no clothes on!''

Why would anyone want to hurt Alvirah Meehan? Scott had hoped she wouldn't get caught up with charlatans trying to invest her money for her, but the thought that anyone might deliberately try to kill her was incredible. ''I'll be right there,'' he said as he slammed down the phone.

The waiting room of the community hospital was open and pleasant, with greenery and an indoor pond, not unlike the lobby of a small hotel. He never saw it without remembering the hours he had sat here, when Jeanie was a patient . . .

He was informed that the doctors were working on Mrs. Meehan, that Dr. Whitley would be available to see him shortly. Elizabeth came in while he was waiting.

''How is she?''

''I don't know.''

''She shouldn't have had those injections. She really *was* afraid. She had a heart attack, didn't she?''

''We don't know yet. How did you get here?''

''Min. We came in her car. She's parking it now. Helmut rode in the ambulance with Mrs. Meehan. This can't be happening.'' Her voice rose. People in nearby chairs turned to stare at her.

Scott forced her to sit on the sofa beside him. ''Elizabeth, get hold of yourself. You only met Mrs. Meehan a few days ago. You can't let yourself get this upset.''

''Where's Helmut?'' Min's voice, coming from behind them, was as flat as though there were no emotion left in her. She too seemed to be in a state of disbelief and shock. She came around the couch and sank into the chair facing them. ''He must be so distraught . . .'' She broke off. ''Here he is.''

To Scott's practiced eye, the Baron looked as though he had seen a ghost. He was still wearing the exquisitely tailored blue smock that was his surgical costume. He sank heavily into the chair beside Min and groped for her hand. ''She is in a coma. They say she had some sort of injection. Min, it is impossible, I swear to you, impossible.''

''Stay here.'' Scott's look included the three of them. From the long corridor that led to the emergency area, he had seen the chief of the hospital beckon to him.

They spoke in the private office. ''She was injected with something that brought on shock,'' Dr. Whitley said flatly. He was a tall, lean sixty-three-year-old whose usual expression was affable and sympathetic. Now it was steely, and Scott remembered that his longtime friend had been an Army fighter pilot in World War II.

''Will she live?''

''Absolutely impossible to say. She's in a coma which may become irreversible. She tried to say something before she went totally under.''

''What was it?''

''It sounded like 'voy.' That's as much as she got out.''

''That's no help. What does the Baron have to say? Does he have any idea how this could have happened?''

''We didn't let him near her, Scott, frankly.''

''I gather you don't think much of the good doctor?''

''I have no reason to doubt his medical capabilities. But there's something about him that shouts 'phony' at me every time I see him. And if *he* didn't inject Mrs. Meehan, then who the hell did?''

Scott pushed back his chair. ''That's just what I intend to find out.''

As he left the office, Whitley called him back. ''Scott, something that might help us—could someone check Mrs. Meehan's rooms and bring in any medication she may have been taking? Until we reach her husband and get her medical history, we don't know what we may be dealing with.''

''I'll take care of it myself.''

Elizabeth drove back to the Spa with Scott. On the way he told her about finding the shred of paper in Cheryl's bungalow. ''Then she did write those letters!'' Elizabeth exclaimed.

Scott shook his head. ''I know it sounds crazy, and I know Cheryl can lie as easily as most of us can breathe, but I've been thinking about this all day, and my gut feeling is she's telling the truth.''

''What about Syd? Did you talk to him?''

''Not yet. She's bound to tell him she admitted that she stole the letter and that he tore it up. I decided to let him stew before I question him. That sometimes works. But I'm telling you, I'm inclined to believe her story.''

''But if *she* didn't write the letters, who did?''

Scott shot a glance at her. ''I don't know.'' He paused, then said, ''What I mean is, I don't know *yet.*''

Min and the Baron followed Scott's car in her convertible. Min drove. ''The only way I can help you is to know the truth,'' she told her husband. ''Did you do something to that woman?''

The Baron lit a cigarette and inhaled deeply. His china-blue eyes watered. The reddish tint in his hair seemed brassy under the late-afternoon sun. The top of the convertible was down. A cool land breeze had dispelled the last of the daytime warmth. A sense of autumn was in the air.

''Minna, what crazy talk is that? I went into the room. She wasn't breathing. I saved her life. What reason would I have to hurt her?''

''Helmut, who is Clayton Anderson?''

He dropped the cigarette. It fell on the leather seat beside him. Min reached over and picked it up. ''You'd better not ruin this car. There won't be a replacement. I repeat: Who is Clayton Anderson?''

''I don't know what you're talking about,'' he whispered.

''Oh, I think you do. Elizabeth came to see me. She read the play. That's why you were so upset this morning, isn't it? It wasn't the appointment book. It was the *play.* Leila had made notes in the margin. She picked up that idiotic phrase you use in the ads. Elizabeth caught it too. So did Mrs. Meehan. She saw one of the previews. That's why you tried to kill her, isn't it? You were still hoping to conceal the fact *you* wrote that play.''

''Minna, I am telling you—you are *crazy!* For all we know that woman was self-injecting.''

''That's nonsense. She talked constantly about her fear of needles.''

''That could have been a cover-up.''

''The playwright put over a million dollars in that play. If you *are* that playwright, where would you have gotten the money?''

They were at the gates of the Spa. Min slowed down and glanced at him, unsmiling. ''I tried to phone Switzerland to check on my balance. Of course, it was after business hours there. I will call tomorrow, Helmut. I hope—for your sake—that money is in my account.''

His expression was as bland as ever, but his eyes were those of a man about to be hanged.

They met on the porch of Alvirah Meehan's bungalow. The Baron opened the door and they went in. Scott saw that Min had clearly taken advantage of Alvirah's naïveté. This was the most expensive of their accommodations—the rooms the First Lady used when she saw fit to seek R-and-R at the Spa. There were a living room, a dining room, a library, a huge master bedroom, two full baths on the first floor. *You sure socked it to her,* Scott thought.

His inspection of the premises was relatively brief. The medicine chest in the bathroom Alvirah used contained only over-the-counter drugs—maximum-strength Bufferin, Allerest, a nasal spray, a jar of Vicks

VapoRub, Ben-Gay. *A nice lady whose nasal passages get stuffed up at night and who probably has a few twinges of arthritis.*

It seemed to him that the Baron was disappointed. Under Scott's careful scrutiny, he insisted on opening all the bottles, spilling out the contents, examining them to see if any extra medication was mixed with the ordinary tablets and pills. Was it an act? How good an actor was the Toy Soldier?

Alvirah's closet revealed well-worn brushed flannel nightgowns side by side with expensive dresses and caftans, most of them carrying labels from Martha Park Avenue and Cypress Point Spa Boutique.

An incongruous note was the expensive Japanese recorder in the carry-on bag that was part of the Louis Vuitton matching luggage. Scott raised his eyes. Sophisticated, professional equipment! He wouldn't have expected it of Alvirah Meehan.

Elizabeth watched as he thumbed through the cassettes. Three of them were marked in numerical sequence. The rest were blank. Scott shrugged, put them back and closed the bag. He left a few minutes later. Elizabeth walked with him to his car. On the ride over, she had not told him her suspicion that Helmut might have written the play. She wanted to be sure first, to demand the truth from Helmut himself. It was still possible that Clayton Anderson existed, she told herself.

It was exactly six o'clock when Scott's car disappeared past the gates. It was getting cool. Elizabeth shoved her hands into her pockets and felt the sunburst pin. She had taken it off Alvirah's robe after the ambulance left. Obviously it had great sentimental value.

They had sent for Alvirah's husband. She would give the pin to him tomorrow.

CHAPTER 10

Ted returned to his bungalow from town at six thirty P.M. He had come back the long way, through the Crocker Woodland, to the service entrance of the Spa. He hadn't missed the cars, half-hidden in the brush beside the road leading to the Cypress Point grounds. Reporters. Like dogs on a scent, following the lead that the *Globe* article suggested. . . .

He peeled off his sweater. It had been too hot to wear—but on the other hand, at this time of year you could be surprised on the Peninsula. The winds could shift and become favorable or unfavorable at a moment's notice.

He drew the shades, switched on the lights and was startled to see the gleam of dark hair that rose over the back of the couch. It was Min. "It is important that I speak with you." The tone was the same he'd always known. Warm and authoritative, a curious blend that at one time had inspired confidence. She was wearing a long, sleeveless jacket over some sort of glittery one-piece outfit.

Ted sat opposite her and lit a cigarette. "I gave these up years ago, but it's amazing how many bad habits you can take on again when you're faced with a lifetime in prison. So much for discipline. I'm not very presentable, Min—but then, I'm not used to having unexpected guests in quite this way."

"Unexpected and uninvited." Min's eyes swept over him. "You've been jogging?"

"No. I've been walking. Quite a long distance. It gives one time to think."

"Your thoughts can't be very pleasant these days."

"No. They're not." Ted waited.

"May I have one of those?" Min indicated the pack of cigarettes he had tossed on the table.

Ted offered her one and lit it for her.

"I too gave them up, but in times of stress . . ." Min shrugged. "I gave up many things in my life while I was clawing my way up. Well, you know how it is . . . launching a model agency and trying to keep it going when there was no money coming in . . . marrying a sick old man and being his nurse, his mistress, his companion for five endless years . . . Oh, I thought I had reached a point of certain security. I thought I had earned it."

"And you haven't?"

Min waved a hand. "It's lovely here, isn't it? This spot is ideal. The Pacific at our feet, the magnificent coastline, the weather, the comfort and beauty of these accommodations, the unparalleled facilities of the Spa . . . Even Helmut's monstrosity of a Roman bath could be a stunning draw. Nobody else would be fool enough to try to build one; nobody else would have the flair to run it."

No wonder she's here, Ted thought. She couldn't risk talking to me with Craig around.

It was as though Min read his mind. "I know what Craig would advise. But Ted, *you're* the entrepreneur, the daring businessman. You and I think alike. Helmut is utterly impractical—I know that; but he also has vision. What he needs, and has always needed, is the money to bring his dreams to fruition. Do you remember a conversation we had—the three of us—when your damn bulldog Craig wasn't around? We talked about your putting a Cypress Point Spa in all your new hotels. It's a fabulous idea. It would work."

"Min, if I'm in prison, there won't *be* new hotels. We've stopped building since the indictment. You know that."

"Then lend me money now." Min's mask dropped. "Ted, I am desperate. I will be bankrupt in weeks. *It need not be!* This place lost something in these past few years. Helmut has not been bringing in new guests. I think I know now why he's been in a terrible state. But it could change. Why do you think I brought Elizabeth here? To help *you.*"

"Min, you saw her reaction to me. If anything, you've made things worse."

"I'm not sure about that. This afternoon I begged her to reconsider. I told her she would never forgive herself if she destroyed you." Min crushed the cigarette into the ashtray. "Ted, I know what I'm saying. Elizabeth is in love with you. She always has been. Make it work for you. It's not too late." She grasped his arm.

He shook off her grip. "Min, you don't know what you're talking about."

"I'm telling you what I *know.* It's something I sensed from the first time she laid eyes on you. Don't you know how difficult it was for her to be around you and Leila, wanting Leila to be happy, loving you both? She was torn in two. That's why she took that play before Leila died. It wasn't a role she wanted. Sammy talked to me about it. She saw it too. Ted, Elizabeth is fighting you because she feels guilty. She knows Leila goaded you beyond endurance. *Make it work for you!* And Ted, I beg you—*help me now!* Please! I beg you."

With naked appeal she looked at him. He had been perspiring, and his dark brown hair was matted in ringlets and waves. A woman would kill for that head of hair, Min thought. His high cheekbones accentuated the narrow, perfectly shaped nose. His lips were even, his jaw just square enough to impart a look of strength to his face. His shirt was clinging to his body. His limbs were tanned and muscular. She wondered where he had been and realized he might not have heard yet about Alvirah Meehan. She did not want to talk about that now.

"Min, I can't go ahead with spas in hotels that won't be built if I go to prison. I can bail you out now, and I will. But let me ask you something: has it ever occurred to you that Elizabeth might be *wrong,* might be mistaken about the time? Has it even occurred to you that I'm telling the truth, when I say I did *not* go back upstairs?"

Min's smile of relief turned to astonishment. "Ted, you can trust me. You can trust Helmut. He hasn't told a soul except me. . . . He never will tell a soul. . . . He *heard* you shouting at Leila. He *heard* her begging for her life."

CHAPTER 11

Should she have told Scott what she suspected about the Baron? Elizabeth wondered as she went into the welcome calm of her bungalow. Her senses absorbed the emerald-and-white color scheme. Splashy print on thick white carpeting. She could almost imagine there was a lingering hint of joy mixed with the salty sea air.

Leila.

Red hair. Emerald eyes. The pale skin of the natural redhead. The billowing white satin pajamas that she'd been wearing when she died. Those yards of material must have floated around her as she fell.

My God. My God. Elizabeth slipped the double lock and huddled on the couch, her head in her hands, appalled at the vision of Leila, floating down through the night to her death. . . .

Helmut. Had he written *Merry-Go-Round*? If so, had he cleaned out Min's untouchable Swiss account to finance it? He would have been frantic when Leila said she was quitting the show. How frantic?

Alvirah Meehan. The ambulance attendants. The speck of blood on Alvirah's face. The incredulous tone when the paramedic spoke to Helmut: ''What do you mean you hadn't started the injections? Who do you think you're kidding?''

Helmut's hands compressed Alvirah's chest . . . Helmut starting the intravenous . . . But Helmut must have been frantic hearing Alvirah talk about ''a butterfly floating on a cloud.'' Alvirah had seen a preview of the play. Leila had made the connection to Helmut. Had Alvirah Meehan made it as well?

She thought about Min's speech to her this afternoon, about Ted. She had virtually acknowledged Ted's guilt, then tried to persuade her that Leila had provoked him over and over again. Was that true?

Was Min right—that Leila would never want to see Ted behind bars for the rest of his life? And why did Min sound so positive about Ted's guilt? Two days ago she'd been saying it must have been an accident.

Elizabeth locked her arms around her knees and laid her head on her hands.

''I don't know what to do,'' she whispered to herself. She had never felt lonelier in her life.

At seven o'clock she heard the faint chimes that indicated ''cocktail'' hour had begun. She decided to have dinner served in the bungalow. It was impossible to envision going through the motions of socializing with any of those people, knowing that Sammy's body was in the morgue awaiting shipment to Ohio, that Alvirah Meehan was fighting for her life in Monterey Hospital. Two nights ago she had been at the table with Alvirah Meehan. Two nights ago Sammy had been in this room with her. Who would be next?

At quarter of eight Min called. ''Elizabeth, everyone is inquiring about you. Are you all right?''

''Of course. I just need to be quiet.''

''You're sure you're not ill? You should know—Ted especially is very concerned.''

Hand it to Min. She never gives up. ''I'm really fine, Min. Would you have them send a tray? I'll take it a bit easy and go for a swim later. Don't worry about me.''

She hung up the phone. Walked around the room restlessly, already longing to be in the water.

''In aqua sanitas,'' the inscription read. For once Helmut was right. Water would soothe her, turn off her mind.

CHAPTER 12

He was reaching for the tank when there was a sharp knock on the door. Frantically he yanked the mask from his face and pulled his arms out of the cumbersome wet suit. He jammed the tank and the mask into the closet, then rushed into the bathroom and turned on the shower.

The knocking was repeated, an impatient staccato. He managed to get free of the suit, dropped it behind the couch and grabbed his robe.

Making is voice sound annoyed, he shouted, ''All right, all right'' and opened the door.

The door was pushed open. ''What took you so long? We've got to talk.''

It was nearly ten o'clock when he was at last able to go to the pool. He reached it just in time to see Elizabeth walking down the path to her bungalow. In his hurry, he brushed against a chair at the edge of the patio. She turned around, and he barely had time to step back into the bushes.

Tomorrow night. There was still a chance to get to her here. If not, a different kind of accident would have to be arranged.

Like Alvirah Meehan, she had picked up the scent and was leading Scott Alshorne along the trail.

That scraping noise. It had been the sound of a chair grating against the patio tiles. The air had become cool but was very still. There was no breeze to set anything in motion. She'd turned quickly and for just an instant had thought she'd seen someone moving. But that was foolish. Why would anyone bother to stand in the shadows of the trees?

Even so, Elizabeth quickened her steps and was glad to be back in the bungalow with the door locked. She phoned the hospital. There was no change in Mrs. Meehan's condition.

It took a long time to fall asleep. What was eluding her? Something that had been said, something she ought to have seized on. Finally she drifted off. . . .

She was searching for someone. . . . She was in an empty building with long, dark halls. . . . Her body was aching with need. . . . Her arms were outstretched. . . . What was that poem she'd read somewhere? ''Is there yet one, oh eyes and lips remembered, who turns and reaches for me in the night?'' She whispered it over and over. . . . She saw a staircase. . . . She hurried down it. . . . He was there. His back to her. She threw her arms around him. He turned and caught her and held her. His mouth was on hers. ''Ted, I love you, I love you,'' she said, over and over again. . . .

Somehow she managed to wake up. For the rest of the night, miserable and despairing, she lay numbly in the bed where Leila and Ted had so often slept together, determined not to sleep.

Not to dream.

Thursday, September 3

QUOTE FOR THE DAY:

The power of beauty, I remember yet.

—Dryden

Dear Cypress Point Spa guest,

A cheery good morning to you. I hope as you read this you are sipping one of our delicious fruit-juice eye-openers. As some of you know, all the oranges and grapefruits are specially grown for the Spa.

Have you shopped in our boutique this week? If not, you must come and see the stunning fashions we have just received for both men and women. One-of-a-kind only, of course. Each of our guests is unique.

A health reminder. By now you may be feeling muscles you'd forgotten you had. Remember, exercise is never pain. Mild discomfort shows you are achieving the stretch. And whenever you exercise, keep your knees relaxed.

Are you looking your very best? For those tiny lines that time and life's experience trace on our face, remember, collagen, like a gentle hand, is waiting to smooth them away.

Be serene. Be tranquil. Be merry. And have a pretty day.

Baron and Baroness Helmut von Schreiber

CHAPTER 1

Long before the first rays of the sun proclaimed yet another brilliant day on the Monterey Peninsula, Ted lay awake thinking about the weeks ahead. The courtroom. The defendant's table where he would sit, feeling the eyes of the spectators on him, trying to get a sense of the impact of the testimony on the jurors. The verdict: Guilty of Murder in the Second Degree. Why Second Degree? he had asked his first lawyer. "Because in New York State, First Degree is reserved for killing a peace officer. For what it's worth, it amounts to about the same, as far as sentencing goes." Life, he told himself. A life in prison.

At six o'clock he got up to jog. The morning was cool and clear, but it would be a hot day. Without a sense of where he wanted to run, he let his feet follow whatever roads they chose and was not surprised to find himself after forty minutes in front of his grandfather's house in Carmel. It was on the ocean block. It used to be white, but the present owners had painted it a moss green—attractive enough, but he preferred the way the white paint used to gleam in the afternoon sun. One of his earliest memories was of this beach. His mother helped him to build a castle; laughing, her dark hair swirling around her face, so happy to be here instead of New York, so grateful for the reprieve. That bloody bastard who was his father! The way he'd ridiculed her, mimicked her, hammered at her. *Why?* What gives anyone a streak of cruelty like that? Or was it simply alcohol that brought out something savage and evil in his father, until he was drinking so much that the savage streak became his personality, all there was, the bottle and the fists? *And had he inherited the same savage streak?*

Ted stood on the beach, staring at the house, seeing his mother and grandmother on the porch, seeing his grandparents at his mother's funeral, hearing his grandfather say, "We should have made her leave him."

His grandmother whispered, "She wouldn't leave him—it would have meant giving up Ted."

Had it been his fault? he wondered as a child. He still asked himself the same question. There was still no answer.

There was someone watching him from a window. Quickly he continued to jog down the beach.

* * *

Bartlett and Craig were waiting in his bungalow. They'd already had breakfast. He went to the phone and ordered juice, toast, coffee. ''I'll be right back,'' he told them. He showered and put on shorts and a T-shirt. The tray was waiting when he came out. ''Quick service here, isn't it? Min really knows how to run a spa! It would have been a good idea to franchise this place for new hotels.''

Neither man answered him. They sat at the library table watching him, seeming to know that he neither expected nor wanted comment. He swallowed the orange juice in one gulp and reached for the coffee. ''I'm going to the spa for the morning,'' he said. ''I might as well have a decent workout. We'll leave for New York tomorrow. Craig, call an emergency board meeting for Saturday morning. I'm resigning as president and chairman of the company, and appointing you in my place.''

His expression warned Craig not to argue. He turned to Bartlett, his eyes ice-cold. ''I've decided to plea-bargain, Henry. Give me the best and worst possible scenarios of what kind of sentence I can expect to get.''

CHAPTER 2

Elizabeth was still in bed when Vicky brought in her breakfast tray. She set it down next to the bed and studied Elizabeth. ''You're not feeling well.''

Elizabeth propped her pillows against the headboard and sat up. ''Oh, I guess I'll survive.'' She attempted a smile. ''One way or another, we have to, don't we?'' She reached over and picked up the vase with the single flower from the tray. ''What's that you always say about carrying roses to fading flowers?''

''I don't mean you.'' Vicky's angular face softened. ''I was off the last two days. I just heard about Miss Samuels. What a nice lady she was. But will you tell me what she was doing in the bathhouse? She once told me just *looking* at that place gave her the creeps. She said it reminded her of a tomb. Even if she wasn't feeling well, that would be the last place she'd go . . .''

After Vicky left, Elizabeth picked up the schedule that was on the breakfast tray. She hadn't intended to go to the Spa for either treatments or exercise, but changed her mind. She was slated for a massage with Gina at ten o'clock. Employees talk. Just now Vicky had underscored her own belief that Sammy would never have gone into the bathhouse on her own. When she had arrived on Sunday and had the massage, Gina had gossiped about the financial problems of the Spa. She might be able to hear more gossip if she asked the right questions.

As long as she was going there, Elizabeth decided to go through the full schedule. The first exercise class helped her to limber up, but it was hard not to look across the room to the place in the front row where Alvirah Meehan had been the other day. She had labored so hard to bend and twist that at the end of the class she had been puffing furiously, her face bright red. "But I kept up!" she had told Elizabeth proudly.

She ran into Cheryl in the corridor leading to the facial rooms. Cheryl was wrapped in a terry-cloth robe. Her finger- and toenails were painted a brilliant bluish-pink. Elizabeth would have passed her without speaking, but Cheryl grasped her arm. "Elizabeth, I've got to talk to you."

"About what?"

"Those poison-pen letters. Is there any chance of finding any more of them?" Without waiting for an answer, she rushed on: "Because if you *have* any more, or *find* any more, I want them analyzed, or tested, or fingerprinted, or whatever you and the world of science can do to trace them back to the sender. *I did not send them!* Got it?"

Elizabeth watched her sweep down the corridor. As Scott had commented, she *sounded* convincing. On the other hand, if she was reasonably sure that those last two letters were the only ones likely to be found, it would be the perfect attitude for her to take. How good an actress was Cheryl?

At ten o'clock Elizabeth was on the massage table. Gina came into the room. "Pretty big excitement around this place," she commented.

"I would say so."

Gina wrapped Elizabeth's hair in a plastic cap. "I know. First Miss Samuels, then Mrs. Meehan. It's crazy." She poured cream on her hands and began to massage Elizabeth's neck. "The tension's there again. This has been a lousy time for you. I know you and Miss Samuels were close."

It was easier not to talk about Sammy. She managed to murmur, "Yes, we were," then asked, "Gina, did you ever have Mrs. Meehan for a treatment?"

"Sure did. Monday and Tuesday. She's some character. What happened to her?"

"They're not sure. They're trying to check her medical history."

"I'd have thought she was sound as a dollar. A little chunky, but good skin tone, good heartbeat, good breathing. She was scared of needles, but that doesn't give anyone cardiac arrest."

Elizabeth felt the soreness in her shoulders as Gina's fingers kneaded the tight muscles.

Gina laughed ruefully. "Do you think there was anyone in the Spa who didn't know Mrs. Meehan was having a collagen injection in treatment room C? One of the girls overheard her ask Cheryl Manning if she'd ever had collagen there. Can you imagine?"

"No, I can't. Gina, the other day you told me the Spa hasn't been the same since Leila died. I know she attracted the celebrity-watchers, but the Baron used to bring in a pretty healthy bunch of new faces every year.''

Gina poured more cream into her palms. ''It's funny. About two years ago that dried up. Nobody can figure out why. He was making enough trips, but most of them were in the New York area. Remember, he used to work the charity balls in a dozen major cities, personally present the certificate for a week at the Spa to whoever came up with the winning ticket, and by the time he got finished talking, the lucky winner had three of her friends going along for the ride—as paying guests.''

''Why do you think it stopped?''

Gina lowered her voice. ''He was up to something. No one could figure out what—including Min, I guess. . . . She started to travel with him a lot. She was getting plenty worried that His Royal Highness, or whatever he calls himself, had something going in New York. . . .''

Something going? As Gina kneaded and pounded her body, Elizabeth fell silent. Was that something a play called *Merry-Go-Round?* And if so, had Min guessed the truth long ago?

CHAPTER 3

Ted left the Spa at eleven o'clock. After two hours of using the Nautilus equipment and swimming laps, he'd had a massage and then sat in one of the private open-air Jacuzzis that dotted the enclosure of the men's spa. The sun was warm; there was no breeze; a flock of cormorants drifted overhead, like a floating black cloud in an otherwise cloudless sky. Waiters were setting up for lunch service on the patio. The striped umbrellas in soft tones of lime green and yellow that shaded the tables complemented the colorful slates on the ground.

Again Ted was aware of how well the place was run. If things were different, he'd put Min and the Baron in charge of creating a dozen Cypress Point Spas all over the world. He almost smiled. Not *completely* in charge—all the Baron's proposed expenditures would be monitored by a hawk-eyed accountant.

Bartlett had probably been on the phone with the district attorney. By now he would have some idea of the kind of sentence he might expect. It still seemed absolutely incredible. Something he had no memory of doing had forced him to become a totally different person, had forced him to lead a totally different life.

He walked slowly to his bungalow, nodding distantly to the guests who'd cut the last exercise class and were lazing by the Olympic pool. He didn't want to get into a conversation with them. He didn't want to face the discussions he would have with Henry Bartlett.

Memory. A word that haunted him. Bits and pieces. Going back up in the elevator. Being in the hall. Swaying. He'd been so goddamn drunk. And then what? Why had he blotted it out? Because he didn't want to remember what he had done?

Prison. Confinement in a cell. It might be better to . . .

There was no one in his bungalow. That, at least, was a break. He'd expected to find them again around the library table. He should have given Bartlett this unit and taken the smaller one himself. At least then he'd have more peace. The odds were they'd be back for lunch.

Craig. He was a good detail man. The company wouldn't grow with him at the helm, but he might be able to keep it on a holding course. He should be grateful for Craig. Craig had stepped in when the plane with eight top company executives had crashed in Paris. Craig had been indispensable when Kathy and Teddy died. Craig was indispensable now. And to think . . .

How many years would he have to serve? Seven? Ten? Fifteen?

There was one more job he needed to do. He took personal stationery from his briefcase and began to write. When he had finished he sealed the envelope, rang for a maid and asked her to deliver it to Elizabeth's bungalow.

He would have preferred to wait until just before he left tomorrow; but perhaps if she knew there wouldn't be any trial, she might stay here a little longer.

When she returned to her bungalow at noon, Elizabeth found the note propped on the table. The sight of the envelope, white bordered in cerise, the flag colors of Winters Enterprises, with her name written in the firm, straight hand that was so familiar, made her mouth go dry. How many times in her dressing room had a note on that paper, in that handwriting, been delivered between acts? *"Hi, Elizabeth. Just got into town. How about late supper—unless you're tied up? First act was great. Love, Ted."* They'd have supper and call Leila from the restaurant. "Watch my guy for me, Sparrow. Don't let some painted bitch try to stake him out."

They'd both have their ears pressed to the phone. "You staked me out, Star," Ted would say.

And she would be aware of his nearness, of his cheek grazing hers, and dig her fingers into the phone, always wishing she'd had the courage not to see him.

She opened the envelope. She read two sentences before she let out a stifled cry and then had to wait before she could force herself to go back to finishing Ted's letter.

Dear Elizabeth,

I can only tell you that I am sorry, and that word is meaningless. You were right. The Baron heard me struggling with Leila that night. Syd saw me on the street. I told him Leila was dead. There's no use any longer in trying to pretend I wasn't there. Believe me, I have absolutely no memory of those moments, but in light of all the facts, I am going to enter a plea of guilty to manslaughter when I return to New York.

At least, this will bring this terrible affair to a conclusion and spare you the agony of testifying at my trial and being forced to relive the circumstances of Leila's death.

God bless and keep you. Long ago Leila told me that when you were a little girl and leaving Kentucky to come to New York, you were frightened and she sang that lovely song to you . . . *''Weep no more, my lady.''*

Think of her as singing that song to you now, and try to begin a new and happier chapter in your life.

Ted

For the next two hours Elizabeth sat hunched up on the couch, her arms locked around her knees, her eyes staring ahead unseeingly. This was what you wanted, she tried to tell herself. He's going to pay for what he did to Leila. But the pain was so intense it gradually retreated into numbness.

When she got up, her legs were stiff, and she moved with the cautious hesitancy of the old. There was still the matter of the anonymous letters. Now she would not rest until she had found out who had sent them and precipitated this tragedy.

It was past one o'clock when Bartlett phoned Ted. ''We have to talk right away,'' Henry said shortly. ''Get over as soon as you can.''

''Is there any reason we can't meet here?''

''I've got some calls from New York coming in. I don't want to risk missing them.''

When Craig opened the door for him, Ted did not waste time on preliminaries. ''What's up?''

''Something you won't like.''

Bartlett was not at the oval dinette table he used as a desk in this suite. Instead, he was leaning back in an armchair, one hand on the phone as though expecting it to leap into his hand. He had a meditative expression, Ted decided, not unlike that of a philosopher confronted with a problem too difficult to solve.

''How bad is it?'' Ted asked. ''Ten years? Fifteen years?''

''Worse. They won't take a plea. A new eyewitness has come forward.''

Briefly, even brusquely, he explained. ''As you know, we put private investigators on Sally Ross. We wanted to discredit her in every way possible. One of the investigators was in her apartment building night before last. A thief was caught red-handed trying to rob the apartment one floor above Mrs. Ross's. He's been making a deal of his own with the district attorney. He was in that apartment once before. The night of March twenty-ninth. *He claims he saw you push Leila off the terrace!*''

He watched the sickly pallor that stole over Ted's face change his deep tan to a muddy beige. ''No plea bargain,'' Ted whispered. His voice was so low that Henry had to lean forward to catch the words.

''Why should they, with a witness like that? From what my people tell me, there's no question that his view was unobstructed. Sally Ross had that eucalyptus tree on the terrace, obscuring her line of vision. One floor higher up, and the tree wasn't in the way.''

''I don't care how many people saw Ted that night,'' Craig blurted. ''He was drunk. He didn't know what he was doing. I'll perjure myself. I'll say he was on the phone with me at nine thirty.''

''You *can't* perjure yourself,'' Bartlett snapped. ''You're already on record as saying you heard the phone ring and didn't pick it up. Don't even think of it.''

Ted jammed clenched fists into his pockets. ''Forget the goddamned phone. What exactly does this witness claim he saw?''

''So far the district attorney has refused to take my calls. I've got a few inside connections there, and from what they've been able to find out, this guy claims Leila was struggling to save herself.''

''Then I could be facing the maximum?''

''The judge assigned to this case is an imbecile. He'll let a throat-slasher from the ghetto off with a slap on the wrist, but he likes to show how tough he is when he deals with important people. And you're important.''

The phone rang. Bartlett had it at his ear before the second ring. Ted and Craig watched as his frown deepened; he moistened his lips with his tongue, then bit his lower lip. They listened as he barked out instructions: ''I want a rap sheet on that guy. I want to know what kind of deal he was offered. I want pictures taken from that woman's terrace on a rainy night. Get on with it.''

When he put down the receiver, he studied Ted and Craig, noticing how Ted had slumped in his chair and Craig had straightened in his. ''We go to trial,'' he said. ''That new eyewitness has been in the apartment before. He described the inside of several of the closets. This time they caught him when he barely got his feet in the entrance hall. He says he *saw* you, Teddy. Leila was clawing at you, trying to save herself. You picked her up, you held her over that railing and you shook her until she let go of your arms. It won't be a pretty scene when it's described in court.''

''I . . . held . . . her . . . over . . . the . . . railing . . . before . . . I . . . dropped . . . her. . . .'' Ted picked up a vase from the table and threw it across the room at the marble fireplace. It smashed, and sprays of delicate crystal cascaded across the carpet. "No! It's not possible!" He turned and ran blindly for the door. He slammed it behind him with a force that shattered the window panel.

They watched as he ran across the lawn to the trees that separated the Spa grounds from the Crocker Woodland.

"He's guilty," Bartlett said. "There's no way I can get him off now. Give me a clean-cut liar and I can work with him. If I put him on the stand, the jury will find Teddy arrogant. If I *don't,* we'll have Elizabeth describing how he shouted at Leila, and two eyewitnesses to tell how he killed her. And I'm supposed to work with that?" He closed his eyes. "By the way, he's just proved to us that he has a violent temper."

"There was a special reason for that outburst," Craig said quietly. "When Ted was eight years old, he saw his father in a drunken rage hold his mother over the terrace of their penthouse."

He paused to catch his breath. "The difference is his father decided not to drop her."

CHAPTER 4

At two o'clock, Elizabeth phoned Syd and asked him to meet her at the Olympic pool. When she got there, a mixed water-aerobics class was starting. Men and women holding beach balls were studiously following the directions of the instructor. "Hold the ball between your palms; swing from side to side . . . no, keep it underwater . . . that's where we get the pull." Music was turned on.

She chose to sit at a table at the far end of the patio. There was no one nearby. Ten minutes later, she heard a scraping sound behind her and gasped. It was Syd. He had cut through the bushes and pushed aside a chair to get onto the patio. He nodded in the direction of the pool. "We had the janitor's apartment in Brooklyn when I was growing up. It's amazing how much muscle tone my mother got swinging a broom."

His tone was pleasant enough, but his manner was guarded. The polo shirt and shorts he was wearing revealed the wiry strength of his arms and the taut muscles in his legs. Funny, Elizabeth thought, I always considered Syd soft-looking, maybe because he has such a poor carriage. That's a mistake.

The scraping sound. Had she heard a chair being moved last night when she was leaving the pool? And Monday night, she thought she had seen something or someone moving. Was it possible she'd been watched while she was swimming? It was a fleeting but upsetting thought.

"For a place that costs so much to relax in, there are quite a few uptight people around here," Syd said. He sat down across from her.

"And I'm the most uptight, I suppose. Syd, you had your own money in *Merry-Go-Round.* You brought the script to Leila. You handled some of the script revisions. I have to talk to the playwright, Clayton Anderson. Where can I get in touch with him?"

"I have no idea. I never met him. The contract was negotiated through his lawyer."

"Tell me the lawyer's name."

"No."

"That's because there *is* no lawyer, right, Syd? Helmut wrote that play, didn't he? He brought it to you, and you brought it to Leila. Helmut knew Min would throw a fit if she found out about it. That play was written by a man obsessed—by Leila. That's why for Leila the play would have worked."

His face turned a dull red. "You don't know what you're talking about."

She handed him the note Ted had written to her. "Don't I? Tell me about meeting Ted the night Leila died. Why didn't you come forward with that information months ago."

Syd scanned the note. "He put that in writing! He's a bigger fool than I realized."

Elizabeth leaned forward. "According to this, the Baron heard Ted struggling with Leila, and Ted told *you* that Leila was dead. Did it ever occur to either of you to see what had happened, if there was any chance to help her?"

Syd shoved his chair back. "I've listened to you long enough."

"No, you haven't. Syd, why did you go to Leila's apartment that night? Why did the Baron go there? She didn't expect either one of you."

Syd stood up. Anger made his face ugly. "Listen, Elizabeth, your sister wiped me out when she quit that play. I went to ask her to reconsider. I never got inside that apartment building. Ted ran past me on the street. I chased him. He told me she was dead. Who lives after a fall like that? I stayed out of it. I never saw the Baron that night." He threw Ted's letter back at her. "Aren't you satisfied? Ted's going to jail. That's what you want, isn't it?"

"Don't leave, Syd. I've still got lots of questions. The letter Cheryl stole. Why did you destroy it? It might have helped Ted. I thought you were so anxious to help him."

Syd sat down heavily. "Look, Elizabeth, I'll make a deal with you. Tearing up that letter was my mistake. Cheryl swears she didn't write that one or any like it. I believe her."

Elizabeth waited. She was not going to concede that Scott believed Cheryl as well.

"You're right about the Baron," Syd continued. "He wrote the play.

You know how Leila put him down. He wanted to have power over her, make her indebted to him. Another guy would want to drag her into bed.'' He waited. ''Elizabeth, if Cheryl can't leave tomorrow and be at her press reception, she'll lose this series. The studio will drop her if they find out she's being detained. You've got Scott's ear. Persuade him to leave Cheryl out of this, and I'll give you a hint about those letters.''

Elizabeth stared at him. Syd seemed to take her silence for assent. As he spoke, he tapped the table with his fingertips. ''The Baron wrote *Merry-Go-Round.* I've got his handwritten changes on the early scripts. Let's play 'Suppose,' Elizabeth. *Suppose* the play is a hit. The Baron doesn't need Min anymore. He's tired of the Spa game. Now he's a Broadway playwright, and constantly with Leila. How could Min prevent that from happening? By making sure the play is a flop. How does she do that? By destroying Leila. And she was just the one who knew how. Ted and Leila were together for three years. If Cheryl wanted to get on their case, why would she have waited that long?''

He did not wait for her response. The chair made the same grating sound as it had when he'd arrived. Elizabeth stared after him. It was possible. It made sense. She could hear Leila say, ''God, Sparrow, Min's really got the hots for the Toy Soldier, hasn't she? I'd hate to be the one who got cozy with him. Min would be on the warpath with a hatchet.''

Or with scissors and paste?

Syd disappeared through the hedges. Watching him, Elizabeth could not see the grim smile he allowed himself as he passed from her vision.

It might work, Syd thought. He'd been wondering how to play this card, and she had made it easy for him. If she fell for it, Cheryl might be in the clear. The smile disappeared. *Might be.*

But what about himself?

CHAPTER 5

Unseeing and motionless, Elizabeth sat at the pool until the brisk voice of the water-aerobics instructor cut through the increasing shock she felt as her mind analyzed the enormity of Min's possible betrayal. She got up and followed the path to the main house.

The afternoon had fulfilled the morning's promise. The sun was golden warm; there was no breeze; even the cypress trees looked mellow, their dark leaves shimmering, the craggy shapes unthreatening. The cheerful clusters of petunias, geraniums and azaleas, perky from recent watering, were now straining toward the warmth, the blossoms open and radiant.

In the office she found a temporary receptionist, a thirtyish, pleasant-faced woman. The Baron and Baroness had gone to the Monterey Peninsula hospital to offer their assistance to Mrs. Meehan's husband. "They're just heartsick about her." The receptionist seemed deeply impressed by their concern.

They'd been heartsick when Leila died, Elizabeth remembered. Now she wondered how much of Min's grief had resulted from guilt. She scribbled a note to Helmut and sealed it. "Please give this to the Baron as soon as he comes back."

She glanced at the copy machine. Sammy had been using that machine when for some reason she'd wandered into the bathhouse. Suppose she really had had some sort of attack that disoriented her. Suppose she had left that letter in the copier. Min had come down early the next morning. Min might have found it and destroyed it.

Wearily, Elizabeth went back to her bungalow. She'd never know who had sent those letters. No one would ever admit it. Why was she staying here now? It was all over. And what was she going to do with the rest of her life? In his note, Ted had told her to start a new and happier chapter. Where? How?

Her head was aching—a dull, steady pounding. She realized that she had skipped lunch again. She'd call and inquire after Alvirah Meehan and then start packing. Funny, how awful it is when there's no place in the world you want to go, no single human being you want to see. She pulled a suitcase out of the closet, opened it, then stopped abruptly.

She still had Alvirah's sunburst pin. It was in the pocket of the slacks she'd been wearing when she'd gone to the clinic. When she took it out and held it, she realized it was heavier than it looked. She was no expert on jewelry, but clearly this was not a valuable piece. Turning it over, she began to study the back. It didn't have the usual safety catch. Instead, there was an enclosed device of some sort. She turned the pin again and studied the face. The small opening in the center was a microphone!

The impact of her discovery left her weak. The seemingly artless questions, the way Alvirah Meehan had fiddled with that pin—she'd been pointing the microphone to catch the voices of the people she was with. The suitcase in her bungalow with the expensive recording equipment, the cassettes there . . . Elizabeth knew she had to get them before anyone else did.

She rang for Vicky.

Fifteen minutes later she was back in her own bungalow, the cassettes and recorder from Alvirah Meehan's suitcase in her possession. Vicky looked flustered and somewhat apprehensive. "I hope no one saw us go in there," she told Elizabeth.

"I'm giving everything to Sheriff Alshorne," Elizabeth assured her. "I just want to be certain they won't disappear if Mrs. Meehan's husband tells anyone about them." She agreed that tea and a sandwich would taste good. When Vicky returned with the tray, she found Elizabeth, earphones on her head, her notebook in her lap, a pen in her hands, listening to the tapes.

CHAPTER 6

Scott Alshorne did not like having a suspicious death and a suspicious near-death unresolved. Dora Samuels had suffered a stroke just before her death. How long before? Alvirah Meehan had had a drop of blood on her face which suggested an injection. The lab report showed a very low blood sugar, possibly the result of an injection. The Baron's efforts had fortunately saved her life. So where did that leave him?

Mrs. Meehan's husband had not been located last night until late evening—one A.M. New York time. He'd chartered a plane and arrived at the hospital at seven A.M. local time. Early in the afternoon, Scott went there to talk to him.

The sight of Alvirah Meehan, ghostly pale, barely breathing, hooked to machines, was incredible to Scott. People like Mrs. Meehan weren't *supposed* to be sick. They were too hearty, too filled with life. The burly man whose back was to him didn't seem to notice his presence. He was bending over, whispering to Alvirah Meehan.

Scott touched his shoulder. "Mr. Meehan, I'm Scott Alshorne, the sheriff of Monterey County. I'm sorry about your wife."

Willy Meehan jerked his head toward the nurses' station. "I know all about how they think she is. But I'm telling you, she's going to be just fine. I told her that if she up and died on me, I was going to take that money and spend it on a blond floozy. She won't let that happen—will you, honey?" Tears began to stream from his eyes.

"Mr. Meehan, I have to speak with you for just a few minutes."

She could hear Willy talking to her, but she couldn't reach him. Alvirah had never felt so weak. She couldn't even move her hand, she was so tired.

And there was something she had to tell them. She *knew* what had happened now. It was so clear. She *had* to make herself talk. She tried moving her lips, but she couldn't. She tried to wiggle her finger. Willy's hand was covering hers, and she couldn't get up the strength to make him understand that she was trying to reach him.

If she could just move her lips, just get his attention. He was talking about the trips they were going to take. A tiny stab of irritation flared through her mind. Keep quiet and *listen* to me, she wanted to shout at him. . . . Oh, Willy, please listen. . . .

* * *

The conversation in the corridor outside the intensive-care unit was unsatisfactory. Alvirah was "healthy as a horse." She was never sick. She was on no medication. Scott did not bother to ask if there was a possibility that she used drugs. There wasn't, and he wouldn't insult this heartbroken man with the question.

"She was looking forward so much to this trip," Willy Meehan said as he put his hand on the door of the intensive-care unit. "She was even writing articles about it for the *Globe*. You should have seen how excited she was when they were showing her how to record people's conversations. . . ."

"She was writing articles!" Scott exclaimed. "She was recording people?"

He was interrupted. A nurse rushed out. "Mr. Meehan, will you come in? She's trying to talk again. We want you to speak to her."

Scott rushed in behind him. Alvirah was straining to move her lips. *"Voi . . . voi . . ."*

Willy grasped her hand. "I'm here, honey, I'm here."

The effort was so much. She was getting so tired. She was going to fall asleep. If she could just get even one word out to warn them. With a terrible effort, Alvirah managed that word. She said it loud enough that she could hear it herself.

She said, "Voices."

CHAPTER 7

The afternoon shadows deepened as, unmindful of time, Elizabeth listened to Alvirah Meehan's tapes. Sometimes she stopped and rewound a segment of the tape and listened to it several times. Her lined pad was filled with notes.

Those questions that had seemed so tactless had actually been so clever. Elizabeth thought of how she had sat at the table with the Countess, wishing she could overhear the conversations at Min's table. Now she could. Some of the talk was muffled, but she could hear enough to detect stress, evasion, attempts to change the subject.

She began to systematize her notations, creating a separate page for everyone at the table. At the bottom of each page she scribbled questions as they came to mind. When she finished the third tape, it seemed to her that she merely had a jumble of confusing sentences.

Leila, how I wish you were here. You were too cynical, but so many times you were right about people. You could see through their facades. Something is wrong, and I'm missing it. What is it?

It seemed to her that she could hear Leila's answer, as if she were in the room. *For heaven's sake, Sparrow, open your eyes! Stop seeing what people want you to see. Start listening. Think for yourself. Didn't I teach you that much?*

She was just about to put the last cassette from Alvirah's sunburst pin into the recorder when the phone rang. It was Helmut. ''You left a note for me.''

''Yes, I did. Helmut, why did you go to Leila's apartment the night she died?''

She heard him gasp. ''Elizabeth, do not talk on the phone. May I come to you now?''

While she waited, she hid the recording equipment and her pad. She had no intention of letting Helmut become aware of the tapes.

For once, his rigid military carriage seemed to have deserted him. He sat opposite her, his shoulders slumped. His voice low and hurried, his German accent more pronounced as he spoke, he told her what he had told Min. He had written the play. He had gone to plead with Leila to reconsider.

''You took the money out of Min's Swiss account.''

He nodded. ''Minna has guessed. What is the use?''

''Is it possible that she always knew? That she sent those letters because she wanted to upset Leila enough to destroy her performance? No one knew Leila's emotional state better than Min.''

The Baron's eyes widened. ''But how magnificent. It is just the sort of thing Minna *would* do. Then she may have known all along that there was no money left. Could she have been simply punishing me?''

Elizabeth did not care if her face showed the disgust she felt. ''I don't share your admiration for that scheme, if it was Min's doing.'' She went to the desk and got a fresh pad. ''You heard Ted struggling with Leila?''

''Yes, I did.''

''Where were you? How did you get in? How long were you there? Exactly what did you hear?''

It helped to be writing, to concentrate on taking down word for word what he said. He had heard Leila pleading for her life, and he had not tried to help her.

When he had finished, perspiration was glistening on his smooth cheeks. She wanted to get him out of her sight, but she could not resist saying, ''Suppose instead of running away, you had gone into that apartment? Leila might be alive right now. Ted might not be plea-bargaining for a lighter sentence if you hadn't been so worried about saving yourself.''

''I don't believe that, Elizabeth. It happened in seconds.'' The Baron's eyes widened. ''But haven't you heard? There is no plea bargain. It's been on the news all afternoon. A second eyewitness saw Ted hold Leila over the terrace before he dropped her. The district attorney wants Ted to get life.''

Leila had not toppled over the railing in a struggle. He had held her, then deliberately dropped her. That Leila's death had taken a few seconds longer seemed to Elizabeth even more cruel than her worst fears. I should be *glad* they're going for the maximum penalty, she told herself. I should be *glad* to have the chance to testify against him.

She wanted desperately to be alone, but she managed to ask the Baron one more question: "Did you see Syd near Leila's apartment that night?"

Could she trust the look of astonishment on his face? "No, I did not," he said firmly. "Was he there?"

It is finished, Elizabeth told herself. She put in a call to Scott Alshorne. The sheriff was out on official business. Could someone else help her? No. She left a message for him to phone her. She would turn over Alvirah Meehan's recording equipment to him and get on the next plane to New York. No wonder they'd all sounded so on edge from Alvirah's relentless questioning. Most of them had something to hide.

The sunburst pin. She started to put it into a bag with the recorder and then realized she hadn't listened to the last cassette. It occurred to her that Alvirah had been wearing the pin in the clinic. . . . She managed to extract the cassette from the tiny container. If Alvirah was so concerned about the collagen injections, would she have left the recorder on during the treatment?

She had. Elizabeth turned up the volume and held the recorder to her ear. The cassette began with Alvirah in the treatment room talking with the nurse. The nurse reassuring her, talking about Valium; the click of the door, Alvirah's even breathing, the click of the door again . . . The Baron's somewhat muffled and indistinct voice, reassuring Alvirah, starting the injection; the click of the door, Alvirah's gasps, her attempt to call for help, her frenzied breath, a click of the door again, the nurse's cheerful voice, "Well, here we are, Mrs. Meehan. All set for your beauty treatment?" And then the nurse, upset, on the edge of panic, saying, "Mrs. Meehan, *what's the matter?* Doctor . . ."

There was a pause, then the voice of Helmut barking orders—"Open that robe!"—calling for oxygen. There was a pounding sound—that must have been when he was compressing her chest; then Helmut called for an intravenous. That was when I was there, Elizabeth thought. He tried to kill her. Whatever he gave her was meant to kill her. Alvirah's persistent references to that sentence about "a butterfly floating on a cloud," her constantly saying that that reminded her of something, her calling him a clever author—did he perceive that as her toying with him? Had he still hoped that somehow Min wouldn't learn the truth about the play, about her Swiss bank account?

She replayed the last tape again and again. There was something about it she didn't understand. What was it? What was she missing?

Not knowing what she was looking for, she reread the notes she had taken when Helmut described Leila's death. Her eyes became riveted on one sentence. But that's *wrong,* she thought.

Unless.

Like an exhausted climber within inches of an icy summit, she reviewed the notes she had made from Alvirah Meehan's tapes.

And found the key.

It had always been there, waiting for her. Did he realize how close she had been to the truth?

Yes, he did.

She shivered, remembering the questions that had seemed so innocent, her own troubled answers that must have been so threatening to him.

Her hand flew to the phone. She would call Scott. And then she withdrew her fingers from the dial. Tell him what? There wasn't a shred of proof. There never would be.

Unless she could force his hand.

CHAPTER 8

For over an hour, Scott sat by Alvirah's bedside, hoping she would say something else. Then, touching Willy Meehan's shoulder, he said, "I'll be right back." He had seen John Whitley at the nurses' station and followed him into his office.

"Have you anything more you can tell me, John?"

"No." The doctor looked both angry and perplexed. "I don't like not knowing what I'm dealing with. Her blood sugar was so low that without a history of severe hypoglycemia we have to suspect that somebody injected her with insulin. She sure as hell has a puncture mark where we found the spot of blood on her cheek. If Von Schreiber claims he didn't inject her face at all, something's screwy."

"What are her chances?" Scott asked.

John shrugged. "I don't know. It's too soon to tell if she has incurred any brain damage. If willpower can bring her back, that husband of hers will manage it. He's doing everything right. Talking to her about chartering a plane to get here, about fixing the house when they go home. If she can hear him, she'll want to stay around."

John's office overlooked the garden. Scott walked to the window, wishing he could spend some time alone, *think* this through. "We can't *prove* Mrs. Meehan was the victim of an attempted murder. We can't prove Miss Samuels was the victim of murder."

"I don't think you can make either one stick, no."

"So that means even if we can make a stab at figuring who would want those women dead—and have the guts to attempt to kill them at a place like the Spa—we still may not be able to prove anything.''

''That's more your line of work than mine, but I'd agree.''

Scott had one parting question: ''Mrs. Meehan has been trying to talk. She finally came out with a single word—'*voices.*' Is it likely that someone in her condition is really trying to communicate something that makes sense?''

Whitley shrugged. ''My impression is that her coma is still too deep to be certain as to her recall. But I could be wrong. It wouldn't be the first time.''

Again Scott conferred with Willy Meehan in the corridor. Alvirah was planning to write a series of articles. The editor of the *New York Globe* had told her to get all the inside information she could on celebrities. Scott remembered her endless questions the night he had been at the Spa for dinner. He wondered what Alvirah might unwittingly have learned. At least it gave some reason for the attack on her—if there had been an attack. And it explained the expensive recording equipment in her suitcase.

He was scheduled to meet with the mayor of Carmel at five o'clock. On his two-way car radio, he learned that Elizabeth had phoned him twice. The second call was urgent.

Some instinct made him cancel his appointment with the mayor for the second time in two days and go directly to the Spa.

Through the picture window, he could see Elizabeth on the phone. He waited until she put the receiver down before he knocked. In the thirty-second interval, he had a chance to study her. The afternoon sun was sending slanted rays into the room which created shadows on her face and revealed the high cheekbones, the wide, sensitive mouth, the luminous eyes. If I were a sculptor, I'd want her to model for me, he thought. She has an elegance that goes beyond beauty.

Eventually she would have surpassed Leila.

Elizabeth turned the tapes over to him. She indicated the writing pad with its lines of notations. ''Do me a favor, Scott,'' she asked him. ''Listen to these tapes very, very carefully. This one''—she indicated the cassette she had taken from the sunburst pin—''is going to shock you. Play it over and see if you don't catch what I think I've heard.''

Now there was a determined thrust to her jaw, a glitter in her eyes. ''Elizabeth, what are you up to?'' he asked.

''Something that I have to do—that *only* I can do.''

Despite Scott's increasingly stern demands for an explanation, she would not tell him more. He did remember to tell her that Alvirah Meehan had managed to utter one word. ''Does 'voices' suggest anything to you?''

Elizabeth's smile was enigmatic.

''You bet it does,'' she said grimly.

CHAPTER 9

Ted had bolted from the Spa grounds in early afternoon. By five o'clock he had still not returned. Henry Bartlett was visibly chafing to go back to New York. "We came here to prepare Ted's defense," he said. "I hope he realized his trial is scheduled to start in five days. If he won't meet with me, I'm not doing any good sitting around here."

The phone rang. Craig jumped to answer it. "Elizabeth. What a nice surprise. . . . Yes, it's true. I'd like to think we can still persuade the district attorney to accept a plea, but that's pretty unrealistic. . . . We hadn't talked about dinner yet, but of course it would be good to be with you. . . . Oh, that! I don't know. It just didn't seem funny anymore. And it always annoyed Ted. Fine. . . . See you at dinner."

Scott drove home with the windows of the car open, appreciating the cool breeze that had begun to blow in from the ocean. It felt good, but he could not shake the sense of apprehension that was overcoming him. Elizabeth was up to something, and every instinct told him that whatever it was, it might be dangerous.

A faint mist was setting in along the shoreline of Pacific Grove. It would develop into a heavy fog later on. He turned the corner and pulled into the driveway of a pleasant narrow house a block from the ocean. For six years now he had been coming home to this empty place and never once not felt that moment of nostalgia that Jeanie was no longer here waiting for him. He used to talk cases through with her. Tonight he would have asked her some hypothetical questions. Would you say that there is a connection between Dora Samuels' death and Alvirah Meehan's coma? Another question jumped into his mind. Would you say that there is a connection between those two women and Leila's death?

And finally: Jeanie, what the hell is Elizabeth up to?

To clear his head, Scott showered, changed into old slacks and a sweater. He made a pot of coffee and put a hamburger on the grill. When he was ready to eat, he turned on the first of Alvirah's tapes.

He began listening at quarter of five. At six o'clock, his notebook, like Elizabeth's, was filled with jottings. At quarter of seven, he heard the tape that documented the attack on Alvirah. "That son of a bitch, Von Schreiber!" he muttered. He *did* inject her with something. But with what? Suppose he had started the collagen and seen her go into some sort of attack? He had returned almost immediately with the nurse.

Scott replayed the tape, then played it a third time and finally realized what Elizabeth had wanted him to hear. There was something odd about the Baron's voice the first time he spoke to Mrs. Meehan. It was hoarse, guttural, startlingly different from his voice a moment or two later, when he was shouting orders to the nurse.

He phoned the hospital and asked for Dr. Whitley. He had one question for him. "Do you think an injection that drew blood is the kind that a doctor would have administered?"

"I've seen some sloppy injections given by topflight surgeons. And if a doctor gave the shot that was meant to harm Mrs. Meehan—he may have had the grace to be nervous."

"Thanks, John."

"Don't mention it."

He was reheating the coffee when his bell rang. In quick strides he reached the door, flung it open to face Ted Winters.

His clothes were rumpled, his face smudged with dirt, his hair matted; vivid fresh scratches covered his arms and legs. He stumbled forward and would have fallen if Scott had not reached out to grasp him.

"Scott, you've got to help me. Somebody's got to help me. It's a trap, I swear it is. Scott, I tried for hours and I couldn't do it. I couldn't make myself do it."

"Easy . . . easy." Scott put his arm around Ted and guided him to the couch. "You're ready to pass out." He poured a generous amount of brandy into a tumbler. "Come on, drink this."

After a few sips, Ted ran his hand over his face, as if trying to erase the naked panic he had shown. His attempt at a smile was a wan failure, and he slumped with weariness. He looked young, vulnerable, totally unlike the sophisticated head of a multimillion-dollar corporation. Twenty-five years vanished, and Scott felt that he was looking at the nine-year-old boy who used to go fishing with him.

"Have you eaten today?" he asked.

"Not that I remember."

"Then sip that brandy slowly, and I'll get you a sandwich and coffee."

He waited until Ted had finished the sandwich before he said, "All right, you'd better tell me all about it."

"Scott, I don't know what's happening, but I *do* know this: I could not have killed Leila the way they're trying to say I did. I don't care how many witnesses come out of the woodwork—something is wrong."

He leaned forward. Now his eyes were pleading. "Scott, you remember how terrified Mother was of heights?"

"She had good cause to be. That bastard of a father of yours—"

Ted interrupted him. "He was disgusted because he could see that I was developing that same phobia. One day when I was about eight, he made her stand out on the terrace of the penthouse and look down. She began to cry. She said, 'Come on, Teddy,' and we started to go inside. He grabbed her and picked her up, and that son of a bitch held her over the railing. It was thirty-eight floors up. She was screaming, begging. I was clawing at him. He didn't pull her in until she'd fainted. Then he just dropped her on the terrace floor and said to me, 'If I ever see you look frightened out here, I'll do the same thing to you.' "

Ted swallowed. His voice broke. "This new eyewitness says I did that to Leila. Today I tried to make myself walk down the cliffs at Point Sur. *I couldn't do it!* I couldn't make my legs go to the edge."

"People under stress can do some pretty funny things."

"No. No. If I'd killed Leila, I'd have done it some other way. I know that. To say that drunk or sober, I could hold her over the railing . . . Syd swears I told him that my *father* pushed Leila off the terrace; he may have known that story about my father. Maybe everybody's lying to me. Scott, I've *got* to remember what happened that night."

With compassionate eyes, Scott studied Ted, taking in the exhausted droop of his shoulders, the fatigue that emanated from his body. He'd been walking all afternoon, trying to make himself stand at the edge of a cliff, battling his own personal demon in search of the truth. "Did you tell them this when they began questioning you about Leila's death?"

"It would have sounded ridiculous. I build hotels where we make people *want* terraces. I've always been able to avoid going out on them without making an issue of it."

Darkness was setting in. Beads of perspiration like unchecked tears were running down Ted's cheeks. Scott switched on a light. The room with its comfortable overstuffed furniture, the pillows Jeanie had embroidered, the tall-backed rocking chair, the pine bookcase came to life. Ted did not seem to notice. He was in a world where he was trapped by other people's testimony, on the verge of being confined to prison for the next twenty or thirty years. He's right, Scott decided. His only hope is to go back to that night. "Are you willing to have hypnosis or sodium pentothal?" he asked.

"Either . . . both . . . it doesn't matter."

Scott went to the phone and called John Whitley at the hospital again. "Don't you ever go home?" he asked.

"I do get there, now and again. In fact, I'm on my way now."

"I'm afraid not, John. We have another emergency. . . ."

CHAPTER 10

Craig and Bartlett walked together toward the main house. They had deliberately skipped the 'cocktail' hour and could see the last of the guests leaving the veranda as the muted gong announced dinner. A cool breeze had come up from the ocean, and the webs of lichen hanging from the giant pines that formed the border of the north end of the property swayed in a rhythmic, solemn movement that was accentuated by the tinted lights scattered throughout the grounds.

"I don't like it," Bartlett told Craig. "Elizabeth Lange is up to something pretty strange when she asks to have dinner with us. I can tell you the district attorney isn't going to like it one damn bit if he hears his star witness is breaking bread with the enemy."

"Former star witness," Craig reminded him.

"Still star witness. That Ross woman is a total nut. The other one is a petty thief. I won't mind being the one to cross-examine those two on the stand."

Craig stopped and grabbed his arm. "You mean you think Ted may still have a chance?"

"Hell, of course not. He's guilty. And he's not a good enough liar to help himself."

There was a placard in the foyer. Tonight there would be a flute-and-harp recital. Bartlett read the names of the artists. "They're first-rate. I heard them in Carnegie Hall last year. You ever go there?"

"Sometimes."

"What kind of music do you like?"

"Bach fugues. And I suppose that surprises you."

"Frankly, I never thought about it one way or another," Bartlett said shortly. Christ, he thought, I'll be glad when this case is over. A guilty client who doesn't know how to lie and a second-in-command with a chip on his shoulder who would never get over his inferiority complex.

Min, the Baron, Syd, Cheryl and Elizabeth were already at the table. Only Elizabeth seemed perfectly relaxed. She, rather than Min, had somehow assumed the role of hostess. The place on either side of her was vacant. When she saw them approaching, she reached out her hands to them in a welcoming gesture. "I saved these seats specially for you."

And what the hell is that supposed to mean? Bartlett wondered sourly.

Elizabeth watched as the waiter filled their glasses with nonalcoholic wine. She said, "Min, I don't mind telling you that when I get home I'll enjoy a good, stiff drink."

"You should be like everyone else," Syd told her. "Where's your padlocked suitcase?"

"Its contents are much more interesting than liquor," she told him. Throughout dinner she led the conversation, reminiscing on the times they had been together at the Spa.

Once dessert was served, it was Bartlett who challenged her. "Miss Lange, I've had the distinct impression that you're playing some sort of game, and I for one don't believe in participating in games unless I know the rules."

Elizabeth was raising a spoonful of raspberries to her lips. She swallowed them, then put down the spoon. "You're quite right," she told him. "I wanted to be with all of you tonight for a very specific reason. You should all know that I no longer believe Ted is responsible for my sister's death."

They stared at her, their faces shocked.

"Let's talk about it," Elizabeth said. "Someone deliberately destroyed Leila by sending those poison-pen letters to her. I think it was you or you." She pointed at Cheryl, then at Min.

"You are absolutely wrong," Min said indignantly.

"I told you to come up with more letters and trace them." Cheryl spat out the words.

"I may do just that," Elizabeth told her. "Mr. Bartlett, did Ted tell you that both Syd and the Baron were around my sister's apartment house the night she died?" She seemed to enjoy his look of astonishment. "There is more to my sister's death than has come out. I know that. One, maybe *two* of you know that. You see, there's another possible scenario. Syd and Helmut had money in that play. Syd knew Helmut was the playwright. They went together to plead with Leila. Something went wrong and Leila died. It would have been considered an accident if it hadn't been for that woman who swore she saw Ted struggling with Leila. At that point, my testimony that Ted had come back trapped him."

The waiter was hovering over them. Min waved him away. Bartlett realized that people at the surrounding tables were watching them, sensing the tension. "Ted doesn't remember anything about going back to Leila's apartment," Elizabeth said, "but suppose he did go back; suppose he left immediately; suppose one of you struggled with Leila. You're all about the same size. It was raining. That Ross woman might have seen Leila struggling, and simply assumed it was Ted. You two agreed to let Ted take the blame for Leila's death and concocted the stories you told him. It's possible, isn't it?"

"Minna, this girl is crazy," the Baron sputtered. "You must know—"

"I deny absolutely that I was in that apartment that night," Syd said.

"You admit you ran after Ted. But from where? The apartment? Because he'd seen you pushing Leila? It would have been a stroke of luck if he was so traumatized that he blocked it out.

"The Baron claims he heard Leila and Ted quarreling. But I heard them too. I was on the telephone. *And I did not hear what he claims he heard!*"

Elizabeth leaned her elbows on the table and looked searchingly from one angry face to the next.

"I'm very grateful for this information," Henry Bartlett told her. "But you seem to have forgotten there's a new witness."

"A very convenient new witness," Elizabeth said. "I spoke to the district attorney this afternoon. This witness turns out not to be very bright. The night he claims he was in that apartment watching Ted drop Leila off the terrace, he was in jail." She stood up. "Craig, would you walk me to my place? I've got to finish packing, and I want to get a swim in. It may be a long time before I'm here again . . . if ever."

Outside, the darkness was now absolute. The moon and stars were again covered with a misty fog; the Japanese lanterns in the trees and bushes were hazy dots of light. Craig put his arm around her shoulders. "That was quite a performance," he said.

"It was just that: a performance. I can't prove anything. If they stick together, there isn't a shred of evidence."

"Do you have any more of those letters that Leila was receiving?"

"No. I was bluffing about that."

"That's a shocker about the new witness."

"I was bluffing about that too. He *was* in jail that evening, but he was released on bond at eight o'clock. Leila died at nine thirty-one. The most they can do is cast doubt on his credibility."

She leaned against him as they reached her bungalow. "Oh, Craig, it's all so crazy, isn't it? I feel as if I'm digging and digging for the vein of truth the way the old prospectors dug for a vein of gold. . . . The only trouble is I'm out of time, so I had to start blasting. But at the very least, I may have upset one of them enough so that he—or she—will make a slip."

His hand smoothed her hair. "You're going back tomorrow?"

"Yes. How about you?"

"Ted still hasn't turned up. He may be on a bender. I can't say I blame him. Though it wouldn't be like him. . . . Obviously, we'll wait for him. But when this is over, when you're ready—promise that you'll call me."

"And get your Japanese-houseboy imitation on the recorder? Oh, I forgot. You said you changed it. Why did you do that, Craig? I always thought it was pretty funny. So did Leila."

He looked embarrassed. She did not wait for him to answer.

"This place used to be such fun," Elizabeth murmured. "Remember when Leila invited you here that first time, before Ted came?"

"Of course I remember."

"How did you meet Leila? I forget."

"She was staying at the Beverly Winters. I sent flowers to her suite. She called to thank me, and we had a drink. She was on her way here, and she invited me along. . . ."

"And then she met Ted. . . ." Elizabeth kissed his cheek. "Pray that whatever I've done tonight works. If Ted is innocent, I want him off just as badly as you do."

"I know you do. You're in love with him, aren't you?"

"I have been from that first day you introduced him to Leila and me."

Inside the bungalow, Elizabeth put on her swimsuit and robe. She went to the desk and wrote a long letter addressed to Scott Alshorne. Then she rang for the maid. It was a new girl, one she'd never seen before, but she had to take the chance. She put the envelope for Scott inside a new one and scribbled a brief note. "Give this to Vicky in the morning," she instructed the girl. "No one else. Is that clear?"

"Of course." The girl was slightly offended.

"Thank you." Elizabeth watched the girl leave and wondered what she would say if she could have read the note to Vicky.

It read: *"In case of my death, deliver this to Sheriff Alshorne immediately."*

At eight o'clock, Ted walked into a private room in the Monterey Peninsula hospital. Dr. Whitley introduced a psychiatrist who was waiting to administer the injection. A video camera had already been set up. Scott and a deputy sheriff were to be witnesses to the statements given under sodium pentothal.

"I still think you ought to have your lawyer here," Scott told him.

Ted was grim-faced. "Bartlett has been the very one urging me not to undergo this test. I don't intend to waste any more time talking about it. Let the truth come out."

He slipped his feet out of his shoes and lay down on the contour couch.

A few minutes after the injection had taken effect he began to answer questions about the last hour he spent with Leila.

"She kept accusing me of cheating on her. Had pictures of me with other women. Group pictures. I told her that that was part of my job. The hotels. I was never with any woman alone. I tried to reason with her. She had been drinking all day. I was drinking with her. Sick of it. I warned her she had to trust me; I couldn't face those scenes the rest of my life. She told me she knew I was trying to break off with her. Leila. Leila. She went wild. I tried to calm her down. She scratched my hands. The phone rang. It was Elizabeth. Leila kept shouting at me. I got out. Went to my apartment downstairs. Looked at myself in the mirror. Blood on my cheek. On my hands. Tried to phone Craig. Knew I couldn't live like that anymore. Knew it was over. But thought maybe Leila would do something to herself. Better stay with her till I can get Elizabeth. God, I'm so drunk. The elevator. Leila's floor. Door open. Leila screaming."

Scott leaned forward intently. "What is she screaming, Ted?"

"Don't. Don't." Ted was trembling, shaking his head, his expression shocked and disbelieving.

"Ted, what do you see? What happened?"

"Push door open. Room is dark. The terrace. Leila. Hold on. Hold on. Help her. Christ, grab her! Don't let her fall! *Don't let Mommy fall!"*

Ted began to sob—deep, racking sounds that filled the room. His body twitched convulsively.

"Ted, who did that to her?"

"Hands. Just see hands. She's gone. *It's my father."* His words became broken. "Leila's dead. Daddy pushed her. Daddy killed her."

The psychiatrist looked at Scott. ''You won't get any more now. Either that's all he knows or he still can't bring himself to face the entire truth.''

''That's what I'm afraid of,'' Scott whispered. ''How soon will he come out of it?''

''Pretty fast. He'd better rest awhile.''

John Whitley stood up. ''I want to look in on Mrs. Meehan. I'll be right back.''

''I'd like to go with you.'' The cameraman was packing his equipment. ''Drop the tape in my office,'' Scott told him. He turned to his deputy. ''Stay here. Don't let Mr. Winters leave.''

The head nurse in the ICU was visibly excited. ''We were just about to send for you, Doctor. Mrs. Meehan seems to be coming out of the coma.''

''She said 'voices' again.'' Willy Meehan's face was alive with hope. ''Just as clear. I don't know what she meant, but she knew what she was trying to say.''

''Does that mean she's out of danger?'' Scott asked Dr. Whitley.

John Whitley studied the chart and reached for Alvirah's pulse. His answer was low enough that Willy Meehan could not hear him. ''Not necessarily. But it sure is a good sign. Whatever prayers you know, start saying them now.''

Alvirah's lids fluttered open. She was looking straight ahead, and as her eyes focused, they rested on Scott. A look of urgency came over her face. ''Voices,'' she whispered. ''Wasn't.''

Scott bent over her. ''Mrs. Meehan, I don't understand.''

Alvirah felt the way she did when she used to clean old Mrs. Smythe's house. Mrs. Smythe was always telling her to push the piano out and get at the dust behind it. It was like trying to push the piano but so much more important. She wanted to tell them who had hurt her but she couldn't think of his name. She could see him plain as plain, but she couldn't remember his name. Desperately she tried to communicate with the sheriff. ''Wasn't the doctor did that to me . . . wasn't his voice. . . . Someone else . . .'' She closed her eyes and felt herself slipping into sleep.

''She's getting better,'' Willy Meehan whispered exultantly. ''She's trying to tell you something.''

''Wasn't the doctor . . . wasn't his voice. . . .'' What the hell did she *mean?* Scott asked himself.

He rushed to the room where Ted was waiting. Ted was sitting up now in the small plastic armchair, his hands folded in front of him. ''I opened the door,'' he said tonelessly. ''Hands were holding Leila over the railing. I could just see the white satin billowing; her arms were flailing. . . .''

''You couldn't see who was holding her?''

''It was so fast. I think I tried to call out, and then she was gone and whoever it was just disappeared. He must have run along the terrace.''

''Have you any idea of his size?''

"No, it was as if I was watching my father when he did that to my mother. I even saw my father's face." He looked up at Scott. "And I haven't helped you, or myself, have I?"

"No, you haven't," Scott said bluntly. "I want a free association from you. *'Voices.'* Say the first thing that comes into your mind."

"Identification."

"Go on."

"Unique. Personal."

"Go on."

Ted shrugged. "Mrs. Meehan. She brought up the subject repeatedly. She apparently had some idea of taking elocution lessons and she got everyone into a discussion about accents and voices."

Scott thought of Alvirah's broken whisper. "Wasn't the doctor . . . wasn't his voice. . . ." Mentally he reviewed the dinner-conversation tapes Alvirah had recorded. Identification. Unique. Personal.

The Baron's voice on the last tape. He drew in his breath sharply. "Ted, do you remember what else Mrs. Meehan said about voices? Something about Craig imitating yours?"

Ted frowned. "She asked me about a story she'd read years ago in *People*—that Craig used to field my phone calls at the fraternity house and the girls couldn't tell the difference between our voices. I told her it was true. In school Craig used to bring down the house with his imitations."

"And she tried to make him demonstrate it for her, but he refused." Scott saw Ted's look of surprise and shook his head impatiently. "Never mind how I know. That's what Elizabeth wanted me to catch when I listened to those tapes."

"I don't know what you're talking about."

"Mrs. Meehan kept pestering Craig to imitate your voice. Don't you see? He didn't want anyone to think about his being a good mimic. *Elizabeth's testimony against you is based solely on hearing your voice.* Elizabeth suspects him, but if she's tipped her hand he'll go after her."

A wild sense of urgency made him grab Ted's arm. "Come on!" he shouted. "We've got to get to the Spa." On the way out, he yelled instructions at the deputy: "Call Elizabeth Lange at the Cypress Point Spa. Tell her to stay in her room with her door locked. Send another car over there."

He ran through the lobby, Ted at his heels. In his car, Scott turned on the siren. It's too late for you, he thought as his mind filled with the image of the murderer. Killing Elizabeth won't help you anymore. . . .

The car raced along the highway between Salinas and Pebble Beach. Scott fired instructions into the two-way radio. As Ted listened, the full impact of what he was hearing penetrated his consciousness; the hands that had held Leila over the terrace became arms, a shoulder, as familiar as his own, and the realization of Elizabeth's danger made him jam his feet on the floor of the car in a futile effort to make contact with an imaginary accelerator.

Had she been toying with him? Of course she had. But like the others, she had underestimated him. And like the others, she would pay for it.

With methodical calm he stripped off his clothes and unlocked his suitcase. The mask was on top of the wet suit and tank. It amused him to remember how at the last moment Sammy had seen his eyes through the mask and known. When he'd called to her in Ted's voice, she had run to him. All the evidence hadn't in the end turned her against Ted. And all the overwhelming evidence he had so carefully laid out, even the new eyewitness he had planted, hadn't convinced Elizabeth.

The wet suit was cumbersome. When this was over, he'd get rid of all this equipment. Just in case anyone questioned Elizabeth's death, it wouldn't be wise to have any visible reminder that he was an expert scuba diver. Ted, of course, should remember. But in all these months it hadn't crossed Ted's mind that he had the special ability to mimic him. Ted—so stupid, so naive. "I tried to phone you; I remember that distinctly." And so Ted had become his impeccable alibi. Until that nosy bitch Alvirah Meehan kept after him. "Let me hear you imitate Ted's voice. Just once. Please. Say anything at all." He'd wanted to throttle her, but then had had to wait until yesterday when he went ahead of her to treatment room C, waited in the closet for her, the hypodermic needle in his hand. Too bad she didn't know she'd sampled his gift for mimicry when she thought she was listening to the Baron.

The wet suit was on. He strapped the tank to his back, turned off the lights and waited. It still chilled him to realize that last night he'd been within seconds of opening the door and confronting Ted. Ted had wanted to talk everything through. "I'm beginning to think you're my only real friend," he'd said.

He opened the door a crack and listened. There was no one in sight, no sound of footsteps. The fog was gathering, and it would be easy to slip behind the trees until he reached the pool. He had to get there before her, be waiting and when she swam past, grab the whistle before she could get it to her lips.

He slipped out, his footsteps noiseless as he cut across the path, avoiding the areas where the lanterns sent out beams of light. If only he'd been able to finish this on Monday night . . . but Ted had been standing near the pool watching Elizabeth.

Ted always in the way. Always the one with money and looks, always the one the girls flocked around. He'd forced himself to accept it, to make himself useful to Ted, first in college, then in the office: the go-fer, the tenacious assistant. He'd had to fight his way up until the executive-plane accident had instantly made him Ted's right hand, and then when Ted lost Kathy and Teddy, he'd been able to take over the reins of the company. . . .

Until Leila.

His loins ached remembering Leila. How it had felt to make love to her. Until he'd brought her here and she'd met Ted. And discarded him, like garbage tossed into a bin.

He had watched those slim arms slide around Ted's neck, that wanton body snuggling against Ted, had helplessly walked away not able to bear the sight of them together, planning revenge, waiting for the time.

And he'd found it with the play. He'd had to prove investing in the play was a mistake. It was already clear that Ted was beginning to ease him out. And it was his chance to destroy Leila. The exquisite pleasure of sending those letters, of watching her fall apart. She'd even shown them to him as she received them. He'd warned her to burn them, to hide them from Ted and Elizabeth. "Ted's getting awfully sick of your jealousy, and if you tell Elizabeth how upset you are, she'll quit her play to be with you. That could ruin her career."

Grateful for his advice, Leila had agreed. "But tell me," she'd begged. "Is it true, Bulldog? Is there someone else?" His elaborate protests had had the effect he wanted. She'd believed the letters.

He hadn't worried about those last two. He'd thought all that unopened mail had been thrown out. But it hadn't mattered. Cheryl burned one, and he had taken the other one from Sammy. Everything was at last working for him. On Saturday he would become chairman and president of Winters Enterprises.

He was at the pool.

He slipped into the dark water and swam to the shallow end. Elizabeth always dived into the deepest area. That night in Elaine's he'd known the time had come to kill Leila. Everyone would believe it was a suicide. He'd let himself in through one of the guest suites on the upper floor of the duplex and listened to them quarrel, listened when Ted stormed out, and then the idea had come to mimic Ted's voice to make Elizabeth think Ted was with Leila just before she died.

He heard the sound of footsteps on the path. She was coming. Soon he would be safe. In those weeks after Leila's death, he'd thought he had lost. Ted hadn't fallen apart. He'd turned to Elizabeth. The death had been considered an accident. Until that unbelievable stroke of luck when that crazy woman had come forward and said she had seen Ted struggling with Leila. And Elizabeth had become the chief witness.

It was destined to be this way. Now the Baron and Syd had become material witnesses against Ted. The Baron wouldn't be able to deny that he had heard Ted struggling with Leila. Syd had seen Ted on the street. Even Ted himself must have glimpsed them on the terrace and because he was drunk and it was dark, relived that episode with his father.

The footsteps were getting closer. He allowed himself to sink to the bottom of the pool. She was so sure of herself, so clever. Waiting for him to come, anxious for him to attack her, ready to outswim him while she blew the whistle and called for help. She wouldn't get the chance.

It was ten o'clock, and there was a difference in the atmosphere of the Spa. Many of the bungalows were already dark, and Elizabeth wondered how many people had actually checked out. The talk-show host was gone; the Countess and her friends must have left before dinner; the tennis player and his girlfriend had not been in the dining room.

Evening fog had settled in, heavy, penetrating, enveloping. Even the Japanese lanterns along the path seemed hooded.

She dropped her robe by the side of the pool and looked carefully into the water. It was absolutely still. There was no one here yet.

She felt for the whistle around her neck. All she would need was to be able to put her lips to it. A blast from this whistle would bring help.

She dived in. The water felt clammy tonight. Or was it because she was afraid? I can outswim anyone, she reassured herself. I had to take this chance. It's the only way. Would the bait be taken?

Voices. Alvirah Meehan had been persistent on that subject. That persistence might have cost her her life. That was what she had been trying to tell them. She'd known it wasn't Helmut's voice.

She'd reached the north end of the pool; she flipped over and began to backstroke. *Voices.* It was her identification of Ted's voice that had placed him in that room with Leila a few minutes before her death.

The night Leila died, Craig had claimed to be in his apartment watching a television show when Ted tried to call him. No one had questioned that *Craig* was home. Ted had been *his* alibi.

Voices.

Craig wanted Ted to be convicted. Ted was about to turn over the running of Winters Enterprises to him.

When she asked Craig about changing the message on his recorder, had she frightened him enough to force him into an overt attack?

Elizabeth began a freestyle breaststroke. From beneath her, arms encircled her, pinning her own arms to her sides. Her startled gasp caused her to swallow a mouthful of water. Choking furiously, she felt herself being dragged to the bottom of the pool. She began to beat with her heels, but they slipped off the heavy rubber wet suit of her assailant. With a desperate burst of strength, she dug her elbows deep into the ribs of her captor. For an instant the grip relaxed, and she began to rise to the surface. Just as her face emerged, as she managed to gulp one breath of air and fumble for the whistle, the arms enclosed her again, and she slipped downward, through the dark waters of the pool.

CHAPTER 11

"After Kathy and Teddy died, I went to pieces." It was as if Ted were talking to himself, not Scott. The car raced past the gate to Pebble Beach without stopping. The roaring siren shattered the peace of the surroundings; the headlights opened only a few feet of visibility in the deepening fog.

"Craig took over running the whole business. He liked it. There were times when he'd answer and say he was me. Imitate my voice. I finally told him to cut it out. Then he met Leila first. I took her away. The reason I was so busy those months before Leila died, I was starting to reorganize. I intended to deemphasize his job; split his responsibilities with two other men. He knew what was happening.

"And he's the one who hired the detective to follow that first witness; the detective who was so conveniently there to make sure the new witness didn't get away."

They were on the grounds of the Spa. Scott drove the car across the lawn and stopped in front of Elizabeth's bungalow. The maid rushed from her station. Ted was banging on the door. "Where is Elizabeth?"

"I don't know," the maid said, her voice faltering. "She gave me a letter. She didn't say she was going out."

"Let me see the letter."

"I don't think—"

"Give me the letter."

Scott read the note to Vicky, ripped open the letter addressed to him and began to read.

"Where is she?" Ted demanded.

"Oh, God, that crazy kid . . . The pool," Scott snapped, "the pool."

The car smashed through hedges and flower beds and roared toward the north end of the property. Inside the bungalows, lights began to go on.

They reached the patio. The fender of the car caught the edge of an umbrella table, knocking it over. The car stopped at the edge of the pool. Scott left the headlights on, and they shone over the water. Waves of gathering fog shimmered in the lights.

They peered down into the pool. "There's no one here," Scott said. A terrible fear grabbed at him. Were they too late?

Ted was pointing at bubbles floating to the surface. "She's down there." Kicking off his shoes, he dived into the pool. He touched bottom and came up. "Get help," he yelled. He went down again and again.

Scott scrabbled in the glove compartment for his flashlight, grabbed it and saw a figure in a scuba-diving outfit begin to climb the ladder out of the pool. Drawing his pistol, he rushed toward the ladder. In a swift, violent gesture, the scuba diver lunged forward and butted him. The gun fell from Scott's hand as he slammed backward onto the patio.

Ted resurfaced. He was holding a limp figure in his arms. He began to swim toward the ladder, and as Scott dazedly pulled himself to a sitting position, the scuba diver fell backward onto Ted, dragging him and Elizabeth under the surface.

Gasping for breath, Scott reached out a groping hand. His numbed fingers closed around his gun. Pointing it upward, he fired two shots, and was rewarded by the insistent sound of sirens racing toward him.

Ted desperately tried to hold on to Elizabeth with one arm as he pummeled his attacker with the other. His lungs were bursting; he was still groggy from the effects of the sodium pentothal; he felt himself losing consciousness. Futilely he tried to punch the thick rubber suit. His blows fell harmlessly on the solid, massive chest.

The oxygen mask. He had to pull it off. He let go of Elizabeth, trying with all his strength to push her toward the surface. For a moment, the grip on him relaxed. A hand stretched past him, reaching to drag Elizabeth back. It gave him the chance to grab at the face mask. But before he could pull it off, a vicious shove sent him reeling backward.

She had held her breath, forcing herself to resist inhaling. She made herself go limp. There was no way she could get away from him. Her only hope was that he would think she was unconscious and leave her. Even from the feel of the arms that pinned her she knew it was Craig. She had forced him into the open—but now he would get away again.

She was slipping into unconsciousness. Hold on, she thought. No, it was *Leila* telling her to hold on. *Sparrow, this is what I've been trying to tell you. Don't let me down now. He thinks he's safe. You can do it, Sparrow.*

She felt the arms begin to release her. She was drifting down, trying to resist the impulse to fight her way to the surface. *Wait, Sparrow, wait. Don't let him see you're still conscious.*

And then she had felt someone grabbing her, pulling her up; other arms, arms that held her to him, cradled her. Ted.

She felt the night air on her face; gasped in one shuddering breath as, his arm around her neck, he dragged her along the top of the pool; heard his own breath, straining, choking, drowning out the sounds she was making.

And then she felt before she saw the heavy figure bear down on them and managed to pull in one great gulp of air before the water again covered her face.

Ted's arm tightened. She felt him flailing out. Craig was trying to kill both of them. Nothing mattered to Craig except to destroy them now. The water pressed against her eardrums. She could not fight Ted's grip. She felt the push as he tried to shove her toward the surface, felt Craig's grasp on her ankle and managed to kick it away.

On the surface she could see the cars pulling up, hear the shouts.

Elizabeth gulped in air, once, twice, filled her lungs and then dived down, down to where Ted was fighting for his life. She knew where Craig was; the arc of her descent was directly over his head. He was squeezing Ted's neck. She reached both hands down. Lights were beaming over the water. She could see the silhouette of Craig's arms, the desperate struggle of Ted's body. She would have only one chance.

Now. She kicked—a sharp, cutting movement of her legs. She was directly over Craig. In a savage thrust, she managed to get her fingers under his face mask. He reached up, and she recoiled from the shove that made her head snap backward, but held on to the mask, held on until she had wrenched it away from his face.

She held it while he groped for it, while his arms grabbed her body, while he tried to pull it from her, held it until she felt him being pulled away from her, held it until, lungs bursting, she found herself being hauled to the surface, still in his grasp.

She could breathe at last. She choked in great gulping sobs as Ted finally relinquished his grip on Craig to the policemen who surrounded them in the water. Then, like two figures drawn by an irresistible magnetic force, she and Ted drifted to each other, and clinging together made their way to the ladder at the end of the pool. . . .

Friday, September 4

QUOTE FOR THE DAY:
For love and beauty and delight.
There is no death nor change.

—Shelley

Dear Spa guests,

Some of you will be leaving us today. Remember, our only concern has been you, your well-being, your health, your beauty. Go into the world knowing that you have been loved and cared for here at Cypress Point Spa, that we are longing for your return. Soon our magnificent Roman bathhouse will be completed. It will be the unparalleled and consummate experience. There will be separate hours for the women and men except between four and six, when we shall enjoy mixed bathing in the European fashion, a very special delight indeed.

Hurry back for another retreat into pampering and health-awareness in the serene atmosphere of Cypress Point Spa.

Baron and Baroness Helmut von Schreiber

CHAPTER 1

The morning dawned clear and bright. The early-morning fog evaporated with the bright warmth of a glowing sun. Sea gulls and blackbirds swept high over the surf and returned to perch on the rocky dunes.

At Cypress Point Spa, the remaining guests followed their schedules. Water classes were held in the Olympic pool; masseurs kneaded muscles and pounded layers of fat; pampered bodies were wrapped in herbal-scented sheets; the business of beauty and luxury continued to function.

Scott had asked Min and Helmut, Syd and Cheryl, Elizabeth and Ted to meet him at eleven. They gathered in the music salon, the door closed, removed from the eyes and ears of the curious guests and staff.

Elizabeth remembered the rest of the night as a blur: Ted holding her . . . someone wrapping the robe around her . . . Dr. Whitley ordering her to bed.

Ted knocked at the door of her bungalow at ten of eleven. They walked up the path together, hands entwined, not needing to say what was between them.

Min and the Baron sat side by side. Min's face was weary but somehow more at peace, Elizabeth thought. There was something of the old Min in the steely determination in her eyes. The Baron, still so absolutely perfect in every hair on his head, his sport shirt resting on him with the ease of an ermine robe, his posture aloof, his assurance regained. For him too, the night had exorcised demons.

Cheryl's eyes moved restlessly toward Ted, narrowed when they found his face. With her sharp-tipped tongue she licked her lips like a cat about to pounce on a forbidden dish of cream.

Next to her, Syd lounged. There was something about him that had been missing: the casual confidence of success.

Ted sat beside her, his arm thrown over the back of her chair, his manner protective and watchful as though he feared she would slip away from him.

"I think we've come to the end of the road." The fatigue in Scott's voice suggested that he had not spent the long hours of the night in bed. "Craig has retained Henry Bartlett, who urged him not to make a statement. However, when I read Elizabeth's letter to him, he admitted everything.

"Let me read that letter to you now." Scott pulled it from his pocket.

Dear Scott,

There is only one way I can prove what I suspect, and I'm about to do that now. It may not work, but if anything happens to me, I think it will be because Craig has decided I'm coming too close to the truth.

Tonight I practically accused Syd and the Baron of causing Leila's death. I hope that will be sufficient bait to make Craig feel secure in attempting to harm me. I believe it will happen at the pool. I think he was there the other night. I can only rely on the fact that I can outswim anyone, and if he tries to attack me, he will have exposed himself. If he succeeds, go after him—for me and for Leila.

By now you will have heard the tapes. Have you caught how upset he sounded when Alvirah Meehan was asking so many questions? He tried to cut Ted off when Ted said that Craig could fool people by imitating him.

I thought I heard Ted shout at Leila to put the phone down. I thought I heard her say, *''You're not a falcon.''* But Leila was sobbing. That's why I misunderstood. Helmut was nearby. He heard her say, *''You're not Falcon.''* He heard accurately. I did not.

That tape of Alvirah Meehan in the treatment room. Listen carefully. That first voice. It sounds like the Baron, but there's something wrong. I think it was Craig imitating the Baron's voice.

Scott, there's no proof of any of this. The only proof will be obtained if Craig has found me too dangerous.

We'll see what happens. There is one thing I know and probably have always known in my heart. Ted is incapable of murder, and I don't care how many witnesses come forward to claim they saw him kill Leila.

Elizabeth

Scott put down the letter and looked sternly at Elizabeth. ''I wish you had trusted me to help you. You almost lost your life.''

''It was the only way,'' Elizabeth said. ''But what did he do to Mrs. Meehan?''

''An insulin injection. As you know, during college he worked summers at the hospital in Hanover. He picked up a lot of medical knowledge those years. But initially the insulin wasn't meant for Alvirah Meehan.'' Scott looked at Elizabeth. ''He had become convinced you were dangerous. He had planned to find a way to do away with you in New York this week, before the trial. But when Ted decided to come here, Craig persuaded Min to invite you too. He persuaded her that you might back off from testifying against Ted once you saw him. What he wanted was a chance to arrange an accident. Alvirah Meehan became a threat. He already had the means to get rid of her.'' Scott stood up. ''And now I'm going home.''

At the door he paused. ''Just one last observation I'd like to make. You, Baron, and you, Syd, were willing to obstruct justice when you thought Ted was guilty. By taking the law into your own hands, you did him no favors and may indirectly have been responsible for Sammy's death and Mrs. Meehan's attack.''

Min jumped up. ''If they had come forward last year, Ted might very well have been persuaded to plead guilty. Ted should be grateful to them.''

''Are *you* grateful, Min?'' Cheryl asked. ''I gather the Baron *did* write the play. You not only married nobility, a doctor, an interior designer, but also an author. You must be thrilled—and broke.''

''I married a Renaissance man,'' Min told her. ''The Baron will resume a full schedule of operations at the clinic. Ted has promised us a loan. All will be well.''

Helmut kissed her hand. Again Elizabeth was reminded of a little boy smiling up at his mother. Min sees him now for what he is, she thought. He'd be lost without her. It cost her a million dollars to find that out, but maybe she'll decide it was worth it.

''Incidentally,'' Scott added, ''Mrs. Meehan is going to make it. We can thank Dr. von Schreiber's emergency treatment for that.'' Ted and Elizabeth followed him out. ''Try to put it behind you,'' Scott told them. ''I have a hunch things are going to be a lot better for you two from now on.''

''They already are.'' Ted's voice was firm.

CHAPTER 2

The noon sun was high overhead. The breeze was coming gently from the Pacific, bringing the scent of the sea. Even the azaleas that had been crushed by the patrol cars seemed to be trying to struggle back. The cypress trees, grotesque in the night, seemed familiar and comforting under the splendid sunshine.

Together Elizabeth and Ted watched Scott drive away, then turned to face each other. ''It really is over,'' Ted said. ''Elizabeth, I'm just starting to realize it. I can breathe again. I'm not going to wake up in the middle of the night and wonder about living in a cell, about losing everything in life I value. I want to get to work again. I want . . .'' His arms went around her. ''I want you.''

Go ahead, Sparrow. This time it's right. No dilly-dallying. Do as I tell you. You're perfect for each other.

Elizabeth smiled up at Ted. She put her hands on his face and brought his lips to hers.

She could almost hear Leila singing again, as she had so long ago, "Weep no more, my lady. . . ."

STILLWATCH

To Pat Myrer, my agent
and
Michael V. Korda, my editor

For their inestimable expertise, support, help and encouragement I joyfully offer "the still small voice of gratitude."

CHAPTER 1

Pat drove slowly, her eyes scanning the narrow Georgetown streets. The cloud-filled sky was dark; streetlights blended with the carriage lamps that flanked doorways; Christmas decorations gleamed against ice-crusted snow. The effect was one of Early American tranquillity. She turned onto N Street, drove one more block, still searching for house numbers, and crossed the intersection. That must be it, she thought—the corner house. Home Sweet Home.

She sat for a while at the curb, studying the house. It was the only one on the street that was unlighted, and its graceful lines were barely discernible. The long front windows were half-hidden by shrubbery that had been allowed to grow.

After the nine-hour drive from Concord her body ached every time she moved, but she found herself putting off the moment when she opened the front door and went inside. It's that damn phone call, she thought. I've let it get to me.

A few days before she'd left her job at the cable station in Boston, the switchboard operator had buzzed her: "Some kind of weirdo insists on talking to you. Do you want me to stay on the line?"

"Yes." She had picked up the receiver, identified herself and listened as a soft but distinctly masculine voice murmured, "Patricia Traymore, you must not come to Washington. You must not produce a program glorifying Senator Jennings. And you must not live in *that* house."

She had heard the audible gasp of the operator. "Who is this?" she asked sharply.

The answer, delivered in the same syrupy murmur, made her hands unpleasantly moist. "I am an angel of mercy, of deliverance—and of vengeance."

Pat had tried to dismiss the event as one of the many crank calls received at television stations, but it was impossible not to be troubled. The announcement of her move to Potomac Cable Network to do a series called *Women in Government* had appeared in many television-news columns. She had read all of them to see if there was any mention of the address where she would live, but there had been none.

The Washington Tribune had carried the most detailed story:

''Auburn-haired Patricia Traymore, with her husky voice and sympathetic brown eyes, will be an attractive addition to Potomac Cable Network. Her profiles of celebrities on Boston Cable have twice been nominated for Emmys. Pat has the magical gift of getting people to reveal themselves with remarkable candor. Her first subject will be Abigail Jennings, the very private senior Senator from Virginia. According to Luther Pelham, news director and anchorman of Potomac Cable, the program will include highlights of the Senator's private and public life. Washington is breathlessly waiting to see if Pat Traymore can penetrate the beautiful Senator's icy reserve.''

The thought of the call nagged at Pat. It was the cadence of the voice, the way he had said ''*that* house.''

Who was it who knew about the house?

The car was cold. Pat realized the engine had been off for minutes. A man with a briefcase hurried past, paused when he observed her sitting there, then went on his way. I'd better get moving before he calls the cops and reports a loiterer, she thought.

The iron gates in front of the driveway were open. She stopped the car at the stone path that led to the front door and fumbled through her purse for the house key.

She paused at the doorstep, trying to analyze her feelings. She'd anticipated a momentous reaction. Instead, she simply wanted to get inside, lug the suitcases from the car, fix coffee and a sandwich. She turned the key, pushed the door open, found the light switch.

The house seemed very clean. The smooth brick floor of the foyer had a soft patina; the chandelier was sparkling. A second glance showed fading paint and scuff marks near the baseboards. Most of the furniture would probably need to be discarded or refinished. The good pieces stored in the attic of the Concord house would be delivered tomorrow.

She walked slowly through the first floor. The formal dining room, large and pleasant, was on the left. When she was sixteen and on a school trip to Washington, she had walked past this house but hadn't realized how spacious the rooms were. From the outside the house seemed narrow.

The table was scarred, the sideboard badly marked, as if hot serving dishes had been laid directly on the wood. But she knew the handsome, elaborately carved Jacobean set was family furniture and worth whatever it would cost to restore.

She glanced into the kitchen and library but deliberately kept walking. All the news stories had described the layout of the house in minute detail. The living room was the last room on the right. She felt her throat tighten as she approached it. Was she crazy to be doing this—returning here, trying to recapture a memory best forgotten?

The living-room door was closed. She put her hand on the knob and turned it hesitantly. The door swung open. She fumbled and found the wall switch. The room was large and beautiful, with a high ceiling, a delicate mantel above the white brick fireplace, a recessed window seat. It was empty except for a concert grand piano, a massive expanse of dark mahogany in the alcove to the right of the fireplace.

The fireplace.

She started to walk toward it.

Her arms and legs began to tremble. Perspiration started from her forehead and palms. She could not swallow. The room was moving around her. She rushed to the French doors at the far end of the left wall, fumbled with the lock, yanked both doors open and stumbled onto the snow-banked patio.

The frosty air seared her lungs as she gulped in short, nervous breaths. A violent shudder made her hug her arms around her body. She began to sway and needed to lean against the house to keep from falling. Light-headedness made the dark outlines of the leafless trees seem to sway with her.

The snow was ankle-deep. She could feel the wetness seep through her boots, but she would not go back in until the dizziness receded. Minutes passed before she could trust herself to return to the room. Carefully she closed and double-locked the doors, hesitated and then deliberately turned around and with slow, reluctant steps walked to the fireplace. Tentatively she ran her hand down the rough whitewashed brick.

For a long time now, bits and pieces of memory had intruded on her like wreckage from a ship. In the past year she had persistently dreamed of being a small child again in this house. Invariably she would awaken in an agony of fear, trying to scream, unable to utter a sound. But coupled with the fear was a pervading sense of loss. The truth is in this house, she thought.

It was here that it had happened. The lurid headlines, gleaned from newspaper archives, flashed through her mind. "WISCONSIN CONGRESSMAN DEAN ADAMS MURDERS BEAUTIFUL SOCIALITE WIFE AND KILLS SELF. THREE-YEAR-OLD DAUGHTER FIGHTS FOR LIFE."

She had read the stories so many times, she knew them by heart. "A sorrowful Senator John F. Kennedy commented, 'I simply don't understand. Dean was one of my best friends. Nothing about him ever suggested pent-up violence.' "

What had driven the popular Congressman to murder and suicide? There had been rumors that he and his wife were on the verge of divorce. Had Dean Adams snapped when his wife made an irrevocable decision to leave him? They must have wrestled for the gun. Both their fingerprints, smudged and overlapping, were found on it. Their three-year-old daughter had been found lying against the fireplace, her skull fractured, her right leg shattered.

Veronica and Charles Traymore had told her that she was adopted. Not until she was in high school and wanted to trace her ancestry had she been given the whole truth. Shocked, she learned that her mother was Veronica's sister. "You were in a coma for a year and not expected to live," Veronica told her. "When you finally did regain consciousness you were like an infant and had to be taught everything. Mother—your grandmother—actually sent an obituary notice to the newspapers. That's how determined she was that the scandal wouldn't follow you all your life. Charles and I were living in England then. We adopted you and our friends were told you were from an English family."

Pat recalled how furious Veronica had been when Pat insisted on taking over the Georgetown house. "Pat, it's wrong to go back there," she'd said. "We should have sold that place for you instead of renting it all these years. You're making a name for yourself in television—don't risk it by raking up the past! You'll be meeting people who knew you as a child. Somebody might put two and two together."

Veronica's thin lips tightened when Pat insisted. "We did everything humanly possible to give you a fresh start. Go ahead, if you insist, but don't say we didn't warn you."

In the end they had hugged each other, both shaken and upset. "Come on," Pat pleaded. "My job is digging for the truth. If I hunt for the good and bad in other people's lives, how can I ever have any peace if I don't do it in my own?"

Now she went into the kitchen and picked up the telephone. Even as a child she had referred to Veronica and Charles by their first names, and in the past few years had virtually stopped calling them Mother and Dad. But she suspected that that annoyed and hurt them.

Veronica answered on the first ring. "Hi, Mother. I'm here safe and sound; the traffic was light all the way."

"Where is *here?*"

"At the house in Georgetown." Veronica had wanted her to stay at a hotel until the furniture arrived. Without giving her a chance to remonstrate, Pat rushed on. "It's really better this way. I'll have a chance to set up my equipment in the library and get my head together for my interview with Senator Jennings tomorrow."

"You're not nervous there?"

"Not at all." She could visualize Veronica's thin, worried face. "Forget about me and get ready for your cruise. Are you all packed?"

"Of course. Pat, I don't like your being alone for Christmas."

"I'll be too busy getting this program together even to think about it. Anyway, we had a wonderful early Christmas together. Look, I'd better unload the car. Love to both of you. Pretend you're on a second honeymoon and let Charles make mad love to you."

"*Pat!*" Disapproval and amusement mingled in her voice. But she managed one more piece of advice before hanging up. "Keep the double locks on!"

Buttoning her jacket, Pat ventured out into the chilly evening, and for the next ten minutes she tugged and hauled the luggage and cartons. The box of linens and blankets was heavy and ungainly; she had to rest every few steps on the way to the second floor. Whenever she tried to carry anything heavy her right leg felt as though it might give way. The carton with dishes and pans and groceries had to be hoisted up to the kitchen counter. I should have trusted the movers to arrive tomorrow on time, she thought—but she had learned to be skeptical of "firm" delivery dates. She had just finished hanging up her clothes and making coffee when the phone rang.

The sound seemed to explode in the quiet of the house. Pat jumped and winced as a few drops of coffee touched her hand. Quickly she put the cup on the counter and reached for the phone. "Pat Traymore."

"Hello, Pat."

She clutched the receiver, willing her voice to sound only friendly. "Hello, Sam."

Samuel Kingsley, Congressman from the 26th District of Pennsylvania, the man she loved with all her heart—the *other* reason she had decided to come to Washington.

CHAPTER 2

Forty minutes later Pat was struggling with the clasp of her necklace when the peal of the door chimes announced Sam's arrival. She had changed to a hunter green wool dress with satin braiding. Sam had once told her that green brought out the red in her hair.

The doorbell rang again. Her fingers were trembling too much to fasten the catch. Grabbing her purse, she dropped the necklace into it. As she hurried down the stairs she tried to force herself to be calm. She reminded herself that during the eight months since Sam's wife, Janice, had died Sam hadn't called once.

On the last step she realized that she was again favoring her right leg. It was Sam's insistence that she consult a specialist about the limp that had finally forced her to tell him the truth about the injury.

She hesitated momentarily in the foyer, then slowly opened the door.

Sam nearly filled the doorway. The outside light caught the silver strands in his dark brown hair. Under unruly brows, his hazel eyes looked wary and quizzical. There were unfamiliar lines around them. But the smile when he looked at her was the same, warm and all-embracing.

They stood awkwardly, each waiting for the other to make the first move, to set the tone for the reunion. Sam was carrying a broom.

Solemnly he handed it to her. "The Amish people are in my district. One of their customs is to carry a new broom and salt into a new home." He reached into his pocket for a salt cellar. "Courtesy of the House dining room." Stepping inside, he put his hands on her shoulders and leaned down to kiss her cheek. "Welcome to our town, Pat. It's good to have you here."

So this is the greeting, Pat thought. Old friends getting together. Washington is too small a town to try to duck someone from the past, so meet her head on and establish the rules. Not on your life, she thought. It's a whole new ball game, Sam, and this time I plan to win.

She kissed him, deliberately, leaving her lips against his just long enough to sense the intensity gathering in him, then stepped back and smiled easily.

"How did you know I was here?" she asked. "Have you got the place bugged?"

"Not quite. Abigail told me you were going to be in her office tomorrow. I called Potomac Cable for your phone number."

"I see." There was something intimate in the way Sam sounded when he mentioned Senator Jennings. Pat felt her heart give a queer twist and looked down, not wanting Sam to see the expression on her face. She made a business of fishing in her purse for her necklace. "This thing has a clasp that Houdini couldn't figure out. Will you?" She handed it to him.

He slipped it around her neck and she felt the warmth of his fingers as he fastened it. For a moment his fingers lingered against her skin.

Then he said, "Okay, that should stay put. Do I get the Cook's Tour of the house?"

"There's nothing to see yet. The moving van delivers tomorrow. This place will have a whole new look in a few days. Besides, I'm starving."

"As I remember, you always were." Now Sam's eyes betrayed genuine amusement. "How a little thing like you can put away hot-fudge sundaes and buttered biscuits and still not put on an ounce . . ."

Very smooth, Sam, Pat thought as she reached into the closet for her coat. You've managed to ticket me as a little thing with a big appetite. "Where are we going?" she asked.

"I made a reservation at Maison Blanche. It's always good."

She handed him her jacket. "Do they have a children's menu?" she asked sweetly.

"*What?* Oh, I see. Sorry—I thought I was paying you a compliment."

Sam had parked in the driveway behind her car. They walked down the path, his hand lightly under her arm. "Pat, are you favoring your right leg again?" There was concern in his tone.

"Just a touch. I'm stiff from the drive."

"Stop me if I'm wrong. But isn't this the house you own?"

She had told him about her parents the one night they had spent together. Now she nodded distractedly. She had often relived that night in the Ebb Tide Motel on Cape Cod. All she needed was the scent of the ocean, or the sight of two people in a restaurant, their fingers linked across the table, smiling the secret smile of lovers. And that one night had ended their relationship. In the morning, quiet and sad at breakfast, on their way to separate planes, they had talked it out and agreed they had no right to each other. Sam's wife, already confined to a wheelchair with multiple sclerosis, didn't deserve the added pain of sensing that her husband was involved with another woman. "And she'd know," Sam had said.

Pat forced herself back to the present and tried to change the subject. "Isn't this a great street? It reminds me of a painting on a Christmas card."

"Almost any street in Georgetown looks like a Christmas card at this time of year," Sam rejoined. "It's a lousy idea for you to try to dredge up the past, Pat. Let go of it."

They were at the car. He opened the door and she slipped in. She waited until he was in the driver's seat and pulling away before she said, "I can't. There's something that keeps nagging me, Sam. I'm not going to have any peace until I know what it is."

Sam slowed for the stop sign at the end of the block. "Pat, don't you know what you're trying to do? You want to rewrite history, remember that night and decide it was all a terrible accident, that your father didn't mean to hurt you or kill your mother. You're just making it harder for yourself."

She glanced over and studied his profile. His features, a shade too strong, a hairbreadth too irregular for classic good looks, were immensely endearing. She had to conquer the impulse to slide over and feel the fine wool of his overcoat against her cheek.

"Sam, have you ever been seasick?" she asked.

"Once or twice. I'm usually a pretty good sailor."

"So am I. But I remember coming back on the *QE 2* with Veronica and Charles one summer. We hit a storm and for some reason I lost my sea legs. I don't ever remember being so miserable. I kept wishing I could be sick and have done with it. And you see, that's the way it's getting to be for me now. Things keep coming back to me."

He turned the car onto Pennsylvania Avenue. "What things?"

"Sounds . . . impressions . . . sometimes so vague; other times, especially when I'm just waking up, remarkably clear—and yet they fade before I can get hold of them. I actually tried hypnosis last year, but it didn't work. Then I read that some adults can remember accurately things that happened when they were as young as two. One study said the best way to recapture the memory is to reproduce the environment. Fortunately or unfortunately, that's something I can do."

"I still think it's a lousy idea."

Pat gazed out the car window. She had studied street maps to get a sense of the city and now tried to test herself on the accuracy of her impressions. But the car was moving too swiftly, and it was too dark to be sure of anything. They didn't speak.

The maître d' at Maison Blanche greeted Sam warmly and escorted them to a banquette.

"The usual?" Sam asked after they were seated.

Pat nodded, acutely aware of Sam's nearness. Was this his favorite table? How many other women had he brought here?

"Two Chivas Regals on the rocks with a splash of soda and a twist of lemon, please," Sam requested. He waited until the maître d' was out of earshot, then said, "All right—tell me about the last few years. Don't leave anything out."

"That's a tall order. Give me a minute to think." She would eliminate those first few months after they had agreed not to see each other, when she'd gotten through the day in a fog of sheer, hopeless misery. She could and did talk about her job, about getting an Emmy nomination for her program on the newly elected woman mayor of Boston, about her growing obsession to do a program about Senator Jennings.

"Why Abigail?" Sam asked.

"Because I think it's high time a woman was nominated for President. In two years there'll be a national election and Abigail Jennings should lead the ticket. Just look at her record: ten years in the House; in her third term in the Senate; member of the Foreign Relations Committee; the Budget Committee; first woman to be Assistant Majority Leader. Isn't it a fact that Congress is still in session because the President is counting on her to get the budget through the way he wants it?"

"Yes, it's true—and what's more, she'll do it."

"What do *you* think of her?"

Sam shrugged. "She's good. She's damn good, as a matter of fact. But she's stepped on a lot of important toes, Pat. When Abigail gets upset, she doesn't care who she blasts, and where and how she does it."

"I assume that's also true of the majority of the men on the Hill."

"Probably."

"Exactly."

The waiter came with menus. They ordered, deciding to share a Caesar salad. And that was another memory. That last day together Pat had made a picnic lunch and asked Sam what salad she should bring. "Caesar," he'd said promptly, "and lots of anchovies, please." "How can you eat those things?" she'd demanded. "How can you not? It's an acquired taste, but once you have it, you'll never lose it." She'd tried them that day and decided they were good.

He remembered too. As they handed back the menus, he commented, "I'm glad you didn't give up on the anchovies." He smiled. "Getting back to Abigail, I'm amazed she agreed to go along with the documentary."

"Frankly, I'm still amazed myself. I wrote to her about three months ago. I'd done a lot of research on her and was absolutely fascinated by what I uncovered. Sam, how much do you know about her background?''

''She's from Virginia. She took her husband's seat in Congress when he died. She's a workaholic.''

''Exactly. That's the way everyone sees her. The truth is that Abigail Jennings comes from Upstate New York, *not* Virginia. She won the Miss New York State beauty contest but refused to go to Atlantic City for the Miss America pageant because she had a scholarship to Radcliffe and didn't want to risk wasting a year. She was only thirty-one when she was widowed. She was so in love with her husband that twenty-five years later she still hasn't remarried.''

''She hasn't remarried, but she hasn't lived in a cloister either.''

''I wouldn't know about that, but judging from the information I've gathered, the vast majority of her days and nights are strictly work.''

''That's true.''

''Anyhow, in my letter I wrote that I'd like to do a program that would give viewers the feeling of knowing her on a personal level. I outlined what I had in mind and got back about the frostiest rejection I've ever read. Then a couple of weeks ago Luther Pelham phoned. He was coming to Boston specifically to take me to lunch and wanted to talk about my coming to work for him. Over lunch he told me the Senator had showed him my letter; he'd already been mulling over the idea of a series called *Women in Government.* He knew and liked my work and felt I was right for the job. He also said that he wanted to make me a regular part of his seven-o'clock news program.

''You can imagine how I felt. Pelham is probably the most important commentator in the business; the network is as big as Turner's; the money's terrific. I'm to kick off the series with a documentary on Senator Jennings and he wants it as fast as possible. But I still don't know why the Senator changed her mind.''

''I can tell you why. The Vice President may be on the verge of resigning. He's much sicker than people realize.''

Pat laid down her fork and stared at him. ''Sam, do you mean . . . ?''

''I mean the President has less than two years left in his second term. How better to make every woman in the country happy than by appointing the first woman Vice President?''

''But that means . . . if Senator Jennings is Vice President, they almost couldn't deny her the nomination for President next time.''

''Hold on, Pat. You're going too fast. All I've said is that *if* the Vice President resigns, there's a damn good chance he'll be replaced by either Abigail Jennings or Claire Lawrence. Claire is practically the Erma Bombeck of the Senate—very popular, very witty, a first-rate legislator. She'd do an excellent job. But Abigail's been there longer. The President and Claire are both from the Midwest, and politically that isn't good. He'd rather appoint Abigail, but he can't ignore the fact that Abigail really isn't well known nationally. And she's made some powerful enemies in Congress."

"They you believe Luther Pelham wants the documentary to let people see Abigail in a warmer, more personal way?"

"From what you've just told me, that's my guess. I think he wants to generate popular support for her. They were pretty cozy for a long time, and I'm sure he'd like to have his dear friend in the Vice President's chair."

They ate silently as Pat mulled the implications of what Sam had told her. Of course it explained the sudden job offer, the need for haste.

"Hey, remember me?" Sam finally said. "You haven't asked me what *I've* been doing these past two years."

"I've been following your career," she told him. "I toasted you when you were reelected—not that I was surprised. I wrote and tore up a dozen notes to you when Janice died. I'm supposed to have a way with words, but nothing sounded right. . . . It must have been very bad for you."

"It was. When it was obvious Janice didn't have much time, I cut my schedule to the bone and spent every possible minute with her. I think it helped."

"I'm sure it did." She had to ask: "Sam, why did you wait so long to call me? In fact, would you ever have called me if I hadn't come to Washington?"

The background sounds of the other diners' voices and the faint clinking of glasses, the tempting aromas of the food, the paneled walls and frosted-glass partitions of the attractive room faded as she waited for his answer.

"I did call you," he said, "a number of times, but I had the guts to break the connection before your phone rang. Pat, when I met you, you were about to become engaged. I spoiled that for you."

"With or without you it wouldn't have happened. Rob is a nice guy, but that's not enough."

"He's a bright young lawyer with an excellent future. You'd be married to him now if it weren't for me. Pat, I'm forty-eight years old. You're twenty-seven. I'm going to be a grandfather in three months. You know you would want to have children, and I simply don't have the energy to raise a new family."

"I see. Can I ask you something, Sam?"

"Of course."

"Do you love me, or have you talked yourself out of that too?"

"I love you enough to give you a chance to meet someone your own age again."

"And have you met someone *your* own age yet?"

"I'm not seeing anyone specifically."

"I see." She managed a smile. "Well, now that we have everything out in the open, why don't you buy me that nice gooey dessert I'm supposed to crave?"

He looked relieved. Had he expected her to badger him? she wondered. He seemed so tired. Where was all the enthusiasm he'd had a few years ago?

An hour later when he was dropping her at home, Pat remembered what she'd been meaning to discuss. "Sam, I had a crazy phone call at the office last week." She told him about it. "Do people in Congress get much hate mail or calls?"

He didn't seem especially concerned. "Not that many, and none of us takes them very seriously." He kissed her cheek and chuckled. "I was just thinking. Maybe I'd better talk to Claire Lawrence and see if she's been trying to scare off Abigail."

Pat watched him drive away, then closed and latched the door. The house reinforced her feeling of emptiness. The furniture will make a difference, she promised herself.

Something on the floor caught her eye: a plain white envelope. It must have been slipped under the door while she was out. Her name was printed in heavy black lettering that was sharply slanted from left to right. Probably someone from the realtor's office, she tried to tell herself. But the usual business name and address were missing from the upper left-hand corner, and the envelope was of the cheapest dime-store sort.

Slowly she ripped it open and pulled out the single sheet of paper. It read: "I TOLD YOU NOT TO COME."

CHAPTER 3

The next morning the alarm went off at six. Pat slipped willingly out of bed. The lumpy mattress had not been conducive to sleep, and she had kept waking, aware of the creaking, settling sounds in the house and the thumping activity of the oil burner as it snapped off and on. Try as she would, she could not dismiss the note as the work of a harmless eccentric. Somebody was observing her.

The movers had promised to arrive by eight. She planned to move the files stored in the basement up to the library.

The basement was dingy, with cement walls and floor. Garden furniture was stacked neatly in the center. The storage room was to the right of the furnace room. A heavy padlock on its door was grimy with the accumulated soot of years.

When Charles had given her the key, he'd warned, "I don't know exactly what you'll find, Pat. Your grandmother instructed Dean's office to send all his personal effects to the house. We never did get around to sorting them."

For a moment it seemed as though the key would not work. The basement was damp, with a vague smell of mildew. She wondered if the lock had rusted. She moved the key back and forth slowly and then felt it turn. She tugged at the door.

Inside the storeroom, a stronger smell of mildew assailed her. Two legal-size filing cabinets were so covered with dust and cobwebs she could barely determine their color. Several heavy cartons, haphazardly piled, stood next to them. With her thumb she rubbed at the grime until the labels appeared: CONGRESSMAN DEAN W. ADAMS, BOOKS. CONGRESSMAN DEAN W. ADAMS, PERSONAL EFFECTS. CONGRESSMAN DEAN W. ADAMS, MEMORABILIA. The inserts on the file drawers read the same: CONGRESSMAN DEAN W. ADAMS, PERSONAL.

"Congressman Dean W. Adams," Pat said aloud. She repeated the name carefully. Funny, she thought, I really don't think of him as a Congressman. I only place him here in this house. What kind of Representative was he?

Except for the formal picture the newspapers used at the time of the deaths, she'd never seen even a snapshot of him. Veronica had shown her albums filled with pictures of Renée as a child, as a young woman at her debut, at her first professional concert, with Pat in her arms. It hadn't been hard to guess why Veronica had kept no reminder of Dean Adams around.

The key to the files was on the ring Charles had given her. She was about to unlock the first one when she began to sneeze. She decided it was crazy to try to examine anything in that cellar. Already her eyes were itching from the dust. I'll wait until it's all in the library, she thought. But first she would wash the outside of the cabinets and get the worst of the dust off the cartons.

It turned out to be a messy, exhausting job. There was no sink in the basement, and she trudged repeatedly upstairs to the kitchen, bringing down a pail of sudsy hot water and returning a few minutes later with both water and sponge blackened.

On the last trip she brought down a knife and carefully scraped the identifying labels from the cartons. Finally she removed the inserts from the fronts of the file drawers. Satisfied, she surveyed her work. The cabinets were olive green and still in decent condition. They would fit along the east wall of the library. The cartons could go there too. No one would have any reason to think they hadn't come from Boston. Veronica's influence again, she thought wryly. "Don't tell anyone, Pat. Think ahead, Pat. When you marry, do you want your children to know that the reason you limp was that your father tried to kill you?"

She had barely time to wash her hands and face before the movers arrived. The three men on the truck hauled in the furniture, unrolled carpets, unpacked china and crystal, brought up the contents of the storage room. By noon they had gone, manifestly pleased with their tip.

Alone again, Pat went directly to the living room. The transformation was dramatic. The fourteen-by-twenty-four-foot Oriental carpet with its brilliant designs of apricot, green, lemon and cranberry against a black background dominated the room. The green velvet love seat stood against the short wall at a right angle to the long apricot satin sofa. The matching high-backed wing chairs flanked the fireplace; the Bombay chest was to the left of the patio doors.

The room was well nigh a restoration of its former self. She walked through it, touching the tops of the tables, adjusting the angle of a chair or lamp, running her hands over the fabric of the upholstered pieces. What was she feeling? She couldn't be sure. Not fear exactly—though she had to force herself to pass the fireplace. What then? Nostalgia? But for what? Was it possible that some of those blurred impressions were memories of happy times spent in this room? If so, what else could she do to retrieve them?

At five minutes to three she stepped out of a cab in front of the Russell Senate Office Building. The temperature had dropped sharply in the last several hours and she was glad to enter the heated foyer. The security guards passed her through the metal detector and directed her to the elevator. A few minutes later she was giving her name to Abigail Jennings' receptionist.

"Senator Jennings is running a little behind," the young woman explained. "She has several constituents who stopped in to see her. It won't be long."

"I don't mind waiting." Pat selected a straight-backed chair and looked around. Abigail Jennings clearly had one of the most desirable of the senatorial offices. It was a corner unit and had a feeling of airiness and space that she knew was in short supply in the overcrowded building. A low railing separated the waiting area from the receptionist's desk. A corridor to the right led to a row of private offices. The walls were covered with framed news photos of the Senator. The small table by the leather couch held pamphlets explaining Senator Jennings' positions on pending legislation.

She heard the familiar voice, softly modulated by the faintest touch of a Southern accent, easing visitors out of an inner office. "I'm delighted you were able to stop by. I only wish we had more time. . . ."

The visitors were a well-dressed sixtyish couple, effusive in their thanks. "Well, at the fund-raiser you did say to stop in anytime, and I said, 'Violet, we're in Washington, let's just do it.' "

"You're sure you're not free for dinner?" the woman visitor interjected anxiously.

"I only wish I were."

Pat watched as the Senator steered her guests to the outer door, opened it and slowly closed it, forcing them out. Well done, she thought. She felt her adrenaline rise.

Abigail turned and paused, giving Pat an opportunity to study her closely. Pat had forgotten how tall the Senator was—about five feet nine, with a graceful, erect carriage. Her gray tweed suit followed the lines of her body; broad shoulders accentuated a taut waistline; angular hips ended in slender legs. Her ash blond hair was cut short around the thin face dominated by extraordinary china-blue eyes. Her nose was shiny, her lips pale and undefined. She seemed to use absolutely no makeup, as though trying deliberately to understate her remarkable beauty. Except for the fine lines around her eyes and mouth, she looked the same as she had six years earlier.

Pat watched as the Senator's glance came to rest on her.

"Hello," the Senator said, moving quickly toward her. With a reproachful glance at the receptionist she said, "Cindy, you should have told me that Miss Traymore was here." Her chiding expression turned rueful. "Well, no harm done. Come inside, please, Miss Traymore. May I call you Pat? Luther has recommended you so highly I feel I know you. And I've seen some of the specials you've done in Boston. Luther ran them for me. They're splendid. And as you mentioned in your letter, we did meet some years ago. It was when I spoke at Wellesley, wasn't it?"

"Yes, it was." Pat followed the Senator into the inner office and looked around. "How lovely!" she exclaimed.

A long walnut console desk held a delicately painted Japanese lamp, an obviously valuable figurine of an Egyptian cat, a gold pen in a holder. The crimson leather chair, wide and comfortable with arched arms and intricate nailheads, was probably seventeenth-century English. An Oriental carpet had predominant tones of crimson and blue. The flags of the United States and the Commonwealth of Virginia were on the wall behind the desk. Blue silk tieback draperies softened the bleakness of the cloudy winter day beyond the windows. One wall was covered with mahogany bookshelves. Pat chose a chair nearest the Senator's desk.

The Senator seemed pleased at Pat's reaction to the office. "Some of my colleagues feel that the shabbier and more cluttered their offices appear, the busier and more down-to-earth their constituents will think they are. I simply can't work in confusion. Harmony is very important to me. I get a lot more accomplished in this atmosphere."

She paused. "There's a vote coming up on the floor within the hour, so I guess we'd better get down to business. Has Luther told you that I really *hate* the idea of this special?"

Pat felt on safe ground. Many people resisted programs about themselves. "Yes, he has," she said, "but I honestly believe you'll be pleased with the result."

"That's the only way I'd even consider this. I'll be perfectly honest: I prefer to work with Luther and you rather than have another network decide to produce an unauthorized story. But even so, I wish the good old days were here when a politician could simply say 'I stand on my record.' "

"They're gone. At least, they are for the people who count."

Abigail reached into her desk drawer and pulled out a cigarette case. "I never smoke in public anymore," she observed. "Just once—*once,* mind you—a paper printed a picture of me with a cigarette in my hand. I was in the House then, and I got dozens of irate letters from parents in my district saying I was setting a bad example." She reached across the desk. "Do you . . . ?"

Pat shook her head. "No, thanks. My father asked me not to smoke till I was eighteen, and by then I'd lost interest."

"And you kept your word? No puffing away behind the garage or whatever?"

"No."

The Senator smiled. "I find that reassuring. Sam Kingsley and I share a great distrust of the media. You know him, don't you? When I told him about this program, he assured me you were different."

"That was kind of him," Pat said, trying to sound casual. "Senator, I suspect the shortest way to go about this is for you to tell me exactly why the idea of the program is so abhorrent to you. If I know in advance what you find objectionable we're bound to save a lot of time."

She watched as the Senator's face became thoughtful. "It's infuriating that no one is satisfied with my personal life. I've been a widow since I was thirty-one years old. Taking my husband's place in Congress after his death, then being elected myself and going on to the Senate—all of it has always made me feel I'm still partners with him. I love my job and I'm married to it. But of course I can't very well tearfully describe little Johnny's first day at school because I never had a child. Unlike Claire Lawrence, I can't be photographed with an army of grandchildren. And I warn you, Pat, I will not allow a picture of me in a bathing suit, high heels and a rhinestone crown to be used in this program."

"But you *were* Miss New York State. You can't ignore that."

"Can't I?" The incredible eyes flashed. "Do you know that shortly after Willard's death, some rag printed that picture of me being crowned Miss New York State with the caption "*And your real prize is to go to Congress for the South?*" The Governor almost changed his mind about appointing me to complete Willard's term. It took Jack Kennedy to persuade him that I'd been working side by side with my husband from the day he was elected. If Jack hadn't been so powerful, I might not be here now. No, thank you, Pat Traymore. No beauty-queen pictures. Start your special when I was a senior at the University of Richmond, just married to Willard and helping him campaign for the first seat in Congress. That's when my life began."

You can't pretend the first twenty years of your life don't exist, Pat thought. And why? Aloud she suggested, ''I came across one picture of you as a child in front of your family home in Apple Junction. That's the kind of early background I plan to use.''

''Pat, I never said that was *my* family home. I said I had *lived* there. In point of fact, my mother was the housekeeper for the Saunders family and she and I had a small apartment in the back. Please don't forget I'm the senior Senator from Virginia. The Jennings family has been prominent in Tidewater Virginia since Jamestown. My mother-in-law always called me Willard's Yankee wife. I've gone to great effort to be considered a Jennings from Virginia and to forget Abigail Foster from Upstate New York. Let's leave it that way, shall we?''

There was a knock at the door. A serious-looking oval-faced man in his early thirties entered, wearing a gray suit with a faint pin stripe that accentuated the leanness of his body. Thinning blond hair carefully combed across his pate failed to conceal his bald spot. Rimless glasses added to the middle-aged effect. ''Senator,'' he said, ''they're about to take the vote. The fifteen-minute bell just went off.''

The Senator stood up abruptly. ''Pat, I'm sorry. Incidentally, this is Philip Buckley, my administrative assistant. He and Toby have put together some material for you—all sorts of stuff: press clippings, letters, photo albums, even some home movies. Why don't you look them over, and then let's talk again in the next few days?''

Pat could do nothing except agree. She would talk to Luther Pelham. Between them, they must convince the Senator that she could not sabotage the program. She realized Philip Buckley was studying her carefully. Did she detect a certain hostility in his manner?

''Toby will drive you home,'' the Senator continued hurriedly. ''Where *is* he, Phil?''

''Right here, Senator. Keep your shirt on.''

The cheerful voice came from a barrel-chested man who immediately gave Pat the impression of being an overage prize-fighter. His big face was beefy, with the flesh beginning to puff under small, deep-set eyes. Fading sandy hair was abundantly mixed with gray. He was wearing a dark blue suit and holding a cap in his hands.

His hands—she found herself staring at them. They were the largest she had ever seen. A ring with an onyx an inch square accentuated the thickness of his fingers.

Keep your shirt on. Had he really said that? Aghast, she looked at the Senator. But Abigail Jennings was laughing.

''Pat, this is Toby Gorgone. He can tell you what his job is as he drives you home. I've never been able to figure it out and he's been with me for twenty-five years. He's from Apple Junction too, and besides me, he's the best thing that ever came out of it. And now I'm off. Come on, Phil.''

They were gone. This special is going to be sheer hell to make, Pat thought. She had three solid pages of points she'd wanted to discuss with the Senator and had gotten to bring up exactly one. Toby had known Abigail Jennings since childhood. That she put up with his insolence was incredible. Maybe he'd answer some questions on the drive home.

She had just reached the reception area when the door was flung open and Senator Jennings rushed back in, followed by Philip. The relaxed manner was gone. "Toby, thank God I caught you," she snapped. "Where did you get the idea I'm not due at the Embassy until seven?"

"That's what you told me, Senator."

"That's what I *may* have told you, but you're supposed to double-check my appointments, aren't you?"

"Yes, Senator," Toby said genially.

"I'm due at *six.* Be downstairs at quarter to." The words were spat out.

"Senator, you'll be late for the vote," Toby said. "You'd better get a move on."

"I'd be late for everything if I didn't have eyes in the back of my head to double-check on you." This time the door slammed behind her.

Toby laughed. "We'd better get started, Miss Traymore."

Wordlessly, Pat nodded. She could not imagine one of the servants at home addressing either Veronica or Charles with such a familiarity or being so unconcerned about a reprimand. What circumstances had created such a bizarre relationship between Senator Jennings and her oxlike chauffeur?

She decided to find out.

CHAPTER 4

Toby steered the sleek gray Cadillac Sedan de Ville through the rapidly gathering traffic. For the hundredth time he brooded on the fact that Washington in the late afternoon was a driver's nightmare. All the tourists in their rented cars who didn't realize that some of the streets became one-way on the dot of four created havoc for the people who worked here.

He glanced into the rearview mirror and liked what he saw. Patricia Traymore was all right. It had taken all three of them—himself, Phil and Pelham—to talk Abby into agreeing to this documentary. So Toby felt even more than usually responsible to see that it worked out.

Still, you couldn't blame Abby for being nervous. She was within an eyelash of everything she'd ever wanted. His eyes met Pat's in the mirror. What a smile that girl had! He'd heard Sam Kingsley tell Abigail that Pat Traymore had a way of making you tell things you never thought you'd share with another human being.

Pat had been considering what approach to take with Toby and had decided the straightforward one was the best. As the car stopped for a light on Constitution Avenue, she leaned forward. There was a chuckle in her voice as she said, "Toby, I have to confess I thought I wasn't hearing straight when you told the Senator to keep her shirt on."

He turned his head to look at her directly. "Oh, I shouldn't a said that first time you met me. I don't usually do that. It's just I knew Abby was uptight about this program business and on her way in for the vote, and a bunch of reporters were going to be all over her about why she wasn't going along with the rest of the party—so I figured if I got her to let down for a minute it'd do her good. But don't misunderstand. I respect the lady. And don't worry about her blowing up at me. She'll forget it in five minutes."

"You grew up together?" Pat prodded gently.

The light turned green. Smoothly the car moved forward; Toby maneuvered into the right lane ahead of a station wagon before answering. "Well, not exactly that. All the kids in Apple Junction go to the same school—'cept, of course, if they go to parochial school. But she was two years ahead of me, so we were never in the same classes. Then when I was fifteen I started doing yard work in the rich part of town. I guess Abby told you she lived in the Saunders house."

"Yes, she did."

"I worked for the people about four places away. One day I heard Abby screaming. The old guy who lived opposite the Saunderses' had taken in his head he needed a watchdog and bought a German shepherd. Talk about vicious! Anyway, the old guy left the gate open and the dog got out just as Abby was coming down the street. Made straight for her."

"And you saved her?"

"I sure did. I started shouting and distracted him. Bad luck for me I'd dropped my rake, 'cause I got half chewed to rags before I got a grip on his neck. And then"—Toby's voice filled with pride—"and then, no more watchdog."

With one hand, Pat slipped her tape recorder out of her shoulder bag and turned it on. "I can see why the Senator must feel pretty strongly about you," she commented. "The Japanese believe that if you save someone's life you become somehow responsible for them. Do you suppose that happened to you? It sounds to me as though you feel responsible for the Senator."

"Well, I don't know. Maybe that did happen, or maybe she stuck her neck out for me when we were kids." The car stopped. "Sorry, Miss Traymore. We should a made that light, but the jerk ahead of me is reading street signs."

"It doesn't matter. I'm not in any hurry. The Senator stuck her neck out for you?"

"I said *maybe* she did. Look, forget it. The Senator doesn't like me to talk about Apple Junction."

"I'll bet she talks about how you helped her," Pat mused. "I can imagine how *I'd* feel if an attack dog was charging at me and someone threw himself in between."

"Oh, Abby was grateful, all right. My arm was bleeding, and she wrapped her sweater around it, then insisted on coming to the emergency room with me and even wanted to sit in while they sewed it. After that we were friends for life."

Toby looked over his shoulder. "*Friends,*" he repeated emphatically, "not boyfriend-girlfriend. Abby's out of my league. I don't have to tell you that. There was no question of any of that stuff. But sometimes in the afternoon she'd come over and talk while I was working around the yard. She hated Apple Junction as much as I did. And when I was flunking English, she tutored me. I never did have any head for books. Show me a piece of machinery and I'll take it apart and put it together in two minutes, but don't ask me to diagram a sentence.

"Anyhow, Abby went off to college and I drifted down to New York and got married and it didn't take. And I took a job running numbers for some bookies and ended up in hot water. After that I started chauffeuring for some fruitcake on Long Island. By then Abby was married and her husband was the Congressman and I read that she'd been in an automobile accident because her chauffeur had been drinking. So I thought, What the hell. I wrote to her and two weeks later her husband hired me and that was going on twenty-five years ago. Say, Miss Traymore, what number are you? We're on N Street now."

"Three thousand," Pat said. "It's the corner house on the next block."

"*That* house?" Too late, Toby tried to cover the shock in his voice.

"Yes. Why?"

"I used to drive Abby and Willard Jennings to that house for parties. Used to be owned by a Congressman named Dean Adams. Did they tell you about him killing his wife and committing suicide?"

Pat hoped her voice was calm. "My father's lawyer arranged the rental. He mentioned there had been a tragedy here many years ago, but he didn't go into it."

Toby pulled up to the curb. "Just as well to forget it. He even tried to kill his kid—she died later on. Cute little thing. Her name was Kerry, I remember. What can you do?" He shook his head. "I'll just park by the hydrant for a minute. Cops won't bother as long as I don't hang around."

Pat reached for the handle of the door, but Toby was too quick for her. In an instant he was out the driver's side, around the car and holding the door open, putting a hand under her arm. "Be careful, Miss Traymore. Plenty icy here."

"Yes, I see that. Thank you." She was grateful for the early dusk, afraid that her expression might send some signal to Toby. He might not have a head for books but she sensed he was extremely perceptive. She had thought of this house only in the context of that one night. Of course there had been parties here. Abigail Jennings was fifty-six. Willard Jennings had been eight or nine years her senior. Pat's father would have been in his early sixties now. They had been contemporaries in those Washington days.

Toby was reaching into the trunk. She longed to ask him about Dean and Renée Adams, about "the cute little kid, Kerry." But not now, she cautioned herself.

Toby followed her into the house, two large cartons in his arms. Pat could see that they were heavy, but he carried them easily. She led him into the library and indicated the area next to the boxes from the storeroom. She blessed the instinct that had made her scrape off the labels with her father's name.

But Toby barely glanced at the boxes. "I'd better be off, Miss Traymore. This box"—he pointed—"has press clippings, photo albums, that sort of thing. The other one has letters from constituents—the personal kind, where you can see the sort of help Abby gives them. It had some home movies too, mostly of when her husband was alive. The usual stuff, I guess. I'll be glad to run the movies for you anytime and tell you who's in them and what was going on."

"Let me sort them out and I'll get back to you. Thanks, Toby. I'm sure you're going to be a big help in this project. Maybe between us, we'll put together something the Senator will be happy about."

"If she's not, we'll both know it." Toby's beefy face lit up in a genial smile. "Good night, Miss Traymore."

"Why not make it 'Pat'? After all, you do call the Senator 'Abby.' "

"I'm the only one who can call her that. She hates it. But who knows? Maybe I'll get a chance to save your life too."

"Don't hesitate for a minute if the opportunity comes your way." Pat reached out her hand and watched it disappear into his.

When he had left, she stood in the doorway, lost in thought. She would have to learn not to show any emotion when Dean Adams was mentioned. She had been lucky that Toby had brought up his name while she was still in the protective darkness of the car.

From the shadow of the house directly opposite, another observer watched Toby drive away. With angry curiosity he studied Pat as she stood in the doorway. His hands were thrust into the pockets of his skimpy overcoat. White cotton pants, white socks and white rubber-soles blended into the snow that was banked against the house. His bony wrists tightened as he closed his fingers into fists, and tension rippled through the muscles in his arms. He was a tall, gaunt man with a stiff, tense stance and a habit of holding his head unnaturally back. His hair, a silvery gray that seemed incongruous over a peculiarly unlined face, was combed forward over his forehead.

She was here. He had seen her unloading her car last night. In spite of his warnings, she was going ahead with that program. That was the Senator's car, and those boxes probably had some kind of records in them. And she was going to stay in that house.

The memory of that long-ago morning sprang into his mind: the man lying on his back, wedged between the coffee table and sofa; the woman's eyes, staring, unfocused; the little girl's hair matted with dried blood . . .

He stood there silently, long after Pat had closed the door, as if he were unable to tear himself away.

Pat was in the kitchen broiling a chop when the phone began to ring. She didn't expect to hear from Sam but . . . With a quick smile she reached for the receiver. "Hello."

A whisper. "Patricia Traymore."

"Yes. Who is this?" But she knew that syrupy, whispering voice.

"Did you get my letter?"

She tried to make her voice calm and coaxing. "I don't know why you're upset. Tell me about it."

"Forget your program on the Senator, Miss Traymore. I don't want to punish you. Don't make me do it. But you must remember the Lord said, 'Whoever harms one of these my little ones, better a millstone be put around his neck and he be drowned in the depth of the sea.' "

The connection went dead.

CHAPTER 5

It was only a crank call—some wacko who probably thought women belonged in the kitchen, not in public office. Pat recalled the character in New York who used to parade on Fifth Avenue with signs quoting Scripture about women's duty to obey their husbands. He had been harmless. So was this caller. She wouldn't believe it was anything more than that.

She brought a tray into the library and ate dinner while she sorted out Abigail's records. Her admiration for the Senator increased with every line she read. Abigail Jennings had meant it when she said she was married to her job. Her constituents *are* her family, Pat thought.

Pat had an appointment with Pelham at the network in the morning. At midnight she went to bed. The master bedroom suite of the house consisted of a large bedroom, a dressing room and bath. The Chippendale furniture with its delicate inlays of fruitwood had been easy to place. It was obvious that it had been purchased for this house. The highboy fitted between the closets; the mirrored dresser belonged in the alcove, the bed with its elaborately carved headboard on the long wall facing the windows.

Veronica had sent a new spring and mattress, and the bed felt wonderfully comfortable. But the trips to the basement to clean the filing cabinets had taken their toll on her leg. The familiar nagging pain was more acute than usual, and even though she was very tired it was hard to fall asleep. Think about something pleasant, she told herself as she stirred restlessly and turned on her side. Then in the dark she smiled wryly. She'd think about Sam.

The offices and studio of the Potomac Cable Network were just off Farragut Square. As she went in, Pat remembered what the news director at the Boston station had told her: "There's no question you should take the job, Pat. Working for Luther Pelham is a once-in-a-lifetime break. When he left CBS for Potomac, it was the biggest upset in the industry."

At the lunch with Luther in Boston, she'd been astonished at the frank stares of everyone in the dining room. She had become used to being recognized in the Boston area and having people come to her table for autographs. But the way virtually every pair of eyes was absolutely riveted on Luther Pelham was something else. "Can you go anywhere without being the center of attention?" she'd asked him.

"Not too many places. I'm happy to say. But you'll find out for yourself. Six months from now, people will be following *you* when you walk down the street and half the young women in America will be imitating that throaty voice of yours."

Exaggerated, of course, but certainly flattering. After the second time she called him "Mr. Pelham," he'd said, "Pat, you're on the team. I have a first name. Use it."

Luther Pelham had certainly been charming, but on that occasion he had been offering her a job. Now he was her boss.

When she was announced, Luther came to the reception area to greet her. His manner was effusively cordial, the familiar well-modulated voice exuding hearty warmth: "Great to have you here, Pat. I want you to meet the gang." He took her around the newsroom and introduced her. Behind the pleasantries, she sensed the curiosity and speculation in the eyes of her new co-workers. She could guess what they were thinking. Would she be able to cut the mustard? But she liked her immediate impressions. Potomac was rapidly becoming one of the largest cable networks in the country, and the newsroom whirred with activity. A young woman was giving on-the-hour headlines live from her desk; a military expert was taping his bi-weekly segment; staff writers were editing copy from the wire services. She well knew that the apparently calm exterior of the personnel was a necessary ploy. Everyone in the business lived with constant underlying tension, always on guard, waiting for something to happen, fearful that somehow a big story might be fumbled.

Luther had already agreed that she could write and edit at home until they were ready for actual taping. He pointed out the cubicle that had been reserved for her, then led her into his private office, a large oak-paneled corner room.

"Make yourself comfortable, Pat," he directed. "There's a call I have to return."

While he was on the phone, Pat had a chance to study him closely. He was certainly an impressive and handsome man. His thick, carefully barbered stone gray hair contrasted with his youthful skin and probing dark eyes. She knew he had just had his sixtieth birthday. The party his wife had given at their Chevy Chase estate had been written up in all the columns. With his aquiline nose and long-fingered hands that tapped impatiently on the desk top, he reminded her of an eagle.

He hung up the phone. "Have I passed inspection?" His eyes were amused.

"With flying colors." Why was it, she wondered, that she always felt at ease in a professional situation and yet so often had a sense of alienation in personal relationships?

"Glad to hear it. If you weren't sizing me up, I'd be worried. Congratulations. You made a great impression on Abigail yesterday."

A quick pleasantry and then he was down to business. She liked that and wouldn't waste his time leading up to the problem. "I was very impressed with her. Who wouldn't be?" Then she added significantly—"for as long as I had the chance to be with her."

Pelham waved his hand as though to remove an unpleasant reality. "I know. I know. Abigail is hard to pin down. That's why I told them to put together some of her personal material for you. Don't expect much cooperation from the lady herself because you won't get it. I've scheduled the program for the twenty-seventh."

"The twenty-seventh? December twenty-seventh!" Pat heard her voice rising. "Next Wednesday! That would mean all the taping, editing and scoring will have to be done in a week!"

"Exactly," Luther confirmed. "And you're the one who can do it."

"But why the rush?"

He leaned back, crossed his legs and smiled with the relish of a bearer of momentous news. "Because this isn't going to be just another documentary. Pat Traymore, you have the chance to be a kingmaker."

She thought of what Sam had told her. "*The Vice President?*"

"The Vice President," he confirmed, "and I'm glad you have your ear to the ground. That triple bypass last year hasn't done the job for him. My spies at the hospital tell me he has extensive heart damage and if he wants to live he's going to have to change his lifestyle. That means he's virtually certain to resign—and now. To keep all factions of the party happy, the President will go through the motions of having the Secret Service check out three or four serious contenders for the job. But the inside bet is that Abigail has the best shot at it. When we air this program we want to motivate millions of Americans to send telegrams to the President in

Abigail's behalf. That's what the program must do for her. And think about what it can do for *your* career.''

Sam had talked about the *possibility* of the Vice President's resignation and Abigail's candidacy. Luther Pelham clearly believed both were imminent *probabilities.* To be at the right place at the right time, to be there when a story was breaking—it was the dream of every newswoman. ''If word leaks out about how sick the Vice President is . . .''

''It's more than leaking out,'' Luther told her. ''I'm carrying it on my newscast tonight, including the rumors that the President is considering a woman replacement.''

''Then the Jennings program could sweep the ratings next week! Senator Jennings isn't that well known to the average voter. Everyone's going to want to find out about her.''

''Exactly. Now you can understand the need to put it together fast and make it something absolutely extraordinary.''

''The Senator . . . If we make this program as bloodless as she seems to want, you won't get fourteen telegrams, never mind millions. Before I proposed this documentary I did some extensive surveying to find out what people think about her.''

''And?''

''Older people compared her to Margaret Chase Smith. They called her impressive, gutsy, intelligent.''

''What's wrong with that?''

''Not one of the older people felt they knew her as a human being. They think of her as being distant and formal.''

''Go on.''

''The younger people have a different approach. When I told them about the Senator being Miss New York State, they thought it was great. They want to know more about it. Remember, if Abigail Jennings is chosen to be Vice President, she'll be second in command of the whole country. A number of people who know she is from the Northeast resent the fact that she never talks about it. I think she's making a mistake. And we'll compound it if we ignore the first twenty years of her life.''

''She'll never let you mention Apple Junction,'' Luther said flatly. ''So let's not waste time on that. She told me that when she resigned her Miss New York State title, they wanted to lynch her there.''

''Luther, she's wrong. Do you seriously think anyone in Apple Junction gives a damn anymore that Abigail didn't go to Atlantic City to try to become Miss America? Right now I'll bet every adult there is bragging that he or she knew Abigail when. As for resigning the title, let's face it head on. Who wouldn't sympathize with an answer like Abigail saying it had been a lark entering the contest but she found she hated the idea of parading around in a bathing suit and having people judge her like a side of beef? Beauty contests are passé now. We'll make her look good for realizing it before anyone else did.''

Luther drummed his fingers on the desk. Every instinct told him Pat was right, but Abigail had been definite on this point. Suppose they talked her into doing some material on her early life and it backfired? Luther was determined to be the power that put Abigail across as Vice President. Of course the party leaders would exact a promise from Abigail not to expect to run for the number one spot next time, but hell, those promises were made to be broken. He'd keep Abigail front and center until the day came when she was sitting in the Oval Office—and she'd owe it to him. . . .

He suddenly realized that Pat Traymore was watching him calmly. Most of the people he hired were trying not to swallow their own spit in the first private session in this office. The fact that she seemed totally at ease both pleased and annoyed him. He had found himself doing a lot of thinking about her in the two weeks since he'd offered her the job. She was smart; she'd asked all the right questions about her contract; she was damn good-looking in an interesting, classy kind of way. She was a born interviewer; those eyes and that raspy voice gave her a kind of sympathetic, even naive quality that created a "tell all" atmosphere. And there was a smoldering sexiness about her that was especially intriguing.

"Tell me how you see the overall approach to her personal life," he ordered.

"First Apple Junction," Pat said promptly. "I want to go there myself and see what I can find. Maybe some shots of the town, of the house where she lived. The fact that her mother was a housekeeper and that she went to college on scholarship is a plus. It's the American dream, only for the first time we're applying it to a national leader who happens to be a woman."

She pulled her notebook from her purse. Flipping it open, she continued. "Certainly we'll emphasize the early years when she was married to Willard Jennings. I haven't run the films yet, but it looks as though we'll pick up quite a bit of both their public and private lives."

Luther nodded affirmatively. "Incidentally, you'll probably see a fair amount of Jack Kennedy in those pictures. He and Willard Jennings were close friends. That's when Jack was a Senator, of course. Willard and Abigail were a part of the pre-Camelot years. People don't realize that about her. Leave in as many clips as you can find of them with any of the Kennedys. Did you know that when Willard died, Jack escorted Abigail to the memorial service?"

Pat jotted a few words on her pad. "Didn't Senator Jennings have any family?" she asked.

"I guess not. It never came up." Luther impatiently reached for the cigarette case on his desk. "I keep trying to give up these damn weeds." He lit one and for the moment looked somewhat relaxed. "I only wish I'd headed to Washington at that time," he said. "I thought New York was where the action was. I've done all right, but those were great Washington years. Crazy, though, how many of those young men died violently. The

Kennedy brothers. Willard in a plane crash. Dean Adams a suicide . . . You've heard about him?''

''Dean Adams?'' She made her voice a question.

''Murdered his wife,'' Luther explained. ''Killed himself. Nearly killed his kid. She did die eventually. Probably better off, too. Brain-damaged, no doubt. He was a Congressman from Wisconsin. Nobody could figure the reason. Just went nuts, I guess. If you come across any pictures of him or his wife in a group shot, edit them out. No one needs to be reminded of that.''

Pat hoped her face didn't betray distress. Her tone remained determinedly brisk as she said, ''Senator Jennings was one of the moving forces in getting the Parental Kidnapping Prevention Act passed. There are some wonderful letters in her files. I thought I'd look up some of the families she's reunited and pick the best one for a segment on the program. That will counteract Senator Lawrence and her grandchildren.''

Luther nodded. ''Fine. Give me the letters. I'll get someone around here to do the legwork. And by the way, in your outline you didn't have anything about the Eleanor Brown case. I absolutely want that in. You know she came from Apple Junction too—the school principal there asked Abigail to give her a job after she'd been caught shoplifting.''

''My instinct is to let that alone,'' Pat said. ''Think about it. The Senator gave a convicted girl a new start. That much is fine. Then Eleanor Brown was accused of stealing seventy-five thousand dollars in campaign funds. She swore she was innocent. Essentially it was the Senator's testimony that convicted her. Did you ever see that girl's pictures? She was twenty-three when she went to prison for the embezzlement but looked about sixteen. People have a natural inclination to feel sorry for the underdog—and the whole purpose of this program is to make everyone love Abigail Jennings. In the Eleanor Brown case, she comes through as the heavy.''

''That case shows that some legislators don't cover up for the crooks on their staff. And if you want Abigail's image softened, play up the fact that thanks to her, that kid got off a lot lighter than anyone else I know who stole that much money. Don't waste your sympathy on Eleanor Brown. She faked a nervous breakdown in prison, was transferred to a psychiatric hospital, was paroled as an outpatient and took off. She was some cool cookie. What else?''

''I'd like to go to Apple Junction tonight. If there's anything worthwhile there, I'll call you and we'll arrange for a camera crew. After that, I want to follow the Senator through a day in her office, plan some shots and then tape her there a day or two later.''

Luther stood up—a signal that the meeting was over. ''All right,'' he said. ''Fly up to . . . What is the place . . . Apple Junction? What a hell of a name! See if you can get good copy. But play it low key. Don't let the natives get the idea they're going to be on camera. The minute they think you might have them on the program, they'll start using all the big words they know and planning what leisure suit to wear.'' He twisted his face into a worried frown, made his voice nasal. ''Myrtle, get the lighter fluid. There's a gravy stain on my jacket.''

''I'm sure I'll find some pretty decent people there.'' Pat forced a faint smile to take the implied rebuke out of her words.

Luther watched her leave, noting the burgundy-and-gray tweed suit, obviously a designer original; the burgundy leather boots with the small gold Gucci trademark; the matching shoulder bag; the Burberry over her arm.

Money. Patricia Traymore had family money. You could always tell. Resentfully, Luther thought of his own humble beginnings on a farm in Nebraska. They hadn't had indoor plumbing until he was ten. No one could sympathize more than he with Abigail about not wanting to resurrect the early years.

Had he done the right thing in allowing Pat Traymore to have her way in this? Abigail would be sore—but she'd probably be a lot sorer when she found out they hadn't told her about the trip.

Luther turned on his intercom. ''Get me Senator Jennings' office.'' Then he hesitated. ''No, hold it; don't bother.''

He put down the phone and shrugged. Why start trouble?

CHAPTER 6

Pat felt the sidelong glances of the people in the newsroom as she left Pelham's office. Deliberately she set her face in a half-smile and made her step brisk. He'd been very cordial; he had risked Senator Jennings' anger by letting her go to Apple Junction. He had expressed his faith in her ability to put the program together on a breakneck schedule.

Then what's the matter? she wondered. I should feel great.

Outside, it was a cold, bright day. The streets were clear, and she decided to walk home. It was a couple of miles, but she wanted the exercise. Why not admit it? she thought. It's what Pelham just said about the Dean Adams mess; it's what Toby said yesterday. It's the feeling of everyone stepping back when Dean Adams' name is mentioned, of no one wanting to admit having known him. What had Luther said about her? Oh, yes—he thought the child had died, and it was better that way; she was probably brain-damaged.

I'm not brain-damaged, Pat thought as she tried to avoid a spray of dirty slush. But I *am* damaged. My leg is the least of it. I hate my father for what he did. He killed my mother and he tried to kill me.

She had come here thinking she only wanted to understand what had caused him to crack up. Now she knew better. She had to face the anger she had been denying all these years.

It was a quarter to one when she got home. It seemed to her that the house was taking on a certain comfortable aura. The antique marble table and Serapi rug in the foyer made the faded paint seem insignificant. The kitchen counters were cheerful now with canisters; the oval wrought-iron table and matching soda-parlor chairs fitted exactly into the area beneath the windows and made it easy to ignore the worn spots on the aging tiles.

Quickly she fixed a sandwich and tea while phoning for a plane reservation. She was fully seven minutes on ''hold'' listening to a particularly poor selection of canned music before a clerk finally came on the line. She arranged for a four-forty flight to Albany and a rental car.

She decided to use the few hours before flight time to begin going through her father's effects.

Slowly she pulled aside the flaps of the first box and found herself staring down at the dust-covered picture of a tall, laughing man with a child on one shoulder. The child's eyes were wide with delight; her mouth half-open and smiling. Her palms were facing each other as though she might have just clapped them. Both man and child were in swimsuits by the water's edge. A wave was crashing behind them. It was late afternoon. Their shadows on the sand were elongated.

Daddy's little girl, Pat thought bitterly. She had seen children on their fathers' shoulders, hanging on to their necks or even twining their fingers in their hair. Fear of falling was a basic instinct. But the child in this picture, the child she had been, clearly had trusted the man holding her, trusted him not to let her fall. She laid the picture on the floor and continued emptying the box.

When she had finished, the carpet was covered with memorabilia from the private office of Congressman Dean Adams. A formal portrait of her mother at the piano. She was beautiful, Pat thought—I resemble him more. There was a collage of snapshots of Pat as a baby and toddler that must have hung on his office wall; his appointment diary, dark green leather with his initials in gold; his silver desk set, now so terribly tarnished; the framed diploma from the University of Wisconsin, a B.A. in English with high honors; his law-school degree from the University of Michigan, proclaiming him an LL.B; a citation from the Episcopal Bishops' Conference for generous and unstinting work for minorities; a Man of the Year plaque from the Madison, Wisconsin, Rotary Club. He must have been fond of seascapes. There were several excellent old prints of sailing vessels, billowing over turbulent waters.

She opened the appointment book. He had been a doodler; almost every page contained swirls and geometric figures. So that's where I got the habit, Pat thought.

Her eyes kept returning to the picture of herself and her father. She looked so blissfully happy. Her father was looking up at her with so much love. His grip on her arm was so firm.

The telephone broke the spell. She scrambled to her feet, alarmed to realize that it was getting late, that she'd have to put all this away and pack a few things in a bag.

"Pat."

It was Sam.

"Hi." She bit her lip.

"Pat, I'm on the run as usual. I've got a committee meeting in five minutes. There's a dinner at the White House Friday night honoring the new Canadian Prime Minister. Would you like to go with me? I'll have to phone your name in to the White House."

"The White House! That would be wonderful. I'd love to go." She swallowed fiercely, trying to suppress the quiver in her voice.

Sam's tone changed. "Pat, is anything wrong? You sound upset. You're not crying, are you?"

At last she could control the tremor in her voice. "Oh, no. Not at all. I guess I'm just getting a cold."

CHAPTER 7

At the Albany airport, Pat picked up her rental car, pored over a road map with the Hertz attendant and worked out the best route to Apple Junction, twenty-seven miles away.

"Better get going, Miss," the clerk warned. "We're supposed to have a foot of snow tonight."

"Can you suggest the best place to stay?"

"If you want to be right in town, the Apple Motel is it." He smirked. "But it's nothing fancy like you'd find in the *Big* Apple. Don't worry about phoning ahead for a reservation."

Pat picked up the car key and her bag. It didn't sound promising, but she thanked the clerk all the same.

The first flakes were falling as she pulled into the driveway of the dreary building with the flickering neon sign APPLE MOTEL. As the Hertz attendant had predicted, the VACANCY sign was on.

The clerk in the tiny, cluttered office was in his seventies. Wire-framed glasses drooped on his narrow nose. Deep lines creased his cheeks. Clumps of gray-white hair sprouted from his skull. His eyes, rheumy and faded, brightened in surprise when Pat pushed open the door.

"Do you have a single for the next night or two?" she asked.

His smile revealed a worn, tobacco-stained dental plate. "Long as you want, Miss; you can have a single, a double, even the Presidential suite." A braying laugh followed.

Pat smiled politely and reached for the registration card. Deliberately she omitted filling the blank spot after PLACE OF BUSINESS. She wanted to have as much chance as possible to look around for herself before the reason for her presence here became known.

The clerk studied the card, his curiosity disappointed. "I'll put you in the first unit," he said. "That way you'll be near the office here in case the snow gets real heavy. We have a kind of dinette." He gestured toward three small tables against the rear wall. "Always have juice and coffee and toast to get you started in the morning." He looked at her shrewdly. "What brings you here, anyway?"

"Business," Pat said, then added quickly, "I haven't had dinner yet. I'll just drop my bag in my room and maybe you can tell me where I can find a restaurant."

He squinted at the clock. "You better hurry. The Lamplighter closes at nine and it's near eight now. Just go out the drive, turn left and go two blocks, then turn left again on Main. It's on the right. Can't miss it. Here's your key." He consulted the registration card. "Miss Traymore," he concluded, "I'm Travis Blodgett. I own the place." Pride and apology blended in his voice. A slight wheeze suggested emphysema.

Except for a dimly lit movie marquee, the Lamplighter was the only establishment open in the two blocks embracing the business district of Apple Junction. A greasy, handprinted menu posted on the front door announced the day's special, sauerbraten and red cabbage for $3.95. Faded linoleum lay underfoot just inside. Most of the checkered cloths on the dozen or so tables were partially covered with unpressed napkins—probably, she guessed, to hide stains caused by earlier diners. An elderly couple were munching on dark-looking meat from overfilled plates. But she had to admit the smell was tantalizing, and she realized she was very hungry.

The sole waitress was a woman in her mid-fifties. Under a fairly clean apron, a thick orange sweater and shapeless slacks mercilessly revealed layers of bulging flesh. But her smile was quick and pleasant. "You alone?"

"Yes."

The waitress looked uncertainly around, then led Pat to a table near the window. "That way you can look out and enjoy the view."

Pat felt her lips twitch. The view! A rented car on a dingy street! Then she was ashamed of herself. That was exactly the reaction she would expect of Luther Pelham.

"Would you care for a drink? We have beer or wine. And I guess I'd better take your order. It's getting late."

Pat requested wine and asked for a menu.

"Oh, don't bother with a menu," the waitress urged. "Try the sauerbraten. It's really good."

Pat glanced across the room. Obviously that was what the old couple were eating. "If you'll give me about half much as . . ."

The waitress smiled, revealing large, even white teeth.

"Oh, sure." She lowered her voice. "I always fill those two up. They can only afford to eat out once a week, so I like to get a decent meal into them."

The wine was a New York State red jug wine, but it was pleasant. A few minutes later the waitress came out of the kitchen carrying a plate of steaming food and a basket of homemade biscuits.

The food was delicious. The meat had been marinated in wines and herbs; the gravy was rich and tangy; the cabbage pungent; the butter melted into the still-warm biscuits.

My God, if I ate like this every night, I'd be the size of a house, Pat thought. But she felt her spirits begin to lift.

When Pat had finished, the waitress took her plate and came over with the coffeepot. "I've been looking and looking at you," the woman said. "Don't I know you? Haven't I seen you on television?"

Pat nodded. So much for poking around on my own, she thought.

"Sure," the waitress continued. "You're Patricia Traymore. I saw you on TV when I visited my cousin in Boston. *I know why you're here!* You're doing a program on Abby Foster—I mean Senator Jennings."

"You knew her?" Pat asked quickly.

"Knew her! I should say I did. Why don't I just have coffee with you?" It was a rhetorical question. Reaching over to the next table for an empty cup, she sank heavily into the chair opposite Pat. "My husband does the cooking; he can take care of closing up. It was pretty quiet tonight, but my feet hurt anyhow. All this standing . . ."

Pat made appropriate sympathetic sounds.

"Abigail Jennings, huh. Ab-by-gail Jennings," the waitress mused. "You gonna put folks from Apple Junction in the program?"

"I'm not sure," Pat said honestly. "Did you know the Senator well?"

"Not well, exactly. We were in the same class at school. But Abby was always so quiet; you could never figure what she was thinking. Girls usually tell each other everything and have best friends and run in cliques. Not Abby. I can't remember her having even one close friend."

"What did the other girls think about her?" Pat asked.

"Well, you know how it is. When someone is as pretty as Abby was, the other kids are kind of jealous. Then everybody got the feeling she thought she was too good for the rest of us, so that didn't make her any too popular either."

Pat considered her for a moment. "Did *you* feel that way about her, Mrs. . . . ?"

"Stubbins. Ethel Stubbins. In a way I guess I did, but I kind of understood. Abby just wanted to grow up and get out of here. The debating club was the only activity she joined in school. She didn't even dress like the rest of us. When everyone else was going around in sloppy joe sweaters and penny loafers, she wore a starched blouse and heels to school. Her mother was the cook at the Saunders house. I think that bothered Abby a lot.''

''I understood her mother was the housekeeper,'' Pat said.

''The *cook,*'' Ethel repeated emphatically. ''She and Abby had a little apartment off the kitchen. My mother used to go the Saunders place every week to clean, so I know.''

It was a fine distinction: saying your mother had been the housekeeper rather than the cook. Pat shrugged mentally. What could be more harmless than Senator Jennings' upgrading her mother's job a notch? She debated. Sometimes taking notes or using a recorder had the immediate effect of causing an interviewee to freeze. She decided to take the chance.

''Do you mind if I record you?'' she asked.

''Not at all. Should I talk louder?''

''No, you're fine.'' Pat pulled out her recorder and placed it on the table between them. ''Just talk about Abigail as you remember her. You say it bothered her that her mother was a cook?'' She had a mental image of how Sam would react to that question. He would consider it unnecessary prying.

Ethel leaned her heavy elbows on the table. ''Did it ever! Mama used to tell me how nervy Abby was. If anyone was coming down the street, she used to walk up the path to the front steps just as though she owned the place and then when no one was looking, she'd scoot around to the back. Her mother used to holler at her, but it didn't do any good.''

''Ethel. It's nine o'clock.''

Pat looked up. A squat man with pale hazel eyes set in a cheerful round face was standing at the table, untying a long white apron. His eyes lingered on the recorder.

Ethel explained what was happening and introduced Pat. ''This is my husband, Ernie.''

Clearly Ernie was intrigued by the prospect of contributing to the interview. ''Tell how Mrs. Saunders caught Abby coming in the front door and told her to know her place,'' he suggested. ''Remember, she made her walk back to the sidewalk and come up the driveway and go around to the back door.''

''Oh, yeah,'' Ethel said. ''That was lousy, wasn't it? Mama said she felt sorry for Abby until she saw the look on her face. Enough to freeze your blood, Mama said.''

Pat tried to imagine a young Abigail forced to walk to the servants' entrance to show that she ''knew her place.'' Again she had the feeling of intruding on the Senator's privacy. She wouldn't pursue that topic. Refusing Ernie's offer of more wine, she suggested, ''Abby—I mean the

Senator—must have been a very good student to get a scholarship to Radcliffe. Was she at the head of her class?''

''Oh, she was terrific in English and history and languages,'' Ethel said, ''but a real birdbrain in math and science. She hardly got by in them.''

''Sounds like me,'' Pat smiled. ''Let's talk about the beauty contest.''

Ethel laughed heartily. ''There were four finalists for Miss Apple Junction. Yours truly was one of them. Believe it or not, I weighed one hundred eighteen pounds then, and I was darn cute.''

Pat waited for the inevitable. Ernie did not disappoint her. ''You're still darn cute, honey.''

''Abby won hands down,'' Ethel continued. ''Then she got into the contest for Miss New York State. You could have knocked everyone over with a feather when she won *that!* You know how it is. Sure, we knew she was beautiful, but we were all so used to seeing her. Was this town ever excited!''

Ethel chuckled. ''I must say Abby kept this town supplied with gossip all that summer. The big social event around here was the country-club dance in August. All the rich kids from miles around went to it. None of *us,* of course. But that year Abby Foster was there. From what I hear, she looked like an angel in a white marquisette gown edged with layers of black Chantilly lace. And guess who took her? Jeremy Saunders! Just home after graduating from Yale. And he was practically engaged to Evelyn Clinton! He and Abby held hands all night and he kept kissing her when they danced.

''The next day the whole town was buzzing. Mama said Mrs. Saunders must have been spitting nails; her only son falling for the cook's daughter. And then''—Ethel shrugged—''it just ended. Abby resigned her Miss New York State crown and took off for college. Said she knew she'd never become Miss America, that she couldn't sing or dance or act for the talent part and there was no way she wanted to parade around in Atlantic City and come back a loser. A lot of people had chipped in for a wardrobe for her to wear to the Miss America contest. They felt pretty bad.''

''Remember Toby threw a punch at a couple of guys who said Abby let the folks around here down?'' Ernie prompted Ethel.

''Toby Gorgone?'' Pat asked quickly.

''The same,'' Ernie said. ''He was always nuts about Abby. You know how kids talk in locker rooms. If any guy said anything fresh about Abby in front of Toby, he was sorry fast.''

''He works for her now,'' Pat said.

''No kidding?'' Ernie shook his head. ''Say hello to him for me. Ask him if he's still losing money on the horses.''

It was eleven o'clock before Pat got back to the Apple Motel, and by then Unit One was chilly. She quickly unpacked—there was no closet, only a hook on the door—undressed, showered, brushed her hair and, propping up the narrow pillows, got into bed with her notebook. As usual, her leg was throbbing—a faint ache that began in her hip and shot down her calf.

She glanced over the notes she had taken during the evening. According to Ethel, Mrs. Foster had left the Saunders home right after the country-club dance and gone to work as a cook in the county hospital. Nobody ever did know whether she'd quit or been fired. But the new job must have been hard on her. She was a big woman—"You think *I'm* heavy," Ethel had said, "you should've seen Francey Foster." Francey had died a long time ago and no one had seen Abigail after that. Indeed, few had seen her for years before that.

Ethel had waxed eloquent on the subject of Jeremy Saunders—"Abigail was lucky she didn't marry him. He never amounted to a hill of beans. Lucky for him he had the family money: otherwise he'd probably have starved. They say his father tied up everything in trusts, even made Evelyn the executor of his will. Jeremy was a big disappointment to him. He always looked like a diplomat or an English lord and he's just a bag of wind."

Ethel had insinuated that Jeremy was a drinker, but suggested that Pat call him: "He'd probably love company. Evelyn spends most of her time with their married daughter in Westchester."

Pat turned out the light. Tomorrow morning she would try to visit the retired principal who'd asked Abigail to give Eleanor Brown a job, and she'd attempt to make an appointment with Jeremy Saunders.

It snowed during the night, some four or five inches, but the plows and sanders had already been through by the time Pat had coffee with the proprietor of the Apple Motel.

Driving around Apple Junction was a depressing experience. The town was a particularly shabby and unattractive one. Half the stores were closed and had fallen into disrepair. A single strand of Christmas lights dangled across Main Street. On the side streets, houses were jammed together, their paint peeling. Most of the cars parked in the street were old. There seemed to be no new building of any kind, residential or business. There were few people out; a sense of emptiness pervaded the atmosphere. Did most of the young people flee like Abigail as soon as they were grown? she wondered. Who could blame them?

She saw a sign reading THE APPLE JUNCTION WEEKLY and on impulse parked and went inside. There were two people working, a young woman who seemed to be taking a want ad over the phone and a sixtyish man who was making an enormous clatter on a manual typewriter. The latter, it developed, was Edwin Shepherd, the editor-owner of the paper and perfectly happy to talk to Pat.

He could add very little to what she already knew about Abigail. However, he willingly went to the files to hunt up issues that might refer to the two contests, local and state, that Abigail had won.

In her research Pat had already found the picture of Abigail in her Miss

New York State sash and crown. But the full-length shot of Abigail with the banner MISS APPLE JUNCTION was new and unsettling. Abigail was standing on a platform at the county fair, the three other finalists around her. The crown on her head was clearly papier-mâché. The other girls had pleased, fluttery smiles—Pat realized that the girl on the end was the youthful Ethel Stubbins—but Abigail's smile was cold, almost cynical. She seemed totally out of place.

"There's a shot of her and her maw inside," Shepherd volunteered, and turned the page.

Pat gasped. Could Abigail Jennings, delicate-featured and bone-slender, possibly be the offspring of this squat, obese woman? The caption read: PROUD MOTHER GREETS APPLE JUNCTION BEAUTY QUEEN.

"Why not take those issues?" Edwin Shepherd asked. "I've got more copies. Just remember to give us credit if you use anything on your program."

It would be awkward to refuse the offer, Pat realized. I can just see using *that* picture, she thought as she thanked the editor and quickly left.

A half-mile down Main Street, the town changed dramatically. The roads became wider, the homes stately, the grounds large and well tended.

The Saunders house was pale yellow with black shutters. It was on a corner, and a long driveway curved to the porch steps. Graceful pillars reminded Pat of the architecture of Mount Vernon. Trees lined the driveway. A small sign directed deliveries to the service entrance in the rear.

She parked and went up the steps, noticing that on closer inspection the paint was beginning to chip and the aluminum storm windows were corroded. She pushed the button and from somewhere far inside could hear the faint sound of chimes. A thin woman with graying hair wearing a half-apron over a dark dress answered the door. "Mr. Saunders is expecting you. He's in the library."

Jeremy Saunders, wearing a maroon velvet jacket, was settled in a high-backed wing chair by the fire. His legs were crossed, and fine dark blue silk hose showed below the cuffs of his midnight-blue trousers. He had exceptionally even features and handsome wavy white hair. A thickened waistline and puffy eyes alone betrayed a predilection for drink.

He stood up and steadied himself against the arm of the chair. "Miss Traymore!" His voice was so pointedly well bred as to suggest classes in elocution. "You didn't tell me on the phone that you were *the* Patricia Traymore."

"Whatever that means," Pat said, smiling.

"Don't be modest. You're the young lady who's doing a program on Abigail." He waved her to the chair opposite his. "You *will* have a Bloody Mary?"

"Thank you." The pitcher was already half-empty.

The maid took her coat.

"Thank you, Anna. That will be all for now. Perhaps a little later Miss

Traymore will join me in a light lunch.'' Jeremy Saunders' tone became even more fatuous when he spoke to the servant, who silently left the room. ''You can close the door if you will, Anna!'' he called. ''Thank you, my dear.''

Saunders waited until the latch clicked, then sighed. ''Good help is impossible to find these days. Not as it was when Francey Foster was presiding over the kitchen and Abby was serving the table.'' He seemed to relish the thought.

Pat did not reply. There was a gossipy kind of cruelty about the man. She sat down, accepted the drink and waited. He raised one eyebrow. ''Don't you have a tape recorder?''

''Yes, I do. But if you prefer I won't use it.''

''Not at all. I prefer that every word I say be immortalized. Perhaps someday there'll be an Abby Foster—forgive me, a *Senator Abigail Jennings*—Library. People will be able to push a button and hear me tell of her rather chaotic coming of age.''

Silently Pat reached into her shoulder bag and pulled out the recorder and her notebook. She was suddenly quite sure that what she was about to hear would be unusable.

''You've followed the Senator's career,'' she suggested.

''Breathlessly! I have the utmost admiration for Abby. From the time she was seventeen and began offering to help her mother with household duties, she had won my utmost respect. She's ingenious.''

''Is it ingenious to help your mother?'' Pat asked quietly.

''Of course not. If you *want* to *help* your mother. On the other hand, if you offer to serve only because the handsome young scion of the Saunders family is home from Yale, it does color the picture, doesn't it?''

''Meaning you?'' Pat smiled reluctantly. Jeremy Saunders had a certain sardonic, self-deprecating quality that was not unattractive.

''You've guessed it. I see pictures of her from time to time, but you can never trust pictures, can you? Abby always photographed very well. How does she look in person?''

''She's absolutely beautiful,'' Pat said.

Saunders seemed disappointed. He'd love to hear that the Senator needs a face lift, Pat reflected. Somehow she could not believe that even as a very young girl Abigail would have been impressed by Jeremy.

''How about Toby Gorgone?'' Saunders asked. ''Is he still playing his chosen role as bodyguard and slave to Abby?''

''Toby works for the Senator,'' Pat replied. ''He's obviously devoted to her, and she seems to count on him very much.'' *Bodyguard and slave,* she thought. It was a good way to describe Toby's relationship to Abigail Jennings.

''I suppose they're still pulling each other's chestnuts out of the fire.''

''What do you mean by that?''

Jeremy raised his hand in a gesture of dismissal. ''Nothing, really. He probably told you how he saved Abby from the jaws of the attack dog our eccentric neighbor kept.''

''Yes, he did.''

''And did he tell you that Abigail was his alibi the night he may have gone joyriding in a stolen car?''

''No, he didn't, but joyriding doesn't seem to be a very serious offense.''

''It is when the police car chasing the 'borrowed' vehicle goes out of control and mows down a young mother and her two children. Someone who looked like him had been observed hanging around the car. But Abigail swore that she had been tutoring Toby in English, right here in this house. It was Abigail's word against an uncertain witness. No charge was brought and the joyrider was never caught. Many people found the possible involvement of Toby Gorgone quite credible. He's always been obsessed with machinery, and that was a new sports car. It makes sense he'd want to give it a spin.''

''Then you're suggesting the Senator may have lied for him?''

''I'm suggesting nothing. However, people around here have long memories, and Abigail's fervent deposition—taken under oath, of course—is a matter of record. Actually, nothing much could have happened to Toby even if he had been in the car. He was still a juvenile, under sixteen. Abigail, however, was eighteen and if she had perjured herself would have been criminally culpable. Oh, well, Toby may very well have spent that evening diligently drilling on participles. Has his grammar improved?''

''It sounded all right to me.''

''You couldn't have spoken to him very long. Now, fill me in on Abigail. The endless fascination she evokes in men. With whom is she involved now?''

''She's not involved with anyone,'' Pat said. ''From what she tells me, her husband was the great love of her life.''

''Perhaps.'' Jeremy Saunders finished the last of his drink. ''And when you consider that she had absolutely no background—a father who drank himself to death when she was six, a mother content among the pots and pans . . .''

Pat decided to try another tack to get some sort of usable material. ''Tell me about this house,'' she suggested. ''After all, Abigail grew up here. Was it built by your family?''

Jeremy Saunders was clearly proud of both house and family. For the next hour, pausing only to refill his glass and then to mix a new pitcher of drinks, he traced the history of the Saunderses from ''not quite the *Mayflower*—a Saunders was supposed to be on that historic voyage, but fell ill and did not arrive till two years later''—to the present. ''And so,'' he concluded, ''I sadly relate that I am the last to bear the Saunders name.'' He smiled. ''You are a most appreciate listener, my dear. I hope I haven't been too long-winded in my recitation.''

Pat returned the smile. ''No, indeed. My mother's family were early settlers and I'm very proud of them.''

''You must let me hear about *your* family,'' Jeremy said gallantly. ''You will stay for lunch.''

''I'd be delighted.''

''I prefer having a tray right here. So much cozier than the dining room. Would that do?''

And so much nearer the bar, Pat thought. She hoped she could soon steer the subject back to Abigail.

Her opportunity came as she made a pretense of sipping the wine Jeremy insisted they have with the indifferently served chicken salad.

''It helps to wash it down, my dear,'' he told her. ''I'm afraid when my wife is away, Anna doesn't put her best foot forward. Not like Abby's mother. Francey Foster took pride in everything she prepared. The breads, the cakes, the soufflés . . . Does Abby cook?''

''I don't know,'' Pat said. Her voice became confidential. ''Mr. Saunders, I can't help feeling that you are angry at Senator Jennings. Am I wrong? I had the impression that at one time you two cared a great deal about each other.''

''Angry at her? Angry?'' His voice was thick, his words slurred. ''Wouldn't *you* be angry at someone who set out to make a fool of you—and succeeded magnificently?''

It was happening now—the moment that came in so many of her interviews when people let down their guard and began to reveal themselves.

She studied Jeremy Saunders. This sleekly overfed, drunken man in his ridiculous formal getup was mulling a distasteful memory. There was pain as well as anger in the guileless eyes, the too soft mouth, the weak, puffy chin.

''Abigail,'' he said, his tone calmer, ''United States Senator from Virginia.'' He bowed elaborately. ''My dear Patricia Traymore, you have the distinction of addressing her former fiancé.''

Pat tried unsuccessfully to hide her surprise. ''You were *engaged* to Abigail?''

''That last summer she was here. Very briefly, of course. Just long enough for her overall scheme. She'd won the state beauty contest but was smart enough to know she wouldn't go any further in Atlantic City. She'd tried to get a scholarship to Radcliffe, but her math and science marks weren't scholarship level. Of course, Abby had no intention of day-hopping to the local college. It was a terrible dilemma for her, and I still wonder if Toby didn't have a hand in planning the solution.

''I had just been graduated from Yale and was due to go into my father's business—a prospect which did not intrigue me; I was about to become engaged to the daughter of my father's best friend—a prospect which did not excite me. And here was Abigail right in my own home, telling me what I could become with her at my side, slipping into my bed in the dark of the night, while poor, tired Francey Foster snored away in their service apartment. The upshot was that I bought Abigail a beautiful gown, escorted her to the country-club dance and proposed to her.

"When we came home we woke our parents to announce the joyous news. Can you imagine the scene? My mother, who delighted in ordering Abigail to use the back door, watching all her plans for her only son dissolving. Twenty-four hours later, Abigail left town with a certified check from my father for ten thousand dollars and her bags filled with the wardrobe the town people had donated. She was already accepted by Radcliffe, you see. She only lacked the money to attend that splendid institution.

"I followed her there. She was quite explicit in letting me know that everything my father was saying about her was accurate. My father to his dying day never let me forget what a fool I'd made of myself. In thirty-five years of married life, whenever Evelyn hears Abigail's name she becomes quite shrewish. As for my mother, the only satisfaction she could get was to order Francey Foster out of the house—and that was cutting off her nose to spite her face. We never had a decent cook after that."

When Pat tiptoed out of the room, Jeremy Saunders was asleep, his head bobbing on his chest.

It was nearly a quarter to two. The day was clouding up again, as though more snow might be in the offing. As she drove toward her appointment with Margaret Langley, the retired school principal, she wondered how accurate Jeremy Saunders' version of Abigail Foster Jennings' behavior as a young woman had been. Manipulator? Schemer? Liar?

Whatever, it didn't jibe with the reputation for absolute integrity that was the cornerstone of Senator Abigail Jennings' public career.

CHAPTER 8

At a quarter of two, Margaret Langley took the unusual step of making a fresh pot of coffee, knowing full well that the burning discomfort of gastritis might plague her later.

As always when she was upset, she walked into her study, seeking comfort in the velvety green leaves of the plants hanging by the picture window. She'd been in the midst of rereading the Shakespeare sonnets with her after-breakfast coffee when Patricia Traymore phoned asking permission to visit.

Margaret shook her head nervously. She was a slightly stooped woman of seventy-three. Her gray hair was fingerwaved around her head, with a small bun at the nape of her neck. Her long, rather horsey face was saved from homeliness by an expression of good-humored wisdom. On her blouse she wore the pin the school had given her when she retired—a gold laurel wreath entwined around the number 45 to signify the years she'd served as teacher and principal.

At ten minutes past two she was beginning to hope that Patricia Traymore had changed her mind about stopping in when she saw a small car coming slowly down the road. The driver paused at the mailbox, probably checking the house number. Reluctantly Margaret went to the front door.

Pat apologized for being late. "I took a wrong turn somewhere," she said, gladly accepting the offer of coffee.

Margaret felt her anxiety begin to subside. There was something very thoughtful about this young woman, the way she so carefully scraped her boots before stepping onto the polished floor. She was so pretty, with that auburn hair and those rich brown eyes. Somehow Margaret had expected her to be terribly aggressive. When she explained about Eleanor, maybe Patricia Traymore would listen. As she poured the coffee she said as much.

"You see," Margaret began, and to her own ears her voice sounded high-pitched and nervous, "the problem at the time the money disappeared in Washington was that everyone talked about Eleanor as though she were a hardened thief. Miss Traymore, did you ever hear the value of the object she supposedly stole when she was a high school senior?"

"No, I don't think so," Pat answered.

"*Six dollars.* Her life was ruined because of a six-dollar bottle of perfume! Miss Traymore, haven't you ever started to walk out of a store and realized you were holding something you meant to buy?"

"A few times," Pat agreed. "But surely no one is convicted of shoplifting for being absentminded about a six-dollar item."

"You are if there's been a wave of shoplifting in town. The shopkeepers were up in arms, and the district attorney had vowed to make an example of the next person caught."

"And Eleanor was the next person?"

"Yes." Find beads of perspiration accentuated the lines in Margaret's forehead. Alarmed, Pat noticed that her complexion was becoming a sickly gray.

"Miss Langley, don't you feel well? May I get you a glass of water?"

The older woman shook her head. "No, it will pass. Just give me a minute." They sat silently as the color began to return to Miss Langley's face. "That's better. I guess just talking about Eleanor upsets me. You see, Miss Traymore, the judge made an example of Eleanor; sent her to the juvenile home for thirty days. After that she was changed. Different. Some people can't take that kind of humiliation. You see, nobody believed her except me. I know young people. She wasn't daring. She was the kind who never chewed gum in class or talked when the teacher was out of the room or cheated on a test. She wasn't only good. She was *timid.*''

Margaret Langley was holding something back. Pat could sense it. She leaned forward, her voice gentle. ''Miss Langley, there's a little more to the story than you're telling.''

The woman's lip quivered. ''Eleanor didn't have enough money to pay for the perfume. She explained that she was going to ask them to wrap it and put it aside. She was going to a birthday party that night. The judge didn't believe her.''

Neither do I, Pat thought. She was saddened she couldn't accept the explanation that Margaret Langley so passionately believed. She watched as the former principal put her hand on her throat as though to calm a rapid pulsebeat. ''That sweet girl came here so many evenings,'' Margaret Langley continued sadly, ''because she knew I was the one person who absolutely believed her. When she was graduated from our school, I wrote and asked Abigail if she could find a job for her in her office.''

''Isn't it true that the Senator gave Eleanor that chance, trusted her, and then Eleanor stole campaign funds?'' Pat asked.

Margaret's face became very tired. The tone of her voice flattened. ''I was on a year's sabbatical when all that happened. I was traveling in Europe. By the time I got home, it was all over. Eleanor had been convicted and sent to prison and had a nervous breakdown. She was in the psychiatric ward of the prison hospital. I wrote to her regularly, but she never answered. Then, from what I understand, she was paroled for reasons of poor health, but only on condition she attend a clinic as an outpatient twice a week. One day she just disappeared. That was nine years ago.''

''And you never heard from her again?''

''I . . . No . . . uh . . .'' Margaret stood up. ''I'm sorry—wouldn't you like a little more coffee? There's plenty in the pot. I'm going to have some. I shouldn't, but I will.'' With an attempt at a smile Margaret walked into the kitchen. Pat snapped off the recorder. She *has* heard from Eleanor, she thought, and can't bring herself to lie. When Miss Langley returned, Pat asked softly, ''What do you know about Eleanor now?''

Margaret Langley set down the coffeepot on the table and walked over to the window. Would she hurt Eleanor by trusting Pat Traymore? Would she in effect point out a trail that might lead to Eleanor?

A lone sparrow fluttered past the window and settled forlornly on the icy branch of an elm tree near the driveway. Margaret made up her mind. She would trust Patricia Traymore, show her the letters, tell her what she believed. She turned and met Pat's gaze and saw the concern in her eyes. ''I want to show you something,'' she said abruptly.

When Margaret Langley returned to the room, she held in each hand a folded sheet of notepaper. ''I've heard from Eleanor twice,'' she said.

''This letter''—she extended her right hand—''was written the very day of the supposed theft. Read it, Miss Traymore; just read it.''

The cream stationery was deeply creased as though it had been handled many times. Pat glanced at the date. The letter was eleven years old. Pat skimmed the contents quickly. Eleanor hoped that Miss Langley was enjoying her year in Europe; Eleanor had received a promotion and loved her job. She was taking painting classes at George Washington University and they were going very well. She had just returned from an afternoon in Baltimore. She'd had an assignment to sketch a water scene and decided on Chesapeake Bay.

Miss Langley had underlined one paragraph. It read:

I almost didn't get there. I had to run an errand for Senator Jennings. She'd left her diamond ring in the campaign office and thought it had been locked in the safe for her. But it wasn't there, and I just made my bus.

This was proof? Pat thought. She looked up, and her eyes met Margaret Langley's hopeful gaze. ''Don't you see?'' Margaret said. ''Eleanor wrote to me the very night of the supposed theft. Why would she make up that story?''

Pat could find no way to soften what she had to say. ''She could have been setting up an alibi for herself.''

''If you're trying to give yourself an alibi, you don't write to someone who may not get the letter for months,'' she said spiritedly. Then she sighed. ''Well, I tried. I just hope you'll have the goodness not to rake up that misery again. Eleanor apparently is trying to make some sort of life for herself and deserves to be let alone.''

Pat looked at the other letter Margaret was holding. ''She wrote you after she disappeared?''

''Yes. Six years ago this came.''

Pat took the letter. The typeface was worn, the paper cheap. The note read:

Dear Miss Langley. Please understand that it is better if I have no contact with anyone from the past. If I am found, I will have to go back to prison. I swear to you I never touched that money. I have been very ill but I am trying to rebuild my life. Some days are good. I can almost believe it is possible to become well again. Other times I am so frightened, so afraid that someone will recognize me. I think of you often. I love and miss you.

Eleanor's signature was wavering, the letters uneven—a stark contrast to the firm and graceful penmanship of the earlier letter.

It took all Pat's persuasive powers to coax Margaret Langley to let her take the letters. ''We are planning to include the case in this program,'' she said, ''but even if Eleanor is recognized and someone turns her in, perhaps we can have her parole reinstated. Then she wouldn't have to hide for the rest of her life.''

''I would love to see her again,'' Margaret whispered. Now tears brightened her eyes. ''She's the nearest thing I ever had to a child of my own. Wait—let me show you her picture.''

On the bottom shelf of the bookcase were stacks of yearbooks. ''I have one for every year I was in school,'' she explained. ''But I keep Eleanor's on top.'' She riffled through the pages. ''She graduated seventeen years ago. Isn't she sweet-looking?''

The girl in the photo had fine, mousy hair; soft, innocent eyes. The caption read:

> Eleanor Brown—Hobby: painting. Ambition: secretary. Activities: choir. Sport: roller skating. Prediction: right-hand gal for executive, marry young, two kids. Favorite thing: Evening in Paris perfume.

''My God,'' Pat said, ''how cruel.''

''Exactly. That's why I wanted her to leave here.''

Pat shook her head, and her glance caught the other yearbooks. ''Wait a minute,'' she said, ''by any chance do you have the book Senator Jennings is in?''

''Of course. Let's see—that would be over here somewhere.''

The second book Margaret Langley checked was the right one. In this photo Abigail's hair was in a pageboy on her shoulders. Her lips were parted slightly as though she had obediently followed the photographer's direction to smile. Her eyes, wide and thick-lashed, were calm and inscrutable. The caption read:

> Abigail Foster (''Abby'')—Hobby: attending state legislature. Ambition: politics. Activities: debating. Prediction: will become state assemblywoman from Apple Junction. Favorite thing: any book in the library.

''State assemblywoman,'' Pat exclaimed; ''that's great!''

A half-hour later she left, the Senator's yearbook under her arm. As she got into the car, she decided that she'd send a camera crew to get some background footage of the town, including Main Street, the Saunders home, the high school and the highway with the bus to Albany. Under the footage she'd have Senator Jennings speak briefly about growing up there and her early interest in politics. They'd close that segment with the picture of the Senator as Miss New York State, then her yearbook picture and her explanation that going on to Radcliffe instead of Atlantic City was the most important decision of her life.

With the unfamiliar and disquieting feeling that somehow she was glossing over the full story, Pat drove around town for an hour and marked locations for the camera crew. Then she checked out of the Apple Motel, drove to Albany, turned in the rental car and with relief got on the plane back to Washington.

CHAPTER 9

Washington is beautiful, Pat thought, from any view, at any hour. By night the spotlights on the Capitol and monuments seem to impart a sense of tranquil agelessness. She'd been gone from here only thirty hours, yet felt as though days had passed since she'd left. The plane landed with a slight bump and taxied smoothly across the field.

As she opened the door to her house, Pat heard the phone ringing and scrambled to answer it. It was Luther Pelham. He sounded edgy.

''Pat, I'm glad I've reached you. You never did let me know where you were staying in Apple Junction. When I finally tracked you down, you had checked out.''

''I'm sorry. I should have phoned you this morning.''

''Abigail is making a major speech before the final vote on the budget tomorrow. She suggested you spend the entire day at her office. She gets in at six-thirty.''

''I'll be there.''

''How did you do in the hometown?''

''Interesting. We can get some sympathetic footage that won't raise the Senator's hackles.''

''I'd like to hear about it. I've just finished dinner at the Jockey Club and can be at your place in ten minutes.'' The phone clicked in her ear.

She had barely time to change into slacks and a sweater before he arrived. The library was cluttered with the Senator's material. Pat brought him back to the living room and offered him a drink. When she returned with it, he was studying the candelabrum on the mantel. ''Beautiful example of Sheffield,'' he told her. ''Everything in the room is beautiful.''

In Boston, she had had a studio apartment similar to those of other young professionals. It had not occurred to her that the costly furnishings and accessories in this house might arouse comment.

She tried to sound casual. ''My folks are planning to move into a condominium soon. We have an attic full of family stuff and Mother told me it's now or never if I want it.''

Luther settled on the couch and reached for the glass she placed in front of him. ''All I know is that at your age I was living at the Y.'' He patted the cushion beside him. ''Sit here and tell me all about Our Town.''

Oh, no, she thought. There'll be no passes tonight, Luther Pelham. Ignoring the suggestion, she sat on the chair across the table from the couch and proceeded to give Luther an accounting of what she had learned in Apple Junction. It was not edifying.

''Abigail may have been the prettiest girl in those parts,'' she concluded, ''but she certainly wasn't the most popular. I can understand now why she's nervous about stirring things up there. Jeremy Saunders will bad-mouth her till the day he dies. She's right to be afraid that calling attention to her being Miss New York State will get the old-timers again talking about how they contributed their two bucks to dress her up for Atlantic City and then she bugged out. Miss Apple Junction! Here, let me show you the picture.''

Luther whistled when he saw it. ''Hard to believe that blimp could be Abigail's mother.'' He thought better of the remark. ''All right. She has a valid reason for wanting to forget Apple Junction and everyone in it. I thought you told me you could salvage some human-interest stuff.''

''We'll cut it to the bone. Background shots of the town, the school, the house where she grew up; then interview the school principal, Margaret Langley, about how Abigail used to go to Albany to sit in on the legislature. Wind up with her school picture in the yearbook. It's not much, but it's something. The Senator's got to be made to understand she's not a UFO who landed on earth at age twenty-one. Anyhow, she agreed to cooperate in this documentary. We didn't give her creative control of it, I hope.''

''Certainly not creative control, but some veto power. Don't forget, Pat. We're not just doing this *about* her; we're doing it *with* her, and her cooperation in letting us use her personal memorabilia is essential.''

He stood up. ''Since you insist on keeping that table between us . . .'' He walked around it, and came over to her, put his hands on hers.

Quickly she jumped to her feet, but she was not fast enough. He pulled her against him. ''You're a beautiful girl, Pat.'' He lifted her chin. His lips pressed down on hers. His tongue was insistent.

She tried to pull away, but his grip was viselike. Finally she managed to dig her elbows into his chest. ''Let go of me.''

He smiled. ''Pat, why don't you show me the rest of the house?''

There was no mistaking his meaning. ''It's pretty late,'' she said, ''but on the way out you can poke your head into the library and dining room. I do sort of wish you'd wait until I've had a chance to get pictures hung and whatever.''

''Where's your bedroom?''

''Upstairs.''

''I'd like to see it.''

''As a matter of fact, even when it's fixed up, I'd like you to think of the second floor of this house the way you had to think about the second floor of the Barbizon for Women in your salad days in New York: offlimits for gentlemen callers.''

''I'd rather you didn't joke, Pat.''

''I'd rather we treat this conversation as a joke. Otherwise I can put it another way. I don't sleep on the job nor do I sleep off the job. Not tonight. Not tomorrow. Not next year.''

''I see.''

She preceded him down the hall. In the foyer she handed him his coat.

As he put it on, he gave her an acid smile. ''Sometimes people who have your kind of insomnia problem find it impossible to handle their responsibilities,'' he said. ''They often discover they're happier at some backwoods station than in the big time. Does Apple Junction have a cable station? You might want to check it out, Pat.''

Promptly at ten to six, Toby let himself in the back door of Abigail's house in McLean, Virginia. The large kitchen was filled with gourmet equipment. Abigail's idea of relaxing was to spend an evening cooking. Depending on her mood, she'd prepare six or seven different kinds of hors d'oeuvres or fish and meat casseroles. Other nights she'd make a half-dozen different sauces, or biscuits and cakes that would melt in your mouth. Then she'd pop everything into the freezer. But when she gave a party she never admitted that she'd prepared everything herself. She hated any association with the word ''cook.''

Abigail herself ate very little. Toby knew she was haunted by the memory of her mother, poor old Francey, that groaning tub of a woman whose trunklike legs settled into fat ankles and feet so wide it was hard to find shoes to fit them.

Toby had an apartment over the garage. Nearly every morning he'd come in and start the coffeepot and squeeze fresh juice. Later on, after he had Abby settled in her office, he'd have a big breakfast, and if she wasn't going to need him, he'd find a poker game.

Abigail came into the kitchen, still fastening a crescent-shaped gold pin on her lapel. She was wearing a purple suit that brought out the blueness of her eyes.

''You look great, Abby,'' he pronounced.

Her smile was quick and instantly gone. Whenever Abby had a big speech planned in the Senate she was like this—nervous as a cat before it, ready to be irritated at anything that went wrong. ''Let's not waste time on coffee,'' she snapped.

''You've got plenty of time,'' Toby assured her. ''I'll have you there by six-thirty. Drink your coffee. You know how crabby you get without it.''

Later he left both cups in the sink, knowing Abby would be irritated if he took time to rinse them out.

The car was at the front entrance. When Abby went to get her coat and briefcase, he hurried outside and turned on the heater.

By six-ten they were on the parkway. Even for a day when she was making a speech, Abby was unusually tense. She'd gone to bed early the night before. He wondered if she'd been able to sleep.

He heard Abby sigh and snap her briefcase closed. "If I don't know what I'm going to say by now I might as well forget it," she commented. "If this damn budget doesn't get voted on soon, we'll still be in session on Christmas Day. But I *won't* let them ax any more of the entitlement programs."

Toby watched in the rearview mirror as she poured some coffee from a thermos. From her attitude he knew she was ready to talk.

"Did you get a good rest last night, Senator?" Once in a while, even when they were alone, he threw in the "Senator." It reminded her that no matter what, he knew his place.

"No, I didn't. I started thinking about this program. I was stupid to let myself get talked into it. It's going to backfire. I feel it in my bones."

Toby frowned. He had a healthy respect for Abby's bones. He still hadn't told Abby that Pat Traymore lived in the Dean Adams house. She'd get real superstitious about that. This wasn't the time for her to lose her cool. Still, at some point she'd have to know. It was bound to come out. Toby was starting to get a lousy feeling about the program himself.

Pat had set the alarm for five o'clock. In her first television job, she'd discovered that being calm and collected kept her energy directed to the project at hand. She could still remember the burning chagrin of rushing breathlessly to interview the Governor of Connecticut and realizing she'd forgotten her carefully prepared questions.

After the Apple Motel, it had felt good to be in the wide, comfortable bed. But she'd slept badly, thinking about the scene with Luther Pelham. There were plenty of men in the television-news business who made the obligatory pass, and some of them were vengeful when rejected.

She dressed quickly, choosing a long-sleeved black wool dress with a suede vest. Once again it looked as though it would be one of the raw, windy days that had characterized this December.

Some of the storm windows were missing, and the panes on the north side of the house rattled as the wind shrieked against them.

She reached the landing of the staircase.

The shrieking sound intensified. But now it was a child screaming. *I ran down the stairs. I was so frightened, and I was crying. . . .*

A momentary dizziness made her grasp the banister. It's starting to happen, she thought fiercely. It *is* coming back.

En route to the Senator's office she felt distracted, out of sync. She could not rid herself of the overwhelming fear that was the result of the fleeting memory.

Why should she experience fear now?

How much had she seen of what happened that night?

Philip Buckley was waiting for her in the office when she arrived. In the gloom of the early morning, his attitude toward her seemed even more cautiously hostile than before. What is he afraid of? Pat wondered. You'd think I was a British spy in a Colonial camp. She told him that.

His small, cold smile was humorless. "If we thought you were a British spy, you wouldn't be anywhere near this Colonial camp," he commented. "The Senator will be here any minute. You might want to have a look at her schedule today. It will give you some idea of her workload."

He looked over her shoulder as she read the crammed pages. "Actually we'll have to put off at least three of these people. It's our thought that if you simply sit in the Senator's office and observe, you'll be able to decide what segments of her day you might want to include in the special. Obviously, if she has to discuss any confidential matters, you'll be excused. I've had a desk put in her private office for you. That way you won't be conspicuous."

"You think of everything," Pat told him. "Come on, how about a nice big smile? You'll have to have one for the camera when we start to shoot."

"I'm saving my smile for the time when I see the final edited version of the program." But he did look a little more relaxed.

Abigail came in a few minutes later. "I'm so glad you're here," she said to Pat. "When we couldn't reach you, I was afraid you were out of town."

"I got your message last night."

"Oh. Luther wasn't sure if you'd be available."

So that was the reason for the small talk, Pat decided. The Senator wanted to know where'd she been. She wasn't going to tell her. "I'm going to be your shadow until the program's completed," she said. "You'll probably get sick of having me around."

Abigail didn't look placated. "I must be able to reach you quickly. Luther told me you had some questions to go over with me. With my schedule the way it is, I don't often know about free time until just before it's available. Now let's get to work."

Pat followed her into the private office and tried to make herself inconspicuous. In a few moments the Senator was in deep discussion with Philip. One report that he placed on her desk was late. Sharply, she demanded to know why. "I should have had that last week."

"The figures weren't compiled."

"Why?"

"There simply wasn't time."

"If there isn't time during the day, there's time in the evening," Abigail snapped. "If anyone on my staff has become a clock-watcher, I want to know about it."

At seven o'clock the appointments started. Pat's respect for Abigail grew with each new person who came into the office. Lobbyists for the oil industry, for environmentalists, for veterans' benefits. Strategy sessions for presenting a new housing bill. A representative from the IRS to register specific objections to a proposed exemption for middle-income taxpayers. A delegation of senior citizens protesting the cutbacks in Social Security.

When the Senate convened, Pat accompanied Abigail and Philip to the chamber. Pat was not accredited to the press section behind the dais and took a seat in the visitors' gallery. She watched as the Senators entered from the cloakroom, greeting one another along the way, smiling, relaxed. They came in all sizes—tall, short; cadaver-slender, rotund; some with manes of hair, some carefully barbered, some bald. Four or five had the scholarly appearance of college professors.

There were two other women Senators, Claire Lawrence of Ohio and Phyllis Holzer of New Hampshire, who had been elected as an independent in a stunning upset.

Pat was especially interested in observing Claire Lawrence. The junior Senator from Ohio wore a three-piece navy knit suit that fitted comfortably over her size 14 figure. Her short salt-and-pepper hair was saved from severity by the natural wave that framed and softened her angular face. Pat noted the genuine pleasure with which this woman was greeted by her colleagues, the burst of laughter that followed her murmured greetings. Claire Lawrence was eminently quotable; her quick wit had a way of taking the rancor out of inflammatory issues without compromising the subject at hand.

In her notebook, Pat jotted "*humor*" and underlined the word. Abigail was rightly perceived to be serious, intense. A few carefully placed light moments should be included in the program.

A long, insistent bell was calling the Senate to order. The senior Senator from Arkansas was presiding in place of the ailing Vice President. After a few short pieces of business had been completed, the Presiding Officer recognized the senior Senator from Virginia.

Abigail stood up and without a trace of nervousness carefully put on blue-rimmed reading glasses. Her hair was pulled back into a simple chignon that enhanced the elegant lines of her profile and neck.

"Two of the best-known sentences in the Bible," she said, "are 'The Lord giveth and the Lord taketh away. Blessed be the name of the Lord.' In recent years our government, in an exaggerated and ill-considered manner, has given and given. And then it has taken away and taken away. But there are few to bless its name.

"Any responsible citizen would, I trust, agree that an overhaul of the entitlement programs has been necessary. But now it is time to examine what we have done. I maintain that the surgery was too radical, the cuts too drastic. I maintain that this is the time for restoration of many necessary programs. Entitlement by definition means 'to have a claim to.' Surely no one in this august chamber will dispute that every human being in this country has a rightful claim to shelter and food. . . .''

Abigail was an excellent speaker. Her address had been carefully prepared, carefully documented, sprinkled with enough specific anecdotes to keep the attention of even these professionals.

She spoke for an hour and ten minutes. The applause was sustained and genuine. When the Senate recessed, Pat saw that the Majority Leader hurried over to congratulate her.

Pat waited with Philip until the Senator finally broke away from her colleagues and the visitors who crowded around her. Together they started back to the office.

''It was good, wasn't it?'' Abigail asked, but there was no hint of question in her voice.

''Excellent, Senator,'' Philip said promptly.

''Pat?'' Abigail looked at her.

''I felt sick that we couldn't record it,'' Pat said honestly. ''I'd love to have had excerpts of that speech on the program.''

They ate lunch in the Senator's office. Abigail ordered only a hard-boiled egg and black coffee. She was interrupted four times by urgent phone calls. One was from an old campaign volunteer. ''Sure, Maggie,'' Abigail said. ''No, you're not interrupting me. I'm always available to you—you know that. What can I do?''

Pat watched as Abigail's face became stern and a frown creased her forehead. ''You mean the hospital told you to come get your mother when the woman can't even raise her head from the pillow? . . . I see. Have you any nursing homes in mind? . . . Six months' wait. And what are you supposed to do in those six months . . . Maggie, I'll call you back.''

She slammed the phone down on the hook. ''This is the kind of thing that drives me wild. Maggie is trying to raise three kids on her own. She works at a second job on Saturdays and now she's told to take home a senile, bedridden mother. Philip, track down Arnold Pritchard. And I don't care if he's having a two-hour lunch somewhere. Find him now.''

Fifteen minutes later the call Abigail was waiting for came through. ''Arnold, good to talk to you. . . . I'm glad you're fine. . . . No, I'm not fine. In fact, I'm pretty upset. . . .''

Five minutes later Abigail concluded the conversation by saying, ''Yes, I agree. The Willows sounds like a perfect place. It's near enough so that Maggie can visit without giving up her whole Sunday to make the trip. And I know I can count on you, Arnold, to make sure the old girl gets settled in. . . . Yes, send an ambulance to the hospital for her this afternoon. Maggie will be so relieved.''

Abigail winked at Pat as she hung up the phone. ''This is the aspect of the job that I love,'' she said. ''I shouldn't take time to call Maggie myself, but I'm going to. . . .'' She dialed quickly. ''Maggie, hello. We're in good shape . . .''

Maggie, Pat decided, would be a guest on the program.

There was an environmental-committee hearing between two and four. At the hearing, Abigail got into a verbal duel with one of the witnesses and quoted from her report. The witness said, ''Senator, your figures are dead wrong. I think you've got the old quotes, not the revised ones.''

Claire Lawrence was also on the committee. ''Maybe I can help,'' she suggested. ''I'm pretty sure I have the latest numbers, and they do change the picture somewhat. . . .''

Pat observed the rigid thrust of Abigail's shoulders, the way she clenched and unclenched her hands as Claire Lawrence read from her report.

The studious-looking young woman seated behind Abigail was apparently the aide who had compiled the inaccurate report. Several times Abigail turned to look at her during Senator Lawrence's comments. The girl was clearly in an agony of embarrassment. Her face was flushed; she was biting her lips to keep them from trembling.

Abigail cut in the instant Senator Lawrence stopped speaking. ''Mr. Chairman, I would like to thank Senator Lawrence for her help, and I would also like to apologize to this committee for the fact that the figures given to me were inaccurate and wasted the valuable time of everyone here. I promise you it will never happen again.'' She turned again to her aide. Pat could read Abigail's lips: ''You're fired.'' The girl slipped out of her chair and left the hearing room, tears running down her cheeks.

Inwardly Pat groaned. The hearing was being televised—anyone seeing the exchange would surely have felt sympathy for the young assistant.

When the hearing was over, Abigail hurried back to her office. It was obvious that everyone there knew what had happened. The secretaries and aides in the outer office did not lift their heads as she roared through. The hapless girl who had made the error was staring out the window, futilely dabbing at her eyes.

''In here, Philip,'' Abigail snapped. ''You too, Pat. You might as well get a full picture of what goes on in this place.''

She sat down at her desk. Except for the paleness of her features and the tight set of her lips, she appeared totally composed. ''What happened, Philip?'' she asked, her tone level.

Even Philip had lost his usual calm. He gulped nervously as he started to explain. ''Senator, the other girls just talked to me. Eileen's husband walked out on her a couple of weeks ago. From what they tell me, she's been in a terrible state. She's been with us three years, and as you know, she's one of our best aides. Would you consider giving her a leave of absence until she pulls herself together? She loves this job.''

''Does she, indeed? Loves it so much she lets me make a fool of myself in a televised hearing? She's finished, Philip. I want her out of here in the next fifteen minutes. And consider yourself lucky you're not fired too. When that report was late, it was up to you to dig for the real reason for the problem. With all the brainy people hungry for jobs, *including mine,* do you think I intend to leave myself vulnerable because I'm surrounded by deadwood?''

''No, Senator,'' Philip mumbled.

''There are no second chances in this office. Have I warned my staff about that?''

''Yes, Senator.''

''Then get out of here and do as you're told.''

''Yes, Senator.''

Wow! Pat thought. No wonder Philip was so on guard with her. She realized the Senator was looking over at her.

''Well, Pat,'' Abigail said quietly, ''I suppose you think I'm an ogre?'' She did not wait for an answer. ''My people know if they have a personal problem and can't handle their job, their responsibility is to report it and arrange for a leave of absence. That policy is in effect to prevent this sort of occurrence. When a staff member makes a mistake, it reflects on me. I have worked too hard, for too many years, to be compromised by anyone else's stupidity. And Pat, believe me, if they'll do it once, they'll do it again. And now, for God's sake, I'm due on the front steps to have my picture taken with a Brownie troop!''

CHAPTER 10

At a quarter to five, a secretary timidly knocked on the door of Abigail's office. ''A call for Miss Traymore,'' she whispered.

It was Sam. The reassuring heartiness of his voice boosted Pat's spirits immediately. She had been unsettled by the unpleasant episode, by the abject misery in the young woman's face.

''Hello, Sam.'' She felt Abigail's sharp glance.

''My spies told me you're on the Hill. How about dinner?''

''Dinner . . . I can't, Sam. I've got to work tonight.''

''You also have to eat. What did you have for lunch? One of Abigail's hard-boiled eggs?''

She tried not to laugh. The Senator was clearly listening to her end of the conversation.

''As long as you don't mind eating fast and early,'' she compromised.

''Fine with me. How about if I pick you up outside the Russell building in half an hour?''

When Pat hung up, she looked over at Abigail.

"Have you reviewed all the material we gave you?—the films?" Abigail demanded.

"No."

"Some of them?"

"No," Pat admitted. Oh, boy, she thought. I'm glad I don't work for you, lady.

"I had thought you might come back to my place for dinner and we could discuss which ones you might be interested in using."

Again a pause. Pat waited.

"However, since you haven't seen the material, I think it would be wiser if I use tonight for some reading I must do." Abigail smiled. "Sam Kingsley is one of the most eligible bachelors in Washington. I didn't realize you knew him so well."

Pat tried to make her answer light. "I really don't." But she couldn't help thinking that Sam was finding it hard to stay away from her.

She glanced out the window, hoping to hide her expression. Outside it was almost dark. The Senator's windows overlooked the Capitol. As the daylight faded, the gleaming domed building framed by the blue silk draperies resembled a painting. "How lovely!" she exclaimed.

Abigail turned her head toward the window. "Yes, it is," she agreed. "That view at this time of day always reminds me of what I'm doing here. You can't imagine the satisfaction of knowing that because of what I did today an old woman will be cared for in a decent nursing home, and extra money may be made available for people who are trying to eke out an existence."

There was an almost sensual energy in Abigail Jennings when she spoke about her work, Pat thought. She means every word.

But it also occurred to her that the Senator had already dismissed from her memory the girl she had fired a few hours earlier.

Pat shivered as she hurried down the few steps from the Senate office building to the car. Sam leaned over to kiss her cheek. "How's the hotshot filmmaker?"

"Tired," she said. "Keeping up with Senator Jennings is not the recipe for a restful day."

Sam smiled. "I know what you mean. I've worked with Abigail on a fair amount of legislation. She never wears down."

Weaving through the traffic, he turned onto Pennsylvania Avenue. "I thought we'd go to Chez Grandmère in Georgetown," he said. "It's quiet, the food is excellent and it's near your place."

Chez Grandmère was nearly empty. "Washington doesn't dine at quarter to six." Sam smiled as the maître d' offered them their choice of tables.

Over a cocktail Pat told him about the day, including the scene in the hearing room. Sam whistled. "That was a rotten break for Abigail. You don't need someone on your payroll to make you look bad."

"Could something like that actually influence the President's decision?" Pat asked.

"Pat, *everything* can influence the President's decision. One mistake can ruin you. Well, figure it out for yourself. If it weren't for Chappaquiddick, Teddy Kennedy might be President today. Then, of course, you have Watergate and Abscam, and way back, vicuña coats and home freezers. It never ends. Everything reflects on the man or woman who holds the office. It's a miracle Abigail survived that scandal about the missing campaign funds, and if she had tried to cover up for her aide, it would have been the end of her credibility. What was the girl's name?"

"Eleanor Brown." Pat thought of what Margaret Langley had said. "*Eleanor couldn't steal. She's too timid.*"

"Eleanor always claimed she was innocent," she told Sam now.

He shrugged. "Pat, I was a county prosecutor for four years. You want to know something? Nine out of ten criminals swear they didn't do it. And at least eight out of nine of them are liars."

"But there is always that one who *is* innocent," Pat persisted.

"Very occasionally," Sam said. "What do you feel like eating?"

It seemed to her that she could watch him visibly unwind in the hour and a half they were together. I'm good for you, Sam, she thought. I can make you happy. You're equating having a child with the way it was when you were doing everything for Karen, because Janice was sick. It wouldn't be that way with me. . . .

Over coffee he asked, "How do you find living in the house? Any problems?"

She hesitated, then decided to tell him about the note she'd found slipped under the door and the second phone call. "But as you say, it's probably just some joker," she concluded.

Sam didn't return her attempt at a smile. "I said that one random call to the Boston station might not be important. But you're saying that in the last three days you've had a second phone call, and a note pushed under the door. How do you think this nut got your address?"

"How did *you* get it?" Pat asked.

"I phoned Potomac Cable and said I was a friend. A secretary gave me your phone number and street address here and told me when you were arriving. Frankly, I was a little surprised they were that casual about giving out so much information."

"I approved it. I'll be using the house as an office for this program, and you'd be surprised how many people volunteer anecdotes or memorabilia when they read about a documentary being prepared. I didn't want to take the chance of losing calls. I certainly didn't think I had anything to worry about."

"Then that creep could have gotten it the same way. By any chance do you have the note with you?"

"It's in my bag." She fished it out, glad to be rid of it.

Sam studied it, frowning in concentration. ''I doubt whether anybody could trace this, but let me show it to Jack Carlson. He's an FBI agent and something of a handwriting expert. And you be sure to hang up if you get another call.''

He dropped her off at eight-thirty. ''You've got to get timers for the lamps,'' he commented as they stood at the door. ''Anybody could come up here and put a note under the door without being noticed.''

She looked up at him. The relaxed expression was gone, and the newly acquired creases around his mouth had deepened again. You've always had to worry about Janice, she thought. I don't want you worrying about me.

She tried to recapture the easy companionship of the evening. ''Thanks for being the Welcome Wagon again,'' she said. ''They're going to make you chairman of the Hospitality Committee on the Hill.''

He smiled briefly and for that moment the tension disappeared from his eyes. ''Mother taught me to be courtly to the prettiest girls in town.'' He closed his hands around hers. For a moment they stood silently; then he bent down and kissed her cheek.

''I'm glad you're not playing favorites,'' she murmured.

''What?''

''The other night you kissed me below my right eye—tonight the left.''

''Good night, Pat. Lock the door.''

Pat had barely reached the library when the telephone began to ring insistently. For a moment she was afraid to answer.

''Pat Traymore.'' To her own ears her voice sounded tense and husky.

''Miss Traymore,'' a woman's voice said, ''I'm Lila Thatcher, your neighbor across the street. I know you just got home, but would it be possible for you to come over now? There's something quite important you should know.''

Lila Thatcher, Pat thought. *Lila Thatcher.* Of course. She was the clairvoyant who had written several widely read books on ESP and other psychic phenomena. Only a few months ago she'd been celebrated for her assistance in finding a missing child.

''I'll be right there,'' Pat agreed reluctantly, ''but I'm afraid I can't stay more than a minute.''

As she threaded her way across the street, taking pains to avoid the worst of the melting slush and mud, she tried to ignore the sense of uneasiness.

She was sure she would not want to hear what Lila Thatcher was about to tell her.

CHAPTER 11

A maid answered Pat's ring and escorted her to the living room. Pat didn't know what kind of person to expect—she'd visualized a turbaned Gypsy; but the woman who rose to greet her could be described simply as cozy. She was gently rounded and gray-haired, with intelligent, twinkling eyes and a warm smile.

"Patricia Traymore," she said, "I'm so glad to meet you. Welcome to Georgetown." Taking Pat's hand, she studied her carefully. "I know how busy you must be with the program you're preparing. I'm sure it's quite a project. How are you getting on with Luther Pelham?"

"Fine so far."

"I hope that continues." Lila Thatcher wore her glasses on a long silver chain around her neck. Absently she picked them up in her right hand and began to tap them against her left palm. "I have only a few minutes myself. I have a meeting in half an hour, and in the morning I have to catch an early flight to California. That's why I decided to phone. This is not the sort of thing I usually do. However, in conscience I can't go away without warning you. Are you aware that twenty-three years ago a murder-suicide took place in the house you're now renting?"

"I've been told that." It was the answer nearest the truth.

"It doesn't upset you?"

"Mrs. Thatcher, many of the houses in Georgetown must be about two hundred years old. Surely people have died in every one of them."

"It's not the same." The older woman's voice became quicker, a thread of nervousness running through it. "My husband and I moved into this house a year or so before the tragedy. I remember the first time I told him that I was beginning to sense a darkness in the atmosphere around the Adams home. Over the next months it would come and go, but each time it returned it was more pronounced. Dean and Renée Adams were a most attractive couple. He was quite splendid-looking, one of those magnetic men who instantly attract attention. Renée was different—quiet, reserved, a very private young woman. My feeling was that being a politician's wife was all wrong for her and inevitably the marriage became affected. But she was very much in love with her husband and they were both devoted to their child."

Pat listened motionless.

"A few days before she died, Renée told me she was going to go back to New England with Kerry. We were standing in front of your house, and I can't describe to you the sense of trouble and danger I experienced. I tried to warn Renée. I told her that if her decision was irrevocable, she should not wait any longer. And then it was too late. I never again felt even a suggestion of trouble concerning your house until this week. But now it's coming back. I don't know why but it's like last time. I sense the darkness involves you. Can you leave that house? *You shouldn't be there.*"

Pat chose her question carefully. "Do you have any reason, other than sensing this aura around the house, for warning me not to stay there?''

''Yes. Three days ago my maid observed a man loitering on the corner. Then she saw footprints in the snow along the side of this house. We thought there might be a prowler and notified the police. We saw footprints again yesterday morning after the fresh snowfall. Whoever is prowling about only goes as far as that tall rhododendron. Standing behind it anyone can watch your house without being observed from our windows or from the street.''

Mrs. Thatcher was hugging herself now as if she were suddenly chilled. The flesh on her face had hardened into deep, grave lines. She stared intently at Pat and then, as Pat watched, her eyes widened; an expression of secret knowledge crept into them. When Pat left a few minutes later, the older woman was clearly upset and again urged Pat to leave the house.

Lila Thatcher knows who I am, Pat thought. I'm sure of it. She went directly to the library and poured a fairly generous brandy. ''That's better,'' she murmured as warmth returned to her body. She tried not to think of the dark outside. But at least the police were on the lookout for a prowler. She tried to force herself to be calm. Lila had begged Renée to leave. If her mother had listened, had heeded the warning, could the tragedy have been averted? Should she take Lila's advice now and go to a hotel or rent an apartment? ''I can't,'' she said aloud. ''I simply can't.'' She had so little time to prepare the documentary. It would be unthinkable to waste any of that time relocating. The fact that, as a psychic, Lila Thatcher *sensed* trouble did not mean she could *prevent* it. Pat thought, If Mother had gone to Boston, Daddy would probably have followed her. If someone is determined to find me, he'll manage it. I'd have to be just as careful in an apartment as here. And I *will* be careful.

Somehow the thought that Lila might have guessed her identity was comforting. She cared about my mother and father. She knew me well when I was little. After the program is finished I can talk to her, probe her memory. Maybe she can help me piece it all together.

But now it was absolutely essential to begin reviewing the Senator's personal files and select some for the program.

The spools of film were jumbled together in one of the cartons Toby had brought in. Fortunately, they were all labeled. She began to sort them. Some were of political activities, campaign events, speeches. Finally she found the personal ones she was most interested in seeing. She started with the film labeled WILLARD AND ABIGAIL—HILLCREST WEDDING RECEPTION.

She knew they had eloped before his graduation from Harvard Law School. Abby had just finished her junior year at Radcliffe. Willard had run for Congress a few months after their wedding. She'd helped him campaign, then completed college at the University of Richmond. Apparently there had been a reception when he brought her to Virginia.

The film opened on the panorama of a festive garden party. Colorful umbrella-covered tables were arranged against the tree-shaded background. Servants moved among the clusters of guests—women in summer gowns and picture hats, men in dark jackets and white flannel trousers.

In the reception line on the terrace, a breathtaking young Abigail wearing a white silk tunic-style gown stood next to a scholarly-looking young man. An older woman, obviously Willard Jennings' mother, was to Abigail's right. Her aristocratic face was set in taut, angry lines. As the guests moved slowly past her, she introduced them to Abigail. Never once did she look directly at Abigail.

What was it the Senator had said? ''My mother-in-law always considered me the Yankee who stole her son.'' Clearly, Abigail had not exaggerated.

Pat studied Willard Jennings. He was only slightly taller than Abigail, with sandy hair and a thin, gentle face. There was something rather endearingly shy about him, a diffidence in his manner as he shook hands or kissed cheeks.

Of the three, only Abigail seemed totally at ease. She smiled constantly, bent her head forward as if carefully committing names to memory, reached out her hand to show her rings.

If there were only a sound track, Pat thought.

The last person had been greeted. Pat watched as Abigail and Willard turned to each other. Willard's mother stared straight ahead. Now her face seemed less angry than thoughtful.

And then she smiled warmly. A tall auburn-haired man approached. He hugged Mrs. Jennings, released her, hugged her again, then turned to greet the newlyweds. Pat leaned forward. As the man's face came into full view, she stopped the projector.

The late arrival was her father, Dean Adams. He looks so young! she thought. He can't be more than thirty! She tried to swallow over the lump in her throat. Did she have a vague memory of him looking like this? His broad shoulders filled the screen. He was like a handsome young god, she thought, towering over Willard, exuding magnetic energy.

Feature by feature she studied the face, frozen on the screen, unwavering, open to minute examination. She wondered where her mother was, then realized that when this film was taken, her mother had still been a student at the Boston Conservatory, still planning a career in music.

Dean Adams was then a freshman Congressman from Wisconsin. He still had the healthy, open look of the Midwest in him, a larger-than-life outdoorsy aura.

She pushed the button and the figures sprang to life—Dean Adams joking with Willard Jennings, Abigail extending her hand to him. He ignored it and kissed her cheek. Whatever he said to Willard, they all began to laugh.

The camera followed them as they walked down the flagstone steps of the terrace and began to circulate among the guests. Dean Adams had his hand under the arm of the older Mrs. Jennings. She was talking to him animatedly. Clearly they were very fond of each other.

When the film ended, Pat reran it, marking off segments that might be used in the program. Willard and Abigail cutting the cake, toasting each other, dancing the first dance. She couldn't use any of the footage from the reception line—the displeasure on the face of the senior Mrs. Jennings was too obvious. And of course there was no question of using the film that involved Dean Adams.

What had Abigail felt that afternoon? she wondered. That beautiful whitewashed brick mansion, that gathering of Virginia gentry and she only a few years removed from the service apartment of the Saunders house in Apple Junction.

The Saunders house. Abigail's mother, Francey Foster. Where was she that day? Had she declined to be at her daughter's wedding reception, feeling she would seem out of place among these people? Or had Abigail made that decision for her?

One by one Pat began to view the other reels, steeling herself against the shock of watching her father regularly appear in those which had been taken on the estate.

Even without the dates, it would have been possible to arrange the films in a time sequence.

The first campaign: professional newsreels of Abigail and Willard hand in hand walking down the street, greeting passersby . . . Abigail and Willard inspecting a new housing development. The announcer's voice . . . "As Willard Jennings campaigned this afternoon for the seat to be made vacant by the retirement of his uncle, Congressman Porter Jennings, he pledged to continue the family tradition of service to the constituency."

There was an interview with Abigail. "How does it feel to spend your honeymoon campaigning?"

Abigail's reply: "I can't think of a better way than being at my husband's side helping him begin his career in public life."

There was a soft lilt in Abigail's voice, the unmistakable trace of a Southern accent. Pat did a rapid calculation. At that point Abigail had been in Virginia less than three months. She marked that segment for the program.

There were clips of five campaigns in all. As they progressed, Abigail increasingly played a major role in reelection efforts. Often her speech would begin "My husband is in Washington doing a job for you. Unlike many others, he is not taking time from the important work of the Congress to campaign for himself. I'm glad to be able to tell you just a few of his accomplishments."

The films of social events at the estate were hardest to watch.

WILLARD'S 35TH BIRTHDAY. Two young couples posing with Abigail and Willard—Jack and Jackie Kennedy and Dean and Renée Adams . . . both recent newlyweds . . .

It was the first time Pat had seen a film of her mother. Renée was wearing a pale green gown; her dark hair fell loosely on her shoulders. There was a hesitancy about her, but when she smiled up at her husband, her expression was adoring. Pat found she could not bear to dwell on it. She was glad to let the film unwind. A few frames later, just the Kennedys and Jenningses were posing together. She made a note on her pad. That will be a wonderful clip for the program, she thought bitterly. The pre-Camelot days minus the embarrassment of Congressman Dean Adams and the wife he murdered.

The last film she viewed was of Willard Jennings' funeral. In it was a newsreel clip that opened outside the National Cathedral. The announcer's voice was subdued. "The funeral cortege of Congressman Willard Jennings has just arrived. The great and the near-great are gathered inside to bid a final farewell to the Virginia legislator who died when his chartered plane crashed en route to a speaking engagement. Congressman Jennings and the pilot, George Graney, were killed instantly.

"The young widow is being escorted by Senator John Fitzgerald Kennedy of Massachusetts. Congressman Jennings' mother, Mrs. Stuart Jennings, is escorted by Congressman Dean Adams of Wisconsin. Senator Kennedy and Congressman Adams were Willard Jennings' closest friends."

Pat watched as Abigail emerged from the first car, her face composed, a black veil covering her blond hair. She wore a simply cut black silk suit and a string of pearls. The handsome young Senator from Massachusetts gravely offered her his arm.

The Congressman's mother was obviously grief-stricken. When she was assisted from the limousine, her eyes fell on the flag-draped casket. She clasped her hands together and shook her head slightly in a gesture of agonized rejection. As Pat watched, her father slid his arm under Mrs. Jennings' elbow and clasped her hand in his. Slowly the procession moved into the cathedral.

She had seen as much as she could absorb in one evening. Clearly the human interest material she had been seeking was amply present in the old film clips. She turned out the lights in the library and went into the hall.

The hall was drafty. There had been no windows open in the library. She checked the dining room, kitchen and foyer. Everything was closed and locked.

But there was a draft.

A sense of apprehension made Pat's breath come faster. The door to the living room was closed. She put her hand on it. The space between the door and the frame was icy cold. Slowly she opened the door. A blast of cold air assaulted her. She reached for the chandelier switch.

The French doors to the patio were open. A pane of glass that had been cut from its frame was lying on the carpet.

And then she saw it.

Lolling against the fireplace, the right leg twisted under it, the white apron soaked with blood, was a Raggedy Ann doll. Sinking to her knees, Pat stared at it. A clever hand had painted downward curves on the stitched mouth, added tears to the cheeks and drawn lines on the forehead so that the typical Raggedy Ann smiling face had been transformed to a pain-filled weeping image.

She held her hand to her mouth to force back a shriek. Who had been here? Why? Half-hidden by the soiled apron was a sheet of paper pinned to the doll's dress. She reached for it; her fingers recoiling at the touch of the crusted blood. The same kind of cheap typing paper as the other note; the same small, slanted printing. *This is your last warning. There must not be a program glorifying Abigail Jennings.*

A creaking sound. One of the patio doors was moving. Was someone there? Pat jumped up. But it was the wind that was pushing the door back and forth. She ran across the room, yanked the doors together and turned the lock. But that was useless. The hand that had cut out the pane could reach through the empty frame, unlock the doors again. Maybe the intruder was still there, still hiding in the garden behind the evergreens.

Her hands shook as she dialed the police emergency number. The officer's voice was reassuring. "We'll send a squad car right away."

As she waited, Pat reread the note. This was the fourth time she'd been warned away from the program. Suddenly suspicious, she wondered if the threats were valid. Was it possible this was some kind of "dirty tricks" campaign to make the Senator's documentary a subject of gossip, to smear it with outlandish, distracting publicity?

What about the doll? Shocking to her because of the memory it evoked, but basically a Raggedy Ann with a garishly painted face. On closer examination, it seemed bizarre rather than frightening. Even the bloodied apron might be a crude attempt to horrify. If I were a reporter covering this story, I'd have a picture of that thing on the front page of tomorrow's newspaper, she thought.

The wail of the police siren decided her. Quickly she unpinned the note and left it on the mantelpiece. Rushing into the library, she dragged the carton from under the table and dropped the doll into it. The grisly apron sickened her. The doorbell was ringing—a steady, persistent peal. Impulsively she untied the apron, pulled it off and buried it deep in the carton. Without it the doll resembled a hurt child.

She shoved the carton back under the table and hurried to admit the policemen.

CHAPTER 12

Two police cars, their dome lights blazing, were in the driveway. A third car had followed them. Don't let it be the press, she prayed. But it was.

Photographs were taken of the broken pane; the grounds were searched, the living room dusted for fingerprints.

It was hard to explain the note. "It was pinned to something," a detective pointed out. "Where did you find it?"

"Right here by the fireplace." That was true enough.

The reporter was from the *Tribune*. He asked to see the note.

"I'd prefer not to have it made public," Pat urged. But he was allowed to read it.

"What does 'last warning' mean?" the detective asked. "Have you had other threats?"

Omitting the reference to "that house," she told them about the two phone calls, about the letter she'd found the first night.

"This one isn't signed," the detective pointed out. "Where's the other one?"

"I didn't keep it. It wasn't signed either."

"But on the phone he called himself an avenging angel?"

"He said something like 'I am an angel of mercy, of deliverance, an avenging angel.' "

"Sounds like a real screwball," the detective commented. He studied her keenly. "Funny he bothered to break in this time. Why not just slip an envelope under the door again?"

Dismayed, Pat watched the reporter scribbling in his notebook.

Finally the police were ready to go. The surfaces of all the living-room tables were smudged with fingerprint powder. The patio doors had been wired together so they couldn't be opened until the pane was replaced.

It was impossible to go to bed. Vacuuming the soot and grit from the living room, she decided, might help her unwind. As she worked, she couldn't forget the mutilated Raggedy Ann doll. *The child had run into the room . . . and tripped . . . the child fell over something soft, and its hands became wet and sticky . . . and the child looked up and saw . . .*

What did I see? Pat asked herself fiercely. What did I see?

Her hands worked unconsciously, vacuuming the worst of the greasy powder, then polishing the lovely old wooden tables with an oil-dampened chamois cloth, moving bric-a-brac, lifting and pushing furniture. The carpet had small clumps of slush and dirt from the policemen's shoes.

What did I see?

She began pushing the furniture back into place. No, not here; that table belongs on the short wall, that lamp on the piano, the slipper chair near the French doors.

It was only when she had finished that she understood what she had been doing.

The slipper chair. The movers had placed it too near the piano.

She'd run down the hall into the room. She'd screamed "Daddy, Daddy . . ." She'd tripped over her mother's body. Her mother was bleeding. She looked up, and then . . .

And then, only darkness . . .

It was nearly three o'clock. She couldn't think about it any more tonight. She was exhausted, and her leg ached. Her limp would have been obvious to anyone as she dragged the vacuum cleaner back to the storage closet and made her way upstairs.

At eight o'clock the telephone rang. The caller was Luther Pelham. Even coming out of the stupor of heavy sleep, Pat realized he was furious.

"Pat, I understand you had a break-in last night. Are you all right?"

She blinked, trying to force the sleep from her eyes and brain. "Yes."

"You made the front page of the *Tribune*. It's quite a caption. 'Anchorwoman's life threatened.' Let me read you the first paragraph:

" 'A break-in at her Georgetown home was the most recent in a series of bizarre threats received by television personality Patricia Traymore. The threats are tied to the documentary program "A Profile of Senator Abigail Jennings," which Miss Traymore will produce and narrate, to be aired next Wednesday night on Potomac Cable Television.'

"That's just the kind of publicity Abigail needs!"

"I'm sorry," Pat stammered. "I tried to keep the reporter away from the note."

"Did it ever occur to you to call *me,* instead of the police? Frankly, I gave you credit for more brains than you displayed last night. We could have had private detectives watch your place. This is probably some harmless nut, but the burning question in Washington will be, Who hates Abigail so much?"

He was right. "I'm sorry," Pat repeated. Then she added, "However, when you realize your home has been broken into, and you're wondering if some nut may be six feet away on the patio, I think it's a fairly normal reaction to call the police."

"There's no use discussing it further until we can assess the damage. Have you reviewed Abigail's films?"

"Yes. I have some excellent material to edit."

"You didn't tell Abigail about being in Apple Junction?"

"No, I didn't."

"Well, if you're smart, you *won't!* That's all she needs to hear now!"

Without saying goodbye, Luther hung up.

It was Arthur's habit to go to the bakery promptly at eight for hot rolls and then pick up the morning paper. Today he reversed the procedure. He was so eager to see if the paper had anything about the break-in that he went to the newsstand first.

There it was, right on the front page. He read the story through, relishing every word, then frowned. Nothing had been said about the Raggedy Ann doll. The doll had been his means of making them understand that violence had been committed in that house and might be again.

He purchased two seeded rolls and walked the three blocks back to the leaning frame house and up to the dreary apartment on the second floor. Only half a mile away King Street had expensive restaurants and shops, but the neighborhood here was run-down and shabby.

The door of Glory's bedroom was open, and he could see she was already dressed in a bright red sweater and jeans. Lately she'd gotten friendly with a girl in her office, a brazen type who was teaching Glory about makeup and had persuaded her to cut her hair.

She did not look up, even though she must have heard him coming in. He sighed. Glory's attitude toward him was becoming distant, even impatient. Like last night when he'd tried to tell her what a hard time old Mrs. Rodriguez had had swallowing her medicine and how he'd had to break up the pill and give her a little bread with it to hide the taste. Glory had interrupted him. "Father, can't we ever talk about anything except the nursing home?" And then she'd gone to a movie with some of the girls from work.

He put the rolls on plates and poured the coffee. "Soup's on," he called.

Glory hurried into the kitchen. She was wearing her coat and her purse was under her arm, as though she couldn't wait to leave.

"Hello," he said softly. "My little girl looks very pretty today."

Gloria didn't smile.

"How was the movie?" he asked.

"It was okay. Look, don't bother getting a roll or bun for me anymore. I'll have mine in the office with the others."

He felt crushed. He liked sharing breakfast with Glory before they left for work.

She must have sensed his disappointment, because she looked right at him and the expression in her eyes softened. "You're so good to me," she said, and her voice sounded a little sad.

For long minutes after she left, he sat staring into space. Last night had been exhausting. After all these years, to have been back in *that* house, in *that* room—to have placed Glory's doll on the exact spot where the child had lain . . . When he'd finished arranging it against the fireplace, the right leg crumpled under it, he had almost expected to turn around and see the bodies of the man and woman lying there again.

CHAPTER 13

After Luther's call, Pat got up, made coffee and began editing the storyboards for the program. She had decided to plan two versions of the documentary, one including an opening segment about Abigail's early life in Apple Junction, the other starting at the wedding reception. The more she thought about it, the more she felt Luther's anger was justified. Abigail was skittish enough about the program without this upsetting publicity. At least I had the sense to hide the doll, she thought.

By nine o'clock she was in the library running off the rest of the films. Luther had already sent over edited segments of the Eleanor Brown case, showing Abigail leaving the courthouse after the Guilty verdict. Her regretful statement: "This is a very sad day for me. I only hope that now Eleanor will have the decency to tell where she has hidden that money. It may have been for my campaign fund, but far more important, it was the donations of people who believed in the goals I embrace."

A reporter asked: "Then, Senator, there is absolutely no truth to Eleanor's insistence that your chauffeur phoned her asking her to look for your diamond ring in the campaign-office safe?"

"My chauffeur was driving me that morning to a meeting in Richmond. The ring was on my finger."

And then the clip showed a picture of Eleanor Brown, a close-up that clearly revealed every feature of her small, colorless face, her timid mouth and shy eyes.

The reel ended with a scene of Abigail addressing college students. Her subject was Public Trust. Her theme was the absolute responsibility of a legislator to keep his or her own office and staff above reproach.

There was another segment Luther had already edited, a compilation of the Senator in airline-safety hearings, with excerpts from her speeches demanding more stringent regulations. Several times she referred to the fact that she had been widowed because her husband had entrusted his life to an inexperienced pilot in an ill-equipped plane.

At the end of each of those segments Luther had marked "*2-minute discussion between Senator J. and Pat T. on subject.*"

Pat bit her lip.

Both those segments were out of sync with what she was trying to do. What happened to my creative control of this project? she wondered. The whole thing is getting too rushed. No, the word is *botched.*

The phone rang as she began to go through Abigail's letters from constituents. It was Sam. "Pat, I read what happened. I've checked with the rental office for my place." Sam lived in the Watergate Towers. "There are several sublets available. I want you to take one on a monthly basis until this character is caught."

"Sam, I can't. You know the kind of pressure I'm under. I have a locksmith coming. The police are going to keep a watch on the place. I have all my equipment set up here.'' She tried to change the subject. ''My real problem is what to wear to the White House dinner.''

''You always look lovely. Abigail is going to be there as well. I bumped into her this morning.''

A short time later, the Senator phoned to express her shock at the break-in. Then she got to the point. ''Unfortunately, the suggestion that you are being threatened because of this program is bound to lead to all sorts of speculation. I really want to get this thing wrapped up, Pat. Obviously, once it's completed and aired, the threats will end even if they are simply from some sort of crank. Have you reviewed the films I gave you?''

''Yes, I have,'' Pat replied. ''There's wonderful material and I've got it marked off. But I'd like to borrow Toby. There are some places where I need names and more specific background.''

They agreed that Toby would come over within the hour. When Pat hung up she had the feeling that in Abigail Jennings' estimation she had become an embarrassment.

Toby arrived forty-five minutes later, his leathery face creased in a smile. ''I wish I'd been here when that joker tried to get in, Pat,'' he told her. ''I'd've made mincemeat of him.''

''I'll bet you would.''

He sat at the library table while she ran the projector. ''That's old Congressman Porter Jennings,'' Toby answered at one point. ''He was the one who said he wouldn't retire if Willard didn't take over his seat. You know that Virginia aristocracy. Think they own the world. But I have to say that he bucked his sister-in-law when he supported Abigail to succeed Willard. Willard's mother, that old she-devil, pulled out all the stops to keep Abigail out of Congress. And between us, she was a lot better Congressman than Willard. He wasn't aggressive enough. You know what I mean?''

While waiting for Toby, Pat had reviewed the newspaper clippings about the Eleanor Brown case. The case seemed almost too simple. Eleanor said that Toby had phoned and sent her to the campaign office. Five thousand dollars of the money had been recovered in her storage area in the basement of her apartment building.

''How do you think Eleanor Brown expected to get away with such a flimsy story?'' Pat now asked Toby.

Toby leaned back in the leather chair, crossing one thick leg over the other, and shrugged. Pat noticed the cigar in his breast pocket. Wincing inwardly, she invited him to smoke.

He beamed, sending his jowly face into a mass of creases. ''Thanks a lot. The Senator can't stand the smell of cigar smoke. I don't dare have even a puff in the car no matter how long I'm waiting for her.''

He lit the cigar and puffed appreciatively.

''About Eleanor Brown,'' Pat suggested. She rested her elbows on her knees, cupping her chin in her hands.

"The way I figure it," Toby confided, "Eleanor didn't think the money would be missed for a while. They've kind of tightened up the law since then, but it really used to be that you could have big money sit in the campaign-office safe for a couple of weeks—even longer."

"But seventy-five thousand dollars in cash?"

"Miss Traymore . . . Pat, you gotta understand how many companies contribute to both sides in a campaign. They want to be sure to be with the winner. Now, of course you can't hand cash to a Senator in the office. *That's* against the law. So what the big shot does is visit the Senator, let him or her know he's planning to make a big donation, and then takes a walk with the Senator's aide on the Capitol grounds and turns over the money there. The Senator never touches it, but *knows* about it. It's put right in the campaign funds. But because it's in cash, if the competition gets elected it isn't so obvious. You know what I mean?"

"I see."

"Don't get me wrong. It's legal. But Phil had taken some big donations for Abigail, and of course Eleanor knew about them. Maybe she had some boyfriend who wanted to make a killing and only borrowed the money. Then when they looked for it so fast, she had to come up with an excuse."

"She just doesn't seem that sophisticated to me," Pat observed, thinking of the high school yearbook picture.

"Well, like the prosecutor said, still water runs deep. I hate to rush you, Pat, but the Senator will be needing me."

"There are just one or two more questions."

The phone rang. "I'll make this fast." Pat picked it up. "Pat Traymore."

"How are you, my dear?" She instantly recognized the precise, overly cultivated voice.

"Hello, Mr. Saunders." Too late she remembered that Toby knew Jeremy Saunders. Toby's head jerked up. Would he associate the name Saunders with the Jeremy Saunders he'd known in Apple Junction?

"I tried to get you several times early last evening." Saunders purred. He was not drunk this time. She was sure of it.

"You didn't leave your name."

"Recorded messages can be heard by the wrong ears. Don't you agree?"

"Just a moment, please." Pat looked at Toby. He was smoking his cigar thoughtfully and seemed indifferent to the call. Maybe he hadn't put together the name Saunders with a man he hadn't seen in thirty-five years.

"Toby, this is a private call. I wonder if . . ."

He stood up quickly before she could finish. "Want me to wait outside?"

"No, Toby. Just hang up when I get to the kitchen extension?" Deliberately she spoke his name again so that Jeremy would hear and not begin talking until he was sure only Pat was on the line.

Toby accepted the receiver casually, but he was certain it was Jeremy Saunders. Why was he calling Pat Traymore? Had she been in touch with him? Abigail would hit the ceiling. From the other end of the phone he heard the faint sound of breathing. That stinking phony, he thought. If he tries to smear Abby . . . !

Pat's voice came on. "Toby, would you mind hanging up?"

"Sure, Pat." He made his voice hearty. He hung up the receiver with a definite click and didn't dare to try to ease it off the hook again.

"*Toby,*" Jeremy Saunders said, his voice incredulous. "Don't tell me you're hobnobbing with Toby Gorgone."

"He's helping me with some of the background material on the program," Pat replied. She kept her voice low.

"Of course. He's been there every step of the way with our stateswoman, hasn't he? Pat, I wanted to call because I realize that the combination of vodka and your sympathy made me rather indiscreet. I do insist that our conversation remain totally confidential. My wife and daughter would not enjoy having the shabby little tale of my involvement with Abigail aired on national television."

"I have no intention of quoting anything you told me," Pat replied. "The *Mirror* might be interested in gossipy personal material, but I assure you, I'm not."

"Very good. I'm greatly relieved." Saunders' voice became friendlier. "I saw Edwin Shepherd at the club. He tells me he gave you a copy of the newspaper showing Abby as the beauty queen. I'd forgotten about that. I do hope you plan to use the picture of Miss Apple Junction with her adoring mother. *That* one's worth a thousand words!"

"I really don't think so," Pat said coldly. His presumption had turned her off. "I'm afraid I'll have to get back to work, Mr. Saunders."

She hung up and went back into the library. Toby was sitting in the chair where she'd left him, but there was something different about him. The genial manner was gone. He seemed distracted and left almost immediately.

After he had gone, she flung open the window to get rid of the cigar smell. But the odor hung in the room. She realized that once again she felt acutely uneasy and jumped at every sound.

Back at the office, Toby went directly to Philip. "How's it going?"

Philip raised his eyes heavenward. "The Senator is in a state about the story. She just gave Luther Pelham hell for ever talking her into that documentary. She'd kill it in a minute if the publicity weren't already out. How did it go with Pat Traymore?"

Toby wasn't ready to talk about Apple Junction, but he did ask Philip to look into the question of the rental of the Adams house, which was also on his mind.

He knocked on the door of Abigail's office. She was quiet now—too quiet. That meant she was worried. She had the afternoon edition of the paper. "Look at this," she told him.

A famous Washington gossip column's lead item began:

> Wags on Capitol Hill are placing bets on the identity of the person who threatened Patricia Traymore's life if she goes ahead with the documentary on Senator Jennings. Seems everyone has a candidate. The beautiful senior Senator from Virginia has a reputation among her colleagues as an abrasive perfectionist.

As Toby watched, Abigail Jennings, her face savage with fury, crumpled the paper in her hand and tossed it into a wastepaper basket.

CHAPTER 14

Sam Kingsley snapped the last stud in his dress shirt and twisted his tie into a bow. He glanced at the clock on the mantel over his bedroom fireplace and decided he had more than enough time for a Scotch and soda.

His Watergate apartment commanded a sweeping view of the Potomac. From the side window of the living room he looked down at the Kennedy Center. Some evenings when he arrived late from the office, he'd go in and catch the second and third acts of a favorite opera.

After Janice died, there'd been no reason to keep the big house in Chevy Chase. Karen was living in San Francisco, and she and her husband spent their holidays with her in-laws in Palm Springs. Sam had given Karen her choice of dishes, silver, bric-a-brac and furniture and sold most of the rest. He had wanted to start with a clean slate in the hope that his pervading sense of weariness might subside.

Sam carried his glass to the window. The Potomac was shimmering from the lights of the apartment building and the floodlights of Kennedy Center. Potomac fever. He had it. So did most of the people who came here. Would Pat catch it as well? he wondered.

He was damn worried about her. His FBI friend Jack Carlson had flatly told him: "First she gets a phone call, then a note under the door, then another phone call and finally a break-in with a warning note left in her home. You figure out what might happen next time.

"You've got a full-blown psycho who's about to explode. That slanted printing is a dead giveaway—and compare these notes. They're written only a few days apart. Some of the letters on the second one are practically illegible. His stress is building to a breaking point. And one way or another, that stress seems to be directed at your Pat Traymore."

His Pat Traymore. In those last months before Janice died, he'd managed to keep Pat from his thoughts. He'd always be grateful for that. He and Janice had managed to recapture something of their early closeness. She had died secure in his love.

Afterward, he had felt drained, exhausted, lifeless, *old.* Too old for a twenty-seven-year-old girl and all that a life with her would involve. He simply wanted peace.

Then he'd read that Pat was coming to work in Washington and he'd decided to phone and invite her to dinner. There was no way he could avoid her, or want to avoid her, and he did not intend their first meeting to be constrained by the presence of others. So he'd asked her out.

He had soon realized that whatever was between them hadn't gone away, but was still simmering, waiting to blaze up—and that was what she wanted.

But what did *he* want?

''I don't know,'' Sam said aloud. Jack's warning rang in his ears: Suppose something happened to Pat?

The house phone rang. ''Your car is here, Congressman,'' the doorman announced.

''Thank you. I'll be right down.''

Sam put his half-empty glass on the bar and went into the bedroom to get his jacket and coat. His movements were brisk. In a few minutes he'd be with Pat.

Pat decided to wear an emerald satin gown with a beaded top to the White House dinner. It was an Oscar de la Renta that Veronica had insisted she purchase for the Boston Symphony Ball. Now she was glad she'd been talked into it. With it she wore her grandmother's emeralds.

''You don't look the part of the girl reporter,'' Sam commented when he picked her up.

''I don't know whether to take that as a compliment.'' Sam was wearing a navy blue cashmere coat and white silk scarf over his dinner jacket. What was it Abigail had called him? One of the most eligible bachelors in Washington?

''It was intended as one. No more phone calls or notes?'' he asked.

''No.'' She had not yet told him about the doll and didn't want to bring it up now.

''Good. I'll feel better when that program is finished.''

''*You'll* feel better.''

In the limousine on the way to the White House, he asked her about her activities.

''Work,'' she said promptly. ''Luther agreed with the film clips I selected and we've completed the storyboard. He's adamant about not crossing the Senator by including her early life. He's turning what's supposed to be a documentary into a paean of praise that's going to be journalistically unsound."

"And you can't do anything about it?"

"I could quit. But I didn't come down here to quit after the first week—not if I can help it."

They were at Eighteenth Street and Pennsylvania Avenue.

"Sam, was there ever a hotel on that corner?"

"Yes, the old Roger Smith. They tore it down about ten years ago."

When I was little I went to a Christmas party there. I wore a red velvet dress and white tights and black patent leather slippers. I spilled chocolate ice cream on the dress and cried and Daddy said, "It's not your fault, Kerry."

The limousine was drawing up to the northwest gate of the White House. They waited in line as each car stopped for the security check. When it was their turn, a respectful guard confirmed their names on the guest list.

Inside, the mansion was festive with holiday decorations. The Marine Band was playing in the marble foyer. Waiters were offering champagne. Pat recognized familiar faces among the assembled guests: film stars, Senators, Cabinet members, socialites, a grande dame of the theater.

"Have you ever been here before?" Sam asked.

"On a school trip when I was sixteen. We took the tour and they told us that Abigail Adams used to hang her wash in what is now the East Room."

"You won't find any laundry there now. Come on. If you're going to have a career in Washington, you'd better get to know some people." A moment later he was introducing her to the President's press secretary.

Brian Salem was an amiable, rotund man. "Are you trying to push us off the front page, Miss Traymore?" he asked, smiling.

So even in the Oval Office the break-in had been discussed.

"Have the police any leads?"

"I'm not sure, but we all think it was just some sort of crank."

Penny Salem was a sharp-eyed wiry woman in her early forties. "God knows Brian sees enough crank letters addressed to the President."

"I sure do," her husband agreed easily. "Anyone in public office is bound to step on toes. The more powerful you are, the madder somebody or some group gets at you. And Abigail Jennings takes positive stands on some mighty volatile issues. Oh, say, there's the lady now." He suddenly grinned. "Doesn't she look great?"

Abigail had just entered the East Room. This was one night she had not chosen to underplay her beauty. She was wearing an apricot satin grown with a bodice covered in pearls. A belled skirt complemented her small waist and slender frame. Her hair was loosely drawn back into a chignon. Soft waves framed her flawless features. Pale blue shadow accentuated the extraordinary eyes, and rose blush highlighted her cheekbones. A deeper apricot shade outlined her perfectly shaped lips.

This was a different Abigail, laughing softly, laying a hand for just an extra moment on the arm of an octogenarian ambassador, accepting the tributes to her appearance as her due. Pat wondered if every other woman in the room felt as she did—suddenly colorless and insignificant.

Abigail had timed her arrival well. An instant later, the music from the Marine Band shifted to a stirring "Hail to the Chief." The President and First Lady were descending from their private quarters. With them were the new Prime Minister of Canada and his wife. As the last notes of "Hail to the Chief" died out, the opening chords of the Canadian national anthem began.

A receiving line was formed. When Pat and Sam approached the President and First Lady, Pat realized that her heart was pounding.

The First Lady was far more attractive in person than in her pictures. She had a long, tranquil face with a generous mouth and pale hazel eyes. Her hair was sandy with traces of gray. There was an air of total self-confidence about her. Her eyes crinkled when she smiled, and her lips parted to reveal strong, perfect teeth. She told Pat that when she was a girl her ambition had been to get a job in television. "And instead"—she laughed, looking up at her husband—"I had no sooner let go of the daisy chain at Vassar than I found myself married."

"I was smart enough to grab her before anyone else did," the President said. "Pat, I'm glad to meet you."

It was a palpable emotion to feel the solid handshake of the most powerful man in the world.

"They're good people," Sam commented as they accepted champagne. "And he's been a strong President. It's hard to believe he's completing his second term. He's young, not sixty yet. It'll be interesting to see what he does with the rest of his life."

Pat was studying the First Lady. "I'd love to do a program on her. She seems comfortable in her own skin."

"Her father was Ambassador to England; her grandfather was Vice President. Generations of breeding and money coupled with a diplomatic background do have a way of instilling self-confidence, Pat."

In the State Dining Room, the tables were set with Limoges china, an intricate green pattern, rimmed with gold. Pale green damask cloths and napkins with centerpieces of red roses and ferns in low crystal containers completed the effect. "Sorry we're not sitting together," Sam commented, "but you seem to have a good table. And please notice where Abigail has been placed."

She was at the President's table between the President and the guest of honor, the Prime Minister of Canada. "I wish I had this on camera," Pat murmured.

She glanced at the first few items on the menu: salmon in aspic, suprême of capon in flamed brandy sauce, wild rice.

Her dinner partner was the Chairman of the Joint Chiefs of Staff. The others at the table included a college president, a Pulitzer Prize-winning playwright, an Episcopal bishop, the director of Lincoln Center.

She glanced around to see where Sam had gone. He was at the President's table directly across from Senator Jennings. They were smiling at each other. With a twinge of pain, Pat looked away.

Near the end of the dinner the President invited everyone to remember in prayer the Vice President, who was so seriously ill. He added, "More than any of us realized, he had been pursuing arduous fourteen-hour days without ever considering the toll they were taking on his health." When the tribute was completed, there was no doubt in anyone's mind that the Vice President would never resume his duties. As he sat down, the President smiled at Abigail. There was something of a public benediction in that glance.

"Well, did you enjoy yourself?" Sam asked on the way home. "That playwright at your table seemed quite taken with you. You danced with him three or four times, didn't you?"

"When you were dancing with the Senator. Sam, wasn't it quite an honor for you to be at the President's table?"

"It's always an honor to be placed there."

An odd constraint came over them. It seemed to Pat that suddenly the evening had gone flat. Was that the true reason Sam had gotten the invitation for her—so that she'd meet Washington people? Did he simply feel he had a certain obligation to help launch her before he withdrew from her life again?

He waited while she unlocked the door, but declined a nightcap. "I've got to get in a long day tomorrow. I'm leaving for Palm Springs on the six-o'clock flight to spend the holiday with Karen and Tom at his family's place. Are you going to Concord for the holiday, Pat?"

She didn't want to tell him that Veronica and Charles had left for a Caribbean cruise. "This will be a working Christmas," she said.

"Let's have a belated celebration after the program is finished. And I'll give you your Christmas present then."

"That'll be fine." She hoped her voice sounded as casually friendly as his. She refused to reveal the emptiness she felt.

"You looked lovely, Pat. You'd be surprised at the number of people I heard commenting about you."

"I hope they were all my own age. Good night, Sam." She pushed the door open and went inside.

"Damn it, Pat!" Sam stepped into the foyer and spun her around. Her jacket fell from her shoulders as he pulled her to him.

Her hands slipped around his neck; her fingertips touched the collar of his coat, found the cool skin above it, twisted his thick, wavy hair. It was as she remembered—the faint good scent of his breath, the feel of his arms enveloping her, the absolute certainty that they belonged together. "Oh, my love," she whispered. "I've missed you so."

It was as if she had slapped him. In an involuntary movement, he straightened up and stepped back. Dumbfounded, Pat dropped her arms.

"Sam . . ."

"Pat, I'm sorry . . ." He tried to smile. "You're just too damn attractive for your own good."

For a long minute they stared at each other. Then Sam grasped her shoulders. "Don't you think I'd like nothing better than to pick up where we left off that day? I'm not going to do it to you, Pat. You're a beautiful young woman. Within six months you'll have your pick of half a dozen men who can give you the kind of life you should have. Pat, my time is past. I damn near lost my seat in the last election. And you know what my opponent said? He said it's time for new blood. Sam Kingsley's been around too long. He's in a rut. Let's give him the rest he needs."

"And you believed it?"

"I believe it because it's true. That last year and a half with Janice left me empty—empty and drained. Pat, it's hard for me to decide where I stand on any issue these days. Choosing what tie to wear is a big effort, for God's sake, but there is one decision I can stick to. I'm not going to foul up your life again."

"Have you ever stopped to think how much you'll foul it up by not coming back into it?"

Unhappily they stared at each other. "I'm simply not going to let myself believe that, Pat." Then he was gone.

CHAPTER 15

Glory was different now. She had begun setting her hair in the morning. She had new clothes, more colorful. The blouses had high ruffled necks instead of button-down collars. And recently she had bought some earrings, a couple of pairs. He'd never seen her wear earrings before.

Every day now she told him not to make her a sandwich for lunch, that she would eat out.

"All by yourself?" he'd asked.

"No, Father."

"With Opal?"

"I'm just eating out"—and there was that unfamiliar note of impatience in her voice.

She didn't want to hear about his work at all anymore. He'd tried a couple of times to tell her how even with the respirator, old Mrs. Gillespie was rasping and coughing and in pain. Glory used to listen so sympathetically when he told her about his patients and agree when he said it would be a mercy if the angels came for the very sick ones. Her agreement helped him carry out his mission.

He'd been so distracted with Glory that when he delivered Mrs. Gillespie to the Lord he'd been careless. He had thought she was asleep, but as he pulled out the respirator plug and prayed over her, she opened her eyes. She had understood what he was doing. Her chin had quivered, and she had whispered, "Please, please oh, . . . sweet Virgin, help me . . ." He'd watched the expression in her eyes change from terrified to glassy to vacant.

And Mrs. Harnick had seen him leaving Mrs. Gillespie's room.

Nurse Sheehan was the one who'd found Mrs. Gillespie. She hadn't accepted the old woman's death as the will of God. Instead she'd insisted that the respirator be checked to make sure it had been functioning properly. Later on he'd seen her with Mrs. Harnick. Mrs. Harnick was very much excited and pointing toward Mrs. Gillespie's room.

Everyone in the Home liked him except Nurse Sheehan. She was always reprimanding him, telling him that he was overstepping. "We have staff chaplains," she would say. "It's not your job to counsel people."

If he'd thought about Nurse Sheehan's being on duty today, he would never have gone near Mrs. Gillespie.

It was his worry over the Senator Jennings documentary that was consuming him, making it impossible for him to think straight. He had warned Patricia Traymore four times that she must not continue to prepare that program.

There would be no fifth warning.

Pat simply wasn't sleepy. After an hour of restless tossing, she gave up and reached for a book. But her mind refused to become involved with the Churchill biography she had been looking forward to reading.

At one o'clock she shut her eyes. At three o'clock she went downstairs to heat a cup of milk. She had left the downstairs foyer light on, but even so, the staircase was dark and she had to reach for the railing where the steps curved.

She used to sit on this step just out of sight of the people in the foyer and watch company come. I had a blue nightgown with flowers on it. I was wearing it that night . . . I had been sitting here and then I was frightened and I went back up to bed. . . .

And then . . . "I don't know," she said aloud. "I don't know."

Even the hot milk did not induce sleep.

At four o'clock she went downstairs again and brought up the nearly completed storyboard.

The program would open with the Senator and Pat in the studio seated in front of an enlarged picture of Abigail and Willard Jennings in their wedding reception line. Mrs. Jennings senior had been edited out of the reel. While the film of the reception ran, the Senator would talk about meeting Willard while she was attending Radcliffe.

At least, that way I get something in about the Northeast, Pat thought.

Then they'd show a montage of Willard's Congressional campaigns with Pat asking about Abigail's growing commitment to politics. Willard's thirty-fifth-birthday party would highlight the pre-Camelot years with the Kennedys.

Then would come the funeral, with Abigail escorted by Jack Kennedy. They'd eliminated the segment that showed her mother-in-law in a separate car. Then Abigail being sworn into Congress in black mourning attire, her face pale and grave.

Next came the footage about the embezzlement of the campaign funds and Abigail's commitment to airline safety. She sounds so strident and sanctimonious, Pat thought, and then you see the picture of that scared kid, Eleanor Brown. And it's one thing to be concerned about airline safety—another to keep pointing the finger at a pilot who also lost his life . . . But she knew she wouldn't be able to persuade Luther to change either segment.

The day after Christmas they would shoot Abigail in her office, with her staff and some carefully selected visitors. Congress had at last adjourned, and the shooting should go quickly.

At least Luther had agreed to a scene of Abigail in her own home with friends. Pat had suggested a Christmas supper party with shots of Abigail arranging the buffet table. The guests would be some distinguished Washington personalities as well as a few of her office staff who could not be with their families on the holiday.

The last scene would be the Senator returning home at dusk, a briefcase under her arm. And then the wrap-up: "Like many of the millions of single adults in the United States, Senator Abigail Jennings has found her family, her vocation, her avocation in the work she loves."

Luther had written that line for Pat to deliver.

At eight o'clock Pat phoned Luther and asked him again to persuade the Senator to allow her early life to be included in the program. "What we have is dull," she said. "Except for those personal films, it's a thirty-minute campaign commercial."

Luther cut her off. "You've examined *all* the film?"

"Yes."

"How about photographs?"

"There were very few."

"Call and see if there are any more. No. I'll call. You're not very high on the Senator's list right now."

Forty-five minutes later she heard from Philip. Toby would be over around noon with photograph albums. The Senator believed Pat would find some interesting pictures in them.

Restlessly Pat wandered into the library. She had jammed the carton with the doll under the library table. She would use this time to go through more of her father's effects.

When she lifted the doll from the carton, she carried it to the window and examined it closely. A skillful pen had shaded the black button eyes, filled in the brows, given the mouth that mournful twist. In the daylight, it seemed even more pathetic. Was it supposed to represent her?

She put it aside and began to unpack the carton: the pictures of her mother and father; the packets of letters and papers; the photo albums. Her hands became soiled and dusty as she sorted the material into piles. Then she sat cross-legged on the carpet and began to go through it.

Loving hands had kept the mementos of Dean Adams' boyhood. Report cards were neatly pasted in sequence. A-pluses, A's. The lowest mark a B-plus.

He had lived on a farm fifty miles from Milwaukee. The house was a medium-sized white frame with a small porch. There were pictures of him with his mother and father. My grandparents, Pat thought. She realized she didn't know their names. The back of one of the pictures was marked *Irene and Wilson with Dean, age 6 months.*

She picked up a packet of letters. The rubber band snapped and they scattered on the carpet. Quickly she gathered and glanced through them. One especially caught her eye.

> *Dear Mom,*
> *Thank you. I guess those are the only words for all the years of sacrifice to put me through college and law school. I know all about the dresses you didn't buy, the outings you never attended with the other ladies in town. Long ago I promised I'd try to be just like Dad. I'll keep that promise. I love you. And remember to go to the doctor please. That cough sounded awfully deep.*
> *Your loving son,*
> *Dean*

An obituary notice for Irene Wagner Adams was beneath the letter. It was dated six months later.

Tears blurred Pat's eyes for the young man who had not been ashamed to express his love for his mother. *She too had experienced that generous love. Her hand in his. Her screaming delight when he came home. Daddy. Daddy. Swung high in the air and tossed up and strong hands catching her. She was riding her tricycle down the driveway . . . her knee scraping along gravel . . . his voice saying, "This won't hurt much, Kerry. We have to make sure it's clean . . . What kind of ice cream should we get? . . ."*

The doorbell rang. Pat swept the pictures and letters together and stood up. Half of them spilled from her arms as she tried to jam them into the carton. The doorbell rang again, this time more insistently. She scrambled to pick up the scattered photos and notes and hide them with the others. She started from the room and realized she'd forgotten to put away the pictures of her parents and the Raggedy Ann doll. Suppose Toby had come in here and seen them! She dropped them into the carton and shoved it under the table.

Toby was about to ring the bell again when she yanked open the door. Involuntarily, she stepped back as his bulky frame filled the doorway.

"I was just giving up on you!" His attempt to sound genial didn't come off.

"Don't give up on me, Toby," she said coldly. Who was he to be annoyed at having to wait a few seconds? He seemed to be studying her. She glanced down and realized how grimy her hands were and that she had been rubbing her eyes. Her face was probably smeared with dirt.

"You look like you were making mud pies." There was a puzzled, suspicious expression on his face. She didn't answer him. He shifted the package under his arm, and the oversized onyx ring moved back and forth on his finger. "Where do you want this stuff, Pat? In the library?"

"Yes."

He followed her so closely that she had the uneasy feeling he would crash into her if she stopped suddenly. Sitting cross-legged for so long had made her right leg numb, and she was favoring it.

"You limping, Pat? You didn't fall on the ice or anything, did you?"

You don't miss a trick, she thought. "Put the box on the table," she told him.

"Okay. I gotta get right back. The Senator wasn't happy about having to figure out where these albums were. I can see myself out."

She waited until she heard the front door close before she went to secure the bolt. As she reached the foyer, the door opened again. Toby seemed startled to see her standing there; then his face creased in an unpleasant smile. "That lock wouldn't keep out anyone who knew his way around, Pat," he said. "Be sure to use the dead bolt."

The Senator's additional material was a hodgepodge of newspaper clippings and fan letters. Most of the pictures were shots of her at political ceremonies, state dinners, ribbon-cutting ceremonies, inaugurations. As Pat turned the pages, several of them fluttered down to the floor.

The back pages of the album were more promising. She came upon an enlarged photo of a young Abigail and Willard seated on a blanket near a lake. He was reading to her. It was an idyllic setting; they looked like lovers on a Victorian cameo.

There were a few more snapshots that might fit into a montage. At last she had gone through everything and bent down to retrieve the pictures that had fallen. Underneath one of them was a folded sheet of expensive notepaper. She opened it. It read:

Billy darling. You were splendid in the hearings this afternoon. I am so proud of you. I love you so and look forward to a lifetime of being with you, of working with you. Oh, my dearest we really are going to make a difference in this world.
A.

The letter was dated May 13. Willard Jennings had been on his way to deliver the commencement address when he met his death on May 20.

What a terrific wrap-up that would make! Pat exulted. It would quiet anyone who thinks of the Senator as cold and uncaring. If she could only persuade Luther to let her read the note on the program. How would it sound? "Billy darling," she read aloud. "I'm so sorry . . ."

Her voice broke. What is the matter with me? she thought impatiently. Firmly, she began again. "Billy darling. You were splendid. . . ."

CHAPTER 16

On the twenty-third of December at 2 P.M. Senator Abigail Jennings sat in the library of her home with Toby and Philip and watched the telecast as the Vice President of the United States formally tendered his resignation to the Chief Executive.

Her lips dry, her fingernails digging into her palms, Abigail listened as the Vice President, propped on pillows in his hospital bed, ashen-faced and obviously dying, said in a surprisingly strong voice, "I had expected to withhold my decision until after the first of the year. However, I feel that it is my clear duty to vacate this office and have the line of succession to Chief Executive of this great country uncompromised. I am grateful for the confidence the President and my party expressed when I was twice chosen to be the Vice Presidential candidate. I am grateful to the people of the United States for having given me the opportunity to serve them."

With profound regret, the President accepted the resignation of his old friend and colleague. When asked if he had decided on a replacement, he said, "I have a few ideas." But he declined to respond to the names suggested by the press.

Toby whistled. "Well, it's happened, Abby."

"Senator, mark my words . . ." Philip began.

"Be quiet and listen!" she snapped. As the scene in the hospital room ended, the camera focused on Luther Pelham in the newsroom of Potomac Cable.

"A historic moment," Luther began. With dignified reticence he recounted a brief history of the Vice Presidency and then came to the point.

"The time has come for a woman to be selected for the high office . . . a woman with the necessary experience and proved expertise. Mr. President, choose *her* now."

Abigail laughed sharply. "Meaning me."

The phone began to ring. "That will be reporters. I'm not in," she said.

An hour later the press was still camped outside Abigail's home. Finally she agreed to an interview. Outwardly she was calm. She said that she was busy with preparations for a Christmas supper for friends. When asked if she expected to be appointed Vice President, she said in an amused tone, "Now, you really can't expect me to comment on that."

Once the door closed behind her, her expression and manner changed. Even Toby did not dare to cross the line.

Luther phoned to confirm the taping schedule. Abigail's raised voice could be heard throughout the house. "Yes, I saw it. You want to know something? I probably have this in the bag right now, without that damn program hanging over my head. I told you it was a rotten idea. Don't tell *me* you only wanted to help me. You wanted to have me obligated to you, and we both know it."

Abigail's voice lowered, and Philip exchanged glances with Toby. "What did you find out?" he asked.

"Pat Traymore was up in Apple Junction last week. She stopped at the newspaper office and got some back issues. She visited Saunders, the guy who was sweet on Abby when she was a kid. He talked his head off to her. Then she saw the retired school principal who knew Abby. I was at Pat's house in Georgetown when Saunders phoned her."

"How much damage could any of those people do to the Senator?" Philip asked.

Toby shrugged. "It depends. Did you find out anything about the house?"

"Some," Philip told him. "We got to the realty company that has been renting it for years. They had a new tenant all lined up, but the bank handling the trust for the heirs said that someone in the family was planning to use it and it wouldn't be for rent again."

"Someone *in* the family?" Toby repeated. "*Who in* the family?"

"I would guess Pat Traymore," Philip said sarcastically.

"Don't get smart with me," Toby snapped. "I want to know *who* owns that place now, and *which* relative is using it."

With mixed emotions Pat watched Potomac Cable cover the Vice President's resignation. At the end of Luther's segment, the anchorman said that it was considered unlikely the President would name a successor before the New Year.

And we air the program on the twenty-seventh, Pat thought.

As Sam had predicted the first night she was in Washington, she might have a hand in the selection of the first woman Vice President.

Once again her sleep had been interrupted by troubled dreams. Did she really remember her mother and father so clearly, or was she confusing the films and pictures she had seen of them with reality? The memory of his bandaging her knee and taking her for ice cream was authentic. She was sure of that. But hadn't there also been times when she had pulled the pillow over her ears because of angry voices and hysterical weeping?

She was determined to finish reviewing her father's effects.

Doggedly she had examined the material and found herself increasingly concerned about the references to her mother. There were letters from her grandmother to Renée. One of them, dated six months before the tragedy, said: "*Renée, dear, the tone of your note troubles me. If you feel you are having onslaughts of depression again, please go into counseling immediately.*"

It had been her grandmother, according to the newspaper articles, who had claimed that Dean Adams was an unstable personality.

She found a letter from her father to her mother written the year before their deaths:

> *Dear Renée,*
> *I am pretty upset that you want to spend the entire summer in New Hampshire with Kerry. You must know how much I miss you both. It is absolutely necessary for me to go to Wisconsin. Why not give it a try? We can rent a Steinway for you while you're there. I certainly understand that Mother's old spinet is hardly appropriate. Please, dear. For my sake.*

Pat felt as though she were trying to remove bandages from a festering wound. The nearer she got to the wound itself, the harder it was to pull the adhesive from it. The sense of pain, emotional and even physical, was increasingly acute.

One of the cartons was filled with Christmas ornaments and strings of lights. They gave her an idea. She would get a small Christmas tree. Why not? Where were Veronica and Charles now? She consulted their itinerary. Their ship would be putting in at St. John tomorrow. She wondered if she could phone them on Christmas Day.

The mail was a welcome respite. She had an abundance of cards and invitations from her friends in Boston. "*Come up just for the day if you possibly can.*" "*We're all waiting for the program.*" "*An Emmy for this one, Pat—not just the nomination.*"

One letter had been forwarded from Boston Cable. The return-address sticker on the envelope read: CATHERINE GRANEY, 22 BALSAM PLACE, RICHMOND, VA.

Graney, Pat thought. That was the name of the pilot who died with Willard Jennings.

The letter was brief:

Dear Miss Traymore:
I have read that you are planning to prepare and narrate a program about Senator Abigail Jennings. As one who has had the opportunity to appreciate several of your fine documentaries, I feel it imperative to notify you that the program about Senator Abigail Jennings may become the subject of a lawsuit. I warn you, do not give the Senator the opportunity to discuss Willard Jennings' death. For your own sake, don't let her assert that pilot error cost her husband his life. That pilot, my husband, died too. And believe me, it is a bitter joke that she dares to affect the pose of a bereaved widow. If you wish to speak with me, you may call me at this number: 804-555-6841.

Pat went to the phone and dialed the number. It rang many times. She was about to hang up when she heard a hurried hello. It was Catherine Graney. The background was noisy, as though a crowd of people were there. Pat tried to make an appointment. ''It will have to be tomorrow,'' the woman told her. ''I run an antiques shop, and I'm having a sale today.''

They agreed on a time, and she hurriedly gave Pat directions.

That afternoon Pat went shopping. Her first stop was an art shop. She left for reframing one of the old sailing prints that had come from her father's office. It would be her Christmas present to Sam.

''Have it for you in a week, Miss. That's a fine print. Worth some money if you ever want to sell it.''

''I don't want to sell it.''

She stopped in the specialty market near the house and ordered groceries, including a small turkey. At the florist's she bought two poinsettias and a garland of evergreen for the mantel. She found a Christmas tree that stood as high as her shoulders. The pick of the trees was gone, but this one was well enough shaped and the pine needles had a luxurious sheen.

By early evening she had finished decorating. The tree was set near the patio doors. The mantel was draped with evergreen. One poinsettia was on the low round table next to the couch, the other on the cocktail table in front of the love seat.

She had hung all the paintings. She had had to guess at placing them, but even so, the living room was now complete. A fire, she thought. There was always a fire.

She laid one, ignited the papers and kindling, and positioned the screen. Then she fixed an omelette and salad and brought the tray to the living room. Tonight she would simply watch television and relax. She felt she had been pushing too hard, that she should let memory unfold in its own way. She had expected this room to be repugnant to her, but despite the terror of that last night, she found it warm and peaceful. Did it harbor happy memories as well?

She turned on the set. The President and First Lady flashed on the screen. They were boarding *Air Force One* en route to their family home for Christmas. Once again the President was being badgered about his choice. "I'll tell you who she or he is by the New Year," he called. "Merry Christmas."

She. Had that been a deliberate slip? Of course not.

Sam phoned a few minutes later. "Pat, how is it going?"

She wished her mouth would not go dry at the sound of his voice. "Fine. Did you see the President on TV just now?"

"Yes, I did. Well, we're surely down to two people. He's committed himself to selecting a woman. I'm going to give Abigail a call. She must be chewing her nails."

Pat raised her eyebrows. "I would be, in her place." She twisted the tassel of her belt. "How's the weather?"

"It's hot as hell. Frankly, I prefer Christmas in a winter setting."

"Then you shouldn't have left. I was trooping around buying a Christmas tree and it was cold enough."

"What are your plans for Christmas Day? Will you be at Abigail's for the supper party?"

"Yes. I'm surprised you weren't invited."

"I was. Pat, it's good to be with Karen and Tom, but—well, this is Karen's family now, not mine. I had to bite my tongue at lunch not to tell off some pompous ass who had a laundry list of all the mistakes this Administration has made."

Pat couldn't resist. "Isn't Tom's mother fixing you up with her available friends or cousins or whatever?"

Sam laughed. "I'm afraid so. I'm not staying till New Year's. I'll be back a few days after Christmas. You haven't had any more threats, have you?"

"Not even one breathless phone call. I miss you, Sam," she added deliberately.

There was a pause. She could imagine his expression—worried, trying to find the right phrase. You care every bit as much about me as you did two years ago, she thought.

"Sam?"

His voice was constrained. "I miss you, too, Pat. You've very important to me."

What a fantastic way to put it. "And you're one of my very dearest friends."

Without waiting for his response, she hung up.

CHAPTER 17

"Father, have you seen my Raggedy Ann doll?"

He smiled at Glory, hoping he didn't look nervous. "No, of course I haven't seen it. Didn't you have it in the closet in your bedroom?"

"Yes. I can't imagine . . . Father, are you sure you didn't throw it away?"

"Why would I throw it away?"

"I don't know." She got up from the table. "I'm going to do a little Christmas shopping. I won't be late." She looked worried, then asked. "Father, are you starting to feel sick again? You've been talking in your sleep the last few nights. I could hear you from my room. Is anything worrying you? You're not hearing those voices again, are you?"

He saw the fear in her eyes. He never should have told Glory about the voices. She hadn't understood. Worse, she had started to be nervous around him. "Oh, no. I was joking when I told you about them." He was sure she didn't believe him.

She put her hand on his arm. "You kept saying Mrs. Gillespie's name in your sleep. Isn't she the woman who just died in the nursing home?"

After Glory went out, Arthur sat at the kitchen table, his thin legs wound around the rungs of the chair, thinking. Nurse Sheehan and the doctors had questioned him about Mrs. Gillespie: had he looked in on her?

"Yes," he'd admitted. "I just wanted to see if she was comfortable."

"How many times did you look in on her?"

"Once. She was asleep. She was fine."

"Mrs. Harnick and Mrs. Drury both thought they saw you. But Mrs. Drury said it was at five after three, and Mrs. Harnick was sure it was later."

"Mrs. Harnick is wrong. I only stopped in once."

They had to believe him. Half the time Mrs. Harnick was almost senile. *But the rest of the time she was very sharp.*

He suddenly picked up the newspaper again. He'd taken the Metro home. An old woman carrying a shopping bag and leaning on a cane had been on the platform. He'd been about to go over and offer to help her with her bag when the express roared into the station. The crowd had surged forward and a young fellow, his arms filled with schoolbooks, had nearly knocked the old lady over as he rushed to get a seat.

He recalled how he had helped her into the train just before the doors closed. "Are you all right?" he had asked.

"Oh, yes. My, I was afraid I'd fall. Young people are so careless. Not like in my day."

"They are cruel," he said softly.

The young man got off at Dupont Circle and crossed the platform. He had followed him, managed to get next to him as he stood at the front of the crowd, right at the edge of the platform. As the train approached he had stepped behind him and jostled his arm so that one of the books began to slip. The young man grabbed for it. Off-balance as he was, it was easy to push him forward. The book and the young man landed on the tracks together.

The newspaper. Yes, here it was on page three: NINETEEN-YEAR-OLD STUDENT KILLED BY METRO. The account called the death an accident. A bystander had seen a book slip from the student's arm. He had bent forward to retrieve it and lost his balance.

The coffee cup in Arthur's hands had grown cold. He would make a fresh cup, then get to work.

There were so many helpless old people in the nursing home waiting for his attention. His mind had been on Patricia Traymore. That was why he hadn't been more careful about Mrs. Gillespie. Tomorrow he'd tell Glory he had to work late and he'd go back to Patricia Traymore's house.

He had to get in again.

Glory wanted her doll back.

At ten o'clock on the twenty-fourth Pat set off for Richmond. The sun had come out strong and golden, but the air was still very cold. It would be a frosty Christmas.

After leaving the highway she took three wrong turns and became thoroughly exasperated with herself. At last she found Balsam Place. It was a street of comfortable medium-sized Tudor-style houses. Number 22 was larger than its neighbors and had a carved sign ANTIQUES on the lawn.

Catherine Graney was waiting in the doorway. She was about fifty, with a square face, deep-set blue eyes and a sturdy, slim body. Her graying hair was straight and blunt-cut. She shook Pat's hand warmly. "I feel as though I know you. I go on buying trips to New England fairly often, and whenever I got the chance I watched your program."

The downstairs was used as a showroom. Chairs, couches, vases, lamps, paintings, Oriental carpets, china and fine glassware were all marked with tags. A Queen Anne breakfront held delicate figurines. A sleepy Irish setter, his dark red hair generously sprinkled with gray, was asleep in front of it.

"I live upstairs," Mrs. Graney explained. "Technically the shop is closed, but someone phoned and asked if she could stop in for a last-minute gift. You will have coffee, won't you?"

Pat took off her coat. She looked around, studying the contents of the room. "You have beautiful things."

"I like to think so," Mrs. Graney looked pleased. "I love searching out antiques and restoring them. My workshop is in the garage." She poured coffee from a Sheffield pot and handed a cup to Pat. "And I have the pleasure of being surrounded by beautiful things. With that auburn hair and gold blouse, you look as though you belong on that Chippendale couch.''

''Thank you.'' Pat realized she liked this outspoken woman. There was something direct and honest about her. It made it possible to get right to the point of the visit. ''Mrs. Graney, you can understand that your letter was quite startling. But will you tell me why you didn't contact the network directly, instead of writing to me?''

Catherine Graney took a sip of coffee. ''As I told you, I've seen a number of your documentaries. I sense integrity in your work, and I didn't think you would willingly help to perpetuate a lie. That's why I'm appealing to you to make sure that George Graney's name is not mentioned on the Jennings program, and that Abigail Jennings does not refer to 'pilot error' in connection with Willard's death. My husband could fly anything that had wings.''

Pat thought of the already-edited segments for the program. The Senator had denounced the pilot—but had she actually mentioned his name? Pat wasn't sure. But she did remember some of the details of the accident. ''Didn't the investigation findings indicate that your husband was flying too low?'' she asked.

''The *plane* was flying too low and went into the mountain. When Abigail Jennings started using that crash as a means for getting her name in the paper as a spokesperson for airline safety regulations, I should have objected immediately.''

Pat watched as the Irish setter, seeming to sense the tension in his mistress' voice, got up, stretched, ambled across the room and settled at her feet. Catherine leaned over and patted him.

''Why *didn't* you speak up immediately?''

''Many reasons. I had a baby a few weeks after the accident. And I suppose I wanted to be considerate of Willard's mother.''

''Willard's mother?''

''Yes. You see, George used to fly Willard Jennings quite often. They became good friends. Old Mrs. Jennings knew that, and she came to me after the crash had been sighted—to *me,* not to her daughter-in-law—and we sat together and waited for the final word. She put a very generous sum of money in trust for my son's education. I didn't want to make her unhappy by using the weapon I could have used against Abigail Jennings. We both had our suspicions, but to her, scandal was anathema.''

Three grandfather clocks simultaneously chimed the hour. It was one o'clock. The sun streamed into the room. Pat noticed that Catherine Graney twisted her gold wedding band as she spoke. Apparently, she had never remarried. ''What weapon could you have used?'' she asked.

''I could have destroyed Abigail's credibility. Willard was miserably unhappy with her and with politics. The day he died he was planning to announce that he was not seeking reelection and that he was accepting the presidency of a college. He wanted the academic life. The last morning he and Abigail had a terrible fight at the airport. She pleaded with him not to announce his resignation. And he told her, right in front of George and me—'Abigail, it won't make a damn bit of difference to you. We're finished.' "

"Abigail and Willard Jennings were on the verge of *divorce?*"

"This 'noble widow' business has always been a posture. My son, George Graney, Junior, is an Air Force pilot now. He never knew his dad. But I'm not going to have him embarrassed by any more of her lies. And whether I win the suit or not, I'll make the whole world realize what a phony she's always been."

Pat tried to choose her words carefully. "Mrs. Graney, I will certainly do what I can to see that your husband isn't referred to in a derogatory way. But I must tell you, I've been going through the Senator's private files and everything I see suggests that Abigail and Willard Jennings were very much in love."

Catherine Graney looked scornful. "I'd like to see the expression on old Mrs. Jennings' face if she ever heard *that!* Tell you what: on your way back, drive an extra mile and pass Hillcrest. That's the Jennings estate. And imagine how strongly a woman must have felt not to leave it—or one red cent—to her own daughter-in-law."

Fifteen minutes later, Pat was looking through high iron gates at the lovely mansion set on the crest of the snow-covered grounds. As Willard's widow, Abigail had had every right to think she might inherit this estate as well as his seat in Congress. As his divorced wife, on the other hand, she would have been the outcast once again. If Catherine Graney was to be believed, the tragedy Abigail spoke so movingly about had, in fact, been the stroke of fortune that twenty-five years ago saved her from oblivion.

CHAPTER 18

"It looks good, Abby," Toby said genially.

"It should photograph well," she agreed. They were admiring the Christmas tree in Abigail's living room. The dining-room table was already set for the Christmas buffet.

"There are bound to be reporters hanging around tomorrow morning," she said. "Find out what time the early services are at the Cathedral. I should be seen there."

She didn't plan to leave a stone unturned. Ever since the President had said, "I'll announce *her,*" Abigail had been sick with nervousness.

"I'm the better candidate," she'd said a dozen times. "Claire is from his own region. That's not good. If only we weren't involved with the damn program.''

''It might help you,'' he said soothingly, though secretly he was as worried as she.

''Toby, it might help if I were running for elective office in a big field of candidates. But I don't think the President is going to see the damn thing and jump up and say '*She's* for me.' But he just might wait to see if there's negative reaction to it before he announces his decision.''

He knew she was right. ''Don't worry. Anyway, you can't pull out. The program's already in the listings.''

She'd carefully selected the guests for the Christmas buffet supper. Among them she had two Senators, three Congressmen, a Supreme Court Justice and Luther Pelham. ''I only wish Sam Kingsley weren't in California,'' she said.

By six o'clock, everything had been arranged. Abby had a goose cooking in the oven. She would serve it cold at the supper the next day. The warm, rich smell filled the house. It reminded Toby of being in the kitchen of the Saunders house when they were high school kids. That kitchen always smelled of good food roasting or baking. Francey Foster had been some cook. You had to give her that!

''Well, I guess I'll be on my way, Abby.''

''Got a heavy date, Toby?''

''Not too heavy.'' The Steakburger waitress was beginning to bore him. Eventually they all did.

''I'll see you in the morning. Pick me up early.''

''Right, Senator. Sleep well. You want to look your best tomorrow.''

Toby left Abby fussing with some strands of tinsel that weren't hanging straight. He went back to his apartment, showered and put on slacks, a textured shirt and a sports jacket. The Steakburger kid had pretty definitely told him she didn't plan to cook tonight. He would take her out for a change and then they'd go back to her apartment for a nightcap.

Toby didn't enjoy spending his money on food—not when the ponies were so interesting. He pulled on his dark green knitted tie and was looking at himself in the mirror when the phone rang. It was Abby.

''Go out and get me a copy of *The National Mirror,*'' she demanded.

''The *Mirror?*''

''You heard me—go out and get it. Philip just phoned. Miss Apple Junction and her elegant mother are on the front page. Who dug out that picture? Who?''

Toby gripped the phone. Pat Traymore had been in the newspaper office at Apple Junction. Jeremy Saunders had phoned Pat Traymore. ''Senator, if someone is trying to put the screws on you, I'll make mincemeat of them.''

* * *

Pat was home by three-thirty and looked forward to an hour's nap. As usual, the extra exertion of standing and climbing to hang the pictures the night before had taken its toll on her leg. The dull, steady ache had been persistent during the drive from Richmond. But she'd scarcely entered the house when the phone rang. It was Lila Thatcher.

"I'm so glad I've caught you, Pat. I've been watching for you. Are you free this evening?"

"As a matter of fact . . ." Caught off guard, Pat could not think of a reasonable excuse. You can't lie easily to a psychic, she thought.

Lila interrupted. "*Don't* be busy. The Ambassador is having people in for his usual Christmas Eve supper and I phoned and told him I'd like to bring you. After all, you are one of his neighbors now. He'd be delighted."

The octogenarian retired Ambassador was perhaps the most distinguished elder statesman of the District. Few world leaders visiting Washington failed to stop at the Ambassador's home.

"I'd love to go," Pat said warmly. "Thank you for thinking of me."

When she hung up, Pat went up to the bedroom. The guests at the Ambassador's home would be a dressy crowd. She decided to wear a black velvet suit with sable-banded cuffs.

She still had time to soak in a hot tub for fifteen minutes and then to take a nap.

As she lay back in the tub, Pat noticed that a corner of the bland beige wallpaper was peeling. A swatch of Wedgwood blue could be seen underneath. Reaching up, she peeled back a large piece of the top layer of paper.

That was what she remembered—that lovely violet and Wedgwood blue. *And the bed had an ivory satin quilted spread,* she thought, *and we had a blue carpet on the floor.*

Mechanically she dried herself and pulled on a terry-cloth caftan. The bedroom was cool and already filled with late-afternoon shadows.

As a precaution, she set the alarm for four-thirty before drifting off to sleep.

The angry voices . . . the blankets pulled over her head . . . the loud noise . . . another loud noise . . . her bare feet silent on the stairs . . .

The insistent pealing of the alarm woke her. She rubbed her forehead trying to recall the shadowy dream. Had the wallpaper triggered something in her head? Oh, God, if only she hadn't set the alarm.

But it's coming closer, she thought. The truth comes closer each time. . . .

Slowly she got up and went to the vanity in the dressing room. Her face was strained and pale. A creaking sound down the hallway made her whirl around, her hand at her throat. But of course, it was just the house settling.

Promptly at five, Lila Thatcher rang the bell. She stood framed in the doorway, almost elfin with her rosy cheeks and white hair. She looked festive in an Autumn Haze mink coat with a Christmas corsage pinned on the wide collar.

"Have we time for a glass of sherry?" Pat asked.

"I think so." Lila glanced at the slender Carrara marble table and matching marble-framed mirror in the foyer. "I always loved those pieces. I'm glad to see them back."

"You know." It was a statement. "I thought so the other night."

She had set out a decanter of sherry and a plate of sweet biscuits on the cocktail table. Lila paused at the doorway of the living room. "Yes," she said, "you've done a very good job. Of course, it's been so long, but it is as I remember it. That wonderful carpet; that couch. Even the paintings," she murmured. "No wonder I've been troubled. Pat, are you sure this is wise?"

They sat down and Pat poured the sherry. "I don't know if it's wise. I *do* know it's necessary."

"How much do you remember?"

"Bits. Pieces. Nothing that hangs together."

"I used to call the hospital to inquire about you. You were unconscious for months. When you were moved, we were given to understand that if you did pull through, you'd be permanently damaged. And then the death notice appeared."

"Veronica . . . my mother's sister and her husband adopted me. My grandmother didn't want the scandal following me . . . or them."

"And that's why they changed your first name as well?"

"My name is Patricia Kerry. I gather the Kerry was my father's idea. Patricia was my grandmother's name. They decided that as long as they were changing my last name they might as well start using my real first name too."

"So Kerry Adams became Patricia Traymore. What are you hoping to find here?" Lila took a sip of sherry and set down the glass.

Restlessly Pat got up and walked over to the piano. In a reflex action she reached toward the keyboard, then pulled her hands back.

Lila was watching her. "You play?"

"Only for pleasure."

"Your mother played constantly. You *know* that."

"Yes. Veronica has told me about her. You see, at first I only wanted to understand what happened here. Then I realized that ever since I can remember I've hated my father; hated him for hurting me so, for robbing me of my mother. I think I hoped to find some indication that he was sick, falling apart—I don't know what. But now, as I begin to remember little things, I realize it's more than that. I'm not the same person I would have become if . . ."

She gestured at the area where the bodies had been found. ". . . if all this hadn't happened. I need to link the child I was with the person I am. I've lost some part of myself back there. I have so many preconceived ideas—my mother was an angel, my father a devil. Veronica hinted that my father destroyed my mother's musical career and then her life. But what about *him?* She married a politician and then refused to share his life. Was that fair? How much was I a catalyst of the trouble between them? Veronica told me once that this house was *too small.* When my mother tried to practice, I'd wake up and start crying."

"Catalyst," Lila said. "That's exactly what I'm afraid you are, Pat. You're setting things in motion that are best left alone." She studied her. "You seem to have recovered very well from your injuries."

"It took a long time. When I finally regained consciousness, I had to be taught everything all over again. I didn't understand words. I didn't know how to use a fork. I wore the brace on my leg till I was seven."

Lila realized she was very warm. Only a moment before she'd felt cool. She didn't want to examine the reason for the change. She knew only that this room had not yet completed its scenario of tragedy. She stood up. "We'd better not keep the Ambassador waiting," she said briskly.

She could see in Pat's face the cheekbones and sensitive mouth of Renée, the wide-spaced eyes and auburn hair of Dean.

"All right, Lila, you've studied me long enough," Pat said, "Which one of them do I resemble?"

"Both," Lila said honestly, "but I think you are more like your father."

"Not in every way, please, God." Pat's attempt at a smile was a forlorn failure.

CHAPTER 19

Well-hidden in the shadows of the trees and shrubs, Arthur observed Pat and Lila through the patio doors. He had been bitterly disappointed to see the lighted house, the car in the driveway. Maybe he wouldn't be able to search for the doll tonight. And he desperately wanted Glory to have it in time for Christmas. He tried to hear what the women were saying but could not catch more than an occasional word. They were both dressed up. Could they be going out? He decided to wait. Avidly he studied Patricia Traymore's face. She was so serious, her expression so troubled. Had she begun to heed his warnings? For her sake he hoped so.

He had been watching only a few minutes when they stood up. They *were* going out. Silently he crept along the side of the house and in a moment heard the sound of the front door opening. They did not take the car. They could not be going too far, maybe to a neighbor's house or a nearby restaurant. He would have to hurry.

Quickly he made his way back to the patio. Patricia Traymore had left the living-room lights on and he could see the strong new locks on the French doors. Even if he cut a pane he would not be able to get in. He had anticipated that and had planned what he would do. There was an elm tree next to the patio, one that would be easy to climb. A thick branch ran just under an upstairs window.

The night he left the doll he'd noticed that window was not completely closed at the top. It sagged as though it didn't hang properly. It would be easy to force it open.

A few minutes later he was stepping over the sill onto the floor. He listened intently. The room had a hollow feeling. Cautiously he turned on his flashlight. The room was empty and he opened the door to the hallway. He was sure he was alone in the house. Where should he begin searching?

He'd gone to so much trouble because of the doll. He'd almost been caught taking the vial of blood from the lab in the nursing home. He'd forgotten how much Glory loved her doll, how when he'd tiptoe into her room just to see if she was sleeping peacefully, she'd always had the doll clutched in her arms.

It was incredible to him that for the second time in a week he was inside this house again. The memory of that long ago morning was still so vivid: the ambulance, lights flashing, sirens blazing, tires screeching in the driveway. The sidewalk crowded with people, neighbors with coats thrown over expensive bathrobes; police cars barricading N Street; cops everywhere. A woman screaming. She was the housekeeper who'd found the bodies.

He and his fellow ambulance attendant from Georgetown Hospital had rushed into the house. A young cop was on guard at the door. "Don't hurry. They don't need you."

The man lying on his back, the bullet in his temple, must have died instantly. The gun was between him and the woman. She had pitched forward and the blood from the chest wound stained the rug around her. Her eyes were still open, staring, unfocused, as though she'd wondered what had happened, how it had happened. She couldn't have been more than thirty. Her dark hair was scattered over her shoulders. Her thin face had delicate nostrils and high cheekbones. A yellow silk robe billowed around her like an evening gown.

He'd been the first to bend over the little girl. Her red hair was so matted with dried blood it had turned auburn; her right leg was jutting from the flowered nightdress, the bone sticking up in a pyramid.

He'd bent closer. "Alive," he'd whispered. Bedlam. I.V. hooked up. They'd hung a bottle of O negative; clamped an oxygen mask on the small, still face; splinted the shattered leg. He'd helped swathe the head, his fingers soothing her forehead, her hair curling around his fingers. Someone said her name was Kerry. "If it is God's will, I'll save you, Kerry," he'd whispered.

"She can't make it," the intern told him roughly, and pushed him out of the way. The police photographers snapped pictures of the little girl; of the corpses. Chalk marks on the carpet outlined the positions of the bodies.

Even then he'd felt the house was a place of sin and evil, a place where two innocent flowers, a young woman and her little girl, had been willfully violated. He'd pointed out the house to Glory once and told her all about that morning.

Little Kerry had remained in an intensive-care unit at Georgetown Hospital for two months. He'd looked in on her as often as he could. She never woke up, just lay there, a sleeping doll. He had come to understand that she was not supposed to live and had tried to find a way to deliver her to the Lord. But before he could act, she was moved to a long-term-care facility near Boston, and after a while he read that she'd died.

His sister had had a doll. "Let me help take care of it," he'd pleaded. "We'll pretend it's sick and I'll make it well." His father's heavy, callused hand had slammed his face. Blood had gushed from his nose. "Make that *well, you sissy."*

He began to search for Glory's doll in Patricia Traymore's bedroom. Opening the closet, he examined the shelves and the floor, but it wasn't there. With sullen anger he observed the many expensive clothes. Silk blouses, and negligées, and gowns, and the kind of suits you see in magazine ads. Glory wore jeans and sweaters most of the time, and she bought them at K-Mart. The people in the nursing home were usually in flannel nightgowns and oversized robes that swaddled their shapeless bodies. One of Patricia Traymore's robes startled him. It was a brown wool tunic with a corded belt. It reminded him of a monk's habit. He took it out of the closet and held it against him. Next he investigated the deep bottom drawers of the dresser. The doll wasn't there either. If the doll was still in the house it was not in her bedroom. He couldn't waste so much time. He glanced into the closets of the empty bedrooms and went downstairs.

Patricia Traymore had left the vestibule light on, as well as a lamp in the library and others in the living room—she had even left on the lights on the Christmas tree. She was sinfully wasteful, he thought angrily. It was unfair to use so much energy, when old people couldn't even afford to heat their own homes. And the tree was already dry. *If a flame touched it, it would ignite and the branches would crackle and the ornaments melt.*

One of the ornaments had fallen from the tree. He picked it up and replaced it. There was really no hiding place in the living room.

The library was the last room he searched. The files were locked—that's where she had probably put it. Then he noticed the carton jammed far back under the library table. And somehow he *knew.* He had to tug hard to get the carton out but when he opened it his heart beat joyfully. There was Glory's precious doll.

The apron was gone, but he couldn't waste time looking for it. He walked through all the rooms, carefully examining them for signs of his presence. He hadn't turned a light on or off or touched a door. He had plenty of experience from his work in the nursing home. Of course if Patricia Traymore looked for the doll, she'd know that someone had come in. But that carton was pushed far under the table. Maybe she wouldn't miss the doll for a while.

He would go out the same way he'd come in—from the second story bedroom window. Patricia Traymore didn't use that bedroom; she probably didn't even glance in it for days at a time.

He had entered the house at five-fifteen. The chimes of the church near the college tolled six as he slid down the tree, made his furtive way through the yard and disappeared into the night.

The Ambassador's house was immense. Stark white walls provided a vivid backdrop for his magnificent art collection. Comfortable, richly upholstered couches and antique Georgian tables caught Pat's eye. A huge Christmas tree decorated with silver ornaments stood in front of the patio doors.

The dining room table was set with an elaborate buffet: caviar and sturgeon, a Virginia ham, turkey en gelée, hot biscuits and salads. Two waiters discreetly refilled the guests' champagne glasses.

Ambassador Cardell, small, trim and whitehaired, welcomed Pat with courtly grace and introduced her to his sister Rowena Van Cleef, who now lived with him. "His baby sister," Mrs. Van Cleef told Pat, her eyes twinkling. "I'm only seventy-four; Edward is eighty-two."

There were some forty other people present. *Soto voce,* Lila pointed out the most celebrated to Pat. "The British Ambassador and his wife, Sir John and Lady Clemens . . . the French Ambassador . . . Donald Arlen—he's about to be appointed head of the World Bank . . . General Wilkins is the tall man by the mantel—he's taking over the NATO command . . . Senator Whitlock—that's *not* his wife with him . . ."

She introduced Pat to the neighborhood people. Pat was surprised to discover she was the center of attention. Was there any indication of who might have been responsible for the break-in? Didn't it seem as though the President was going to appoint Senator Jennings Vice President? Was the Senator easy to work with? Did they tape the entire program in advance?

Gina Butterfield, the columnist from *The Washington Tribune,* had drifted over and was listening avidly to what Pat was saying.

"It's so extraordinary that someone broke into your house and left a threatening note," the columnist observed. "Obviously you didn't take it seriously."

Pat tried to sound offhand. "We all feel it was the work of a crank. I'm sorry so much was made of it. It really is unfair to the Senator."

The columnist smiled. ''My dear, this is Washington. Surely you don't believe that anything this newsy can be ignored. You seem very sanguine, but if I were in your shoes I'd be quite upset to find my home broken into and my life threatened.''

''Especially in that house,'' another volunteered. ''Were you told about the Adams murder-suicide there?''

Pat stared at the bubbles in her champagne glass. ''Yes, I'd heard the story. But it was so long ago, wasn't it?''

''Must we discuss that subject?'' Lila broke in. ''It is Christmas Eve.''

''Wait a minute,'' Gina Butterfield said quickly. ''*Adams. Congressman Adams.* Do you mean that Pat is living in the house where he killed himself? How did the press miss that?''

''What possible connection does it have to the break-in?'' Lila snapped.

Pat felt the older woman touch her arm in a warning gesture. Was her expression revealing too much?

The Ambassador stopped at their group. ''Please, help yourselves to some supper,'' he urged.

Pat turned to follow him, but the columnist's question to another guest stopped her.

''You were living here in Georgetown at the time of the deaths?''

''Yes, indeed,'' the woman answered. ''Just two houses down from them. My mother was alive then. We knew the Adams couple quite well.''

''That was before I came to Washington,'' Gina Butterfield explained, ''but of course I heard all the rumors. Is it true there was a lot more to the case than came out?''

''Of course it's true.'' The neighbor's lips parted in a crafty smile. ''Renée's mother, Mrs. Schuyler, played the *grande dame* in Boston. She told the press that Renée had realized her marriage was a mistake and planned to divorce Dean Adams.''

''Pat, shall we get something to eat?'' Lila's arm urged her away.

''Wasn't she getting the divorce?'' Gina asked.

''I doubt it,'' the other snapped. ''She was insane about Dean, crazy jealous of him, resentful of his work. A real dud at parties. Never opened her mouth. And the way she'd practice that damn piano eight hours a day. In warm weather we all went wild listening to it. And believe me, she was no Myra Hess. Her playing was altogether pedestrian.''

I won't believe this, Pat thought. I don't want to believe it. What was the columnist asking now? Something about Dean Adams having a reputation as a womanizer?

''He was so attractive that women always made a play for him.'' The neighbor shrugged her shoulders. ''I was only twenty-three then, and I had a huge crush on him. He used to walk with little Kerry in the evening. I made it my business to bump into them regularly, but it didn't do me any good. I think we'd better get on that buffet line. I'm starved.''

''Was Congressman Adams visibly unstable?'' Gina asked.

''Of course not. Renée's mother started that talk. She knew what she was doing. Remember, both their fingerprints were on the gun. My mother and I always thought Renée was probably the one who flipped and shot up the place. And as far as what happened to Kerry . . . Listen, those bony pianist's hands were mighty powerful! I wouldn't have put it past her to have hit that poor child that night.''

CHAPTER 20

Sam sipped a light beer as he stared aimlessly across the crowd at the Palm Springs Racquet Club. Turning his head, he glanced at his daughter and smiled. Karen had inherited her mother's coloring; her deep tan only made her blond hair seem that much lighter. Her hand rested on her husband's arm. Thomas Walton Snow, Jr., was a very nice fellow, Sam thought. A good husband; a successful businessman. His family was too boringly social for Sam's taste, but he was happy that his daughter had married well.

Since his arrival, Sam had been introduced to several extremely attractive women in their early forties—widows, grass widows, career types, each ready to select a man for the rest of her life. All of this only caused Sam to feel a cumulative restlessness, an inability to settle down, an aching, pervasive sense of not belonging.

Where in the merry hell *did* he belong?

In Washington. That was where. It was good to be with Karen, but he simply didn't give a damn about the rest of the people she found so intensely satisfying.

My child is twenty-four years old, he thought. She's happily married. She's expecting a baby. I don't want to be introduced to all the eligible forty-plus women in Palm Springs.

''Daddy, will you please stop scowling?''

Karen leaned across the table, kissed him and then settled back with Tom's arm around her. He surveyed the bright, expectant faces of Tom's family. In another day or so they'd start to get fed up. He'd become a difficult guest.

''Sweetheart,'' he said to Karen, making his voice confidential. ''You asked me if you thought the President would appoint Senator Jennings Vice President, and I said I didn't know. I should be more honest. I think she'll get it.''

All eyes were suddenly focused on him.

''Tomorrow night the Senator is having a Christmas supper party at her home; you'll see some of it on the television program. She'd like me to be there. If you don't mind, I think I should attend."

Everyone understood. Karen's father-in-law sent out for a timetable. If Sam left L.A. the next morning on the 8 A.M. flight, he'd be at National Airport by four-thirty East Coast time. How interesting to be a guest at the televised dinner party. Everyone was looking forward to the program.

Only Karen was quiet. Then, laughing, she said, "Daddy, cut the baloney. I've heard the rumors that Senator Jennings has her eye on you!"

CHAPTER 21

At nine-fifteen, Pat and Lila walked silently together from the Ambassador's party. It was only when they were within reach of their own houses that Lila said quietly, "Pat, I can't tell you how sorry I am."

"How much of what that woman said was true and how much was exaggeration? I must know." Phrases kept running through her mind: neurotic . . . long, bony fingers . . . womanizer . . . We think she hit that poor kid . . . "I really need to know how much is true," she repeated.

"Pat, she's a vicious gossip. She knew perfectly well what she was doing when she started to talk about the background of the house with that woman from *The Washington Tribune.*"

"She was mistaken, of course," Pat said tonelessly.

"Mistaken?"

They were at Lila's gate. Pat looked across the street at her own house. Even though she'd left several lights burning downstairs, it still seemed remote and shadowy. "You see, there's one thing that I'm quite sure I remember. When I ran through the foyer into the living room that night I tripped over my mother's body." She turned to Lila. "So you see what that gets me: a neurotic mother who apparently found me a nuisance and a father who went berserk and tried to kill me. Quite a heritage, isn't it?"

Lila didn't answer. The sense of foreboding that had been nagging at her was becoming acute. "Oh, Kerry, I want to help you."

Pat pressed her hand. "You are helping me, Lila," she said. "Good night."

In the library, the red button on the answering machine was flashing. Pat rewound the tape. There was a single call on the unit. "This is Luther Pelham. It is now seven-twenty. We have a crisis. No matter what time you get in, call me at Senator Jennings' home, 703/555-0143. It is imperative that we meet there tonight."

Her mouth suddenly dry, Pat phoned the number. It was busy. It took three more attempts before she got through. Toby answered.

"This is Pat Traymore, Toby. What's wrong?"

"Plenty. Where are you?"

"At home."

"All right. Mr. Pelham has a car standing by to pick you up. It should be there in ten minutes."

"Toby, what's wrong?"

"Miss Traymore, maybe that's something you're going to have to explain to the Senator."

He hung up.

A half-hour later the network staff car that Luther had sent pulled up in front of Senator Jennings' home in McLean. On the drive over, Pat had worried herself with endless suppositions, but all her thoughts led to the same chilling conclusion: something had happened to further upset or embarrass the Senator, and whatever it was, she was being blamed.

A grim-faced Toby opened the door and led her into the library. Silent shapes were seated around the table in a council of war, the atmosphere oddly at variance with the poinsettia plants flanking the fireplace.

Senator Jennings, icy calm, her sphinxlike expression cast in marble, stared through Pat. Philip was to the Senator's right, his long, thin strands of colorless hair no longer combed carefully over his oval skull.

Luther Pelham's cheekbones were mottled purple. He appeared to be on the verge of a stroke.

This isn't a trial, Pat thought. It's an inquisition. My guilt has already been decided. But for what? Without offering her a seat, Toby dropped his heavy bulk into the last chair at the table.

"Senator," Pat said, "something is terribly wrong and it's quite evident it has to do with me. Will someone please tell me what's going on?"

There was a newspaper in the middle of the table. With one gesture, Philip flipped it over and pushed it at Pat. "Where did they get that picture?" he asked coldly.

Pat stared down at the cover of *The National Mirror.* The headline read: "WILL MISS APPLE JUNCTION BE THE FIRST WOMAN VEEP?" The picture, which took up the entire cover, was of Abigail in her Miss Apple Junction crown standing with her mother.

Enlarged, the picture revealed even more cruelly the massive dimensions of Francey Foster. Bulging flesh strained against the splotchy print of her badly cut dress. The arm around Abigail was dimpled with fat; the proud smile only emphasized the double-chinned face.

"You've seen this picture before," Philip snapped.

"Yes." How horrible for the Senator, she thought. She remembered Abigail's stern observation that she had spent more than thirty years trying to put Apple Junction behind her. Ignoring the others, Pat addressed the Senator directly. ''Surely you can't believe I had anything to do with the *Mirror* getting this picture?''

''Listen, Miss Traymore,'' Toby answered, ''don't bother lying. I found out that you were snooping around Apple Junction, including digging up back issues of the newspaper. I was at your place the day Saunders called.'' There was nothing deferential about Toby now.

''I have told the Senator you went to Apple Junction against my explicit orders,'' Luther thundered.

Pat understood the warning. She was not to let Abigail Jennings know that Luther had acceded to her trip to Abigail's birthplace. But that didn't matter now. What mattered was Abigail. ''Senator,'' she began, ''I understand how you must feel . . .''

The effect of her words was explosive. Abigail jumped to her feet. ''Do you indeed? I thought I'd been plain enough, but let me start again. I hated every minute of my life in that stinking town. Luther and Toby have finally gotten around to letting me in on your activities up there, so I know you saw Jeremy Saunders. What did that useless leech tell you? That I had to use the back door and that my mother was the cook? I'll *bet* he did.

''I believe you released that picture, Pat Traymore. And I know why. You're bound and determined you're going to profile me *your* way. You *like* Cinderella stories. In your letters to me you insinuated as much. And when I was bloody fool enough to let myself get talked into this program, you decided that it had to be done *your* way so everyone could talk about that poignant, moving Patricia Traymore touch. Never mind that it could cost me everything I've been working for all my life.''

''You believe I would send out that picture to somehow further my own career?'' Pat looked from one to the other. ''Luther, has the Senator seen the storyboard yet?''

''Yes, she has.''

''How about the alternative storyboard?''

''Forget that one.''

''What alternative storyboard?'' Philip demanded.

''The one I've been begging Luther to use—and I assure you it has no mention of the first beauty contest or picture from it. Senator, in a way you're right. I do want to see this production done my way. But for the best possible reason. I have admired you tremendously. When I wrote to you, I didn't know there was any chance that you might soon be appointed Vice President. I was looking ahead and hoping you would be a serious contender for the Presidential nomination next year.''

Pat paused for breath, then rushed on. ''I wish you'd dig out that first letter I sent you. I meant what I said. The one problem you have is that the American public considers you cold and remote. That picture is a good example. Obviously you're ashamed of it. But look at the expression on your mother's face. She's so *proud* of you! She's fat—is that what bothers you? Millions of people are overweight, and in your mother's generation a lot more older people were. So if I were you, when you get inquiries, I'd tell whoever asked me that that was the first beauty contest and you entered because you knew how happy it would make your mother if you won. There isn't a mother in the world who won't like you for that. Luther can show you the rest of my suggestions for the show. But I can tell you this. If you're not appointed Vice President, it won't be because of this picture; it will be because of your reaction to it and your being ashamed of your background.

''I'll ask the driver to take me home,'' she said. Then, eyes blazing, she turned to Luther. ''You can call me in the morning and let me know if you still want me on this program. Good night, Senator.''

She turned to go. Luther's voice stopped her. ''Toby, get your ass out of that chair and make some coffee. Pat, sit down and let's start fixing this mess.''

It was one-thirty when Pat got home. She changed into a nightgown and robe, made tea, brought it into the living room and curled up on the couch.

Staring at the Christmas tree, she reflected on the day. If she accepted what Catherine Graney said, all the talk about the great love between Abigail and Willard Jennings was a lie. If she believed what she had heard at the Ambassador's party, her mother had been a neurotic. If she believed Senator Jennings, everything Jeremy Saunders had told her was a twisted complaint.

It was he who must have sent the picture of Abigail to the *Mirror*. It was just the sort of mean-spirited thing he would do.

She swallowed the last sip of tea and got up. There was no use trying to think about it anymore. Walking over to the Christmas tree, she reached for the switch to turn off the lights, then paused. When she and Lila were having sherry, she thought she'd noticed that one of the ornaments had slipped from its branch and was lying on the floor. My mistake, she thought.

She shrugged and went to bed.

CHAPTER 22

At nine-fifteen on Christmas morning, Toby was standing at the stove in Abigail Jennings' kitchen waiting for the coffee to perk. He hoped that he'd be able to have a cup himself before Abby appeared. True, he'd known her since they were kids, but this was one day he couldn't predict what her mood was likely to be. Last night had been some mess. There'd been only two other times he'd seen her so upset, and he never let himself think of either of them.

After Pat Traymore left, Abby and Pelham and Phil had sat around for another hour still trying to decide what to do. Or, rather, Abby had shouted at Pelham, telling him a dozen times that she still thought Pat Traymore was working for Claire Lawrence, that maybe Pelham was too.

Even for her, Abigail had gone pretty far, and Toby was amazed that Pelham had taken it. Later Phil supplied the answer: "Listen, he's the biggest TV news personality in the country. He's made millions. But he's sixty years old, and he's bored stiff. Now he wants to be another Edward R. Murrow. Murrow capped his career as head of the U.S. Information Agency. Pelham wants that job so bad he can taste it. Tremendous prestige and no more competing for ratings. The Senator will deliver for him if he delivers for her. He knows she's got a right to scream about the way this program is going."

Toby had to agree with what Pelham said. Like it or not, the damage was done. Either the program was produced from the angle of including Apple Junction and the beauty contests or it would seem like a farce.

"You can't ignore the fact you're on the cover of *The National Mirror*," Pelham kept telling Abby. "It's read by four million people and handed away to God knows how many more. That picture is going to be reprinted by every sensational newspaper in this country. You've got to decide what you're going to tell them about it."

"Tell them?" Abby had stormed. "I'll tell them the truth: my father was a lush and the only decent thing he ever did was die when I was six. Then I can say that my fat mother had the viewpoint of a scullery maid and her highest ambition for me was that I'd be Miss Apple Junction and a good cook. Don't you think that's exactly the background a Vice President is supposed to have?" She had cried tears of rage. Abigail was no crybaby. Toby could remember only those few occasions. . . .

He had said his piece. "Abby, listen to me. You're stuck with Francey's picture, so get your act together and go along with Pat Traymore's suggestion."

That had calmed her down. She trusted him.

He heard Abby's steps in the hall. He was anxious to see what she'd be wearing. Pelham had agreed that she should show up at Christmas services at the Cathedral and wear something photogenic but not too luxurious. "Leave your mink home," he'd said.

"Good morning, Toby. Merry Christmas." The tone was sarcastic but under control. Even before he turned around he knew Abby had recovered her cool.

"Merry Christmas, Senator." He swung around. "Hey, you look great."

She was wearing a double-breasted bright red walking suit. The coat came to her fingertips. The skirt was pleated.

"Like one of Santa's helpers," she snapped. But even though she sounded crabby, there was a sort of joke in her voice. She picked up her cup and held it out in a toast. "We're going to bring this one off too, aren't we, Toby?"

"You bet we are!"

They were waiting for her at the Cathedral. As soon as Abigail got out of the car, a television correspondent held up a microphone to her.

"Merry Christmas, Senator."

"Merry Christmas, Bob." Abby was smart, Toby reflected. She made it her business to know all the press and TV people, no matter how unimportant they were.

"Senator, you're about to go into Christmas services at the National Cathedral. Is there a special prayer you'll be offering?"

Abby hesitated just long enough. Then she said, "Bob, I guess we're all praying for world peace, aren't we? And after that my prayer is for the hungry. Wouldn't it be wonderful if we knew that every man, woman and child on this earth would be eating a good dinner tonight?" She smiled and joined the people streaming through the portal of the Cathedral.

Toby got back into the car. Terrific, he thought. He reached under the driver's seat and pulled out the racing charts. The ponies hadn't been too good to him lately. It was about time his luck changed.

The service lasted an hour and fifteen minutes. When the Senator came out another reporter was waiting for her. This one had some hard questions to ask. "Senator, have you seen *The National Mirror* cover this week?"

Toby had just gotten around the car to open the door. He held his breath, waiting to see how she'd handle herself.

Abby smiled—a warm, happy smile. "Yes, indeed."

"What do you think of it, Senator?"

Abby laughed. "I was astonished. I must say I'm more used to being mentioned in the *Congressional Record* than in *The National Mirror.*"

"Did the appearance of that picture upset or anger you, Senator?"

"Of course not. Why should it? I suppose that, like most of us, on holidays I think about the people I loved who aren't with me anymore. That picture made me remember how happy my mother was when I won that contest. I entered it to please her. She was widowed, you know, and brought me up alone. We were very, very close."

Now her eyes became moist, her lips trembled. Quickly she bent her head and got into the car. With a decisive snap, Toby closed the door behind her.

The recorder light was blinking when Pat returned from the morning service. Automatically she pressed the rewind button until the tape screeched to a halt, then switched to playback.

The first three calls were disconnects. Then Sam came on, his voice edgy. "Pat, I've been trying to reach you. I'm just boarding a plane for D.C. See you at Abigail's this evening."

How loving can you get? Sam had planned to spend the week with Karen and her husband. And now he's rushing home. Abigail had obviously summoned him to be one of her close and intimate friends at her Christmas supper. There *was* something between them! Abigail was eight years older, but didn't look it. Plenty of men married older women.

Luther Pelham had also phoned. "Continue to work on the second version of the storyboard. Be at the Senator's home at four P.M. If you are called by newspapers about the *Mirror* picture, claim you haven't seen it."

The next message began in a soft, troubled voice: "Miss Traymore—er, Pat—you may not remember me. [A pause.] Of course you will; it's just you meet so many people, don't you? [Pause.] I must hurry. This is Margaret Langley. I am the principal . . . retired, of course . . . of Apple Junction High School."

The message time had run out. Exasperated, Pat bit her lip.

Miss Langley had called back. This time she said hurriedly, "To continue, please call me at 518/555-2460." There were sounds of tremulous breathing. Then Miss Langley burst out, "Miss Traymore, I heard from Eleanor today."

The phone rang only once before Miss Langley answered. Pat identified herself and was interrupted immediately. "Miss Traymore, after all these years I've heard from Eleanor. Just as I came in from church the phone was ringing and she said hello in that sweet, shy voice and we both started to cry."

"Miss Langley, where is Eleanor? What is she doing?"

There was a pause; then Margaret Langley spoke carefully, as though trying to choose exactly the right words. "She didn't tell me where she is. She said she is much better and doesn't want to be hiding forever. She said she is thinking of turning herself in. She knows she'll go back to jail—she did violate her parole. She said that this time she'd like me to visit her."

"Turning herself in!" Pat thought of the stunned, helpless face of Eleanor Brown after her conviction. "What did you tell her?"

"I begged her to call you. I thought you might be able to get her parole reinstated." Now Margaret Langley's voice broke. "Miss Traymore, please don't let that girl go back to prison."

"I'll try," Pat promised. "I have a friend, a Congressman, who will help. Miss Langley, please, for Eleanor's sake, do you know where I can reach her?"

"No, honestly, I don't."

"If she calls back, beg her to contact me before she surrenders. Her bargaining position will be so much stronger."

"I knew you'd want to help. I knew you were a good person." Now Margaret Langley's tone changed. "I want you to know how happy I am that that nice Mr. Pelham phoned and invited me to be on your program. Someone is coming to interview and tape me tomorrow morning.''

So Luther had taken that suggestion too. ''I'm so glad.'' Pat tried to sound enthusiastic. ''Now, remember to tell Eleanor to call me.''

She lowered the receiver slowly. If Eleanor Brown was the timid girl Miss Langley believed her to be, turning herself in would be a tremendous act of courage. But for Abigail Jennings, it could be mortally embarrassing if, in the next few days, a vulnerable young woman was marched back to prison still protesting her innocence of the theft from Abigail's office.

CHAPTER 23

As he walked down the corridor of the nursing home, Arthur sensed the tension and was immediately on guard. The place seemed peaceful enough. Christmas trees and Hanukkah candles stood on card tables covered with felt and make-believe snow. All the doors of the patients' rooms had greeting cards taped to them. Christmas music was playing on the stereo in the recreation room. But something was wrong.

''Good morning, Mrs. Harnick. How are you feeling?'' She was advancing slowly down the hall on her walker, her birdlike frame bent over, her hair scraggly around her ashen face. She looked up at him without raising her head. Just her eyes moved, sunken, watery, afraid.

''Stay away from me, Arthur,'' she said, her voice aquiver. ''I told them you came out of Anita's room, and I know I'm right.''

He touched Mrs. Harnick's arm, but she shrank away. ''Of course I was in Mrs. Gillespie's room,'' he said. ''She and I were friends.''

''She wasn't your friend. She was afraid of you.''

He tried not to show his anger. ''Now, Mrs. Harnick . . .''

''I mean what I say. Anita wanted to stay alive. Her daughter, Anna Marie, was coming to see her. She hadn't been East for two years. Anita said she didn't care when she died as long as she saw her Anna Marie again. She didn't just stop breathing. I told them that.''

The head nurse, Elizabeth Sheehan, sat at a desk halfway down the corridor. He hated her. She had a stern face, and blue-gray eyes that could turn steel gray when she was angry. ''Arthur, before you make your rounds please come to the office.''

He followed her into the business office of the nursing home, the place where families would come to make arrangements to jettison their old people. But today there weren't any relatives, only a baby-faced young man in a raincoat with shoes that needed a shine. He had a pleasant smile and a very warm manner, but Arthur wasn't fooled.

"I'm Detective Barrott," he said.

The superintendent of the home, Dr. Cole, was also there.

"Arthur, sit down," he said, trying to make his voice friendly. "Thank you, Nurse Sheehan; you needn't wait."

Arthur chose a straight chair and remembered to fold his hands in his lap and look just a little puzzled, as though he had no idea what was going on. He'd practiced that look in front of the mirror.

"Arthur, Mrs. Gillespie died last Thursday," Detective Barrott said.

Arthur nodded and made his expression regretful. He was suddenly glad he'd met Mrs. Harnick in the hall. "I know. I was so hoping she'd live just a little longer. Her daughter was coming to visit her and she hadn't seen her for two years."

"You knew that?" Dr. Cole asked.

"Of course. Mrs. Gillespie told me."

"I see. We didn't realize she'd discussed her daughter's visit."

"Doctor, you know how long it took to feed Mrs. Gillespie. Sometimes she'd need to rest and we'd just talk."

"Arthur, were you glad to see Mrs. Gillespie die?" Detective Barrott asked.

"I'm glad she died before that cancer got much worse. She would have been in terrible pain. Isn't that right, Doctor?" He looked at Dr. Cole now, making his eyes wide.

"It's possible, yes," Dr. Cole said unwillingly. "Of course one never knows. . . ."

"But I wish Mrs. Gillespie had lived to see Anna Marie. She and I used to pray over that. She used to ask me to read prayers from her *Saint Anthony Missal* for a special favor. That was her prayer."

Detective Barrott was studying him carefully. "Arthur, did you visit Mrs. Gillespie's room last Monday?"

"Oh, yes, I went in just before Nurse Krause made her rounds. But Mrs. Gillespie didn't want anything."

"Mrs. Harnick said she saw you coming out of Mrs. Gillespie's room at about five of four. Is that true?"

Arthur had figured out his answer. "No, I didn't go in her room. I *looked* in her room, but she was asleep. She'd had a bad night and I was worried about her. Mrs. Harnick saw me look in."

Dr. Cole leaned back in his chair. He seemed relieved.

Detective Barrott's voice got softer. "But the other day you said Mrs. Harnick was wrong."

"No, somebody asked me if I'd *gone into* Mrs. Gillespie's room twice. I hadn't. But then, when I thought about it, I remembered I'd looked in. So Mrs. Harnick and I were both right, you see."

Dr. Cole was smiling now. "Arthur is one of our most caring helpers," he said. "I told you that, Mr. Barrott."

But Detective Barrott wasn't smiling. "Arthur, do many of the orderlies pray with the patients or is it just you?"

"Oh, I think it's just me. You see, I was in a seminary once. I was planning to become a priest but got sick and had to leave. In a way I think of myself as a clergyman."

Detective Barrott's eyes, soft and limpid, encouraged confidences. "How old were you when you went into that seminary, Arthur?" he asked kindly.

"I was twenty. And I stayed until I was twenty and a half."

"I see," Detective Barrott said. "Tell me, Arthur, what seminary were you in?"

"I was at Collegeville, Minnesota, with the Benedictine community."

Detective Barrott pulled out a notebook and wrote that down. Too late Arthur realized he had told too much. Suppose Detective Barrott got in touch with the community and they told that after Father Damian's death, Arthur had been requested to leave.

Arthur worried about that all day. Even though Dr. Cole told him to go back to work, he could feel the suspicious glances from Nurse Sheehan. All the patients were looking at him in a peculiar way.

When he went to look in on old Mr. Thoman, his daughter was there and she said, "Arthur, you don't have to worry about my dad anymore. I've asked Nurse Sheehan to appoint another orderly to help him."

It was a slap in the face. Only last week Mr. Thoman had said, "I can't put up with feeling so sick much longer." Arthur had comforted him saying, "Maybe God won't ask you to, Mr. Thoman."

Arthur tried to keep his smile bright as he crossed the recreation room to help Mr. Whelan, who was struggling to his feet. As he walked Mr. Whelan down the hall to the lavatory and back, he realized that he was getting a headache, one of those blinding ones that made lights dance in front of his eyes. He knew what would happen next.

As he eased Mr. Whelan back into his chair, he glanced at the television set. The screen was all cloudy and then a face began to form, the face of Gabriel as he would look on Judgment Day. Gabriel spoke only to him. "Arthur, you are not safe here anymore."

"I understand." He didn't know he'd said the words out loud until Mr. Whelan said, "Shhh."

When he went down to his locker, Arthur carefully packed his personal effects but left his extra uniform and old shoes. He was off tomorrow and Wednesday, so they might not realize he wouldn't return on Thursday morning unless for some reason they searched his locker and found it empty.

He put on his sports jacket, the brown-and-yellow one he'd bought at J. C. Penney's last year. He kept it here so that if he was meeting Glory for a movie or something, he could look nice.

In the pocket of his raincoat he put the pair of socks that had three hundred dollars stuffed in the toes. He always kept emergency money available, both here and at home, just in case he had to leave suddenly.

The locker room was cold and dingy. There was no one around. They'd given the day off to as many of the staff as possible. *He* had volunteered to work.

His hands were restless and dry; his nerves were screaming with resentment. They had no right to treat him like this. Restlessly his eyes roamed around the barren room. Most of the supplies were locked up in the big storage room, but there was a kind of catchall closet near the stairs. It was filled with opened bottles and cans of cleaning agents and unwashed dust rags. He thought of those people upstairs—Mrs. Harnick accusing him, Mr. Thoman's daughter telling him to stay away from her father, Nurse Sheehan. How dared they whisper about him, question him, reject him!

In the closet he found a half-empty can of turpentine. He loosened the cap, then turned the can on its side. Drops of turpentine began to drip onto the floor. He left the closet door open. Right next to it, a dozen bags of trash were piled together waiting to be carried out to the dump site.

Arthur didn't smoke, but when visitors left packs of cigarettes around the nursing home, he always picked them up for Glory. Now he took a Salem from his pocket, lit it, puffed until he was sure it wouldn't go out, unfastened the tie on one of the trash bags and dropped it in.

It would not take long. The cigarette would smolder; then the whole bag would catch fire; then the other bags would go, and the dripping turpentine would cause the fire to burn out of control. The rags in the closet would cause dense smoke, and by the time the staff tried to get the old people out, the whole building would be gone. It would seem to be a careless accident—an ignited cigarette in the trash; a fire caused by an overturned can of turpentine that had dripped from the shelf—if the investigators could even piece that much together.

He retied the bag as the faint, good burning smell made his nostrils quiver and his loins tighten, then hurried from the building and down the lonely street toward the Metro.

Glory was on the couch in the living room reading a book when Arthur got home. She was wearing a very pretty blue wool housecoat, with a zipper that came up to her neck and long, full sleeves. The book she was reading was a novel on the best-seller list that had cost $15.95. Arthur had never in his life spent more than a dollar for a book. He and Glory would go to second-hand stores and browse and come home with six or seven titles. And it was their pleasure to sit companionably reading. But somehow the dog-eared volumes with the stained covers that they had delighted in purchasing seemed poor and shabby next to this book with the shiny jacket and crisp new pages. The girls in the office had given it to her.

Glory had fixed a roast chicken for him, and cranberry sauce and hot muffins. But it was no pleasure eating Christmas dinner alone. She'd said she wasn't hungry. She seemed to be thinking so deeply. Several times he caught her staring at him, her eyes questioning and troubled. They reminded him of the way Mrs. Harnick had looked at him. He didn't want Glory to be afraid of him.

"I have a present for you," he told her. "I know you'll like it." Yesterday, at the big discount store in the mall, he'd bought a frilly white apron for the Raggedy Ann doll, and except for a few spots on the dress, the doll looked just the same. And he'd bought Christmas paper and wrappings and made it look like a real present.

"And I have a present for you, Father."

They exchanged the gifts solemnly. "You open first," he said. He wanted to see her expression. She'd be so happy.

"All right." She smiled, and he noticed that her hair seemed lighter. Was she coloring it?

She untied the ribbon carefully, pushed back the paper, and the frilly apron showed first. "What . . . oh, Father." She was startled. "You found her. What a pretty new apron." She looked pleased, but not as exquisitely happy as he'd expected. Then her face became very thoughtful. "Look at that poor, sad face. And that's the way I thought of myself. I remember the day I painted it. I was so sick, wasn't I?"

"Will you take her to bed with you again?" he asked. "That's why you wanted her, isn't it?"

"Oh, no. I just wanted to look at her. Open your present. It will make you happy, I think."

It was a handsome blue-and-white wool sweater with a V-neck and long sleeves. "I knitted it for you, Father," Glory told him happily. "Would you believe I finally was able to stick with something and finish it? I guess I'm getting my act together. It's about time, don't you think?"

"I like you just as you are," he said. "I like taking care of you."

"But pretty soon it may be impossible," she said.

They both knew what she meant.

It was time to tell her. "Glory," he said carefully. "Today I was asked to do something very special. There are a number of nursing homes in Tennessee that are badly understaffed and need the kind of help I can give to very sick patients. They want me to go there right away and select one of them to work in."

"Move? Again?" She looked dismayed.

"Yes, Glory. I do God's work, and now it's my turn to ask for your help. You're a great comfort to me. We will leave Thursday morning."

He was sure he'd be safe until then. At the very least, the fire would have caused great confusion. At best, his personnel records might be destroyed. But even if the fire was put out before it burned the place down, it would probably be at least a few days before the police could check his references and find the long gaps between employment, or learn the reason he'd been asked to leave the seminary. By the time that detective wanted to question him again, he and Glory would be gone.

For a long time Glory was silent. Then she said, "Father, if my picture is on that program Wednesday night, I'm going to turn myself in. People all over the country will see it, and I can't go on any longer wondering if someone is staring at me because he or she knows who I am. Otherwise I will go with you to Tennessee." Her lip quivered, and he knew she was near tears.

He went to her and patted her cheek. He could not tell Glory that the only reason he was waiting until Thursday to go away was because of that program.

"Father," Glory burst out, "I've started to be happy here. I don't think it's fair the way they expect you to just pick up and go all the time."

CHAPTER 24

At 1:30 P.M. Lila rang Pat's doorbell. She was carrying a small package. "Merry Christmas!"

"Merry Christmas. Come in." Pat was genuinely pleased by the visit. She had been trying to decide whether or not to confide in Luther that Eleanor might turn herself in to the police. And how could she broach the subject of Catherine Graney to him? The prospect of a lawsuit would send him into orbit.

"I won't stay but a minute," Lila said. "I just wanted to give you some fruitcake. It's a specialty of mine."

Pat hugged her impulsively. "I'm glad you did come. It's terribly odd to be so quiet on Christmas afternoon. How about a glass of sherry?"

Lila looked at her watch. "I'll be out of here by quarter of two," she announced.

Pat led her back to the living room; got a plate, a knife and glasses; poured the sherry and cut thin slices of the cake. "Marvelous," she pronounced after sampling it.

"It is good, isn't it?" Lila agreed. Her eyes darted around the living room. "You've changed something in here."

"I switched a couple of paintings. I realized they were in the wrong place."

"How much is coming back to you?"

"Some." Pat admitted. "I was in the library working. Then something just made me come in here. As soon as I did, I knew that the still life and the landscape should be reversed."

"What else, Pat? There's more."

"I'm so darn edgy," Pat said simply. "And I don't know why."

"Pat, please don't stay here. Move to an apartment, a hotel." Lila clasped her hands imploringly.

"I can't," Pat said. "But help me now. Were you ever in here on Christmas Day? What was it like?"

"That last year, you were three and a half and able to really understand Christmas. They were both so delighted with you. It was a day of genuine happiness."

"I sometimes think I remember a little of that day. I had a walking doll and was trying to make it walk with me. Could that have been true?"

"You did have a walking doll that year, yes."

"My mother played the piano that afternoon, didn't she?"

"Yes."

Pat walked over to the piano, opened it. "Do you remember what she played that Christmas?"

"I'm sure it was her favorite Christmas carol. It's called 'Bells of Christmas.' "

"I know it. Veronica wanted me to learn it. She said my grandmother loved it." Slowly her fingers began to run over the keys.

Lila watched and listened. When the last notes faded away, she said, "That was very much like your mother playing. I told you you resemble your father, but I never realized until this minute how startling the resemblance is. Somebody who knew him well is bound to make the connection."

At three o'clock the television crew from Potomac Cable Network arrived at Senator Jennings' house to tape her Christmas supper.

Toby watched them with a hawk's eye as they set up in the living room and dining rooms, making it his business to be sure nothing got broken or scratched. He knew how much everything in the place meant to Abby.

Pat Traymore and Luther Pelham came within a minute or two of each other. Pat was wearing a white wool dress that showed off her figure. Her hair was twisted in a kind of bun. Toby had never seen her wear it like that. It made her look different and yet familiar. Who the hell did she remind him of? Toby wondered.

She seemed relaxed, but you could tell Pelham wasn't. As soon as he walked in, he started snapping at one of the cameramen. Abigail was uptight, and that didn't help either. Right away she tangled with Traymore. Pat wanted to set the food out on the buffet table and tape the Senator inspecting it and making little changes in the way it was placed. Abigail didn't want to put the food out so early.

"Senator, it takes time to get exactly the feeling we want," Pat told her. "It will be much easier to do now than when your guests are standing around watching."

"I won't have my guests standing around like extras in a B movie," Abigail snapped.

"Then I suggest we photograph the table now."

Toby noticed that Pat didn't back down when she wanted something done. Luther remarked that Abigail had prepared all the food herself, and that was another hassle. Pat wanted a shot of her in the kitchen working.

"Senator, everybody thinks you just phone a caterer when you have a party. That you actually do everything yourself will endear you to all the women who are stuck preparing three meals a day, to say nothing of the men and women whose hobby is cooking."

Abigail flatly rejected the idea, but Pat kept insisting. "Senator, the whole purpose of our being here is to make people see you as a human being."

In the end it was Toby who persuaded Abigail to go along. "Come on, show them you're a regular Julia Child, Senator," he coaxed.

Abby refused to put an apron over her designer shirt and slacks, but when she began to put hors d'oeuvres together, she made it clear she was a gourmet cook. Toby watched as she rolled batter for pastry shells, chopped ham for quiche, seasoned crabmeat, those long, slender fingers working miraculously. No messy kitchen for Abby. Well, you had to give a tip of the hat to Francey Foster for that.

Once the crew started taping, Abigail began to relax. They had done only a couple of takes when Pat said, "Senator, thank you. I'm sure we have what we want. That came over very well. Now, if you don't mind changing to whatever you're planning to wear at the party, we can get the footage at the table."

Toby was anxious to see what Abigail would wear. She'd been hemming and hawing between a couple of outfits. He was pleased when she came back, wearing a yellow satin blouse that matched the yellow in her plaid taffeta skirt. Her hair was soft around her face and neck. Her eye makeup was heavier than usual. She looked stunning. Besides, she had a glow about her. Toby knew why. Sam Kingsley had phoned to say he'd be at the party.

There was no question Abby had set her cap for Sam Kingsley. Toby hadn't missed the way she'd suggested to her friends that they put Sam next to her at dinner parties. There was something about him that reminded Toby of Billy, and of course that was the big attraction for Abby. She'd put on a good show in public, but she'd been a basket case when Billy died.

Toby knew Sam didn't like him. But that wasn't a problem. Sam wouldn't last any longer than the others had. Abby was too domineering for most men. Either they got sick of adjusting to her schedule and moods, or if they knuckled under, she got sick of them. He, Toby, would be a part of Abby's life until one or the other of them died. She'd be lost without him, and she knew it.

As he watched her posing at the buffet table, a tinge of regret made him swallow hard. Every once in a while he daydreamed about how it would have been if he'd been smart in school instead of just having the smarts; if he'd gone on to become an engineer instead of a jack-of-all-trades. And if he'd been good-looking like that wimp Jeremy Saunders, instead of rough-faced and burly—well, who knew? Somewhere along the line, Abby might have fallen for him.

He dismissed the thought and got back to work.

Promptly at five the first car drove up. The retired Supreme Court Justice and his wife entered a minute or two later. "Merry Christmas, Madam Vice President," the Justice said.

Abigail returned his kiss warmly. "From your lips to God's ear," she laughed.

Other guests began to flow in. Hired waiters poured champagne and punch. "Keep the hard stuff for later," Luther had suggested. "The Bible Belt doesn't like to be reminded that its public officials serve booze."

Sam was the last to arrive. Abigail opened the door for him. Her kiss on his cheek was affectionate. Luther was directing the other camera toward them. Pat felt her heart sink. Sam and Abigail made a stunning couple—both tall, her ash blond hair contrasting with his dark head, the streaks of gray in his hair a subtle balance to the fine lines around her eyes.

Pat could see everyone clustering around Sam. I only think about him as *Sam,* she thought. I've never seen him in his professional element. Was that the way it had been with her mother and father? They'd met when they were both vacationing on Martha's Vineyard. They'd married within a month, never really knowing or understanding each other's worlds—and then the clash had begun.

Except I wouldn't clash with you, Sam. I like your world.

Abigail must have said something amusing; everyone laughed. Sam smiled at her.

"That's a nice shot, Pat," the cameraman said. "A little sexy—you know what I mean? You never see Senator Jennings with a guy. People *like* that." The cameraman was beaming.

"All the world loves a lover," Pat replied.

"We've got enough," Luther suddenly announced. "Let the Senator and her guests have some peace. Pat, you be at the Senator's office for the taping in the morning. I'll be in Apple Junction. You know what we need." He turned his back, dismissing her.

Did his attitude result from the picture in the *Mirror* or from her refusal to sleep with him? Only time would tell.

She slipped past the guests, down the hallway and into the den, where she'd left her coat.

"Pat."

She turned around. "Sam!" He was standing in the doorway, looking at her. "Ah, Congressman. Season's greetings." She reached for her coat.

"Pat, you're not leaving?"

"No one invited me to stay."

He came over, took the coat from her. "What's this about the *Mirror* cover?"

She told him. "And it seems the senior Senator from Virginia believes I slipped that picture to that rag just to get my way about this program."

He put his hand on her shoulder. "You didn't?"

"That sounds like a question!" Could he really believe she'd had anything to do with the *Mirror* cover? If so, he didn't know her at all. Or maybe it was time she realized that the man she thought she knew didn't exist.

"Pat, I can't leave yet, but I should be able to get away in an hour. Are you going home?"

"Yes, I am. Why?"

"I'll be there as soon as I can. I'll take you to dinner."

"All the decent restaurants will be closed. Stay; enjoy yourself." She tried to pull away from him.

"Miss Traymore, if you give me your keys, I'll bring your car around."

They sprang apart, both embarrassed. "Toby, what the hell are *you* doing here?" Sam snapped.

Toby looked at him impassively. "The Senator is about to ask her guests in to supper, Congressman, and told me to round them up. She particularly told me to look for you."

Sam was still holding Pat's coat. She reached for it. "I can get my own car, Toby," she said. She looked at him directly. He was standing in the doorway, a large, dark mass. She tried to pass him, but he didn't move. "*May* I?"

He was staring at her, his expression distracted. "Oh, sure. Sorry." He stepped aside, and unconsciously she shrank against the wall to avoid brushing against him.

Pat drove at breakneck speed trying to escape the memory of how warmly Abigail and Sam had greeted each other, of the subtle way in which the others seemed to treat them as a couple. It was a quarter to eight when she got home. Grateful that she'd had the foresight to cook the turkey, she made a sandwich and poured a glass of wine. The house felt dark and empty. She turned on the lights in the foyer, library, dining room and living room, then plugged in the tree.

The other day the living room had somehow seemed warmer, more livable. Now, for some reason, it was uncomfortable, shadowy. Why? Her eye caught a strand of tinsel almost hidden on a brilliant apricot-hued section of the carpet. Yesterday when she and Lila were here, she thought she'd seen an ornament with a piece of tinsel lying on this area of the carpet. Perhaps it had been just the tinsel.

The television set was in the library. She carried the sandwich and the wine there. Potomac Cable had hourly news highlights. She wondered if they'd show Abigail at church.

They did. Pat watched dispassionately as Abigail stepped from the car, the bright red suit dramatic against her flawless skin and hair, her eyes soft as she voiced her prayer for the hungry. This was the woman Pat had revered. The newscaster announced, ''Later Senator Jennings was questioned about her picture as a young beauty queen, which is on the cover of this week's *National Mirror.*'' A postage-stamp-size picture of the *Mirror* cover was shown. ''With tears in her eyes the Senator recalled her mother's desire to have her enter that contest. Potomac Cable Network wishes Senator Abigail Jennings a very merry Christmas; and we're sure that her mother, were she aware of her success, would be terribly proud of her.''

''Good Lord,'' Pat cried. Jumping up, she pushed the button that turned off the set. ''And Luther has the gall to call that news! No wonder the media are criticized for bias.''

Restlessly she began to jot down the conflicting statements she had been hearing all week:

Catherine Graney said that Abigail and Willard were about to divorce.
Senator Jennings claims she loved her husband very much.

Eleanor Brown stole $75,000 from Senator Jennings.
Eleanor Brown swears she did not steal that money.

George Graney was a master pilot; his plane was carefully inspected before takeoff.
Senator Jennings said George Graney was a careless pilot with second-rate equipment.

Nothing adds up, Pat thought, absolutely nothing!

It was nearly eleven o'clock before the door chimes signaled Sam's arrival. At ten-thirty, ready to give up on him, Pat had gone to her room, then told herself that if Sam were not coming, he would have called. She changed into silk pajamas that were comfortable for lounging but technically still suitable for receiving guests. She washed her face, then touched her eyelids lightly with shadow and her lips with gloss. No point looking like a mouse, she thought—not when he'd just left the beauty queen.

Swiftly she hung up the clothes she had left scattered over the room. Was Sam neat? I don't even know that, she thought. The one night they had stayed together certainly hadn't been any barometer of either of their personal habits. When they'd checked into the motel she'd brushed her teeth with the folding toothbrush she always carried in her cosmetic case. ''I wish I had one of those,'' he'd said. She'd smiled up at his reflection in the mirror. ''One of my favorite lines from *Random Harvest* was when the minister asks Smithy and Paula if they're so in love they use the same toothbrush.'' She ran hers under hot water, spread toothpaste across the bristles and handed it to him. ''Be my guest.''

That toothbrush was now in a velvet jeweler's box in the top drawer of the vanity. Some women press roses or tie ribbons around letters, Pat thought. I kept a toothbrush.

She had just come down the stairs when the chimes rang again. ''Come in, come in, whoever you are,'' she said.

Sam's expression was contrite. ''Pat, I'm sorry. I couldn't get away as fast as I'd hoped. And then I cabbed to my place, dropped my bags and picked up my car. Were you on your way to bed?''

''Not at all. If you mean this outfit, its technically called lounging pajamas and, according to the Saks brochure, is perfect for that evening at home when entertaining a few friends.''

''Just be careful which friends you entertain,'' Sam suggested. ''That's a pretty sexy-looking getup.''

She took his coat; the fine wool was still cold from the icy wind.

He bent down to kiss her.

''Would you like a drink?'' Without waiting for his answer, she led him into the library and silently pointed to the bar. He poured brandy into snifters and handed one to her. ''I assume this is still your after-dinner choice?''

She nodded and deliberately chose the fan-back chair across from the couch.

Sam had changed when he stopped at his apartment. He was wearing an Argyle sweater with a predominantly blue-and-gray pattern that complemented the blueness of his eyes, the touches of gray in his dark brown hair. He settled on the couch, and it seemed to her there was a weariness in the way he moved and in the lines around his eyes.

''How did it go after I left?''

''About as you saw it. We did have one high point, however. The President phoned to wish Abigail a merry Christmas.''

''*The President phoned!* Sam, does that mean . . . ?''

''My bet is he's milking this for all it's worth. He probably phoned Claire Lawrence as well.''

''You mean he hasn't made his decision?''

''I think he's still sending up trial balloons. You saw the way he featured Abigail at the White House dinner last week. But he and the First Lady also went to a private supper in Claire's honor the next night.''

''Sam, how badly did that *Mirror* cover hurt Senator Jennings?''

He shrugged. ''Hard to say. Abigail has done the Southern-aristocracy scene a little too heavily for a lot of people around here. On the other hand, it just may make her sympathetic. Another problem: that publicity about the threats to you has made for a lot of locker-room jokes on Capitol Hill—and they're all on Abigail.''

Pat stared at her untouched brandy. Her mouth suddenly felt dry and brackish. Last week Sam had been worried about *her* because of the break-in. Now he was sharing Abigail's reaction to the publicity. Well, in a way it made things easier. "If this program causes any more unfavorable publicity to Senator Jennings, could it cost her the Vice Presidency?"

"Perhaps. No President, particularly one who's had a spotless administration, is going to risk having it tarnished."

"That's exactly what I was afraid you'd say." She told him about Eleanor Brown and Catherine Graney. "I don't know what to do," she concluded. "Should I warn Luther to keep away from those subjects on the program? If I do, he'll have to tell the Senator the reason."

"There's no way Abigail can take any more aggravation," Sam said flatly. "After the others left she was really wired."

"After the others left!" Pat raised an eyebrow. "You mean you stayed?"

"She asked me to."

"I see." She felt her heart sink. It confirmed everything she had been thinking. "Then I shouldn't tell Luther."

"Try it this way. If that girl . . ."

"Eleanor Brown."

"Yes—if she calls you, persuade her to wait until I see if we can plea-bargain on her parole. In that case there'd be no publicity, at least until the President announces his selection."

"And Catherine Graney."

"Let me look into the records of that crash. She probably doesn't have a leg to stand on. Do you think either one of these women might have made those threats to you?"

"I've never met Eleanor. I'm sure it wasn't Catherine Graney. And don't forget it was a man's voice."

"Of course. He hasn't called again?"

Her eyes fell on the carton under the table. She considered, then rejected, the idea of showing the Raggedy Ann doll to Sam. She did not want him concerning himself about her anymore. "No, he hasn't."

"That's good news." He finished the brandy and set the glass on the table. "I'd better be on my way. It's been a long day and you must be bushed."

It was the opening she was waiting for. "Sam, on the way home from the Senator's tonight, I did some hard thinking. Want to hear about it?"

"Certainly."

"I came to Washington with three specific and rather idealistic goals in mind. I was going to do an Emmy-winning documentary on a wonderful, noble woman. I was going to find an explanation for what my father did to my mother and me. And I was going to see you and it would be the reunion of the century. Well, none of these turned out as I expected. Abigail Jennings is a good politician and a strong leader, but she isn't a nice person. I was suckered into this program because my preconceived notions about Abigail suited Luther Pelham, and whatever reputation I've achieved in the industry gives credibility to what is essentially P.R. fluff. There's so much about that lady that doesn't hang together that it frightens me.

"I've also been here long enough to know that my mother wasn't a saint, as I'd been led to believe, and very possibly goaded my father into some form of temporary insanity that night. That's not the full story—not yet; but it's close.

"And as for us, Sam, I do owe you an apology. I certainly was terribly naive to think that I was anything more to you than a casual affair. The fact that you never called me after Janice died should have been the tip-off, but I guess I'm not a quick study. You can stop worrying now. I don't intend to embarrass you with any more declarations of love. It's very clear you've got something going with Abigail Jennings."

"I don't have anything going with Abigail!"

"Oh, yes, you do. Maybe you don't know it yet, but you do. That lady *wants* you, Sam. Anyone with half an eye can see that. And you didn't cut short your vacation and come rushing across the country at her summons without good reason. Just forget about having to let me down easy. Really, Sam, all that talk about being worn out and not able to make decisions isn't very becoming. You can drop it now."

"I told you that because it's *true.*"

"Then snap out of it. It doesn't become you. You're a handsome, virile man with twenty or thirty good years ahead of you." She managed a smile. "Maybe the prospect of becoming a grandfather is a little shocking to your ego."

"Are you finished?"

"Quite."

"Then if you don't mind, I've overstayed my welcome." He got up, his face flushed.

She reached out her hand. "There's no reason not to be friends. Washington is a small town. That *is* the reason you called me in the first place, isn't it?"

He didn't answer.

With a certain degree of satisfaction, Pat heard him slam the front door as he left.

CHAPTER 25

"Senator, they'll probably want you to be anchorwoman on the *Today* show," Toby volunteered genially. He glanced into the rearview mirror to see Abby's reaction. They were on their way to the office. At 6:30 A.M. on December 26 it was still dark and bone-chilling.

"I have no desire to be anchorwoman on the *Today* show or any other show," Abigail snapped. "Toby, what the hell do I look like? I never closed an eye last night. Toby, the President *phoned* me . . . he *phoned* me personally. He said to have a good rest over the Christmas recess because it was going to be a busy year ahead. What could he have meant by that? . . . Toby, I can taste it. The Vice Presidency. Toby, *why* didn't I follow my instincts? *Why* did I let Luther Pelham talk me into this program? Where was my head?"

"Senator, listen. That picture may be the best thing that ever happened to you. It's for sure that wallflower Claire Lawrence never won any contests. Maybe Pat Traymore is right. That kind of makes you more accessible . . . is that the word?"

The were going over the Roosevelt Bridge, and traffic was picking up. Toby concentrated on the driving. When he looked again into the rearview mirror, Abby's hands were still in her lap. "Toby, I've worked for this."

"I know you have, Abby."

"It isn't fair to lose it just because I've had to claw my way up."

"You're not going to lose it, Senator."

"I don't know. There's something about Pat Traymore that disturbs me. She's managed to give me two bouts of embarrassing publicity in one week. There's more to her than we know."

"Senator, Phil checked her out. She's been touting you since she was in college. She wrote an essay on you her senior year at Wellesley. She's on the level. She may be bad luck, but she's on the level."

"She's trouble. I warn you, there's something else about her."

The car swung past the Capitol and pulled up at the Russell Senate Office Building. "I'll be right up, Senator, and I promise you, I'll keep an eye on Pat Traymore. She won't get in your way." He hopped out of the car to open the door for Abby.

She accepted his hand, got out, then impulsively squeezed his fingers. "Toby, look at that girl's eyes. There's something about them . . . something secretive . . . as though . . ."

She didn't finish the sentence. But for Toby, it wasn't necessary.

At six o'clock Philip was waiting in the office to admit Pat and the network camera crew.

Sleepy-eyed guards and cleaning women with weary, patient faces were the only other people in evidence in the Russell building. In Abigail's office, Pat and the cameramen bent over the storyboard. "We'll only give three minutes to this segment,'' Pat said. ''I want the feeling of the Senator arriving at an empty office and starting work before anyone shows up. Then Philip coming in to brief her . . . a shot of her daily calendar, but don't show the date . . . then office help arriving; the phones starting; a shot of the daily mail; the Senator greeting visitors from her state; the Senator talking to a constituent; Phil in and out with the messages. You know what we want—a sense of behind-the-scenes in a Senator's workday office.''

When Abigail arrived, they were ready for her. Pat explained the first shot she wanted, and the Senator nodded and returned to the vestibule. Cameras rolled, and her key turned in the latch. Her expression was preoccupied and businesslike. She slipped off the gray cashmere cape that covered a well-cut but restrained pin-striped gray suit. Even the way she ran her fingers through her hair as she tossed off her hat was natural, the gesture of someone who cares about her appearance but is preoccupied with more important matters.

''Cut,'' Pat said. ''Senator, that's fine, just the feeling I wanted.'' Her spontaneous praise sounded patronizing even to her own ears.

Senator Jennings' smile was enigmatic. ''Thank you. Now what?''

Pat explained the scene with the mail, Phil and the constituent, Maggie Sayles.

The taping went smoothly. Pat quickly realized that Senator Jennings had a natural instinct for presenting herself at the best camera angle. The pin-striped suit gave her an executive, businesslike appearance that would be a nice contrast to the taffeta skirt at the Christmas supper party. Her earrings were silver; she wore a silver tie pin, stark and slim against the ascot of a soft gray silk blouse. It was the Senator's idea to photograph her office in a long shot showing the flags of both the United States and Virginia and then to have only the flag of the United States behind her in close-ups.

Pat watched the camera angle in as Abigail carefully selected a letter from the mound of mail on her desk—a letter in a childish handwriting. Another touch of theater, Pat thought. How smart of her. Then the constituent, Maggie, came in—the one whom Abigail had helped to find a nursing home for her mother. Abigail sprang up to meet her, kissed her affectionately, led her to a chair . . . all animation, warmth, concern.

She does mean the concern, Pat thought. I was here when she got that woman's mother into a home; but there's so much showmanship going on now. Are all politicians like this? Am I simply too damn naive?

By ten o'clock they had finished. Having reassured Abigail that they had everything they needed, Pat and the camera crew got ready to leave. ''We'll do the first rough edit this afternoon,'' Pat told the director. ''Then go over it with Luther tonight.''

''I think it's going to turn out great,'' the cameraman volunteered.

''It's turning into a good show. That much I'll grant,'' Pat said.

CHAPTER 26

Arthur's night had been filled with dreams of Mrs. Gillespie's eyes as they'd started to glaze over. In the morning he was heavy-eyed and tired. He got up and made coffee and would have gone out for rolls, but Glory asked him not to. "I won't have any, and after I go to work, you should get some rest. You didn't sleep well, did you?"

"How did you know?" He sat across from her at the table, watching as she perched at the edge of her chair.

"You kept calling out. Did Mrs. Gillespie's death worry you so much, Father? I know how often you used to talk about her."

A chill of fear went through him. Suppose they asked Glory about him? What would she say? Nothing ever to hurt him, but how would she know? He tried to choose his words carefully.

"It's just I'm so sad she didn't get to see her daughter before she died. We both wanted that."

Glory gulped her coffee and got up from the table. "Father, I wish you would take some time off and rest. I think you're working too hard."

"I'm fine, Glory. What was I saying in my sleep?"

"You kept telling Mrs. Gillespie to close her eyes. What were you dreaming about her?"

Glory was looking at him as if she were almost frightened of him, he thought. What did she know, or guess? After she had gone, he stared into his cup worried and suddenly tired. He was restless and decided to go out for a walk. It didn't help. After a few blocks he turned back.

He had reached the corner of his street when he noticed the excitement. A police car was stopped in front of his home. Instinctively he ducked into the doorway of a vacant house and watched from the foyer. Whom did they want? Glory? Himself?

He would have to warn her. He'd tell her to meet him somewhere and they'd go away again. He had the $300 in cash, and he had $622 in Baltimore in a savings account under a different name. They could make that last until he had a new job. It was easy to get work in a nursing home. They were all desperate for orderlies.

He slipped along the side of the house, cut through the adjacent yard, hurried to the corner and phoned Glory's office.

She was on another line. "Get her," he told the girl angrily. "It's important. Tell her Father says it's important."

When Glory got on the phone, she sounded impatient. "Father, what *is* it?"

He told her. He thought she'd cry or get upset, but there was nothing from her—just silence. "Glory . . . ?"

"Yes, Father." Her voice was quiet, lifeless.

"Leave right now, don't say anything, act like you're going to the ladies' room. Meet me at Metro Central, the Twelfth and G exit. We'll be gone before they have a chance to put out an alert. We'll pick up the money at the bank in Baltimore and then go South.''

''No, Father.'' Now Glory's voice sounded strong, sure. ''I'm not running anymore. Thank you, Father. You don't have to run anymore for me. I'm going to the police.''

''Glory. No. Wait. Maybe it will be all right. Promise me. *Not yet.*''

A police car was cruising slowly down the block. He could not lose another minute. As she whispered, ''I promise,'' he hung up the phone and ducked into a doorway. When the squad car had passed, he shoved his hands into his pockets and with his stiff, unyielding gait made his way to the Metro station.

It was a subdued Abigail who returned to the car at ten-thirty. Toby started to speak, but something told him to keep his mouth shut. Let Abby be the one to decide if she wanted to get things off her chest.

''Toby, I don't feel like going home yet,'' Abigail said suddenly. ''Take me over to Watergate. I can get a late breakfast there.''

''Sure, Senator.'' He made his voice hearty, as though the request were not unusual. He knew why Abby had selected that place. Sam Kingsley lived in the same building as the restaurant. The next thing, she'd probably phone upstairs and if Sam was in, ask him to join her for coffee.

Fine, but that hadn't been a casual chat in the den between Kingsley and Pat Traymore last night. There was something between those two. He didn't want to see Abby get hurt again. He wondered if he should tip her off.

Glancing over his shoulder, he noticed that Abigail was checking her makeup in her hand mirror. ''You look fantastic, Senator,'' he said.

At the Watergate complex the doorman opened the car door, and Toby noticed the extra-large smile and respectful bow. Hell, there were one hundred Senators in Washington but only one Vice President. I want it for you, Abby, he thought. Nothing will stand in your way if I have anything to say about it.

He steered the car to where the other drivers were parked and got out to say hello. Today the talk was all about Abigail. He overheard a Cabinet member's driver say, ''It's practically all sewed up for Senator Jennings.''

Abby, you're almost there, girl, he thought exultantly.

Abby was gone more than an hour, so he had plenty of time to read the newspaper. Finally he opened the Style section to glance at the columns. Sometimes he could pick up useful tidbits to pass on to Abby. She was usually too busy to read gossip.

Gina Butterfield was the columnist everyone in Washington read. Today her column had a headline that ran across the two center pages of the section. Toby read it, then read it again, trying to deny what he was seeing. The headline was ADAMS DEATH HOUSE SCENE OF THREATS.

SENATOR ABIGAIL JENNINGS INVOLVED. The first couple of paragraphs of the story were in extra-large type:

> Pat Traymore, the fast-rising young television newswoman hired by Potomac Cable to produce a documentary about Senator Jennings, has been harassed by letters, phone calls and a break-in threatening her life if she continues to work on the program.
>
> A guest at the exclusive Christmas Eve supper of Ambassador Cardell, winsome Pat revealed that the house she is renting was the scene of the Adams murder-suicide twenty-four years ago. Pat claims not to be disturbed by the sinister history of the house, but other guests, long-time residents of the area, were not so complacent. . . .

The rest of the column was devoted to details of the Adams murder. On the pages were blown-up file photos of Dean and Renée Adams, the garish picture of the sacks in which their bodies were bundled, a close-up of their small daughter being carried out swathed in bloody bandages. ''SIX MONTHS LATER KERRY ADAMS LOST HER VALIANT FIGHT FOR LIFE'' was the caption under that picture.

The article hinted at a whitewash in the murder-suicide verdict:

> Aristocratic Patricia Remington Schuyler, mother of the dead woman, insisted that Congressman Adams was unstable and about to be divorced by his socialite wife. But many old-timers in Washington think Dean Adams may have been given a bum rap, that it was Renée Adams who held the gun that night. ''She was clearly besotted by him,'' one friend told me, ''and he had a roving eye.'' Did her jealousy reach the breaking point that night? *Who* may have triggered that tragic outburst? Twenty-four years later, Washington still speculates.

Abigail's picture in her Miss Apple Junction crown was prominent. The copy under it read:

> Most specials profiling celebrities are ho-hum material, rehashes of the old Ed Murrow format. But the upcoming program on Senator Abigail Jennings will probably win the Nielsen ratings for the week. After all, the Senator may become our first woman Vice President. The smart money is on her. Now everyone's hoping that the footage will include more pictures of the distinguished senior Senator from Virginia in the rhinestone crown she picked up as a beauty queen along the way. And on the serious side, no one can agree on who hates Abigail Jennings enough to

> threaten the life of the newswoman who conceived the idea of the program.

Half of the right-hand page was subcaptioned THE PRE-CAMELOT YEARS. It was filled with photographs, most of them informal snapshots. The accompanying text read:

> In a bizarre coincidence, Senator Abigail Jennings was at one time a frequent guest at the Adams house. She and her late husband, Congressman Willard Jennings, were close friends of Dean and Renée Adams and the John Kennedys. The three stunning young couples could not have guessed that the dark shadow of fate was hovering over that house and all their lives.

There were pictures of the six together and in mixed groups in the garden of the Georgetown house, on the Jennings estate in Virginia and at the Hyannis Port compound. And there were a half-dozen photos of Abigail alone in the group after Willard's death.

Toby uttered a savage, angry growl. He started to crumple the paper between his hands, willing the sickening pages to disintegrate under his sheer physical strength, but it was no use. It wouldn't go away.

He would have to show this to Abby as soon as he got her home. God only knew what her reaction would be. She *had* to keep her cool. Everything depended on that.

When Toby pulled the car up to the curb, Abigail was there, Sam Kingsley at her side. He started to get out, but Kingsley quickly opened the door for Abigail and helped her into the car. ''Thanks for holding my hand, Sam,'' she said. ''I feel a lot better. I'm sorry you can't make dinner.''

''You promised me a rain check.''

Toby drove quickly, frantic to get Abigail home, as though he needed to insulate her from public view until he could nurse her through the first reaction to the article.

''Sam is special,'' Abby said suddenly, ending the heavy silence. ''You know how it's been with me all these years—but Toby, in a crazy way he reminds me of Billy. I have this feeling—just a feeling, mind you—that there could be something developing between Sam and me. It would be like having a second chance.''

It was the first time she'd ever talked like this. Toby looked into the rearview mirror. Abigail was leaning against the seat, her body relaxed, her face soft and with a half-smile.

And he was the son-of-a-bitch who was going to have to destroy that hope and confidence.

''Toby, did you buy the paper?''

There was no use lying. ''Yes, I did, Senator.''

''Let me see it, please.''

He handed back the first section.

''No, I don't feel like the news. Where's the section with the columns?''

''Not now, Senator.'' The traffic was light; they were over Chain Bridge. In a few minutes, they'd be home.

''What do you mean, *not now?*''

He didn't answer, and there was a long pause. Then Abigail said, her tone cold and brittle, ''Something bad in one of the columns . . . something that could hurt me?''

''Something you won't like, Senator.''

They drove the rest of the way in silence.

CHAPTER 27

Over the Christmas holiday official Washington was a ghost town. The President was in his private vacation residence in the Southwest; Congress was in recess; the universities were closed for vacation. Washington became a sleepy city, a city waiting for the burst of activity that signaled the return of its Chief Executive, lawmakers and students.

Pat drove home through the light traffic. She wasn't hungry. A few nibbles of turkey and a cup of tea were as much as she wanted. She wondered how Luther was making out in Apple Junction. Had he turned on the courtly charm he had once used to woo her? All of that seemed long ago.

Apropos of Apple Junction, she wondered if Eleanor Brown had ever called Miss Langley back. *Eleanor Brown.* The girl was a pivotal figure in Pat's growing doubt about the integrity of the television program. What were the facts? It was Eleanor's word against Toby's. *Had* he phoned and requested her to go to the campaign office to look for the Senator's ring? The Senator supported Toby's claim that he had been driving her at the time of the supposed call. And part of the money had been found in Eleanor's storage area. How had she expected to get away with such a flimsy alibi?

I wish I had a transcript of the trial, she thought.

She opened her pad and studied the sentences she had written down the night before. They still didn't add up. On the next page she wrote *Eleanor Brown.* What had Margaret Langley said about the girl? Tapping her pen on the desk and frowning in concentration, she began to jot her impressions of their conversation:

Eleanor was timid . . . she never chewed gum in class or talked when the teacher was out of the room . . . she loved her job in the Senator's office . . . she had just been promoted . . . she was taking art classes . . . she was going to Baltimore that day to sketch . . . .

Pat read and reread her notes. A girl doing well at a responsible job who had just been given a promotion, but so stupid she had hidden stolen money in her own storage room.

Some stolen money. The bulk of it—$70,000—was never found.

A girl as timid as that would be a poor witness in her own defense.

Eleanor had had a nervous breakdown in prison. She would have had to be a consummate actress to fake that. But she had violated her parole.

And what about Toby? He had been the witness who contradicted Eleanor's story. He had sworn he never phoned her that morning. Senator Jennings had confirmed that Toby was driving her at the time of the alleged call.

Would Senator Jennings deliberately lie for Toby, deliberately allow an innocent girl to go to prison?

But suppose someone who *sounded* like Toby had phoned Eleanor? In that case all three—Eleanor, Toby and the Senator—had been telling the truth. Who else would have known about Eleanor's storage space in her apartment building? What about the person who had made the threats, broken in here, left the doll? Could he be the *x* factor in the disappearance of the campaign funds?

The doll. Pat pushed back her chair and reached for the carton jammed under the library table, then changed her mind. There was nothing to be gained by looking at the doll now. The sight of that weeping face was too unsettling. After the program was aired, if there were no more threats, she'd throw it away. If there were any more letters or phone calls or attempted break-ins, she'd have to show the doll to the police.

On the next page in her pad she wrote *Toby,* then fished through the desk drawer for the cassettes of her interviews.

She had recorded Toby in the car that first afternoon. He hadn't realized she was taping him, and his voice was somewhat muffled. She turned the sound as high as possible, pushed the "play" button and began to take notes.

Maybe Abby stuck her neck out for me . . . I was working for a bookie in New York and almost got in trouble . . . I used to drive Abby and Willard Jennings to that house for parties . . . cute little kid, Kerry.

She was glad to switch to the interview with the waitress, Ethel Stubbins, and her husband, Ernie. They had said something about Toby. She found the segment, Ernie saying, "Say hello to him for me. Ask him if he's still losing money on the horses."

Jeremy Saunders had discussed Toby. She listened to his derisive remarks about the joyriding incident, his story about his father's buying off Abigail: "I always thought Toby had a hand in it."

After hearing the last of the cassettes, Pat read and reread her transcriptions. She knew what she had to do. If Eleanor turned herself in and was sent back to prison, Pat vowed she would stay with the case until she had satisfied herself as to Eleanor's guilt or innocence. And if it turns out I believe her story, Pat thought, I'll do everything I can to help her. Let the chips fall where they may—including Abigail Jennings' chips.

Pat wandered from the library into the foyer, and then to the staircase. She glanced up, then hesitated. *The step above the turn. That's where I used to sit.* Impulsively she hurried up the stairs, sat on that step, leaned her head against the baluster and closed her eyes.

Her father was in the foyer. She had shrunk deeper into the shadows, knowing that he was angry, that this time he would not joke about finding her here. She had run back to bed.

She hurried up the rest of the staircase. Her old room was past the guest room, across the back of the house, overlooking the garden. It was empty now.

She'd walked in here that first morning as the moving men were scurrying through the house, but it had evoked absolutely no memories. Now it seemed she could remember the bed with the frilly white canopy, the small rocking chair near the window with the music box, the shelves of toys.

I came back to bed that night. I was frightened because Daddy was so angry. The living room is right underneath this room. I could hear voices; they were shouting at each other. Then the loud noise and Mother screaming, "No . . . No!"

Mother screaming. After the loud noise. Had she been able to scream after she was shot or had she screamed when she realized she had shot her husband?

Pat felt her body begin to shake. She grasped the door for support, felt the dampness in her palms and forehead. Her breath was coming in short, hard gasps. She thought, I am afraid. But it's over. It was so long ago.

She turned and realized she was running down the hall; she was rushing down the staircase. I am back there, she thought. I am going to remember. "*Daddy, Daddy,*" she called softly. At the foot of the stairs, she turned and began to stumble through the foyer, her arms outstretched. *Daddy . . . Daddy!*

At the living-room door she crumpled to her knees. Vague shadows were around her but would not take form. Burying her face in her hands, she began to sob . . . "Mother, Daddy, come home."

She had awakened and there had been a strange baby-sitter. Mother.

Daddy. I want my mother. I want my daddy. And they had come. Mother rocking her. Kerry, Kerry it's all right. Daddy patting her hair; his arms around both of them. Shhh, Kerry, we're here.

After a while Pat slid into a sitting position and leaned against the wall, staring into the room. Another memory had broken through. She was sure it was accurate. No matter which one was guilty that last night, she thought fiercely, I know that both of them loved me. . . .

CHAPTER 28

There was a movie theater on Wisconsin Avenue that opened at ten. Arthur went into a cafeteria near it and dawdled over coffee, then walked around the neighborhood until the box office opened.

Whenever he was upset, he liked to go to the movies. He would choose a seat near the back and against the wall. And he'd buy the tallest bag of popcorn and sit and eat and watch unseeingly as the figures moved on the screen.

He liked the feeling of people near him but not conscious of him, the voices and music on the soundtrack, the anonymity of the darkened auditorium. It gave him a place to think. Now he settled in and stared blankly at the screen.

It had been a mistake to set the fire. There had been no mention of it in the newspaper. When he got off the Metro, he'd phoned the nursing home and the operator had answered at once. He'd muffled his voice: "I'm Mrs. Harnick's son. How serious was the fire?"

"Oh, sir, it was discovered almost at once. A smoldering cigarette in the trash bag. We didn't know any of the guests were even aware of it."

That meant they must have seen the overturned can of turpentine. No one would believe it had tipped accidentally.

If only he hadn't mentioned the monastery. Of course, the office there might simply say: "Yes, our records indicate Arthur Stevens was with us for a short time."

Suppose they were pressed for details? "He left at the suggestion of his spiritual director."

"May we speak to the spiritual director?"

"He died some years ago."

Would they tell why he had been asked to leave? Would they study the records of the nursing home and see which patients had died in these few years and how many of them he had helped to nurse? He was sure they wouldn't understand that he was only being kind, only alleviating suffering.

Twice before he'd been questioned when patients he had cared for had slipped away to the Lord.

''Were you glad to see them die, Arthur?''

''I was glad to see them at peace. I did everything possible to help them get well or at least be comfortable.''

When there was no hope, no relief from pain, when old people became too weak to even whisper or moan, when the doctors and relatives agreed it would be a blessing if God took them, then, and only then, did he help them slip away.

If he had known that Anita Gillespie was looking forward to seeing her daughter, he would have waited. It would have given him so much joy to know Mrs. Gillespie died happy.

That was the problem. She had been fighting death, not reconciled to it. That was why she had been too frightened to understand he was only trying to help her.

It was his concern for Glory that had made him so careless. He could remember the night the worry had begun. They were having dinner at home together, each reading a section of the newspaper, and Glory had cried, ''Oh, dear God!'' She was looking at the television page of the *Tribune* and had seen the announcement of the Senator Jennings program. It would include the highlights of her career. He had begged Glory not to be upset; he was sure it would be all right. But she hadn't listened. She'd started to sob. ''Maybe it's better to face it,'' she'd said. ''I don't want to live my life like this any longer.''

Right then her attitude began to change. He stared ahead, heedlessly chewing on the popcorn. He had not been given the privilege of formally taking his vows. Instead, he had sworn them privately. Poverty, chastity, and obedience. Never once had he broken them—but he used to get so lonely . . .

Then nine years ago he'd met Glory. She'd been sitting in the dreary waiting room of the clinic, clutching the Raggedy Ann doll and waiting her turn to see the psychiatrist. The doll was what had caught his attention. Something made him wait around outside for her.

They'd started walking toward the bus stop together. He'd explained he was a priest but had left parish work to work directly with the sick. She'd told him all about herself, how she'd been in prison for a crime she didn't commit and she was on parole and lived in a furnished room. ''I'm not allowed to smoke in my room,'' she told him, ''or even have a hot plate so I can fix coffee or soup when I don't want to go out to the drugstore to eat.''

They went for ice cream and it began to get dark. She said she was late and the woman where she lived would be angry. Then she started to cry and said she'd rather be dead than go back there. And he had taken her home with him. ''You will be a child in my care,'' he'd told her. And she was like a helpless child. He gave her his bedroom and slept on the couch, and in the beginning she would just lie in bed and cry. For a few weeks the cops came around the clinic to see if she'd shown up again, but then they lost interest.

They'd gone to Baltimore. That was when he told her he was going to tell everyone that she was his daughter. "You call me Father anyhow," he said. And he had named her Gloria.

Slowly she had started to get better. But for nearly seven years she had left the apartment only at night; she was so sure that a policeman would recognize her.

He'd worked in different nursing homes around Baltimore, and then two years ago it was necessary to leave and they'd come to Alexandria. Glory loved being near Washington, but she was afraid she might run into people who knew her. He convinced her that was foolish. "None of the people from the Senator's office would ever come near this neighborhood." Even so, whenever Glory went out, she wore dark glasses. Gradually her spells of depression began to ease. She needed less and less of the medicine he brought from the nursing home, and she'd gotten the typing job.

Arthur finished the popcorn. He would not leave Washington until tomorrow night, after he'd seen the program about Senator Jennings. He never helped people slip away until there was absolutely nothing the doctors could do for them, until his voices directed him that their time had come. Neither would he condemn Patricia Traymore without evidence. If she did not talk about Glory on the program or show her picture, Glory would be safe. He would arrange to meet her and they'd go away together.

But if Glory was exposed to the world as a thief, she would give herself up. This time she would die in prison. He was sure of it. He had seen enough people who had lost the will to live. But if it happened, Patricia Traymore would be punished for that terrible sin! He would go to the house where she lived and mete out justice to her.

Three Thousand N Street. Even the house where Patricia Traymore lived was a symbol of suffering and death.

The movie was ending. Where could he go now?

You must hide, Arthur.

"But where?" He realized he had spoken aloud. The woman in the seat ahead of him turned and glanced back.

Three Thousand N Street, the voices whispered. *Go there, Arthur. Go in the window again. Think about the closet.*

The image of the closet in the unused bedroom filled his mind. He would be warm and safe concealed behind the rows of shelves in that closet. The lights were on in the theater and he stood up quickly. He must not draw attention to himself. He would go to another movie now and another after that. By then it would be dark. Where better to spend the hours until the broadcast tomorrow evening than in Patricia Traymore's own home? No one would dream of looking for him there.

She must have her chance to be exonerated, Arthur. You must not be too hasty. The words swirled in the air above his head. ''I understand,'' he said. If there was no reference to Glory on the program, Patricia Traymore would never know that he had been staying with her. But if Glory was shown and identified, Patricia would be punished by the angels.

He would light the avenging torch.

CHAPTER 29

At one o'clock Lila Thatcher's maid returned from grocery shopping. Lila was in her study working on a lecture she was planning to give the following week at the University of Maryland. The subject was ''Harness Your Psychic Gift.'' Lila bent over the typewriter, her hands clasped.

The maid knocked on the door. ''Miss Lila, you don't look too happy.'' The maid spoke with the comfortable familiarity of an employee who had become a trusted friend.

''I'm not, Ouida. For someone who's trying to teach people to use their psychic skills, my own are pretty scrambled today.''

''I brought in the *Tribune.* Do you want to see it now?''

''Yes, I think so.''

Five minutes later, in angry disbelief, Lila was reading the Gina Butterfield spread. Fifteen minutes later, she was ringing Pat's doorbell. With dismay she realized Pat had been weeping. ''There's something I have to show you,'' she explained.

They went into the library. Lila laid the paper on the table and opened it. She watched as Pat saw the headline and the color drained from her face.

Helplessly Pat skimmed the copy, glanced at the pictures. ''My God, it makes me sound as though I was blabbing about the break-in, the Senator, this house, *everything.* Lila, I can't tell you how upset they'll all be. Luther Pelham had every single picture of my mother and father edited out of the old films. He didn't want any connection between the Senator and, I quote him, 'the Adams mess.' It's as though there's a force in action I can't stop. I don't know whether to try to explain, to resign or what.'' She tried to hold back angry tears.

Lila began to fold the newspaper. ''I can't advise you about the job, but I can tell you that you must not look at this again, Kerry. I had to show it to you, but I'm taking it home with me. It's not wise for you to see yourself as you were that day, like a broken doll.''

Pat grabbed the older woman's arm. ''Why did you say that?''

"Say what? You mean why did I call you Kerry? That just slipped out."

"No, I mean why did you compare me to a broken doll?"

Lila stared at her and then looked down at the newspaper. "It's in here," she said. "I just read it. Look." In the lead column Gina Butterfield had reprinted some of the original *Tribune* story about the murder-suicide.

> Police Chief Collins, commenting on the grisly scene, said, "It's the worst I've ever come across. When I saw that poor little kid like a broken doll, I wondered why he hadn't shot her too. It would have been easier for her."

"A broken doll," Pat whispered. "Whoever left it knew me then."

"Left *what?* Pat, sit down. You look as though you're going to faint. I'll get you a glass of water." Lila hurried from the room.

Pat leaned her head against the back of the couch and closed her eyes. When she had looked up the newspaper accounts of the tragedy, she had seen the pictures of the bodies being carried out; of herself, bandaged and bloody on the stretcher. But seeing them juxtaposed against those of the smiling, apparently carefree young couples was worse. She didn't remember reading that quote from the police chief. Maybe she hadn't seen the issue in which it appeared. But it proved that whoever had threatened her knew who she was, had known her then.

Lila came back. She had filled a glass with cold water.

"I'm all right," Pat said. "Lila, the night someone broke in here, he didn't just leave a note." She tugged at the carton to try to get it out from under the library table. It was wedged in so tightly that it wouldn't budge. I can't believe I jammed it in like this, Pat thought. As she struggled, she told Lila about finding the doll.

Shocked, Lila absorbed what she was hearing. The intruder had left a bloodied doll against the fireplace? Pat was in danger here. She had sensed it all along. She was still in danger.

Pat freed the carton. She opened it, going through it rapidly. Lila watched as her expression changed from surprise to alarm. "Pat, what is it?"

"The doll. It's gone."

"Are you sure . . ."

"I put it here myself. I looked at it again just the other day. Lila, I took its apron off. It was sickening to look at. I shoved it way down. Maybe it's still here." Pat fished through the box. "Look, here it is."

Lila stared at the crumpled piece of white cotton, soiled with reddish-brown stains, the strings of the sash hanging limply from the sides.

"When was the last time you saw the doll?"

"Saturday afternoon. I had it out on the table. The Senator's chauffeur came with more of her photograph albums. I hid it in the carton again. I didn't want him to see it.'' Pat paused.

''Wait. There was something about Toby when he came in. He was brusque and kept eyeing everything in this room. I hadn't answered the bell right away and I think he wondered what I'd been up to. And then he said he'd let himself out. When I heard the door close, I decided to slide the bolt, and Lila, the door was opening again. Toby had something that looked like a credit card in his hand. He tried to pass it off by insinuating that he was just testing the lock for me, and that I should be sure to keep the bolt on.

''He knew me when I was little. Maybe he's the one who's been threatening me. But why?''

It was not yet midafternoon, but the day had turned gray and cloudy. The dark wood paneling and the fading light made Pat seem small and vulnerable. ''We must call the police immediately,'' Lila said. ''They'll question the chauffeur.''

''I can't do that. Can you imagine what the Senator would think? And it's only a possibility. But I do know someone who can have Toby investigated quietly.'' Pat saw the distress on Lila's face. ''It's going to be all right,'' she assured her. ''I'll keep the bolt on the door—and Lila, if everything that's happened is an attempt to stop the program, it's really too late. We're taping the Senator arriving home this evening. Tomorrow we do some in-studio scenes and tomorrow night it will be aired. After that there won't be any point in trying to scare me. And I'm beginning to think that's what this is about—just an attempt to scare me off.''

Lila left a few minutes later. Pat had to be at the studio at four o'clock. She promised she would phone her Congressman friend—Sam Kingsley—and ask him to have the chauffeur investigated. To Lila's consternation, Pat insisted on keeping the newspaper. ''I'll have to read it carefully and know exactly what it says. If you don't give me this, I'll go out and buy another one.''

Lila's maid had the door open when she came up the steps. ''I've been watching for you, Miss Lila,'' she explained. ''You never finished your lunch and you looked real upset when you left.''

''You've been watching for me, Ouida?'' Lila went into the dining room and walked over to the windows facing the street. From there she could see the entire frontage and the right side of Pat's house and property. ''It won't work,'' she murmured. ''He broke in through the patio doors and I can't see them from here.''

''What did you say, Miss Lila?''

''It's nothing. I'm going to keep a stillwatch and I had thought of setting my typewriter on a table just back from the windows.''

''A stillwatch?''

''Yes, it's an expression that means if you believe something is wrong, you keep a vigil.''

"You think something is wrong at Miss Traymore's? You think that prowler may come back again?"

Lila stared at the unnatural darkness surrounding Pat's house. With an acute sense of foreboding she answered somberly, "That's just what I think."

CHAPTER 30

From the moment Father phoned her, Glory had been waiting for the police to come. At ten o'clock it happened. The door of the real estate office opened and a man in his mid-thirties came in. She looked up and saw a squad car parked out front. Her fingers dropped from the typewriter.

"Detective Barrott," the visitor said, and held up a badge. "I'd like to speak with Gloria Stevens. Is she here?"

Glory stood up. Already she could hear his questions: *Isn't your real name Eleanor Brown? Why did you violate parole? How long did you think you could get away with it?*

Detective Barrott came over to her. He had a frank, chubby face with sandy hair that curled around his ears. His eyes were inquisitive but not unfriendly. She realized he was about her own age, and somehow he seemed a little less frightening than the scornful detective who had questioned her after the money was found in her storage room.

"Miss Stevens? Don't be nervous. I wonder if I could speak to you privately?"

"We could go in here." She led the way into Mr. Schuller's small private office. There were two leather chairs in front of Mr. Schuller's desk. She sat in one of them and the detective settled in the other.

"You looked scared," he said kindly. "You have nothing to worry about. We just want to talk to your dad. Do you know where we can reach him?"

Talk to her dad. Father! She swallowed. "When I left for work he was home. He probably went to the bakery."

"He didn't come back. Maybe when he saw the police car in front of your house, he decided not to. Do you think he might be with some relatives or friends?"

"I . . . I don't know. Why do you want to talk to him?"

"Just to ask a few questions. By any chance has he called you this morning?"

This man thought Arthur was her father. He wasn't interested in her.

"He . . . he did call. But I was on the phone with my boss."

"What did he want?"

"He . . . wanted me to meet him and I said I couldn't."

"Where did he want you to meet him?"

Father's words rang in her ears. *Metro Central . . . Twelfth and G exit* . . . Was he there now? Was he in trouble? Father had taken care of her all these years. She could not hurt him now.

She chose her words carefully. "I couldn't stay on the phone. I . . . I just said I couldn't leave the office and practically hung up on him. Why do you want to talk to him? What's wrong?"

"Well, maybe nothing." The detective's voice was kind. "Does your dad talk to you about his patients?"

"Yes." It was easy to answer that question. "He cares so much about them."

"Has he ever mentioned Mrs. Gillespie to you?"

"Yes. She died last week, didn't she? He felt so bad. Something about her daughter coming to visit her." She thought about the way he had cried out in his sleep, "Close your eyes, Mrs. Gillespie. Close your eyes." Maybe he had made a mistake when he was helping Mrs. Gillespie and they were blaming him for it.

"Has he seemed different lately—nervous or anything like that?"

"He is the kindest man I know. His whole life is devoted to helping people. In fact, they just asked him at the nursing home to go to Tennessee and help out there."

The detective smiled. "How old are you, Miss Stevens?"

"Thirty-four."

He looked surprised. "You don't look it. According to the employment records, Arthur Stevens is forty-nine." He paused, then in a friendly voice added, "He's not your real father, is he?"

Soon he would be pinning her down with questions. "He used to be a parish priest but decided to spend his whole life caring for the sick. When I was very ill and had no one, he took me in."

Now he would ask her real name. But he didn't.

"I see. Miss . . . Miss Stevens, we do want to talk to, er . . . Father Stevens. If he calls you, will you contact me?" He gave her his card. DETECTIVE WILLIAM BARROTT. She could sense him studying her. Why wasn't he asking her more questions about herself, about her background?

He was gone. She sat alone in the private office until Opal came in. "Gloria, is anything wrong?"

Opal was a good friend, the best friend she'd ever had. Opal had helped her think of herself as a woman again. Opal was always after her to go to parties, saying her boyfriend would fix her up with a blind date. She'd always refused.

"Gloria, what's wrong?" Opal repeated. "You look terrible."

"No, nothing's wrong. I have a headache. Do you think I could go home?"

"Sure; I'll finish your typing. Gloria, if there's anything I can do . . ."

Glory looked into her friend's troubled face. "Not anymore, but thank you for everything."

She walked home. The temperature was in the forties, but even so, the day was raw with a chill that penetrated her coat and gloves. The apartment, with its shabby, rented furniture, seemed strangely empty, as though it sensed they would not be returning. She went to the hall closet and found the battered black suitcase that Father had bought at a garage sale. She packed her meager supply of clothing, her cosmetics and the new book Opal had given her for Christmas. The suitcase wasn't large, and it was hard to force the locks to snap.

There was something else—her Raggedy Ann doll. At the mental-health clinic the psychiatrist had asked her to draw a picture of how she felt about herself, but somehow she couldn't do that. The doll was with some others on a shelf, and he had given it to her. "Do you think you could show me how this doll would look if it were you?"

It hadn't been hard to paint the tears and to sketch in the frightened look about the eyes and to change the thrust of the mouth so that instead of smiling it seemed about to scream.

"That bad?" the doctor had said when she was finished.

"Worse."

Oh, Father, she thought, I wish I could stay here and wait until you call me. But they're going to find out about me. That detective is probably having me checked right now. I can't run away anymore. While I have the courage, I have to turn myself in. Maybe it will help me get a lighter sentence for breaking parole.

There was one promise she could keep. Miss Langley had begged her to call that television celebrity Patricia Traymore before she did anything. Now she made the call, told what she planned and listened impassively to Pat's emotional pleading.

Finally at three o'clock she left. A car was parked down the street. Two men were sitting in it. "That's the girl," one of them said. "She was lying about not planning to meet Stevens." He sounded regretful.

The other man pressed his foot on the pedal. "I told you she was holding back on you. Ten bucks she'll lead us to Stevens now."

CHAPTER 31

Pat sped across town to the Lotus Inn Restaurant on Wisconsin Avenue. Desperately she tried to think of some way she could persuade Eleanor Brown not to surrender herself yet. Surely she could be persuaded to listen to reason.

She had tried to reach Sam, but after five rings had slammed down the phone and run out. Now as she rushed into the restaurant she wondered if she would recognize the girl from her high school picture. Was she using her own name? Probably not.

The hostess greeted her. "Are you Miss Traymore?"

"Yes, I am."

"Miss Brown is waiting for you."

She was sitting at a rear table sipping chablis. Pat slipped into the chair opposite her, trying to collect herself to know what to say. Eleanor Brown had not changed very much from her high school picture. She was obviously older, no longer painfully thin and prettier than Pat had expected, but there was no mistaking her.

She spoke softly. "Miss Traymore? Thank you for coming."

"Eleanor, please listen to me. We can get you a lawyer. You can be out on bail while we work something out. You were in the midst of a breakdown when you violated parole. There are so many angles a good lawyer can work."

The waiter came with an appetizer of butterfly shrimp. "I used to dream of these," Eleanor said. "Do you want to order something?"

"No. Nothing. Eleanor, did you understand what I said?"

"Yes, I did." Eleanor dipped one of the shrimp in the sweet sauce. "Oh, that's good." Her face was pale but determined. "Miss Traymore, I hope I can get my parole reinstated, but if I can't, I know I'm strong enough now to serve the time they gave me. I can sleep in a cell, and wear a prison uniform, and eat that slop they call food, and put up with the strip searches and the boredom. When I get out I won't have to hide anymore, and I'm going to spend the rest of my life trying to prove my innocence."

"Eleanor, wasn't the money found in your possession?"

"Miss Traymore, half the people in the office knew about that storeroom. When I moved from one apartment to the other, six or eight of them helped. We made a party of it. The furniture I couldn't use was carried down to the storage room. *Some* of the money was found there, but seventy thousand dollars went into someone else's pocket."

"Eleanor, you claim Toby phoned you and he said he didn't. Didn't you think it unusual to be asked to go to the campaign office on Sunday?"

Eleanor pushed aside the shells on her plate. "No. You see the Senator was up for reelection. A lot of mailings were sent from the campaign office. She used to drop by and help just to make the volunteers feel important. When she did that she would take off her big diamond ring. It was a little loose and she really was careless with it. A couple of times she left without it."

"And Toby or someone sounding like Toby said she'd lost or mislaid it again."

"Yes. I knew she'd been in the campaign office on Saturday helping with the mailings, so it sounded perfectly natural that she might have forgotten it again and one of the senior aides might have put it in the safe for her.

"I believe Toby was driving the Senator at the time the call was made. The voice was muffled and whoever spoke to me didn't say much. It was something like, 'See if the Senator's ring is in the campaign safe and let her know.' I was annoyed because I wanted to go to Richmond to sketch and I even said something like 'she'll probably find it under her nose.' Whoever it was who phoned sort of laughed and hung up. If Abigail Jennings hadn't talked so much about the second chance she had given me, called me a convicted thief, I would have had a better chance of reasonable doubt. I've lost eleven years of my life for something I didn't do and I'm not losing another day." She stood up and laid money on the table. "That should cover everything." Bending down, she picked up her suitcase, then paused. "You know what's hardest for me now? I'm breaking my promise to the man I've been living with, and he's been so good to me. He begged me not to go to the police yet. I wish I could explain to him, but I don't know where he is."

"Can I call him for you later? What's his name? Where does he work?"

"His name is Arthur Stevens. I think there's some problem at his job. He won't be there. There's nothing you can do. I hope your program is very successful, Miss Traymore. I was terribly upset when I read the announcement about it. I knew that if even one picture of me was shown I'd be in jail within twenty-four hours. But you know, that made me realize how tired I was of running. In a crazy way, it gave me the courage to face going back to prison so that someday I really will be free. Father, I mean Arthur Stevens, just couldn't accept that. And now I'd better go before I run out of courage."

Helplessly Pat watched her retreating back.

As Eleanor left the restaurant two men at a corner table got up and followed her out.

CHAPTER 32

"Abby, it's not as bad as it could be." In the forty years he had known her, it was only the third time he had had his arms around her. She was sobbing helplessly.

"Why didn't you tell me she was staying in that house?"

"There was no reason to."

They were in Abigail's living room. He'd shown her the article when they arrived, then tried to calm the inevitable explosion.

"Abby, tomorrow this newspaper will be lining garbage cans."

"I don't want to line garbage cans!" she'd screamed.

He poured a straight Scotch and made her drink it. "Come on, Senator, pull yourself together. Maybe there's a photographer hiding in the bushes."

"Shut up, you bloody fool." But the suggestion had been enough to shock her. And after the drink, she'd started to cry. "Toby, it looks like the old penny-dreadful scandal sheets. And that picture. Toby, *that picture.*" She didn't mean the one of her and Francey.

He put his arms around her, clumsily patted her back and realized with the dullness of a long-accepted pain that he was nothing more to her than a railing to grab when your feet gave way underneath you.

"If anyone really studies the pictures! Toby, look at *that* one."

"Nobody's going to bother."

"Toby, that girl—that Pat Traymore. How did she happen to lease that house? It can't be a coincidence."

"The house has been rented to twelve different tenants in the past twenty-four years. She's just another one of them." Toby tried to make his voice hearty. He didn't believe that; but on the other hand, Phil still hadn't been able to uncover the details of the rental. "Senator, you gotta hang in there. Whoever made those threats to Pat Traymore . . ."

"Toby, *how do we know there were threats?* How do we know this isn't a calculated attempt to embarrass me?"

He was so startled he stepped back. In a reflex action she pulled away from him, and they stared at each other. "God Almighty, Abby, do you think she *engineered* this?"

The ring of the telephone made them both jump. He looked at her. "You want me . . ."

"Yes." She held her hands up to her face. "I don't give a goddamn who's calling. I'm not here."

"Senator Jennings' residence." Toby put on his butler's voice. "May I take a message for the Senator? She's not available at the moment." He winked at Abby and was rewarded by the trace of a smile. "The President. . . . Oh, just a minute, sir." He held his hand over the mouthpiece. "Abby, the President is calling you. . . ."

"Toby, don't you dare . . ."

"Abby, for chrissake, it's the *President!*"

She clasped her hands to her lips, then came over and took the phone from him. "If this is your idea of a joke . . ." She got on. "Abigail Jennings."

Toby watched as her expression changed. "Mr. President. I'm so sorry. . . . I'm sorry . . . Some reading . . . That's why I left word. . . . I'm sorry. . . . Yes, sir, of course. Yes, I can be at the White House tomorrow evening . . . eight-thirty, of course. Yes, we've been quite busy with this program. Frankly, I'm not comfortable being the subject of this sort of thing. . . . Why, how kind of you. . . . Sir, you mean . . . I simply don't know what to say. . . . Of course, I understand. . . . Thank you, sir."

She hung up. Dazed, she looked at Toby. "I'm not to tell a soul. He's announcing his appointment of me tomorrow night after the program. He said it isn't a bad idea the whole country gets to know me a little better. He laughed about the *Mirror* cover. He said his mother was a big gal too, but that I'm much prettier now than when I was seventeen. Toby, I'm going to be Vice President of the United States!" She laughed hysterically and flung herself at him.

"Abby, you *did* it!" He lifted her off her feet.

An instant later her face twisted with tension. "Toby, nothing can happen . . . Nothing must stop this. . . ."

He put her down and covered both her hands in his. "Abby, I *swear* nothing will keep this from you."

She started to laugh and then began to cry. "Toby, I'm on a roller coaster. You and that damn Scotch. You know I can't drink. Toby—*Vice President!*"

He had to ease her down. His voice soothing, he said, "Later on we'll take a ride over and just kind of cruise past your new house, Abby. You're finally getting a mansion. Next stop Massachusetts Avenue."

"Toby, shut up. Just make me a cup of tea. I'm going to take a shower and try to collect myself. Vice President! My God, my God!"

He put the kettle on and then, not bothering with a coat, walked to the roadside mailbox and flipped it open. The usual collection of junk—coupons, contests, "You may have won two million dollars". . . . Ninety-nine percent of Abby's personal mail went through the office.

Then he saw it. The blue envelope with the hand-written address. A personal note to Abby. He looked at the upper left-hand corner and felt the blood drain from his face.

The note was from Catherine Graney.

CHAPTER 33

Sam drove across town on 7th Street, already a little late for his noon appointment with Larry Saggiotes of the National Transportation Safety Board.

After he left Pat, he'd gone home and lain awake most of the night, his emotions shifting from anger to a sober examination of Pat's charges.

"Can I help you, sir?"

"What? Oh, sorry." Sheepishly Sam realized he'd been so deep in thought, he had arrived in the lobby of the FAA building without realizing he had come through the revolving door. The security guard was looking at him curiously.

He went up to the eighth floor and gave his name to the receptionist. "It will be just a few minutes," she said.

Sam settled into a chair. Had Abigail and Willard Jennings been having a violent argument that last day? he wondered. But that didn't have to mean anything. He remembered there were times when he'd threatened to quit Congress, to get a job that would provide some of the luxuries that Janice deserved. She'd argued with him and stormed at him, and anyone who heard them would have thought they couldn't stand each other. Maybe the pilot's widow did hear Abigail arguing with Willard Jennings that day. Maybe Willard was disgusted about something and ready to give up politics and she didn't want him burning his bridges.

Sam had called his FBI friend Jack Carlson to trace the report of the crash.

"Twenty-seven years ago? That could be a tough one," Jack had said. "The National Transportation Safety Board handles investigations into crashes now, but that many years ago the Civil Aeronautics Administration was in charge. Let me call you back."

At nine-thirty Jack had phoned back. "You're in luck," he'd said laconically. "Most records are shredded after ten years, but when prominent people are involved, the investigation reports are stored in the Safety Board warehouse. They've got the data on accidents involving everyone from Amelia Earhart and Carole Lombard to Dag Hammarskjöld and Hale Boggs. My contact at the board is Larry Saggiotes. He'll get the report sent to his office, look it over. He suggests you come by about noon. He'll review it with you."

"Excuse me, sir. Mr. Saggiotes will see you now."

Sam looked up. He had a feeling the receptionist had been trying to get his attention. I'd better get with it, he thought. He followed her down the corridor.

Larry Saggiotes was a big man whose features and coloring reflected his Greek heritage. They exchanged greetings. Sam gave a carefully edited explanation of why he'd wanted to investigate the crash.

Larry settled back in his chair, frowning. "Nice day here, isn't it?" he commented. "But it's foggy in New York, icy in Minneapolis, pouring in Dallas. Yet in the next twenty-four hours one hundred twenty thousand commercial, military and private planes will take off and land in this country. And the odds against any of them crashing are astronomical. That's why when a plane that's been checked out by an expert mechanic and flown by a master pilot on a day with good visibility suddenly crashes into a mountain and is scattered over two square miles of rocky landscape, we're not happy."

"The Jennings plane!"

"The Jennings plane," Larry confirmed. "I've just read the report.

What happened? We don't know. The last contact with George Graney was when he left traffic control in Richmond. There was no suggestion of trouble. It was a routine two-hour flight. And then he was overdue.''

''And the verdict was pilot error?'' Sam asked.

''*Probable* cause, pilot error. It always ends up like that when we can't come up with other answers. It was a fairly new Cessna twin-engine, so their engineers were around to prove the plane was in great shape. Willard Jennings' widow cried her eyes out about how she'd had a horror of small charter planes, that her husband had complained about rough landings with Graney.''

''Did the possibility of foul play ever come up?''

''Congressman, the possibility of foul play is *always* investigated in a case like this. First we look for how it might have been done. Well, there are plenty of ways that are pretty hard to trace. For example, with all the magnetic tape being used today, a strong magnet hidden in the cockpit could screw up all the instruments. Twenty-seven years ago that wouldn't have happened. But if anybody had fooled with the generator of Graney's plane, maybe, frayed or cut a wire, Graney would have had a complete loss of power right as he's flying over a mountain. The chances of recovering usable evidence would have been negligible.

''The fuel switch would be another possibility. That plane had two tanks. The pilot switched to the second tank when the first tank's needle indicated it was empty. Suppose the switch wasn't working? He wouldn't have had a chance to use the second tank. Then, of course, we have corrosive acid. Somebody who doesn't want a plane to make it safely could have put a leaky container of the stuff on board. It could be in the luggage area, under a seat—wouldn't matter. That would eat through the cables within half an hour and there'd be no controlling the plane. But that would be easier to discover.''

''Did any of this come up at the hearing?'' Sam asked.

''There weren't enough pieces of that plane recovered to play Pick Up Sticks. So the next thing we do is look for motive. And found absolutely none. Graney's charter line was doing well; he hadn't taken out any recent insurance. The Congressman was so poorly insured it was amazing, but when you have family dough, you don't need insurance, I guess. Incidentally, this is the second request I've had for a copy of the report. Mrs. George Graney came in for one last week.''

''Larry, if it's at all possible, I'm trying to keep Senator Jennings from being embarrassed by having this rehashed—and of course I'll study the report myself, but let me get this straight: was there any suggestion that George Graney was an inexperienced or careless pilot?''

''Absolutely none. He had an impeccable record, Congressman. He had been in air combat through the Korean War, then worked for United for a couple of years. This kind of flying was child's play to him.''

''How about his equipment?''

''Always in top shape. His mechanics were good.''

''So the pilot's widow has a valid reason to be upset that the blame for the crash got laid at George Graney's doorstep.''

Larry blew a smoke ring the size of a cruller. ''You bet she does—*more* than valid.''

CHAPTER 34

At ten minutes past four, Pat managed to reach Sam from the lobby of the Potomac Cable Network building. Without mentioning their quarrel, she told him about Eleanor Brown. ''I couldn't stop her. She was determined to turn herself in.''

''Calm down, Pat. I'll send a lawyer to see her. How long will you be at the network?''

''I don't know. Have you seen the *Tribune* today?''

''Just the headlines.''

''Read the second section. A columnist I met the other night heard where I lived and rehashed everything.''

''Pat, I'll be here. Come over when you finish at the network.''

Luther was waiting for her in his office. She had expected to be treated as a pariah. Instead, he was fairly restrained. ''The Apple Junction shooting went well,'' he told her. ''It snowed there yesterday and that whole cruddy backwoods looked like the American dream. We caught the Saunders house, the high school with the crèche in front and Main Street with its Christmas tree. We put a sign in front of the town hall: 'Apple Junction, Birthplace of Senator Abigail Foster Jennings.' ''

Luther puffed on a cigarette. ''That old lady, Margaret Langley, was a good interview. Kind of classy-looking and quaint. Nice touch having her talk about what a dedicated student the Senator was and showing the yearbook.''

Pat realized that somehow it had become *Luther's* idea to do background shots in Apple Junction. ''Have you seen the footage from last night and this morning?'' she asked.

''Yes. It's okay. You might have gotten a little more of Abigail actually working at her desk. The sequence at Christmas dinner was fine.''

''Surely you've seen today's *Tribune?*''

''Yes.'' Luther ground his cigarette into the ashtray and reached for another one. His voice changed. Tell-tale red spots appeared in his cheeks. ''Pat, would you mind laying your cards on the table and explaining why you gave out that story?''

"Why I *what?*"

Now the restraint in Luther's manner disappeared. "Maybe a lot of people would consider it coincidence that so much has happened this week to give the Senator sensational publicity. I happen not to believe in coincidence. I agree with what Abigail said after that first picture came out in the *Mirror.* You've been out from day one to force us to produce this program *your* way. And I think you've used every trick in the books to get personal publicity for yourself. There isn't anyone in Washington who isn't talking about Pat Traymore."

"If you believe that, you ought to fire me."

"And give you more headlines? No way. But just as a matter of curiosity, will you answer a few questions for me?"

"Go ahead."

"The first day in this office, I told you to edit out any reference to Congressman Adams and his wife. Did you know you were renting their house?"

"Yes, I did."

"Wouldn't it have been natural to mention it?"

"I don't think so. I certainly edited out every single picture of them from the Senator's material—and incidentally, I did a damn good job of it. Have you run through all those films?"

"Yes. You did do a good job. Then suppose you tell me your reasoning for the threats. Anyone who knows the business would realize that whether or not you worked on the program it was going to be completed."

Pat chose her words carefully. "I think the threats were just that—*threats.* I don't think anyone ever meant to harm me, just scare me off. I think that someone is afraid to have the program made and thought that if I didn't do it the project would be dropped." She paused, then added deliberately. "That person couldn't know I'm just a figurehead in a campaign to make Abigail Jennings Vice President."

"Are you trying to insinuate . . . ?"

"No, not insinuate: state. Look, I fell for it. I fell for being hired so fast, for being rushed down here to do three months' work in a week, for having the material for the program spoon-fed to me by you and the Senator. The little claim this program will have to being an honest documentary is because of the segments I had to force down your throats. It's only because of the rotten publicity I've inadvertently caused Abigail Jennings that I'm going to do my best to make this program work for her. But I warn you, when it's over, there are some things I intend to investigate."

"Such as . . . ?"

"Such as Eleanor Brown, the girl who was convicted of embezzling the campaign funds. I saw her today. She was about to turn herself in to the police. And she swears she never touched that money."

''Eleanor Brown turned herself in?'' Luther interrupted. ''We can make a plus out of that. As a parole violator, she won't get bail.''

''Congressman Kingsley is trying to have bail set.''

''That's a mistake. I'll see that she stays put until the President makes his appointment. After that, who cares? She had a fair trial. We'll talk about the case on the program just as we've written it, only we'll add the fact that because of the program she turned herself in. That'll spike her guns if she wants to make trouble.''

Pat felt that somehow she had betrayed her trust. ''I happen to think that girl is innocent, and if she is, I'll fight to get her a new trial.''

''She's guilty,'' Luther snapped. ''Otherwise why did she break parole? She's probably gone through that seventy thousand bucks now and wants to be able to stop running. Don't forget: a panel of jurors convicted her unanimously. You still believe in the jury system, I hope? Now, is there anything else? Any single thing that you know that could reflect badly on the Senator?''

She told him about Catherine Graney.

''So she's talking about suing the network?'' Luther looked immensely pleased. ''And you're worried about that?''

''If she starts gossiping about the Jennings marriage . . . the very fact that the Senator wasn't left a penny by her mother-in-law. . . .''

''Abigail will have the wholehearted support of every woman in America who's put up with a miserable mother-in-law. As far as the Jennings marriage goes, it's this Graney woman's word against the Senator and Toby . . . don't forget he was a witness to their last time together. And what about the letter you gave me that the Senator wrote to her husband? That's dated only a few days before he died.''

''We *assume* that. Someone else could point out that she never filled in the *year.*''

''She can fill it in now if necessary. Anything else?''

''To the best of my knowledge those are the only two places where the Senator might have unfavorable publicity. I'm prepared to give my word of honor on that.''

''All right.'' Luther seemed appeased. ''I'm taking a crew to tape the Senator going into her home this evening—that end-of-the-day working scene.''

''Don't you want me at that taping?''

''I want you as far away from Abigail Jennings as you can get until she has time to calm down. Pat, have you read your contract with this network carefully?''

''I think so.''

''Then you do realize we have the right to cancel your employment here for a specified cash settlement? Frankly, I don't buy the cock-and-bull story that someone is trying to keep this program from being made. But I almost admire you for having made yourself a household word in

Washington, and you've done it by piggybacking onto a woman who's dedicated her whole life to public service.''

''Have *you* read my contract?'' Pat asked.

''I wrote it.''

''Then you do know you gave me creative control of the projects to which I'm assigned. Do you think you've fulfilled my contract this week?'' She opened the door of Luther's office, sure that everyone in the newsroom was listening to them.

Luther's last words echoed through the room: ''By this time next week the terms of your contract will be moot.''

It was one of the few times in her life that Pat slammed a door.

Fifteen minutes later she was giving her name to the desk clerk in Sam's apartment building.

Sam was waiting in the hallway when the elevator stopped at his floor. ''Pat, you look bushed,'' he told her.

''I am.'' Wearily she looked up at him. He was wearing the same Argyle sweater he'd had on the night before. With a stab of pain she noted again how it brought out the blueness of his eyes. He took her arm and they walked down the long corridor.

Inside the apartment, her immediate impression was surprise at the decor. Charcoal gray sectional furniture was grouped in the center of the room. The walls had a number of good prints and a few first-class paintings. The carpet was wall-to-wall in a tweedy gray-black-and-white combination.

Somehow in Sam's home she'd expected a more traditional look—a couch with arms, easy chairs, family pieces. An Oriental, however worn, would have been a distinct improvement over the carpet. He asked her what she thought of the place and she told him.

Sam's eyes crinkled. ''You sure know how to get invited back, don't you? You're right, of course. I wanted to make a clean sweep, start over, and naturally outdid myself. I agree. This place does look like a motel lobby.

''Then why stay here? I gather you have other options.''

''Oh, the apartment is fine,'' Sam said easily. ''It's just the furniture that bugs me. I rang out the old but didn't know exactly what the new was supposed to be.''

It was a half-joking statement that suddenly assumed too much weight. ''By any chance, do you have a Scotch for a tired lady?'' she asked.

''Sure do.'' He went over to the bar. ''Lots of soda, one ice cube, twist of lemon if possible, but don't worry if you're out of lemon.'' He smiled.

''I'm sure I don't sound that wimpy.''

''Not wimpy, just considerate.'' He mixed the drinks and placed them on the cocktail table. ''Sit down and don't be so fidgety. How did the studio go?''

"By this time next week I probably won't have a job. You see, Luther really thinks I'm pulling all this as a publicity stunt and he rather admires my moxie for trying it."

"I think Abigail has somewhat the same view."

Pat raised an eyebrow. "I'm sure you'd be the first to know. Sam, I hardly expected to call you so quickly after last night. In fact, my guess would have been a nice three-month cooling-off period before we met as disinterested friends. But I do need some help fast, and I certainly can't look to Luther Pelham for it. So I'm afraid you're elected."

"Not exactly the reason I'd choose to hear from you, but I'm glad to be of service."

Sam was different today. She could feel it. It was as though that vacillating aimlessness was missing. "Sam, there was something else about the break-in." As calmly as possible, she told him about the Raggedy Ann doll. "And now the doll is gone."

"Pat, are you telling me that someone has been back in your house without you knowing it?"

"Yes."

"Then you're not going to spend another minute there."

Restlessly she got up and walked over to the window. "That isn't the answer. Sam, in a crazy way the fact that the doll is gone is almost reassuring. I don't think whoever has been threatening me really intends to hurt me. Otherwise he certainly would have done it. I think he's afraid of what the program might do to *him.* And I've got some ideas." Quickly she explained her analysis of the Eleanor Brown case. "If Eleanor Brown wasn't lying, Toby was. If Toby was lying, the Senator was covering up for him, and that seems incredible. But suppose another person was involved who could imitate Toby's voice, who knew about Eleanor's storeroom and planted just enough of the money to make her look guilty?"

"How do you explain the doll and the threats?"

"I think someone who knew me when I was little, and may have recognized me, is trying to scare me and stop this program. Sam, what do you make of this? *Toby* knew me when I was little. Toby has become truly hostile toward me. I thought at first it was because of the Senator and all the bad publicity, but the other day he kept eyeing the library as though he was casing it. And after he left, he let himself back in. He didn't realize I intended to follow him to slide the safety bolt. He tried to say he was just testing the lock and that anyone could get in and I should be careful. I fell for that—but Sam, I really am nervous about him. Could you have him checked out and see if he's ever been in trouble? I mean real trouble?"

"Yes, I can. I never liked that bird myself." He came up behind her, put his arms around her waist. In an instinctive reaction she leaned back against him. "I've missed you, Pat."

"Since last night?"

"No, since two years ago."

"You could have fooled me." For a moment she gave herself up to the sheer joy of being close to him; then she turned and faced him. "Sam, a little residual affection doesn't add up to what I want. So why don't you just . . ."

His arms were tight around her. His lips were no longer tentative. "I'm fresh out of residual affection."

For long moments they stood there, silhouetted against the window.

Finally Pat stepped back. Sam let her go. They looked at each other. "Pat," he said, "everything you said last night was true except one thing. There is absolutely nothing between Abigail and me. Can you give me a little time to find myself again? I didn't know until I saw you this week that I've been functioning like a zombie."

She tried to smile. "You seem to forget, I need some time too. Memory Lane isn't as simple as I expected it to be."

"Do you think you're getting honest impressions of that night?"

"Honest, perhaps, but not particularly desirable. I'm beginning to believe my mother may have been the one who went crazy that night, and somehow that's harder."

"Why do you think that?"

"It's not why I *think* it, but why she may have snapped that interests me now. Well, one more day and 'The Life and Times of Abigail Jennings' will be presented to the world. And at that point I start doing some real investigating. I just wish to God this whole thing wasn't so rushed. Sam, there's too much that doesn't hang together. And I don't care what Luther Pelham thinks. That segment about the plane crash is going to blow up in Abigail's face. Catherine Graney means business."

She declined his invitation to dinner. "This has been a grueling day. I was up at four o'clock to get ready for the Senator's office, and tomorrow we finish taping. I'm going to fix a sandwich and be in bed by nine o'clock."

At the door, he held her once more. "When I'm seventy, you'll be forty-nine."

"And when you're one hundred and three, I'll be eighty-two. You'll get a trace on Toby and you'll let me know when you hear anything about Eleanor Brown?"

"Of course."

When Pat left, Sam phoned Jack Carlson and quickly told him what Pat had confided.

Jack whistled. "You mean that guy's been back? Sam, you really have a loony. Sure we can check this Toby character, but do me a favor. Get me a sample of his handwriting, can you?"

CHAPTER 35

Detective Barrott was kind. He believed she was telling the truth. But the older detective was hostile. Over and over Eleanor answered the same questions from him.

How could she tell them where she was keeping seventy thousand dollars that she'd never even seen?

Was she angry at Patricia Traymore for preparing the program that might force her out of hiding? No, of course not. At first she was afraid and then she knew she couldn't hide anymore, that she'd be glad if it were over.

Did she know where Patricia Traymore lived? Yes, Father had told her that Patricia Traymore lived in the Adams house in Georgetown. He'd shown her that house once. He'd been on the ambulance squad of Georgetown Hospital when that awful tragedy had happened. Break into that house? Of course not. How could she?

In the cell she sat on the edge of the bunk wondering how she could have thought she was strong enough to go back into this world. The steel bars and the insulting intimacy of the open toilet, the sense of entrapment, the haunting depression that like a black fog was beginning to envelop her.

She lay on the bunk and wondered where Father had gone. It was impossible that they seemed to be suggesting he would deliberately hurt anyone. He was the kindest man she had ever known. But he had been terribly nervous after Mrs. Gillespie died.

She hoped he wouldn't be angry that she had given herself up. They would have arrested her anyway. She was sure Detective Barrott was planning to investigate her.

Had Father gone away? Probably. With growing concern Eleanor thought of the many times he had changed jobs. Where was he now?

Arthur had an early dinner in a cafeteria on 14th Street. He chose beef stew, lemon meringue pie and coffee. He ate slowly and carefully. It was important that he eat well now. It might be days before he had a hot meal again.

His plans were made. After dark he would go back to Patricia Traymore's house. He'd slip in through the upstairs window. He'd settle himself in the closet in the guest room. He'd bring cans of soda; he still had one of the Danish pastries and two of the rolls from this morning in his pocket. He'd better pick up some cans of juice too. And maybe he should get some peanut butter and rye bread. That would be enough to hold him over until he saw the program the next night.

He had to spend ninety of his precious dollars on a miniature black-and-white TV with a headset. That way he could watch the program right in Patricia Traymore's house.

On the way to her house, he'd buy caffeine pills in the drugstore. He couldn't take the chance of crying out in his sleep. Oh, she'd probably never hear him from her room, but he couldn't risk it.

Forty minutes later he was in Georgetown, two streets from Patricia Traymore's home. The whole area was quiet, more quiet than he would have liked. Now that the Christmas shopping was over, a stranger was more likely to be noticed. The police might even be keeping a watch on Miss Traymore's house. But the fact that she had the corner property helped. The house behind hers was dark.

Arthur slipped into the yard of the unlighted house. The wooden fence that separated the backyards wasn't high. He dropped his shopping bag over the fence, making sure that it slid down onto a snowbank, and then easily climbed over.

He waited. There wasn't a sound. Miss Traymore's car wasn't in the driveway. Her house was totally dark.

It was awkward getting up the tree with the shopping bag. The trunk was icy and hard to grasp; he could feel its rough coldness through his gloves. Without the tiers of branches, he could not have made it. The window was stiff and hard to raise. When he stepped over the sill into the room, the floorboards creaked heavily.

For agonizing minutes he waited by the window, ready to bolt out again, to clamber down the tree and run across the yard. But there was only silence in the house. That and the occasional rumble of the furnace.

He began to organize his hiding place in the closet. To his satisfaction he realized that the shelves were not attached to the walls. If he spread them out just a little, they would look as though they were touching the walls and no one would realize how much space he had in the triangular area behind him.

Carefully he began to set up his secret place. He selected a thick quilt and laid it on the floor. It was large enough to use as a sleeping bag. He set up his supplies of food and his television set. There were four king-size pillows on the lowest shelf.

In a few minutes he was settled. Now he needed to explore.

Unfortunately, she hadn't left any lights on. It meant he could move around only by holding his flashlight very low to the floor so no gleam could show out the window. Several times he practiced going back and forth between the guest bedroom and the master suite. He tested the floorboards and found the one that creaked.

It took him twelve seconds to make his way down the hall from his closet to Pat's room. He crept into her room and over to the vanity table. He had never seen such pretty objects. Her comb and mirror and brushes were all decorated with ornate silver. He took the stopper from the perfume bottle and inhaled the subtle fragrance.

Then he went into the bathroom, noticed her negligee on the back of the door and tentatively touched it. Angrily he thought that this was the kind of clothing Glory would enjoy.

Had the police gone to Glory's office to question her? She should be home now. He wanted to talk to her.

He made his way over to the bed, found the phone on the night table and dialed. After the fourth ring he began to frown. She had talked about turning herself in to the police, but she would never do that after having promised she'd wait. No, she was probably lying in bed, trembling, waiting to see if her picture was shown on the program tomorrow night.

He replaced the phone on the night table but sat crouched by Pat's bed. Already he missed Glory. He was keenly aware of the solitary quiet of the house. But he knew that soon his voices would come to join him.

CHAPTER 36

"That was fine, Senator," Luther said. "Sorry I had to ask you to change. But we did want the look of a single working day, so you had to be wearing the same outfit coming home as going out."

"It's all right. I should have realized that," Abigail said shortly.

They were in her living room. The camera crew were packing their equipment. Toby could see that Abigail had no intention of offering Pelham a drink. She just wanted to be rid of him.

Luther was obviously getting the message. "Hurry up," he snapped at the crew. Then he smiled ingratiatingly. "I know it's been a long day for you, Abigail. Just one more session in the studio tomorrow morning and we'll wrap it up."

"That will be the happiest moment in my life."

Toby wished Abigail could relax. They'd gone for a drive and passed the Vice President's mansion a couple of times. Abby had even joked about it: "Can you imagine what the columnists would say if they saw me casing the place?" But as soon as the camera crew arrived, she'd tensed up again.

Pelham was putting on his coat. "The President has called a news conference for nine P.M. in the East Room tomorrow night. Are you planning to be there, Abigail?"

"I believe I've been invited," she said.

"That makes our timing excellent. The program will run between six-thirty and seven, so there won't be a schedule conflict for the viewers."

"I'm sure all of Washington is fainting with anticipation," Abigail said. "Luther, I really am terribly tired."

"Of course. Forgive me. I'll see you in the morning. Nine o'clock, if that's all right."

''One minute more and I'd have gone mad,'' Abigail said when she and Toby were finally alone. ''And when I think all this is absolutely unnecessary . . .''

''No, it's not unnecessary, Senator,'' Toby said soothingly. ''You still have to be confirmed by Congress. Sure, you'll get a majority, but it would be nice if a lot of people sent telegrams cheering your nomination along. The program can do that for you.''

''In that case it will be worth it.''

''Abby, is there anything more you want me for tonight?''

''No, I'm going to bed early and read until I fall asleep. It's been a long day.'' She smiled, and he could see she was starting to unwind. ''Which waitresses are you chasing now? Or is it a poker game?''

Pat got home at six-thirty. She switched on the foyer light, but the stairs past the turn remained in shadow.

Her father's angry words suddenly echoed in her ears: ''You shouldn't have come.''

That last night the bell had run insistently; her father had opened the door; someone had brushed past him; that person had been looking up—that is why she was so scared; Daddy was angry and she was afraid she'd been seen.

Her hand shook as she placed it on the banister. There's no use getting upset, she thought. It's just that I'm overtired and it's been a rough day. I'll get comfortable and fix some dinner.

In her bedroom she undressed quickly and reached for the robe on the back of the door, then decided she would wear the brown velour caftan instead. It was warm and comfortable.

At her dressing table she tied back her hair and began to cream her face. Mechanically her fingertips moved over her skin, rotating in the pattern the beautician had taught her, pressing for an instant against her temples, touching the faint scar near her hairline.

The furniture behind her was reflected in the mirror; the posts of the bed seemed like tall sentinels. She looked intently into the mirror. She had heard that if you picture an imaginary dot on your forehead and stare into it you can hypnotize yourself and retreat back into the past. For a full minute she concentrated on the imaginary dot, and had the odd sensation of watching herself walking backward into a tunnel . . . and it seemed she was not alone. She had a sense of another presence.

Ridiculous. She was getting lightheaded and fanciful.

Going downstairs to the kitchen, she fixed an omelette, coffee and toast and forced herself to eat.

The kitchen had a cozy, calming warmth. She and her mother and father must sometimes have eaten together here. Did she have a vague recollection of sitting on her father's lap at this table? Veronica had shown her their last Christmas card. It was signed Dean, Renée and Kerry.

She said the names aloud, ''Dean, Renée and Kerry'' and wondered why the cadence seemed wrong.

Rinsing the dishes and putting them in the dishwasher was a reason for delaying what she knew must be done. She had to study that newspaper article and see if it divulged any new facts about Dean and Renée Adams.

The paper was still on the library table. Opening it to the center spread, she forced herself to read every line of the text. Much of it she already knew but that did not help to deaden the pain . . . ''The gun smeared with both their fingerprints . . . Dean Adams had died instantly from the bullet wound in his forehead . . . Renée Adams might have lived a short time. . . .'' One column emphasized the rumors her neighbors had gleefully picked up at the party: the marriage was clearly unhappy, Renée had urged her husband to leave Washington, she despised the constant round of receptions, she was jealous of the attention her husband attracted from other women. . . .

That quote from a neighbor: ''She was clearly besotted with him—and *he* had a roving eye.''

There were persistent rumors that Renée, not Dean, had fired the gun. At the inquest, Renée's mother had attempted to squelch that speculation. ''It is not a mystery,'' she said, ''it is a tragedy. Only a few days before she was murdered, my daughter told me she was coming home with Kerry and would file for divorce and custody. I believe that her decision triggered his violence.''

She could have been right, Pat thought. I remember tripping over a body. Why am I sure it was Mother's, not his? *She wasn't sure.*

She studied the informal snapshots that covered most of the second page. Willard Jennings was so scholarly-looking. Catherine Graney had said that he wanted to give up Congress and accept a college presidency. And Abigail had been an absolutely beautiful young woman. There was one rather blurred snapshot sandwiched in among the others. Pat glanced at it several times, then moved the paper so that the light shone directly on it.

It was a candid shot that had been taken on the beach. Her father, her mother and Abigail were in a group with two other people. Her mother was absorbed in a book. The two strangers were lying on blankets, their eyes closed. The camera had caught her father and Abigail looking at each other. There was no mistaking the air of intimacy.

There was a magnifying glass in the desk. Pat found it and held it over the picture. Magnified, Abigail's expression became rapturous. Her father's eyes were tender as they looked down at her. Their hands were touching.

Pat folded the newspaper. What did the pictures mean? A casual flirtation? Her father had been attractive to women, probably encouraged their attention. Abigail had been a beautiful young widow. Maybe that was all it amounted to.

As always when she was troubled, Pat turned to music. In the living room she plugged in the Christmas-tree lights and impulsively switched off the chandelier. At the piano she let her fingers rove over the keys until she found the soft notes of Beethoven's *Pathétique.*

Sam had been himself again today, the way she'd remembered him, strong and confident. He needed time. Of course he did. So did she. Two years ago they'd felt so torn and guilty about their relationship. Now it could be different.

Her father and Abigail Jennings. Had they been involved? Had she just been one in a string of casual affairs? Her father might have been a ladies' man. Why not? He was certainly attractive, and it was the style among rising young politicians then—look at the Kennedys. . . .

Eleanor Brown. Had the lawyer been able to arrange bail for her? Sam hadn't phoned. Eleanor is innocent, Pat told herself—I am sure of it.

Liszt's *Liebestraum.* That was what she was playing now. And the Beethoven. She had unconsciously chosen both those pieces the other night as well. Had her mother played them here? The mood of both of them was the same, plaintive and lonely.

"Renée, listen to me. Stop playing and listen to me." "I can't. Let me alone." The voices—his troubled and urgent, hers despairing.

They quarreled so much, Pat thought. After the quarrels she would play for hours. But sometimes, when she was happy, she'd put me on the bench next to her. *"No, Kerry, this way. Put your fingers here. . . . She can pick out the notes when I hum them. She's a natural."*

Pat felt her hands beginning the opening notes of Mendelssohn's *Opus 30, Number 3,* another piece that suggested pain. She stood up. There were too many ghosts in this room.

Sam phoned just as she was starting up the stairs again. "They won't release Eleanor Brown. They're afraid she'll jump bail. It seems the man she's living with is a suspect in some nursing-home deaths."

"Sam, I can't stand thinking of that girl in a cell."

"Frank Crowley, the lawyer I sent, thinks she's telling the truth. He's getting a transcript of her trial in the morning. We'll do what we can for her, Pat. It may not be much, I'm afraid. . . . How are you?"

"Just about to turn in."

"The place locked up?"

"Bolted tight."

"Good. Pat, it may be all over but the shouting. Quite a few of us have been invited to the White House tomorrow night. The President's making an important announcement. Your name is on the media list. I checked."

"Sam, do you think . . . ?"

"I just don't know. The money's on Abigail, but the President is really playing it close. None of the possible appointees has been given Secret Service protection yet. That's always a tip-off. I guess the President wants to keep everyone guessing until the last minute. But no matter who gets it, you and I will go out and celebrate."

"Suppose you don't agree with his choice?"

"At this point I don't give a damn whom he chooses. I've got other things in mind. I want to celebrate just being with you. I want to catch up on the last two years. After we stopped seeing each other, the only way I could get over missing you was to tell myself why it wouldn't have worked even if I was free. After a while, I guess I started to believe my own lies."

Pat's laugh was shaky. She blinked back the sudden moisture in her eyes. "Apology accepted."

"Then I want to talk about not wasting any more of our lives."

"I thought you needed more time. . . ."

"Neither of us does." Even his voice was different—confident, strong, the way she had remembered it all those nights she had lain awake thinking about him. "Pat, I fell hopelessly in love with you that day on Cape Cod. Nothing will ever change that. I'm so damn grateful you waited for me."

"I had no choice. Oh, God, Sam, it's going to be marvelous. I love you so."

For minutes after they said goodbye, Pat stood with her hand resting on the telephone as though by touching it, she could hear again every single word Sam had uttered. Finally, still smiling softly, she started up the stairs. A sudden creaking sound overhead startled her. She knew what it was. That one board on the upstairs landing which always moved when she stepped on it.

Don't be ridiculous, she told herself.

The hallway was poorly lit by flame-shaped bulbs in wall sconces. She started to go into her bedroom, then impulsively turned and walked toward the back of the house. Deliberately she stepped on the loose board and listened as it responded with a distinct creaking. I'd swear that's the sound I heard. She went into her old bedroom. Her footsteps echoed on the uncarpeted floor. The room was stuffy and hot.

The door of the guest bedroom was not quite closed. It was much cooler in there. She felt a draft and walked over to the window. The window was open from the top. She tried to close it, then realized the sash cord was broken. That's what it is, she thought; there's probably enough draft to make the door sway. Even so, she opened the closet and glanced at the shelves of bedding and linen.

In her room she undressed quickly and got into bed. It was ridiculous to still feel so jittery. Think about Sam; think about the life that they would have together.

Her last impression before she began to doze was the strange feeling that she was not alone. It didn't make sense, but she was too tired to think about it.

With a sigh of relief, Catherine Graney reversed the sign on the shop door from "OPEN" to "CLOSED." For the day after Christmas, business had been unexpectedly brisk. A buyer from Texas had bought the pair of Rudolstadt figura candelabra, the marquetry game tables and the Stouk carpet. It had been a most impressive sale.

Catherine turned off the lights in her shop and went upstairs to her apartment, Sligo at her heels. She had laid a fire that morning. Now she touched a match to the paper under the kindling. Sligo settled in his favorite spot.

Going into the kitchen, she began to fix dinner. Next week when young George was here she'd enjoy cooking big meals. But a chop and a salad were all she wanted now.

George had called her the day before to wish her a merry Christmas and to tell her the news. He'd been promoted to major. "Twenty-seven years old and an oak leaf already!" she'd exclaimed. "By God, would your Dad be proud."

Catherine put her chop under the broiler. One more good reason not to let Abigail Jennings smear George senior's name any longer. She wondered what Abigail had thought of the letter. She had worked and reworked it before mailing it Christmas Eve.

> *I must insist you take the opportunity on the upcoming program to publicly acknowledge that there has never been a shred of proof to indicate that pilot error caused your husband's fatal accident. It is not enough to no longer smear George Graney's reputation: you must set the record straight. If you do not, I will sue you for libel and reveal your true relationship with Willard Jennings.*

At eleven o'clock she watched the news. At eleven-thirty Sligo nuzzled her hand. "I know," she groaned. "Okay, get your leash."

The evening was dark. Earlier there'd been some stars, but now the sky was clouded over. The breeze was raw, and Catherine pulled up the collar of her coat. "This is going to be one quick walk," she told Sligo.

There was a path through the woods near her house. Usually she and Sligo cut through there and then walked back around the block. Now he strained at the leash, rushing her through the path to his favorite bushes and trees. Then he stopped abruptly and a low growl came from his throat.

"Come on," Catherine said impatiently. All that she'd need would be for him to go after a skunk.

Sligo leaped forward. Bewildered, Catherine watched as a hand shot out and grabbed the old animal in a lock around the neck. There was a sickening cracking sound, and Sligo's limp body dropped onto the hardened snow.

Catherine tried to scream, but no sound came. The hand that had snapped Sligo's neck was raised over her head, and in the instant before she died, Catherine Graney finally understood what had happened that long-ago day.

CHAPTER 37

On the morning of December 27, Sam got up at seven, reread the transcript of the CAA investigation into the crash that had killed Congressman Willard Jennings, underlined a particular sentence and phoned Jack Carlson. "How are you coming with that report on Toby Gorgone?"

"I'll have it by eleven."

"Are you free for lunch? I have something to show you." It was the sentence from the transcript: *"Congressman Jennings' chauffeur, Toby Gorgone, placed his luggage on the plane."* Sam wanted to read the report on Toby before discussing it.

They agreed to meet at the Gangplank Restaurant at noon.

Next Sam phoned Frank Crowley, the attorney he'd hired to represent Eleanor Brown, and invited him to the same lunch. "Can you have the transcript of Eleanor Brown's trial with you?"

"I'll make sure I have it, Sam."

The coffee was perking. Sam poured a cup and turned on the kitchen radio. Most of the nine-o'clock news was over. The weatherman was now promising a partly sunny day. The temperature would be in the low thirties. And then the headlines were recapped, including the fact that the body of a prominent antiques dealer, Mrs. Catherine Graney of Richmond, had been found in a wooded area near her home. Her dog's neck had been broken. Police believed the animal had died trying to defend her.

Catherine Graney dead! Just as she'd been about to blow open a potential scandal involving Abigail. "I don't believe in coincidence," Sam said aloud. "I just don't believe in it."

For the rest of the morning he agonized over his suspicions. Several times he reached for the phone to call the White House. Each time he withdrew his hand.

He had absolutely no proof that Toby Gorgone was anything but what he appeared to be, a devoted bodyguard-chauffeur for Abigail. Even if Toby was guilty of the crime, he had absolutely no proof that Abigail was aware of his activities.

The President would announce the appointment of Abigail that night. Sam was sure of it. But the confirmation hearings were several weeks away. There would be time to launch a thorough investigation. And this time I'll make sure there's no whitewash, he thought grimly.

Somehow Sam was sure that Toby was responsible for the threats to Pat. If he had anything to hide, he wouldn't want her digging into the past.

If he turned out to be the one who had threatened her . . .

Sam clenched his hands into fists. He was no longer thinking of himself as a grandfather-to-be.

* * *

Abigail twisted her hands nervously. "We should have left earlier," she said, "we're in all the traffic. Step on it."

"Don't worry, Senator," Toby said soothingly. "They can't start taping without you. How did you sleep?"

"I kept waking up. All I could think of was 'I am going to be Vice President of the United States.' Turn on the radio. Let's see what they're saying about me. . . ."

The eight-thirty CBS news was just beginning. "Rumors persist that the reason the President has called a news conference for this evening is to announce his choice of either Senator Abigail Jennings or Senator Claire Lawrence as Vice President of the United States, the first woman to be so honored." And then: "In a tragic coincidence, it has been learned that Mrs. Catherine Graney, the Richmond antiques dealer found murdered while walking her dog, is the widow of the pilot who died twenty-seven years ago in a plane crash with Congressman Willard Jennings. Abigail Jennings began her political career when she was appointed to complete her husband's term. . . ."

"Toby!"

He glanced into the rearview mirror. Abigail looked shocked. "Toby, how awful."

"Yeah, it's lousy." He watched as Abigail's expression hardened.

"I'll never forget how Willard's mother went to that woman and sat with her when the plane was overdue. She never even called to see how *I* was."

"Well, they're together now, Abby. Look how fast the traffic is moving. We'll be at the studio right on time."

As they pulled into the private parking area, Abigail asked quietly, "What did you do last night, Toby—play poker or have a date?"

"I saw the little lady from Steakburger and spent the evening with her. Why? You checking on me? You want to talk to her, Senator?" Now his tone had an indignant edge.

"No, of course not. You're welcome to your cocktail waitresses, on your own time. I hope you enjoyed yourself."

"I did. I haven't been taking much personal time lately."

"I know. I've kept you awfully busy." Her voice was conciliatory. "It's just . . ."

"Just *what,* Senator?"

"Nothing . . . nothing at all."

At eight o'clock Eleanor was taken for a lie-detector test. She had slept surprisingly well. She remembered that first night in a cell eleven years ago when she had suddenly started to scream. "You expressed acute claustrophobia that night," a psychiatrist had told her after the breakdown. But now there was a curious peacefulness about not running anymore.

Could Father have hurt those old people? Eleanor racked her brain, trying to remember a single example of his being anything but kind and gentle. There was none.

''This door.'' The matron led her into a small room near the cellblock. Detective Barrott was reading the newspaper. She was glad he was there. He didn't treat her as though she were a liar. He looked up at her and smiled.

Even when another man came in and hooked her to the lie-detector machine, she didn't start to cry the way she had after her arrest for stealing from the Senator. Instead, she sat in the chair, held up her doll and a little embarrassed, asked if they'd mind if she kept it with her. They didn't act as though it were a crazy request. Frank Crowley, that nice fatherly-looking man who was her lawyer, came in. She had tried to explain to him yesterday that she couldn't pay him more than the nearly five hundred dollars she'd saved, but he told her not to worry about it.

''Eleanor, you can still refuse to take this test,'' he told her now, and she said that she understood.

At first the man who was giving her the test asked simple, even silly questions about her age and education and her favorite food. Then he started asking the ones she'd been gearing herself to hear.

''Have you ever stolen anything?''

''No.''

''Not even anything small, like a crayon or a piece of chalk when you were little?''

The last time she'd been asked that, she'd started sobbing, ''I'm not a thief. I'm *not* a thief.'' But now it wasn't that hard. She pretended she was talking to Detective Barrott, not this brusque, impersonal stranger. ''I've never, ever stolen anything in my life,'' she said earnestly. ''Not even a crayon or a piece of chalk. I couldn't take anything that belonged to anyone else.''

''What about the bottle of perfume when you were in high school?''

''*I did not steal it.* I swear to you. I forgot to give it to the clerk!''

''How often do you drink? Every day?''

''Oh, no. I just have wine sometimes, and not very much. It makes me sleepy.'' She noticed that Detective Barrott smiled.

''Did you take the seventy-five thousand dollars from Senator Jennings' campaign office?''

Last time during the test, she'd gotten hysterical at that question. Now she simply said, ''No, I did not.''

''But you put five thousand dollars of that money in your storage room, didn't you?''

''No, I did not.''

''Then how do you think it got there?''

The questions went on and on. ''Did you lie when you claimed Toby Gorgone phoned?''

''No, I did not.''

''You're sure it was Toby Gorgone?''

''I thought it was. If it wasn't, it sounded just like him.''

Then the incredible questions began: ''Did you know Arthur Stevens was a suspect in the death of one of his patients, a Mrs. Anita Gillespie?''

She almost lost control. ''No, I did not. I can't believe that.'' Then she remembered the way he'd yelled in his sleep: *''Close your eyes, Mrs. Gillespie. Close your eyes!''*

''You do believe it's possible. It shows up right in this test.''

''No,'' she whispered. ''Father could never have hurt anyone, only help them. He takes it so to heart when one of his patients is in pain.''

''Do you think he might try to stop the pain?''

''I don't know what you mean.''

''I think you do. Eleanor, Arthur Stevens tried to set fire to the nursing home on Christmas Day.''

''That's impossible.''

The shock of what she was hearing made Eleanor blanch. Horrified, she stared at the interrogator as he asked his last question: ''Did you ever have any reason to suspect that Arthur Stevens was a homicidal maniac?''

During the night Arthur swallowed caffeine pills every two hours. He could not risk falling asleep and calling out. Instead he sat crouched in the closet, too tense to lie down, staring into the dark.

He'd been so careless. When Patricia Traymore came home, he'd listened at the door of the closet to the sounds of her moving around the house. He'd heard the roar of the pipes when she'd showered; she'd gone back downstairs and he'd smelled coffee perking. Then she had begun playing the piano. Knowing it was safe to go out, he'd sat on the landing listening to the music.

That was when the voices started talking to him again, telling him that when this was over he must find a new nursing home where he could continue his mission. He'd been so deep in meditation that he hadn't realized that the music had stopped, hadn't thought about where he was until he heard Patricia Traymore's footsteps on the stairs.

In his rush to get to his hiding place he'd stepped on the loose board, and she had known something was wrong. He hadn't dared to breathe when she opened the door of the closet. But of course it never occurred to her to look behind the shelves.

And so he had kept watch all night, straining for the sounds of her awakening, glad when she finally left the house, but afraid to leave the closet for more than a few minutes at a time. A housekeeper might come in and hear him.

The long hours passed. Then the voices directed him to take the brown robe from Patricia Traymore's closet and put it on.

If she had betrayed Glory, he would be suitably clothed to mete out her punishment.

CHAPTER 38

Pat arrived at the network building at nine thirty-five and decided to have coffee and an English muffin in the drugstore. She wasn't ready for the charged atmosphere, underlying irritability and explosive nerves that she knew would be waiting on this final day of taping and editing. Her head was vaguely throbbing, her whole body sore. She knew that she had slept restlessly and that her dreams had been troubled. At one point she had cried out, but she couldn't remember what she had said.

In the car she had turned on the news and learned about Catherine Graney's death. She couldn't put the image of the woman out of her mind. The way her face had brightened when she talked about her son; the affectionate pat she had given her aging Irish setter. Catherine Graney would have followed through on her threat to sue Senator Jennings and the network after the program was aired. Her death had ended that threat.

Had she been the random victim of a mugger? The report had said she was walking her dog. What was his name? Sligo? It seemed unlikely that a criminal would choose to attack a woman with a large dog.

Pat pushed back the English muffin. She wasn't hungry. Only three days ago she had shared coffee with Catherine Graney. Now that attractive, vibrant woman was dead.

When she reached the studio, Luther was already on the set, his face mottled, his lips bloodless, his eyes constantly roving, hunting for flaws. "I said to get rid of those flowers!" he was shouting. "I don't give a damn whether they were just delivered or not. They look dead. Can't anybody do anything right around here? And that chair isn't high enough for the Senator. It looks like a goddamn milking stool." He spotted Pat. "I see you're finally here. You heard about that Graney woman? We'll have to redo the segment of Abigail talking about traffic safety. She comes across a little too heavy on the pilot. There's bound to be backlash when people find out his widow is a crime victim. We start taping in ten minutes."

Pat stared at Luther. Catherine Graney had been a good and decent person and all this man cared about was that her death had caused a setback in the taping. Wordlessly she turned and went into the dressing room.

Senator Jennings was seated in front of a mirror, a towel wrapped around her shoulders. The makeup artist was anxiously hovering over her, dabbing a touch of powder on her nose.

The Senator's fingers were tightly locked together. Her greeting was cordial enough. "This is it, Pat. Will you be as glad to be finished as I?"

"Yes, I think so, Senator."

The makeup girl picked up the can of hair spray and tested it.

"Don't use that stuff on me," the Senator snapped. "I don't want to look like a Barbie doll."

"I'm sorry." The girl's tone faltered. "Most people . . ." Her voice trailed off.

Aware that Abigail was watching her in the mirror, Pat deliberately avoided eye contact.

"There are a few points we should discuss." Now Abigail's tone was brisk and businesslike. "I'm just as glad we're redoing the air-safety segment, even though of course it's terrible about Mrs. Graney. But I want to come off more emphatically on the necessity for better facilities at small airports. And I've decided we should talk more about my mother. There's no use not meeting that *Mirror* picture and that spread in yesterday's *Tribune* head on. And we should certainly emphasize my role in foreign affairs. I've prepared some questions for you to ask me."

Pat put down the brush she was holding and turned to face the Senator. "*Have* you?"

Four hours later, over sandwiches and coffee, a small group sat in the projection room viewing the completed tape. Abigail was in the first row, Luther and Philip on either side of her. Pat sat several rows behind them with the assistant director. In the last row, Toby kept his solitary vigil.

The program opened with Pat, Luther and the Senator sitting in a semicircle. "Hello, and welcome to the first program in our series *Women in Government. . . .*" Pat studied herself critically. Her voice was huskier than usual; there was something in the rigid way she was sitting that suggested tension. Luther was totally at ease, and on the whole, the opening sounded all right. She and Abigail complemented each other well. Abigail's blue silk dress had been a good choice; it expressed femininity without frills. Her smile was warm, her eyes crinkled. Her acknowledgment of the flattering introduction had no hint of coyness.

They discussed her position as senior Senator from Virginia. Abigail: "It's a tremendously demanding and satisfying job. . . ." The montage of shots of Apple Junction. The shot of Abigail with her mother. Pat watched the screen as Abigail's voice became tender. "My mother faced the same problem as so many working mothers today. She was widowed when I was six. She didn't want to leave me alone and so she took a job as a housekeeper. She sacrificed a hotel-management career so that she'd be there when I came home from school. We were very close. She was always embarrassed about her weight. She had a glandular problem. I guess a lot of people can understand. When I tried to get her to live with Willard and me, she'd laugh and say, 'No way is the mountain coming to Washington.' She was a funny, dear lady." At that point Abigail's voice trembled. And then Abigail explained the beauty contest: "Talk about win it for the Gipper . . . I won that for Mommy. . . ."

Pat found herself caught in the spell of Abigail's warmth. Even the scene in Abigail's den when the Senator had called her mother a fat tyrant seemed unreal now. But it *was* real, she thought. Abigail Jennings is a consummate actress. The clips of the reception and the first campaign. Pat's questions to Abigail: ''Senator, you were a young bride; you were completing your last year in college and you were helping your husband campaign for his first seat in Congress. Tell us how you felt about that.'' Abigail's answer: ''It was wonderful. I was very much in love. I'd always pictured myself getting a job as an assistant to someone in public office. To be there right at the beginning was thrilling. You see, even though a Jennings had always held that seat, Willard's competition was stiff. The night we heard Willard had been elected—I can't describe it. Every election victory is exciting, but the first one is unforgettable.''

The clip with the Kennedys at Willard Jennings' birthday party . . . Abigail said, ''We were all so young. . . . There were three or four couples who used to get together regularly and we'd sit around for hours talking. We were all so sure we could help to change the world and make life better. Now those young statesmen are gone. I'm the only one left in government and I often think of the plans Willard and Jack and the others were making.''

And my father was one of the ''others,'' Pat reflected as she watched the screen.

There were several genuinely touching scenes. Maggie in the office with Abigail thanking her for finding her mother a place in the nursing home; a young mother tightly holding her three-year-old daughter and telling how her ex-husband had kidnapped the child. ''No one would help me. No one. And then someone said, 'Call Senator Jennings. She gets things done.' ''

Yes, she does, Pat agreed.

But then, with Luther interviewing her, Abigail discussed the embezzled campaign funds. ''I'm so glad that Eleanor Brown has turned herself in to complete her debt to society. I only hope that she may also be honest enough to return whatever is left of that money, or tell who shared in spending it.''

Something made Pat turn around. In the semi-darkness of the screening room, Toby's thick bulk loomed in his chair, his hands folding under his chin, the onyx ring gleaming on his finger. His head was nodding approval. Quickly she looked back at the screen, not wanting to meet his gaze.

Luther questioned Abigail about her commitment to airline safety. ''Willard was constantly asked to speak at colleges and he accepted every possible date. He said that college was the time when young people were beginning to form mature judgments about the world, about government. We were living on a Congressman's salary and had to be very careful. I am a widow today because my husband chartered the cheapest plane he could find. . . . Do you know the statistics on how many army pilots bought a second-hand plane and tried to start a charter airline on a shoestring? Most of them went out of business. They hadn't the funds to keep the planes in proper condition. My husband died over twenty-five years ago and I've been fighting ever since to bar those small planes from busy fields. And I've always worked closely with the Airline Pilots Association to tighten and maintain rigid standards for pilots."

No mention of George Graney, but once again the implied reason for Willard Jennings' death. After all these years Abigail won't stop underscoring the blame for that accident, Pat thought. As she watched herself on the screen, she realized that the documentary had turned out exactly as she had planned it; it portrayed Abigail Jennings as a sympathetic human being and a dedicated public servant. The realization brought no satisfaction.

The program ended with Abigail walking into her home in the near-dark and Pat's commentary that like so many single adults, Abigail was going home alone, and she would spend the evening at her desk studying proposed legislation.

The screen went dark, and as the room brightened, they all stood up. Pat watched for Abigail's reaction. The Senator turned to Toby. He nodded approvingly, and with a relaxed smile Abigail pronounced the program a success.

She glanced at Pat. "In spite of all the problems, you've done a very good job. And you were right about using my early background. I'm sorry I gave you so much grief. Luther, what do you think?"

"I think you come across terrific. Pat, what's your feeling?"

Pat considered. They were all satisfied, and the ending was technically all right. Then what was it that was forcing her to press for an additional scene? The letter. She wanted to read the letter Abigail had written to Willard Jennings. "I have one problem," she said. "The personal aspects of this program are what make it special. I wish we hadn't ended on a business note."

Abigail raised her eyes impatiently. Toby frowned. The atmosphere in the room suddenly became strained. The projectionist's voice came over the loudspeaker. "Is that a wrap?"

"No. Run the last scene again," Luther snapped.

The room darkened and an instant later the closing two minutes of the program were replayed.

They all watched intently. Luther was the first to comment. "We can leave it, but I think Pat may be right."

"That's wonderful," Abigail said. "What are you going to do about it? I've got to be at the White House in a few hours and I don't intend to arrive there at the last second."

Can I get her to go along with me? Pat wondered. For some reason she desperately wanted to read the "Billy darling" letter and she wanted the Senator's spontaneous reaction to it. But Abigail had insisted on seeing every inch of the storyboard before they taped. Pat tried to sound casual. "Senator, you've been very generous in opening your personal files to us.

In the last batch Toby brought over I found a letter that might just give the final personal touch we want. Of course you can read it before we tape, but I think it would have a more natural quality if you don't. In any case, if it doesn't work, we'll go with the present close.''

Abigail's eyes narrowed. She looked at Luther. ''Have you read this letter?''

''Yes, I have. I agree with Pat. But it's up to you.''

She turned to Philip and Toby. ''You two went over everything you released for possible use on the program?''

''Everything, Senator.''

She shrugged. ''In that case . . . Just make sure you don't read a letter from someone saying she was Miss Apple Junction the year after me.''

They all laughed. There is something changed about her, Pat thought. She's surer of herself.

''We'll shoot in ten minutes,'' Luther said.

Pat hurried into the dressing room. She dabbed fresh powder on the beads of perspiration that had formed on her forehead. What is the matter with me? she asked herself fiercely.

The door opened and Abigail came in. She opened her purse and pulled out a compact. ''Pat, that program is pretty good, isn't it?''

''Yes, it is.''

''I was so against it. I had such a bad feeling about it. You've done a great job making me look like a pretty nice person.'' She smiled. ''Seeing the tape, I liked myself better than I have in a long time.''

''I'm glad.'' Here again was the woman she had admired so much.

A few minutes later they were back on the set. With her hand, Pat was covering the letter she was about to read. Luther began to speak. ''Senator, we want to thank you for sharing your time with us in this very personal way. What you have accomplished is certainly an inspiration to everyone and surely an example of how good can come from tragedy. When we were planning this program, you gave us many of your private papers. Among them we found a letter you wrote to your husband, Congressman Willard Jennings. I think this letter sums up the young woman you were and the woman you became. May I allow Pat to read it to you now?''

Abigail tilted her head, her expression questioning.

Pat unfolded the letter. Her voice husky, she read it slowly. ''Billy, darling.'' Her throat tightened. She had to force herself to go on. Again her mouth was hopelessly dry. She glanced up. Abigail was staring at her, the color draining from her face. ''You were splendid in the hearings this afternoon. I am so proud of you. I love you so and look forward to a lifetime of being with you, of working with you. Oh, my dearest, we really are going to make a difference in this world.''

Luther interjected, ''That note was written on May thirteenth, and on May twentieth Congressman Willard Jennings died and you went on alone to make a difference in this world. Senator Abigail Jennings, thank you.''

The Senator's eyes were shining. A tender half-smile played at the corners of her mouth. She nodded and her lips formed the words ''Thank you.''

''Cut,'' the director called.

Luther jumped up. ''Senator, that was perfect. Everybody will . . .''

He stopped in mid-sentence as Abigail lunged forward and grabbed the letter from Pat's hand. ''Where did you *get* that?'' she shrieked. ''What are you trying to *do* to me?''

''Senator, I told you, we don't have to use it,'' Luther protested.

Pat stared as Abigail's face twisted into a mask of anger and pain. Where had she seen that expression, on *that* face, once before?

A bulky figure rushed past her. Toby was shaking the Senator, almost shouting at her: ''Abby, get hold of yourself. That was a great way to end the program. *Abby, it's okay to let people know about your last letter to your husband.''*

''My . . . last . . . letter?'' Abigail raised one hand to cover her face as though she were trying to remold her expression. ''Of course . . . I'm sorry . . . It's just that Willard and I used to write little notes to each other all the time. . . . I'm so glad you found—the last one. . . .''

Pat sat immobilized. ''Billy darling, Billy darling . . .'' The words had a drumroll cadence, hammering in her mind. Gripping the arms of the chair, she looked up and met Toby's savage stare. She shrank back in mindless terror.

He turned back to Abigail and, with Luther and Phil assisting, escorted her from the studio. One by one the floodlights were turned off. ''Hey, Pat,'' the cameraman called. ''That's a wrap, isn't it?''

At last she was able to get up. ''It's a wrap,'' she agreed.

CHAPTER 39

Whenever Sam was wrestling with a problem, a long walk had a way of clearing his head and helping him think. That was why he elected to walk the several miles from his apartment to the Southwest section of the District. The Gangplank Restaurant was on the Washington Channel, and as he neared it, he studied the restless pattern of the whitecaps.

Cape Cod. Nauset Beach. Pat walking beside him, her hair tossed by the wind, her arm tucked in his, the incredible sense of freedom, as though it were just the two of them and sky and beach and ocean. Next summer we'll go back, he promised himself.

The restaurant resembled a ship moored to the dock. He hurried up the gangplank, enjoying the faint undulating feeling.

Jack Carlson was already seated at a window table. Several crushed cigarettes were in the ashtray in front of him, and he was sipping a Perrier. Sam apologized for being late.

"I'm early," Jack said simply. He was a trim, gray-haired man with bright, inquisitive eyes. He and Sam had been friends for more than twenty years.

Sam ordered a gin martini. "Maybe that will quiet me down or pick me up," he explained with an attempt at a smile. He felt Jack's eyes studying him.

"I've seen you looking more cheerful," Jack commented. "Sam, what made you ask us to check on Toby Gorgone?"

"Only a hunch." Sam felt himself tense. "Did you come up with anything interesting?"

"I'd say so."

"Hello, Sam." Frank Crowley, his normally pale face ruddy from the cold, his heavy white hair somewhat disheveled, joined them. He introduced himself to Jack, adjusted his silver-rimmed glasses, opened his briefcase and pulled out a bulky envelope. "I'm lucky to be here," he announced. "I started going through the trial transcript and almost forgot the time." The waiter was at his elbow. "Vodka martini, very dry," he ordered. "Sam, you seem to be the only one I know who can still drink gin martinis."

Without waiting for a reply, he continued. *"United States* versus *Eleanor Brown.* Makes interesting reading and boils down to one simple issue: which member of Senator Jennings' official family was lying, Eleanor or Toby? Eleanor took the stand in her own defense. A big mistake. She started talking about the shoplifting connection and the prosecutor blew it up until you'd think she'd robbed Fort Knox. The Senator's testimony didn't help any. She talked too damn much about giving Eleanor a second chance. I've marked the most relevant pages." He handed Carlson the transcript.

Jack took an envelope from his pocket. "Here's the fact sheet you wanted on Gorgone, Sam."

Sam skimmed it, raised his eyebrows and reread it carefully.

> Apple Junction: Suspect in car theft. Police chase resulted in death of three. No indictment.
> Apple Junction: Suspect in bookmaking operation. No indictment.
> New York City: Suspect in firebombing of car resulting in death of loan shark. No indictment.
> Thought to be on fringe of Mafia.
> May have settled gambling debts by performing services for mob.
> Other relevant fact: Exceptional mechanical aptitude.

''A perfectly clean record,'' he said sarcastically.

Over sliced-steak sandwiches they discussed, compared and evaluated the fact sheet on Toby Gorgone, Eleanor Brown's trial transcript, the CAA findings on the plane crash and the news of Catherine Graney's murder. By the time coffee was served, they had separately and jointly arrived at disturbing possibilities: Toby was a mechanical whiz who had left a suitcase on the Jennings plane minutes before takeoff and the plane had crashed under mysterious circumstances. Toby was a gambler who might have been in debt to bookies at the time the campaign funds disappeared.

''It seems to me that Senator Jennings and this character Toby take turns exchanging favors,'' Crowley commented. ''She alibis for him and he pulls her chestnuts out of the fire.''

''I can't believe Abigail Jennings would deliberately send a young girl to prison,'' Sam said flatly. ''And I certainly don't believe she'd be party to the murder of her husband.'' He realized they were all whispering now. They were talking about a woman who in a few hours might become Vice President-designate of the United States.

The restaurant was starting to empty. The diners, most of them government people, were hurrying back to their jobs. Probably at one point during lunch every one of them had speculated about the President's conference tonight.

''Sam, I've seen dozens of characters like this Toby,'' Jack said. ''Most of them in the mob. They're devoted to the head guy. They smooth his path—and take care of themselves at the same time. Perhaps Senator Jennings wasn't involved in Toby's activities. But look at it this way: Let's say Toby knew Willard Jennings wanted to give up his seat in Congress and get a divorce from Abigail. Jennings wasn't worth fifty thousand bucks in his own right. Mama held the purse strings. So Abigail would have been out of the political scene, dropped by Willard Jennings' circle of friends and back to being an ex-beauty queen from a hick town. And Toby decided not to let that happen.''

''Are you suggesting she returned the favor by lying for him about the campaign money?'' Sam asked.

''Not necessarily,'' Frank said. ''Here—read the Senator's testimony on the stand. She admitted that they stopped at a gas station around the time Eleanor received the call. The engine had developed a knock and Toby wanted to check it. She swears he was never out of her sight. But she *was* on her way to deliver a speech and probably studying her notes. One minute she probably saw Toby in front of the car tinkering at the engine; the next maybe he was behind it getting a tool out of the trunk. How long does it take to scoot around to the public phone, dial a number and leave a two-second message? I'd have torn that testimony apart. But even assuming we're right, I can't understand why Toby picked Eleanor.''

"That's easy," Jack said. "He knew about her record. He knew how sensitive she was. Without that open-and-shut case, there'd have been a full-blown investigation into the missing funds. He'd have been a suspect and his background investigated. He's smart enough to have gotten away with another 'no indictment' on his fact sheet, but the Senator would have been pressured by the party to get rid of him."

"If what we believe about Toby Gorgone checks out," Sam concluded, "Catherine Graney's death becomes too timely, too convenient to be a case of random murder."

"If Abigail Jennings gets the nod from the President tonight," Jack said, "and it comes out that her chauffeur murdered the Graney woman, those confirmation hearings will be a worldwide scandal."

The three men sat at the table, each somberly reflecting on the possible embarrassment to the President. Sam finally broke the silence.

"One bright note is if we can prove Toby wrote those threatening notes and arrest him, I can stop worrying about Pat."

Frank Crowley nodded at Jack. "And if your people get enough on him, Toby might be persuaded to tell the truth about the campaign funds. I tell you, to see that poor girl Eleanor Brown taking that lie-detector test this morning and swearing she'd never even stolen a piece of chalk would break your heart. She doesn't look eighteen, never mind thirty-four. That prison experience almost killed her. After her breakdown a shrink had her paint a doll's face to show how she felt. She still carries that doll around with her. The damn thing would give you the creeps. It looks like a battered child."

"A doll!" Sam exclaimed. "She has a *doll.* By any chance, is it a Raggedy Ann doll?"

At Frank's astonished nod, he signaled for more coffee. "I'm afraid we're barking up the wrong tree," he said wearily. "Let's start all over again."

CHAPTER 40

Toby poured a Manhattan into the chilled cocktail glass and set it down in front of Abigail. "Drink this, Senator. You need it."

"Toby where did she get that letter? Where did she get it?"

"I don't know, Senator."

"It couldn't have been in anything you gave her. I never saw it again after I wrote it. *How much does she know?* Toby, if she could prove I was there that night . . ."

"She can't, Senator. No one can. And no matter what she may have dug up, she hasn't any proof. Come on, she did you a favor. That letter will clinch sympathy for you. Wait and see."

He finally appeased her the only way that worked. "*Trust* me! Don't worry about it. Have I ever let you down?" He calmed her a little, but even so, she was still a bundle of nerves. And in a few hours she was due at the White House.

"Listen, Abby," he said. "While I fix you something to eat, I want you to belt two Manhattans. After that have a hot bath and sleep for an hour. Then get yourself in your best-looking outfit. This is the biggest night of your life."

He meant it. She had reason to be upset—plenty of reason. The minute he heard the letter being read, he'd been on his feet. But as soon as Pelham said, "Your husband was lost a week later," he'd known it would be all right.

Abby almost blew it. Once again he'd been there to stop her from making a terrible mistake.

Abby reached for her glass. "Bottoms up," she said, and a touch of a smile lingered around her lips. "Toby, in a little while we'll have it."

The Vice Presidency. "That's right, Senator." He was sitting on a hassock across from the couch.

"Ah, Toby," she said. "What would I have become without you?"

"State assemblywoman from Apple Junction."

"Oh, sure." She tried to smile.

Her hair was loose around her face and she didn't look more than thirty years old. She was so slim. Slim the way a woman should be. Not a bag of bones, but firm and sleek.

"Toby, you look as though you're thinking. That would be a first."

He grinned at her, glad she was starting to loosen up. "You're the smart one. I leave the thinking to you."

She sipped the drink quietly. "The program turned out all right?"

"I keep telling you . . . it wouldn't have made sense for you to carry on about the letter. She did you a favor."

"I know. . . . It's just . . ."

The Manhattan was hitting her. He had to get some food into her. "Senator, you relax. I'll fix a tray for you."

"Yes . . . that would be a good idea. Toby, do you realize that a few hours from now I'm going to be Vice President-designate of the United States?"

"I sure do, Abby."

"We all know how ceremonial the office is. But Toby, if I do a good job, they may not be able to deny me the top spot next year. That's what I intend to have happen."

"I know that, Senator." Toby refilled her glass. "I'm going to fix you an omelette. Then you're going to take a nap. This is your night."

Toby got up. He couldn't look anymore at the naked yearning on her face. He'd seen it the day she got the news that she wouldn't be eligible for a scholarship to Radcliffe. She'd come over to where he was mowing the lawn and shown him the letter, then sat on the porch steps, hugged her legs and dropped her head in her lap. She'd been eighteen years old. "Toby, I want to go there so bad. I can't rot in this stinking town. I can't. . . ."

And then he'd suggested she romance that jerk Jeremy Saunders. . . . He'd helped her other times, helped her to find her destiny.

And now, once again, somebody was trying to ruin everything for her.

Toby went into the kitchen. As he prepared the dinner he tried to envision how interesting it would be when Abby was one heartbeat away from the Presidency.

The phone rang. It was Phil. "The Senator okay?"

"She's fine. Look, I'm getting her dinner."

"I have a piece of information you wanted. Guess who owns Pat Traymore's house."

Toby waited.

"Pat Traymore, that's who. It's been in trust for her since she was four years old."

Toby whistled soundlessly. Those eyes, that hair, a certain look about her . . . Why hadn't he figured it out before this? He could have blown everything by being so dumb.

Phil's voice was querulous. "Did you hear me? I said . . ."

"I heard you. Just keep it under your hat. What the Senator don't know won't hurt her."

A short time later he went back to his apartment above the garage. Under his urging, Abigail decided to watch the program while resting in her room. At eight o'clock he would bring the car around and they'd leave for the White House.

He waited until the program had been on a few minutes, then quietly left his apartment. His car, a black Toyota, was in the driveway. He pushed it until he could roll it down to the street. He didn't want Abby to know he was going out. He had a little less than an hour and a half for the round trip to Pat Traymore's house.

It was enough to do what was needed.

CHAPTER 41

Pat drove across Massachusetts Avenue, up Q Street, over the Buffalo Bridge and into Georgetown. Her head was aching now —a steady throbbing. She drove by rote, observing traffic lights subconsciously.

Presently she was on 31st Street, turning the corner, pulling into her driveway. She was on the steps, the slap of the wind on her face. Her fingers were fumbling in her purse for her key. The lock was clicking; she was pushing the door open, going into the shadowy quiet of the foyer.

In a reflex action, she closed the door and leaned against it. The coat was heavy on her shoulders. She shrugged it off, tossed it aside. She raised her head; her eyes became riveted on the step at the bend of the staircase. *There was a child sitting there. A child with long reddish-brown hair, her chin leaning on the palms of her hands; her expression curious.*

I wasn't asleep, she thought. I heard the doorbell ring and I wanted to see who was coming. *Daddy opened the door and someone pushed past him. He was angry. I ran back to bed.* When I heard the first shot, I didn't come right down. I stayed in bed and screamed for Daddy.

But he didn't come. And I heard another loud bang and ran down the stairs to the living room. . . .

And then . . .

She realized she was trembling and light-headed. Going into the library, she poured brandy into a tumbler and sipped it quickly. Why had Senator Jennings been so devastated by that letter? She'd been panicky, furious, frightened.

Why?

It didn't make sense.

And why did I get so upset reading it? Why has it upset me every time I've read it?

The way Toby looked at me as though he hated me. The way he shouted at the Senator. He wasn't trying to calm her down. He was trying to warn her about something. But what?

She sat huddled in the corner of the sofa, her arms clasped around her knees. I used to sit in here like this when Daddy was working at his desk. "You can stay, Kerry, as long as you promise to be quiet." Why was her memory of him so vivid now? She could see him, not as he'd looked in the film clips but as he'd been here in this room, leaning back in the chair, tapping his fingers on the desk when he was concentrating.

The newspaper article was still open on the desk. On a sudden impulse she went over to it, reread it carefully. Her eyes kept coming back to the picture of her father and Abigail Jennings on the beach. There was an undeniably intimate quality there. A summer-afternoon flirtation or more? Suppose her mother had looked up and caught that glance between them?

Why was she so afraid? She'd slept so badly last night. A hot bath and a brief rest would help calm her down. Slowly she went upstairs to her room. Again she had the eerie feeling she was being watched. She had had the same sensation the night before, before she fell asleep, but again she brushed it from her mind.

The phone rang just as she reached her room. It was Lila.

''Pat, are you all right? I'm worried about you. I don't want to alarm you, but I must. I sense danger around you. Won't you please come over here now and stay with me?''

''Lila, I think the impression you're getting is that I'm really quite close to a breakthrough in remembering that night. Something happened today, during the final taping, that seems to be triggering it. But don't worry—no matter what it is, I can handle it.''

''Pat, *listen* to me. You shouldn't be in that house now!''

''It's the only way I'll be able to piece it together.''

She's nervous because of the break-ins, Pat told herself as she lay in the tub. She's afraid I can't face the truth. She slipped on her terry-cloth robe. Sitting at the dressing table, she unpinned her hair and began to brush it. She'd been wearing it in a chignon most of the week. She knew Sam liked it best when it was loose. Tonight she'd wear it that way.

She got into bed and turned the radio on low. She hadn't expected to doze, but she soon drifted off. The sound of Eleanor's name startled her into consciousness.

The bedside clock read six-fifteen. The program would be on in fifteen minutes.

''Giving as her motive that she could no longer endure the fear of being recognized, Miss Brown has surrendered and was taken into custody. She still steadfastly maintains her innocence of the theft for which she was convicted. A police spokesman said that in the nine years since she violated parole, Miss Brown had been living with a paramedic Arthur Stevens. Stevens is a suspect in a series of nursing-home deaths and a warrant has been issued for his arrest. A religious fanatic, he has been dubbed the 'nursing home angel.' ''

''The Nursing Home Angel!'' The first time he phoned, the caller had referred to himself as an angel of mercy, of deliverance, of vengeance. Pat bolted up and grabbed the phone. Frantically she dialed Sam's number, let the phone ring ten, twelve, fourteen times before she finally replaced it. If only she had realized what Eleanor was saying when she talked about Arthur Stevens! *He had begged Eleanor not to give herself up. To save Eleanor he might have tried to stop the program.*

Could Eleanor have been aware of those threats? No, I'm sure she wasn't, Pat decided. Her lawyer should know about this before we tell the police.

It was twenty-five past six. She got out of bed, tightened the belt of her robe and put on her slippers. As she hurried down the stairs, she wondered where Arthur Stevens was now. Was he aware that Eleanor was under arrest? Would he see the program and blame her when Eleanor's picture was shown? Blame her because Eleanor had not kept her promise to wait before going to the police?

In the living room she turned the chandelier to the brightest setting and took a moment to light the Christmas tree before switching on the set. Even so, the room had an oddly cheerless quality. Settling herself on the couch, she watched intently as the credits rolled after the six-o'clock news.

She had wanted the chance to watch the program alone. In the studio she'd been conscious of tuning into everyone else's reactions to it. Even so, she realized she was dreading seeing it again. It was much more than the usual apprehension of launching a new series.

The furnace rumbled and a hissing of air came from the heat risers. The sound made her jump. It's crazy what this place is doing to me, she thought.

The program was beginning. Critically Pat studied the three of them—the Senator, Luther and herself, sitting in the semicircle. The background was good. Luther had been right about changing the flowers. Abigail showed none of the tension she'd exhibited off-camera. The footage on Apple Junction was well chosen. Abigail's reminiscences about her early life had just the right touch of human interest. And it's all such a lie, Pat thought.

The films of Abigail and Willard Jennings at their wedding reception, at parties on the estate, during his campaigns. Abigail's tender memories of her husband as the clips were shown. "Willard and I . . . ," "My husband and I . . ." Funny she never once referred to him as Billy.

With growing awareness, Pat realized that the films of Abigail as a young woman had an oddly familiar quality. They were evoking memories that had nothing to do with her having viewed them so many times. Why was that happening now?

There was a commercial break.

The segment about Eleanor Brown and the embezzled funds would come next.

Arthur heard Patricia Traymore go down the stairs. Cautiously he tiptoed until he was sure he was listening to the faint sounds of the television broadcast coming from downstairs. He had been afraid that friends might join her to view the program. But she was alone.

For the first time in all these years he felt as though he were dressed in the garb God intended him to wear. With moist, open palms, he smoothed the fine wool against his body. This woman even defiled sacred garments. What right had she to wear the raiment of the chosen?

Returning to his secret place, he put on the earphones, turned on the set and adjusted the picture. He had tapped into the cable antenna, and the screen was remarkably clear. Kneeling as before an altar, his hands locked in the posture of prayer, Arthur began to watch the program.

Lila sat watching the documentary, her dinner on a tray before her. It was hard to make even a pretense of eating. Her absolute certainty that Pat was in serious danger only heightened as she saw Pat's image on the screen.

Cassandra's warnings, she thought bitterly. Pat won't listen to me. She simply has to get out of that house *or she will suffer a death more violent than her parents endured. She is running out of time.*

Lila had met Sam Kingsley just once and liked him very much. She sensed that he was important to Pat. Would it be of any use to try to talk to Congressman Kingsley, share her apprehension with him? Could she possibly persuade him to insist that Pat leave her home until this dark aura around it dissolved?

She pushed the tray aside, got up and reached for the green book. She would call him immediately.

Sam went directly to his office from the restaurant. He had several meetings scheduled, but found it impossible to concentrate on any of them. His mind kept returning to the luncheon discussion.

They had built a strong circumstantial case against Toby Gorgone, but Sam had been a prosecutor long enough to know that strong circumstantial evidence can be upset like a house of cards. And the Raggedy Ann doll was upsetting the case against Toby. If Toby was innocent of involvement in the plane crash and the embezzled funds, if Catherine Graney had been the victim of a random mugging, then Abigail Jennings was what she seemed to be—above reproach and a worthy candidate for the job most people expected her to get. But the more Sam thought about Toby, the more uneasy he got.

At twenty after six he was finally free and immediately dialed Pat. Her phone was busy. Quickly he locked his desk. He wanted to get home in time to watch the documentary.

The sound of the telephone stopped him as he was rushing out of the office. Some instinct warned him not to ignore it.

It was Jack Carlson. "Sam, are you alone?"

"Yes."

"We have some new developments in the Catherine Graney case. Her son found a draft of a letter she wrote to Senator Jennings. A letter that probably arrived at the Senator's house yesterday. It's pretty strong stuff. Mrs. Graney intended to attack Senator Jennings' version of her relationship with her husband, and she was going to sue her for libel if she didn't retract her statements about pilot error on the program."

Sam whistled. "Are you saying that Abigail may have received that letter yesterday?"

"Exactly. But that isn't the half of it. Mrs. Graney's neighbors had a party last night. We got a list of the guests and checked them all out. One young couple who came late, about eleven-fifteen or so, had trouble locating the exact street. They'd asked directions from a guy who was getting in his car two blocks away. He brushed them off fast. The car was a black Toyota, with Virginia plates. They described someone who sounds like Gorgone. The girl even remembers he was wearing a heavy, dark ring. We're picking Toby up for questioning. Do you think you ought to phone the White House?

Toby might have been seen near the site of Catherine Graney's murder. If he had killed Catherine Graney, everything else they suspected of him was possible, even logical. "Abigail has to know about this immediately," Sam said. "I'll go to her now. She should have the chance to withdraw her name from consideration. If she refuses, I'll call the President myself. Even if she had no idea of what Toby was up to, she's got to accept the moral responsibility."

"I don't think that lady has ever worried about moral responsibility. If J. Edgar were alive, she wouldn't have gotten this far toward the Vice Presidency. You saw that article in the *Trib* the other day about what great pals she was with Congressman Adams and his wife."

"I saw it."

"Like the paper said, there was always a rumor that another woman was the direct cause of the fatal quarrel. I was new in the Bureau when that case broke, but when I read that article, something started bugging me. On a hunch I pulled the Adams file. We have a memo in it about a freshman Congresswoman named Abigail Jennings. All the indications were that *she* was that other woman."

Try as she would, Abigail couldn't rest. The knowledge that in a few hours she would be nominated to be Vice President of the United States was too exhilarating to bear.

Madam Vice President. *Air Force Two* and the mansion on the grounds of the old Naval Observatory. Presiding over the Senate and representing the President all over the world.

In two years the Presidential nomination. I'll win, she promised herself. Golda Meir. Indira Gandhi. Margaret Thatcher. Abigail Jennings.

The Senate had been a mighty step up. The night she was elected Luther had said, "Well, Abigail, you're a member of the world's most exclusive club."

Now another vast step was impending. No longer one of one hundred Senators, but the second-highest official in the land.

She had decided to wear a three-piece outfit, a silk blouse and a skirt with a knitted jacket, in tones of pink and gray. It would show up well on the television sets.

Vice President Abigail Jennings . . .

It was six-fifteen. She got up from the chaise, went over to her dressing table and brushed her hair. With deft strokes she applied a touch of eye shadow and mascara. Excitement had flushed her cheeks; she didn't need blush. She might as well get dressed now, watch the program and practice her acceptance speech until it was time to leave for the White House.

She slipped into the suit and fastened a gold-and-diamond sunburst pin to her jacket. The library television set had the biggest screen. She'd watch her program in there.

"Stay tuned for *Women in Government.*"

She had already seen everything but the last few minutes of the program. Even so, it was reassuring to watch it again. Apple Junction under a fresh coating of snow had a down-home country look that concealed its shabby dreariness. Thoughtfully she studied the Saunders home. She remembered when Mrs. Saunders had ordered her to retrace her steps and take the path to the service entrance. She'd made that miserable witch pay for that mistake.

If it weren't for Toby's figuring out how to get the money for Radcliffe, where would she be now?

The Saunderses *owed* me that money, she told herself. Twelve years of humiliations in that house!

She watched the clips of the wedding reception, the early campaigns, Willard's funeral. She remembered the exultation she had felt when in the funeral car Jack Kennedy had agreed to urge the Governor to appoint her to complete Willard's term.

The insistent ring of the doorbell startled her. No one ever dropped in. Could someone from the press be brazen enough to ring like that? She tried to ignore it. But the peal became a steady, unbroken intrusion. She hurried to the door. "Who is it?"

"Sam."

She pulled open the door. He stepped in, his face grim, but she barely glanced at him. "Sam, why aren't you watching *This Is Your Life?* Come on." Grabbing his hand, she ran ahead into the library. On the program, Luther was asking her about her commitment to airline safety.

"Abigail, I have to talk to you."

"Sam, for heaven's sake. Don't you want me to see my own program?"

"This won't wait." Against the background of the documentary, he told her why he had come. He watched the disbelief grow in her eyes.

"You're trying to say Toby may have killed the Graney woman? You're crazy."

"Am I?"

"He was out on a date. That waitress will vouch for him."

"Two people described him accurately. The letter Catherine Graney wrote you was the motive."

"What letter?"

They stared at each other, and her face paled.

''He picks up your mail, doesn't he, Abigail?''

''Yes.''

''Did he get it yesterday?''

''Yes.''

''And what did he bring in?''

''The usual junk. Wait a minute. You can't make these accusations about him. You make them *to* him.''

''Then call him in here now. He's going to be picked up for questioning anyway.''

Sam watched as Abigail dialed the phone. Dispassionately he observed the beautiful outfit she was wearing. She was dressed up to become Vice President, he thought.

Abigail held the receiver to her ear, listening to the bell ring. ''He's probably just not answering. He certainly wouldn't expect me to be calling.'' Her voice trailed off, then became resolutely brisk. ''Sam, you can't believe what you're saying. Pat Traymore put you up to this. She's been out to sabotage me from the beginning.''

''Pat has nothing to do with the fact that Toby Gorgone was seen near Catherine Graney's home.''

On the television screen Abigail was discussing her leadership in airline safety regulations. ''I am a widow today because my husband chartered the cheapest plane he could find.''

Sam pointed to the set. ''That statement would have been enough to send Catherine Graney to the newspapers tomorrow morning, and Toby knew it. Abigail, if the President has called this news conference tonight to introduce you as Vice President-designate, you've got to ask him to postpone the announcement until this is cleared up.''

''Have you taken leave of your senses? I don't care if Toby was two blocks from where that woman was killed. What does it prove? Maybe he has a girlfriend or a floating card game in Richmond. He's probably just not answering the phone. I wish to God I hadn't bothered to answer the door.''

A sense of urgency overwhelmed Sam. Yesterday Pat had told him that she felt Toby had become hostile to her; that she was becoming nervous when he was around. Only a few minutes ago Abigail had said that Pat was trying to sabotage her. Did Toby believe that? Sam grasped Abigail's shoulders. ''Is there any reason that Toby might consider Pat a threat to you?''

''Sam, stop it! Let go of me! He was just as upset as I about the publicity she's caused, but even that turned out all right. In fact, he thinks that in the long run she did me a favor.''

''Are you *sure?''*

''Sam, Toby never laid eyes on Pat Traymore before last week. You're not being rational.''

He never laid eyes on her before last week? That wasn't true. Toby had known Pat well as a child. Could he have recognized her? Abigail had been involved with Pat's father. Was Pat becoming aware of that? Forgive me, Pat, he thought. I have to tell her. "Abigail, Pat Traymore is Dean Adams' daughter, Kerry."

"Pat Traymore is—Kerry?" Abigail's eyes widened with shock. Then she shook herself free. "You don't know what you're talking about. Kerry Adams is dead."

"I'm telling you Pat Traymore is Kerry Adams. I've been told that you were involved with her father, that you may have triggered that last quarrel. Pat is starting to remember bits and pieces of that night. Would Toby try to protect you or himself from anything she might find out?"

"No," Abigail said flatly. "I don't care if she remembers seeing me. Nothing that happened was my fault."

"Toby—what about *Toby?* Was he there?"

"She never saw him. When he went back for my purse he told me she was already unconscious."

The implications of what she had said burst upon both of them. Sam ran for the door, Abigail stumbling behind him.

Arthur watched the film clips of Glory in handcuffs being led from the courtroom after the Guilty verdict. There was one close-up of her. Her face was dazed and expressionless, but her pupils were enormous. The uncomprehending pain in her eyes brought tears to his own. He buried his face in his hands as Luther Pelham talked about Glory's nervous breakdown, her parole as a psychiatric outpatient, her disappearance nine years ago. And then, not wanting to believe what he was hearing, he listened as Pelham said, "Yesterday, citing her overwhelming fear of being recognized, Eleanor Brown surrendered to the police. She is now in custody and will be returned to federal prison to complete her sentence."

Glory had surrendered to the police. She had broken her promise to him.

No. She had been *driven* to break her promise—driven by the certainty that this program would expose her. He knew he would never see her again.

His voices, angry and vengeful, began speaking to him. Clenching his fists, he listened intently. When they were silent, he tore off the headset. Without bothering to push the shelves together to conceal his hiding place, he hurried out to the landing and descended the stairs.

Pat sat motionless, studying the program. She watched herself begin to read the letter. "Billy, darling."

"Billy," she whispered. "Billy."

Raptly she studied Abigail Jennings' shocked expression, the involuntary clenching of her hands before she managed with iron control to assume a pleasant misty-eyed demeanor as the letter was read to her.

She had seen that anguished expression on Abigail's face before.

"Billy, darling. Billy, darling."

"You must not call Mommy 'Renée.' "

"But Daddy calls you 'Renée' . . ."

The way Abigail had lunged at her when the cameras stopped rolling. *"Where did you get that letter? What are you trying to do to me?"*

Toby's shout: "It's all right, Abby. It's all right to let people hear the last letter you wrote your husband." *"Your husband."* That's what he'd been trying to tell her.

The picture of Abigail and her father on the beach, their hands touching.

Abigail was the one who had rung the bell that night, who had pushed past her father, her face ravaged with grief and anger.

"You must not call me 'Renée,' and you must not call Daddy 'Billy.' "

Dean *Wilson* Adams. Her *father*—not Willard Jennings—was Billy!

The letter! She had found it on the floor in the library the day she had tried to hide her father's personal papers from Toby. That letter must have fallen from *his* files, not Abigail's.

Abigail had been here that night. She and Dean Adams—*Billy* Adams—had been lovers. Had she precipitated that final quarrel?

A little girl was crouched in bed, her hands over her ears to drown out the angry voices.

The shot.

"Daddy! Daddy!"

Another loud bang.

And then I ran downstairs. I tripped over Mother's body. Someone else was there. Abigail? Oh, God, could Abigail Jennings have been there when I ran into the room?

The patio door had opened.

The phone began to ring, and in the same instant, the chandeliers went off. Pat jumped up and spun around. Illuminated by the twinkling lights of the Christmas tree an apparition was rushing toward her, the tall, gaunt figure of a monk with a vacant unlined face and silvery hair that fell forward over glittering china blue eyes.

Toby drove toward Georgetown, careful to keep his car below the speed limit. This was one night he didn't need a ticket. He'd waited until the documentary was on before he left. He knew Abby would be glued to the set for that half-hour. If she did phone him after the program, he could always say he'd been outside checking the car.

From the beginning he'd known there was something weirdly familiar about Pat Traymore. Years ago he hadn't shed any tears when he'd read that Kerry Adams had "succumbed to her injuries." Not that anything a three-or-four-year-old kid said stood up in court; but even so, it wasn't the kind of grief he needed.

Abby had been right. Pat Traymore had been out to put the screws on them from the beginning. But she wasn't going to get away with it.

He was on M Street in Georgetown. He turned onto 31st Street and drove to N, then turned right. He knew where to park. He'd done it before.

The right side of the property extended halfway down the block. He left the car just around the next corner, walked back and ignoring the padlocked gate, easily scaled the fence. Silently he melted into the shadowy area beyond the patio.

It was impossible not to think about the other night in this place—dragging Abby out, holding his hand over her mouth to keep her from crying out, laying her on the back seat of the car, hearing her terrified moan, "My purse is in there" and going back.

Edging his way under cover of the tree trunks, Toby pressed against the back of the house until he was on the patio a few inches from the doors. Turning his head, he glanced cautiously inside.

His blood froze. Pat Traymore was lying on the couch, her hands and legs tied behind her. Her mouth was taped. A priest or monk, his back to the door, was kneeling beside her and lighting the candles in a silver candelabrum. What in hell was he up to? The man turned, and Toby had a better chance to see him. He wasn't a real priest. That wasn't a habit—it was some sort of robe. The look on his face reminded Toby of a neighbor who years before had gone berserk.

The guy was yelling at Pat Traymore. Toby could barely make out the words. "You did not heed my warnings. You were given the choice."

Warnings. They thought Pat Traymore had made up that story about the phone calls and the break-in. But if she hadn't . . . As Toby watched, the man carried the candelabrum over to the Christmas tree and set it under the lowest branch.

He was setting fire to the place! Pat Traymore would be trapped in there. All he had to do was get back into the car and go home.

Toby flattened against the wall. The man was heading toward the patio doors. *Suppose he was found in there?* Everyone knew Pat Traymore had been getting threats. If this place burned and she was found with the guy who had been threatening her, that would be the end of it. No more investigations, no possibility that someone would talk about having seen a strange car parked in the neighborhood.

Toby listened for the click of the lock. The robed stranger pushed open the patio doors, then turned back to look into the room.

Silently Toby moved over and stood behind him.

As the closing credits of the program rolled onto the screen, Lila redialed Sam's number. But it was useless. There was still no answer. Again she tried to phone Pat. After a half-dozen rings she hung up and walked over to the window. Pat's car was still in the driveway. Lila was positive she was home. As Lila watched, it seemed there was a reddish glow behind the dark aura surrounding the house.

Should she call the police? Suppose Pat was simply coming close to the memory of the tragedy; suppose the danger Lila was sensing was of an emotional not physical nature. Pat wanted so desperately to understand how one of her parents had hurt her so badly. Suppose the truth was even worse than she had envisioned?

What could the police do if Pat simply refused to answer the door? They would never break it down just because Lila had told them about her premonitions. Lila knew exactly how scornful of parapsychology the policemen could be.

Helplessly she stood at the window staring at the whirling clouds of blackness which were enveloping the house across the street.

The patio doors. They had opened that night. She had looked up and seen him and run to him, wrapping her arms around his legs. Toby, her friend who always gave her piggy-back rides. And he had picked her up and thrown her . . .

Toby . . . it had been *Toby.*

And he was there now, standing behind Arthur Stevens. . . .

Arthur sensed Toby's presence and whirled around. The blow from Toby's hand caught him directly on the throat, sending him reeling backward across the room. With a gasping, strangling cry he collapsed near the fireplace. His eyes closed; his head lolled to the side.

Toby came into the room. Pat shrank from the sight of the thick legs in the dark trousers, the massive body, the powerful hands, the dark square of the onyx ring.

He bent over her. "You know, don't you, Kerry? As soon as I figured out who you were, I was sure you'd get around to doping it out. I'm sorry about what happened, but I had to take care of Abby. She was crazy about Billy. When she saw your mother shoot him, she fell apart. If I hadn't come back for her purse, I swear I wouldn't of touched you. I just wanted to shut you up for a while. But now you're out to get Abby, and that can't happen.

"You made it easy for me this time, Kerry. Everyone knows you've been getting threats. I didn't expect to be so lucky. Now this kook will be found with you and no more questions asked. You ask too many questions—you know that?"

The branches directly above the candelabrum suddenly ignited. They began to crackle, and gusts of smoke surged toward the ceiling. "The whole room will be gone in a few minutes, Kerry. I've got to get back now. It's a big night for Abby."

He patted her cheek. "Sorry."

The entire tree burst into flame. As she watched him closing the patio doors behind him, the carpet began to smolder. The pungent odor of evergreen mingled with the smoke. She tried to hold her breath. Her eyes stung so painfully that it was impossible to keep them open. She'd suffocate here. Rolling to the edge of the couch, she threw herself to the floor. Her forehead banged against the leg of the cocktail table. Gasping at the sudden pain, she began to wriggle toward the hall. With her hands tied behind her, she could barely move. She managed to flip over onto her back, brace her hands under her and use them to propel herself forward. The heavy terry-cloth robe hampered her. Her bare feet slid helplessly over the carpet.

At the threshold of the living room, she stopped. If she could manage to close the door, she'd keep the fire from spreading, at least for a few minutes. She dragged herself over the doorsill. The metal plate broke the skin on her hands. Squirming around the door, she propped herself against the wall, wedged her shoulder behind the door and leaned backward until she heard the latch click. The hallway was already filling with smoke. She couldn't tell any longer which way she was going. If she made a mistake and wandered into the library, she wouldn't have a chance.

Using the baseboard for guidance, she inched her way toward the front door.

CHAPTER 42

Lila tried once again to reach Pat. This time she asked the operator to check the number. The phone was in working order.

She could not wait any longer. Something was terribly wrong. She dialed the police. She could ask them to check Pat's house, tell them she thought she had seen the prowler. But when the desk sergeant answered, she could not speak. Her throat closed as though she was choking. Her nostrils filled with the smell of acrid smoke. Pain shot through her wrists and ankles. Her body suffused with heat. The sergeant repeated his name impatiently. At last Lila found her voice.

''Three thousand N Street,'' she shrieked. ''Patricia Traymore is dying! Patricia Traymore is dying!''

Sam drove at a frenzied pace, running red lights, hoping to pick up a police escort. Beside him Abigail sat, her clenched hands pressing against her lips.

''Abigail, I want the truth. What happened the night Dean and Renée Adams died?''

''Billy had promised he'd get a divorce. . . . That day he called me and said he couldn't do it. . . . That he had to make a go of his marriage . . .

That he couldn't leave Kerry. I thought Renée was in Boston. I went there to plead with him. Renée went wild when she saw me. She had found out about us. Billy kept a gun in the desk. She turned it on herself. . . . He tried to get it from her . . . the gun went off. . . . Sam, it was a nightmare. He died before my eyes!"

"Then who killed *her?*" Sam demanded. "Who?"

"She killed herself," Abigail sobbed. "Toby knew there'd be trouble. He was watching from the patio. He dragged me out to the car. Sam, I was in shock. I didn't know what was happening. The last I saw was Renée standing there, holding the gun. Toby had to go back for my purse. Sam, I heard that second shot before he went back into the house. I swear it. He didn't tell me about Kerry until the next day. He said she must have come down right after we left, that Renée must have shoved her against the fireplace to get her out of the way. But he didn't realize she'd been seriously injured."

"Pat remembers tripping over her mother's body."

"No. That's impossible. She can't have."

The tires screeched as they turned onto Wisconsin Avenue.

"You've always believed Toby," he accused her, "because you *wanted* to believe him. It was better for you that way. Did you believe the plane crash was an accident, Abigail—a fortunate accident? Did you believe Toby when you alibied for him for the campaign funds?"

"Yes . . . yes. . . ."

The streets were packed with pedestrians. Wildly he honked the horn. The dinner crowd was drifting into the restaurants. He raced the car down M Street, across 31st Street to the corner of N and floored the brake pedal. They were both thrown forward.

"Oh, my God," Abigail whispered.

An elderly woman, screaming for help, was banging her fists against the front door of Pat's house. A police car, its siren wailing, was racing down the block.

The house was in flames.

Toby hurried through the yard toward the fence. It was all over now. No more loose ends. No pilot's widow to stir up trouble for Abigail. No Kerry Adams to remember what happened in the living room that night.

He'd have to hurry. Pretty soon Abby would be looking for him. She was due at the White House in an hour. *Someone was yelling for help. Someone must have spotted smoke.* He heard the police siren and he began to run.

He'd just reached the fence when a car roared past, spun around the corner and screeched to a stop. Car doors slammed and he heard a man shouting Pat Traymore's name. Sam Kingsley! He had to get out of here. The whole back of the house was starting to go. Someone would see him.

''Not the front door, Sam, back here, back here.'' Toby dropped from the fence. Abby. It was Abby. She was running along the side of the house, heading for the patio. He ran to her, overtook her. ''Abby, for Christ sake, stay away from there.''

She looked at him wildeyed. The smell of smoke permeated the night air. A side window blew out and flames whooshed across the lawn.

''Toby, is Kerry in there?'' Abby grabbed his lapels.

''I don't know what you're talking about.''

''Toby, you were seen near the Graney woman's house last night.''

''Abby, shut up! Last night I had dinner with my Steakburger friend. You saw me come in at ten-thirty.''

''No I didn't.''

''Yes, you did, Senator!''

''Then it's true. . . . What Sam told me . . .''

''Abby, don't pull that shit on me. I take care of you. You take care of me. It's always been like that, and you know it.''

A second police car, its dome light blinking, sped past. ''Abby, I've got to get out of here.'' There was no fear in his voice.

''Is Kerry in there?''

''I didn't start the fire. I didn't do a thing to her.''

''Is she in there?''

''Yes.''

''You oaf! You stupid, homicidal oaf! Get her *out* of there!'' She pounded on his chest. ''You heard me. Get her out of there.'' Flames shot through the roof. ''Do as I say,'' she shouted.

For several seconds they stared at each other. Then Toby shrugged, giving in, and ran clumsily along the snow-covered side lawn, through the garden and onto the patio. The sound of fire engines wailed down the street as he kicked in the patio doors.

The heat inside was withering. Pulling off his coat, Toby wrapped it around his head and shoulders. She had been on the couch, somewhere to the right of the doors. It's because she's Billy's girl, he thought. It's all over for you, Abby. We can't pull this one off now. . . .

He was at the couch, running his hands along it. He couldn't see. She wasn't there.

He tried to feel the floor around the couch. A crackling sound exploded overhead. He had to get out of here—the whole place was going to cave in.

He stumbled toward the doors, guided only by the cold draft. Pieces of plaster fell on him and he lost his balance and fell. His hand touched human flesh. A face, but not a woman's face. It was the crazy.

Toby pulled himself up, felt himself shaking, felt the room shaking. A moment later the ceiling collapsed.

With his last breath he whispered, ''Abby!'' But he knew she couldn't help him this time. . . .

* * *

In a pushing, crawling motion, Pat moved inch by inch along the hallway. The tightly knotted rope had cut off the circulation in her right leg. She had to drag her legs, use only her fingers and palms to propel herself. The floorboards were becoming unbearably hot. The acrid smoke stung her eyes and skin. She couldn't feel the baseboard any longer. She was disoriented. It was hopeless. She was choking. She was going to burn to death.

Then it began . . . the pounding . . . the voice . . . Lila's voice shouting for help. . . . Pat twisted her body, tried to move toward the sound. A roar from the back of the house shook the floor. The whole house was collapsing. She felt herself losing consciousness. . . . She had been meant to die in this house.

As blackness overwhelmed her, she heard a cacophony of hammering, splintering noises. They were trying to break the door down. She was so near it. A rush of cold air. Funnels of flames and smoke roaring toward the draft . . . Men's angry voices shouting, *''It's too late. You can't go in there.''* Lila's screams: *''Help her, help her.''* Sam's desperate, furious *''Let go of me.''*

Sam . . . Sam . . . Footsteps running past her . . . Sam yelling her name. With the last of her strength, Pat lifted her legs and smashed them against the wall.

He turned. In the light of the flames, he saw her, scooped her up, and ran out of the house.

The street was crowded with fire engines and squad cars. Onlookers huddled together in shocked silence. Abigail stood statuelike as the ambulance attendants worked over Pat. Sam was kneeling at the side of the stretcher, his hands caressing Pat's arms, his face bleak with apprehension. A trembling, ashen-faced Lila was standing a few feet away, her eyes riveted on Pat's still body. Around them, hot sooty debris drifted from the wreckage of the house.

''Her pulsebeat is getting stronger,'' the attendant said.

Pat stirred, tried to push aside the oxygen mask. ''Sam . . .''

''I'm here, darling.'' He looked up as Abigail touched his shoulder. Her face was smudged with grimy smoke. The suit she had planned to wear to the White House was soiled and wrinkled. ''I'm glad Kerry's all right, Sam. Take good care of her.''

''I intend to.''

''I'll get a policeman to drive me to a phone. I don't feel quite up to telling the President in person that I must resign from public life. Let me know what I need to do to help Eleanor Brown.''

Slowly she began to walk to the nearest police car. Recognizing her, the onlookers broke into astonished comments and parted to open a path for her. Some of them began clapping. ''Your program was great,

Senator,'' someone yelled. ''We love you.'' ''We're rooting for you to be Vice President,'' another one shouted.

As she stepped into the car, Abigail Jennings turned, and with a tortured half-smile forced herself to acknowledge their greetings for the last time.

CHAPTER 43

On December 29 at 9 P.M. the President strode into the East Room of the White House for the news conference he had summarily postponed two nights earlier. He walked to the lecturn where the microphones had been placed. ''I wonder why we're all here,'' he remarked. There was a burst of laughter.

The President expressed regret at the untimely resignation of the former Vice President. Then he continued, ''There are many outstanding legislators who would fill the role with great distinction and could complete my second term in office if for any reason I were unable to. However, the person I have chosen to be Vice President, with the hearty approval of the leaders of all branches of the government and subject to confirmation by the Congress, is one who will fill a unique place in the history of this country. Ladies and gentlemen, it is my pleasure to present to you the first woman Vice President of the United States, Senator Claire Lawrence of Wisconsin.''

A roar of applause erupted as the White House audience jumped to its feet.

Nestled together on the couch in his apartment, Sam and Pat watched the news conference. ''I wonder if Abigail is seeing this,'' Pat said.

''I imagine she is.''

''She never needed Toby's kind of help. She could have done it on her own.''

''That's true. And it's the saddest part of it.''

''What will happen to her?''

''She'll leave Washington. But don't count her out. Abigail's tough. She'll fight her way back. And this time without that goon in the background.''

''She did so much good,'' Pat said sadly. ''In so many ways, she *was* the woman I believed her to be.''

They listened to Claire Lawrence's acceptance speech. Then Sam helped Pat to her feet. ''With your eyebrows and lashes singed, you have the most incredible surprised look.'' He cupped her face in his hands. ''Feel good to be out of the hospital?''

"You know it!"

He had come so close to losing her. Now she was looking up at him, her face trusting but troubled.

"What will happen to Eleanor?" she asked. "You haven't said anything and I've been afraid to ask."

"I didn't mean *not* to tell you. The revised statement from Abigail coupled with everything else we have on Toby will exonerate her. How about you? Now that you know the truth, how do you feel about your mother and father?"

"Happy that it wasn't my father who pulled the trigger. Sorry for my mother. Glad that neither one of them hurt me that night. They were absolutely wrong for each other, but so much that happened was nobody's fault. Maybe I'm starting to understand people better. At least I hope so."

"Think about this. If your parents hadn't gotten together, you wouldn't be around, and I might be spending the rest of my life in a place that's decorated . . . how did you put it . . . like a motel lobby?"

"Something like that."

"Have you decided about the job?"

"I don't know. Luther does seem sincere about wanting me to stay. I guess for what it's worth the program was well received. He's asked me to start planning one on Claire Lawrence and thinks we might even be able to get the First Lady. It's mighty tempting. He swears this time I'll have creative control of my projects. And with you around, he certainly won't try any more passes at me."

"He'd better not!" Sam put his arm around her and saw the faint beginning of a smile. "Come on. You like a water view." They walked to the window and looked out. The night had clouded over but the Potomac gleamed in the lights of the Kennedy Center.

"I don't think I've ever experienced anything like seeing that house on fire, knowing you were inside," he said. His arm tightened around her. "I can't lose you, Pat, not now, not ever." He kissed her. "I'm dead serious about not wasting any more time. Would a honeymoon in Caneel Bay next week suit you?"

"Save your money. I'd rather go back to the Cape."

"And the Ebb Tide?"

"You guessed it. With just one change." She looked up at him and her smile became radiant. "This time when we leave we'll take the same plane home."

A CRY IN THE NIGHT

Acknowledgment

My very special thanks to Dr. John T. Kelly, M.D., M.P.H., Professor of Psychiatry and Professor and Associate Head of the Department of Family Practice and Community Health, University of Minnesota Medical School, for his generous and expert assistance in helping me design and interpret the psychopathic personalities found in this book and in *The Cradle Will Fall*.

Prologue

Jenny began looking for the cabin at dawn. All night she had lain motionless in the massive four-poster bed, unable to sleep, the stillness of the house oppressive and clutching.

Even after weeks of knowing it would not come, her ears were still tuned for the baby's hungry cry. Her breasts still filled, ready to welcome the tiny, eager lips.

Finally she switched on the lamp at the bedside table. The room brightened and the leaded crystal bowl on the dresser top caught and reflected the light. The small cakes of pine soap that filled the bowl cast an eerie green tint on the antique silver mirror and brushes.

She got out of bed and began to dress, choosing the long underwear and nylon Windbreaker that she wore under her ski suit. She had turned on the radio at four o'clock. The weather report was unchanged for the area of Granite Place, Minnesota; the temperature was twelve degrees Fahrenheit. The winds were blowing at an average of twenty-five miles per hour. The wind-chill factor was twenty-four below zero.

It didn't matter. Nothing mattered. If she froze to death in the search she would try to find the cabin. Somewhere in that forest of maples and oaks and evergreens and Norwegian pines and overgrown brush it was there. In those sleepless hours she had devised a plan. Erich could walk three paces to her one. His naturally long stride had always made him unconsciously walk too fast for her. They used to joke about it. "Hey, wait up for the city girl," she'd protest.

Once he had forgotten his key when he went to the cabin and immediately returned to the house for it. He'd been gone forty minutes. That meant that for him the cabin was usually about a twenty-minute walk from the edge of the woods.

He had never taken her there. "Please understand, Jenny," he'd begged. "Every artist needs a place to be totally alone."

She had never tried to find it before. The help on the farm was absolutely forbidden to go into the woods. Even Clyde, who'd been the farm manager for thirty years, claimed he didn't know where the cabin was.

The heavy, crusted snow would have erased any path, but the snow also made it possible for her to try to search on cross-country skis. She'd have to be careful not to get lost. With the dense underbrush and her own miserable sense of direction, she could easily go around in circles.

Jenny had thought about that, and decided to take a compass, a hammer, tacks and pieces of cloth. She could nail the cloth to trees to help her find her way back.

Her ski suit was downstairs in the closet off the kitchen. While water boiled for coffee, she zipped it on. The coffee helped to bring her mind into focus. During the night she had considered going to Sheriff Gunderson. But he would surely refuse help and would simply stare at her with that familiar look of speculative disdain.

She would carry a thermos of coffee with her. She didn't have a key to the cabin, but she could break a window with the hammer.

Even though Elsa had not been in for over two weeks, the huge old house still glistened and shone with visible proof of her rigid standards of cleanliness. Her habit as she left was to tear off the current day from the daily calendar over the wall phone. Jenny had joked about that to Erich. ''She not only cleans what was never dirty, she eliminates every weekday evening.''

Now Jenny tore off Friday, February 14, crumpled the page in her hand and stared at the blank sheet under the bold lettering, Saturday, February 15. She shivered. It was nearly fourteen months since that day in the gallery when she'd met Erich. No that couldn't be. It was a lifetime ago. She rubbed her hand across her forehead.

Her chestnut-brown hair had darkened to near-black during the pregnancy. It felt drab and lifeless as she stuffed it under the woolen ski cap. The shell-edged mirror to the left of the kitchen door was an incongruous touch in the massive, oak-beamed kitchen. She stared into it now. Her eyes were heavily shadowed. Normally a shade somewhere between aqua and blue, they reflected back at her wide-pupiled and expressionless. Her cheeks were drawn. The weight loss since the birth had left her too thin. The pulse in her neck throbbed as she zipped the ski suit to the top. Twenty-seven years old. It seemed to her that she looked at least ten years older, and felt a century older. If only the numbness would go away. If only the house weren't so quiet, so fearfully, frighteningly quiet.

She looked at the cast-iron stove at the east wall of the kitchen. The cradle, filled with wood, was beside it again, its usefulness restored.

Deliberately she studied the cradle, made herself absorb the constant shock of its presence in the kitchen, then turned her back on it and reached for the thermos bottle. She poured coffee into it, then collected the compass, hammer and tacks and strips of cloth. Thrusting them into a canvas knapsack she pulled a scarf over her face, put on her cross-country ski shoes, yanked thick, fur-lined mittens on her hands and opened the door.

The sharp, biting wind made a mockery of the face scarf. The muffled lowing of the cows in the dairy barn reminded her of the exhausted sobs of deep mourning. The sun was coming up, dazzling against the snow, harsh in its golden-red beauty, a far-off god that could not affect the bitter cold.

By now Clyde would be inspecting the dairy barn. Other hands would be pitching hay in the polebarns to feed the scores of black Angus cattle, which were unable to graze beneath the hard-packed snow and would habitually head there for food and shelter. A half-dozen men working on this enormous farm, yet there was no one near the house—all of them were small figures, seen like silhouettes, against the horizon. . . .

Her cross-country skis were outside the kitchen door. Jenny carried them down the six steps from the porch, tossed them on the ground, stepped into them and snapped them on. Thank God she'd learned to ski well last year.

It was a little after seven o'clock when she began looking for the cabin. She limited herself to skiing no more than thirty minutes in any direction. She started at the point where Erich always disappeared into the woods. The overhead branches were so entangled that the sun barely penetrated through them. After she'd skied in as straight a line as possible, she turned right, covered about one hundred feet more, turned right again and started back to the edge of the forest. The wind covered her tracks almost as soon as she passed any spot but at every turning point she hammered a piece of cloth into the tree.

At eleven o'clock she returned to the house, heated soup, changed into dry socks, forced herself to ignore the tingling pain in her forehead and hands, and set out again.

At five o'clock, half frozen, the slanting rays of the sun almost vanishing, she was about to give up for the day when she decided to go over one more hilly mound. It was then she came upon it, the small bark-roofed log cabin that had been built by Erich's great-grandfather in 1869. She stared at it, biting her lips as savage disappointment sliced her with the physical impact of a stiletto.

The shades were drawn; the house had a shuttered look as though it had not been open for a time. The chimney was snow-covered; no lights shone from within.

Had she really dared to hope that when she came upon it, that chimney would be smoking, lamps would glow through the curtains, that she'd be able to go up to the door and open it?

There was a metal shingle nailed to the door. The letters were faded but still readable: ABSOLUTELY NO ADMITTANCE. VIOLATORS WILL BE PROSECUTED. It was signed by Erich Fritz Krueger and dated 1903.

There was a pump house to the left of the cabin, an outhouse discreetly half-hidden by full-branched pines. She tried to picture the young Erich coming here with his mother. "Caroline loved the cabin just as it was," Erich had told her. "My father wanted to modernize the old place but she wouldn't hear of it."

No longer aware of the cold, Jenny skied over to the nearest window.

Reaching into the knapsack, she pulled out the hammer, raised it and smashed the pane. Flying glass grazed her cheek. She was unaware of the trickle of blood that froze as it ran down her face. Careful to avoid the jagged peaks, she reached in, unfastened the latch and shoved the window up.

Kicking off her skis, she climbed over the low sill, pushed aside the shade and stepped into the cabin.

The cabin consisted of a single room about twenty feet square. A Franklin stove on the north wall had wood piled neatly next to it. A faded Oriental rug covered most of the white pine flooring. A wide-armed, high-backed velour couch and matching chairs were clustered around the stove. A long oak table and benches were near the front windows. A spinning wheel looked as though it might still be functional. A massive oak sideboard held willowware china and oil lamps. A steep stairway led to the left. Next to it, rows of file baskets held stacks of unframed canvases.

The walls were white pine, unknotted, silk-smooth and covered with paintings. Numbly Jenny walked from one to the other of them. The cabin was a museum. Even the dim light could not hide the exquisite beauty of the oils and watercolors, the charcoals and pen-and-ink drawings. Erich had not even begun to show his best work yet. How would the critics react when they saw these masterpieces? she wondered.

Some of the paintings on the walls were already framed. These must be the next ones he planned to exhibit. The polebarn in a winter storm. What was so different about it? The doe, head poised, listening, about to flee into the woods. The calf reaching up to its mother. The fields of alfalfa, blue-flowered, ready for harvest. The Congregational Church with worshipers hurrying toward it. The main street of Granite Place suggesting timeless serenity.

Even in her desolation, the sensitive beauty of the collection gave Jenny a momentary sense of quietude and peace.

Finally she bent over the unframed canvases in the nearest rack. Again admiration suffused her being. The incredible dimensions of Erich's talent, his ability to paint landscapes, people and animals with equal authority; the playfulness of the summer garden with the old-fashioned baby carriage, the . . .

And then she saw it. Not understanding, she began to race through the other paintings and sketches in the files.

She ran to the wall from one canvas to the next. Her eyes widened in disbelief. Not knowing what she was doing, she stumbled toward the staircase leading to the loft and rushed up the stairs.

The loft sloped with the pitch of the roof and Jenny had to bend forward the top stair before she stepped into the room.

As she straightened up, a nightmarish blaze of color from the back wall assaulted her vision. Shocked, she stared at her own image. A mirror?

No. The painted face did not move as she approached it. The dusky light from the slitlike window played on the canvas, shading it in streaks, like a ghostly finger pointing.

For minutes she stared at the canvas, unable to wrench her eyes from it, absorbing every grotesque detail, feeling her mouth slacken in hopeless anguish, hearing the keening sound that was coming from her own throat.

Finally she forced her numbed, reluctant fingers to grasp the canvas and yank it from the wall.

Seconds later, the painting under her arm, she was skiing away from the cabin. The wind, stronger now, gagged her, robbed her of breath, muffled her frantic cry.

"Help me," she was screaming. "Somebody, please, please help me."

The wind whipped the cry from her lips and scattered it through the darkening wood.

CHAPTER 1

It was obvious that the exhibition of paintings by Erich Krueger, the newly discovered Midwest artist, was a stunning success. The reception for critics and specially invited guests began at four, but all day long browsers had filled the gallery, drawn by *Memory of Caroline,* the magnificent oil in the showcase window.

Deftly Jenny went from critic to critic, introducing Erich, chatting with collectors, watching that the caterers kept passing fresh trays of hors d'oeuvres and refilling champagne glasses.

From the moment she'd opened her eyes this morning, it had been a difficult day. Beth, usually so pliable, had resisted leaving for the day-care center. Tina, teething with two-year molars, awakened a half-dozen times during the night, crying fretfully. The New Year's Day blizzard had left New York a nightmare of snarled traffic and curbsides covered with mounds of slippery, sooty snow. By the time she'd left the children at the center and made her way across town she was nearly an hour late for work. Mr. Hartley had been frantic.

"Everything is going wrong, Jenny. Nothing is ready. I warn you. I need someone I can count on."

"I'm so sorry." Jenny tossed her coat in the closet. "What time is Mr. Krueger due?"

"About one. Can you believe three of the paintings weren't delivered until a few minutes ago?"

It always seemed to Jenny that the small, sixtyish man reverted to being about seven years old when he was upset. He was frowning now and his mouth was trembling. "They're all here, aren't they?" she asked soothingly.

"Yes, yes, but when Mr. Krueger phoned last night I asked if he'd sent those three. He was terribly angry at the prospect they'd been lost. And he insists that the one of his mother be exhibited in the window even though it's not for sale. Jenny, I'm telling you. You could have posed for that painting."

"Well, I didn't." Jenny resisted the impulse to pat Mr. Hartley on the shoulder. "We've got everything. Let's get on with hanging them."

Swiftly she helped with the arrangement, grouping the oils, the watercolors, the pen-and-ink sketches, the charcoals.

"You've got a good eye, Jenny," Mr. Hartley said, visibly brightening as the last canvas was placed. "I knew we'd make it."

Sure you did! she thought, trying not to sigh.

The gallery opened at eleven. By five of eleven the featured painting was in place, the handsomely lettered, velvet-framed announcement beside it: FIRST NEW YORK SHOWING, ERICH KRUEGER. The painting immediately began to attract the passersby on Fifty-seventh Street. From her desk, Jenny watched as people stopped to study it. Many of them came into the gallery to see the rest of the exhibit. Not a few of them asked her, "Were you the model for that painting in the window?"

Jenny handed out brochures with Erich Krueger's bio:

> Two years ago, Erich Krueger achieved instant prominence in the art world. A native of Granite Place, Minnesota, he has painted as an avocation since he was fifteen years old. His home is a fourth-generation family farm where he breeds prize cattle. He is also president of the Krueger Limestone Works. A Minneapolis art dealer was the first to discover his talent. Since then he has exhibited in Minneapolis, Chicago, Washington, D.C., and San Francisco. Mr. Krueger is thirty-four years old and is unmarried.

Jenny studied his picture on the cover of the brochure. And he's also marvelous-looking, she thought.

At eleven-thirty, Mr. Hartley came over to her. His anxious, fretful look had almost disappeared. "Everything's all right?"

"Everything's fine," she assured him. Anticipating his next question she said, "I reconfirmed the caterer. *The Times, The New Yorker, Newsweek, Time* and *Art News* critics are definitely coming. We can expect at least eight at the reception, and allowing for gate-crashers about one hundred. We'll close to the public at three o'clock. That will give the caterer plenty of time to set up."

"You're a good girl, Jenny." Now that everything was in order, Mr. Hartley was relaxed and benign. Wait till she told him that she couldn't stay till the end of the reception! "Lee just got in," Jenny continued, referring to her part-time assistant, "so we're in good shape." She grinned at him. "Now please stop worrying."

"I'll try. Tell Lee I'll be back before one to have lunch with Mr. Krueger. You go out and get yourself something to eat now, Jenny."

She watched him march briskly out the door. For the moment there was a lull in the number of new arrivals. She wanted to study the painting in the window. Without bothering to put on a coat, she slipped outside. To get perspective on the work she backed up a few feet from the glass. Passersby on the street, glancing at her and the picture, obligingly walked around her.

The young woman in the painting was sitting in a swing on a porch, facing the setting sun. The light was oblique, shades of red and purple and mauve. The slender figure was wrapped in a dark green cape. Tiny tendrils of blue-black hair blew around her face, which was already half-shadowed. I see what Mr. Hartley means, Jenny thought. The high forehead, thick brows, wide eyes, slim, straight nose and generous mouth were very like her own features. The wooden porch was painted white with a slender corner column. The brick wall of the house behind it was barely suggested in the background. A small boy, silhouetted by the sun, was running across a field toward the woman. Crusted snow suggested the penetrating cold of the oncoming night. The figure in the swing was motionless, her gaze riveted on the sunset.

Despite the eagerly approaching child, the solidity of the house, the sweeping sense of space, it seemed to Jenny that there was something peculiarly isolated about the figure. Why? Perhaps because the expression in the woman's eyes was so sad. Or was it just that the entire painting suggested biting cold? Why would anyone sit outside in that cold? Why not watch the sunset from a window inside the house?

Jenny shivered. Her turtleneck sweater had been a Christmas gift from her ex-husband Kevin. He had arrived at the apartment unexpectedly on Christmas Eve with the sweater for her and dolls for the girls. Not one word about the fact that he never sent support payments and in fact owed her two hundred dollars in "loans." The sweater was cheap, its claim to warmth feeble. But at least it was new and the turquoise color was a good background for Nana's gold chain and locket. Of course one asset of the art world was that people dressed to please themselves and her too-long wool skirt and too-wide boots were not necessarily an admission of poverty. Still she'd better get inside. The last thing she needed was to catch the flu that was making the rounds in New York.

She stared again at the painting, admiring the skill with which the artist directed the gaze of the viewer from the figure on the porch to the child to the sunset. "Beautiful," she murmured, "absolutely beautiful." Unconsciously she backed up as she spoke, skidded on the slick pavement and felt herself bump into someone. Strong hands gripped her elbows and steadied her.

"Do you always stand outside in this weather without a coat and talk to yourself?" The tone of voice combined annoyance and amusement.

Jenny spun around. Confused, she stammered, "I'm so sorry. Please excuse me. Did I hurt you?" She pulled back and as she did realized that the face she was looking at was the one depicted on the brochure she'd been passing out all morning. Good God, she thought, of all people I have to go slamming into Erich Krueger!

She watched as his face paled; his eyes widened, his lips tightened. He's angry, she thought, dismayed. I practically knocked him down. Contritely she held out her hand. "I'm so sorry, Mr. Krueger. Please forgive me. I was so lost in admiring the painting of your mother. It's . . . It's indescribable. Oh, do come in. I'm Jenny MacPartland. I work in the gallery."

For a long moment his gaze remained on her face as he studied it feature by feature. Not knowing what to do, she stood silently. Gradually his expression softened.

"Jenny." He smiled and repeated, *"Jenny."* Then he added, "I wouldn't have been surprised if you told me . . . Well, never mind."

The smile brightened his appearance immeasurably. They were practically eye to eye and her boots had three-inch heels so she judged him to be about five nine. His classically handsome face was dominated by deep-set blue eyes. Thick, well-shaped brows kept his forehead from seeming too broad. Bronze-gold hair, sprinkled with touches of silver, curled around his head, reminding her of the image on an old Roman coin. He had the same slender nostrils and sensitive mouth as the woman in the painting. He was wearing a camel's hair cashmere coat, a silk scarf at his throat. What had she expected? she wondered. The minute she'd heard the word *farm,* she had had a mental image of the artist coming into the gallery in a denim jacket and muddy boots. The thought made her smile and snapped her back to reality. This was ludicrous. She was standing here shivering. "Mr. Krueger . . ."

He interrupted her. "Jenny, you're cold. I'm so terribly sorry." His hand was under her arm. He was propelling her toward the gallery door, opening it for her.

He immediately began to study the placement of his paintings, remarking how fortunate it was that the last three had arrived. "Fortunate for the shipper," he added, smiling.

Jenny followed him around as he made a meticulous inspection, stopping twice to straighten canvases that were hanging a hairbreadth off-center. When he was finished, he nodded, seemingly satisfied. "Why did you put *Spring Plowing* next to *Harvest*?" he asked.

"It's the same field, isn't it?" Jenny asked. "I felt a continuity between plowing the ground and then seeing the harvest. I just wish there was a summer scene as well."

"There *is,*" he told her. "I didn't choose to send it."

Jenny glanced at the clock over the door. It was nearly noon. "Mr. Krueger, if you don't mind, I'm going to settle you in Mr. Hartley's private office. Mr. Hartley's made a luncheon reservation for you and him at the Russian Tea Room for one o'clock. He'll be along soon and I'm going to go out now for a quick sandwich."

Erich Krueger helped her on with her coat. "Mr. Hartley is going to have to eat alone today," he said. "I'm very hungry and I intend to go to lunch with you. Unless, of course, you're meeting someone?"

"No, I'm going to get something fast at the drugstore."

"We'll try the Tea Room. I imagine they'll find room for us."

She went under protest, knowing Mr. Hartley would be furious, knowing that her hold on her job was becoming increasingly more precarious. She was late much too often. She'd had to stay home two days last week because Tina had croup. But she realized she wasn't being given a choice.

In the restaurant he brushed aside the fact they had no reservation and succeeded in being placed at the corner table he wanted. Jenny turned down the suggestion of wine. "I'd be drowsy in fifteen minutes. I was a bit short on sleep last night. Perrier for me, please."

They ordered club sandwiches, then he leaned across the table. "Tell me about yourself, Jenny MacPartland."

She tried not to laugh. "Did you ever take the Dale Carnegie course?"

"No, I didn't. Why?"

"That's the kind of question they teach you to ask on a first meeting. Be interested in the other fellow. I *want* to *know* about *you*."

"But it happens that I do want to know about you."

The drinks came and they sipped as she told him: "I am the head of what the modern world calls 'the single parent family.' I have two little girls. Beth is three and Tina just turned two. We live in an apartment in a brownstone on East Thirty-seventh Street. A grand piano, if I had one, would just about take up the whole place. I've worked for Mr. Hartley for four years."

"How could you work for him four years with such young children?"

"I took a couple of weeks off when they were born."

"Why was it necessary to go back to work so quickly?"

Jenny shrugged. "I met Kevin MacPartland the summer after I finished college. I'd been a fine arts major at Fordham University in Lincoln Center. Kev had a small part in an off-Broadway show. Nana told me I was making a mistake but naturally I didn't listen."

"Nana?"

"My grandmother. She raised me since I was a year old. Anyhow Nana was right. Kev's a nice enough guy but he's a—lightweight. Two children in two years of marriage wasn't on his schedule. Right after Tina was born he moved out. We're divorced now."

"Does he support the children?"

"The average income for an actor is three thousand dollars a year. Actually Kev is quite good and with a break or two might make it. But at the moment the answer to the question is no."

"Surely you haven't had those children in a day-care center from the time they were born?"

Jenny felt the lump start to form in her throat. In a minute her eyes would be filling with tears. She said hurriedly, "My grandmother took care of them while I worked. She died three months ago. I really don't want to talk about her now."

She felt his hand close over hers. "Jenny, I'm sorry. Forgive me. I'm not usually so dense."

She managed a smile. ''My turn. *Do* tell *me* all about *you*.''

She nibbled on the sandwich while he talked. ''You probably read the bio on the brochure—I'm an only child. My mother died in an accident on the farm when I was ten . . . on my tenth birthday to be exact. My father died two years ago. The farm manager really runs the place. I spend most of my time in my studio.''

''It would be a waste if you didn't,'' Jenny said. ''You've been painting since you were fifteen years old, haven't you? Didn't you realize how good you were?''

Erich twirled the wine in his glass, hesitated, then shrugged. ''I could give the usual answer, that I painted strictly as an avocation, but it wouldn't be the whole truth. My mother was an artist. I'm afraid she wasn't very good but her father was reasonably well known. His name was Everett Bonardi.''

''Of *course* I know of him,'' Jenny exclaimed. ''But why didn't you include that in your bio?''

''If my work is good, it will speak for itself. I hope I've inherited something of his talent. Mother simply sketched and enjoyed doing it, but my father was terribly jealous of her art. I suppose he'd felt like a bull in a china shop when he met her family in San Francisco. I gather they treated him like a Midwest hunky with hayseed in his shoes. He reciprocated by telling mother to use her skill to do useful things like making quilts. Even so he idolized her. But I always knew he would have hated to find me 'wasting my time painting,' so I kept it from him.''

The noonday sun had broken through the overcast sky and a few stray beams, colored by the stained-glass window, danced on their table. Jenny blinked and turned her head.

Erich was studying her. ''Jenny,'' he said suddenly, ''you must have wondered about my reaction when we met. Frankly I thought I was seeing a ghost. Your resemblance to Caroline is quite startling. She was about your height. Her hair was darker than yours and her eyes were a brilliant green. Yours are blue with just a suggestion of green. But there are other things about you. Your smile. The way you tilt your head when you listen. You're so slim, just as she was. My father was always fretting over her thinness. He'd keep trying to make her eat more. And I find myself wanting to say, 'Jenny, finish that sandwich. You've barely touched it.' ''

''I'm fine,'' Jenny said, ''But would you mind ordering a quick coffee? Mr. Hartley will be having a heart attack as it is that you arrived when he was out. And I have to sneak away from the reception early which won't endear me to him.''

Erich's smile vanished. ''You have plans for tonight?''

''Big ones. If I'm late picking up the girls at Mrs. Curtis' Progressive Day Care Center, I'm in trouble.''

Jenny raised her eyebrows, pursed her lips, imitated Mrs. Curtis. " 'My usual time for closing is five P.M. but I make an exception for working mothers, Mrs. MacPartland. But five-thirty is the finish. I don't want to hear anything about missed buses or last-minute phone calls. You be here by five-thirty, or you keep your kids home the next morning. Understan?' "

Erich laughed. "I *understan*. Now tell me about your girls."

"Oh, that's easy," she said. "Obviously they're brilliant and beautiful and lovable and . . ."

"And walked at six months and talked at nine months. You sound like my mother. People tell me that's the way she used to talk about me."

Jenny felt an odd catch on her heart at the wistful expression that suddenly came over his face. "I'm sure it was true," she said.

He laughed. "And I'm sure it wasn't. Jenny, New York staggers me. What was it like growing up here?"

Over coffee they talked. She about city life: "There isn't a building in Manhattan I don't love." He, drily, "I can't imagine that. But then you've never really experienced the other way of life." They talked about her marriage. "How did you feel when it was over?"

"Surprisingly, only the same degree of regret that I imagine I'd have for the typical first love. The difference is I have my children. For that I'll always be grateful to Kev."

When they got back to the gallery Mr. Hartley was waiting. Nervously Jenny watched the angry red points on his cheekbones, then admired the way Erich placated him. "As I'm sure you'll agree, airline food is not fit to eat. Since Mrs. MacPartland was just leaving for lunch, I prevailed on her to allow me to join her. I merely nibbled and now look forward to lunching with you. And may I compliment you on the placement of my work."

The red points receded. Thinking of the thick sandwich Erich had consumed, Jenny said demurely, "Mr. Hartley, I recommended the chicken Kiev to Mr. Krueger. Please make him order it."

Erich quirked one eyebrow and as he passed her he muttered, "Thanks a lot."

Afterward she regretted her impulsive teasing. She hardly knew the man. Then why this sense of rapport? He was so sympathetic and yet gave an impression of latent strength. Well, if you're used to money all your life and have good looks and talent thrown in, why wouldn't you feel secure?

The gallery was busy all afternoon. Jenny watched for the important collectors. They'd all been invited to the reception but she knew many of them would come in early to have a chance to study the exhibit. The prices were steep, very steep, for a new artist. But Erich Krueger seemed to be quite indifferent whether or not they sold.

Mr. Hartley got back just as the gallery was closed to the public. He told Jenny that Erich had gone to his hotel to change for the reception. ''You made quite an impression on him, Jenny,'' he said, sounding rather puzzled. ''He did nothing but ask questions about you.''

By five o'clock the reception was in full swing. Efficiently Jenny escorted Erich from critics to collectors, introducing him, making small talk, giving him a chance to chat, then extricating him to meet another visitor. Not infrequently they were asked, ''Is this young lady your model for *Memory of Caroline*?''

Erich seemed to enjoy the question. ''I'm beginning to think she is.''

Mr. Hartley concentrated on greeting guests as they arrived. From his beatific smile, Jenny could surmise that the collection was a major success.

It was obvious that the critics were equally impressed by Erich Krueger, the man. He had changed his sports jacket and slacks for a well-tailored dark blue suit; his white French-cuffed shirt was obviously custom-made; a maroon tie against the crisp white collar brought out his tanned face, blue eyes and the silver tints in his hair. He wore a gold band on the little finger of his left hand. She'd noticed it at lunch. Now Jenny realized why it looked familiar. The woman in the painting had been wearing it. It must be his mother's wedding ring.

She left Erich talking with Alison Spooner, the elegant young critic from *Art News* magazine. Alison was wearing an off-white Adolfo suit that complemented her ash-blond hair. Jenny became suddenly aware of the drooping quality of her own wool skirt, the fact that her boots still looked scuffed even though she'd had them resoled and shined. She knew that her sweater looked just what it was, a cheap, misshapen, polyester rag.

She tried to rationalize her sudden depression. It had been a long day and she was tired. It was time for her to leave and she almost dreaded picking up the girls. When Nana was still with them, going home had been a pleasure.

''Now sit down, dear,'' Nana would say, ''and get yourself relaxed. I'll fix us a nice little cocktail.'' She'd enjoyed hearing what was going on at the gallery, and she'd read the children a bedtime story while Jenny got dinner. ''From the time you were eight years old, you were a better cook than I am, Jen.''

''Well, Nana,'' Jenny would tease, maybe if you didn't cook hamburgers so long they wouldn't look like hockey pucks. . . .''

Since they'd lost Nana, Jenny picked up the girls at the day-care center, bused them to the apartment and placated them with cookies while she threw a meal together.

As she was reaching for her coat, one of the most important collectors cornered her. Finally at 5:25 she managed to get away. She debated about saying good night to Erich but he was still deep in conversation with Alison Spencer. What possible difference would it make to him that she was going? Shrugging away the renewed sensation of depression, Jenny quietly left the gallery by the service door.

CHAPTER 2

Patches of ice on the sidewalk made the going treacherous. Avenue of the Americas, Fifth, Madison, Park, Lexington, Third. Second. Long, long blocks. Whoever said Manhattan was a narrow island had never run across it on slick pavements. But the buses were so slow, she was better off on foot. Still she'd be late.

The day-care center was on Forty-ninth Street near Second Avenue. It was quarter of six before, panting from running, Jenny rang the bell of Mrs. Curtis' apartment. Mrs. Curtis was clearly angry, her arms folded, her lips a narrow slash in her long, unpleasant face. ''Mrs. MacPartland!''

''We had a terrible day,'' the grim lady continued. ''Tina wouldn't stop crying. And you told me that Beth was terlet-trained, but let me tell you she isn't.''

''She is terlet-, I mean toilet-trained,'' Jenny protested. ''It's probably that the girls aren't used to being here yet.''

''*And they won't get the chance.* Your kids are just too much of a handful. You try to understand my position; a three-year-old who isn't trained and a two-year-old who never stops crying are a full-time job by themselves.''

''Mommy.''

Jenny ignored Mrs. Curtis. Beth and Tina were sitting together on the battered couch in the dark foyer that Mrs. Curtis grandly referred to as the ''play area.'' Jenny wondered how long they'd been bundled in their outside clothes. With a rush of tenderness, she hugged them fiercely. ''Hi, Mouse. Hello, Tinker Bell.'' Tina's cheeks were damp with tears. Lovingly, she smoothed back the soft auburn hair that spilled over their foreheads. They'd both inherited Kev's hazel eyes and thick, sooty lashes as well as his hair.

''Her was scared today,'' Beth reported, pointing at Tina. ''Her cried and cried.''

Tina's bottom lip quivered. She reached up her arms to Jenny.

''And you're late again,'' Mrs. Curtis accused.

''I'm sorry.'' Jenny's tone was absentminded. Tina's eyes were heavy, her cheeks flushed. Was she starting another siege of coup? It was this place. She never should have settled on it.

She picked up Tina. Fearful of being left behind, Beth slid off the couch. ''I'll keep both girls until Friday, which is a favor,'' Mrs. Curtis said, ''but that's *it*.''

Without saying good night, Jenny opened the door and stepped out into the cold.

It was completely dark now and the wind was sharp. Tina burrowed her head in Jenny's neck. Beth tried to shield her face in Jenny's coat. ''I only wet once,'' she confided.

Jenny laughed. ''Oh, Mouse, love! Hang on. We'll be in the nice warm bus in a minute.''

But three buses went by full. At last she gave up and began walking downtown. Tina was a dead weight. Trying to hurry meant she had to half-drag Beth. At the end of two blocks, she bent down and scooped her up. "I can walk, Mommy," Beth protested. "I'm big."

"I know you are," Jenny assured her, "but we'll make better time if I carry you." Locking her hands together, she managed to balance both small bottoms on her arms. "Hang on," she said, "the marathon is under way."

She had ten more blocks to go downtown, then two more across town. They're not heavy, she told herself. They're your children. Where in the name of God would she find another day care by next Monday? Oh, Nana, Nana, we need you so much! She couldn't dare take more time off from the gallery. Had Erich asked Alison Spencer to have dinner with him? she wondered.

Someone fell in step beside her. Jenny looked up startled as Erich reached down and took Beth from her arms. Beth's mouth formed a half-surprised, half-frightened circle. Seeming to realize she was about to protest, he smiled at her. "We'll get home a lot faster if I carry you and we race Mommy and Tina." His tone was conspiratorial.

"But . . ." Jenny began.

"Now surely you're going to let me help you, Jenny?" he said, "I'd like to carry the little one too but I'm sure she wouldn't come to me."

"She wouldn't," Jenny agreed, "and I'm grateful, of course, Mr. Krueger, but . . ."

"Jenny, will you please stop calling me Mr. Krueger? Why did you leave me stuck with that tiresome woman from *Art News?* I kept expecting you to rescue me. When I realized you were gone, I remembered the day-care center. That awful woman told me you'd left but I got your address from her. I decided to walk down to your apartment and ring your bell. Then right in front of me I see a pretty girl in need of help, and here we are."

She felt his arm tuck firmly under her elbow. Suddenly instead of feeling fatigued and depressed, she was absurdly happy. She glanced at his face.

"Do you go through this every night?" he asked. His tone was both incredulous and concerned.

"We usually manage to get a bus in bad weather," she said. "Tonight they were so full, there was hardly room for the driver."

The block between Lexington and Park was filled with high-stooped brownstones. Jenny pointed to the third house on the uptown side. "That's it." She eyed the street affectionately. To her the rows of brownstones offered a sense of tranquillity: houses nearly one hundred years old, built when Manhattan still had large neighborhoods of single-family homes. Most of them were gone now, reduced to rubble to make way for skyscrapers.

Outside her building, she tried to say good night to Erich but he refused to be dismissed.

"I'll see you in," he told her.

Reluctantly she preceded him into the ground-level studio. She'd made slipcovers in a cheerful yellow-and-orange pattern for the battered secondhand upholstery; a piece of dark brown carpet covered most of the scarred parquet floor; the cribs fit into the small dressing room off the bathroom and were almost concealed by the louver door. Chagall prints hid some of the peeling wall paint and her plants brightened the ledge over the kitchen sink.

Glad to be released Beth and Tina ran into the room. Beth spun around. "I'm very glad to be home, Mommy," she said. She glanced at Tina. "Tina is glad to be home too."

Jenny laughed. "Oh, Mouse, I know what you mean. You see," she explained to Erich, "it's a little place but we love it."

"I can see why. It's very pleasant."

"Well, don't look too hard," Jenny said. "The management is letting it run down. The building is going co-op so they're not spending any more money on it now."

"Are you going to buy your apartment?"

Jenny began to unzip Tina's snowsuit. "I haven't a prayer. It will cost seventy-five thousand dollars, if you can believe it, for this room. We'll just hang in till they evict us and then find someplace else."

Erich picked up Beth. "Let's get out of those heavy clothes." Quickly he unfastened her jacket, then said, "Now we've got to make up our minds. I've invited myself to dinner, Jenny. So if you have plans for the evening, kick me out. Otherwise point me to a supermarket."

They stood up together and faced each other. "Which is it, Jenny," he asked, "the supermarket or the door?"

She thought she detected a wistful note in the question. Before she could answer, Beth tugged at his leg. "You can read to me if you want," she invited.

"That settles it," Erich said decisively. "I'm staying. You have nothing more to say about it, Mommy."

Jenny thought, He really wants to stay. He honestly wants to be with us. The realization sent unexpected waves of delight through her. "There's no need to go shopping," she told him. "If you like meatloaf we're in great shape."

She poured Chablis, then turned on the evening news for him while she bathed and fed the children. He read a story to them while she prepared dinner. As she set the table and made a salad she stole glances at the couch. Erich was sitting, one little girl under each arm, reading *The Three Bears* with appropriate histrionics. Tina began to doze and quietly he pulled her on his lap. Beth listened rapturously, her eyes never leaving his face. "That was very, very good," she announced when he finished. "You read almost as good as Mommy."

He lifted one eyebrow to Jenny, smiling triumphantly.

After the children were in bed they ate at the dinette table that overlooked the garden. The snow in the yard was still white. The bare-limbed trees glistened in the reflection of the lights from the house. Thick, high evergreens almost hid the fence that separated the property from the adjacent yards.

"You see," Jenny explained, "country within the city. After the girls are settled, I linger over coffee here and imagine I'm gazing at my acreage. Turtle Bay, about ten blocks uptown, is a beautiful area. The brownstones have magnificent gardens. This is sort of mock turtle bay but I'll be very sorry when moving day arrives."

"Where will you go?"

"I'm not sure yet but I've got six months to worry about it. We'll find something. Now how about coffee?"

The bell rang. Erich looked annoyed. Jenny bit her lip. "It's probably Fran from upstairs. She's between boyfriends now and pops in to visit every couple of nights."

But it was Kevin. He filled the doorway, boyishly handsome in his expensive ski sweater, a long scarf casually knotted over his shoulder, his dark red hair well-barbered, his face evenly tanned.

"Come in, Kevin," she said, trying not to sound exasperated. Timing, she thought. By heaven, he's got it.

He strode into the room, kissing her quickly. She felt suddenly embarrassed, knowing Erich's eyes were on them.

"Kids in bed, Jen?" Kevin asked. "Too bad. I was hoping to see them. Oh, you have company."

His voice changed, became formal, almost English. Ever the actor, Jenny thought. The former husband meeting the ex-wife's new friend in a drawing-room comedy. She introduced the men and they nodded to each other without smiling.

Kevin apparently decided to lighten the atmosphere. "Smells good in here, Jen. What have you been cooking?" He examined the stove top. "My word, what a fancy meatloaf." He sampled it. "Excellent. I can't imagine why I let you get away from me."

"It was a dreadful mistake," Erich said, his voice chipped with ice.

"It surely was," Kevin agreed easily. "Well, look I won't delay. Just thought I'd pop by on my way past. Oh, Jen, could I speak with you outside for a minute?"

She knew exactly why he wanted to speak with her. It was payday. Hoping Erich wouldn't notice she slipped her purse under her arm as she went out to the foyer. "Kev, I really haven't . . ."

"Jen, it's just that going overboard for Christmas for you and the kids left me short. My rent is due and the landlord is getting nasty. Just lend me thirty dollars for a week or so."

"*Thirty dollars*. Kevin, I can't."

"Jen, I *need* it."

Reluctantly she took out her wallet. "Kevin, we've got to talk. I think I'm going to lose my job."

Quickly he took the bills. Stuffing them in his pocket, he turned toward the outside door. "That old joker would never let you go, Jen. He knows a good thing when he has it. Call his bluff and strike for a raise. He'll never hire anyone for what he's paying you. You'll see."

She went back into the apartment. Erich was clearing the table, running water in the sink. He picked up the pan with the remaining meatloaf and walked over to the garbage can.

"Hey, hold it," Jenny protested. "The kids can have that tomorrow night for dinner."

Deliberately he dumped it out. "Not after that actor-ex of yours touched it they won't!" He looked directly at her. "How much did you give him?"

"Thirty dollars. He'll pay me back."

"You mean to say you allow him to walk in here, kiss you, joke about abandoning you and breeze out with your money to spend at some expensive bar?"

"He's short on his rent."

"Don't kid yourself, Jenny; how often does he pull that? Every payday, I suppose."

Jenny smiled wearily. "No, he missed one last month. Look, Erich, please leave those dishes. I can do them myself."

"You've got far too much work to do as it is."

Silently Jenny picked up a towel. Why had Kevin chosen just this evening to walk in? What a fool she was to hand him money.

The rigid disapproval in Erich's face and stance began to ease. He took the towel from her hands. "That's enough of that," he smiled.

He poured wine into fresh glasses and brought it over to the couch. She sat beside him, keenly aware of a deep but vague intensity about him. She tried to analyze her feelings and could not. In a little while Erich would leave. Tomorrow morning he was going back to Minnesota. Tomorrow night at this time she'd be here by herself again. She thought of the happiness on the children's faces when Erich read to them, the blessed relief she'd felt when he appeared beside her and took Beth from her. Lunch and dinner had been such fun, as though by his very presence he could dispel worry and loneliness.

"Jenny." His voice was tender. "What are you thinking?"

She tried to smile. "I don't think I was thinking. I was . . . just content, I suppose."

"And I don't know when I've been this content. Jenny, you're sure you're not still in love with Kevin MacPartland."

She was astonished enough to laugh. "Good Lord, no."

"Then why are you so willing to give him money?"

"A misguided feeling of responsibility, I suppose. The worry that maybe he does need his rent."

''Jenny, I have an early flight tomorrow morning. But I can get back to New York for the weekend. Are you free on Friday night?''

He was coming back to see her. The same delicious sense of relief and pleasure that had been hers when he suddenly appeared on Second Avenue filled her. ''I'm free. I'll find a sitter.''

''How about Saturday? Do you think the children would enjoy going to the Central Park zoo if it isn't too cold? And then we could take them to Rumpelmayer's for lunch.''

''They'd love it. But, Erich, really . . .''

''I'm not only sorry I can't just stay in New York for a while. But I've got a meeting in Minneapolis about some investments I'm planning to make. Oh, may I . . .?''

He had spotted the photo album on the shelf under the cocktail table.

''If you wish. It's not terribly exciting.''

They sipped wine as he inspected the book. ''That's me being picked up at the children's home,'' she told him. ''I was adopted. Those are my new parents.''

''They're a nice-looking young couple.''

''I don't remember them at all. They were in an automobile accident when I was fourteen months old. After that it was just Nana and me.''

''Is that a picture of your grandmother?''

''Yes. She was fifty-three when I was born. I remember when I was in the first grade and came home with a long face because the kids were making Father's Day cards and I didn't have a father. She said, 'Listen, Jenny, I'm your mother, I'm your father, I'm your grandmother, I'm your grandfather. I'm all you need. You make *me* a card for Father's Day!''

She felt Erich's arm around her shoulders. ''No wonder you miss her so.''

Hurriedly Jenny went on: ''Nana worked in a travel agency. We took some terrific trips. See, here we are in England. I was fifteen. This is our trip to Hawaii.''

When they came to the pictures of her wedding to Kevin, Erich closed the album. ''It's getting late,'' he said. ''You must be tired.''

At the door he took both her hands in his and held them to his lips. She had kicked off her boots and was in her stocking feet. ''Even this way you are so like Caroline,'' he said, smiling. ''You look tall in heels and quite small without them. Are you a fatalist, Jenny?''

''What is to be will be. I suppose I believe that.''

''That will do.'' The door closed behind him.

CHAPTER 3

At exactly eight o'clock the phone rang. "How did you sleep, Jenny?"

"Very well." It was true. She had drifted off to sleep in a kind of euphoric anticipation. Erich was coming back. She would see him again. For the first time since Nana's death she did not wake up around dawn with the sickening feeling of heavyhearted pain.

"I'm glad. So did I. And I might add I enjoyed some very pleasant dreams. Jenny, starting this morning, I've arranged for a limousine to come for you and the girls at eight-fifteen. He'll take them to the day-care center and you to the gallery. And he'll pick you up evenings at ten after five."

"Erich, that's impossible."

"Jenny, *please*. It's such a little thing for me. I simply can't be worrying about you struggling with those babies in this weather."

"But, Erich!"

"Jenny, I have to run. I'll call you later."

At the day-care center Mrs. Curtis was elaborately pleasant. "Such a distinguished boyfriend you have, Mrs. MacPartland. He phoned this morning. And I want you to know that you don't have to transfer the children. I think we just need to get to know each other better and give them a chance to settle in. Isn't that right, girls?"

He called her at the gallery. "I just landed in Minneapolis. Did the car get there?"

"Erich, it was a blessing. Not having to rush the girls out made such a difference. Whatever did you say to Mrs. Curtis? She was oozing sweetness and light."

"I'll bet she was. Jenny, where do you want to eat Friday night?"

"It doesn't matter."

"Choose a restaurant that you've always wanted to try . . . someplace you've never been with anyone else."

"Erich, there are thousands of restaurants in New York. The ones on Second Avenue and in Greenwich Village are my speed."

"Have you ever been to Lutèce?"

"Good Lord, no."

"Fine. We'll eat there Friday night."

In a daze Jenny got through the day. It didn't help to have Mr. Hartley repeatedly comment how taken Erich had been with her. "Love at first sight, Jenny. He's got it."

Fran, the flight attendant who lived in apartment 4E of the brownstone, dropped in that evening. She was consumed with curiosity. "I saw that gorgeous guy in the foyer last night. I figured he had to have been here. And you have a date with him Friday. Wow!"

She volunteered to mind the girls for Jenny. "I'd love to meet him. Maybe he has a brother or a cousin or an old college pal."

Jenny laughed. ''Fran, he'll probably think this through and call to tell me to forget it.''

''No, he won't.'' Fran shook her tightly curled head. ''I've got a hunch.''

The week dragged. Wednesday. Thursday. And then miraculously it was Friday.

Erich came for her at seven-thirty. She had decided to wear a long-sleeved dress she'd bought on sale. The gold locket was set off by the oval neckline and its center diamond gleamed brilliantly against the black silk. She had twisted her hair into a French braid.

''You're lovely, Jenny.'' He looked quietly expensive in a dark blue suit with a faint pinstripe, a dark blue cashmere coat, a white silk scarf.

She phoned Fran to come down, caught the amused gleam in Erich's eye at Fran's open approval.

Tina and Beth were enchanted with the dolls Erich had brought them. Jenny looked at the beautiful painted faces on the dolls, the eyelids that opened and closed, the dimpled hands, the curling hair and compared them with the shabby gifts Kevin had chosen for Christmas.

She caught Eric's frown as she handed him her well-worn thermal coat and for a moment wished that she'd accepted Fran's suggestion that she borrow her fur jacket. But Nana always told her not to borrow.

Erich had hired a limousine for the evening. She leaned back against the upholstery and he reached for her hand. ''Jenny, I've missed you. These were the longest four days of my life.''

''I've missed you too.'' It was the simple truth but she wished she hadn't sounded so fervent.

In the restaurant she glanced around at the other tables, spotting celebrity faces.

''Why are you smiling, Jenny?'' Erich asked.

''Culture shock. Jet lag from one life-style to another. Do you realize not one person in this room is even aware of Mrs. Curtis' Day Care Center.''

''Let's hope not.'' His eyes had a look of amused tenderness.

The waiter poured champagne. ''You were wearing that locket the other day, Jenny. It's quite lovely. Did Kevin give it to you?''

''No. It was Nana's.''

He leaned across the table; his slender, sculptured fingers entwined around hers. ''I'm glad. Otherwise it would have been bothering me all night. Now I can enjoy seeing it on you.''

In excellent French he discussed the menu with the captain. She asked him where he had acquired the language.

''Abroad. I did quite a bit of traveling. Finally I realized I was happiest and least lonely when I was at the farm, painting. But these last few days were pretty bad.''

''Why?''

"I was lonely for you."

On Saturday they went to the zoo. Endlessly patient, Erich rotated having the girls on his shoulders and at their entreaties returned to the monkey section three times.

At lunch he cut Beth's food as Jenny prepared Tina's plate. He talked Tina into finishing her milk by promising to finish his Bloody Mary and with mock solemnity shook his head at Jenny's twitching lips.

Over Jenny's protests he insisted the girls each select one of Rumpelmayer's famed stuffed animals and seemed blissfully unaware of the interminable time Beth took to make her decision.

"Are you sure you don't have six kids on your Minnesota farm?" Jenny asked him as they stepped onto the street. "Nobody comes naturally by that kind of patience with children."

"But I was raised by someone who had that kind of patience and it's all I know."

"I wish I'd known your mother."

"I wish I'd known your grandmother."

"Mommy," Beth asked, "why do you look so happy?"

On Sunday Erich arrived with double-runner ice skates for Tina and Beth and took them all to the rink at Rockefeller Center to skate.

That evening he took Jenny to the Park Lane for a quiet dinner. Over coffee they both became silent. Finally he said, "It's been a very happy two days, Jenny."

"Yes."

But he didn't say anything about coming back. She turned her head and looked out at Central Park, now sparkling from the combination of streetlights, headlights, and the windows of the apartments that bordered it. "The park is always so pretty, isn't it?"

"Would you miss it very much?"

"Miss it?"

"Minnesota has a different kind of beauty."

What was he saying? She turned to face him. In a spontaneous gesture their hands met, their fingers entwined. "Jenny, it's fast but it's right. If you insist I'll come to New York every weekend for six months—for a year—and court you. But is it necessary?"

"Erich, you hardly know me!"

"I've always known you. You were a solemn baby; you swam when you were five; you won the general excellence medal in the fifth, sixth and seventh grades."

"Seeing an album doesn't mean you know me."

"I think it does. And I know myself. I've always understood what I was looking for, was confident that when it came I would recognize it. You feel it too. Admit it."

"I've already made one mistake. I thought I felt all the right things for Kevin."

"Jenny, you're not fair to yourself. You were very young. You told me he was the first date you ever cared about. And don't forget, wonderful as your grandmother was, you have to have missed having a man in your life, a father, a brother. You were *ready* to fall in love with Kevin."

She considered. "I suppose that's true."

"And the girls. Don't lose their childhood, Jenny. They're so happy when you're with them. I think they could be happy with me. Marry me, Jenny. Soon."

A week ago she hadn't known him. She felt the warmth of his hand, looked into his questioning eyes, felt that her own reflected the same blaze of love.

And she knew without a doubt what her answer would be.

They sat up till dawn in the apartment and talked. "I want to adopt the girls, Jenny. I'll have my lawyers prepare forms for MacPartland to sign."

"I don't think he'll give up the children."

"My guess is that he will. I want them to have my name. When we have a family of our own I don't want Beth and Tina to feel like outsiders. I'll be a good father to them. He's worse than a bad one. He's indifferent to them. By the way, what kind of engagement ring did you get from MacPartland?"

"I didn't."

"Good. I'll have Caroline's ring reset for you."

Wednesday evening on the phone he told her that he'd arranged to meet Kevin on Friday afternoon. "I think it's best if I see him alone, dear."

All week Tina and Beth kept asking when "Mr. Kruer" would come back. When he arrived at the apartment on Friday evening they flew into his arms. Jenny felt happy tears in her eyes at their whoops of joy as he hugged them.

Over dinner at The Four Seasons he told her about his session with Kevin. "He wasn't too friendly. I'm afraid he's something of a spoiler, darling. He doesn't want you or the children, but he doesn't want anyone else to have you. But I persuaded him it was in their best interest. We'll complete the formalities by the end of the month. Then the adoption will take about six months to finalize. Let's get married on February third; that will be almost a month to the day we met.

"Which reminds me." He opened his attaché case. She'd been surprised that he brought that case to the dinner table. "Let's see how this fits."

It was an emerald-cut solitaire. As Erich slipped it on her finger, Jenny stared down into the fiery beauty of the perfect stone.

"I decided not to have it reset," he told her. "It really is perfect just as it is."

"It's beautiful, Erich."

"And, darling—let's get this out of the way too." He pulled out a sheaf of papers. "When my lawyers prepared the adoption papers, they also insisted on taking care of the premarital agreement."

"The premarital agreement?" Jenny asked absently. She was absorbed in admiring her ring. It was not all a dream. It was real. It was happening. She was going to marry Erich. She almost laughed thinking of Fran's reaction. "Jenny, he's too perfect. He's handsome; he's rich; he's talented; he worships you. God, he can't take his eyes off you; he's crazy about the kids. Let me tell you there's got to be something wrong. He's gotta be a gambler or a drinker or a bigamist."

She'd almost told Erich that and then decided against it. She knew Fran's brash humor didn't go over very well with him. What was he saying?

"It's just that I'm a rather—wealthy—man. . . . My lawyers weren't happy about the way things have moved so rapidly. This simply says that if we were to break up before ten years have passed the Krueger interests will remain intact."

She was taken aback. "If we broke up, I wouldn't want anything from you, Erich."

"I would rather die that lose you, Jen. This is just a formality." He laid the papers by her plate. "Of course you may want your lawyers to go over these carefully. In fact I was instructed to tell you that even if you or they are satisfied with all the clauses, you should not mail them back before you've held them two days."

"Erich, I don't have a lawyer." She glanced at the top page, was aghast at the legal jargon and shook her head. Incongruously she remembered Nana's habit of carefully checking the grocery tape, her occasional triumphant, "He charged me *twice* for the lemons." Nana would scrutinize any document like this before she signed it.

"Erich, I don't want to wade through all this. Where shall I sign?"

"I've marked the places for you, darling."

Quickly Jenny scrawled her name. Obviously, Erich's lawyers feared that she might be marrying him for his money. She supposed she couldn't blame them but even so it felt uncomfortable.

"And, darling, besides that one provision, this sets up a trust fund for each of the girls which they'll inherit at twenty-one. It goes into effect as soon as the adoption is complete. It also provides that you will inherit everything I have on my death."

"Don't even *talk* about that, Erich."

He put the papers back in his case. "What a terribly unromantic thing to have to do," he said. "What do you want for our fiftieth anniversary, Jen?"

"Darby and Joan?"

"What?"

"They're Royal Doulton figurines. An old man and an old woman sitting contentedly side by side. I've always loved them."

The next morning when Erich came to the house he had a gift box under his arm. The two figurines were in it.

Even more than the ring, they made Jenny sure about the rest of her life.

CHAPTER 4

"I appreciate this, Jen. Three hundred bucks is a big help. You were always a good sport."

"Well, you and I collected this stuff together. The money is rightfully half yours, Kev."

"God, when I think of how we'd go around late at night to pick up the furniture people were leaving out with their garbage. Remember how we just beat someone to the love seat? You sat on it before the other guy could get to it."

"I remember," Jenny said. "He was so mad I thought he'd pull a knife on me. Look, Kevin, I wish you'd come earlier. Erich will be here in a few minutes and I don't think he'll be pleased to run into you."

They were standing in the dismantled apartment. The furniture had been taken out—Jenny had sold everything for just under six hundred dollars. The walls, now bare of the cheerful prints, looked soiled and cracked. The basic shabbiness of the apartment was cruelly revealed without the furniture and carpet to hide its nakedness. The handsome new suitcases were the only items in the room.

Kevin was wearing an Ultrasuede jacket. No wonder he's always broke, she thought. Dispassionately she studied him, noticing the puffy lines under his eyes. Another hangover, she guessed. With guilt she realized that she felt more nostalgia at leaving this tiny apartment than she did at the prospect of not seeing Kevin again.

"You look beautiful, Jen. That blue is a great color on you."

She was wearing a two-piece blue silk dress. On one of his visits, Erich had insisted on outfitting her and the children at Saks. She'd protested but he'd overridden her objection. "Look at it this way. By the time the bill comes in you'll be my wife."

Now her Vuitton bags were filled with designer suits and blouses and sweaters and slacks and evening skirts, Raphael boots and Magli shoes. After her first uneasiness about having Erich paying for them before they were married, she'd had a marvelous time. And what joy it had been to shop for the girls. "You're so good to us." It became a constant refrain.

"I love you, Jenny. Every penny I spend is pleasure for me. I've never been happier."

He'd helped her select the clothes. Erich had an excellent sense of style. "The artist's eye," she joked.

"Where are the girls?" Kevin asked. "I'd like to say good-bye to them."

"Fran took them for a walk. We'll pick them up after the ceremony. Fran and Mr. Hartley are having lunch with us. Then we'll go right to the airport."

"Jen, I think you've rushed into this too fast. You've only known Krueger a month."

"That's long enough when you're sure, when you're very sure. And we both are."

"Well, *I'm* still not sure about the adoption. I don't want to give up my kids."

Jenny tried not to show irritation. "Kevin, we've been through this. You've signed the papers. You don't bother with the girls. You don't support them. In fact whenever you're interviewed you deny having a family."

"How are they going to feel when they're grown and understand that I gave them up?"

"Grateful for giving them the chance to be with a father who wants them. You seem to forget I'm adopted. And I'll always be grateful to whoever gave me up. Being raised by Nana was mighty special."

"I agree Nana was mighty special. But I don't like Erich Krueger. There's something about him . . ."

"Kevin!"

"All right. I'll go. I'll miss you, Jen. I still love you. You know that." He took her hands. "And I love my kids too."

Act three, curtain, Jenny thought. Not a dry eye in the house. "Please, Kevin. I don't want Erich to find you here."

"Jen, there's a chance I may be coming to Minnesota. I've got a good crack at getting in the repertory company at the Guthrie Theater in Minneapolis. If I do, I'll look you up."

"Kevin, don't look me up!"

Firmly she opened the apartment door. The buzzer rang. "That must be Erich," Jenny said nervously. "Darn it. I didn't want him to see you here. Come on, I'll walk you out."

Erich was waiting behind the locked French-glass foyer doors. He was holding a large gift-wrapped box. Dismayed, she watched his expression change from anticipation to displeasure as he saw her coming down the hall with Kevin.

She opened the outer door to admit him and said quickly, "Kevin stopped over for just a minute. Good-bye, Kevin."

The two men stared at each other. Neither spoke. Then Kevin smiled and bent over Jenny. Kissing her on the mouth, he said, his tone intimate, "It was wonderful being with you. Thanks again, Jen. See you in Minnesota, darling."

CHAPTER 5

"We are crossing over Green Bay, Wisconsin. Our altitude is thirty thousand feet. We'll be landing at the Twin Cities Airport at five-fifty-eight P.M. The temperature in Minneapolis is eight degrees Fahrenheit. It's a clear, beautiful afternoon. Hope you're enjoying your flight, folks. Thanks again for flying Northwest."

Erich's hand covered Jenny's. "Enjoying your flight?"

She smiled at him. "Very much." They both looked down at his mother's gold wedding band now on her finger.

Beth and Tina had fallen asleep. The flight attendant had removed the center arm and they were curled up together, auburn ringlets overlapping, their new green velvet jumpers and white turtleneck pullovers somewhat rumpled now.

Jenny turned to study the cushion of clouds that floated outside the plane window. Underneath her happiness she was still furious with Kevin. She'd known he was weak and irresponsible but she's always thought of him as being casually good-natured. But he was a spoiler. He'd managed to cloud their wedding day.

In the apartment after he left, Erich had said, "Why did he thank you and what did he mean? Did you invite him to our home?"

She'd tried to explain but the explanation felt hollow in her own ears.

"You gave him three hundred dollars?" Erich asked incredulously. "How much does he owe you in support payments and loans?"

"But I don't need that and the furniture was half his."

"Or maybe you wanted to be sure he had fare to come visit you?"

"Erich, how can you believe that?" She'd forced back the tears that threatened to fill her eyes but not before Erich had seen them.

"Jenny, forgive me. I'm sorry. I'm jealous of you. I admit that. I hate the fact that man ever touched you. I don't want him to ever put a finger on you again."

"He won't. I can promise you that. God, if anything I'm so grateful to him for signing the adoption papers. I kept my fingers crossed right to the last minute on that."

"Money talks."

"Erich you didn't pay him?"

"Not much. Two thousand dollars. A thousand per girl. A very cheap price to get rid of him."

"He sold you his children." Jenny had tried to keep the contempt from showing in her voice.

"I'd have paid fifty times more."

"You should have told me."

"I wouldn't have told you now except I don't want any leftover pity for him. . . . Let's forget him. This is our day. How about opening your wedding present?"

It was a Blackglama mink coat. "Oh, Erich."

"Come on—try it on."

It felt luxurious, soft, lightweight, warm. "It's exactly right with your hair and eyes," Erich said, pleased. "Do you know what I was thinking this morning?"

"No."

He'd put his arms around her. "I slept so badly last night. I hate hotels and all I could think is that tonight Jenny will be with me in my own home. Do you know that poem, 'Jenny Kissed Me'?"

"I'm not sure."

"I could only remember a couple of the lines. 'Say I'm weary, say I'm sad' . . . and then the triumphant last line is 'Jenny kissed me.' I was thinking that as I rang the bell and then a minute later I have to watch Kevin MacPartland kiss you."

"Please, Erich."

"Forgive me. Let's get out of this place. It's depressing."

She hadn't had time to take a final look before he rushed her to the limousine.

Even during the ceremony Kevin had been on her mind, especially her marriage to him at St. Monica's four years ago. They'd chosen that church because Nana had been married there. Nana sat beaming in the first row. She hadn't approved of Kevin but put her doubts behind her when she couldn't dissuade Jen. What would she think of this ceremony before a judge instead of a priest? "I, Jennifer, take you . . ." She hesitated. Dear God, she'd almost said *Kevin*. She felt Erich's questioning eyes and began again. Firmly, "I, Jennifer, take you, Erich . . ."

"What God has joined together, man must not separate."

The judge had spoken the words solemnly.

But they'd said that at her wedding to Kevin.

They arrived in Minneapolis one minute ahead of schedule. A large sign said, WELCOME TO THE TWIN CITIES. Jenny studied the airport with avid interest. "I've been all over Europe but never farther west than Pennsylvania," she laughed. "I had a mental image of landing in the midst of a prairie."

She was holding Beth by the hand. Erich was carrying Tina. Beth looked backward at the ramp that led to the plane. "More plane, Mommy," she begged.

"You may have started something, Erich," Jenny said. "They seem to be developing a taste for first-class travel."

Erich was not listening. "I told Clyde to have Joe waiting for us," he said. "He should have been at the arrival gate."

"Joe?"

"One of the farmhands. He's not too bright but he's excellent with horses and a good driver. I always have him chauffeur me when I don't want to leave the car at the airport. Oh, here he is."

Jenny saw rushing toward them a straw-haired, slenderly built young man of about twenty, with wide innocent eyes and rosy cheeks. He was neatly dressed in a thermal coat, dark knit trousers, heavy boots and gloves. A chauffeur's cap sat incongruously on his thick hair. He pulled it off as he stopped in front of Erich, and she had time to reflect that for such a handsome young man he looked awfully worried.

"Mr. Krueger, I'm sorry I'm late. The roads are pretty icy."

"Where's the car?" Erich asked brusquely. "I'll get my wife and children settled, then you and I can attend to the luggage."

"Yes, Mr. Krueger." The worried look deepened. "I'm really sorry I'm late."

"Oh, for heaven's sake," Jenny said. "We're early, one minute early." She held out her hand. "I'm Jenny."

He took it, holding it gingerly as though he feared hurting it. "I'm Joe, Mrs. Krueger. Everybody's looking forward to seeing you. Everybody's been talking about you."

"I'm sure they have," Erich said shortly. His arm urged Jenny forward. Joe fell back behind them. She realized Erich was annoyed. Maybe she wasn't supposed to have been so friendly. Her life in New York and Hartley gallery and the apartment on Thirty-seventh Street suddenly seemed terribly far away.

CHAPTER 6

Erich's maroon Fleetwood was mint-new and the only car in the parking area not spattered with crusted snow. Jenny wondered if Joe had taken precious minutes to have it washed before arriving at the airport. Erich settled her and Tina in the back seat, gave permission to Beth to ride in front, and hurried away to help Joe collect the baggage.

A few minutes later they were pulling onto the highway. "It's nearly a three-hour drive to the farm," Erich told her. "Why don't you lean against me and nap?" He seemed relaxed, even genial now, the spasm of anger forgotten.

He reached for Tina, who willingly settled in his lap. Erich had a way with the little girl. Seeing the contentment on Tina's face snapped Jenny out of her momentary homesickness.

The car sped into the country. The lights along the highway began to disappear. The road darkened and narrowed. Joe switched on the high beams of the headlights and she could discern clumps of graceful maples and irregular, poorly shaped oaks. The land seemed absolutely flat. It was all so different from New York. That was why she'd felt that terrible sense of alienation as they left the airport.

She needed time to think, to get in focus, to adjust. Settling her head on Erich's shoulder, she murmured, "You know something, I am tired." She didn't want to talk any more, not right now. But, oh, how good it was to lean against him, to know that their time together wouldn't ever again be rushed and frantic. He had suggested that they defer an official honeymoon. "You don't have anyone to leave with the girls," he'd said. "Once they're comfortably settled on the farm, we'll find a reliable sitter and take a trip." How many other men would have been that thoughtful? she wondered.

She felt Erich looking down at her.

"Awake, Jenny?" he asked but she didn't answer. His hand smoothed back her hair; his fingers kneaded her temple. Tina was asleep now; her breathing came soft and measured. In the front seat, Beth had stopped chattering to Joe so she too must be napping.

Jenny made her own breath rise and fall evenly. It was time to plan ahead, to turn away from the life she had left and begin to anticipate the one that was waiting for her.

Erich's home had been without a woman's touch for a quarter of a century. It probably needed a massive overhaul. It would be interesting to see how much of Caroline's influence remained in it.

Funny, she mused, I never think of Erich's mother as his mother. I think of her as Caroline.

She wondered if his father hadn't referred to her that way. If instead of saying "your mother" to Erich, when he reminisced he'd say, "Caroline and I used to . . ."

Redecorating would be a joy. How many times had she studied the apartment and thought, if I could afford it, I'd do this . . . and this . . . and this . . .

What a sense of freedom it would be to wake up in the morning and know she didn't have to rush off to work. Just to be with the children, to spend time with them, real time, not end-of-the-day exhausted time! She'd already lost the best part of their baby years.

And to be a wife. Just as Kevin had never been a real father to the children, he'd never been a real husband to her. Even in their most intimate moments, she'd always felt that Kevin had a mental image of himself playing the romantic lead in an M-G-M film. And she was certain that he'd been unfaithful to her even during the short time they lived together.

Erich was mature. He could have married long before now but he'd waited. He welcomed responsibility. Kevin had shunned it. Erich was so reticent. Fran said she thought he was a bit stodgy and Jenny knew that even Mr. Hartley wasn't comfortable with him. They didn't realize that his seeming aloofness was simply a cover for an innately shy nature. "I find it easier to paint my sentiments than to express them," he'd told her. There was so much love expressed in everything he painted. . . .

She felt Erich's hand stroking her cheek. "Wake up, darling, we're nearly home."

"What? Did I fall asleep?" She pulled herself up.

"I'm glad you slept, darling. But look out the window now. The moon is so bright you should be able to see quite a bit." His voice was eager. "We're on county road twenty-six. Our farm begins at that fence, on both sides of the road. The right side eventually ends at Gray's Lake. The other side winds and twists. The woods take up nearly two hundred acres alone; they end at the river valley that slopes into the Minnesota River. Now, watch, you'll see some of the outer buildings. Those are the polebarns, where we feed the cattle in the winter. Beyond them are the grainery and stables and the old mill. Now as we come around this bend you can see the west side of the house. It's set on that knoll."

Jenny pressed her face against the car window. From the background glimpses she'd seen in some of Erich's paintings, she knew that at least part of the exterior of the house was pale red brick. She'd imagined a Currier and Ives kind of farmhouse. Nothing Erich had said had prepared her for what she was looking at now.

Even viewed from the side, it was obvious that the house was a mansion. It was somewhere between seventy and eighty feet long and three stories high. Lights streamed from the long graceful windows on the first floor. Overhead the moon blanched the roof and gables into glistening tiaras. The snow-covered fields shone like layers of white ermine, framing the structure, enhancing its flowing lines.

"Erich!"

"Do you like it, Jenny?"

"Like it? Erich, it's magnificent. It's twice, no five times larger than I expected. Why didn't you warn me?"

"I wanted to surprise you. I told Clyde to be sure and have it lighted for your first impression. I see he took me at my word."

Jenny stared, trying to absorb every detail as the car moved slowly along the road. A white wooden porch with slender columns began at the side door and extended to the rear of the house. She recognized it as the setting of *Memory of Caroline*. Even the swing in the painting was still there, the only piece of furniture on the porch. A gust of wind was making it sway gently to and fro.

The car turned left and drove through open gates. A sign, KRUEGER FARM, was lighted by the torchères that topped the gateposts. The car followed the driveway skirting snow-covered fields. To their right the woods began, a thick heavy forest of trees whose branches were bare and skeletal against the moon. The car turned left and completed the arc, stopping in the driveway in front of wide stone steps.

Massive, ornately carved double doors were illuminated by the fan window arching over them. Joe hurried to open Jenny's door. Quickly

Erich handed the sleeping Tina to him. ''You bring in the girls, Joe,'' he said.

Taking Jenny's hand, he hurried up the steps, turned the latch and pushed open the doors. Pausing, he looked directly into her eyes. ''I wish I could paint you now,'' he said. ''I could call the painting *Coming Home*. Your long, lovely dark hair, your eyes so tender looking at me . . . You do love me, don't you, Jenny?''

''I love you, Erich,'' she said quietly.

''Promise you'll never leave me. Swear that, Jenny.''

''Erich, how can you even think that now?''

''Please promise, Jenny.''

''I'll never leave you, Erich.'' She put her arms around his neck. His need is so great, she thought. All this month she'd been troubled by the one-sided aspect of their relationship, he the giver, she the taker. She was grateful to realize it wasn't that simple.

He picked her up. ''Jenny kissed me.'' Now he was smiling. As he carried her into the house he kissed her lips, at first tentatively, then with gathering emotion. ''Oh, Jenny!''

He set her down in the entrance hall. It had gleaming parquet floors, delicately stenciled walls, a crystal and gold chandelier. A staircase with an ornately carved balustrade led to the second floor. The walls were covered with paintings, Erich's bold signature in the right-hand corner. For a moment Jenny was speechless.

Joe was coming up the steps with the girls. ''Now don't run,'' he was cautioning them. But the long nap had revived them and they were eager to explore. Keeping one eye on them, Jenny listened as Erich began to show her through the house. The main parlor was to the left of the entry foyer. She tried to absorb everything he was telling her about the individual pieces. Like a child showing off his toys, he pointed out the walnut étagère, kidney-shaped and marble-based. ''It's early eighteenth century,'' he said. Ornate oil lamps, now wired, stood on either side of a massive high-backed couch. ''My grandfather had that made in Austria. The lamps are from Switzerland.''

Memory of Caroline was hung above the couch. An overhead light revealed the face in the portrait more intimately than it had appeared in the gallery window. It seemed to Jenny that in this lighting, in this room, her own resemblance to Caroline was accentuated. The woman in the painting seemed to be looking directly at her. ''It's almost like an icon,'' Jenny whispered. ''I feel as though her eyes are following me.''

''I always feel that way,'' Erich said. ''Do you think they might be?''

An immense rosewood reed organ on the west wall immediately attracted the children. They climbed onto the velvet-cushioned bench and began to press the keys. Jenny saw Erich wince as the buckle of Tina's shoe scratched the leg of the bench. Quickly she lifted the protesting girls down. ''Let's see the rest of the house,'' she suggested.

The dining room was dominated by a banquet table large enough to accommodate twelve chairs. An elaborate heart motif was carved out of each of the chairbacks.

A quilt was hung like a tapestry on the far wall. Pieced entirely of hexagons with a scalloped border and stitched in flower motifs, it added a bright note to the austerely handsome room. "My mother made it," Erich said. "See her initials."

All the walls of the large library were covered with walnut bookcases. Each shelf held an even row of precisely placed books. Jenny glanced at some of the titles. "Am I going to have a good time!" she exclaimed. "I can't wait to catch up on reading. About how many books have you got?"

"Eleven hundred and twenty-three."

"You know *exactly* how many?"

"Of course."

The kitchen was huge. The left wall contained the appliances. A round oak table and chairs were placed exactly in the center of the room. On the east wall, a giant old iron stove with highly polished nickel chrome and isinglass windows looked capable of heating the whole house. An oak cradle next to the stove held firewood. A couch covered in a colonial print and matching chair were at rigid right angles to each other. In this room, as in others she had seen, absolutely nothing was out of place.

"It's a little different from your apartment, isn't it, Jenny?" His tone was proud. "You see why I didn't tell you. I wanted to enjoy your reaction."

Jenny felt an urge to defend the apartment. "It's certainly bigger," she agreed. "How many rooms are there?"

"Twenty-two," Erich said proudly. "Let's just have a quick look at our bedrooms. We'll finish the tour tomorrow."

He put his arm around her as they walked up the stairs. The gesture was comforting and helped to relieve some of the strangeness she was feeling. All right, she thought, I do feel as though I'm on a guided tour: Look but don't touch.

The master bedroom was a large corner room in the front of the house. Dark mahogany furniture gleamed with a fine velvet patina. The massive four-poster bed was covered with a spread of cranberry-colored brocade. The brocade was repeated in the canopy and draperies. A leaded crystal bowl on the left side of the dresser was filled with small bars of pine soap. An initialed silver dressing set, each piece an inch apart, was to the right of the bowl. The dressing set had been Erich's great-grandmother's; the bowl was Caroline's and had come from Venice. "Caroline never wore perfume but loved the scent of pine," Erich said. "That soap is imported from England."

The pine soap. That was what she had detected as she came into the room—the faint aroma of pine, so subtle it was almost impossible to distinguish.

"Is this where Tina and I sleep, Mommy?" Beth asked.

Erich laughed. "No, Mouse. You and Tina will be across the hall. But do you want to see my room first? It's right next door."

Jenny followed, expecting to see the room of a bachelor in the family home. She was anxious to experience Erich's personal taste in furnishing. Almost everything she had seen so far seemed to have been left to him.

He threw open the door of the room next to the master bedroom. Here too the overhead light was already on. She saw a single maple bed covered by a colorful quilt. A rolltop desk, half-open, revealed pencils and crayons and sketch pads. A three-shelf bookcase contained the *Book of Knowledge*. A Little League trophy stood on the dresser. A high-backed rocker was in the left corner near the door. A hockey stick was propped against the right wall.

It was the room of a ten-year-old child.

CHAPTER 7

"I never slept here after Mother died," Erich explained. "When I was little I used to love lying in bed, listening to the sound of her moving around in her room. The night of the accident I couldn't stand to come in here. To calm me down, Dad and I both moved to the two back bedrooms. We never moved back."

"Are you saying that this room and the master bedroom haven't been slept in in nearly twenty-five years?"

"That's right. But we didn't close them off. We just didn't use them. But someday our son will use this room, sweetheart."

Jenny was glad to go back into the foyer. Despite the cheerful quilt and warm maple furniture there was something disquieting about Erich's boyhood room.

Beth tugged at her restlessly. "Mommy, we're hungry," she said positively.

"Oh, Mouse, I'm sorry. Let's go to the kitchen." Beth raced down the long hall, her footsteps noisy for such little feet. Tina ran behind her. "Wait for me, Beth."

"Don't run," Erich called after them.

"Don't break anything," Jenny warned, remembering the delicate porcelain in the parlor.

Erich lifted the mink off her shoulders, dropped it over his arm. "Well, what do you think?"

Something about the way he asked the question was disturbing. It was as though he was too eager for approval, and she reassured him now the same way she answered a similar question from Beth. ''It's perfect. I love it.''

The refrigerator was well-stocked. She heated milk for cocoa and made ham sandwiches. ''I have champagne for us,'' Erich said. He put his arm over the back of her chair.

''I'll be ready for it in a little while.'' Jenny smiled at him and tilted her head toward the girls. ''As soon as I clear the decks.''

They were just about to get up when the doorbell rang. Erich's scowl changed to a look of pleasure when he opened the door. ''Mark, for heaven sake! Come on in.''

The visitor filled the entry. His windblown sandy hair almost touched the top of the doorway. Rangy shoulders were not hidden by his heavy hooded parka. Piercing blue eyes dominated his strong-featured face. ''Jenny,'' Erich said. ''This is Mark Garrett. I've told you about him.''

Mark Garrett, *Dr.* Garrett, the veterinarian, who had been Erich's closest friend since boyhood. ''Mark's like a brother,'' Erich had told her. ''If fact if anything had happened to me before I married, he would have inherited the farm.''

Jenny extended her hand, felt his, cold and strong, cover hers.

''I've always said you had good taste, Erich,'' Mark commented. ''Welcome to Minnesota, Jenny.''

She liked him immediately. ''It's lovely to be here.'' She introduced the girls to him. They were both unexpectedly shy. ''You're very, very big,'' Beth told him.

He refused coffee. ''I hate to barge in,'' he told Erich, ''but I wanted you to hear it from me. Baron pulled a tendon pretty badly this afternoon.''

Baron was Erich's horse. Erich had talked about him. ''A thoroughbred, flawless breeding, nervous, bad-tempered. A remarkable animal. I could have raced him but prefer having him for myself.''

''Were any bones broken?'' Erich's voice was absolutely calm.

''Positively not.''

''What happened?''

Mark hesitated. ''Somehow the stable door was left open and he got out. He stumbled when he tried to jump the barbed-wire fence on the east field.''

''The stable door was open?'' Each word was precisely enunciated. ''Who *left* it open?''

''No one admits to it. Joe swears he closed it when he left the stable after he fed Baron this morning.''

Joe. The driver. No wonder he had looked so frightened, Jenny thought. She looked at the girls. They were sitting quietly at the table. A minute ago they'd been ready to scamper away. Now they seemed to sense the change in the atmosphere, the anger Erich wasn't bothering to hide.

''I told Joe not to discuss it with you until I had a chance to see you.

Baron will be fine in a couple of weeks. I think Joe probably didn't pull the door fast when he left. He'd never be deliberately careless. He loves that animal.''

''Apparently no one in his family inflicts harm *deliberately,*'' Erich snapped. ''But they certainly manage to inflict it. If Baron is left lame . . .''

''He won't be. I've hosed him down and bandaged him. Why don't you walk out and see him now? You'll feel better.''

''I might as well.'' Erich reached into the kitchen closet for his coat. His expression was coldly furious.

Mark followed him out. ''Again, welcome, Jenny,'' he said. ''My apologies for being the bearer of bad news.'' As the door closed behind them, she heard his deep, calm voice: ''Now, Erich, don't get upset.''

It took a warm bath and bedtime story before the children finally settled down. Jenny tiptoed out of the room exhausted. She'd pushed the beds together with one against the wall. Then she'd shoved the steamer trunk against the exposed side of the other one. The room that an hour before had been in perfect order was a mess. The suitcases were open on the floor. She'd rifled through them hunting for pajamas and Tina's favorite old blanket, but had not bothered to unpack properly. She was too tired now. It could wait till morning. Erich was there just as she came out. She watched his expression change as he surveyed the untidiness inside.

''Let's leave it, darling,'' she said wearily. ''I know it's every which way but I'll put it right tomorrow.''

It seemed to her that he made a deliberate attempt to sound casual. ''I'm afraid I couldn't go to bed and leave this.''

It took him only a few minutes to completely unpack, to stack underwear and socks in furniture drawers, to hang dresses and sweaters in the closet. Jenny gave up trying to help. If they wake up they'll be around for hours, she thought, but was suddenly too tired to protest. Finally Erich pushed the outer bed so that it was lined exactly with its twin, straightened the small shoes and boots, stacked the suitcases on the upper shelf and closed the closet door which Jenny had left ajar.

When he was finished, the room was infinitely neater and the children hadn't awakened. Jenny shrugged. She knew she should be grateful but could not help feeling that the risk of waking the children should have overcome the need for a clean-up session, particularly on a wedding night.

In the hall, Erich put his arms around her. ''Sweetheart, I know what a long day this has been. I drew a tub for you. It should be about the right temperature now. Why don't you get changed and I'll fix a tray for us. I've got champagne cooling and a jar of the best caviar I could find in Bloomingdale's. How does that sound?''

Jenny felt a rush of shame at her feeling of irritation. She smiled up at him. ''You're too good to be true.''

The bath helped. She soaked in it, enjoying the unaccustomed length and depth of the tub, which was still mounted on its original brass claw feet. As the hot water soothed the muscles in her neck and shoulders she determined to relax.

She realized now that Erich had carefully avoided describing the house to her. What had he said? Oh, yes, things like, "Nothing much has been changed since Caroline died. I think the extent of the redecorating was to replace some curtains in the guest bedroom."

Was it just that nothing had worn out in these years or was Erich religiously preserving intact everything that reminded him of his mother's presence here? The scent she loved was still lingering in the master bedroom. Her brushes and combs and nail buffer were on the dresser. She wondered if there might not still be a few strands of Caroline's hair caught in one of the brushes.

His father had been desperately wrong to have allowed Erich's childhood bedroom to be left intact, frozen in time, as though growth in this house had stopped with Caroline's death. The thought made her uneasy and she deliberately pushed it aside. Think of Erich and yourself, she told herself. Forget the past. Remember that you belong to each other now. Her pulse quickened.

She thought of the lovely new nightgown and peignoir inside her new suitcase. She'd bought them in Bergdorf Goodman with her last paycheck, splurging extravagantly, but wanting to truly look like a bride tonight.

Suddenly lighthearted, she got out of the tub, released the stopper and reached for a towel. The mirror above the sink was clouded over. She started to dry herself then paused and began to wipe away the steam. She felt that in the midst of all the newness she needed to see herself, find her own image. As the glass dried, she glanced into it. But it was not her own blue-green eyes that she saw reflected back.

It was Erich's face, Erich's midnight-blue eyes meeting hers in the reflection. He had opened the door so silently she hadn't heard him. Spinning around, she instinctively clutched the towel in front of her, then deliberately let it fall.

"Oh, Erich, you scared me," she said. "I didn't hear you come in."

His eyes never left her face. "I thought you'd want your gown, darling," he said. "Here it is."

He was holding an aquamarine satin nightgown with a deep V cut in the front and back.

"Erich, I have a new gown. Did you just buy this one for me?"

"No," Erich said, "it was Caroline's." He ran his tongue nervously over his lips. He was smiling strangely. His eyes as they rested on her were moist with love. When he spoke again his tone was pleading. "For my sake, Jenny, wear it tonight."

CHAPTER 8

For minutes Jenny stood staring at the bathroom door, not knowing what to do. I don't want to wear a dead woman's nightgown, she protested silently. The satin felt soft and clinging under her fingers.

After Erich handed her the gown he'd abruptly left the room. She began to shiver as she looked at the suitcase. Should she simply put on her own gown and peignoir, simply say, "I prefer this, Erich."

She thought of his expression when he handed his mother's gown to her.

Maybe it won't fit, she hoped. That would solve everything. But when she pulled it over her head, it might have been made for her. She was thin enough for the tapered waist, the narrowly cut hips, the straight line to the ankles. The V cut accentuated her firm breasts. She glanced in the mirror. The steam was evaporating now and tiny driblets of water were running down. That must be why she looked different. Or was it that something in the aqua tone of the gown emphasized the green in her eyes?

She could not say the gown did not fit and certainly it was becoming. But I don't want to wear it, she thought uneasily. I don't feel like myself in it.

She was about to pull it over her head when there was a soft tap on the door. She opened it. Erich was wearing gray silk pajamas and a matching dressing gown. He had turned off all the lights except for the one on the night table and his burnished gold hair was a counterpoint to the glow of the lamp.

The brocaded cranberry-colored spread was off the bed. The sheets were turned back. Lace embroidered pillows were propped against the massive headboard.

Erich was holding two glasses of champagne. He handed one of them to her. They walked to the center of the room and he touched his glass to hers. "I looked up the rest of the poem, darling." His voice soft, he spoke the words slowly:

"Jenny kissed me when we met,
Jumping from the chair she sat in;
Time, you thief, who love to get
Sweets into your list, put that in:
Say I'm weary, say I'm sad,
Say that health and wealth have missed me,
Say I'm growing old, but add,
Jenny kissed me."

Jenny felt tears in her eyes. This was her wedding night. This man who had offered so much love to her and whom she loved so much was her husband. This beautiful room was theirs. What difference what nightgown she wore! It was such a little thing to do for him. She knew her smile was as happy as his as they toasted each other. When he took the glass from her hand and set it down, she joyfully went into his arms.

Long after Erich slept, his arm pillowing her head, his face buried in her hair, Jenny lay awake. She was so accustomed to the street noises that were part of the night sounds of the New York apartment that she was not yet able to absorb the absolute stillness of this room.

The room was very cool. She liked that and reveled in the clear fresh air. But it was so quiet, so absolutely still, except for the even breathing that rose and fell against her neck.

I am so happy, she thought. I didn't know it was possible to be this happy.

Erich was a shy, tender and considerate lover. She had always suspected that there were far deeper emotions possible than Kevin had ever aroused in her. It was true.

Before Erich fell asleep they had talked. ''Was Kevin the only one before me, Jenny?''

''Yes, he was.''

''There's never been anyone before for me.''

Did he mean he'd never *loved* anyone before or he'd never slept with anyone before? Was that possible?

She drifted off to sleep. Light was just beginning to trickle into the room when she felt Erich stir and slip out of bed.

''Erich.''

''Darling, I'm sorry to wake you. I never sleep more than a few hours. In a little while I'll go to the cabin and paint. I'll be back around noon.''

She felt his kiss on her forehead and lips as she drifted back to sleep. ''I love you,'' she murmured.

The room was flooded with light when she awoke again. Quickly she ran to the window and pulled up the shade. As she watched she was surprised to see Erich disappearing into the woods.

The scene outside was like one of his paintings. The tree branches were white with frozen snow. Snow covered the gambrel roof of the barn nearest the house. Far back in the fields she could catch glimpses of cattle.

She glanced at the porcelain clock on the night table. Eight o'clock. The girls would be waking up soon. They might be startled to find themselves in a strange room.

Barefoot she hurried out of the bedroom and started down the wide foyer. As she passed Erich's old room, she glanced into it, then stopped. The coverlet was tossed back. The pillows were bunched up. She went into the room and touched the sheet. It was still warm. Erich had left their room and come in here. Why?

He doesn't sleep much, she thought. He probably didn't want to toss and turn and wake me up. He's used to sleeping alone. Maybe he wanted to read.

But he said he'd never slept in this room since he was ten years old.

Footsteps were running down the hall. "Mommy. Mommy."

Quickly she hurried to the foyer, bent down and opened her arms. Beth and Tina, their eyes shining from the long sleep, ran to her.

"Mommy, we were looking for you," Beth said accusingly.

"Me like it here," Tina chirped in.

"And we have a present," Beth said.

"A present? What have you got, love?"

"Me too," Tina cried. "Thank you, Mommy."

"It was on our pillows," Beth explained.

Jenny gasped and stared. Each little girl was holding a small round cake of pine soap.

She dressed the children in new red corduroy overalls and striped tee shirts. "No school," Beth said positively.

"No school," Jenny agreed happily. Quickly she put on slacks and a sweater and they went downstairs. The cleaning woman had just arrived. She had a scrawny frame with incongruously powerful arms and shoulders. Her small eyes set in a puffy face were guarded. She looked as though she rarely smiled. Her hair, too tightly braided, seemed to be pulling up the skin around her hairline, robbing her of expression.

Jenny held out her hand. "You must be Elsa. I'm . . ." She started to say "Jenny" and remembered Erich's annoyance at her too friendly greeting to Joe. "I'm Mrs. Krueger." She introduced the girls.

Elsa nodded. "I do my best."

"I can see that," Jenny said. "The house looks lovely."

"You tell Mr. Krueger that stain on the dining-room paper was not my fault, Maybe he had paint on his hand."

"I didn't notice a stain last night."

"I show you."

There was a smudge on the dining-room paper near the window. Jenny studied it. "For heaven sake, you almost need a microscope to see it."

Elsa went into the parlor to begin cleaning and Jenny and the girls breakfasted in the kitchen. When they were finished she got out their coloring books and crayons. "Tell you what," she proposed, "let me have a cup of coffee in peace and then we'll go out for a walk."

She wanted to think. Only Erich could have put those cakes of soap on the girls' pillows. Of course it was perfectly natural that he'd look in on them this morning and there was nothing wrong with the fact that he obviously liked the smell of pine. Shrugging, she finished her coffee and dressed the children in snowsuits.

The day was cold but there was no wind. Erich had told her that winter in Minnesota could range from severe to vicious. "We're breaking you in easy this year," he'd said. "It's just middlin bad."

At the doorway she hesitated. Erich might want to show them around the stables and barns and introduce her to the help. "Let's go this way," she suggested.

She led Tina and Beth around the back of the house and toward the open fields on the east side of the property. They walked on the crunching snow until the house was almost out of sight. Then as they strolled toward the country road that marked the east boundary of the farm, Jenny noticed a fenced-off area and realized they had come upon the family cemetery. A half-dozen granite monuments were visible through the white pickets.

"What's that, Mommy?" Beth asked.

She opened the gate and they went inside the enclosure. She walked from one to the other of the tombstones, reading the inscriptions. Erich Fritz Krueger, 1843–1913, and Gretchen Krueger, 1847–1915. They must have been Erich's great-grandparents. Two little girls: Marthea, 1875–1877, and Amanda, 1878–1890. Erich's grandparents, Erich Lars and Olga Krueger, both born in 1880. She died in 1941, he in 1948. A baby boy, Erich Hans, who lived eight months in 1911. So much pain, Jenny thought, so much grief. Two little girls lost in one generation, a baby boy in the next one. How do people bear that kind of hurt? At the next monument, Erich John Krueger, 1915–1979. Erich's father.

There was one grave at the south end of the plot, as separate from the others as it was possible to be. It was the one she realized she had been looking for. The inscription read Caroline Bonardi Krueger, 1924–1956.

Erich's father and mother were not buried together. Why? The other monuments were weathered. This one looked as though it had been recently cleaned. Did Erich's love for his mother extend to taking extraordinary care of her tombstone? Inexplicably Jenny felt a stab of anxiety. She tried to smile. "Come on, you two. I'll race you across the field."

Laughing, they ran after her. She let them catch and then pass her, pretending to try to keep up with them. Finally they all stopped breathless. Clearly Beth and Tina were elated to have her with them. Their cheeks were rosy, their eyes sparkled and glowed. Even Beth had lost her perpetually solemn look. Jenny hugged them fiercely.

"Let's walk as far as that knoll," she suggested, "then we'll turn back."

But when they reached the top of the embankment, Jenny was surprised to see a fair-sized white farmhouse nestled on the other side. She realized it had to be the original family farmhouse now used by the farm manager.

"Who lives there?" Beth asked.

"Some people who work for Daddy."

As they stood looking at the house, the front door opened. A woman came out on the porch and waved to them, clearly indicating she wanted them to come up to the house. "Beth, Tina, come on," Jenny urged. "It looks as though we're about to meet our first neighbor."

It seemed to her that the woman stared at them unrelentingly as they walked across the field. Unmindful of the cold day she stood in the doorway, the door wide open behind her. At first Jenny thought from her slight frame and sagging body that she was elderly. But as she got closer, she realized that the woman was no more than in her late fifties. Her brown hair was streaked with gray and twisted high on her head in a carelessly pinned knot. Her rimless glasses magnified sad gray eyes. She wore a long, shapeless sweater over baggy, double-knit slacks. The sweater accentuated her bony shoulders and acute thinness.

Still there were vestiges of prettiness about the face, and the drooping mouth had well-shaped lips. There was a hint of a dimple in her chin, and somehow Jenny visualized this woman younger, more joyous. The woman stared at her as she introduced herself and the girls.

"Just like Erich told me," the woman said, her voice low and nervous. " 'Rooney,' he said, 'wait till you meet Jenny, you'll think you're looking at Caroline.' But he didn't want me talking about it." She made a visible effort to calm herself.

Impulsively Jenny held out both her hands. "And Erich has told me about you, Rooney, how long you've been here. I understand your husband is the farm manager. I haven't met him yet."

The woman ignored that. "You're from New York City?"

"Yes, I am."

"How old are you?"

"Twenty-six."

"Our daughter Arden is twenty-seven. Clyde said she went to New York. Maybe you met her?" The question was asked with fierce eagerness.

"I'm afraid I haven't," Jenny said. "But of course New York is so big. What kind of work does she do? Where does she live?"

"I don't know. Arden ran away ten years ago. She didn't have to run away. Could just as easily have said, 'Ma, I want to go to New York.' I never denied her. Her dad was a bit strict with her. I guess she knew he wouldn't let her go so young. But she was such a good girl, why she was president of the 4-H club. I didn't know she wanted to go so bad. I thought she was really happy with us."

The woman's gaze was fixed on the wall. She seemed to be in a reverie of her own, as though explaining something she had explained many times before. "She was our only one. We waited a long time for her. She was such a pretty baby, and so *wanting,* you know what I mean. So active, right from the minute she was born. So I said, let's call her Arden, short for ardent. It suited her real nice."

Beth and Tina shrank against Jenny. There was something about this woman, about the staring eyes and slight tremor, that frightened them.

My God, Jenny thought. Her only child and she hasn't heard from her in ten years. I would go mad.

"See her picture here." Rooney indicated a framed picture on the wall. "I took that just two weeks before she left."

Jenny studied the picture of a sturdy, smiling teenager with curly blond hair.

''Maybe she's married and has babies too,'' Rooney said. ''I think about that a lot. That's why when I saw you coming along with the little ones, I thought maybe that's Arden.''

''I'm sorry,'' Jenny said.

''No, it's all right. And please don't tell Erich I've been talking about Arden again. Clyde said Erich is sick of listening to me always going on about Arden and Caroline. Clyde said that's why Erich retired me from my job at the house when his dad died. I took real good care of that house, just like my own. Clyde and I came here when John and Caroline were married. Caroline liked the way I did things and even after she died I kept everything just so for her, as though she'd be walking in any minute. But come on in the kitchen. I made doughnuts and the coffeepot's on.''

Jenny could smell the perking coffee. They sat around the white enamel table in the cheerful kitchen. Hungrily Tina and Beth munched at still-warm powdered doughnuts and drank milk.

''I remember when Erich was that age,'' Rooney said. ''I used to make those doughnuts for him all the time. I was the only one Caroline ever left him with if she went out shopping. Felt almost like he was my own. Still do, I guess. I didn't have Arden for ten years after we wuz married but Caroline had Erich that first year. Never saw a little boy loved his mother more. Never wanted her out of his sight. Oh, you do look like her, you do.''

She reached for the coffeepot and refilled Jenny's cup. ''And Erich's been so good to us. He spent ten thousand dollars on private detectives trying to find where Arden went.''

Yes, Jenny thought, Erich would do that. The clock over the kitchen sink began to chime. It was noon. Hastily Jenny got up. Erich would be home. She wanted terribly to be with him. ''Mrs. Toomis, we'd better run. I do hope you'll come and visit us.''

''Call me Rooney. Everybody does. Clyde don't want me to go to the big house anymore. But I fool him. I go up there a lot to make sure everything's nice. And you come back here again and visit. I like having company.''

A smile made a remarkable transformation in her face. For a moment the drooping, sad lines disappeared and Jenny knew she'd been right in guessing that at one time Rooney Toomis had been a very pretty woman.

Rooney insisted they take a plate of doughnuts home. ''They're good for an afternoon snack.'' As she held open the door for them she started to turn up the collar of her sweater. ''I think I'll start looking for Arden now,'' she sighed. Once again her voice had become vague.

The noon sun was brilliant, high in the heavens, shining on the snow-covered fields. As they turned the bend, the house came into view. The pale red of the brick glowed under the sun's rays. Our home, Jenny thought. She held the girls by the hand. Was Rooney going to walk aimlessly around these acres looking for her lost child?

"That was a very nice lady," Beth announced.

"Yes, she was," Jenny agreed. "Come on, now. On the double. Daddy's probably waiting for us."

"Which daddy?" Beth asked matter-of-factly.

"The only one."

Just before she opened the kitchen door, Jenny whispered to the children, "Let's tiptoe in and surprise Daddy."

Eyes sparkling, they nodded.

Noiselessly she turned the handle. The first sound they heard was Erich's voice. It was coming from the dining room, each angry word pitched slightly higher than its predecessor. "How dare you tell me that I might have caused that stain! It's obvious that you let the oil rag touch the wallpaper when you dusted the windowsill. Do you realize the entire room will have to be repapered now? Do you know how difficult it will be to get that pattern again? How many times have I warned you about those oil rags?"

"But Mr. Krueger . . ." Elsa's protest, nervously loud, was cut off.

"I want you to apologize for blaming that mess on me. Either apologize or get out of this house and don't come back."

There was silence.

"Mommy," Beth whispered, frightened.

"Sshh," Jenny said. Erich couldn't be that upset over that little smudge on the paper, could he? she wondered. Stay out of it, some instinct warned. There's nothing you can do.

As she heard Elsa's sullen, unhappy voice say, "I apologize, Mr. Krueger," she pulled the children outside and closed the door.

CHAPTER 9

"Why is Daddy mad?" Tina asked.

"I'm really not sure, love. But we'll pretend that we didn't hear him. All right?"

"But we did hear him," Beth said seriously.

"I know," Jenny agreed, "but it doesn't have anything to do with us. Now, come on. Let's go in again."

This time she called, "Erich, hi," before they were even in the house. Not pausing to allow an answer she called again, "Is there a husband in this place?"

"Sweetheart!" Erich hurried into the kitchen, his smile welcoming, his entire manner relaxed. "I've just been asking Elsa where you were. I'm disappointed you went out. I wanted to show you around myself."

His arms were around her. His cheek, still cold from the outdoors, rubbed against hers. Jenny blessed the instinct that had kept her from visiting the farm buildings.

"I knew you'd want to give us the tour," she said, "so we just walked across the east fields and got some fresh air. You can't imagine how wonderful it is not to stop for a traffic light every few feet."

"I'll have to teach you to be sure to avoid the fields where the bulls are kept," Erich smiled. "Believe me, you'd prefer the traffic lights." He became aware of the plate she was holding. "What's that?"

"Mrs. Toom gave that to Mommy," Beth told him.

"Mrs. Toomis," Jenny corrected.

"Mrs. Toomis," Erich said. His arms dropped to his sides. "Jenny, I hope you're not going to tell me you were in Rooney's house?"

"She waved to us," Jenny explained. "It would have been so rude . . ."

"She waves to anyone who passes," Erich interrupted. "This is why you really ought to have waited for me to take you around, darling. Rooney is a very disturbed woman and if you give her an inch she'll take a stranglehold on you. I finally had to lay it to Clyde that he must keep her away from this house. Even after I retired her, I'd come home and find her puttering in here. God help her, I'm sorry for her, Jenny, but it got pretty rough waking up in the middle of the night and hearing her walking around the hall or even standing in my room." He turned to Beth. "Come on, Mouse. Let's get that snowsuit off." He lifted Beth in the air and to her delight sat her on top of the refrigerator.

"Me too, me too," Tina cried.

"You too, you too," he mimicked. "Now isn't this a good way to get your boots off?" he asked them. "Just the right height isn't it, Mommy?"

Apprehensively Jenny moved nearer to the refrigerator to make sure that one of the girls didn't lean forward too far and topple off it but she realized there was no need to worry. Erich quickly yanked the small overshoes off and lifted the girls down. Before he put them on the ground he said, "Okay, you two, what's my name?"

Tina looked at Jenny. "Daddy?" she said, her voice a question.

"Mommy said you're the only daddy," Beth informed him.

"Mommy said that?" Erich put the girls down and smiled at Jenny. "Thank you, Mommy."

Elsa came into the kitchen. Her face was flushed and set in angry, defensive lines. "Mr. Krueger, I finish upstairs. You want me to do something special now?"

"Upstairs?" Jenny asked quickly. "I meant to tell you. I hope you didn't bother to separate the beds in the children's room. They're on their way up for a nap."

"I told Elsa to straighten the room," Erich said.

"But, Erich, they can't sleep on those high beds the way they are," Jenny protested. "I'm afraid we'll really have to get them youth beds." A thought occurred to her. It was a gamble but it would be a natural request. "Erich, couldn't the girls nap in your old room? That bed is quite low."

She studied his face, waiting for his reaction. Even so she did not miss the sly look Elsa threw at him. She's enjoying this, Jenny thought. She knows he wants to refuse.

Erich's expression became closed. "As a matter of fact, Jenny," he said, his tone suddenly formal, "I intended to speak to you about allowing the children to use that room. I thought I made myself plain about the fact that that room is not to be occupied. Elsa tells me she found the bed unmade this morning."

Jenny gasped. Of course it had never occurred to her that Tina and Beth might have gotten into that bed when they were wandering around before she woke up.

"I'm sorry."

His face softened. "It's all right, darling. Let the girls nap in the beds they used last night. We'll order youth beds for them immediately."

Jenny prepared soup for the children, then took them upstairs. As she pulled down the shades, she said, "Now, look, you two, when you wake up, I don't want you getting into any other beds. Understand?"

"But we always get into your bed at home," Beth said, her tone injured.

"That's different. I mean any other beds in this house." She kissed them gently. "Promise. I don't want Daddy to get upset."

"Daddy yelled loud," Tina murmured, her eyes closing. "Where's my present?"

The cakes of soap were on the night table. Tina slipped hers under her pillow. "Thank you for giving that to me, Mommy. We didn't get into your bed, Mommy."

Erich had begun slicing turkey for sandwiches. Deliberately Jenny closed the door that shut the kitchen off from the rest of the house.

"Hi," she said. Putting her arms around him, she whispered, "Look, we had our wedding dinner with the children. At least let me fix our first by-ourselves meal on Krueger Farm and you pour us some of that champagne we never got around to finishing last night."

His lips were on her hair. "Last night was beautiful for me, Jenny. Was it for you?"

"It was beautiful."

"I didn't get much done this morning. All I could think of is how you look when you're asleep."

He made a fire in the cast-iron stove and they sipped the champagne and ate the sandwiches, curled up together on the couch in front of it.

''You know,'' Jenny said, ''walking around today made me realize the sense of continuity this farm has. I don't know my roots. I don't know if my people lived in the city or country. I don't know if my birth mother liked to sew or paint or if she could carry a tune. It's so wonderful that you know everything about your people. Just looking at the burial plot made me appreciate that.''

''You went to the burial plot?'' Erich asked quietly.

''Yes, do you mind?''

''Then you saw Caroline's grave?''

''Yes, I did.''

''And you probably wondered why she and my father aren't together the way the others are?''

''I was surprised.''

''It isn't any mystery. Caroline had those Norwegian pines planted. At that time she told my father she wanted to be buried at the south end of the graveyard where the pines would shelter her. He never really approved, but he respected her wishes. Before he died he told me he'd always expected to be placed in the grave next to his parents. Somehow I felt that was the right thing to do for both of them. Caroline always wanted more freedom than my father would give her anyway. I think that afterward he regretted the way he ridiculed her art until she threw out her sketch pad. What difference would it have made if she'd painted instead of making quilts? He was wrong. *Wrong!*''

He paused, staring into the fire. Jenny felt that Erich seemed to be unaware of her presence. ''But so was she,'' he whispered.

With a tremor of anxiety Jenny realized that for the first time Erich was hinting that the relationship between his mother and father had been troubled.

Jenny settled into a daily routine that she found immensely satisfying. Each day she realized how much she had missed by being away from the children so much. She learned that Beth, the practical, quiet child, had a definite musical talent and could pick out simple tunes on the spinet in the small parlor after hearing them played only a few times. Tina's whiny streak vanished as she blossomed in the new atmosphere. She who had always cried so easily became positively sunny-dispositioned and showed signs of a natural sense of humor.

Erich usually left for the studio by dawn and never returned until noon. Jenny and the girls had breakfast around eight and at ten o'clock, when the sun was becoming stronger, bundled up in snowsuits and went for a walk.

The walks soon assumed a pattern. First the chicken house, where Joe taught the girls to collect the fresh-laid eggs. Joe had decided that Jenny's presence had saved his job after Baron's accident. ''I bet if Mr. Krueger wasn't so happy about your being here, he'd have fired me. My maw says he's not a forgiving man, Mrs. Krueger.''

"I really didn't have a thing to do with it," Jenny protested.

"Dr. Garrett says I'm taking real good care of Baron's leg. When the weather gets warmer and he can exercise a little it will be fine. And, Mrs. Krueger, I tell you, now I check that stable door ten times every day."

Jenny knew what he meant. Unconsciously she had begun to check so many little things a second time, things she never would have dreamed of noticing before. Erich was more than tidy, he was a perfectionist. She quickly learned to tell by a certain tenseness in his face and body if something had upset him—a closet door left open, a glass standing in the sink.

The mornings Erich didn't go to the cabin, he worked in the farm office next to the stable with Clyde Toomis, the farm manager. Clyde, a stocky man of about sixty with a leathery, wrinkled face, and thick, yellow-white hair, had a matter-of-fact manner that approached brusqueness.

When he introduced Jenny to him, Erich said, "Clyde really runs the farm. Sometimes I think I'm just window dressing around here."

"Well, you're certainly not window dressing in front of an easel," she laughed, but was surprised that Clyde did not make even a perfunctory effort to contradict Erich.

"Think you'll like it here?" Clyde asked her.

"I do like it here," she smiled.

"It's quite a change for a city person," Clyde said abruptly. "Hope it isn't too much for you."

"It isn't."

"Funny business," Clyde said. "The country girls hanker after the city. The city girls claim they love the country." She thought she heard a note of bitterness in his voice and wondered if he was thinking about his own daughter. She decided he was when he added, "My wife's all excited about having you and the children here. If she starts dropping in on you, just let me know. Rooney don't mean to bother people but sometimes she kind of forgets herself."

It seemed to Jenny there was a defensive tone in his voice when he spoke of Rooney. "I enjoyed visiting with her," she said sincerely.

The brusque manner softened. "That's good to hear. And she's looking up patterns to make jumpers or some such things for your girls. Is that all right?"

"It's fine."

When they left the office Erich said, "Jenny, Jenny, don't encourage Rooney."

"I promise I won't let it get out of hand. Erich, she's just lonely."

Every afternoon after lunch while the children napped, she and Erich put on cross-country skis and explored the farm. Elsa was willing to mind the children as they slept. In fact it was she who suggested the arrangement. It occurred to Jenny that Elsa was trying to make up for accusing Erich of damaging the dining-room wall.

And yet she wondered if it weren't possible that he *had* caused the stain. Often when he came in for lunch his hands would still have paint or charcoal smudges. If he noticed anything out of order, a curtain not centered on the rod, bric-a-brac not exactly in place, he would automatically adjust it. Several times Jenny stopped him before he touched something with paint-spattered fingers.

The paper in the dining room was replaced. When the paperhanger and his assistant came in, they were incredulous. ''You mean to say that he bought eight double rolls at these prices and he's replacing exactly what he has?''

''My husband knows what he wants.''

When they were finished, the room looked exactly the same except that the smudge was gone.

During the evenings she and Erich liked to settle in the library reading, listening to music, talking. He asked her about the faint scar at her hairline. ''An automobile accident when I was sixteen. Someone jumped the divider and plowed into us.''

''You must have been frightened, darling,''

''I don't remember a thing about it,'' Jenny laughed. ''I'd just leaned my head back and fallen asleep. The next thing I was aware of was being in the hospital three days later. I had a pretty bad concussion—enough to give me amnesia for those days. Nana was frantic. She was sure I'd be brain-damaged or something. I did have headaches for a while and even did some sleepwalking around final exam time. Stress brought it on according to the doctor. But gradually it stopped.''

At first hesitantly, then the words tumbling out, Erich talked about his mother's accident. ''Caroline and I had just gone into the dairy barn to see the new calf. It was being weaned and Caroline held the nursing bottle to its lips. The stock tank—that's the thing that looks like a bathtub in the calving pen—was full of water. It was muddy underfoot and Caroline slipped. She tried to grab something to keep from falling. The something was the lamp cord. She fell into the tank, pulling the lamp with her. That fool of a workman, Joe's uncle incidentally, was rewiring the barn and he'd left the lamp slung over a nail on the wall. In a minute it was all over.''

''I hadn't realized you were with her.''

''I don't like to talk about it. Luke Garrett, Mark's father, was here. He tried to revive her but it was hopeless. And I stood there holding the hockey stick she'd just given me for my birthday. . . .''

Jenny was sitting on the hassock at the foot of Erich's leather easy chair. She raised his hands to her lips. Leaning down he lifted her up and held her tightly against him. ''For a long time I hated the sight of that hockey stick. Then I started to think of it as her last present to me.'' He kissed her eyelids. ''Don't look so sad, Jenny. Having you makes up for everything. Please, Jenny, promise me.''

She knew what he wanted to hear. With a wrench of tenderness, she whispered, ''I'll never leave you.''

CHAPTER 10

One morning when she was walking with Tina and Beth, Jenny spotted Rooney leaning over the picket fence at the southern end of the graveyard. She seemed to be looking down at Caroline's grave.

"I was just thinking of all the nice times I had when Caroline and I were young and Erich was little and then when Arden was born. Caroline drew a picture of Arden once. It was so pretty. I don't know what happened to it. It disappeared right out of my room. Clyde says I was probably carrying it around like I used to do sometime. Why don't you come visit me again?"

Jenny had braced herself for the question. "It's just we've been so busy settling. Beth, Tina, aren't you going to say hello to Mrs. Toomis?"

Beth said hello, shyly. Tina ran forward and raised her face for a kiss. Rooney bent down and smoothed Tina's hair from her forehead. "She reminds me of Arden, this one. Always jumping from one place to the next. Erich probably told you to keep away from me. Well, I can't say I blame him. I guess I am an awful nuisance sometimes. But I found the pattern I was looking for. Can I make the jumpers for the girls?"

"I'd like that," Jenny said, deciding that Erich would have to get used to the idea that she would become friendly with Rooney. There was something infinitely appealing about the woman.

Rooney turned so that once again she was gazing into the graveyard. "Do you get lonesome here yet?" she asked.

"No," Jenny said honestly. "It's different, of course. I was used to a busy job and talking to people all day, and the phones ringing and friends popping into my apartment. Some of that I miss, I suppose. But mostly I'm just so glad to be here."

"So was Caroline," Rooney said. "So happy for a while. And then it changed." She stared down at the simple headstone on the other side of the fence. There were snow clouds in the air and the pines threw restless shadows across the pale pink granite. "Oh, indeed it changed for Caroline," she whispered, "and after she was gone, it started right then to change for us all."

"You're trying to get rid of me," Erich protested. "I don't want to go."

"Sure I'm trying to get rid of you," Jenny agreed. "Oh, Erich, this is perfectly beautiful." She held up a three-by-four-foot oil to examine it more closely. "You've caught the haze that comes around the trees just before they start to bud. And that dark spot circling the ice in the river. That shows the ice is about to break up, that there's moving water below, doesn't it?"

"You've got a good eye, darling. That's right."

"Well, don't forget I was a fine arts major. *Changing Seasons* is a lovely title. The change is so subtle here."

Erich draped an arm across her shoulders and studied the painting with her. ''Remember, anything you want us to keep, I won't exhibit.''

''No, that's foolish. This is the time to keep building your reputation. I won't mind at all eventually being known as the wife of the most prestigious artist in America. They'll point me out and say, 'See, isn't she lucky? And he's gorgeous too!' ''

Erich pulled her hair. ''Is that what they'll say?''

''Uh-huh, and they'll be right.''

''I could just as easily send word that I can't make the show.''

''Erich, don't do it. They've already planned a reception for you. I just wish I could go but I can't leave the kids yet and dragging them with us won't work. Next time.''

He began to stack the canvases. ''Promise you'll miss me, Jenny.''

''I'll miss you lots. It's going to be a lonesome four days.'' Unconsciously Jenny sighed. In nearly three weeks, she'd spoken only to a handful of people: Clyde, Joe, Elsa, Rooney and Mark.

Elsa was taciturn almost to the point of absolute silence. Rooney, Clyde and Joe were hardly companions. She'd only chatted with Mark briefly once since that first evening, even though she knew from Joe that he'd checked on Baron at least half a dozen times.

She'd been on the farm a week before she realized that the telephone never rang. ''Haven't they heard about the 'reach out and touch someone' campaign around here?'' she joked.

''The calls all go through the office,'' Erich explained. ''I only have them come directly to the house if I'm expecting a particular one. Otherwise whoever is in the office will buzz me.''

''But suppose no one's in the office?''

''Then the Phone-Mate will take messages.''

''But Erich, *why*?''

''Darling, if I have one quirk, it's that I despise the intrusion of a telephone ringing constantly. Of course whenever I'm away, Clyde will set the line to ring through to the house at night so I can call you.''

Jenny wanted to protest, then decided against it. Later on when she had friends in the community it would be time enough to coax Erich into normal phone service.

He finished separating the canvases. ''Jenny, I was thinking. It's about time I showed you off a bit. Would you like to go to church next Sunday?''

''I swear you can read my mind,'' she laughed. ''I was just thinking that I'd like to meet some of your friends.''

''I'm better at donating money than attending services, Jen. How about you?''

''I never missed Sunday Mass growing up. Then after Kev and I were married, I got careless. But as Nana always said the apple doesn't fall far from the tree. I'll probably be back at Mass regularly one of these days.''

They attended Zion Lutheran the following Sunday. The church was old and not very large, actually chapel-sized. The delicate stained-glass windows diffused the winter light so that it shone blue and green and gold and red on the sanctuary. She could read the names on some of the windows: DONATED BY ERICH AND GRETCHEN KRUEGER, 1906 . . . DONATED BY ERICH AND OLGA KRUEGER, 1930.

The window over the alter, an Adoration of the Magi scene, was particularly beautiful. She gasped at the inscription: IN LOVING MEMORY OF CAROLINE BONARDI KRUEGER, DONATED BY ERICH KRUEGER.

She tugged at his arm. ''When did you give that window?''

''Last year when the sanctuary was renovated.''

Tina and Beth sat between then, sedately conscious of their new blue coats and bonnets. People looked over at the children throughout the service. She knew Erich was aware of the glances too. He had a contented smile on his face and during the sermon slipped his hand into hers.

Midway through the sermon he whispered, ''You're beautiful, Jenny. Everybody is looking at you and the girls.''

After the service he introduced her to Pastor Barstrom, a slight man in his late sixties with a gentle face. ''We're happy to have you with us, Jenny,'' he said warmly. He looked down at the girls. ''Now who's Beth and who's Tina?''

''You know their names,'' Jenny commented, pleased.

''Indeed I do. Erich told me all about you when he stopped by the parsonage. I hope you realize what a very generous husband you have. Thanks to him our new senior citizen center will be very comfortable and well-equipped. I've known Erich since he was a boy and we're all very happy for him now.''

''I'm mighty happy too,'' Jenny smiled.

''There's a meeting of the women in the parish Thursday night. Perhaps you'd like to join them? We want to get to know you.''

''I'd love to,'' Jenny agreed.

''Darling, we'd better start,'' Erich said. ''There are others who want to visit with the pastor.''

''Of course.'' As she extended her hand, the pastor said, ''It certainly must have been very difficult for you to be widowed so young with such little babies, Jenny. Both you and Erich are surely deserving of much good fortune and many blessings now.''

Erich propelled her forward before she could do more than gasp. In the car she exclaimed, ''Erich, surely you didn't tell Pastor Barstrom that I was widowed, did you?''

Erich steered the car from the curb. ''Jenny, Granite Place isn't New York. It's a small town in the Midwest. People around here were shocked to hear I was getting married a month after I met you. At least a young widow is a sympathetic image; a New York divorcée says something quite different in this community. And I never exactly said you were a widow. I told Pastor Barstrom you had lost your husband. He surmised the rest.''

''So you didn't lie but in effect I've lied for you by not correcting him,'' Jenny said. ''Erich, don't you understand the kind of position that places me in?''

''No, I don't, dear. And I won't have people around here wondering if I had my head turned by a sophisticated New Yorker taking advantage of a hayseed.''

Erich had a mortal fear of looking ridiculous, so much so that he would lie to his clergyman to avoid the possibility.

''Erich, I will have to tell Pastor Barstrom the truth when I go to the meeting Thursday night.''

''I'll be gone Thursday.''

''I know. That's why I think it would be pleasant to be there. I'd like to meet the people around here.''

''Are you planning to leave the children alone?''

''Of course not. Surely there are baby-sitters?''

''Surely you don't intend to leave the children with just anyone?''

''Pastor Barstrom could recommend . . .''

''Jenny, please wait. Don't start getting involved in activities. And don't tell Pastor Barstrom you're a divorcée. Knowing him, he'll never bring up the subject again unless you introduce it.''

''But why do you object to my going?''

Erich took his eyes from the road and looked at her. ''Because I love you so much I'm not ready to share you with other people, Jenny. I *won't* share you with anyone, Jenny.''

CHAPTER 11

Erich was leaving for Atlanta on February 23. On the twenty-first, he told Jenny he had an errand to do and would be late for lunch. It was nearly one-thirty when he returned. ''Come over to the stable,'' he invited. ''I've got a surprise for you.'' Grabbing a jacket, she ran out with him.

Mark Garrett was waiting there, smiling broadly. ''Meet the new tenants,'' he said.

Two Shetland ponies stood side by side in the stalls nearest the door. Their manes and tails were full and lustrous, their copper bodies gleaming. ''My present to my new daughters,'' Erich said proudly. ''I thought we'd call them Mouse and Tinker Bell. Then the Krueger girls will never forget their pet names.''

He hurried her to the next stall.

"And this is your gift."

Speechless, Jenny stared at a bay Morgan mare who returned her gaze amiably.

"She's a treasure," Erich exulted. "Four years old, impeccable breeding, gentle. She's already won half a dozen ribbons. Do you like her?"

Jenny reached a hand to pat the mare's head and was thrilled that the animal did not draw back. "What's her name?"

"The breeder called her Fire Maid. Claims she has fire and heart as well as heritage. Of course you can call her anything you want."

"Fire and heart," Jenny whispered. "That's a lovely combination. Erich, I'm so delighted."

He looked pleased. "I don't want you riding yet. The fields are still too icy. But if you and the girls start making friends with the horses and visiting them every day, by next month you can get started on lessons. Now if you don't mind, how about lunch?"

Impulsively Jenny turned to Mark. "You can't have had lunch either. Won't you join us? It's just cold meat and a salad."

She caught Erich's frown but was relieved to see it disappear as fast as it came. "Please do, Mark," he urged.

Over lunch Jenny realized that she was constantly thinking about Fire Maid. Finally Erich said, "Darling, you have the most happy-child smile on your face. Is it me or the bay mare?"

"Erich, I have to say I'm so darn delighted about that horse I haven't even begun to think about thanking you."

"Have you ever had a pet, Jenny?" Mark asked.

There was something sturdy and easygoing about Mark that made her feel instantly at home in his presence. "I *almost* had a pet," she laughed. "One of our neighbors in New York had a miniature poodle. When puppies were born I used to stop every afternoon on my way home from school to help take care of them. I was about eleven or twelve. But we weren't allowed to have pets in our apartment."

"So you always felt cheated," Mark guessed.

"I certainly felt as though I missed something growing up."

They finished coffee and Mark pushed back his chair. "Jenny, thank you. This has been very pleasant."

"I wish you'd come to dinner when Erich gets back from Atlanta. Bring a date."

"That's a good idea," Erich agreed, and she thought he sounded as though he meant it. "How about Emily, Mark? She's always had an eye for you."

"She always had an eye for *you*," Mark corrected. "But yes, I will ask her."

* * *

Before Erich left, he held her tightly. "I'll miss you so, Jenny. Be sure to lock the doors at night."

"I will. We'll be fine."

"The roads are icy. If you want something from the store let Joe drive you."

"Erich, I'm a big girl," she protested. "Don't worry about me."

"I can't help it. I'll call you tonight, darling."

That night Jenny felt a guilty sense of freedom as she lay propped up in bed reading. The house was still except for the occasional hum of the furnace as it went off and on. From across the hallway she could hear Tina occasionally talking in her sleep. She smiled, realizing that Tina never woke up crying anymore.

Erich should have gotten to Atlanta by now. He'd be calling soon. She glanced around the room. The closet door was half open and she'd left her robe tossed over the slipper chair. Erich would have objected, of course, but tonight she didn't have to worry.

She returned to her book. An hour later the telephone rang. She reached for the receiver eagerly. "Hello, darling," she said.

"What a nice way to be greeted, Jen."

It was Kevin.

"Kevin." Jenny pulled herself up from the pillows so suddenly that her book slid from the bed onto the floor. "Where are you?"

"In Minneapolis. The Guthrie Theater. I'm auditioning."

Jenny felt acute uneasiness. "Kevin, that's wonderful." She tried to sound convincing.

"We'll see what happens. How's it going with you, Jen?"

"Very, very well."

"And the kids?"

"They're simply fine."

"I'm coming down to see them. You gonna be home tomorrow?" His words were slurred, his tone aggressive.

"Kevin, no."

"I want to see my kids, Jen. Where's Krueger?"

Something warned Jenny not to admit that Erich would be gone for four days.

"He's out at the moment. I thought he was calling now."

"Give me directions for getting to your place. I'll borrow a car."

"Kevin, you can't do that. Erich would be furious. You have no right here."

"I have every right to see my children. That adoption isn't final yet. I can stop it by snapping my fingers. I want to be sure Tina and Beth are happy. I want to be sure you're happy, Jen. Maybe we both made a mistake. Maybe we should talk about it. Now how do I get to your place?"

"You're not coming!"

"Jen, Granite Place is on the map. And I guess everybody there knows where Mr. High and Mighty lives."

Jenny felt her palms become sticky as she gripped the phone. She could imagine the gossip in town if Kevin showed up asking directions to Krueger Farm. It would be just like him to say he'd been married to her. She remembered the look in Erich's face when he'd seen Kevin in the foyer of the apartment on their wedding day.

"Kev," she pleaded, "don't come here. You'll spoil everything for us. The girls and I are very happy. I've always been pretty decent to you. Have I ever once turned you down when you asked me for money even when I hardly had my own rent? That should count for something."

"I know you did, Jen." Now his voice took on the intimate, coaxing tone she knew so well. "As a matter of fact I'm a little short right now and you're loaded. How about giving me the rest of the furniture money?"

Jenny felt relief flood her. He was just looking for money. That would make it a lot easier. "Where do you want me to send it?"

"I'll come down for it."

He was obviously determined to see her. There was no way she could allow him to come to this house, even to this town. She shuddered, thinking how painstakingly Erich had been teaching the girls to say Beth Krueger, Tina Krueger.

There was a small restaurant in the shopping center twenty miles away. It was the only place she could think of to suggest. Quickly she gave Kevin directions and agreed to meet him at one o'clock the next day.

After he hung up she leaned back on the pillows. The relaxed pleasure of the evening was gone. Now she dreaded Erich's call. Should she tell him that she was going to see Kevin?

When Erich's call came she still was not sure what to do. Erich sounded tense. "I miss you. I'm sorry I came, darling. Did the girls ask for me tonight?"

She still hesitated to tell him about Kevin. "Of course they did. And Beth is starting to call her dolls 'critters.' "

Erich laughed. "They'll end up talking like Joe yet. I should let you go to sleep."

She had to tell him. "Erich . . ."

"Yes, darling."

She paused, suddenly remembering Erich's astonishment when she admitted giving Kevin half the furniture money, his suggestion that maybe she wanted him to have plane fare to Minnesota. She *couldn't* tell him about meeting Kevin. "I . . . I love you so much, Erich. I wish you were here right now."

"Oh, darling, so do I. Good night."

She could not sleep. The moonlight flooded into the room, reflecting against the crystal bowl. Jenny thought that the bowl seemed almost urn-shaped as it stood silhouetted on the dresser. Could ashes be pine-scented? she wondered. What a crazy, horrible thought, she chided herself restlessly. Caroline was buried in the family cemetery. Even so, Jenny suddenly felt uneasy enough to want to go in and check the girls. They were deeply asleep. Beth had her cheek pillowed on her hand. Tina was fetal-positioned, the satin binding of the blanket hugged against her face.

Jenny kissed them softly. They looked so content. She thought about how happy they were to have her home with them all day, about their ecstasy when Erich had shown them the ponies. Silently she vowed that Kevin was not going to spoil this new life for them.

CHAPTER 12

The keys to the Cadillac were in the farm office, but Erich kept spare keys to all the buildings and machines in the library. It would make sense that the extra Cadillac keys were there as well.

Her guess was right. Slipping them in the pocket of her slacks, she fed the girls an early lunch and settled them down for a nap. ''Elsa, I have an errand to do. I'll be back by two o'clock.''

Elsa nodded. Was Elsa naturally this taciturn? She didn't think so. Sometimes when she'd come in after skiing with Erich, Tina and Beth would be already awake and she'd hear Elsa chatting with them, her Swedish accent more pronounced when she spoke quickly. But when Jenny or Erich was around, she was silent.

The country roads had a few patches of ice but the highway was completely clear. Jenny realized how good it felt to drive again. She smiled to herself, remembering the weekend jaunts she and Nana took in her secondhand Beetle. But after she and Kevin were married she'd had to sell it; the upkeep had become too expensive. Now she would ask Erich to pick up a small car for her.

It was twenty of one when she got to the restaurant. Surprisingly Kevin was already there, a nearly empty carafe of wine in front of him. She slid into the booth and looked across the table. ''Hello, Kev.'' Incredible that in less than a month he could seem older, less buoyant. His eyes were puffy. Was Kevin drinking too much? she wondered.

He reached for her hand. ''Jenny, I've missed you. I've missed the kids.''

She disengaged her fingers. ''Tell me about the Guthrie.''

''I'm pretty sure I've got the job. I'd better have it. Broadway is tight as a drum. And I'll be that much nearer you and the kids out here. Jen, let's try again.''

''Kev, you're crazy.''

"No, I'm not. You're beautiful, Jenny. I like that outfit. That jacket must have cost a fortune."

"I guess it was expensive."

"You're classy, Jen. I always knew it but didn't think about it. I always believed you'd be there for me."

Again he covered her hand with his. "Are you happy, Jen?"

"Yes, I am. Look, Erich would be terribly upset about my seeing you. I have to tell you you didn't make much of an impression on him the last time you met."

"And he didn't make much of an impression on me when he stuck a piece of paper in front of me and told me you'd sue me for nonsupport and attach every nickel I ever made if I didn't sign."

"Erich said that!"

"*Erich said that.* Come on, Jen. That was a lousy trick. I was up for a part in the new Hal Prince musical. That would have really queered me. Too bad I didn't know I'd already been eliminated. Believe me, there wouldn't have been any adoption papers signed."

"It isn't that simple," Jenny said. "I know Erich gave you two thousand dollars."

"That was just a loan."

She was torn between pity for Kevin and the nagging certainty that he would always use the girls as a wedge for staying in her life. She opened her pocketbook. "Kev, I must get back. Here's the three hundred dollars. But after today, please don't contact me; don't try to see the children. If you do, you'll make trouble for them, for you, for me."

He took the money, flipped his fingers idly through the bills, then put them in his wallet. "Jen, you want to know something. I have a bad feeling about you and the kids. It's something I can't explain. But I do."

Jenny got up. In an instant Kevin was beside her, his arms were pulling her to him. "I still love you, Jenny." His kiss was harsh and demanding.

She could not pull away without creating a scene. It was fully half a minute before she felt his arms loosen and she could step back. "Leave us alone," she whispered. "I beg you, I *warn* you, Kevin, leave us alone."

She almost bumped into the waitress who was standing behind her, order pad in hand. The two women at the window table were staring at them.

As Jenny fled from the restaurant she realized why one of the women seemed familiar. She had sat across the aisle from them at church on Sunday morning.

CHAPTER 13

After that first evening, Erich did not call again. Jenny tried to rationalize her uneasiness. Erich had a thing about telephones. But he had planned to call every night. Should she try to reach him at the hotel? A half-dozen times she put her hand on the phone and then removed it.

Did Kevin get hired by the Guthrie? If he did, he'd be trying the same thing here that he'd done at the apartment, dropping in when he was broke or feeling sentimental. Erich would never stand for it and it was no good for the children.

Why didn't Erich phone?

He was due home on the twenty-eighth. Joe was picking him up at the airport. Should she ride up to Minneapolis with Joe? No, she'd wait at the farm and have a good dinner ready. She missed him. She hadn't realized how totally she and the girls had embraced their new life in these past weeks.

If it weren't for the miserable feeling of guilt over meeting Kevin, Jenny knew she wouldn't be troubled that Erich hadn't phoned. Kevin was the spoiler. Suppose when the three hundred dollars was gone, he came back? It would be twice as bad if Erich learned she'd met him and said nothing.

She flew into Erich's arms when he opened the door. He held her against him. In the short distance from the car to the porch the chill of the evening had caught in his coat and his lips were cool. They warmed quickly as he kissed her. With a half-sob she thought, *It will be all right.*

"I've missed you so." They said it together.

He hugged the girls, asked them if they'd been good, and at their enthusiastic response presented them with brightly wrapped packages. He smiled indulgently at their squeals of delight over their new dolls.

"Thank you very, very much," Beth said solemnly.

"Thank you, Daddy," he corrected.

"That's what I mean," Beth said, her tone puzzled.

"What did you bring Mommy?" Tina asked.

He smiled at Jenny. "Has Mommy been a good girl?"

They agreed that she had.

"You're sure, Mommy?"

Why was it that the most ordinary teasing seemed double-edged when you have something to hide? Jen thought of Nana shaking her head about an acquaintance. "That one's bad news; she'd lie even when the truth would serve her better."

Was that what she'd done? "I've been a good girl." She tried to make her voice sound amused, casual.

"Jenny, you're blushing." Erich shook his head.

She knew her smile was forced. "Where's my present?"

He reached into his suitcase. "Since you like Royal Doulton figurines, I thought I'd try to find another one for you in Atlanta. This one leaped out at me. It's called *The Cup of Tea.*"

She opened the box. The figurine was of an old woman sitting in a rocking chair, a cup of tea in her hand, a look of contentment on her face.

"It even looks like Nana," she sighed.

His eyes were tender as he watched her examine the figurine. Her eyes were bright with tears, she smiled at him. And Kevin would spoil this for me, she thought.

She had made a fire in the stove; a carafe of wine and wedge of cheese were on the table. Linking her fingers in his, she brought him over to the couch. Smiling, she poured wine into his glass and handed it to him. "Welcome home." She sat beside him, turning so that her knee touched his. She was wearing a green, ruffle-necked Yves St. Laurent silk blouse and tweed slacks in a brown-and-green weave. She knew it was one of Erich's favorite outfits. Her hair was growing longer and fell loosely on her shoulders. Except when it was bitterly cold she liked to go bareheaded and the winter sun had bleached gold highlights in her dark hair.

Erich studied her, his face inscrutable. "You're a beautiful woman, Jen. Aren't you quite dressed up?"

"It isn't every night my husband comes home after being away four days."

"If I hadn't come home tonight, it would have been a waste getting all dolled up, I hope."

"If you hadn't come home tonight, I'd have worn this for you tomorrow." Jenny decided to change the subject. "How did it go in Atlanta?"

"It was miserable. The gallery people spent most of their time trying to persuade me to sell *Memory of Caroline*. They had a couple of big offers for it and could smell the commission."

"You ran into the same thing in New York. Maybe you'll have to stop showing that painting."

"And maybe I choose to show it because it's still my best work," Erich said quietly. Was there an implied criticism of her suggestion in his voice?

"Why don't I finish putting dinner together?" As she got up, Jenny leaned over and kissed him. "Hey," she whispered, "I love you."

While she was tossing the salad and stirring a hollandaise sauce, he called Beth and Tina over. A few minutes later he had both girls on his lap and was animatedly telling them the story of the Peachtree Hotel in Atlanta where the elevators were glass and went up outside the building just like a magic carpet. Someday he'd take them there.

"Mommy too?" Tina asked.

Jenny turned, smiling, but the smile ended when Erich said, "If Mommy wants to come with us."

She'd cooked a rib roast. He ate well but his fingers drummed restlessly on the table and no matter what she said he answered in monosyllables. Finally Jenny gave up and started talking only to the children. "Did you tell Daddy that you sat on the ponies' backs?"

Beth put down her fork and looked at Erich. "It was fun. I said giddyap but Mouse didn't go."

"I said giddyap too," Tina chimed in.

"Where were the ponies?" Erich asked.

"Right in the stalls," Jenny said hastily, "and Joe lifted them up for just a minute."

"Joe takes too much on himself," Erich interrupted. "I want to be there when the girls are put on the ponies. I want to be sure he's watching them carefully. How do I know he's not as careless as that fool of an uncle was?"

"Erich, that was so long ago."

"It doesn't seem long ago when I bump into that drunken sot. And Joe tells me he's back in town again."

Was that the reason Erich was so upset? "Beth, Tina, if you're finished you can excuse yourselves and play with your new dolls." When the children were out of earshot she said, "Is Joe's uncle the problem, Erich, or is it something else?"

He reached across the table in that familiar gesture of entwining their fingers. "It's that. It's the fact that I think Joe has been tootling around in the car again. It has at least forty extra miles on it. Of course he denies driving it but he used it once in the fall without permission. He didn't drive you anywhere, did he?"

She clenched her fist. "No."

She had to say something about Kevin. She wouldn't have Erich believe that Joe had deceived him.

"Erich . . . I . . ."

He interrupted her. "And it's the damn art galleries. For four days I had to keep telling that fool in Atlanta that *Memory of Caroline* was not for sale. I think it's still my best work and I want to exhibit it but . . ." His voice stopped. When he spoke again, it was calmer. "I'll be doing more painting, Jen. You don't mind, do you? It means I'll have to hole up in the cabin for three or four days at a stretch. But it's necessary."

Dismayed, Jenny thought how these last days had dragged. She tried to make her voice sound casual. "If it's necessary, of course."

When she came back to the library from putting the girls to bed, Erich's eyes were filled with tears.

"Erich, what is it?"

Hastily he brushed his eyes with the back of his hand. "Forgive me, Jenny. It's just I was so depressed. I missed you so much. And Mother's anniversary is next week. You can't know how hard a time that always is for me. Every year it's still as though it's just happened. When Joe told me his uncle is around, it was like a punch in the stomach. I felt so lousy. Then the car turned in from the road and the house was lighted. I was so afraid it would be dark and empty; and I opened the door and you were there, so beautiful, so glad to see me. I was so afraid that maybe while I was away somehow I'd lost you.''

Jenny slipped to her knees. She smoothed the hair back from his forehead.

''Glad to see you. You can't guess!''

His lips silenced her.

When they went up to bed, Jenny reached for one of her new nightgowns then stopped. Reluctantly she opened the dresser drawer that held the aqua gown. The bosom of the gown felt too small. Well, maybe that's one solution, she thought. I'll outgrow the damn thing.

Later just before she fell asleep she realized what it was that had been teasing her subconscious. The only times Erich made love to her was when she was wearing this gown.

CHAPTER 14

She heard Erich walking around the bedroom before dawn. ''Are you going to the cabin?'' she murmured, trying to pull herself from sleep.

''Yes, darling.'' His whisper was barely audible.

''Will you be back for lunch?'' As she started to wake up she remembered that he had talked about staying at the cabin.

''I'm not sure.'' The door closed behind him.

She and the girls took their usual walk after breakfast. The ponies had replaced the chickens as first attraction for Beth and Tina. They ran ahead of her now. ''Hold it, you two,'' she called. ''Make sure Baron is locked up.''

Joe was already in the stable. ''Good morning, Mrs. Krueger.'' His round face broke into a smile. The soft, sandy hair spilled out from under his cap. ''Hello, girls.''

The ponies were immaculate. Their thick manes and tails were brushed and shining. ''Just groomed them for you,'' Joe said. ''Did you bring some sugar with you?''

He held the girls up to feed the sugar. ''Now how about sitting on their backs for a couple of minutes?''

''Joe, I'm afraid not,'' Jenny said. ''Mr. Krueger didn't approve of putting the girls on the ponies.''

''I want to sit on Tinker Bell's back,'' Tina said.

''*Daddy* will let us,'' Beth said positively. ''Mommy, you're mean.''

"Beth!"

"Mean Mommy," Tina said. Her lip trembled.

"Don't cry, Tina," Beth said. She looked up at Jenny. "Mommy, *please*."

Joe was looking at her too.

"Well . . ." Jenny wavered, then thought of Erich's face when he said that Joe took too much on himself. She could not have Erich accuse her of deliberately ignoring his wishes.

"Tomorrow," she said positively. "I'll talk to Daddy. Now let's go see the chickens."

"I want to ride my pony," Tina cried. Her small hand slapped Jenny's leg. "You're a bad mommy."

Jenny reached down. In a reflex action she swatted Tina's bottom. "And you're a very fresh little girl."

Tina ran from the barn, crying. Beth was right behind her.

Jenny hurried after the girls. They were holding hands, walking toward the barn. As she caught up with them she heard Beth say soothingly, "Don't be sad, Tina. We'll tell Daddy on Mommy."

Joe was at her side. "Mrs. Krueger."

"Yes, Joe." Jenny turned her face from him. She did not want him to see the tears that were swimming in her eyes. In her bones she knew that when they asked him, Erich would give permission to the girls to sit on the ponies in the stable.

"Mrs. Krueger, I was wondering. We have a new puppy at our place. We're just down the road about half a mile. Maybe the girls would like to see Randy. It might take their minds off the ponies."

"Joe, that would be nice." Jenny caught up with the children. She crouched in front of Tina. "I'm sorry I spanked you, Tinker Bell. I want to ride Fire Maid just as much as you want to ride your pony, but we have to wait till Daddy says okay. Now Joe wants to take us to see his puppy. Want to go?"

They walked together, Joe pointing out the first signs of the approaching spring. "See how the snow is going. In a couple of weeks the ground will be real muddy. That's because all the frost will be coming out of it. Then the grass starts to grow. Your dad wants me to build a ring for you to ride in."

Joe's mother was home; his father had died five years ago. She was a heavyset woman in her late fifties with a practical, no-nonsense approach. She invited them in. The small house was comfortably shabby. Souvenir knickknacks covered the tables. The walls were strewn with family pictures indiscriminately hung.

"Nice to meet you, Mrs. Krueger. My Joe talks about you all the time. No wonder he says you're pretty. You sure are. And oh, my land, how you look like Caroline! I'm Maude Ekers. You call me Maude."

"Where's Joe's dog?" Tina asked.

"Come on in the kitchen," Maude told them.

They followed her eagerly. The puppy looked to be a combination of German shepherd and retriever. Awkwardly it struggled up on ungainly legs. "We found it on the road," Joe explained. "Somebody must have pushed it out of a car. If I hadn't come along it probably would have frozen to death."

Maude shook her head. "He's always bringing home stray animals. My Joe has the kindest heart I ever come across. Never was one for schoolwork, but let me tell you, he's magic with animals. You shoulda seen his last dog. He was a beauty. Smart as a whip too."

"What happened to him?" Jenny asked.

"We don't know. We tried to keep him fenced in but sometimes he'd get away. He used to want to trail after Joe to your farm. Mr. Krueger didn't like it."

"I don't blame Mr. Krueger," Joe said hastily. "He had a purebred bitch and he didn't want Tarpy to get near her. But one day Tarpy did follow me and was on Juna. Mr. Krueger was real mad."

"Where's Juna now?" Jenny asked.

"Mr. Krueger got rid of her. Said she wouldn't be any use if she carried a litter from a mongrel."

"What happened to Tarpy?"

"We don't know," Maude said. "He got out again one day and never came back. I've got my suspicions," she hinted darkly.

"Maw," Joe said hastily.

"Erich Krueger threatened to shoot that dog," she continued simply. "If Tarpy ruined his expensive bitch I don't much blame him for getting sore. But least he coulda told you. Joe hunted high and low for that dog," she told Jenny. "I thought he'd get sick."

Tina and Beth squatted on the floor beside Randy. Tina's face was rapturous. "Mommy, can we have a dog, please?"

"We'll ask Daddy," she promised.

The children played with the puppy while she had coffee with Maude. The woman immediately began interrogating her. How did she like the Krueger home? Pretty fancy, wasn't it? Must be tough to come out from New York City to a farm. Jenny replied that she was sure she'd be happy.

"Caroline said that too," Maude hinted darkly. "But the Krueger men aren't very sociable. Kind of makes it hard on their wives. Everybody around here thought the world of Caroline. And they respected John Krueger. Same as they do Erich. But the Kruegers aren't warm even with their own. And they're not forgiving people. When they get angry, they stay angry."

Jenny knew Maude was referring to her brother's role in Caroline's accident. Quickly she finished her coffee. "We'd better get back."

The kitchen door was pushed open just as she stood up. "Well, who's this?'' The voice was raspy, as though the vocal cords had been strained. The man was in his mid-fifties. His eyes were bloodshot and faded with the bleary expression of the heavy drinker. He was painfully thin, so that the waist of his pants settled somewhere around his hips.

He stared at Jenny, then his eyes narrowed thoughtfully. ''You gotta be the new Mrs. Krueger I've been hearing about.''

''Yes, I am.''

''I'm Josh Brothers, Joe's uncle.''

The electrician who had been responsible for the accident. Jenny sensed immediately that Erich would be furious if he heard about this meeting.

''I can see why Erich picked you,'' Josh said heavily. He turned to his sister. ''Swear it was Caroline, wouldn't you, Maude?'' Without waiting for an answer he asked Jenny, ''Heard all about the accident, I suppose?''

''Yes, I did.''

''The Krueger version. Not mine.'' Clearly Josh Brothers was about to tell an often-repeated story. Jenny got the smell of whiskey from his breath. His voice took on a reciting quality. ''In spite of the fact they were divorcing, John was crazy about Caroline. . . .''

''Divorcing!'' Jenny interrupted. ''Erich's father and mother *divorcing*!''

The bleary eyes became crafty. ''Oh, Erich didn't tell you that? He likes to pretend it didn't happen. Lots of gossip here, let me tell you, when Caroline didn't even *try* to get custody of her only child. Anyhow the day of the accident I was working in the dairy barn and Caroline and Erich came in. She was leaving for good that afternoon. It was his birthday and he was holding his new hockey stick and crying his eyes out. She waved me away; that's why I hung the lamp over the nail. I heard Caroline say, 'Just like this little calf has to be weaned away from its mother . . .' Then I pulled the door closed behind me so they could say good-bye to each other and a minute later Erich began screaming. Luke Garrett pounded on her chest and did that mouth-to-mouth breathing, but we all knew it was no good. When she slipped and fell into the stock tank, she grabbed the cord and pulled the lamp in with her. That voltage went right through her. . . . She never had no chance.''

''Josh, keep quiet,'' Maude said sharply.

Jenny stared at Josh. Why had Erich never told her that his parents were divorcing, that Caroline was leaving him and his father? And to have witnessed that ghastly accident! No wonder Erich was so terribly insecure now, so afraid of losing her.

Deep in thought, she collected the girls and murmured good-byes.

As they walked back home, Joe spoke timidly to Jenny. ''Mr. Krueger wouldn't be pleased to hear my mom talked so much and that you met my uncle.''

''I'm not going to discuss it, Joe, I promise,'' she reassured him.

The country road back to Krueger Farm was peaceful in the late morning. Beth and Tina ran ahead of them, happily scooping up loose snow. Jenny felt depressed and frightened. She thought of the countless times Erich had talked about Caroline. Never once had he even hinted about the fact that she had been planning to leave him.

If only I had a friend here, Jenny thought, someone I could talk to. She remembered how she and Nana had been able to talk through any problem that came up in their lives, how she and Fran would have coffee after the girls were in bed and exchange confidences.

"Mrs. Krueger," Joe said softly, "you look as though you feel real bad. I hope my uncle didn't upset you. I know Mom talks kind of mean about the Kruegers but please don't take offense."

"I won't," Jenny promised. "But, Joe, will you please do one thing for me?"

"Anything."

"For God sake when Mr. Krueger isn't around, call me Jenny. I'm beginning to forget my own name around here."

"I call you Jenny whenever I think about you."

"Terrific," Jenny laughed, feeling better, then glanced at Joe. The open worship on his face was unmistakable.

Oh, dear God, she thought, if he ever looks at me like that in front of Erich there'll be hell to pay.

CHAPTER 15

As they neared the big house Jenny thought she saw someone watching them from the window of the farm office. Erich often stopped there on his way back from the cabin.

She hurried the girls into the house and began preparing grilled cheese sandwiches and hot cocoa. Tina and Beth perched at the table, expectantly watching the toaster oven as the bubbling smell of melting cheese filled the kitchen.

What could have made Caroline so desperately unhappy that she would leave Erich? How much resentment was mixed in with Erich's love for her? Jenny tried to visualize any circumstance under which she'd leave Beth and Tina. There was none.

The children were tired from the long walk and fell asleep as soon as she put them in for their nap. She watched as their eyes drooped and closed. She was reluctant to leave the room. She sat on the window seat for a moment, realizing she felt lightheaded. Why?

Finally she went downstairs, pulled on a jacket and walked over to the office. Clyde was working at the big desk. Trying to sound casual, she remarked, "Erich hasn't come in yet for lunch. I thought he might have been delayed over here."

Clyde looked puzzled. "He just stopped in for a couple of minutes on his way back from getting supplies. He told me you knew he's planning to stay up at the cabin and paint."

Wordlessly Jenny turned to leave. Then her eye spotted the incoming mail basket. "Oh, Clyde, if I get any mail while Erich is at the cabin, will you be sure that someone brings it over to me?"

"Sure will. Usually I just give anything for you to Erich."

Anything for you . . . In the month she'd been here, even though she'd written to Fran and Mr. Hartley, she hadn't received a single piece of mail. "I'm afraid he forgot about it." She could hear the strain in her voice. "How much has come in?"

"A letter last week, a couple of postcards. I don't know."

"I see." Jenny looked at the telephone. "How about phone calls?"

"Someone from church phoned last week about a meeting. And the week before you got a call from New York. You mean Erich didn't give you those messages?"

"He was so concerned with getting ready for the trip," Jenny murmured. "Thanks, Clyde."

Slowly she started back to the house. The sky was overcast now. Snow was beginning to fall in stinging, slapping gusts. The ground that had begun to thaw had hardened again. The temperature was dropping swiftly.

I won't share you, . . . Jenny. Erich had meant that literally. Who had phoned from New York? Kevin to say he was coming to Minnesota? If so, why didn't Erich warn her?

Who had written? Mr. Hartley? Fran?

I can't let this happen, Jenny thought. I've got to do something.

"Jenny!" Mark Garrett was hurrying from the barn. With his long strides he covered the distance between them in seconds. His sandy hair was rumpled. He was smiling but his eyes were serious. "Haven't had a chance to say hello for a while. How's everything?"

How much did he suspect? Could she discuss Erich with him? No, that wouldn't be fair to Erich. But there was one thing she could do.

She tried to make her smile seem natural. "I'm fine," she replied. "And you're just the person I wanted to see. Remember we talked about having you and your friend . . . is it Emily? . . . for dinner?"

"Yes."

"Let's make it March eighth. That's Erich's birthday. I want to have a little party for him."

Mark frowned. "Jenny, I have to warn you. Erich still finds his birthday a pretty rough day."

"I know," Jenny said. She looked up at Mark, aware of his tallness. "Mark, that was twenty-five years ago. Isn't it about time that Erich got over losing his mother?"

Mark seemed to be choosing his words. ''Go easy, Jenny,'' he suggested. ''It takes time to wean someone like Erich off imprinted reactions.'' He smiled. ''But I must say it shouldn't take him very long to start to appreciate what he has now.''

''Then you will come?''

''Definitely. And Emily's been dying to meet you.''

Jenny laughed wistfully. ''I've been dying to meet some people too.''

She said good-bye and went into the house. Elsa was just ready to leave. ''The girls are still asleep. Tomorrow I can shop on my way in. I have the list.''

''List?''

''Yes, when you were out with the girls this morning, Mr. Krueger came in. He said I should do the shopping from now on.''

''That's nonsense,'' Jenny protested. ''I can go or Joe can take me.''

''Mr. Krueger said he was taking the keys to the car.''

''I see. Thank you, Elsa.'' Jenny would not let the woman see the dismay she felt.

But when the door closed behind Elsa, she realized she was trembling. Had Erich taken the keys to make sure Joe didn't use the car? Or was it possible he guessed that *she* had used it? Nervously she glanced around the kitchen. In the apartment whenever she'd been upset she'd calmed herself by tackling some big cleaning job that needed to be done. But this house was immaculate.

She stared at the canisters on the counter space. They took up so much room and were so seldom used. Every room here was formal, cold, overcrowded. It was her home. Surely Erich would be pleased if she put her own stamp on this place?

She made room for the canisters on a pantry shelf. The round oak table and chairs were exactly centered in the middle of the room. Placed under the window on the south wall, they'd be infinitely more convenient to the buffet bar, and at meals it would be pleasant to look out at the far fields. Not caring if the table legs scuffed the floor, Jenny dragged it over.

The hook rug that had been in the girls' bedroom had been taken up to the attic. She decided that placing it near the cast-iron stove and grouping the couch, its matching chair and a slipper chair from the library on it would create a pleasant den area in the kitchen.

Fired now with nervous energy, she went into the parlor, swept some of the bric-a-brac into her arms and carried it to a cupboard. Tugging and straining, she managed to pull down the lace curtains that blocked sunlight and view from the parlor and the dining room. The couch in the parlor was almost too heavy to push. Somehow she managed to reverse it with the mahogany trestle table. When she was finished the room seemed airier, more inviting.

She went through the rest of the downstairs rooms, making mental notes. A little at a time, she promised herself. She folded the curtains neatly and carried them up to the attic. The braided rug was there. If she couldn't manage to bring that down by herself she'd call Joe.

She yanked at the rug she wanted, realized there was no way she could manage it alone and with idle curiosity glanced at the other pieces in the room.

A small blue leather vanity case with the initials C.B.K. caught her eye. She pulled it out to examine it. Was it unlocked? Hesitating for only an instant, she deflected one then the other of the catches. The lid swung up.

Toilet articles were set in a traylike holder. Creams and makeup and pine-scented soap. A leather-bound daily reminder notebook was under the tray. The date on the cover was twenty-five years old. Jenny opened the book and flipped through the pages. January 2, 10 A.M., teacher conference, Erich. January 8: dinner, Luke Garrett, the Meiers, the Behrends. January 10: return library books. She skimmed through the entries. February 2: judges chambers, 9 A.M. Would that have been the divorce hearing? Feb. 22: order hockey stick for E. The last entry, March 8: Erich b-day. That had been written in light blue ink. Then with a different pen, 7 P.M.. Northwest flight 241, Minneapolis to San Francisco. A ticket unused, one-way, clipped to that page, a note under it.

The named printed across the top of the note: EVERETT BONARDI. Caroline's father, Jenny thought. Quickly she read the uneven handwriting: ''Caroline, dear. Your mother and I are not surprised to learn you are leaving John. We are deeply concerned about Erich but after reading your letter agree it is best if he stays with his father. We had no idea of the true circumstances. Neither of us has been well but are looking forward to having you with us. Our love to you.''

Jenny folded the letter, slipped it back in the notebook and closed the lid of the vanity case. What had Everett Bonardi meant when he wrote ''We had no idea of the true circumstances''?

Slowly she went down the attic stairs. The girls were still asleep. Lovingly she looked down at them, then her mouth went dry. The girls' dark red hair was tumbled out on their pillows. On the top of each pillow, positioned so it almost seemed to be a hair ornament, was a small round cake of pine soap. The faint scent of pine permeated the air.

''Aren't they little beauties?'' a voice sighed in her ear. Too startled to scream, Jenny spun around. A thin, bony arm encircled her waist. ''Oh, Caroline,'' Rooney Toomis sighed, her eyes vacant and moist, ''don't we just love our babies?''

Somehow Jenny got Rooney out of the room without waking the girls. Rooney went willingly although she kept her arm wrapped around Jenny's waist. Awkwardly they descended the stairs.

''Let's have a cup of tea,'' Jenny suggested, trying to keep her voice normal. How had Rooney gotten in? She must still have a house key.

Rooney sipped the tea silently, never taking her gaze from the window.

"Arden used to love those woods," she said. "Course she knew she wasn't to go any farther than the edge. But she was always climbing trees. She'd perch up there in that one"—Rooney pointed vaguely to a large oak—"and watch the birds. Did I tell you she was president of the 4-H club one year?"

Her voice was calming. Her eyes were clearer when she turned to look at Jenny. "You're not Caroline," she said, puzzled.

"No, I'm not. I'm Jenny."

Rooney sighed. "I'm sorry. I guess I forgot. Something came over me, one of my spells. I was thinking I was late getting to work. Thought I'd overslept. Course Caroline would never care but Mr. John Krueger was so exacting."

"And you had a key?" Jenny asked.

"I forgot my key. The door was unlocked. But I don't have a key anymore, do I?"

Jenny was positive the lock had been on the kitchen door. On the other hand . . . She decided not to try to pin Rooney down.

"And I went upstairs to make the beds," Rooney said. "But they were all finished. And then I saw Caroline. No, I mean I saw you."

"And you put the pine soap on the children's pillows?" Jenny asked.

"Oh, no. Caroline must have done that. She was the one who loved that scent."

It was useless. Rooney's mind was too confused to attempt to separate imagination from reality. "Rooney, do you ever go out to church or to any meetings? Do you ever have friends in?"

Rooney shook her head. "I used to go to all the activities with Arden, the 4-H, the school plays, her band concerts. But no more."

Her eyes were clear now. "I shouldn't be here. Erich won't like it." She looked fearful. "You won't tell him or Clyde, will you? Promise you won't tell."

"Of course I won't."

"You're like Caroline, pretty and gentle and sweet. I hope nothing happens to you. That would be such a shame. Toward the end Caroline was so anxious to get away. She used to say, 'I just have a feeling, Rooney, that something terrible is going to happen. And I'm so helpless.' " Rooney got up to go.

"Didn't you wear a coat?" Jenny asked.

"I guess I didn't notice."

"Wait a minute." Jenny dug her thermal coat out of the foyer closet. "Put this on. Look, it fits you perfectly. Button it up around the neck. It's cold out."

Hadn't Erich said practically the same thing to her at that first lunch in the Russian Tea Room? Was that really less than two months ago?

Rooney glanced around uncertainly. "If you want I'll help you move the table back before Erich comes."

"I don't intend to move the table back. It's staying right where it is."

"Caroline had it at the window once but John said she was just trying to show herself off to the men on the farm."

"What did Caroline say?"

"Nothing. She just put on her green cape and went outside and sat on the porch swing. Just like in the picture. Once she told me she used to like to sit out there and face west because that's where her folks were. She got awful homesick for them."

"Didn't they ever come here to visit?"

"Never. But Caroline still loved the farm. She was raised in the city but she'd always say, 'This country is so beautiful, Rooney, so special in what it does for me.' "

"And then she left?"

"Something happened and she decided she had to go."

"What was that?"

"I don't know." Rooney glanced down. "This coat is nice. I like it."

"Please keep it," Jenny told her. "I've hardly worn it since I came here."

"If I do, can I make the girls jumpers like you promised?"

"Of course you can. And, Rooney, I'd like to be your friend."

Jenny stood at the kitchen door, watching the slight figure, now warmly wrapped, bend forward against the wind.

CHAPTER 16

It was the waiting that was so hard. Was Erich angry? Had he simply become so involved in painting that he hadn't wanted to break his concentration? Did she dare go into the woods, try to find the cabin and confront him?

No, she must not do that.

The days seemed endlessly long. Even the children became restless. Where's Daddy? was a constant inquiry. In this short time, Erich had become terribly important to them.

Let Kevin stay away, Jenny prayed. Make him leave us alone.

She spent her time concentrating on the house. Room by room she rearranged furniture, sometimes switching only a chair or table, sometimes making radical adjustments. Unwillingly Elsa helped her take down the rest of the heavy lace curtains. "Look, Elsa," Jenny finally said firmly, "these curtains are coming down and I don't want any more talk about checking with Mr. Krueger first. Either help me or don't."

Outside, the farm seemed gray and depressing. When the snow was on the ground, it had a Currier and Ives beauty. When spring came, she was sure the lush green of the fields and trees would be magnificent. But now the frozen mud, the brown fields, the dark tree trunks and overcast skies chilled and depressed her.

Would Erich come back to the house for his birthday? He'd told her that he was always on the farm that day. Should she cancel his birthday dinner?

The evenings alone were interminable. In New York when the children were settled for the night, she'd often gone to bed with a book and a cup of tea. The library on the farm was excellent. But the books in this library didn't invite leisurely reading. They were placed in exact rows, seemingly by size and color rather than author or subject. To her, they had the same effect as furniture with plastic covers; she hated to touch them. Her problem was solved when on one of her trips to the attic she noticed a box marked BOOKS—CBK. Happily she helped herself to a couple of the comfortably shabby, well-read volumes.

But even though she read far into the night, she was finding it harder and harder to sleep. All her life she'd only had to close her eyes and instantly she'd be in a sound sleep for hours. Now she began to wake up frequently, to dream vague, frightening dreams in which shadowy figures slithered through her subconscious.

On March 7, following a particularly restless night, she made up her mind. She needed more exercise. After lunch she went out to hunt for Joe and found him in the farm office. His unaffected pleasure at the visit was reassuring. Quickly she explained: "Joe, I want to start riding lessons today."

Twenty minutes later she was sitting astride the mare, trying to keep Joe's instructions straight in her head.

She realized she was enjoying herself thoroughly. She forgot the chill, the sharp wind, the fact that her thighs were getting sore, that her hands were tingling against the reins. Softly she spoke to Fire Maid. "Now you at least give me a chance, old girl," she suggested. "I'll probably make mistakes but I'm new at this business."

By the end of an hour she was getting the feel of moving her body in cadence with the horse. She spotted Mark watching her and waved to him. He came over.

"You look pretty good. This your first time on a horse?"

"The very first." Jenny started to dismount. Quickly Mark took the horse's bridle. "The other side," he said.

"What, oh, sorry." She slid down easily.

"You did real good, Jenny," Joe told her.

"Thank you, Joe. Monday okay with you?"

"Anytime, Jenny."

Mark walked with her to the house. "You've got a fan in Joe."

Was there some kind of warning in his voice?

She tried to sound matter-of-fact. "He's a good teacher and I think Erich will be pleased that I'm learning to ride. It will be a surprise for him that I've started taking lessons."

"I hardly think so," Mark commented. "He was watching you for quite a while."

"Watching me?"

"Yes, for nearly half an hour from the woods. I thought he didn't want to make you nervous."

"Where is he now?"

"He went up to the house for a minute and then started back to the cabin."

"Erich was in the house?" I sound stupid, Jenny thought, hearing the astonishment in her voice.

Mark stopped, took her arm and turned her to him. "What's the matter, Jenny?" he asked. Somehow she could imagine him examining an animal, searching for the source of pain.

They were almost at the porch. She said stiffly, "Erich has been staying at the cabin since he came back from Atlanta. It's just that it's rather lonely for me now. I'm used to being terribly busy and around people and now . . . I guess I feel out of touch all around."

"See if it doesn't get much better after tomorrow," Mark advised. "By the way, are you sure you want us for dinner?"

"No. I mean, I'm not even sure Erich will be home. Could we make it the thirteenth instead? That will separate his birthday party from the anniversary. If he still hasn't come back by then, I'll give you a call and you two can decide if you want to come just to visit me or go out and enjoy yourselves."

She was afraid she sounded resentful. What's the matter with me? she thought, dismayed.

Mark took both her hands in his. "We'll come, Jenny, whether Erich is home or not. For what it's worth I've had Erich turn on me when he gets in one of his moods. The rest of the picture is that when he comes out of them, he's all the good things—intelligent, generous, talented, kind. Give him a chance to get through tomorrow and see if he isn't the real Erich again."

With a quick smile, he squeezed her hands, released them and left her. Sighing, Jenny entered the house. Elsa was ready to go. Tina and Beth were cross-legged on the floor, crayons in hand. "Daddy brought us new coloring books," Beth announced. "Aren't they good?"

"Mr. Krueger left note for you." Elsa pointed to a sealed envelope on the table.

Jenny felt the curiosity in the woman's eyes. She slipped the note into her pocket. "Thank you."

As the door closed behind the cleaning woman, Jenny pulled the envelope from her pocket and ripped it open. The sheet of paper, covered by oversized letters in Erich's bold handwriting, held one sentence: *You should have waited for me to ride with you.*

"Mommy, Mommy." Beth was tugging at her jacket. "You look sick, Mommy." Trying to smile, Jenny looked down at the woebegone face. Tina was next to Beth now, her face puckered, ready to cry.

Jenny crumbled the note and shoved it in her pocket. "No, love, I'm fine. I just didn't feel so well for a minute."

She was not reassuring Beth. A wave of nausea had come over her as she read the note. Dear God, she thought, he can't mean this. He won't let me go to the church meetings. He won't let me use the car. Now he won't let me even learn to ride when he's painting.

Erich, don't spoil it for us, she protested silently. You can't have it both ways. You can't hole up and paint and expect me to sit with my hands folded waiting for you. You can't be so jealous that I'm afraid to be honest with you.

She glanced around wildly. Should she take a stand, pack and go back to New York? If there was any chance to keep their relationship from being destroyed, he'd have to get counseling, get some help to overcome this possessiveness. If she left, he'd know she meant it.

Where could she go? And with what?

She didn't have a dollar in her pocketbook. She had no money for fare, no place to go, no job. And she didn't want to leave him.

She was afraid she was going to be sick. "I'll be right back," she whispered and hurried upstairs. In the bathroom she wrung out a cold cloth and washed her face. Her reflection had a sickly, unnatural pallor.

"Mommy, Mommy." Beth and Tina were in the hallway. They had followed her upstairs.

She knelt down, swooped them to her, hugging them fiercely.

"Mommy, you're hurting me," Tina protested.

"I'm sorry, Moppet." The warm, wiggling bodies close to hers restored her balance. "You two certainly got yourselves one brilliant mother," she said.

The afternoon dragged slowly. To pass the time, she sat with the girls at the spinet and began to teach them to pick out notes. Without the curtains it was possible to look out the parlor windows and see the sunset. The clouds had been blown away and the sky was coldly beautiful in shades of mauve and orange, gold and pink.

Leaving the children banging on the keyboard, she walked to the kitchen door that opened onto the west porch. The wind was making the porch swing move gently. Ignoring the cold, Jenny stood on the porch and admired the last of the sunset. When the final lights were ebbing into grayness, she turned to go back into the house.

A movement in the woods caught her attention. She stared. Someone was watching her, a shadowy figure, nearly concealed by the double trunk of the oak tree that Arden used to climb.

''Who's there?'' Jenny called sharply.

The shadow receded into the woods as though trying to step back into the protection of the underbrush.

''Who's there?'' Jenny called again sharply. Aware only of her anger at the intrusion on her privacy, she started down the porch steps toward the woods.

Erich stepped out from the shelter of the oak and with outstretched arms started running toward her.

''But, darling, I was only joking. How could you have thought for a minute that I wasn't joking?'' He took the crumbled note from her. ''Here, let's throw that out.'' He shoved it in the stove. ''There, it's gone.''

Bewildered, Jenny looked at Erich. There wasn't a trace of nervousness about him. He was smiling easily, shaking his head at her in amusement. ''It's hard to believe you took that seriously, Jenny,'' he said, then he laughed. ''I thought you'd be flattered that I pretended to be jealous.''

''Erich!''

He locked his arms around her waist, rubbed his cheek against hers. ''Umm, you feel good.''

Nothing about the fact that they hadn't seen each other for a week. And that note *wasn't* a joke. He was kissing her cheek. ''I love you, Jen.''

For a moment she held herself rigid. She had vowed that she would have it out with him, the absences, the jealousy, her mail. But she didn't want to start an argument. She'd missed him. Suddenly the whole house seemed cheerful again.

The girls heard his voice and came running back into the room. ''Daddy, Daddy.'' He picked them up.

''Hey, you two sounded great on the piano. Guess we'll have to start lessons for you pretty soon. Would you like that?''

Jenny thought, Mark's right. I've got to have patience, give him time. Her smile was genuine when he looked at her over the children's heads.

Dinner had a festive air. She prepared carbonara and an endive salad. Erich brought a bottle of Chablis from the wine rack. ''It gets harder and harder to work in the cabin, Jen,'' he said. ''Especially when I know I'm missing dinners like this.'' He tickled Tina. ''And it's no fun being away from my family.''

''And your home,'' she said. It seemed a good moment to bring up the changes she'd made. ''You haven't mentioned how you like the way I've moved things around.''

''I'm slow to react,'' he said lightly. ''Let me think about it.''

It was better than she'd hoped for. She got up, walked around the table and put her arms around his neck. ''I was so afraid you might be upset.''

He reached up and smoothed her hair. As always the feel of his nearness thrilled her, pushed away the doubts and uncertainties.

Beth had just left the table. Now she came running back. ''Mommy, do you love Daddy better than our other daddy?''

Why in the name of God had she thought to ask that question now? Jenny wondered despairingly. Desperately she tried to frame an answer. She could only find the truth. ''I loved your first daddy mostly because of you and Tina. Why do you want to know that?'' To Erich she said, ''They haven't mentioned Kevin for weeks.''

Beth pointed at Erich. ''Because *this daddy* asked me if I love him better than our first daddy.''

''Erich, I wouldn't discuss that with the girls.''

''I shouldn't,'' he said contritely. ''I guess I was just anxious to see if their memory of him was beginning to fade.'' He put his arms around her. ''How about your memory, darling?''

She took a long time with the children's baths. Somehow it was calming to watch their uncomplicated pleasure splashing in the tub. She wrapped them in thick towels, rejoicing in the sturdy little bodies and brushing back the freshly shampooed ringlets. Her hands trembled as she buttoned their pajamas. I'm getting so nervous, she fumed at herself. It's just I feel so dishonest that the smallest thing Erich says I take the wrong way. *Damn* Kevin.

She heard the girls' prayers. ''God bless Mommy and Daddy,'' Tina intoned. She paused then looked up. ''Should we say God bless both daddies?''

Jenny bit her lip. Erich had started this. She wasn't going to tell the children not to pray for Kevin. Still . . . ''Why not tonight say God bless everyone?'' she suggested.

''And Fire Maid and Mouse and Tinker Bell and Joe. . . .'' Beth added.

''And Randy,'' Tina reminded her. ''Can we have a puppy too?''

Jenny tucked them into bed, realizing how every night she was becoming more and more reluctant to go downstairs again. When she was alone, the house seemed too big, too silent. On windy nights there was a mournful wail from the trees that penetrated the quiet.

And now when Erich was here she didn't know what to expect. Would he stay overnight or go back to the cabin?

She went downstairs. He had made the coffee. ''They must have been pretty dirty for you to be so long with them, sweetheart.''

She had planned to ask him for the keys to the car but he didn't give her a chance. He picked up the tray with the coffee service. ''Let's sit in the front parlor and let me absorb your changes.''

As she followed him she realized how well the white cable-knit sweater he was wearing set off his dark, gold hair. My handsome, successful, talented husband, she thought, and with a tinge of irony remembered Fran saying, "He's too perfect."

In the parlor she pointed out to him how moving some furniture and putting away the excessive bric-a-brac made it possible to appreciate the lovely pieces in the room.

"Where did you put everything?"

"The curtains are in the attic. The small pieces are in the cupboard in the pantry. Don't you think having the trestle table under *Memory of Caroline* is better? I always felt the pattern in the couch was distracting so near the painting."

"Perhaps."

She couldn't be sure of his reaction. Nervously she tried to fill the silence with conversation. "And don't you think with the light that way, we see more of the little boy—of you? Before this your face was rather shadowed."

"That's a bit fanciful. The child's face was never meant to be defined. As a fine arts major who worked in a prominent gallery, you should realize that, Jenny."

He laughed.

Was he intending to joke? Was it just that no matter what he said tonight, there seemed to be a sting in it? Jenny picked up her coffee cup and realized her hand was shaking. The cup slipped from her hand and the coffee splattered on the couch and Oriental rug.

"Jenny, darling. Why are you so nervous?" Erich's face creased into worried lines. With his napkin he began to swab the stain.

"Don't rub it in," Jenny cautioned. Rushing into the kitchen, she grabbed a bottle of club soda from the refrigerator.

With a sponge she dabbed furiously at the spots. "Thank God I hadn't put cream in yet," she murmured.

Erich said nothing. Would he consider the couch and carpet destroyed as he had the dining-room wallpaper?

But the club soda did the trick. "I think I've got it all." She got up slowly. "I'm sorry, Erich."

"Sweetheart, don't worry about it. But can't you tell me why you're so upset? You *are* upset, Jen. That note for example. A few weeks ago you would have known I was teasing you. Darling, your sense of humor is one of the most delightful parts of your personality. Please don't lose it."

She knew he was right. "I'm sorry," she said miserably. She was going to tell Erich about meeting Kevin. No matter what, she had to clear the air. "The reason I'm so . . ."

The phone rang.

"Answer it, please, Jenny."

"It won't be for me."

It rang again.

"Don't be so sure. Clyde tells me in the last week there have been a dozen disconnects where someone didn't want to leave a taped message. That's why I told him to let it ring through tonight.''

With a sense of fatality she preceded him into the kitchen. The phone rang a third time. She knew even before she picked it up that it was Kevin.

''Jenny, I can't believe I finally got through to you. That damn answering machine! How are you?'' Kevin's voice was buoyant.

''I'm all right, Kev.'' She felt Erich's eyes on her face; he bent over the phone so he could hear the conversation. ''What do you want?'' *Would Kevin talk about their meeting?* If only she'd told Erich first.

''To share the good news. I'm officially in the repertory company at the Guthrie, Jen.''

''I'm glad for you,'' she said stiffly. ''But, Kevin, I don't want you calling me. I forbid you to call me. Erich is right here and he's very upset that you're contacting me.''

''Listen, Jen, I'll call all I want. You tell Krueger for me that he can tear up those adoption papers. I'm going to court to stop the adoption. You can have custody, Jen, and I'll pay support, but those kids are MacPartlands and that's the way it's going to be. Who knows? Someday Tina and I might be doing a Tatum and Ryan O'Neal number. She's a real little actress. Oh, Jen. Gotta run. They're calling for me. I'll get back to you. Bye.''

Slowly Jenny hung up the phone. ''Can he stop the adoption?'' she asked.

''He can try. He won't succeed.'' Erich's eyes were cold, his tone icy.

''A Tatum and Ryan O'Neal number, my God,'' Jenny said disbelievingly. ''I'd almost admire him if I thought he wanted the children, really wanted them. But this!''

''Jenny, I predicted you were making a mistake letting him sponge off you,'' Erich said. ''If you'd been yanking him into court for support payments, you'd have been finished with him two years ago.''

As usual, Erich was right. Suddenly she felt infinitely weary and the faint nausea she'd experienced earlier was coming back. ''I'm going to bed,'' she said abruptly. ''Are you staying here tonight, Erich?''

''I'm not sure.''

''I see.'' She started down the foyer from the kitchen to the staircase. She had gone only a few feet when he caught up with her.

''Jenny.''

She turned. ''What is it, Erich?''

His eyes were warm now, his face concerned and gentle. ''I know it isn't your fault that MacPartland is bothering you. I promise I know that. I shouldn't get upset with you.''

''It makes it so much harder for me when you do.''

''We'll work this out. Let me get through these next few days. I'll feel better then. Try to understand. Maybe it's because Mother promised me just before she died that she'd always be here on my birthday. Maybe that's why I'm so depressed around this time. I feel her presence—and her loss—so much. Try to understand me; try to forgive me when I hurt you. I don't *mean* it, Jenny. I love you."

They were wrapped in each other's arms. "Erich, *please*," Jenny begged, "let this be the last year you react like this. Twenty-five years. *Twenty-five years*. Caroline would be fifty-seven years old. You still see her as a young woman whose death was a tragedy. It was, but it's over. Let's get on with life. It could be good for us. Let me share your life, really share it. Bring your friends in. Take me to see your studio. Get me a small car so I can go shopping or to an art gallery or take the kids to a movie when you're painting."

"You want to be able to meet Kevin, don't you?"

"Oh, my God." Jenny pulled away. "Let me go to bed, Erich. I really don't feel well."

He did not follow her up the stairs. She looked in on the girls. They were fast asleep. Tina stirred when she kissed her.

She went into the master bedroom. The faint scent of pine that always lingered in the room seemed heavier tonight. Was it because she felt queasy? Her eyes fell on the crystal bowl. Tomorrow she'd move that bowl to a guest bedroom. Oh, Erich, stay tonight, she pleaded silently. Don't go away feeling like this. Suppose Kevin started pestering them with calls? Suppose he stopped the adoption? Suppose he had regular visitation rights? It would be unbearable for Erich. It would destroy their marriage.

She got into bed and determinedly opened her book. But it was impossible to concentrate. Her eyes were heavy and her body ached in unaccustomed places. Joe had warned her the riding would cause that. "You'll hear from muscles you didn't know you had," he'd grinned.

Finally she turned off the light. A little later she heard footsteps in the hall. Erich? She pulled herself up on one elbow but the footsteps continued up the stairs to the attic. What was he doing there? A few minutes later she heard him coming down. He must be dragging something. There was a thudding sound every few steps. What was he doing?

She was about to get up and investigate when she heard sounds from downstairs, the sounds of furniture being moved.

Of course, she thought.

Erich had gone upstairs for the carton of curtains. Now he was rearranging the furniture, putting it back in its original places.

In the morning when Jenny went downstairs, the curtains were rehung; every table and chair and piece of bric-a-brac was in place and her plants were missing. Later she found them in the trash container behind the barn.

CHAPTER 17

Slowly Jenny walked through the downstairs rooms a second time. Erich had not failed to return a single vase or lamp or footstool to its original exact spot. He'd even found the ornately ugly owl sculpture that she'd poked away in an unused cabinet over the stove.

She had known what to expect but even so the absolute rejection of her wishes and taste shocked her. Finally she made coffee and went back to bed. Shivering, she pulled the covers around her and leaned back on the pillows propped against the massive headboard. It would be another cold and gloomy day. The sky was gray and misty; a sharp wind rattled the window-panes.

The eighth of March, Erich's thirty-fifth birthday, Caroline's twenty-fifth anniversary. That last morning of her life had Caroline awakened in this bed, heartsick that she was leaving her only child? Or had she awakened counting the hours until she could leave this house?

Jenny rubbed her forehead. It ached dully. Once again her sleep had been restless. She'd been dreaming of Erich. Always he had that same expression on his face, an expression she could never quite understand. Once this anniversary was over and he came back to the house she'd talk to him quietly. She would ask him to go with her for counseling. If he refused she'd have to consider taking the children to New York.

Where?

Maybe her job would be available again. Maybe Kevin would lend her a few hundred dollars for airfare. *Lend*. He owed her hundreds. Fran would let her and the girls bunk in her place for a short time. It was a terrible inconvenience to ask of anyone but Fran was a good scout.

I don't have a cent, Jenny thought, but it isn't that. I don't want to leave Erich. I love him. I want to spend the rest of my life with him.

She was still so chilled. A hot shower might help. And she'd wear that warm argyll sweater. It was in the closet.

Jenny glanced at the closet and understood what had been subconsciously bothering her.

When she got up she'd taken her robe from the closet. But last night she had left the robe thrown over the vanity bench. The bench had been pulled back from the dressing table. Now it was precision-straight.

No wonder she dreamed of Erich's face. She must have subconsciously realized he was in the room. Why hadn't he stayed? She shivered. Her skin felt prickly. But it wasn't the cold. She was afraid. Afraid of Erich, of her own husband? Of course not, she told herself. I am afraid of his rejection. He came to me and then left me. Had Erich gone back to the cabin during the night or had he slept in the house?

Quietly she put on her robe and slippers and went into the hall. The door of Erich's boyhood room was closed. She listened at the door. There was no sound. Slowly she turned the handle and opened the door.

Erich was curled up in bed, the gaily patterned patchwork quilt wrapped around him. Only his ear and hairline showed. His face was buried in folds of soft material. Silently Jenny entered the room and became aware of a familiar faint scent. She bent over Erich. In his sleep he was nuzzling the aqua nightgown to his face.

She and the children had almost finished breakfast when Erich came downstairs. He refused even coffee. He was already wearing one of his heavy parkas and was carrying what was obviously an expensive hunting rifle, even to Jenny's inexperienced eye. Jenny eyed it nervously.

"I don't know if I'll be back tonight," he told her. "I don't know what I'll do. I'll just be around the farm today."

"All right."

"Don't go changing any of the furniture again, Jenny. I didn't like it your way."

"I gathered that," Jenny said evenly.

"It's my birthday, Jen." His tone sounded high-pitched, *young*, like the voice of a boy. "Aren't you going to wish me a happy birthday?"

"I'd rather wait until Friday night. Mark and Emily are coming to dinner. We'll celebrate it with them. Wouldn't you prefer that?"

"Maybe." He came over to her. The cold steel of the rifle brushed her arm. "Do you love me, Jenny?"

"Yes."

"And you'll never leave me?"

"I'd never want to leave you."

"That's what Caroline said, those very words." His eye became reflective.

The children had been silent. "Daddy, can I go with you?" Beth begged.

"Not now. Tell me your name."

"Beth Crew-grr."

"Tina, what's your name?"

"Tina Crew-grr."

"Very good. I'll get both of you presents." He kissed them, and came back to Jenny. Propping the rifle against the stove, he took her hands and ran them through his hair. "Do it like that," he whispered. "Please, Jen."

His eyes were on her intently now. They looked as they had in her dream. With a wrench of tenderness she obeyed. He looked so vulnerable, and last night he had not been able to come to her for comfort.

"That's good," he smiled. "That feels so good. Thank you."

He picked up the rifle and walked to the door. "Good-bye, girls."

He smiled at Jenny, then hesitated. "Sweetheart, I have an idea. Let's go out together for dinner tonight, just the two of us. I'll ask Rooney and Clyde to stay with the children for a few hours."

"Oh, Erich, I'd love that!" If he began to share this date with her . . . it's a breakthrough, she thought, a good omen.

"I'll phone and make reservations for eight o'clock at the Groveland

Inn. I've been promising to take you there, darling. It's the best food around.''

The Groveland Inn where she had met Kevin. Jenny felt her face pale.

When she and the girls got to the stable, Joe was waiting for them. His usually sunny smile was missing; his young face was set in unfamiliar lines of worry.

''Uncle Josh came over this morning. He was pretty drunk and Maw told him to get lost. He left the door open and Randy got out. I just hope nothing happens to him. He's not used to cars.''

''Go look for him,'' Jenny said.

''Mr. Krueger won't like . . .''

''It will be all right, Joe. I'll see it is. The girls would be heartsick if anything happened to Randy.''

She watched him hurry down the dirt road, then said, ''Come on, girls. Let's take our walk now. You can visit the ponies later.''

They ran ahead of her across the fields. Their rubber boots made soft squishing sounds. The ground was thawing. Maybe it would be an early spring after all. She tried to imagine these fields fleshed out with alfalfa and grass, those spare empty trees weighted with leaves.

Even the wind had lost something of its biting edge. In the south pastures she could see that the cattle had their heads down and were sniffing at the ground as though anticipating the shoots of grass that would soon be coming.

I'd like to start a garden, Jenny thought. I don't know a thing about it but I could learn. Maybe it was because she needed exercise that she was feeling physically rotten. It wasn't just nerves; once again the clammy, queasy feeling was back. She stopped abruptly. Was it possible? Dear God, was it possible?

Of course it was.

She'd felt this way when she was carrying Beth.

She was pregnant.

That explained why the nightgown felt too tight in the bodice; it explained the light-headedness, the queasiness; it even explained the periods of depression.

What a marvelous gift to tell Erich tonight that she believed she was expecting a child! He wanted a son to inherit this farm. Surely the night staff at the restaurant was different from the lunchtime help? It would be all right. *Erich's son.*

''Randy,'' Tina called. ''Look, Mommy, there's Randy.''

''Oh, good,'' Jenny said. ''Joe was so worried.'' She called to him. ''Randy come here.''

The puppy must have cut through the orchard. He stopped, turned and looked at her. Squealing, Beth and Tina began running toward him. With a bark of delight he turned tail and began to run toward the south fields.

''Randy, stop,'' Jenny shouted. Now barking noisily, the puppy loped ahead. Don't let Erich hear him, she prayed. Don't let him run toward the cow pastures. Erich would be furious if he upset the cows. Nearly a dozen of them were coming to term with calves.

But he wasn't heading toward the pastures. Instead he veered and started running along the east line of the property.

The cemetery. He was heading straight for it. Jenny remembered how Joe joked about Randy digging around their house. ''Swear he's trying to get to China, Jenny. You should just see him. Every spot that shows a bit of thawing, he's into.''

If the dog ever started digging in the graves . . .

Jenny passed the girls, running as fast as she could on the mushy ground. ''Randy,'' she called again. ''Randy, *come here*.''

Suppose Erich heard her? Puffing heavily as she ran around the line of Norwegian pines that screened the graveyard and into the clearing. The gate was open and the puppy was leaping among the tombstones. In its isolated corner Caroline's grave was covered with a blanket of fresh roses. Randy romped over it, crushing the flowers.

Jenny saw the glint of metal coming from the woods. Instantly she realized what it was. ''No, no,'' she screamed, ''don't shoot! Erich, don't shoot him!''

Erich stepped from the shelter of the trees. With slow-motion precision he raised it to his shoulder. ''Don't, please!'' she screamed.

The sharp crack of the rifle sent sparrows squawking from the trees. With a howl of pain the puppy crumbled to the ground, his small body sinking into the roses. As Jenny watched in disbelieving horror, Erich worked the bolt with a well-oiled click, and shot the whimpering animal again. As the echo of the blast died away, the whimpering ceased.

CHAPTER 18

Later Jenny remembered the hours after the shooting as a nightmare, blurred and difficult to piece together. She remembered her own frantic rush to head off the girls before they saw what had happened to Randy, yanking their hands. ''We have to go home now.''

''But we want to play with Randy.''

She thrust them in the house. ''Wait here. Don't come out again.''

A shirt-sleeved, grave Erich was carrying Randy's still form; the parka he had wrapped the animal in was soaked with blood. Joe tried to blink back tears.

''Joe, I thought it was one of those damn strays. You know half of them are rabid. If I'd only realized . . .''

"You shouldn't have put him on your good coat, Mr. Krueger."

"Erich, how can you be so cruel? You shot him twice. You shot him after I called you."

"I had to, darling," he insisted. "The first bullet shattered his spine. Do you think I could have left him like that? Jenny, I was frantic when I thought the girls were chasing a stray. A child nearly died last year after being bitten by one of them."

Clyde, looking uncomfortable, shifted from one foot to the other. "You just can't go around petting animals on a farm, Miz Krueger."

"I'm sorry to give you so much trouble, Mr. Krueger," Joe said apologetically.

Her own anger dissipated into confusion. Erich smoothed her hair. "Joe, I'll replace him with a good hunter."

"You don't need to do that, Mr. Krueger." But there was hope in his voice.

Joe took Randy to bury him on his own property. Taking her back to the house, Erich insisted she lie on the couch, bring her a steaming cup of tea. "I forget my darling is still a city girl." And then he left her.

Finally she got up and got the girls' lunch. While they napped she rested, forcing herself to read, willing her mind to stop squirming about in hopeless worry.

"It will be a fast dinner for you tonight," she told Beth and Tina. "Daddy and I are going out."

"Me too," Tina volunteered.

"No, not you too," Jenny said, hugging her. "For once Daddy and I have a date." But no wonder the girls expected to be included. The few places she and Erich had gone to in this last month, he'd always insisted on bringing them along. How many stepfathers would be so considerate?

She took elaborate care with her own preparations. Soaking in a steaming tub took some of the soreness from her body. Hesitating only a minute, she filled the tub with the pine-scented bath crystals that she'd so far ignored in the bathroom cabinet.

She washed her hair and pulled it back in a Psyche knot. When she'd been in the restaurant with Kevin her hair had been loose on her shoulders.

She studied the contents of her closet, choosing a long-sleeved, hunter-green wraparound silk that accentuated her narrow waist and the green in her eyes.

Erich came into the room just as she was fastening her locket. "Jenny, you dressed especially for me. I love you in green."

She cupped his face in her hands. "I always dress for you. I always will."

He was carrying a canvas. ''Miraculous as it might seem, I managed to finish it this afternoon.''

It was a spring scene, a new calf half-hidden in a hollow, the mother watchfully beside it, eyeing the other cattle, seeming to warn them to stay away. The sunlight filtered through pine trees; the sun was a five-pointed star. The painting had the aura of a Nativity scene.

Jenny studied it and felt all her senses quickening to its profound beauty. ''It's magnificent,'' she said quietly. ''There's so much tenderness there.''

''Today you told me I was cruel.''

''Today I was terribly stupid and terribly wrong. Will this be for the next exhibit?''

''No, darling, this is my gift to you.''

She pulled the collar of her coat around her face as they went into the restaurant. The other time she'd been so anxious to escape quickly that she'd hardly noticed the details of the place. Now she realized that with its bright red carpeting, pine furniture, mellow lighting, colonial curtains and blazing fire, the inn was immensely appealing. Her eyes slid to the booth where she'd sat with Kevin.

''Right this way.'' The hostess led them in that direction. Jenny held her breath but mercifully the hostess sailed past it and led them to a window table. There was a bottle of champagne already in the cooler beside the table.

When their glasses had been filled Jenny held hers up to Erich. ''Happy birthday, darling.''

''Thank you.''

Quietly they sipped.

Erich was wearing a dark gray tweed jacket, a narrow black tie, charcoal gray trousers. His thick charcoal eyebrows and lashes intensified the blue of his eyes. His bronze-gold hair was highlighted by the flickering candle on the table. He reached for her hand.

''I enjoy taking you to places for the first time, darling.''

Her mouth went dry. ''I enjoy being everywhere . . . anywhere with you.''

''I think that's why I left that note. You're right, sweetheart. I wasn't only teasing. I *was* jealous watching Joe teach you to ride. All I could think was that I wanted to share the first minute you were on Fire Maid. I suppose it's as though I'd bought you a piece of jewelry and you'd worn it for someone else.''

''Erich,'' Jenny protested. ''I just thought it would be nice for you not to be bothered with the ABCs of the learning process.''

''It's not unlike the house, is it, Jenny? You came in, and in four weeks you try to transform a historical treasure into a New York studio complete with bare windows and spider plants. Darling, may I suggest a birthday present for me? Take a little time to find out who I am . . . who we are. You accused me of cruelty when I shot an animal I thought might attack our children. May I suggest that you in a different way shoot from the hip utterly without justification? And, Jenny, I have to say this, you have the distinction of being the first Krueger woman in four generations to create a scene in front of a hired hand. Caroline would have fainted dead away before she would publicly criticize my father.''

''I'm not Caroline,'' Jenny said quietly.

''Darling, just understand that I'm not cruel to animals. I'm not unreasonably rigid. That first night in your apartment I could see you didn't understand why I was astonished that you gave MacPartland money; the same thing on our wedding day. But it's come back to haunt us, hasn't it?''

If you only knew, Jenny thought.

The maître d' was heading toward them with menus, a professional smile plastered on his face. ''And now, my sweet,'' Erich said, ''let's consider that we've cleared the air a bit. Let's have a wonderful dinner together and please know that I'd rather be here with you in this place at this moment than anywhere else with anyone else in the world.''

When they arrived home she deliberately put on the aqua gown. She had not told Erich at dinner about her possible pregnancy. She'd been too shaken by the truth of his observations. When they were in bed, his arms around her, she would tell him.

But he did not stay with her. ''I need to be completely alone. I'll be back by Thursday but not before then.''

She did not dare to protest. ''Now don't get into a creative haze and forget that Mark and Emily are coming to dinner on Friday.''

He looked down at her as she lay in bed. ''I won't forget.'' Without kissing her, he left. Once again she was alone in the cavernous bedroom to fall into the uneasy, dream-filled sleep that was becoming a way of life.

CHAPTER 19

In spite of everything, planning the dinner party was a pleasant diversion. She wanted to shop herself but would not make driving the car an issue. Instead she compiled a long list for Elsa. ''Coquilles St. Jacques,'' she told Erich when he came to the house on Friday morning. ''Mine is really good. And you say Mark likes a rib roast?'' She chatted on, determined to bridge the perceptible estrangement. He'll get over it, she thought, especially when he knows about the baby.

Kevin had not called again. Maybe he had met a girl in the cast and had become involved. If so, they wouldn't hear from him for a while. If necessary, as soon as the adoption became final they could take legal steps to make him stay away. Or if he did try to block the adoption, Erich might as a last resort buy him off. Silently, she prayed: Please let the children have a home, a real family. Let it be good again between Erich and me.

The night of the dinner she set out the Limoges china, delicately beautiful with its gold-and-blue border. Mark and Emily were due at eight. Jenny found herself eagerly looking forward to meeting Emily. All her life she'd had girlfriends. She'd lost touch with most of them because of lack of time to keep up contacts after Beth and Tina came along. Maybe Emily and she would hit it off.

She said as much to Erich. "I doubt it," he told her. "There was a time when the Hanovers looked very fondly at the prospect of having me as a son-in-law. Roger Hanover is the president of the bank in Granite Place and has a good idea of my net worth."

"Did you ever go out with Emily?"

"A little. But I wasn't interested and didn't want to get into a situation that would prove uncomfortable. I was waiting for the perfect woman, you see."

She tried to make her voice teasing. "Well, you found her, dear."

He kissed her. "I certainly hope so."

She flinched. He's joking, she told herself fiercely.

After she got Beth and Tina into bed, Jenny changed into a white silk blouse with lace cuffs and a multicolored, ankle-length skirt. She studied her reflection in the mirror and realized she was deathly pale. Adding a touch of rouge helped.

Erich had set up the tea table in the parlor as a bar. When she came into the room he studied her carefully. "I like that costume, Jen."

"That's good," she smiled. "You certainly paid enough for it."

"I thought you didn't like it. You've never worn it before."

"It seemed kind of dressed up for just sitting around."

He came over to her. "Is that a spot on your sleeve?"

"That? Oh, it's just a speck of dust. It must have happened in the store."

"Then you haven't worn this outfit before?"

Why did he ask that? Was he simply too sensitive not to know she was hiding something from him?

"First time, girl scout's honor."

The door chimes were a welcome interruption. Her mouth had begun to go dry. It's getting so that no matter what Erich says, I'm afraid of giving myself away, she thought.

Mark was wearing a pepper-and-salt jacket that suited him well. It brought out the gray in his hair, accentuated his broad shoulders, the lean strength of his tall frame. The woman with him was about thirty, small-boned, with wide inquisitive eyes and dark blond hair that skimmed the collar of her well-cut brown velvet suit. Jenny decided that Emily had the air of someone who never had experienced an instant of self-doubt. She made no secret of looking Jenny over from head to toe. ''You do realize I have to report to everyone in town what you're like; the curiosity is overwhelming. My mother gave me a list of twenty questions I'm to discreetly toss in. You haven't exactly made yourself available to the community.''

Before Jenny could answer, she felt Erich's arm slip around her waist. ''If we'd taken a two-month honeymoon cruise nobody would have thought a thing of it. But as Jenny says, because we chose to honeymoon in our own home, Granite Place is outraged not to be camped in our living room.''

I never said that! Jenny thought helplessly as she watched Emily's eyes narrow.

Over cocktails, Mark waited until Erich and Emily were deep in conversation before he commented, ''You look pale, Jenny. Are you all right?''

''Fine!'' she tried to sound as though she meant it.

''Joe told me about his dog. I understand you were pretty upset.''

''I guess I have to learn to understand that things are different here. In New York we cliff dwellers weep collectively over the picture of a stray about to be destroyed. Then somebody shows up to adopt him and we all cheer.''

Emily was looking around the room. ''You haven't changed anything, have you?'' she asked. ''I don't know whether Erich has mentioned it but I am an interior designer and if I were you, I'd get rid of those curtains. Sure they're beautiful but the windows are so overdressed and you lose that glorious view.''

Jenny waited for Erich to defend her. ''Apparently, Jen doesn't agree with you,'' he said smoothly. His tone and smile were indulgent.

Erich, that's unfair, Jenny thought furiously. Should she contradict him? *The first Krueger woman in four generations to create a scene in front of a hired hand*. How about a scene in front of friends? What was Emily saying?

''. . . and I happen to be never at peace if I'm not switching things around but maybe that isn't your interest. I understand you're an artist too.''

The moment had passed. It was not too late to correct the impression Erich had left. ''I'm not an artist,'' Jenny said. ''My degree is in fine arts. I worked in a gallery in New York. That's where I met Erich.''

''So I've heard. Your whirlwind romance has created quite a stir in these parts. How does our rustic life compare with the Big Apple?''

Jenny chose her words carefully. She had to undo the impression that she felt Erich had given that she was scornful of the local people. ''I miss my friends, of course. I miss bumping into people who know me and comment on how big the children are getting. I like people and I make friends easily. But once,'' she glanced at Erich, ''once our honeymoon is officially over, I hope to be active in the community.''

''Report that to your mother, Emily,'' Mark suggested.

Jenny thought, Bless you for underscoring. Mark knew what she was trying to do.

Emily laughed, a brittle, mirthless sound. ''From what I hear you've got at least one friend to keep you amused.''

She had to be referring to the meeting with Kevin. The woman from church had been gossiping. She felt Erich's questioning look and did not meet his eyes.

Jenny murmured something about seeing to the dinner and went into the kitchen. Her hands were shaking so she could hardly lift the roasting pan from the oven. Suppose Emily followed through on her insinuations? Emily believed she was a widow; now her telling the truth would in effect be branding Erich as a liar. What about Mark? The question had not come up but undoubtedly he too thought she had been a widow.

Somehow she managed to get the food onto serving dishes, to light the candles and call them to the table. At least I'm a good cook, she reflected. Emily can tell her mother that.

Erich carved and served the rib roast. ''One of our own steers,'' he said proudly. ''Are you sure that doesn't repel you, Jenny?''

He was teasing her. She mustn't overreact. The others didn't seem to notice. ''Think, Jenny,'' he continued in the same bantering tone, ''the yearling you pointed out to me in the field last month, the one you said looked so wistful. You're eating him now.''

Her throat closed. She was afraid she would gag. Please, God, please don't let me get sick.

Emily laughed. ''Erich, you are so mean. Remember you used to bait Arden like that and have her in tears?''

''Arden?'' Jenny asked. She reached for her water glass. The knot in her throat started to dissolve.

''Yes. What a nice kid she was. Talk about the all-American girl. Crazy about animals. At sixteen she wouldn't touch meat or poultry. Said it was barbaric and that she was going to be a vet when she grew up. But I guess she changed her mind. I was in college when she ran away.''

''Rooney's never given up hope that she'll come back,'' Mark commented. ''It's incredible, the mother instinct. You see it from the first moment of birth. The dumbest animal knows its own calf and will protect it to the death.''

''You're not eating your meat, darling,'' Erich commented.

A flash of anger made it possible for her to square her shoulders and look across the table directly into his eyes. ''And you're not eating your vegetables, darling,'' she told him.

He winked at her. He *was* just teasing. ''Touché,'' he smiled.

The peal of the door chimes startled all of them. Erich frowned. ''Now, who could that . . .'' His voice trailed off as he stared at Jenny. She knew what he was thinking. Don't let it be Kevin, she prayed, and realized as she pushed back her chair that all evening she'd been sending frantic prayers for divine intervention.

A heavily built man of about sixty, with massive shoulders, a bulging leather jacket and narrow, heavy-lidded eyes, was there. His car was parked directly in front of the house, an official car with a red dome top.

''Mrs. Krueger?''

''Yes.'' Relief made her weak. No matter what this man wanted, at least Kevin hadn't come.

''I'm Wendel Gunderson, sheriff of Granite County. May I come in?''

''Of course. I'll get my husband.''

Erich was hurrying down the hall, into the foyer. Jenny noticed the instant respect that came into the sheriff's face. ''Sorry to bother you, Erich. Just have to ask your wife a few questions.''

''Ask me a few questions?'' But even as she spoke, Jenny knew that this visit had to do with Kevin.

''Yes, ma'am.'' From the dining room they could hear the sound of Mark's voice. ''Could we speak quietly for a few minutes?''

''Why don't you come and join us for coffee?'' Erich suggested.

''Perhaps your wife would rather answer my questions privately, Erich.''

Jenny felt clammy perspiration on her forehead. She realized her palms were damp. The queasiness was so strong, she had to clamp her lips together. ''There's certainly no reason we can't talk at the table,'' she murmured helplessly.

She led the way into the dining room, listened as Emily greeted the sheriff with quickly concealed surprise, watched as Mark leaned back in his chair, an attitude she had begun to realize meant he was diagnosing a situation. As Erich offered the sheriff a drink which was refused ''because of being on official business,'' she set out the coffee cups.

''Mrs. Krueger, do you know a Kevin MacPartland?''

''Yes.'' She knew her voice was trembling. ''Has Kevin been in an accident?''

''When and where did you last see him?''

She put her hands in her pockets, clenched them into fists. Of course it had to come out. But why this way? Oh, Erich, I'm so sorry, she thought. She could not look at Erich. ''On February twenty-fourth at the shopping center in Raleigh.''

''Kevin MacPartland is the father of your children?''

''He is my former husband and the father of my children.'' She heard Emily gasp.

''When did you last speak with him?''

''He phoned on the evening of March seventh about nine o'clock. Please tell me. Has anything happened to him?''

The sheriff's eyes narrowed into slits. ''On Monday afternoon, March ninth, Kevin MacPartland received a telephone call during a rehearsal at the Guthrie Theater. He said his former wife had to see him about the children. He borrowed a car from one of the other actors and left a half an hour later, about four-thirty P.M., promising to return in the morning. That was four days ago and he hasn't been heard from since. The car he borrowed was only six weeks old and the actor who lent it had just met MacPartland so you can understand that he's pretty concerned. Are you saying that you did not ask him to meet you?''

''No, I did not.''

''May I ask why you've been in touch with your former husband? We understood around here that you were a widow.''

''Kevin wanted to see the girls,'' Jenny said. ''He was talking about stopping the adoption.'' It surprised her how lifeless her voice sounded. She could see Kevin as though he were in the room: the expensive ski sweater, the long scarf draped over his left shoulder, the dark red hair so carefully barbered, the poses and posturing. Had he deliberately staged a disappearance to embarrass her? She had warned him that Erich was upset. Did Kevin hope to destroy their marriage before it had a chance?

''And what did you tell him?''

''When I saw him, and when he called, I told him to leave us alone.'' Her voice was getting higher.

''Erich, were you aware of this meeting, of the phone call on March seventh?''

''I was aware of the phone call on March seventh. I was here when it came. I was not aware of the meeting. But I can understand it. Jenny knew my feelings about Kevin MacPartland.''

''You were home with your wife on the evening of March ninth?''

''No, as a matter of fact, I stayed in the cabin that night. I was just completing a new canvas.''

''Did your wife know you were planning to be away?''

There was a long silence. Jenny broke it. ''Of course I knew.''

''What did you do that evening, Mrs. Krueger?''

''I was very tired and went to bed shortly after I had settled my little girls in their room.''

''Did you speak to anyone on the phone?''

''No one. I went to sleep almost immediately.''

''I see. And you are very sure you did not invite your former husband to visit you during Erich's absence?''

''No, I did not . . . I would never ask him to come here.'' It was as though she could read their minds. Of course they didn't believe her.

Her untouched plate was on the serving buffet. Congealed fat was forming a narrow rim around the beef. The beef had a crimson center. She thought of Randy's body turning crimson with blood as he collapsed among the roses; she thought of Kevin's dark red hair.

Now the plate was going around and around. She had to get fresh air. She was spinning too. Pushing back her chair, she tried to struggle to her feet. Her last conscious recollection was Erich's expression—was it concern or annoyance?—as her chair slammed against the buffet behind her.

When she woke up she was lying on the couch in the parlor. Someone was holding a cold cloth on her head. It felt so good. Her head hurt so much. There was something she didn't want to think about.

Kevin.

She opened her eyes. ''I'm all right. I'm so sorry.''

Mark was bending over her. There was so much concern in his face. It was oddly comforting. ''Take it easy,'' he said.

''Can I get something for you, Jenny?'' There was an undercurrent of excitement in Emily's voice. She's enjoying this, Jenny thought. She's the kind of person who wants to be in on everything.

''Darling!'' Erich's tone was solicitous. He came over and took both her hands.

''Not too close,'' Mark warned. ''Give her air.''

Her head started to clear. Slowly she sat up, the taffeta skirt rustling as she moved. She felt Mark slip pillows behind her head and back.

''Sheriff, I can answer any questions you have. I'm sorry. I don't know what came over me. I've not felt quite well these past few days.''

His eyes seemed wider and shinier now, as though they'd locked into an intense focus on her. ''Mrs. Krueger, I'll make this brief. You did not phone your former husband on the ninth of March to request a meeting, nor did he arrive here that night?''

''That's correct.''

''Why would he have told his colleagues that you had called him? What purpose would he have in lying?''

''The only thought I have is that sometimes Kevin used to say he was visiting me and the children when he wanted to get out of other plans. If he was in the process of dropping one girlfriend for another, he'd often use us as an excuse.''

''Then may I ask why you're so upset at his disappearance if you think he might be off with some woman?''

Her lips were so stiff it was hard to form words. She spoke slowly, like a teacher enunciating for a first-year language class. ''You must understand there is something terribly wrong. Kevin *had* been accepted by the Guthrie Theater for the repertory company. That is true, isn't it?''

"Yes, it is."

"You must look for him," she said. "He would never jeopardize that opportunity. Kevin's acting is the most important thing in his life."

They all left a few minutes later. She insisted on walking with them to the front door. Jenny could imagine the conversation that would take place when Emily reported back to her mother. "*She's* not a widow . . . that was her ex-husband she was kissing in the restaurant . . . and now he's missing . . . the sheriff obviously thinks she's lying . . . poor Erich . . ."

"I'll treat this as a missing person. . . . Get out some flyers. . . . We'll be back to you, Mrs. Krueger."

"Thank you, Sheriff."

He was gone. Mark pulled on his coat. "Jenny, you ought to go right to bed. You still look mighty rocky."

"Thanks for coming you two," Erich said, "Sorry our evening ended so badly." His arm was around Jenny. He kissed her cheek. "Shows what happens when you marry a woman with a past, doesn't it?"

His tone was amused. Emily laughed. Mark's face showed no emotion. When the door closed behind him, Jenny wordlessly started up the staircase. All she wanted to do was go to bed.

Erich's astonished voice stopped her. "Jenny, surely you're not planning to leave the house in this condition overnight?"

CHAPTER 20

Rooney let herself in as Jenny was sipping a second cup of tea after breakfast. Jenny spun around at the faint click of the door. "Oh!"

"Did I scare you?" Rooney sounded pleased. Her eyes were vague; her thin hair, scattered by the wind, blew around her birdlike face.

"Rooney, that door was locked. I thought you said you're not supposed to have a key."

"I must have found one."

"Where? Mine is missing."

"Did I find yours?"

Of course, Jenny thought. The coat I gave her. It was in the pocket. Thank God I didn't admit to Erich that I lost it. "May I have my key, please?" She held out her hand.

Rooney looked puzzled. "I didn't know there was a key in your coat. We gave you back your coat."

"I don't think so."

"Yes. Clyde made me. He put it back himself. I saw you wear it."

"It's not in the closet," Jenny said. What difference? she thought. She tried a new approach. "Let me see your key, Rooney, please."

Rooney pulled a heavy key ring out of her pocket. The large bunch of keys were all individually tagged: house, barn, office, grainery . . .

"Rooney, aren't these Clyde's keys?"

"I guess so."

"You must put them back. Clyde will be angry if you take his keys."

"He says I shouldn't take them."

So that was how Rooney got into the house. I'll have to tell Clyde to hide his keys, Jenny thought. Erich would have a fit if he knew she could get at them.

Jenny looked at Rooney with pity. In the three weeks since the sheriff had come, she hadn't visited Rooney and in fact had tried to avoid running into her. "Sit down and let me pour you a cup of tea," she urged. For the first time she noticed that Rooney had a package tucked under her arm. "What have you got there?"

"You said I could make the girls jumpers. You promised."

"Yes, I did. Let me see."

Hesitantly Rooney opened the brown paper and shook two violet-blue corduroy jumpers from tissue wrapping. The stitching was fine; the strawberry-shaped pockets were embroidered in red and green. Jenny could see that the sizes would be perfect.

"Rooney, these are lovely," she said sincerely. "You sew beautifully."

"I'm glad you like them. I made Arden a skirt with this material and had some left over. I was going to make her a jacket too but then she ran away. Don't you think this is a pretty shade of blue?"

"Yes, I do. It will be wonderful with their hair."

"I wanted you to see the material before I started, but when I came that night you were on your way out and I didn't want to interfere."

On the way out at night? Not likely, Jenny thought, but let it go. She found herself glad for Rooney's company. These weeks had dragged so. Ceaselessly she thought about Kevin. What had happened to him? He was a fast driver. He'd been driving a strange car. The roads were icy that day. Could he have been in an accident, maybe not hurt himself but have wrecked the borrowed car? Would that have panicked him into leaving Minnesota? Always she got back to one irrefutable fact. Kevin would never walk away from the Guthrie Theater.

She felt so rotten. She should tell Erich she was pregnant. She should see a doctor.

But not yet. Not until something was resolved about Kevin. The news of the baby should be joyful. It shouldn't be told in this tense, hostile atmosphere.

The night of the dinner party Erich had insisted that every piece of china and crystal be handwashed, every pot scrubbed before they went upstairs.

As they got into bed, he'd commented, "I must say you look pretty upset, Jenny. I didn't realize that MacPartland meant that much to you. No, I'll correct myself. Maybe I've sensed it; maybe that's why I'm not even surprised that you had a clandestine meeting with him."

She'd tried to explain but to her own ears the justification seemed feeble and halting. Finally she'd been too tried, too upset, to discuss it any further. As she'd drifted off to sleep, he'd put his arm around her. "I'm your husband, Jenny," he said. "No matter what, I'll stand by you as long as you tell me the truth."

". . . Like I said, I didn't want to interfere with your visit," Rooney was saying.

"What . . . Oh, I'm sorry." Jenny realized she had not been listening to Rooney. She looked across the table. Rooney's eyes were clearer. How much of her problem was her absolute obsession with Arden? How much was the loneliness of no outside contacts? "Rooney, I've always wanted to learn to sew. Do you think you could teach me?"

Rooney brightened. "Oh, I'd love that. I can teach you to sew and knit and crochet if you want."

She left a few minutes later. "I'll get everything together and come back tomorrow afternoon," she promised. "It will be like old times. Caroline didn't know how to do none of those things neither. I was the one who taught her. Maybe you can make a nice quilt before something happens to you."

"Hal-lo, Jenny," Joe called cheerfully.

Oh, God, Jenny thought. Erich was just a few steps behind her with the girls but had not turned the corner into the stable.

"How are you, Joe?" she asked nervously. Something in her voice made him look up quickly. He saw Erich and reddened. "Oh, good morning, Mr. Krueger. Didn't expect you, I guess."

"I'm sure you didn't." Erich's icy tone made Joe blush several shades deeper. "I want to see how my girls are doing with their lessons."

"Yes, sir, I'll tack up the ponies right away." He scurried into the tack room.

"Is he in the habit of addressing you as Jenny?" Erich asked quietly.

"It's my fault," Jenny said, then wondered how many times in the last weeks she'd used those words.

Joe came back with the tack. As the girls squealed impatiently, he put the saddles on. "We'll each lead one of the ponies," Erich told him.

"How about you, Mrs. Krueger?" Joe asked. "You up to riding today?"

"Not yet, Joe."

"Haven't you been riding?" Erich asked.

"No. My back has been hurting quite a bit."

"You didn't tell me that."

"It will be fine."

She still couldn't tell him about the baby. Nearly four weeks had passed since Sheriff Gunderson had come and there hadn't been a single word more.

Spring was about to break. The trees all had a red haze around them. Joe told her that that happened just before the budding started. There were shoots of green coming through the mud in the fields. The chickens were wandering out of the chicken house and exploring the territory around them. The boastful crowing of the roosters could be heard from behind the grainery and polebarn and stable. One of the hens had selected a corner of the stable for her own nest and was brooding her unhatched eggs.

"Since when have you had a backache, Jenny? Do you want to see a doctor?" Erich's tone was loving and concerned.

"No. Let's see if it doesn't just go away. I've had them before." She had had mild backaches during her other pregnancies.

Someone fell into step with them. It was Mark. She hadn't run into Mark since the night of the dinner.

"Hello, you two," Mark said. His manner was easy. There was nothing to indicate he was thinking of what had happened at the dinner party.

"Stay a minute and watch the way my girls sit their ponies," Erich invited.

In the past weeks Tina and Beth had made rapid progress on the ponies. Jenny smiled unconsciously at their delighted faces as they sat straight up, holding the reins with rapt concentration.

"They look good," Mark commented. "They'll grow to be fine riders."

"They love those animals."

Erich left them to lead one of the ponies.

"I've never seen Erich happier. He was showing their pictures to everyone at the Hanovers' the other night. Emily was sorry you couldn't make it."

"Couldn't make it?" Jenny repeated. "Couldn't make what?"

"The Hanovers' party. Erich said you weren't feeling up to par. Have you seen a doctor yet? I just overheard you mentioning your back. And that fainting spell that night, Jenny. Was that unusual? Do you have any history of weak spells?"

"No. I never faint. And I will see a doctor soon."

She felt rather than saw Mark studying her. Somehow she didn't mind. Whatever conclusion he had reached about Kevin's possible visit and her supposed widow status, he had not condemned her.

Should she tell him that she had no idea about Emily's party? What good would it do? Erich left us together here because he knew Mark would probably bring up the party, she thought. Erich wanted me to know about it. Why? Was it simply another way of trying to hurt her, to punish her, for the gossip around the Krueger name? How much did people in this community know? She was sure Emily had told her family and friends about the sheriff's visit.

If Erich believed people thought he had made a mistake and were pitying him, he'd be furious. She remembered his anger when Elsa suggested he had made the smudge on the wall.

Erich was a perfectionist.

As Mark turned to leave, Erich called, "See you tonight." Tonight? Jenny wondered. Another party? Business of some kind? Whatever it was, she wouldn't hear about it.

The girls ran to her when they dismounted. "Daddy is going to ride Baron with us soon," Beth said. "Don't you like to ride with us, Mommy?"

Joe led the ponies into the barn. "See you, Mrs. Krueger," he said. She was very sure he would not call her Jenny again.

"Come along, dear." Erich took her arm. "Didn't my little princesses do beautifully?"

My princesses. *My* girls. *My* daughters. Not *our,* only *my*. When had that begun? Jenny realized that the emotion she was experiencing was stark jealousy. Good Lord, she thought. Don't let me start getting upset about that. The one good thing in my life right now is that the children are so happy.

They were almost to the house when a car pulled into the driveway, a car with a dome light on the roof. Sheriff Gunderson.

Did he have news about Kevin? She forced herself not to hurry, not to let her face show anxiety. As the sheriff got out of the car, Erich linked his arm in hers. He was holding Tina by the other hand. Beth was running in front of them. The devoted husband standing by his wife in time of trouble, Jenny thought. That had to be the impression the sheriff was getting.

Wendell Gunderson's face was grim. There was a trifle more formality in his manner even when he greeted Erich. He wanted to speak with Jenny alone.

They went into the library. Jenny thought how in the first weeks this had been her favorite room. The meeting with Kevin had changed everything. The sheriff ignored the couch and chose the one straight chair.

"Mrs. Krueger, there has been absolutely no sign of your ex-husband. The Minneapolis police are treating his disappearance as possible foul play. There is no evidence he planned to stay away. There was two hundred dollars in cash in a desk drawer; he took only a small overnight bag with him when he left. Everyone he worked with at the Guthrie agreed that he wouldn't walk away from that opportunity. I realize that last time it would have been much easier if I insisted on speaking with you alone. Please tell the truth, because once this investigation is in full swing, I promise you the truth will come out. Did you phone Kevin MacPartland on the afternoon of Monday, March ninth?"

''I did not.''

''Did you see him on the night of Monday, March ninth?''

''I did not.''

''He left Minneapolis about five-thirty. Driving straight through, that would get him here about nine. We'll assume he might have stopped along the way to get something to eat. Where were you between nine-thirty and ten that Monday night?''

''I was in bed. I turned out the light before nine o'clock. I was very tired.''

''You insist you did not see him?''

''I did not.''

''The Guthrie operater confirmed that he received a call from a woman. Is there any woman who might have called him in your name? Any close friend?''

''I don't have any close friends here,'' Jenny said, ''man or woman.'' She stood up. ''Sheriff, no one wants more than I do to find Kevin MacPartland. He is the father of my children. There's never been even a hint of animosity between us. So will you please explain to me what you're driving at? Are you suggesting that I invited or enticed Kevin here knowing that my husband planned to be away? And if you believe that, are you insinuating I had something to do with his disappearance?''

''I'm not suggesting anything, Mrs. Krueger. I'm only asking you to tell us everything you know. If MacPartland was definitely on his way here and didn't show up, it gives us a starting point. If he was here and we knew what time he left, it gives us something else. Can you see what I'm getting at? I can understand why that might be embarrassing for you but . . .''

''I don't think we have anything more to discuss,'' Jenny said. Turning abruptly, she left the library. Erich was in the kitchen with the girls. He'd made ham and cheese sandwiches. The three of them were eating companionably. Jenny saw there was no place set for her.

''Erich, I think the sheriff is ready to leave,'' she said. ''You might want to see him out.''

''Mommy.'' Beth looked anxious.

Oh, Mouse, Jenny thought, that antenna of yours. She tried to smile. ''Say, you two looked terrific on the ponies today.'' Going to the refrigerator, she poured a glass of milk.

''Don't you know better, Mommy?'' Beth asked.

''Know what better?'' Jenny picked up Tina, sat at the table with the little girl on her lap.

''Daddy told Joe when we were on our ponies that even if you don't know better than to have Joe call you Mrs. Krueger, Joe should know better.''

''Daddy said that?''

"Yes." Beth was positive. "You know what else he said?"

Jenny sipped her milk. "No, what?"

"He said that when Joe got home for lunch today, he'd find a brand-new puppy Daddy bought for him because Randy runned away. Can we see the puppy, Mommy?"

"Sure. Let's walk over there after your nap."

So Randy "runned away," she thought. That's the official version of what happened to that poor little puppy.

CHAPTER 21

The new puppy was a golden retriever. Even to Jenny's unpracticed eye, the long nose, thin face and slender body indicated good breeding.

The thick old quilt on the kitchen floor was the same one Randy had curled up on. The bowl with water still had his name in the jaunty red letters Joe had painted on it.

Even Joe's mother seemed mollified by the gift. "Erich Krueger is a fair man," she conceded to Jenny. "Feel as though I was wrong of accusing him of maybe doing away with Joe's dog last year. Seems as though if he got rid of that dog he'd a come out and said so."

Except that this time I saw him, Jenny thought, and then felt unfair to Erich.

Beth patted the sleek head. "You must be very careful because he's so little," she instructed Tina. "You must not hurt him."

"They sure are pretty little girls," Maude Ekers said. "They favor you except for the hair."

To Jenny there was something different about the woman's attitude today. Her welcome had been restrained. She had hesitated before inviting them in. Jenny would not have accepted a cup of coffee from the ever-present percolator but was surprised when it wasn't offered.

"What's the puppy's name?" Beth asked.

"Randy," Maude said. "Joe's decided he's another Randy."

"Naturally," Jenny commented. "Somehow I knew Joe wouldn't just forget that other little dog so quickly. He's much too good-hearted."

They were sitting at the kitchen table. She smiled at the other woman.

But to her astonishment Maude's face showed worried hostility. "*You leave my boy alone,* Mrs. Krueger," she burst out. "He's a simple farm boy and I already got enough worries with the way that brother of mine is bringing Joey to the bars with him at night. Joe moons about you too much as it is. Maybe it's not for me to say but you're married to the most important man in this community and you should realize your position.''

Jenny pushed the chair back and stood up. ''What do you mean?''

''I think you know what I mean. With a woman like you there's bound to be trouble. My brother's life was spoiled because of that accident in the dairy barn. You got to have heard that John Krueger felt my brother was careless with the work light 'cause he got so flustered around Caroline. Joe's all I got. He means the world to me. I don't want accidents or problems.''

Now that she had started, the words tumbled from her mouth. Beth and Tina stopped playing with the puppy. Uncertainly they clasped their hands. ''And something else, it may not be my place but you're awful foolish to have your ex-husband sneaking around here when everyone knows Erich is in his cabin painting.''

''What are you talking about?''

''I'm no gossip and this ain't passed my lips but one night last month that actor ex-husband of yours came here looking for directions. He's a talky one. Introduced himself. Boasted you invited him down. Said he'd just been hired by the Guthrie. I pointed the road to your place myself but let me tell you I wasn't happy about doing it.''

''You must immediately phone Sheriff Gunderson and tell him what you know,'' Jenny said, keeping her voice as steady as she could. ''Kevin never arrived at our house that night. The sheriff is inquiring for him. He's officially listed as a missing person.''

''He never got to your house?'' Maude's normally strong voice became louder.

''No, he did not. Please call Sheriff Gunderson immediately. And thank you for letting us visit the puppy.''

Kevin had been in Maude's house!

He had specifically told Maude that she, Jenny, had called him.

Maude had pointed the way to the Krueger farmhouse, a three-minute drive away.

And Kevin had not arrived.

If Sheriff Gunderson had been insolent with his insinuations today, what would he be like now?

''Mommy, you're hurting my hand,'' Beth protested.

''Oh, sorry, love. I didn't mean to squeeze it.''

She had to get out of here. No, that was impossible. She couldn't leave until she knew what had happened to Kevin.

And beyond that. She was carrying in her womb the microcosm of a human being who was a fifth-generation Krueger, who belonged to this place, whose birthright was this land.

Afterward Jenny thought of that evening of April 7 as the final calm hours. Erich was not in the house when she and the girls got home.

I'm glad, she thought. At least she would not have to keep up some sort of pretense. The next time she saw him she would tell him what Maude had told her.

Maude had probably called the sheriff already. Would he come back here tonight? Somehow she didn't think so, but why would Kevin tell people she'd called him? What had happened to him?

''What do you want for dinner, ladies,'' she asked.

''Frankfurters,'' Beth said positively.

''Ice cream,'' was Tina's hopeful contribution.

''Sounds terrific,'' Jenny said. Somehow she'd felt the girls slipping away from her. That wouldn't happen tonight.

Recklessly she let the girls bring their plates to the couch. *The Wizard of Oz* was on. Companionably nibbling frankfurters and sipping Cokes they huddled together as they watched it.

By the time it was over Tina was asleep in Jenny's lap and Beth's head was drooping on her shoulder. She carried them both upstairs.

Just over three months had passed since that wintry evening when she'd been carrying them home from the day-care center and Erich had caught up with them. There was no use thinking about that. He probably would stay in the cabin again. Even so she didn't want to sleep in the master bedroom.

She undressed the children, buttoned them into pajamas, patted their faces and hands with a warm washcloth and tucked them into bed. Her back hurt. She should not carry them anymore. Too much weight, too much of a strain. It didn't take long to stack the dishwasher. Carefully she examined the couch for signs of crumbs.

She remembered the nights in the apartment when if she was very tired she left the dishes stacked and rinsed in the sink and got into bed with a cup of tea and a good book. I didn't know when I was well off, she thought. And then she remembered the leaky ceiling, rushing the girls to the day-care center, the constant worry about money, the relentless loneliness.

When she was finished straightening up it was not quite nine o'clock. She went through the downstairs rooms, checking that no lights had been left on. In the dining room she stopped under Caroline's quilt. Caroline had wanted to paint and had been shamed and ridiculed away from her art. She'd ''done something useful.''

It had taken Caroline eleven years before she'd been driven away. Had she too experienced the sensation of being the outsider who did not belong?

Slowly climbing the stairs, Jenny realized how close she felt to the woman who had lived in this house. She wondered if Caroline had entered the master bedroom with the same sense of hopeless entrapment that she now felt.

* * *

It was midmorning before Sheriff Gunderson came back to the house. Again Jenny had had fitful dreams, dreams of walking in the forest and smelling the pine trees. Was she looking for the cabin?

When she woke up she became ill. How much of the early-morning nausea had to do with the physical aspect of pregnancy and how much was the result of the anxiety over Kevin's disappearance?

Elsa came in as usual at nine o'clock: dour, silent, vanishing upstairs with vacuum and window cleaners and polishing rags.

She was still reading to the girls when Wendell Gunderson came. She had not yet dressed but was wearing a warm wool robe over her nightgown. Would Erich object to her talking to the sheriff in her robe? No, how could he? The robe zipped up to her neck.

She knew she was pale. She'd tied her hair at the nape of her neck. The sheriff came to the front door.

"Mrs. Krueger." She detected a pitch of excitement. "Mrs. Krueger," he repeated, his voice deepening. "Last night I received a call from Maude Ekers."

"I asked her to phone you," Jenny said.

"So she claims. I didn't talk to you right away because I decided to figure out where Kevin MacPartland might have driven if he didn't come here."

Was it possible the sheriff did believe her? His face, his voice, were so serious. No. He looked like a poker player about to play his winning card.

"I realized it could happen that a stranger might miss your gate if he turned off on the bend that leads to the riverbank."

The riverbank. Oh, dear God, Jenny thought. Could Kevin have made that turn and kept driving, maybe driving quickly, and then gone over the bank. That road was so dark.

"We investigated and I'm sorry to say that's what happened," the sheriff said. "We found a late-model white Buick in the water near the shoreline. It's crusted by ice and that thick brush keeps anyone walking on the bank from seeing it. We pulled it out."

"Kevin?" She knew what he would tell her. Kevin's face flashed before her mind.

"A man's body is in the car, Mrs. Krueger. It's badly decomposed but generally answers the description of the missing Kevin MacPartland, including the clothing he was wearing when last seen. The driver's license in his pocket is MacPartland's."

Oh, Kevin, Jenny mourned silently, oh, Kevin. She tried to speak, but could not.

"We will need you to give us positive identification as soon as possible."

No, she wanted to shriek, no. Kevin was so vain. He worried about a blemish. Badly decomposed! Oh, God.

''Mrs. Krueger, you may want to engage a lawyer.''

''Why?''

''Because there'll be an inquest into MacPartland's death and some tough questions will be asked. You don't have to say anything more.''

''I'll answer any questions you have now.''

''All right. I'm going to ask you again. Did Kevin MacPartland come to this house that Monday night, March ninth?''

''No, I told you *no*.''

''Mrs. MacPartland, do you own a full-length maroon thermal winter coat?''

''Yes, I do. No, I mean I did. I gave it away. Why?''

''Do you remember where you purchased it?''

''Yes, in Macy's in New York.''

''I'm afraid you have a lot of explaining to do, Mrs. Krueger. A woman's coat was found on the seat next to the body. A maroon thermal coat with the label of Macy's department store. We'll need you to look at it and see if it's the one you claim you gave away.''

CHAPTER 22

The inquest was held a week later. For Jenny the week was a blur of unfocused pain.

In the morgue, she stared down at the stretcher. Kevin's face was mutilated but still recognizable, with the long straight nose, the curve of the forehead, the thick, dark red hair. Memories of their wedding day in St. Monica's kept flashing back to her. ''I, Jennifer, take thee Kevin . . . Till death do us part.'' Never had her life been more entwined with his than now. Oh, Kevin, why did you follow me here?

''Mrs. Krueger?'' Sheriff Gunderson's voice urging the identification.

Her throat closed. She hadn't even been able to swallow tea this morning.

''Yes,'' she whispered, ''that's my husband.''

A low, harsh laugh behind her. ''Erich, oh, Erich, I didn't mean . . .''

But he was gone, his footsteps decisively slapping the tiled floor. When she got to the car he was there, stony-faced, and did not speak to her on the way home.

During the inquest the same questions were asked a dozen different ways. ''Mrs. Krueger, Kevin MacPartland told a number of people you had invited him to come to your home in your husband's absence.''

''I did not.''

''Mrs. Krueger what is the phone number of your home?''

She gave it.

"Do you know the telephone number of the Guthrie Theater?"

"I do not."

"Let me tell you or perhaps refresh your memory. It is 555-2824. Is it familiar to you?"

"No."

"Mrs. Krueger, I am holding a copy of the March telephone bill from Krueger Farm. A call to the Guthrie Theater appears on this bill dated March *ninth.* Do you still deny making that call?"

"Yes, I do."

"Is this your coat, Mrs. Krueger?"

"Yes, I gave it away."

"Do you have a key to the Krueger residence?"

"Yes, but I've mislaid it." The coat, she thought. Of course it was in the pocket of the coat. She told the prosecutor that.

He held up something, a key; the ring had her initials, J.K. The key Erich had given her.

"Is this your key?"

"It looks like it."

"Did you give it to anyone, Mrs. Krueger? Please tell us the truth."

"No, I did not."

"This key was found in Kevin MacPartland's hand."

"That's impossible."

On the stand Maude unhappily, doggedly, repeated the story she had told Jenny. "He said his ex-wife wanted to see him and I pointed the road. I'm very sure of the date. He came the night after my son's dog was killed."

Clyde Toomis on the stand was embarrassed, tongue-tied, but patently honest. "I told my wife she had her own good everyday winter coat. I scolded her for accepting it. I put that maroon coat back in the closet in the hall off the kitchen of Krueger farmhouse myself, put it there the very day my wife wore it home."

"Did Mrs. Krueger know that?"

"Don't know how she coulda missed it. The closet ain't that big and I hung it right next to that ski jacket she wears all the time."

I didn't notice, Jenny thought, but knew it was possible she simply hadn't paid attention.

Erich testified. The questions were brief, respectful. "Mr. Krueger, were you at home the night of Monday, March ninth?"

"Did you make known your plans to paint in your cabin that night?"

"Were you aware your wife had been in contact with her former husband?"

Erich might have been talking about a stranger. He answered with detachment, weighing his words, unemotional.

Jenny sat in the first row watching him. Not for a second did his glance meet hers. Erich, who hated even talking on the phone, Erich, who was one of the most private people she had ever known, who had become estranged from her because he was upset about Kevin's phone call and her meeting with him.

The inquest was over. When he summed up, the coroner said that a severe bruise on the right temple of the deceased might have been incurred during the impact of the crash or might have been inflicted previous to it.

The official verdict was death by drowning.

But as Jenny left the courthouse she knew the verdict that the community had passed. At the least she was a woman who had been seeing her former husband clandestinely.

At the worst she had murdered him.

In the three weeks that followed the inquest, the dinners Erich ate with her fell into a pattern. He never spoke directly to her, only to the girls. He would say, "Ask Mommy to pass the rolls, Tinker Bell." His tone was always warm and affectionate. It would have taken sensitive ears to pick up the tension between them.

When she put the girls to bed, she never knew whether she would find him still in the house when she came downstairs. She wondered where he went. To the cabin? To the home of friends? She dared not ask. If he did sleep in the house, it was in the rear bedroom that his father had used for so many years.

There was no one she could talk to. Something told her that he would get over it. There were times she caught him looking at her with such tenderness in his face that she had to restrain herself from putting her arms around him, begging him to believe in her.

Quietly she mourned the waste of Kevin's life. He could have accomplished so much; he had been so talented. If only he had disciplined himself, stayed away from involvements with women, drunk less.

But how did her coat get in the car?

One night she came downstairs to find Erich sipping coffee at the kitchen table.

"Jenny," he said, "we have to talk."

Not sure whether the emotion she felt was relief or anxiety, she sat down. After the girls were settled, she'd showered and put on her nightgown and the robe Nana had given her. She watched as Erich studied her.

"That red is perfect against your hair. Dark cloud on scarlet. Symbolic, isn't it? Like dark secrets in a scarlet woman. Is that why you wear it?"

So this was to be the "talk." "I put it on because I was cold," Jenny said.

"It's very becoming. Maybe you're expecting someone?"

Odd, she thought, in the midst of all this I can still feel sorry for him.

What had been worse for him, she wondered suddenly, Caroline's death or the fact that Caroline had been planning to leave him?

"I'm not expecting anyone, Erich. If you think I am, why not stay with me every night and reassure yourself?" She knew she should be outraged and furious but there was no emotion left in her except pity for him. He looked so troubled, so vulnerable. Always when he was upset he seemed younger, almost boyish.

"Erich, I'm so sorry about all this. I know people are gossiping and how distressing this must be for you. I don't have any logical explanation for what happened."

"Your coat."

"I don't know how it got in that car."

"You expect me to believe that."

"I would believe you."

"Jenny, I want to believe you and I can't. But I do believe this. If you agreed to let MacPartland come here, maybe you did want to warn him to stay away from us. I can accept that. But I can't live with the lie. Admit you invited him down here and I'll put this behind us. I can see how it happened. You didn't want to bring him in the house so you had him drive to the dead end at the riverbank. You warned him and you had your key in your hand. Maybe he made a pass at you. Did you struggle? You slid out of your coat and got out of the car. Maybe when he went to reverse he went forward. *Jenny, it's understandable*. But say so. Just don't look at me with those wide, innocent eyes. Don't look thin and wan like some kind of wounded victim. Admit you're a liar and I promise I'll never mention this again. We love each other so much. It's still there, all that love."

At least he was being totally honest. She felt as though she were sitting on a mountain looking down into a valley, observing what was going on, a disinterested spectator.

"It would almost be easier to do what you wanted," she observed. "But it's funny; we're all the sum total of our lives. Nana despised liars. She was contemptuous of even the social lie. 'Jenny,' she used to say, 'don't evade. If you don't want to go on a date with someone just say no thank you, not that you have a headache or have to do math homework. Truth serves everyone best.' "

"We're not talking about math homework," Erich said.

"I'm going to bed, Erich," she said. "Good night." There was no point in continuing like this.

Such a short time ago they'd gone upstairs arms around each other. To think she'd objected to wearing the aqua nightgown. It was so unimportant in retrospect.

Erich did not answer her even though she went up the stairs slowly, giving him the chance to respond.

She dropped off to sleep quickly, the exhaustion weighing her down, forcing her into weary dreams. She slept restlessly, always just under the conscious level, aware of herself moving around the bed. She was dreaming again; this time she was in the car, struggling with Kevin; he wanted the key. . . .

Then she was in the woods, walking in them, searching. She flung up her arm to push away the nearness of the trees and touched flesh.

Her fingers felt the outline of a forehead, the soft membrane of an eyelid. Long hair brushed her cheek.

Biting her lips over the scream that tried to escape her throat, she bolted up and fumbled for the night-table light. She snapped it on and looked around wildly. There was no one there. She was alone in bed, in the room.

She sank back on the pillows, her body trembling helplessly. Even her facial muscles were twitching.

I'm going crazy, she thought. I'm losing my mind. For the rest of the night, she did not turn off the light and the first rays of dawn were filtering through the drawn shades before she finally fell asleep.

CHAPTER 23

Jenny awoke to bright sunlight and instantly remembered what had happened. A bad dream, she thought, a nightmare. Embarrassed, she snapped off the table lamp and got out of bed.

The weather was finally breaking. She stood at the window looking out into the woods. The trees were a mass of opening buds. From the chicken house she heard the strident crowing of the largest roosters. Opening the windows, she listened to the sounds of the farm, smiled as she heard the new calves bawling for their mothers.

Of course it had been a nightmare. Even so the vivid memory made her perspire, a cold, clammy sweat. It had seemed so real, the feeling of touching a face. Could she be hallucinating?

And the dream about being in the car with Kevin, struggling with him. Could she have phoned Kevin? She'd been so upset that day thinking about what Erich said at the birthday dinner, realizing that Kevin could destroy her marriage. Could she have forgotten that she called Kevin and asked to see him?

The concussion from the accident. The doctor had warned her to take any future headaches seriously.

She'd been having headaches.

She showered, tied her hair in a knot at the top of her head, pulled on jeans and a heavy wool sweater. The girls weren't awake yet. Maybe if she was very calm, she'd be able to eat some breakfast. She must have lost ten pounds in these three months. It was bound to be bad for the baby.

Just as she put the kettle on, she saw Rooney's head bob past the window. This time Rooney knocked.

Rooney's eyes were clear, her face composed. "I had to see you."

"Sit down, Rooney. Coffee or tea?"

"Jenny!" Today Rooney had none of the vagueness. "I've hurt you but I'll try to make amends."

"How could you hurt me?"

Rooney's eyes filled with tears. "I've been feeling so much better with you here. A young, pretty girl to talk to, teaching you to sew. It's made me so happy. And I didn't blame you a bit for meeting him. Krueger men aren't easy to live with. Caroline found that out. So I understand. And I never was going to talk about it, not ever."

"Talk about what? Rooney, there can't be anything to be so upset about."

"There, is, oh, Jenny, there is. Last night I got one of my spells. You know I just keep talking but this time I told Clyde how I came to show you the blue corduroy that Monday night after Caroline's anniversary to see if you liked the color. It was late. Near ten o'clock. But being it was so near the anniversary I was restless. And I thought I'd just look and see if your light was on in the kitchen. And you were just getting in the white car. I saw you get in. I saw you drive away with him down the road to the riverbank but I swear, Jenny, I never planned to tell. I couldn't hurt you."

Jenny put her arms around the trembling woman. "I know you wouldn't hurt me." I did go with Kevin, she thought. I did go. No, I don't believe that. I can't believe that.

"And Clyde said it was his duty to tell Erich and the sheriff," Rooney sobbed. "This morning I told Clyde I made it up, that I got all mixed up, but Clyde said he remembers he woke up that night and I'd just come in with the material under my arm and he was mad I'd gone out. He's going to talk to Erich and the sheriff. Jenny, I'm going to lie for you. I don't care. But I'm causing trouble for you."

"Rooney," Jenny said carefully, "try to understand. I think you are mistaken. I was in bed that night. I never asked Kevin to come here. You wouldn't be lying if you tell them you got confused. I promise you that."

Rooney sighed. "I'd like that coffee now. I love you, Jenny. Sometimes when you're here I can start to believe that Arden may never come back and that I'll get over it someday."

It was later in the morning that they came into the house together, the sheriff, Erich and Mark. Why Mark?

"You know why we're here, Mrs. Krueger."

She listened attentively. They were talking about someone else, someone she didn't know who had been seen getting into a car, driving away.

Erich didn't look angry anymore, only sorrowful. ''Apparently Rooney is trying to retract her statement but we couldn't keep this information from Sheriff Gunderson.'' He came over to her now, put his hands on her face, smoothed her hair.

Jenny wondered why she felt as though she were being stripped in public. ''My darling,'' Erich said, ''these are your friends. Tell the truth.''

She reached up, grasped his hands, pulling them from her face. Otherwise she would suffocate.

''I have told the truth as I know it,'' she said.

''You ever had spells of any kind, Mrs. Krueger?'' The sheriff's voice was not unkind.

''I did have a concussion once.'' Briefly she told them about the accident. All the time she was aware of Mark Garrett's eyes studying her. He probably thinks I'm making this up, she thought.

''Mrs. Krueger, were you still in love with Kevin MacPartland?''

What a terrible question to ask in front of Erich, Jenny thought. How humiliating this is for him. If only she could go away. Take the girls. Leave him to his own life.

But she was carrying his child. Erich would love his son. It would be a boy. She was certain of that.

''Not in the way I presume you mean,'' she said.

''Isn't it true that you showed public affection for him to the point where the waitress and two patrons of the Groveland Inn were shocked.''

For a moment Jenny thought she would laugh. ''They shock easily. Kevin kissed me when I left. I didn't kiss him.''

''Perhaps I should ask it this way, Mrs. Krueger. Weren't you pretty upset about your ex-husband showing up? Wasn't he a threat to your marriage?''

''What do you mean?''

''Initially you gave out to Mr. Krueger that you were a widow. Mr. Krueger's a wealthy man. He's adopting your kids. MacPartland coulda ruined your pretty setup.''

Jenny looked at Erich. She was about to say that the adoption papers would show that Kevin had signed them, that Erich knew about Kevin before their marriage. But what point? This was hard enough on Erich without having his friends and neighbors know that he had deliberately lied to them. She evaded the direct question.

''My husband and I were in complete agreement. We did not want Kevin to come to the house and upset the children.''

''But the waitress heard him tell you that he wasn't giving up, that he wasn't letting the adoption go through. She heard you say, 'I warn you, Kevin.' So he was a threat to your marriage, wasn't he, Mrs. Krueger?''

Why didn't Erich help her? She looked at him and watched his face darken with anger. ''Sheriff, I think this has gone far enough,'' he said firmly. ''Nothing could ever upset our marriage, certainly not Kevin

MacPartland, alive or dead. We all know Rooney is mentally ill. My wife denies being in that car. Are you prepared to press charges? If not I demand that you stop harassing her.''

The sheriff nodded. ''Okay, Erich. But I have to warn you. There's a possibility the inquest will be reopened.''

''If it is, we'll face it.''

To a degree he had defended her. Jenny realized she was surprised at his matter-of-fact attitude. Was he becoming resigned to notoriety?

''I'm not saying it *will* be. Whether or not Rooney's testimony would change anything, I'm not sure. Until Mrs. Krueger starts remembering exactly what happened, we're not much further along than we were up till now. I don't think there was much doubt in any juror's mind that she was in that car at some point.''

Erich walked the sheriff to his car. They stood for a few minutes deep in conversation.

Mark lingered behind them. ''Jenny, I'd like to make an appointment for you with a doctor.''

There was deep concern in his face. Was it for her or for Erich. ''A shrink, I suppose?''

''No, a good old-fashioned family doctor. I know one in Waverly. You don't look well. This certainly has been a strain for you.''

''I'll hold off a bit, I think, but thanks.''

She had to get out of the house. The girls were playing in their room. She went upstairs and got them. ''Let's go for a walk.''

It was springlike outside. ''Can we ride?'' Tina asked.

''Not now,'' Beth said positively. ''Daddy said he'll take us.''

''I want to give Tinker Bell, sugar.''

''Sure, let's go to the stable,'' Jenny agreed. For a moment she allowed herself to daydream. Wouldn't it be wonderful if Erich were saddling Baron and she were on Fire Maid and they could go riding together on a beautiful day like this? They'd planned that, looked forward to it.

A somber-faced Joe was in the stable. Since she'd become aware that Erich was angry and jealous about her friendship with Joe, she'd made it a point to avoid him as much as possible. ''How's Randy the second?'' she asked.

''He's fine. He and I live in town now with my uncle. We've got a place over the post office. You'll have to come and see him there.''

''You left your mother?''

''You bet I did.''

''Joe, tell me. Why did you move out of your mother's place?''

''Because she's a troublemaker. I'm just sick, Mrs. Krueger, *Jenny,* about the things she said to you. I told her if you say you didn't see that fellow Kevin that night, it's because it was necessary for you to say it. I told her you been so good to me, I'd a lost my job when Baron got away 'cept for you. If Maw'd minded her business, you wouldn't a had all that awful talk round here. That ain't the first time a car went off that road down the riverbank. People woulda said 'That's a shame' and somebody woulda said we need a better sign. Instead everybody in this county is snickering about you and Mr. Krueger and saying shows what happens when you get your head turned by a gold digger from New York.''

''Joe, please.'' Jenny put her hand on his arm. ''I've caused enough trouble here. Your mother must be upset. Joe, please move back home.''

''No way. And, Mrs. Krueger, if you want a ride anywhere or if the girls want to see Randy, I'll be happy to bring you on my own time. You just say the word.''

''Sshh, Joe, that kind of talk doesn't help.'' She gestured toward the open doors. ''Please, someone might hear you.''

''I don't care who hears me.'' The anger died from his face. ''Jenny, I'd do anything to help you.''

''Mommy, let's go now.'' Beth pulled at her. But what was it Joe had said that was nagging at her?

She remembered. ''Joe, whatever you said to your mother about it being necessary for me to say I wasn't in the car? Joe, why did you put it that way?''

His face flamed red. Awkwardly he thrust his hands in his pocket, half-turned from her. When he spoke, his voice was a near-whisper. ''Jenny, you don't have to pretend with me. I was there. I was worried that maybe I hadn't locked Baron's stall door tight. I was just cutting across the orchard when I saw Rooney. She was almost at the big house. I stopped 'cause I didn't want to get stuck talking to her. Then the car pulled up, that white Buick, and the front door opened and you ran out of the house. I saw you get in the car, Jenny, but I swear to God I'll never tell anyone. I . . . I love you, Jenny.'' Tentatively he took his hand from his pocket and closed it over her arm.

CHAPTER 24

Erich came in just as the sun began to send slanting rays across the fields. Jenny had decided that no matter what, it was time to tell him about the baby.

He made it unexpectedly easy. He had brought canvases from the cabin, the ones he was planning to exhibit in San Francisco.

''What do you think of them?'' he asked her. There was nothing in his voice or manner to suggest that the exchange with Sheriff Gunderson had taken place this morning.

''They're wonderful, Erich.'' *Shall I tell him what Joe said? Should I wait? When I go to a doctor, maybe I can find out if amnesia spells can happen to pregnant women.*

Erich was looking at her curiously.

"Do you want to come to San Francisco with me, Jenny?"

"Let's talk about it later."

He put his arms around her. "Don't be afraid, darling. I'll take care of you. Today when Gunderson was badgering you I realized that no matter what happened that night, you're my whole life. I need you."

"Erich, I'm so confused."

"Why is that, darling?"

"Erich, I don't remember going out with Kevin but Rooney wouldn't lie."

"Don't worry. She's not a reliable woman. It's a good thing. Gunderson told me that he'd reopen the inquest in a shot if she were."

"You mean if someone else came forward and claimed to have seen me get in that car, they'd reopen the inquest and maybe charge me with a crime?"

"There's no need to talk about it. There's no other witness."

Oh, yes, there is, Jenny thought. Could anyone have overheard Joe today? His voice was loud. Joe's mother was starting to worry that Joe, like his uncle, had a tendency to drink. Suppose sometime in a bar he confided that he'd seen her get in the car with Kevin?

"Could I have forgotten that I went out?" she asked Erich.

He put his arms around her. His hands stroked her hair. "It would have been a shocking experience. Your coat was off. He had the key in his hand when he was found. Maybe, as I suggested to you, Kevin made a pass at you, grabbed the key. Maybe you resisted him. The car started to roll. You got out before it went over the bank."

"I don't know," Jenny said. "I can't believe it."

Later when it was time to go upstairs, Erich said, "Wear the aqua gown, darling."

"I can't."

"Can't? Why not?"

"It's too small for me. I'm going to have a baby."

Kevin had responded with dismay the first time she told him she thought she was pregnant. "Hell, Jen, we can't afford it. Get rid of it."

Now Erich shouted with joy. "My darling! Oh, Jen, that's the reason you've been looking so ill. Oh, my sweet. Will it be a boy?"

"I'm sure it is." Jenny laughed, savoring the momentary release from anxiety. "He's already given me a harder time in three months than both girls did in nine."

"We'll have to get you right to a good doctor. My *son*. Do you mind if we call him Erich? It's the family tradition."

"I want it that way."

With her wrapped in his arms on the couch, all the mistrust between them was forgotten. "Jen, we've had a rotten break. We'll put all this misery behind us. We'll have a big party when I come back from San Francisco. You shouldn't travel now, should you, not if you haven't been feeling well? We'll face this community down. We'll be a real family. The adoption will be complete by the summer. I'm sorry for MacPartland, but at least he's not a threat anymore. Oh, Jen. . . ."

Not a threat, Jenny thought. Should she tell Erich about Joe? No, this was the baby's night.

Finally they went upstairs. Erich was already in bed when she came out of the bathroom. "I've missed sleeping with you, Jen," he said. "I've been so lonely."

"I've been so lonely too." The intense physical relationship between them, heightened and fired by separation, helped her forget the weeks of suffering. "I love you, Jenny. I love you so."

"Erich, I thought I'd go crazy, feeling so estranged from you. . . ."

"I know."

"Jen?"

"Yes, darling."

"I'm anxious to see whom the baby looks like."

"Mmm, I hope like you. . . . Just like you."

"How much I hope that too." His breathing became even.

She began to drift off to sleep, then felt that she'd been slapped with ice water. Oh, God, Erich couldn't doubt that he was the baby's father, could he? Of course not. It was just that her nerves were so shot. Everything upset her. But it was the way he'd put it . . .

In the morning, he said, "I heard you crying in your sleep last night, darling."

"I wasn't aware of it."

"I love you, Jenny."

"Love is trust, Erich. Please, darling, remember love and trust go hand in hand."

Three days later he took her to an obstetrician in Granite Place. When she met Dr. Elmendorf she liked him instantly. He was anywhere between fifty and sixty-five, small and bald with knowing eyes.

"You've been spotting, Mrs. Krueger?"

"Yes, but that happened both times before and I was fine."

"Did you lose so much weight at the beginning of your first two pregnancies?"

"No."

"Were you always anemic?"

"No."

"Were there any complications about your own birth?"

"I don't know. I was adopted. My grandmother never mentioned anything. I was born in New York City. That's about all I know of my background."

"I see. We've got to build you up. I'm aware you've been under a great strain."

What a delicate way of putting it, Jenny thought.

"I'll want to start you on vitamins. Also no lifting, no pushing or hauling. Get a great deal of rest."

Erich was sitting beside her. He reached for her hand and stroked it. "I'll take good care of her, Doctor."

The eyes rested on Erich speculatively. "I think it would be well if you abstain from marital relations for the next month at least and possibly through the pregnancy if the spotting continues. Will that be too much of a problem?"

"Nothing is too much of a problem if it means that Jenny will have a healthy child."

The doctor nodded approvingly.

But it is a problem, Jenny thought, dismayed. You see, Doctor, our marital relations give us the one area where we are simply two people who love and want each other and we manage to close the door on jealousy and suspicion and outside pressures.

CHAPTER 25

The late spring was warm with afternoon showers and the rich abundant land became thick and green. The tough, heady alfalfa plants, now decorated with blue blossoms, were ready for the first cutting of the season.

Cattle strayed far away from the polebarns, happy with the grazing in the sloping fields that led to the riverbank. Tree branches rustled against each other, dressed in the leaves that made a solid green wall of the edge of the woods. Deer sometimes ran through that wall, paused, listened, then escaped back into the protective arms of the trees.

Even the house brightened with the fair weather. Rigid as they were, the heavy curtains could not withstand the delicate breezes that brought the scent of irises and violets and sunflowers and roses indoors.

For Jenny the change was welcome. The warmth of the spring sun seemed to penetrate the constant chill of her body. The scent of flowers in the house almost overcame the pervasive hint of pine. In the mornings she would get out of bed, open the windows and lie back against the pillows, enjoying the fresh, delicate breeze.

The pills for morning sickness weren't helping. Every morning she was racked by nausea. Erich insisted she stay in bed. He brought her tea and saltines, and after a while the feeling would subside.

He stayed in the house every night now. "I don't want you to be alone, darling, and I'm all ready for the San Francisco exhibit." He was leaving on the twenty-third of May. "By then Dr. Elmendorf said you'll probably be feeling a lot better."

"I hope so. Are you sure you're not interrupting your painting?"

"Very sure. It's good to spend more time with the girls. And face it, Jen. Between Clyde on the farm and the manager at the limeworks and Emily's father at the bank, I can manage my time my way."

Now it was Erich who took the girls to the stable during the mornings and led them on their ponies. Rooney came over regularly. The sweater Jenny was knitting was going well and she was already starting Jenny on a patchwork quilt.

Jenny was still helpless to explain how her coat got in Kevin's car. Suppose Kevin did come down, and tried that door on the west porch? It could have been unlocked. Suppose he came in? The closet door was right there. He might have panicked. After all, he didn't know whether or not a housekeeper slept in. Perhaps he took her coat, planning to insinuate that he'd seen her, started driving away, took the wrong turn, put his hand in the pocket in the hope of finding money, pulled out the key and with that the car went off the bank.

It still didn't explain the phone call.

After their nap the girls loved to roam in the fields. Jenny sat on the west porch watching them as her fingers knitted the rows of wool or made patchwork squares. Rooney had dug up material from the attic, leftover goods that had been used for dresses long ago, a bag of scraps, a bolt of dark blue cotton. "John brought that blue material for me to make curtains for the back bedroom when he took it over. I warned him they'd be too dark. He hated to admit it but he had me take them down after a couple of months. Then I made the ones that are there now."

Somehow Jenny could not bring herself to sit in Caroline's swing. Instead she chose a wicker chair, high-backed with comfortable cushions. Nevertheless Caroline had sat on this porch, sewing, watching her child play in these fields.

She no longer felt the lack of company. Now she always refused Erich's suggestions of dinner at one of the local restaurants. "Not yet, Erich. I don't even like the smell of food."

He began taking the children with him when he went out on errands. They came back chatting about the people they'd met, the places where they'd stopped to visit and stayed for cookies and milk.

Now Erich always slept in the back bedroom. "Jen, it's easier this way. I can stay away from you if I'm not too near you but I can't lie beside you night after night and not have my hands on you. Besides, you're a restless sleeper. You'll probably sleep better alone."

She should be grateful but she wasn't. The nightmares happened regularly; over and over again she'd had that sensation of touching flesh, a face in the dark, of feeling long hair against her cheek. She didn't dare tell him that. He'd surely think she was mad.

The day before he was to leave for San Francisco, he suggested she go to the stable with him. The morning nausea hadn't occurred for two days.

"I'd rather you be there when the girls ride. I'm getting pretty unhappy with Joe."

A quick thrill of worry. "Why?"

"I've heard rumors he's boozing it up every night with his uncle. Josh Brothers is exactly the wrong influence on Joe at this stage. Anyhow if you think he seems hung over, I don't want the girls out with him. I may have to get rid of him."

Mark was in the stable. His normally calm voice was raised and icy. "Don't you know how dangerous it is to leave rat poison five feet from the oat supply? Suppose some of it got mixed in with the feed? Those horses would go crazy. What the hell is the matter with you lately, Joe? Let me tell you, if this happens again, I'll recommend that Erich fire you. Those children ride the ponies every day. Erich's horse is hard enough to handle even for an experienced rider like him. Give Baron a taste of the strychnine in that stuff and he'd trample anyone who came near him."

Erich dropped Jenny's arm. "What's this all about?"

A red-faced Joe who seemed on the verge of tears admitted, "I was going to put the poison in the traps. I pulled the box in here when it started to rain and I forgot it."

"You're fired," Erich said evenly.

Joe looked at Jenny. Was their something significant in his expression or simple pleading? She wasn't sure.

She stepped forward, took Erich's hand. "*Please,* Erich. Joe's been wonderful with the children. He's so patient teaching them to ride. They'd miss him terribly."

Erich studied her face. "If it means that much to you," he said shortly, then turned back to Joe. "Any mistake, Joe, *any* mistake, a stall door open, a dog running around my property, this sort of thing . . ." He glanced contemptuously at the box of rat poison. "That's *it.* Got it?"

"Yes, sir," Joe whispered. "Thank you, sir. Thank you, Mrs. Krueger."

"And make sure it's *Mrs. Krueger,*" Erich snapped. "Jenny, I don't want the girls riding till I come back. Is that clear?"

"Yes." She agreed with him. Joe looked ill. There was a bruise on his forehead.

Mark left the stable with them. "You've got a new calf in the dairy barn, Erich. That's why I'm here. Keep an eye on Joe. He was in another fight last night."

"What the hell is he fighting about?" Erich asked irritably.

Mark's face closed. "Give people not used to liquor a couple of boilermakers and you don't need much excuse."

"Come back to lunch with us," Erich suggested. "We haven't seen much of you."

"Please come," Jenny murmured.

They walked up to the house together.

"You two go in," Erich suggested. "Mark, pour us a sherry, will you? I want to pick up the mail at the office."

"Sure thing."

He waited until Erich was out of earshot then said quickly, "Two things, Jenny. I heard the good news about the baby. Congratulations. How do you feel?"

"Much better now."

"Jenny, I have to warn you. It was very good of you to save Joe's job for him but it's a mistaken kindness. The reason he's getting into fights is that he's too open about his feelings for you. He worships you and the guys who hang around the bars at night are teasing him about it. Joe would be better off far away from this farm."

"And from me?"

"Bluntly, yes."

CHAPTER 26

When Erich was leaving for San Francisco he decided to drive the Cadillac to the airport and leave it there. "Unless you particularly want to use it, darling?"

Was there an edge to the question? The last time he'd been away she'd used the car to meet Kevin. "I don't want it," she said quietly. "Elsa can pick up anything I need."

"You have your vitamins."

"Plenty of them."

"If you don't feel well, Clyde will drive you to the doctor." They were at the door. "Girls," Erich called, "come give Daddy a kiss."

They ran to him. "Bring me a present," Beth begged.

"Me too," Tina chimed in.

"Oh, Erich, before you go, tell the girls you don't want them on the ponies until you get back."

"Daddy!" There were two wails of protest.

"Oh, I don't know. Joe came to apologize to me. Says he knows he's been off-base. He's even going to move back in with his mother. I think it's all right to let him take the girls out. You just be sure to be with them every minute, Jen."

"I'd rather not," she said evenly.

"Any reason?" His eyebrows quirked.

She thought of what Mark had told her. But there was no way she could discuss that with Erich. "If you're sure it's safe."

His arms were around her. "I'll miss you."

"I'll miss you too."

She walked with him to the car. Clyde had driven it out of the garage. Joe was polishing it with a soft cloth. Rooney was standing by it, ready to come in and sew with Jenny. Mark had come over to say good-bye.

"I'll call you as soon as I get to the hotel," Erich told Jenny. "That will be ten your time."

That night she lay in bed waiting for the phone to ring. This house is too large, she thought. Anyone could come in the front door, the west door, the back door, come up the back staircase and I'd never hear him or her. The keys were hanging in the office. They were locked up at night but often during the day the office was empty. Suppose someone took a house key, made a copy and returned the first key to the office? No one would ever know.

Why am I worrying about that now? she wondered.

It was just that dream, that recurring dream of touching flesh, of her fingers grazing a cheek, an ear, hair. It was happening almost nightly now. And always the same. The heavy scent of pine, the feeling of a presence, the touching, and then a faint sighing sound. And always when she turned on the light the room was empty.

If only she could talk to someone about it. But who? Dr. Elmendorf would suggest she see a psychiatrist. She was sure of that. That's all Granite Place would need, she thought. Now that Krueger woman is going to have her head examined.

It was not quite ten o'clock. The phone rang. Quickly she picked it up. "Hello."

The line was dead. No, she could hear something. Not breathing but something.

"Hello." She felt herself start to tremble.

"Jenny." The voice was a whisper.

"Who is this?"

"Jenny, are you alone?"

"Who is this?"

"Have you got another boyfriend from New York with you yet, Jenny? Does he like to swim?"

"What are you talking about?"

Now the voice burst forth, a shriek, a scream, half-laugh, half-sob, unrecognizable. "Whore. Murderer. Get out of Caroline's bed. Get out of it *now*."

She slammed the phone down. Oh, God, help me. She held her hands against her cheek feeling a tic under her eye. Oh, God.

The phone rang. I won't pick it up. I won't.

Four times, five times, six times. It stopped. It began to ring again. Erich, she thought. It was after ten o'clock. She grabbed the receiver.

''Jenny,'' Erich's voice was concerned, ''what's the matter? I called a few minutes ago and the line was busy. Then no answer. Are you all right? Who was on the phone?''

''I don't know. It was just a voice.'' Her own voice was near hysteria.

''You sound upset. What did whoever called you say?''

''I . . . I couldn't make out the words.'' She couldn't tell him.

''I see.'' A long pause, then in a resigned tone, Erich said, ''We won't discuss it now.''

''What do you mean we won't discuss it?'' Shocked, Jenny heard the shriek in her own voice. She sounded exactly like the caller. ''I want to discuss it. Listen, listen to what they said.'' Sobbing, she told him. ''Who would accuse me like that? Who could hate me so much?''

''Darling, calm yourself, please.''

''But, Erich, *who*?''

''Darling, *think*. It was Rooney, of course.''

''But *why*? Rooney likes me.''

''She may *like* you but she *loved* Caroline. She wants Caroline back and when she gets upset she sees you as an intruder. Darling, I warned you about her. Jenny, please don't cry. It's going to be all right. I'll take care of you. I'll always take care of you.''

Sometime during the long, sleepless night the cramps began. First they were shooting pains in her abdomen. Then they settled into a steady off-on pattern. At eight she phoned Dr. Elmendorf. ''You'd better come in,'' he told her.

Clyde had left early for a cattle auction and had taken Rooney with him. She didn't dare ask Joe to drive her. There were a half-dozen other men on the farm, the daily help who came in the morning and went to their own homes at night. She knew their names and faces but Erich had always cautioned her ''not to get familiar.''

She didn't want to ask one of them. She called Mark and explained. ''By any chance . . .?''

His answer was prompt. ''No problem. If you don't mind waiting until after office hours for me to drive you back. Or better still my dad can do it. He just got up from Florida. He'll stay most of the summer with me.''

Mark's father, Luke Garrett. Jenny was anxious to meet him.

Mark came for her at nine-fifteen. The morning was warm and hazy. It would be a hot day. Jenny had gone to her closet for something to wear and realized that all the new clothes Erich bought her when they were married were for cool weather. She'd had to rummage to find a summer cotton from last year in New York. Putting it on she'd felt peculiarly herself again. The two-piece pink-checked dress was an Albert Capraro, one she'd bought at an end-of-the-season sale. The soft, wide skirt was only a little tight at the waist; the blouse on top concealed her thinness.

Mark's car was a four-year-old Chrysler station wagon. His bag was tossed in the back. A stack of books was scattered next to it on the seat. The car had an air of comfortable untidiness.

It was the first time she'd ever really been alone with Mark. I'll bet even the animals know instinctively he'll make things better when he's around, she thought. She told him that.

He glanced over at her. "I'd like to think so. And I hope Elmendorf is having the same effect on you. He's a good doctor, Jenny. You can trust him."

"I do."

They drove down the dirt road that led past the farm into Granite Place. Acre on acre of Krueger land, she thought. All those animals grazing on the fields. Krueger prize cattle. And I really had visualized a pleasant farmhouse and some cornfields. I never understood.

Mark said, "I don't know whether you heard that Joe is moving back in with his mother."

"Erich told me."

"The best possible situation. Maude is a smart woman. Drink runs in that family. She'll keep a tight rein on Joe."

"I thought her brother started drinking because of the accident?"

"I wonder. I heard my father and John Krueger talk about it afterward. John always said that Josh Brothers had been drinking that day. Maybe the accident was his excuse for coming out in the open with his boozing."

"Will Erich ever forgive me for all this gossip? It's destroying our marriage." She hadn't expected to ask the question. She heard it come from her flat and lifeless. Did she dare tell Mark about the phone call, about Erich's response to it?

"Jenny." There was a long silence then Mark began to speak. She'd already noticed that his voice had a tendency to deepen when he was particularly intent on what he was saying. "Jenny, I can't tell you what a different person Erich is since the first day he came back here after meeting you. He's always been a loner. He's always spent a lot of time in that cabin. Now of course we understand why. But even so . . . picture it. I doubt whether John Krueger ever so much as kissed Erich when he was a child. Caroline was the kind who'd scoop you up, hug you when you came in, run her fingers through your hair when she talked to you. People around here aren't like that. We're not outwardly expressive. Caroline was half-Italian, as you know. I remember my father teasing her about that Latin warmth in her. Can you imagine what it must have been like for Erich to know she was planning to leave him? No wonder he was so upset about your former husband. Just give him time. The gossip will die down. By next month people will have something else to chew on."

"You make it sound so easy."

"Not easy, but maybe not as bad as you think."

He dropped her at the doctor's office. "I'll just sit out here and catch up on some reading. You shouldn't be too long."

The obstetrician did not mince words. "You've had false labor and I certainly don't like it at this stage. You haven't been exerting yourself?"

"No."

"You've lost more weight."

"I just can't eat."

"For the sake of the baby, you've got to try. Malted milks, ice cream, just get something down. And stay off your feet as much a possible. Are you worried about anything?"

Yes, Doctor, she wanted to say. I'm worried because I don't know who calls me when my husband is away. Is Rooney sicker than I realize? How about Maude? She resents the Kruegers, particularly resents me. Who else knows so much about when Erich is away?

"Are you worried about anything, Mrs. Krueger?" he repeated.

"Not really."

She told Mark what the doctor had said. His arm was slung around the back of the seat. He's so big, she thought, so overpoweringly, comfortably male. She could not imagine him exploding in fury. He had been reading. Now he tossed the book in the backseat, and started the car. "Jenny," he suggested, "don't you have a friend or a cousin or someone who could come out and spend a couple of months with you? You seem so alone here. I think that might help to take your mind off things."

Fran, Jenny thought. With absolute longing she wanted Fran to come and visit. She thought of the amusing evenings they had spent together while Fran expounded on her latest boyfriend. But Erich disliked Fran intensely. He'd told her to make sure that Fran didn't visit. Jenny thought of some of her other friends. None of them could spend nearly four hundred dollars to fly out for a weekend visit. They had jobs and families. "No," she said, "I don't have anyone who can come."

The Garrett farm was on the north end of Granite Place. "We're small potatoes next to Erich," Mark said. "We have a section, six hundred and forty acres. I have my clinic right on the property."

The farmhouse was like the one she'd pictured Erich would have. Large and white, black-shuttered, with a wide front porch.

The parlor was lined with bookshelves. Mark's father was reading in an easy chair there. He looked up when they came in. Jenny watched as a startled expression came over his face.

He was a big man too, with rangy shoulders. The thick hair was pure white but the part broke at the same place as his son's. His reading glasses enhanced his blue-gray eyes, and his lashes were gray-white. Mark's were dark. But Luke's eyes had that same quizzical expression.

"You have to be Jenny Krueger."

"Yes, I am." Jenny liked him at once.

"No wonder Erich . . ." He stopped. "I've been anxious to meet you. I'd hoped to get the chance when I was here in late February."

"You were here in February?" Jenny turned to Mark. "Why didn't you bring your father over?"

Mark shrugged. "Erich pretty well sent out signals you two were doing an at-home honeymoon. Jenny, I've got ten minutes before the clinic opens. What would you like? Tea? Coffee?"

Mark disappeared into the kitchen and she was alone with Luke Garrett. She felt as though she were being looked over by the school counselor, as though any minute he'd ask, "And how do you like your courses? Are you comfortable with your teachers?"

She told him that.

He smiled. "Maybe I am analyzing. How is it going?"

"How much have you heard?"

"The accident? The inquest?"

"You've heard." She raised her hands as though pushing away a weight that was closing in on her. "I can't blame people for thinking the worst. My coat was in the car. A woman did call the Guthrie Theater from our telephone that afternoon.

"I keep thinking there's a reasonable explanation and once I find out, everything will be all right again."

She hesitated, then decided against discussing Rooney with him. If Rooney had made that call last night in one of her spells, she'd probably have forgotten it by now. And Jenny did not want to repeat what the caller had said to her.

Mark came in followed by a short, stocky woman carrying a tray. The warm, enticing scent of coffee cake reminded Jenny of Nana's one great baking success, a Bisquick coffee cake. A wave of nostalgia made her blink back tears.

"You're not very happy here, are you, Jenny?" Luke asked.

"I expected to be. I could be," she replied honestly.

"That's exactly what Caroline said," Luke commented softly. "Remember, Mark, when I was putting her bags in the car that last afternoon?"

A few minutes later Mark left for the clinic and Luke drove her home. He seemed quiet and distracted and after a few efforts at conversation, Jenny became quiet too.

Luke steered the station wagon through the main gate. They circled around to the west entrance. She saw Luke's eyes rest on the porch swing. "The problem," he said suddenly, "is that this place doesn't change. If you took a picture of this house and compared it to one that was thirty years old, it would be the same. Nothing is added, nothing is renovated, nothing is moved. Maybe that's why everyone here has that same feeling of her presence, as though the door might fling open and she'd come running out, always glad to see you, always urging you to stay for dinner.

After Mark's mother and I were divorced she had Mark here so much. Caroline was a second mother to him."

"And to you?" Jenny asked. "What was she to you?"

Luke looked at her through eyes that were suddenly anguished. "Everything I ever wanted in a woman." He cleared his throat abruptly as though fearing he had revealed too much of himself. As she got out of the car Jenny said, "When Erich comes back, promise you'll come for dinner with Mark."

"I'd enjoy that, Jenny. Sure you have everything?"

"Yes." She started to walk toward the house.

"Jenny," he called.

She turned. Luke's face was filled with pain. "Forgive me. It's just that you resemble Caroline so strongly. It's rather frightening. Jenny, be careful. Be careful of accidents."

CHAPTER 27

Erich was due home on June third. He called the night of the second. "Jen, I've been miserable. Darling, I'd give anything not to have you so upset."

She felt the hard knot of tension ease. It was as Mark said, eventually the gossip would blow over. If only she could hang on to that thought. "It's all right. We're going to get through all this."

"How do you feel, Jen?"

"Pretty good."

"Eating better?"

"Trying to. How did the exhibit go?"

"Very, very well. The Gramercy Trust bought three oils. Stiff prices too. The reviews were fine."

"I'm so glad. What time does your plane get in?"

"Around eleven. I should be home between two and three. I love you so much, Jen."

That night the room seemed less threatening. Maybe it will be all right, she promised herself. For the first time in weeks she slept without dreaming.

She was sitting at the breakfast table with Tina and Beth when the screaming started, a hideous cacophony of wild neighing and frantic sounds of human pain.

"Mommy!" Beth jumped off her chair and ran for the door.

"Stay there," Jenny ordered. She ran toward the sounds. They were coming from the stable. Clyde was rushing from the office, a rifle in his hand. "Stay back, Miz Krueger, stay back."

She could not. Joe. It was Joe who was screaming.

He was in the stall, crouched against the back wall, trying frantically to dodge the flying hooves. Baron was rearing on his hind legs, his eyes rolling in his head, the sharp metal-shod hoofs flailing in the air. Joe was bleeding from the head; one arm hung limply at his side. As she watched he slumped onto the floor and Baron's front legs trampled his chest.

"Oh, God, oh, God, oh, God!" She heard her own voice weeping, praying, entreating. She was shoved aside. "Get out of his way, Joe. I'm gonna shoot." Clyde took aim as the hooves reared up again. There was a sharp crack of the rifle, followed by a screeching, protesting neighing; Baron stood poised statuelike in midair, then crumbled into the straw in the stall.

Somehow Joe managed to press against the wall, to avoid the crushing weight of the falling animal. Joe lay still, his breath coming in sharp gasps, his eyes glazed with shock, his arm twisted grotesquely. Clyde threw down the rifle and ran over to him.

"Don't move him!" Jenny shouted. "Call for an ambulance. Hurry."

Trying to avoid Baron's body, she kneeled beside Joe, her hand smoothing his forehead, wiping the blood from his eyes, pressing against the gaping tear in his hairline. Men came running from the fields. She could hear the sounds of a woman sobbing. Maude Ekers. "Joey, Joey."

"Maw . . ."

"Joey."

The ambulance arrived. Efficient white-clad attendants ordered everyone back. Then Joe was on the stretcher, his eyes closed, his face ashen. An attendant's low voice whispered, "I think he's going."

There was a shriek from Maude Ekers.

Joe's eyes opened, fastening on Jenny. His voice was bewildered, amazingly clear. "I'd never a told anyone I saw you get in the car that night, honest I wouldn't," he said.

Maude turned on Jenny, as she climbed in the ambulance after her son. "If my boy dies, it's your fault, Jenny Krueger," she screamed. "I *curse* the day you came here! God *damn* you Krueger women for what you've done to my family! God damn the baby you're carrying, whoever it belongs to!"

The ambulance sped away, the wail of its siren shattering the peace of the summer morning.

Erich arrived home a few hours later. He chartered a plane to fly a chest surgeon down from the Mayo Clinic, and phoned for private nurses. Then he walked into the stable and crouched beside Baron, his hand patting the sleek, beautiful head of the dead animal.

Mark had already analyzed the bucket of oats. The report: strychnine mixed with oats.

Later Sheriff Gunderson showed up at the front door with his now familiar car. ''Mrs. Krueger, a half-dozen people heard Joe say he wouldn't have told that he saw you get in the car that night. What did he mean by that?''

''I don't understand what he meant.''

''Mrs. Krueger, you were present a short time ago when Dr. Garrett admonished Joe for leaving the rat poison near the oats. You knew what effect it would have on Baron. You heard Dr. Garrett warn Joe that strychnine would drive Baron wild.''

''Did Dr. Garrett tell you that?''

''He told me that Joe had been careless with the rat poison and that you and Erich were present when he dressed Joe down.''

''What are you trying to say?''

''Nothing I can say, Mrs. Krueger. Joe claims he got the boxes mixed up. I don't believe him. No one does.''

''Will Joe live?''

''Too soon to tell. Even if he does, he'll be a mighty sick boy for a long time. If he makes it through the next three days, they're moving him up to Mayo.'' The sheriff turned to go. ''Like his maw said, at least he'll be safe up there.''

CHAPTER 28

Caught up in the rhythm of her pregnancy, Jenny began counting the days and weeks until the baby was due. In twelve weeks, in eleven weeks, in ten weeks, Erich would have a son. He would move back into their room. She would be well again. The talk of the town would die out for lack of fresh fuel. The baby would look exactly like Erich.

The operation on Joe's chest had been successful, though he would not leave Mayo Clinic until the end of August. Maude was staying in a furnished apartment near the hospital. Jenny knew that Erich was paying all the bills.

Now Erich rode Fire Maid when he took the girls riding. He never mentioned Baron to her. She did hear from Mark that Joe had persisted in his story that he must have mixed the poison in with the oats himself and that he had no idea what he'd meant when he talked about seeing Jenny that night.

She didn't need Mark to tell her that no one believed him.

Erich was working less at the cabin and more on the farm with Clyde and the men. When she asked him about that he said, ''I can't quite get in the mood for painting.''

He was kind to her but remote. Always she felt that he was watching her. In the evenings they'd sit in the parlor and read. He rarely spoke to her, but when she glanced up, she'd see his eyes drop as though he didn't want to be caught studying her.

About once a week Sheriff Gunderson would drop by, seemingly just to chat. "Let's go over the night Kevin MacPartland came here, Mrs. Krueger." Or he would speculate: "Joe has a real big crush on you, don't he? Enough to make him pretty protective. Anything you feel like talking about, Mrs. Krueger?"

The sensation of someone being in the room with her at night was constant. Always the pattern was the same. She would start dreaming of being in the woods; something would come toward her, hover over her; she'd push out her hand and feel long hair, a woman's hair. The sighing sound came next. She would fumble for the light and when she turned it on she'd be alone in the room.

Finally she told Dr. Elmendorf about the dream.

"How do you explain it?" he asked.

"I don't know." She hesitated. "No, that's not quite true. I always think it has something to do with Caroline." She told him about Caroline, told him that everyone close to her seemed to have a sense of her presence.

"I'd guess that your imagination is playing tricks on you. Would you like me to arrange counseling?"

"No. I'm sure you're right."

She started to sleep with the light on in the room, then determinedly snapped it off. The bed was to the right of the door. The massive headboard was against the north wall. One side of the bed was close to the east wall of the room. She wondered if Erich would move the bed for her so that it was between the windows on the south wall. There would be more moonlight there. She'd be able to look out when she wasn't sleeping. The corner where the bed was placed was terribly dark.

She knew better than to make the request.

One morning Beth asked, "Mommy, why didn't you talk to me when you came into my room last night?"

"I didn't come to you, Mouse."

"Yes, you did!"

Was she sleepwalking?

The tiny flutters of life inside her seemed unlike the sturdy kicks she'd known with Beth and Tina. Let the baby be healthy, she pleaded in silent prayer. Let me give Erich his son.

The hot August afternoons dissolved into cool evenings. The woods held the first touches of gold. "It will be an early fall," Rooney commented. "And by the time the leaves are all turned, your quilt will be finished. You can hang it in the dining room too."

Jenny avoided Mark as much as possible, staying in the house whenever she glimpsed his station wagon parked near the office. Did he too believe she might have deliberately put poison in Baron's feed? She felt she could not stand it if she sensed accusation from him too.

In early September, Erich invited Mark and Luke Garret for dinner. He told her about it casually. ''Luke's going back to Florida until the holidays. I haven't seen enough of him. Emily's coming too. I can have Elsa stay and cook.''

''No, that's the one thing I get to do around here.''

The first dinner party since the night Sheriff Gunderson had come to tell her Kevin was missing. She found herself looking forward to seeing Luke again. She knew Erich went over to the Garrett farm regularly. He'd taken Tina and Beth with him. He never cleared the outings with her anymore. He'd simply announce, ''I'll keep the girls out of your hair for the afternoon. Get a good rest, Jen.''

It wasn't that she wanted to go. She didn't want to run the risk of seeing any of the townspeople. How would they treat her? Smile to her face and gossip about her as she passed?

When Erich was away with the girls, she would take long walks on the farm. She would wander along the river and try not to think that Kevin's car plunged over the bank just around that bend. She walked past the cemetery. Caroline's grave was planted with summer flowers.

She found herself longing to slip into the woods, to find Erich's cabin. Once she went fifty yards into them. The thick branches blotted out the sun. A fox passed her, brushing her legs, in pursuit of a rabbit. Startled, she'd turned back. Birds nesting in the trees sent up a flutter of protest as she passed.

She'd ordered some maternity clothes from a Dayton's catalog. Nearly seven months pregnant, she thought, and my own clothes aren't that much too tight. But the new blouses and slacks and skirts buoyed her spirits. She remembered how carefully she'd shopped when she was pregnant with Beth. She'd worn those same clothes for Tina. For this baby Erich had said, ''Order as much as you want.''

The night of the dinner she wore an emerald-green two-piece silk dress with a white lace collar. It was simple and well-cut. She knew Erich liked her to wear green. It did something to her eyes. Like the aqua gown.

The Garretts and Emily came together. Jenny decided there seemed to be a new intimacy between Mark and Emily. They sat side by side on the couch. At one point Emily's hand rested on Mark's arm. Maybe they are engaged, she thought. The possibility brought a queer stab of pain. Why?

Emily was making a distinct effort to be pleasant. But it was hard to find common ground. She talked about the county fair. ''Corny as they are, I always enjoy them. And everyone was talking about how darling your girls are.''

''Our girls,'' Erich smiled. ''Oh, by the way, you'll all be glad to know the adoption is complete. The girls are legally and bindingly Kruegers.''

Jenny'd expected that, of course. But how long had Erich known? A few weeks ago he'd stopped asking her if she minded if he took the girls out. Was that the reason: they were "legally and bindingly Kruegers?"

Luke Garrett was very quiet. He had chosen to sit in the wing chair. After a while Jenny understood why. It gave the clearest view of Caroline's portrait. His eyes seldom strayed from it. What had he meant by that warning about accidents?

The dinner turned out well. She'd made tomato bisque from a recipe she found in an old cookbook in the kitchen. Luke raised his eyebrows. "Erich, if I'm not mistaken that must be the recipe your grandmother used when I was a boy. Excellent, Jenny."

As though to make up for his earlier silence, Luke began reminiscing about his youth. "Your dad," he said to Erich, "was as close to me growing up as you and Mark ever were."

At ten o'clock they went home. Erich helped her to clear the table. He seemed pleased the way the evening had gone. "Looks as though Mark and Emily are getting close to an engagement," he said. "Luke would be glad. He's been after Mark to settle down."

"I thought so too," Jenny agreed. She tried to sound pleased but knew the effort was a failure.

In October it became sharply colder. Biting winds stripped the trees of their autumn finery; frost dulled the grass to brown; rain became icy. The furnace hummed constantly now. Every morning Erich started a fire in the kitchen stove. Beth and Tina came to breakfast wrapped in warm robes, eagerly anticipating the first snowfall.

Jenny seldom left the house. The long walks were too tiring and Dr. Elmendorf advised against them. Her legs cramped frequently and she was afraid of falling. Rooney came to visit every afternoon. Between them they'd made a layette for the baby. "I'll never sew properly," Jenny sighed, but even so it was gratifying to make simple kimonos from the flowered cloth that Rooney ordered from town.

It was Rooney who showed Jenny the corner of the attic where the Krueger bassinet was covered with sheets. "I'll make a new skirt for it," Rooney said. The activity seemed to brighten her and for days at a time she was never confused.

"I'll put the bassinette in Erich's old room," she told Rooney. "I don't want to move the girls and the other rooms are too far away. I'd be afraid I wouldn't hear the baby at night."

"That's what Caroline said," Rooney volunteered. "You know Erich's room used to be part of the master bedroom, kind of an alcove of it. Caroline put the bassinette and baby dresser there. John didn't like having the baby in his room. Said he didn't have a big house so he'd have to tiptoe around an infant. That's when they put the partition in."

"The partition?"

''Didn't Erich ever tell you that? Your bed used to be on the south wall. Behind the headboard where it is now is the sliding wall.''

''Show me, Rooney.''

They went upstairs to Erich's old room. ''Course you can't open it from your side with the headboard there,'' Rooney said, ''but look-see.'' She pushed the high-back rocker aside and pointed to a recessed handle in the wallpaper. ''Just watch how easy it works.''

Noiselessly the panel slid open. ''Caroline had it made like that so when Erich was bigger you could just close off the two rooms. My Clyde made the partition and Josh Brothers helped him. Didn't they do a good job? Would you ever guess it was there?''

Jenny stood in the opening. She was behind the headboard of her bed. She leaned over. That was why she had felt a presence, reached out, touched a face. She remembered the constant sensation of long hair. Rooney's hair removed from the tight bun was surely quite long. ''Rooney,'' she tried to sound casual, ''do you ever come into this room and open the partition at night? Maybe look in at me?''

''I don't think I do. But, Jenny . . .'' Rooney put her lips to Jenny's ear. ''I wouldn't tell Clyde because he'd think I'm crazy. Sometimes he scares me. He talks about putting me away for my own good. But, Jenny, I've seen Caroline walking around the farm at night these last few months. Once I followed her here to the house and she came up the back stairs. That's why I keep thinking if Caroline is able to come back, maybe my Arden will be here soon too.''

CHAPTER 29

This time it wasn't false labor. Quietly Jenny lay in bed timing the contractions. From ten minutes apart for two hours, they suddenly accelerated to five-minute intervals. Jenny patted the small mound in her abdomen. We've made it, young Mr. Krueger, she thought. For a while I wasn't sure we would.

Dr. Elmendorf had been cautiously pleased on her last visit. ''The baby is about five pounds,'' he said. ''I'd wish it bigger but that's a comfortable weight. Frankly I was sure you were going to deliver prematurely.'' He'd done a scan. ''You're right, Mrs. Krueger. You're going to have a boy.''

She went down the hall to call Erich. The door of his bedroom was closed. She never went there. Hesitating she knocked. ''Erich,'' she called softly.

There was no answer. Could he have gone to the cabin during the night? He'd started painting again but always came home for dinner. Even if he went back to the cabin for the evening he returned to the house at some point.

She'd asked him about the panel that separated his old room from the master bedroom. ''My God, Jen, I'd forgotten all about it. Why do you get the idea someone has been opening it? I'll bet Rooney is in and out of this place more than we realize. I warned you against getting so cozy with her.''

She hadn't dared tell him that Rooney talked about seeing Caroline.

Now she pushed open the door to the room he'd been using and reached for the light. The bed was made. Erich wasn't here.

She'd have to get to the hospital. It was only four o'clock. There wouldn't be anyone up until seven. Unless . . .

Padding softly on bare feet down the wide foyer, Jenny passed the closed doors of the other bedrooms. Erich would never use any of those except . . .

Cautiously she opened the door of his old room. The Little League trophy on the dresser glistened in the moonlight. The bassinette, now frothy with a yellow silk skirt overlaid with white net, was next to the bed.

The bedcovers were rumpled. Erich was asleep, his body hunched in his favorite fetal position. His hand was thrown over the bassinette as though he'd fallen asleep holding it. Something Rooney had said came back to her. ''I can see Caroline rocking that bassinette by the hour with Erich fussing in it. I used to tell him he was lucky to have had such a patient mother.''

''Erich,'' Jenny whispered, touching his shoulder.

His eyes flew open. He jumped up. ''Jenny, what's the matter?''

''I think I'd better get to the hospital.'' He got out of bed quickly, put his arms around her. ''Something told me to come in here tonight, to be near you. I fell asleep thinking how wonderful it will be when our little boy is in that bassinette.''

It had been weeks since he had touched her. She had not realized how starved she had been for the feeling of arms around her. She reached up her hands to his face.

In the dark her fingers felt the curve of his face, the softness of his eyelids.

She shivered.

''What is it, dear? Are you all right?''

She sighed. ''I don't know why but just for a minute I was so frightened. You'd think this was my first baby, wouldn't you?''

The overhead light in the delivery room was very bright. It hurt her eyes. She was slipping in and out of consciousness. Erich, masked and coated like the doctors and nurses, was watching her. Why did Erich watch her all the time?

A last rush of pain. Now, she thought, now. Dr. Elmendorf held up a small, limp body. All of them bending over it. "Oxygen."

The baby had to be all right. "Give him to me." But her lips didn't form the words. She couldn't move her lips.

"Let me see him," Erich said. He sounded anxious, nervous. Then she heard his dismayed whisper. "He has hair like the girls, *dark red hair!*"

When she opened her eyes again the room was dark. A nurse was sitting by the bed.

"The baby?"

"He'll be fine," the nurse said soothingly. "He just gave us a little scare. Try to sleep."

"My husband?"

"He's gone home."

What was it Erich had said in the delivery room? She couldn't remember.

She drifted in and out of sleep. In the morning a pediatrician came in. "I'm Dr. Bovitch. The baby's lungs aren't fully developed. He's in trouble but we'll pull him through, Mother. I promise you that. However, since you gave your religion as Roman Catholic we thought it best to have him baptized last night."

"Is he that sick? I want to see him."

"You can walk down to the nursery in a little while. We can't take him out of the oxygen yet. Kevin's a beautiful little baby, Mrs. Krueger."

"*Kevin!*"

"Yes. Before the priest baptized him he asked your husband what you planned to call him. That is right, isn't it? Kevin MacPartland Krueger?"

Erich came in with an armful of long-stemmed red roses. "Jenny, Jenny, they say he'll make it. The baby will make it. When I went home I spent the night crying. I thought it was hopeless."

"Why did you tell them his name was Kevin MacPartland?"

"Darling, they said they didn't think he'd survive more than a few hours. I thought we'd save the name Erich for a son who would live. It was the only other name that came to my mind. I thought you'd be pleased."

"Change it."

"Of course, darling. He'll be Erich Krueger the fifth on his birth certificate."

The week she was in the hospital Jenny forced herself to eat, husbanded her strength, pushed back the depression that sapped her energy. After the fourth day they took the baby out of oxygen and let her hold him. He was so frail. Her being ached with tenderness as his mouth reached for her breast. She had not nursed Beth or Tina. It had been too important to get back to work. But to this child she could give all her time, all her energy.

She was discharged from the hospital when the baby was five days old. For the next three weeks she went back there every four hours during the day to nurse him. Sometimes Erich drove her. Other times he gave her the car. "Anything for the baby, darling."

The girls got used to her leaving them. At first they fussed, then became resigned. "It's all right," Beth told Tina. "Daddy will mind us and we have fun with him."

Erich heard. "Who do you like best, Mommy or me?" He tossed them in the air.

"You, Daddy," Tina giggled. Jenny realized she'd learned the answers Erich wanted to hear.

Beth hesitated, glanced at Jenny. "I like you both the same."

Finally, the day after Thanksgiving, she was allowed to bring the baby home. Tenderly, she dressed the small body, glad to hand back the coarse hospital shirt and replace it with a new one, washed once to soften the cotton fibers. A long flowered nightgown, the blue woolen sacque and bonnet, a receiving blanket, the brushed wool bunting lined in satin.

It was bitterly cold out. November had brought snow, ice-tipped, constant. Wind whispered through the trees, stirring the naked branches into restless movement. Smoke wisped constantly from the chimneys in the house, from the office, blew over the ridge from Clyde and Rooney's home near the cemetery.

The girls were ecstatic over their little brother, each pleading to hold him. Sitting beside them on the couch, Jenny let them have a turn. "Gently, gently. He's so tiny."

Mark and Emily dropped by to see him. "He's beautiful," Emily declared. "Erich is showing his picture to everyone."

"Thank you for your flowers," Jenny murmured, "and your father and mother sent a beautiful arrangement. I phoned to thank your mother but apparently she wasn't home."

The "apparently" was a deliberate choice of words. She was certain that Mrs. Hanover was home when she called.

"They're so happy for you . . . and for Erich, of course," Emily said hastily. "I'm just hoping I'm giving someone over here ideas." She laughed in Mark's direction.

He smiled back at her.

You don't make remarks like that until you're pretty sure of yourself, Jenny thought.

She tried to make conversation. "Well, Dr. Garrett, how do you judge my son? Would he win a prize at the county fair?"

"A thoroughbred, for sure," Mark replied. What was there in his voice? A worried tone? Pity? Did he see something as fragile in the baby as she did?

She was sure of it.

* * *

Rooney was a born nurse. She loved to give the baby the supplemental bottle after Jenny breast-fed him. Or she would read to the girls when the baby was sleeping.

Jenny was grateful for the help. The baby worried her. He slept too much; he was so pale. His eyes began to focus. They would be wide with the hint of almond shaping that Erich's had. They were china blue now. "But I swear I see some green lights in them. I bet they're like your mother's eyes, Erich. You'd like that?"

"I'd like that."

He moved the four-poster to the south wall of the master bedroom. She left the partition open between that room and the small one. The bassinette was kept there. She could hear every sound the baby made.

Erich still hadn't moved back into their room. "You need your rest a little longer, Jenny."

"You can come in with me. I'd like that."

"Not yet."

Then she realized she was relieved. The baby consumed her every thought. At the end of the first month he had lost six ounces. The pediatrician looked grave. "We'll increase the formula in the supplemental bottle. I'm afraid your milk isn't rich enough for him. Are you eating properly? Is anything upsetting you? Remember a relaxed mother has a happier baby."

She forced herself to eat, to nibble, to drink milk shakes. The baby would start to nurse eagerly then tire and fall asleep. She told the doctor that.

"We'd better do some tests."

The baby was in the hospital three days. She slept in a room near the nursery. "Don't worry about my girls, Jenny. I'll take care of them."

"I know you will, Erich."

She lived for the moment she could hold the baby.

One of the valves in the baby's heart was defective. "He'll need an operation later on, but we can't risk it yet."

She thought of Maude Ekers' curse: "God damn the baby you're carrying." Her arms tightened around the sleeping infant.

"Is the operation dangerous?"

"Any operation has potential risk. But most babies come through nicely."

Again she brought the baby home. The tiny birth fuzz started to fall out. Fine golden shades of down began to replace it. "He'll have your hair, Erich."

"I think he'll stay red like the girls."

December came. Beth and Tina made up long lists for Santa Claus. Erich set up a huge tree in the corner near the stove. The girls helped him. Jenny held the baby as she watched. She hated to put him down. "He sleeps better this way,'' she told Erich. ''He always feels so cold. His circulation is poor.''

''Sometimes I don't think you care about anyone except him,'' Erich observed. ''I have to tell you, Tina and Beth and I are feeling pretty left out, aren't we?''

He took the girls to see Santa Claus in a nearby shopping mall. ''What a list,'' he commented indulgently. ''I had to write everything down that they were ordering. The big things they seem to want are bassinettes and baby dolls.''

Luke had come back to Minnesota for the holidays. He, Mark and Emily stopped in on Christmas afternoon. Emily looked subdued. She showed an exquisite leather pocketbook. ''Mark's present. Isn't it lovely?''

Jenny wondered if she had been expecting an engagement ring.

Luke asked to hold the baby. ''He's a little beauty.''

''And he's put on eight ounces,'' Jenny announced joyfully. ''Didn't you, Pumpkin?''

''Do you always call him Pumpkin?'' Emily asked.

''I suppose it sounds silly. It's just that Erich sounds like too much name for such a tiny little scrap. He'll have to grow into it.''

She looked up smiling. Erich looked impassive. Mark, Luke and Emily were exchanging startled glances. Of course. They'd probably seen the birth notice in the paper the day after the baby was born, the notice that listed his name as Kevin. But hadn't Erich explained?

Emily rushed to fill the awkward silence. Bending over the baby again, she said, ''I think he'll have the same coloring as the girls.''

''Oh, I'm sure he's going to be blond like Erich,'' Jenny smiled again. ''Just give him six months. We'll have a Krueger towhead.'' She took him from Luke. ''You'll look just like your daddy, won't you, Pumpkin?''

''That's what I've been saying right along,'' Erich commented.

Jenny felt the smile freeze on her face. Did he mean what she thought he meant? She looked searchingly from one face to the other. Emily looked acutely embarrassed. Luke stared straight ahead. Mark was stony-faced. She felt the anger in him. Erich was smiling warmly at the baby.

She knew with absolute certainty that Erich had not changed the name on the birth certificate.

The baby began to whimper. ''My poor little darling,'' she said. She stood up. ''If you'll excuse me, I have to . . .'' She paused, then finished quietly, ''I have to take care of Kevin.''

Long after the baby fell asleep she sat by the bassinette. She heard Erich bring the girls upstairs, his voice soft. ''Don't wake up the baby. I'll kiss Mommy good night for you. Didn't we have a wonderful Christmas?''

Jenny thought: I can't live like this.

At last she went downstairs. Erich had closed the gift boxes and stacked them neatly around the tree. He was wearing the new velvet jacket she'd ordered from Dayton's for him. The deep blue suited him. All strong colors suit him, she thought objectively.

''Jen, I'm really happy with my present. I hope you're as pleased with yours.'' He'd bought her a white mink jacket.

Without waiting for a reply, he continued to straighten the gifts, then said, ''The girls really went for those bassinettes, didn't they? You'd never guess they got anything else. And the baby. Well, he's a little too young to appreciate them but before long he'll have fun with those stuffed animals.''

''Erich, where is the baby's birth certificate?''

''It's on file in the office, dear. Why?''

''What name is on it?''

''The baby's name. Kevin.''

''You told me you'd changed that.''

''I realized it would have been a terrible mistake to change it.''

''Why?''

''Jenny, hasn't there been enough talk about us? What do you think the people around here would say if we corrected the baby's name? My God, that would give them fuel for the next ten years. Don't forget we weren't married quite nine months when he was born.''

''But *Kevin.* You called him *Kevin.*''

''I explained the reason for that. Jenny, already the talk is dying down. When people talk about the accident, they don't mention Kevin's name. They talk about Jenny Krueger's first husband, the guy who followed her to Minnesota and somehow went over the riverbank. But I can tell you this. If we changed the baby's name now, they'd be trying to figure out why for the next fifty years. And by God, then they'd remember Kevin MacPartland.''

''Erich,'' she asked fearfully, ''is there a better reason you didn't change the birth certificate? Is the baby sicker than I realize? Is it because you're saving your name for a child who will live? Tell me, Erich, please. Are you and the doctor hiding anything from me?''

''No, no, no.'' He came over to her, his eyes tender. ''Jenny, don't you see? Everything will be fine. I want you to stop worrying. The baby is getting stronger.''

There was another question she had to ask him. ''Erich, there was something you said in the delivery room, that the baby had dark red hair like the girls. Kevin had dark red hair. Erich, tell me, promise me, that you're not suggesting that Kevin was the baby's father. You can't believe that?''

''Jenny, why would I believe that?''

''Because of what you said about his hair.'' She felt her voice quivering. ''The baby's going to be the image of you. Wait and see. All his new hair is blond. But when the others were here . . . The way you picked me up when I said he'll look just like his daddy. The way you said, 'That's what I've been saying right along.' Erich, surely you can't think Kevin is the baby's father?''

She stared at him. The blue velvet gave an almost burnished look to his blond hair. She'd never really appreciated how dark his lashes and brows were. She was reminded of the paintings in the palace in Venice where generations of lean-faced, smoldering-eyed doges looked disdainfully down on the tourists. There was something of that contempt in Erich's eyes now.

His facial muscles tightened. ''Jenny, is there any end to the ways you misunderstand me? I've been good to you. I brought you and the children out of that miserable apartment to this beautiful home. I gave you jewelry and clothes and furs. You could have had anything you wanted and still you allowed Kevin MacPartland to contact you and cause a scandal. I'm sure there isn't a house in this community that doesn't discuss us over the dinner table every night. I forgive you but you have no right to be angry with me, to question every word out of my mouth. Now let's go upstairs. I think it's time I moved back in with you.''

His hands tightened on her arms. His entire body was so rigid. There was something frightening about him. Confused, she looked away.

''Erich,'' she said carefully, ''we're both very tired. We've been under a strain for a long time. I think what you should do is start painting again. Do you realize how few times you've gone to the cabin since the baby was born? Go to your own room tonight and get an early start in the morning. But bundle up; it's probably very cold there now.''

''How do you know it's cold? When did you go there?'' His voice was quick and suspicious.

''Erich, you know I've never been there.''

''Then how did you know. . . ?''

''Sshh, listen.'' From upstairs they heard a wailing.

''It's the baby.'' Jenny turned and ran up the stairs, Erich behind her. The baby's arms and legs were flailing. His face was damp. As they watched he began to suck his clenched fist.

''Oh, Erich, look, he's crying real tears.'' Tenderly she bent over and picked him up. ''There, there, Pumpkin. I know you're hungry, my precious lamb. Erich, he is getting stronger.''

From behind her, she heard the door close. Erich had left the room.

CHAPTER 30

She dreamed of a pigeon. Somehow it seemed terribly ominous. It was flying through the house and she had to catch it. It mustn't be allowed in the house. It sailed into the girls' room and she followed it. It flew frantically round and round the room. It escaped her hands and fluttered past her into the baby's room. It settled on the bassinette. She began to cry, no, no, no.

She woke up with tears drenching her face and rushed in to the baby. He was sleeping contentedly.

Erich had left a note on the kitchen table. "Taking your advice. Will be at cabin painting for a few days."

At breakfast, Tina paused over her cereal and said, "Mommy, why didn't you talk to me when you came into my room last night?"

That afternoon Rooney stopped in to visit and it was she who first realized that the baby had a fever.

She and Clyde had had Christmas dinner with Maude and Joe. "Joe's doing fine," Rooney informed Jenny. "Going down to Florida right from the hospital did wonders for him and for Maude too. Both of them that tanned and healthy. Joe gets rid of the brace next month."

"I'm so glad."

"Course Maude says she's happy to be home now. She told me Erich was real generous to them. But I guess you know that. He paid every cent of the medical bills and gave them a check for five thousand dollars beside. He wrote Maude that he felt responsible."

Jenny was stitching the last of her quilt together. She looked up. "*Responsible?*"

"I don't know what he means. But Maude told me she feels real bad that the baby hasn't been well. Says she remembers saying awful things to you."

Jenny remembered the awful things Maude had said.

"Guess Joe admitted that he'd had a pretty good hangover that morning; insists it was likely he'd mixed up the poison and oats."

"Joe said that?"

"He did. Anyhow I think Maude wanted me to give you her apologies. I know when they got back last week Joe went down and spoke to the sheriff himself. Joe's real upset about all the rumors flying around his accident. You know, because of the wild thing he said about seeing you. He said he don't know why he ever said anything like that."

Poor Joe, Jenny thought. Trying to undo irreparable harm and then making it worse by stirring it up again.

"My, Jenny, do you realize that your quilt is just about finished? Real lovely too. That took patience."

"I was glad to have it to do," she said.

"Will you hang it in the dining room near Caroline's?"

"I haven't thought about it."

She hadn't thought about very much today except the possibility that she was sleepwalking. In her dream she'd been trying to chase a pigeon out of the girls' room. But had she actually been in the room?

There were too many episodes like that now over the past few months. The next time she went in to see Dr. Elmendorf, she'd talk to him about them. Maybe she did need some counseling.

I am so afraid, she thought.

She had begun to doubt whether Erich would ever forgive her for the notoriety that she had caused. No matter how hard they both tried, it would never be right again. And no matter what Erich said, she believed that subconsciously he was not sure that the baby was his son. She couldn't live her life out with that between them.

But the baby was a Krueger and deserved the best medical attention Erich's wealth could obtain for him. After the baby had the operation and was well, if things hadn't gotten much better, she'd leave. She tried to visualize living in New York, working in the gallery, the day-care center, picking up the children, hurrying home to start dinner. It wouldn't be easy. But nothing was easy and many women managed it. And anything would be better than this terrible feeling of isolation, this sense of losing touch with reality.

Nightmares. Sleepwalking. Amnesia. Was even amnesia possible? She'd never had any trouble in the apartment in New York. She'd be bone-tired at the end of the day but always slept. She might not have had nearly enough time for the girls but now it seemed she had no time. She was so worried about the baby and Erich kept whisking Tina and Beth off on outings that she couldn't or wouldn't attend.

I want to go home, she thought. Home wasn't a place, maybe not even a house or apartment. Home was where you could close your door and be at peace.

This land. Even now. The snow falling, the wind blowing. She liked the savageness of winter. She imagined the house as she had started to arrange it. The heavy curtains down, this table at the window, the friends she'd expected to make, the parties she would have given over the holidays.

"Jenny, you look so sad," Rooney said suddenly.

She tried to smile. "It's just . . ." Her voice trailed off.

"This is the best Christmas I've had since Arden went. Just watching the children so happy and being able to help you with the baby . . ."

Jenny realized that Rooney never called the baby by name.

She held up the quilt. "Here it is, Rooney, complete."

Beth and Tina were playing with their new picture puzzles. Beth looked up. "That is very pretty, Mommy. You're a very good sewer."

Tina volunteered, "I like it better than the one on the wall. Daddy said that yours won't be as nice as the one on the wall and I thought that was mean.''

She bent her head over her book. Every line of her body suggested injury.

Jenny could not help smiling. ''Oh, Tinker, you're such an actress.'' She went over, knelt down and hugged her.

Tina returned the hug fiercely. ''Oh, Mommy.''

I've given them so little time since the baby came, Jenny thought. ''Tell you what,'' she said, ''we're going to bring Pumpkin down in a few minutes. If you two wash your hands you can have a chance to hold him.''

Rooney interrupted their squeals of delight. ''Jenny, may I get him?''

''Of course. I'll fix his cereal.''

Rooney was back downstairs in a few minutes, carefully holding the blanketed baby. She looked concerned. ''I think he has a fever.''

At five o'clock Dr. Bovitch came. ''We'd better take him to the hospital.''

''No, please.'' Jenny tried not to have her voice quiver.

The pediatrician hesitated. ''We could give it till morning,'' he said. ''Trouble is—with infants the fever can go high pretty fast. On the other hand, I'm not crazy about taking him out in the cold. All right. Let's see how he is in the morning.''

Rooney stayed and prepared supper for them. Jenny gave the baby aspirin. She was chilled herself. Was she catching cold or was she simply numb with anxiety? ''Rooney, hand me my shawl, please.''

She wrapped it around her shoulders, sheltered the baby in it as she held him.

''Oh, dear.'' Rooney's face was ashen.

''What is it, Rooney?''

''It's just that the shawl, I didn't realize when I made it that the color . . . with your dark hair . . . for just a minute it was like watching that painting of Caroline. Made me feel kind of queer.''

Clyde was coming at seven-thirty to walk Rooney home. ''He won't have me out of the house alone at night,'' Rooney confided. ''Says he doesn't like my wild talk after I've been out alone.''

''What kind of wild talk?'' Jenny asked absently. The baby was sleeping. His breathing sounded heavy.

''You know,'' Rooney said, her tone lowered to a whisper. ''Once in one of my spells, when I just spill out words, I told Clyde I've been seeing Caroline around an awful lot. Clyde got real mad.''

Jenny shivered. Rooney had seemed so well. She hadn't talked about seeing Caroline since before the baby was born.

There was a sharp knock at the door and Clyde stepped into the kitchen foyer. ''Come on, Rooney,'' he said, ''let's get started. I want my dinner.''

Rooney brought her lips to Jenny's ear. ''Oh, Jenny, you have to believe me, she's here. Caroline's come back. I can understand, can't you? She just wants to see her grandchild.''

For the next four night Jenny kept the bassinette by the side of her bed. A vaporizer circulated warm, moist air; a dim nightlight made it possible for her, between snatches of sleep, to see that the baby was covered, that he was breathing easily.

The doctor came every morning. ''Just have to watch for any signs of pneumonia,'' he said. ''In an infant a cold can go into the lungs in a few hours.''

Erich did not come back from the cabin. During the day, Jenny brought the baby down and put him in the cradle near the stove. That way she could watch him all the time and still be with Beth and Tina.

The possibility that she was sleepwalking haunted Jenny. Dear God, could she be wandering outside at night? From a distance she would look like Caroline, especially if she had the shawl wrapped around her.

If she were sleepwalking, it would explain Rooney's claims of seeing Caroline, Tina's, ''Why didn't you talk to me when you came into my room,'' Joe's absolute certainty that he had watched her get in Kevin's car.

On New Year's Eve, the doctor's smile was genuine. ''I think he's just about over it. You're a good nurse, Jenny. Now you've got to get some rest yourself. Put him back in his own room. If he doesn't look for a feeding during the night, don't wake him up.''

After she nursed the baby at ten o'clock, Jenny rolled the bassinette back. ''I'm going to miss you as my bunky, Pumpkin,'' she said. ''But it's awfully nice to have you over that cold.''

The baby's eyes, deep midnight blue, looked solemnly up at her from under long sooty lashes. The incoming blond fuzz sent silken gold lights through his dark strands of birth hair. ''Do you know you're eight weeks old?'' she asked. ''What a great big boy.''

She tied the drawstring on the long nightgown. ''Now kick all you want,'' she smiled. ''You're going to be covered in spite of yourself.''

For a long minute she held him against her, sniffing the faint scent of talcum. ''You smell so good,'' she whispered. ''Good night, Pumpkin.''

She left the sliding panel open only a crack and got into bed. The new year would begin in a few hours. A year ago tonight, Fran and some of the other people in the brownstone had stopped in. They'd known that she was bound to be feeling low; the first new year Nana hadn't been with her.

Fran had joked about Nana. ''She's probably up in heaven, leaning out the window rattling a noisemaker.''

They'd laughed together. ''It's going to be a good year for you, Jen,'' Fran had said. ''I feel it in my bones.''

Good year! When she finally got back to New York she'd tell Fran to get her bones checked. They were sending out the wrong vibes.

But the baby! He made everything else that had happened this year unimportant. I take it back, she thought quickly. It *was* a good year.

When she awakened, the sun was streaming in, a clear, cold light that warned of a frigid day outside. The small porcelain clock on the night table said five minutes of eight.

The baby had slept through the night, slept through his six o'clock feeding. She bolted out of bed, shoved the panel aside and rushed to the bassinette.

The long lashes cast tranquil shadows on the pale cheeks. A blue vein on the side of the tiny nose was dark against the translucent skin. The baby's arms were flung over his head; his tiny hands were open, the fingers spread so they resembled stars.

The baby was not breathing.

Afterward she remembered screaming, remembered running with the baby in her arms; running out in her nightgown, barefoot, across the snow to the office. Erich, Clyde, Luke and Mark were there. Mark grabbed the baby from her, putting his mouth down to the tiny lips.

"Crib death, Mrs. Krueger," Dr. Bovitch said. "He was a very sick infant. I don't know how he could have survived the operation. This is so much easier for him."

Rooney intoned over and over again, "Oh, no, oh, no!"

"Our little boy," Erich wailed. *My* little boy, she thought fiercely. You denied him your name.

"Why did God take our baby to heaven?" Tina and Beth asked.

Why indeed.

"I'd like to bury him with your mother, Erich," Jenny said. "Somehow it would be less lonesome leaving him there." Her arms ached and felt empty.

"I'm sorry, Jenny," Erich said firmly. "I can't disturb Caroline's grave."

After a Mass of the Angels, Kevin MacPartland Krueger was placed next to the three babies who had been lost in other generations. Dry-eyed, Jenny watched as the small casket was lowered. That first morning on this farm she'd looked at those tombstones and wondered how anyone could bear the grief of losing a child.

Now that grief was hers.

She began to weep. Erich put his arm around her. She shook it off.

They filed back to the house, Mark, Luke, Clyde, Emily, Rooney, Erich, herself. It was so cold. Elsa was inside. She had made sandwiches. Her eyes were red and swollen. So Elsa has feelings, Jenny thought bitterly, and then was ashamed.

Erich led them into the front parlor. Mark was beside her. "Jenny, drink this. It will warm you up.'' The brandy burned her throat. She hadn't touched liquor from the moment she knew she was pregnant. Now it didn't matter.

Numbly she sat down, sipped the brandy. It was so hard to swallow.

''You're trembling,'' Mark said.

Rooney heard him. ''I'll get your shawl.''

Not the green one, Jenny thought, not the one I wrapped the baby in. But Rooney was laying it over her shoulders, tucking it around her.

Luke's eyes were riveted on her. She knew why. She tried to shrug off the shawl.

Erich had allowed Tina and Beth to bring their bassinettes into the parlor so they could be with everyone. They looked frightened.

Beth said, ''Look, Mommy, this is the way God will cover our baby in heaven.'' Lovingly she tucked the blanket under her doll's chin.

There was absolute silence in the room.

Then Tina's voice, sweet and clear: ''And this is the way that lady''—she pointed to the painting—''covered the baby the night God took him to heaven.''

Slowly, deliberately, she opened her palms and pressed them over her doll's face.

Jenny heard a harsh, drawn-out gasp. Had it come from her own lips? Everyone was staring at the painting now, and then in a single gesture, every head turned and eyes that burned and questioned stared at her.

CHAPTER 31

''Oh, no, no.'' Rooney's voice was singsong. ''Caroline would never hurt the baby, love.'' She rushed over to Tina. ''You see Caroline always used to cup her hands on Erich's face when he was little. Like this.'' Gently she placed her palms on the doll's cheeks. ''And she would laugh and say, '*Caro, caro.*' That means dear one.''

Rooney straightened up and looked around. Now her pupils were enormous. ''Jenny, it's just like I told you. She came back. Maybe she knew the baby was sick and wanted to help.''

Erich's voice was low. ''Get her out of here, Clyde.''

Clyde grasped Rooney's arm. ''Come on. And be quiet.''

Rooney pulled away. ''Jenny, tell them how I've been seeing Caroline. Tell them I told you that. Tell them I'm not crazy.''

Jenny tried to get up from the chair. Clyde was hurting Rooney. His fingers were digging into the thin arm. But her legs wouldn't hold her up. She tried to speak but no words came. Tina's small hands over the doll's mouth and nostril. . . .

It was Luke who pried Clyde's fingers loose. "Leave her alone, man. For God sake, can't you see this has been too much for her?" His tone was soothing. "Rooney, why don't you go home and lie down? It's been a terrible day for you too."

Rooney did not seem to hear. "I've been seeing her and seeing her. Sometimes at night I sneak out after Clyde's asleep because I want to talk to her. I bet she knows where Arden went. And I see her coming into the house. Once I saw her at the window of the baby's room. The moonlight was shining on her, just as clear as day. I wish she'd talk to me sometimes. Maybe she thinks I'm afraid of her. But why would I be? If Caroline is here that means that even if Arden is dead she might be able to come back. Isn't that right?"

She pulled away from Clyde and ran over to Jenny. Sinking on her knees she put her arms around her. "That means maybe the baby will come back too. Won't that be nice? Jenny, will you let me hold him when he comes back?"

It was nearly two o'clock. Her breasts were heavy with milk. Dr. Elmendorf had bound them to stop the lactation but at the hours she'd fed the baby they still filled. They hurt, but she was glad to have a physical pain. It balanced the agony of grief. Rooney's frail body was shaking. Jenny reached out, put her arms around the thin shoulders. "He isn't coming back, Rooney," she said. "Neither is Caroline or Arden. Tina was dreaming."

"Of course she was," Mark said brusquely.

Luke and Clyde lifted Rooney up. "She needs a sedative," Luke said. "I'll drive with you to the hospital." Luke looked ill himself.

Emily and Mark stayed a little longer. Emily made halfhearted attempts to talk to Erich about his painting.

"I have an exhibit in Houston in February," Erich told her. "I'll take Jenny and the girls with me. The change will do us all good."

Mark sat next to her. There was something so quietly comforting about him. She could feel his compassion and it helped.

After he and Emily left, Jenny managed to prepare dinner for the girls and Erich. Somehow she found the strength to get the children ready for bed. Tina splashed in the tub. Jenny thought about holding the baby in the crook of her arm while she bathed him. She brushed Beth's long, thick curls. The baby was losing that dark hair. His would have been golden. She heard their prayers. "God bless Nana and our baby in heaven." She closed her eyes as waves of pain washed over her.

Downstairs Erich had brandy waiting. "Drink this, Jenny. It will help you relax." He pulled her down beside him. She did not resist. His hands ran through her hair. Once that gesture had thrilled her. "Jen, you heard the doctor. The baby wouldn't have made it through the surgery. He really was much sicker than you knew.''

She listened, waiting for the numbness to wear off. Don't try to make it easier, Erich, she thought. Nothing you can say matters.

''Jenny, I'm worried. I'll take care of you. But Emily is a gossip. By now what Tina said is going to be all over town.'' He put his arms around her. ''Thank God, Rooney is an unreliable witness and Tina is so small. Otherwise . . .''

She tried to pull away from him. His hands held her fast. His voice so soft, so hypnotically gentle. ''Jenny, I'm terribly afraid for you. Everyone has remarked how much you resemble Caroline. They're going to hear what Tina said. Oh, my darling, don't you see what they're going to say?''

Soon she would wake up and be back in the apartment. Nana would be there. ''Now, Jen, you're talking in your sleep again. You must have had a nightmare. You've got too much on your mind, dear.''

But she was not in the apartment. She was in this cold, overfurnished parlor listening to the incredible suggestion that people might think she had killed her own baby.

''The trouble is, Jen, you *have* been sleepwalking. How many times have the girls asked why you don't speak to them when you go into their room at night? It's entirely possible you were in the baby's room, maybe patting the baby's face. Tina didn't understand what she saw. You yourself told Dr. Elmendorf you've been hallucinating. He called me about that.''

''He called *you?*''

''Yes. He's quite concerned. He says you've refused to see a psychiatrist.''

Jenny stared past him at the curtains. The lace seemed weblike. Once she had taken those curtains down, blindly trying to change the stifling atmosphere of this house. Erich had put them back up.

Now the curtains seemed to be closing in on her, enmeshing her, smothering her.

Smothering. She closed her eyes against the memory of Tina's small hands covering her doll's face, pressing down.

Hallucinating. Had she imagined the face, the feeling of hair hanging over the bed? All those nights, had she been imagining that?

''Erich, I'm so confused. I don't know what reality is anymore. Even before this. But now. I've got to get away. I'll take the girls.''

''Impossible, Jenny. You're much too upset. For your sake, for their sake, you can't be alone. And don't forget. The girls are legally Kruegers. They're just as much my children as yours.''

''I'm their mother, their natural mother and guardian.''

''Jenny, please remember this. In the eyes of the law I have every bit as much right to them as you. And believe me if you ever tried to leave me, I'd get custody. Do you think any court would award them to you with your reputation in this community?''

''But they're *mine!* The baby was yours and you wouldn't give him your name. The girls are mine and you want them. Why?''

''Because I want you. No matter what you've done, no matter how sick you are, I want you. Caroline was willing to leave me but I know you, Jenny. You'd never leave your children. That's why we'll be together always. We're going to start over as of right now. I'm moving back in with you tonight.''

''No.''

''You have no choice. We'll put the past behind. I'll never mention the baby again. I'll be there to help if you start to sleepwalk. I'll take care of you. If they investigate the baby's death, I'll hire a lawyer.''

He was pulling her to her feet. Helplessly she allowed him to propel her up the stairs. ''Tomorrow we'll put the room back the old way,'' he told her. ''Just pretend the baby never was born.''

She had to humor him until she could plan. They were in the bedroom; he opened the bottom drawer of the large dresser. She knew what he was reaching for. The aqua gown. ''Wear it for me, Jen. It's been so long.''

''I can't.'' She was so afraid. His eyes were so strange. She didn't know this man who could tell her that people believed she was a murderer, tell her to forget the baby she'd buried a few hours ago.

''Yes, you can. You're very thin now. You're lovely.''

She took it from him and went into the bathroom. She changed and the nightgown did fit her again. She stared into the mirror over the sink. And understood why people thought she looked like Caroline.

Her eyes had the same sad, haunted look as those of the woman in the painting.

In the morning Erich slid out of bed quietly and began to tiptoe around the room. ''I'm awake,'' she told him. It was six o'clock. It should have been time to feed the baby.

''Try to go back to sleep, darling.'' He pulled on a heavy ski sweater. ''I'm going to the cabin. I've got to finish the paintings for the Houston exhibition. We'll go together, darling, the two of us and the girls. We'll have a wonderful time.'' He sat down on the edge of the bed. ''Oh, Jen, I love you so.''

She stared up at him.

''Tell me you love me, Jen.''

Dutifully she said, ''I love you, Erich.''

It was a bleak morning. Even by the time the girls had had breakfast, the sun was still hidden by patches of wintry clouds. The air had a chilly, dark feeling as before a storm.

She dressed Tina and Beth for a walk. Elsa was going to take down the Christmas tree and Jenny broke small branches from it.

"What are you going to do with those, Mommy?" Beth asked.

"I thought we'd put them on the baby's grave."

The fresh dirt had frozen during the night. The luminous pine needles softened the starkness of the little mound.

"Mommy, don't look so sad," Beth begged.

"I'll try not to, Mouse." They turned away. If I could only feel something, she thought. I am so empty, so terribly empty.

On the way back to the house, she saw Clyde drive into the farm road. She waited for him to find out about Rooney.

"They won't let her come home for a while," he said. "They're doing all kinds of tests and they say maybe I should put her in a special hospital for a while. I said no way. She's been a lot better since you came here, Miz Krueger. I guess I never knew how lonesome Rooney was. She's always afraid to leave the farm for long. Just in case Arden suddenly called or came back. But then lately she's been worse again. You saw."

He swallowed, fiercely blinking back tears.

"And, Miz Krueger, what Tina said, got out. The sheriff . . . he's been talking to Rooney. He had a doll out with him. Told her to show him the way Caroline used to pat the baby's face, and how Tina said the lady in the painting touched the baby. I don't know what he's up to."

I do, Jenny thought. Erich's right. Emily couldn't wait to spill that story to the people in town.

Sheriff Gunderson came out three days later. "Mrs. Krueger, I have to warn you there's been talk. I have an order to exhume your baby's body. The medical examiner wants to do an autopsy."

She stood and watched as sharp spades opened the newly frozen earth, as the small casket was loaded onto the funeral car.

She felt someone standing beside her. It was Mark. "Why torture yourself, Jenny? You shouldn't be here."

"What are they looking for?"

"They want to make sure there are no bruises or signs of pressure on the baby's face."

She thought of the long lashes throwing shadows on the pale cheeks, the tiny mouth, the blue vein on the side of his nose. The blue vein. She'd never noticed it before that morning when she'd found him.

"Did you notice any bruises on him?" she asked. Mark would have known the difference between a bruise and a vein.

"When I tried the mouth-to-mouth resuscitation I held his face pretty hard. There could be some."

"You told them that."

"Yes."

She turned to him. The wind wasn't strong but every stir of air sent fresh shivers through her. "You told them that to protect me. It wasn't necessary."

''I told them the truth,'' he said.

The hearse drove onto the dirt road. ''Come back to the house,'' Mark urged.

She tried to analyze her feelings as she trudged by his side through the fresh fallen snow. He was so tall. She'd never realized how used she'd become to Erich's relatively small stature. Kevin had been tall, over six feet. Mark. What would he be? Six four or five?

She had a headache. Her breasts were burning. Why didn't the milk stop flowing? It wasn't needed. She could feel her blouse getting damp. If Erich was in the house he'd be mortified. He hated untidiness. He was so neat. And so private. If he hadn't married her, the Krueger name wouldn't have been dragged through the mud.

Erich believed she had scandalized his name and still he claimed he loved her. He liked her to look like his mother. That's why he always asked her to wear the aqua gown. Maybe when she was sleepwalking she tried to look like his mother to please him.

''I guess I'm trying,'' she said. Her voice startled her. She didn't know she'd spoken aloud.

''What did you say, Jenny? *Jenny!*''

She was falling; she could not stop herself from falling. But something stopped her just as her hair brushed the snow.

''Jenny!'' Mark was holding her, was carrying her. She hoped she wasn't too heavy.

''Jenny, you're burning up.''

Maybe that was why she couldn't keep her thoughts straight. It wasn't just the house. Oh, God, how she hated the house.

She was riding in a car. Erich was holding her. She remembered this car. It was Mark's station wagon. He had books in it.

''Shock, milk fever,'' Dr. Elmendorf said. ''We'll keep her here.''

It was so nice to float away, so nice to wear one of those rough hospital gowns. She hated the aqua gown.

Erich was in and out of her room. ''Beth and Tina are fine. They send their love.''

Finally Mark brought the message she needed to have. ''The baby is back in the cemetery. They won't disturb him again.''

''Thank you.''

His fingers closing over her hands. ''Oh, Jenny.''

That night she had two cups of tea, a piece of toast.

''Good to see you feeling better, Mrs. Krueger.'' The nurse was genuinely kind. Why was it that kindness made her want to weep? She used to take for granted that people liked her.

The fever was low-grade persistent. ''I won't allow you to go home until we've licked it,'' Dr. Elmendorf insisted.

She cried a lot. Often when she'd dozed off, she'd wake up to find her cheeks wet with tears.

Dr. Elmendorf said, "While you're here, I'd like Dr. Philstrom to have a few talks with you."

Dr. Philstrom was a psychiatrist.

He sat by her bed, a tidy little man who looked like a bank clerk. "I understand you had a series of pretty bad nightmares."

They all wanted to prove that she was crazy. "I don't have them anymore."

And it was true. In the hospital she was starting the sleep through the night. Each day she began to feel stronger, more like herself. She realized she was joking with the nurse in the morning.

The afternoon was the hardest. She didn't want to see Erich. The sound of his footsteps in the hall made her hands clammy.

He brought the girls to see her. They weren't allowed inside the hospital but she stood at the window and waved to them. Somehow they seemed so forlorn, waving back up at her.

That night she ate a full dinner. She had to get her strength back. There was nothing to hold her on Krueger Farm any longer. There was no way she and Erich could recapture what they once had. She could plan to get away. And she knew how she could manage it. On the trip to Houston. Somehow on that trip, she and Beth and Tina would leave Erich and get on a plane for New York. Erich might be able to get custody of the children in Minnesota but New York would never give it to him.

She could sell Nana's locket to get some money. A jeweler had offered Nana eleven hundred dollars for it a few years ago. If she got anything like that, it would be enough to buy airline tickets and tide her over until she got a job.

Away from Caroline's house, Caroline's portrait, Caroline's bed, Caroline's nightgown, Caroline's *son,* she'd be herself again—able to think calmly, to try to capture all the awful thoughts that kept rising almost to the surface of her mind and then slipping away. There were so many of them—so many impressions that seemed to be eluding her.

Jenny fell asleep, the hint of a smile on her lips, her cheeks pillowed in her hands.

The next day she phoned Fran. Oh, blessed, blessed freedom, knowing no one would pick up the extension in the office.

"Jenny, you haven't answered my letters. I thought you'd jettisoned me into outer space."

She didn't bother to explain that she'd never received them. "Fran, I need you." As quickly as possible she explained: "I have to get out of here."

Fran's usual matter-of-fact laughter disappeared. "It's been bad, Jenny. I can hear it in your voice."

Later she could tell Fran everything. Now she simply agreed, "It's been bad."

"Trust me. I'll get back to you."

''Call after eight o'clock. That's when visiting hours end.''

Fran called at ten after seven the next night. The minute the phone rang, Jenny knew what had happened. Fran had not allowed for the time difference. It was ten after eight in New York. Erich was sitting by her bed. His eyebrows raised as he handed her the receiver. Fran's voice was vibrant, carrying. ''I've got great plans!''

''Fran, how good to hear from you.'' Turning to him: ''Erich, it's Fran, say hello.''

Fran caught on. ''Erich, how are you? So sorry to hear Jenny hasn't been well.''

After they hung up, Erich's question: ''What plans, Jenny?''

CHAPTER 32

She went home on the last day in January. Beth and Tina seemed like strangers, curiously quiet, curiously petulant. ''You're always gone, Mommy.''

She'd spent more time with them in the evenings and weekends in New York than she had here this past year.

How much did Erich suspect about Fran's calls? She'd been evasive. ''I just realized I hadn't spoken to Fran in ages and picked up the phone. Wasn't it dear of her to call me back?''

She'd called Fran after Erich left the hospital that night. Fran had exulted: ''I have a friend who runs a nursery school near Red Bank, New Jersey. It's marvelous and goes right through kindergarten. I told her you can teach music and art and she has a job for you if you want it. She's looking for an apartment for you.''

Jenny bided her time.

Erich was preparing for the Houston exhibition. He began bringing in paintings from the cabin.

''I call this one *The Provider,*'' he said, holding up an oil on canvas in tones of blue and green. High on the branches of an elm, a nest could be seen. The mother bird was flying toward the tree, a worm in its beak. The leaves sheltered the nest so it was impossible to see the baby birds. But somehow the viewer sensed their presence.

''The idea for that painting came to me that first night on Second Avenue, when I came on you carrying the girls,'' Erich said. ''You had a purposeful look on your face and you could just tell you were anxious to get the kids home and fed.''

His tone was affectionate. He put his arm around her. ''How do you like it?''

"It's beautiful."

The one time she was not nervous with Erich was when she studied his work. This was the man with whom she had fallen in love, the artist whose wondrous talent at once could capture the simplicity of daily life and the complicated emotions that attended that simplicity.

The trees in the background. She recognized the line of Norwegian pines that grew near the graveyard. "Erich, you just finished this painting?"

"Yes, darling"

She pointed. "But that tree is gone. You had most of the elms near the cemetery taken down because of the Dutch elm disease last spring."

"I started a painting using that tree in the background but couldn't make it express what I wanted to say. Then one day I saw a bird flying with food for its young and thought of you. You inspire everything I do, Jenny."

In the beginning, a statement like that would have melted her heart. Now it only caused her fear. Invariably it was followed by a remark that would reduce her to trembling nerves for the rest of the day.

The remark wasn't long in coming. Erich covered the painting. "I'm sending thirty canvases. The shippers will pick them up in the morning. Will you be here to make sure they take them all?"

"Of course I'll be here. Where else would I be?"

"Don't be edgy, Jenny. I thought Mark might try to see you before he goes."

"What do you mean?"

"Luke had a heart attack just after he got back to Florida. But that doesn't give him the right to try to break up our marriage."

"Erich, what are you talking about?"

"Luke called me last Thursday. He's out of the hospital. He suggested that you and the girls visit him in Florida. Mark is leaving today to spend a week with him. Luke had the nerve to think I'd let you travel down there with Mark."

"How kind of him." Jenny knew the offer had been refused.

"It wasn't kind of him. Luke just wanted to get you down there away from me. I told him so."

"Erich!"

"Don't be surprised, Jenny. Why do you think Mark and Emily have stopped seeing each other?"

"Have they stopped?"

"Jenny, why are you always so blind? Mark told Emily he realized he wasn't interested in getting married and that it wasn't fair to take her time."

"I didn't know that."

"A man doesn't do that unless he has some other woman in mind."

"Not necessarily."

''Mark's crazy about you, Jenny. If it weren't for him the sheriff would have ordered an inquest into the baby's death. You know that, don't you?''

''No, I don't.'' All the hard-won calm of the hospital was deserting her. Her mouth was dry; her hands were sweaty. She felt herself trembling. ''Erich, what are you saying?''

''I'm saying that there was a bruise near the baby's right nostril. The coroner said that it probably preceded death. Mark insisted that he was rough when he was trying to resuscitate the baby.''

The memory of Mark holding the tiny form flashed through her mind.

Erich was standing next to her now, his lips against her ear. ''Mark knows. You know. I know. The baby was bruised, Jenny.''

''What are you telling me?''

''Nothing, darling. I'm just warning you. We both know how delicate the baby's skin was. That last night the way he was flailing his fists. He probably bruised himself. But Mark lied. He's just like his father. Everyone knew the way Luke felt about Caroline. Even now whenever he's here he sits in the wing chair so he can see her portrait. He was driving Caroline to the airport that last day. All she had to do was snap her fingers and he was there.

''And now Mark thinks he can pull the same thing. Well he can't. I called Lars Ivanson, the veterinarian from Hennepin Grove. He'll start caring for my animals. Mark Garrett will never set foot on this farm again.''

''Erich, you can't mean that.''

''Oh, but I can. I know you didn't mean to but you encouraged him, Jenny. I saw it. How many times did he come to the hospital?''

''He came twice. Once to tell me that the baby was back in his grave. Once to bring fruit Luke had ordered for me from Florida. Erich, don't you see? You read so much into the simplest, most innocent situation. Where does it end?''

She did not wait for a reply. She walked out of the room and opened the door onto the west porch. The last of the sun was slipping behind the woods. The evening wind was making Caroline's swing rock. No wonder Caroline had sat out here. She had been driven from the house too.

That night Erich came into the bedroom shortly after her. She held herself rigid, not wanting to be close to him. But he simply turned on his side and went to sleep. She felt her body go limp with relief.

She would not see Mark again. By the time he returned from Florida she would be in New Jersey. Was Erich right? Had she been sending out some kind of signal to Mark? Or was it simply that he and Emily had decided they weren't right for each other and Erich, always suspicious, was reading more into it?

For once, she thought, Erich may be right.

* * *

The next morning she prepared a list of odds and ends she needed for the trip. She expected Erich to argue about her requesting the car but he was unexpectedly indifferent. ''But leave the girls with Elsa,'' he told her.

After he left for the cabin she circled a jewelry store listed in the classified ad section that advertised HIGHEST PRICE$ PAID FOR YOUR GOLD. It was in a shopping center two towns away. She called and described Nana's locket. Yes, they'd be interested in buying it. Immediately she phoned Fran. Fran wasn't home but her recorder was on. She left a message. ''We'll be in New York on the seventh or eighth. Don't phone here.''

While the children napped she rushed to the jewelry store.

She was offered eight hundred dollars for the locket. It wasn't enough but she had no choice.

She bought makeup and underwear and panty hose with the credit card Erich had given her. She made a point of showing the things to him.

Their first wedding anniversary was February third. ''Why don't we celebrate in Houston, darling?'' Erich asked. ''I'll give you your present there.''

''That will be fine.'' She wasn't a good enough actress to keep up the farce of celebrating this marriage. But, oh, God, soon, soon it would be over. The anticipation put a sparkle in her eye that had not been there in months. Tina and Beth responded to it. They had become so quiet. Now they brightened as she chatted with them. ''Do you remember when we were on the plane and had that lovely ride? We're going on a plane again to a big city.''

Erich came in. ''What are you talking about?''

''I'm telling them about our trip to Houston, what fun it will be.''

''You're smiling, Jenny. Do you know how long it's been since you looked happy?''

''Too long.''

''Tina, Beth, come on with Daddy to the store. I'll buy you ice cream.''

Beth put her hand on Jenny's arm. ''I want to stay with Mommy.''

''I do too,'' Tina said positively.

''Then I won't go,'' Erich said.

He seemed unwilling to leave her alone with the children.

On the night of the fifth she packed. She only took what would appear reasonable for three days. ''What fur should I take, my coat or jacket?'' she asked Erich. ''What's the weather like in Houston?''

''The jacket would be enough, I think. Why are you so nervous, Jenny?''

''I'm not nervous. It's just that I'm out of the habit of traveling. Will I need a long dress?''

''Maybe one. That taffeta skirt and blouse would do. Wear your locket with it.''

Was there an edge in his voice; was he toying with her? She tried to sound natural. ''That's a good idea.''

They had a two o'clock flight from Minneapolis. ''I've asked Joe to drive us to the airport,'' Erich said.

''Joe!''

''Yes, he's able to start working again. I'm going to rehire him.''

''But, Erich, after all that happened.''

''Jenny, we've put all that behind us.''

''Erich, after all the gossip you propose to rehire him!'' She bit her lip. What difference who was here?

Rooney would be coming back from the hospital around the fourteenth. They had persuaded Clyde to let her stay a full six weeks. Jenny wished she could say good-bye to her. Maybe she could write and have Fran mail the letter for her from some city on one of her flights. There was nothing else she could do.

At last it was time to go. The girls were dressed in their velvet coats and matching hats. Jenny's heart surged. I'm going to take them to the Village for linguine the night we get to New York, she decided.

From the bedroom window she could barely see a corner of the cemetery. After breakfast she'd slipped over to the baby's grave to say good-bye.

Erich had packed the car. ''I'll get Joe,'' he told her. ''Come with me, girls. Give Mommy a chance to finish dressing.''

''I am finished,'' she said. ''Hold a minute. I'll go with you.''

He seemed not to have heard. ''Hurry up, Mommy,'' Beth called as she and Tina clattered down the stairs behind Erich. Jenny shrugged. Just as well to have ten minutes to be sure she had everything. The locket money was in the inside jacket pocket of the suit she had packed.

On her way downstairs she glanced into the girls' room. Elsa had made the beds and straightened the room. Now it seemed inordinately neat, with a quality of emptiness as though it sensed that the girls would not be returning.

Had Erich sensed the same thing?

Suddenly troubled, Jenny ran down the stairs, pulling on her jacket. Erich should be back any minute.

Ten minutes later, she went out on the porch. She was getting so warm. Surely he'd be along any second now? He always left so much time to get to the airport. She stared at the road, straining to see the first sign of the car coming.

At the end of half an hour, she phoned the Ekers'. Her fingers fumbled with the dial. Twice she had to break the connection and start again.

Maude answered. ''What do you mean have they left yet? I saw Erich drive past here over forty minutes ago with the girls in the car. . . . Joe? Joe wasn't driving them to the airport. Where did you get that idea?''

Erich had gone without her. Taken the girls and gone without her. The money was in the luggage he'd taken. Somehow he had guessed her plans.

She phoned the hotel in Houston. "I want to leave a message for Erich Krueger. Tell him to call his wife as soon as he arrives."

The reservation clerk's hearty Texan voice: "There must be a misunderstanding. Those reservations were cancelled nearly two weeks ago."

At two o'clock Elsa came in to her. "Good-bye, Mrs. Krueger."

Jenny was sitting in the parlor, studying Caroline's painting. She did not turn her head. "Good-bye, Elsa."

Elsa did not go at once. Her long frame hovered in the doorway. "I'm sorry to leave you."

"Leave me?" Yanked from lethargy, Jenny jumped up. "What do you mean?"

"Mr. Krueger said that he and the girls would be going away. He said he'd let me know when to come back."

"When did he tell you that, Elsa?"

"This morning, when he was getting in the car. Are you staying here alone?"

There was a curious mixture of emotion in the stolid face. Ever since the baby's death Jenny had felt a compassion in Elsa that she would not have expected. "I guess I am," she said quietly.

For hours after Elsa left, she sat in the parlor waiting. Waiting for what? A phone call. Erich would phone. She was certain of that.

How would she handle the call? Admit she'd been planning to leave him? He already knew that. She was sure of it. Promise to stay with him? He wouldn't trust the promise.

Where had he taken the girls?

The room grew dark. She should turn on some lamps. But somehow the effort was too great. The moon came up. It shone in through the lace of the curtains, throwing a weblike beam on the painting.

Finally Jenny went into the kitchen, made coffee, sat by the telephone. At nine o'clock it began to ring. Her hand trembled so she could barely pick up the receiver. "Hello." Her voice was so low she wondered if it could be heard.

"Mommy!" Beth sounded so far away. "Why didn't you want to come with us today? You promised."

"Bethie, where are you?"

The sound of the phone being moved.

Beth's voice changing to a protest. "I want to talk to Mommy."

Tina interrupted. "Mommy, we didn't go for a plane ride and you said we would."

"Tina, where are you?"

"Hello, darling." Erich's voice was warmly solicitous. Tina and Beth were wailing in the background.

"Erich, where are you? Why did you do this?"

"Why did I do what, darling? Prevent you from taking my children from me? Keep them from danger?"

"Danger? What are you talking about?"

"Jenny, I told you I'd take care of you. I mean it. But I'll never let you leave me and take my girls away."

"I won't, Erich. Bring them home."

"That's not good enough. Jenny, go over to the desk. Get writing paper and a pen. I'll hold on."

The girls were still crying. But she could hear something else. Road sounds. A truck in gear. He must be calling from a phone booth on a highway. "*Erich, where are you?*"

"I said get paper and pen. I'll dictate. You write. Hurry up, Jenny."

The Edwardian desk was held closed by a large gold key. As she tried to turn it, she pulled it out and dropped it. Awkwardly she bent down, scooped it up. The sudden rush of blood to her head made her dizzy. Tripping in her rush to return to the phone, she had to steady herself against the wall.

"I'm ready, Erich."

"It's a letter to me. *Dear Erich* . . ."

Wedging the receiver between her shoulder and ear, she scrawled the two words.

He spoke slowly:

> "I realize I am very ill. I know I sleepwalk constantly. I think I do terrible things that I can't remember. I lied when I said I didn't get in the car with Kevin. I asked him to come down here so I could persuade him to leave us alone. I didn't mean to hit him so hard."

Mechanically she was writing, anxious not to make him angry. The meaning of the words filtered through.

"Erich, I won't write that. That's not true."

"Let me finish. Just listen." He spoke rapidly now.

> "Joe was threatening to tell me he saw me get in the car. I couldn't let him talk. I dreamed I mixed the poison with the oats. But I know it wasn't a dream. I thought you would accept the baby but you knew it wasn't yours. I thought it would be better for our marriage if the baby didn't live. He was taking all my attention. Tina saw me go in to the baby. She saw me press my hands on his face. Erich, promise you will never trust me alone with the children. I am not responsible for what I do."

The pen dropped from her fingers. "*No!*"

''When you write and sign that statement, Jenny, I'll come back. I'll put it in the safe. No one will ever know about it.''

''Erich, please. You can't mean this?''

''Jenny, I can be gone months at a time, years if necessary. You know that. I'll call you in a week or two. Think it over.''

''I won't.''

''Jenny, I know what you've done.'' His voice became warm. ''We love each other, Jenny. We both know it. But I can't risk losing you and I can't risk the girls with you.''

The phone clicked. She stared into it, stared at the crumbled paper in her hand.

''Oh, God,'' she said, ''please help me. I don't know what to do.''

She called Fran. ''We're not coming.''

''Jenny, why not? What's wrong?'' The connection was poor. Even Fran's normally strong voice sounded so remote.

''Erich's taken the girls on a trip. I'm not sure when they'll be back.''

''Jenny, do you want me to come out? I've got four days off.''

Erich would be furious if Fran came. It was the phone call from Fran in the hospital that had alerted him to her plans.

''No, Fran, don't come. Don't even call. Just pray for me. Please.''

She could not sleep in the master bedroom. She could not sleep anywhere upstairs: the long dark hallway, the closed doors, the girls' room across from the master bedroom, the room where the baby had slept those few short weeks.

Instead she lay down on the couch by the iron stove and covered herself with the shawl Rooney had made. The heat automatically went off at ten. She decided to make a fire in the stove. The wood was in the cradle. The cradle moved as she touched it. Oh, Pumpkin, she mourned, remembering the solemn eyes that had gazed steadily back at her, the small fist that had curled around her finger.

She could not write that letter. The next time Erich had an outburst of jealousy he might give it to the sheriff. How long would he stay away?

She heard the clock strike one . . . two . . . three . . . Sometime after that she dozed off. A sound awakened her. The house creaking and groaning as it settled. No, she was hearing footsteps. Someone was walking upstairs.

She had to know. Slowly, step by step, she made herself go up the stairs. She clutched the shawl around her against the chill. The hallway was empty. She made herself go into the master bedroom, switch on a lamp. There was no one there.

Erich's old room. The door was open a crack. Hadn't it been closed? She went into it, flipped on the overhead light. No one.

And yet, there was something, a feeling of presence. What was it? The pine scent. Was it stronger again? She couldn't be sure.

She walked over to the window. She needed to open it, to breathe fresh air. Her hands on the sill, she looked down.

A figure was standing outside in the yard, the figure of a man gazing up at the house. The moonlight flickered on his face. It was Clyde. What was he doing there? She waved to him.

He turned and ran.

CHAPTER 33

For the rest of the night she lay on the couch, listening.

Sometimes she fancied she heard sounds, footsteps, a door closing. Imagination. All of it.

At six o'clock she got up and realized she hadn't undressed. The printed silk suit she'd planned to wear on the trip was hopelessly wrinkled. No wonder I couldn't sleep, she thought.

A long, hot shower cleared some of the numbing fatigue. With the heavy bath towel wrapped around her she went into the bedroom and opened the drawer. A faded pair of jeans were there, a pair she used to wear in New York. She put them on and rummaged until she found one of her old sweaters. Erich had wanted her to give everything away. But she'd hung onto a few things. It was important to wear something of her own now, something she'd bought herself. She remembered how badly dressed she'd felt that day she met Erich. She'd been wearing that cheap sweater Kevin gave her and Nana's gold locket.

She'd come here with that one piece of jewelry of her own and the girls. Now she didn't have Nana's locket and Erich had the girls.

Jenny stared at the dark oak floor. Something was shining on it, just outside the closet. She bent down and picked it up. It was a scrap of mink. She yanked open the closet door. The mink coat was half off the hanger. One sleeve drooped raggedly around the hem. What was the matter? Jenny went to adjust it, then pulled back. Her fingers had slid through to the skin beneath the fur at the collar line. Bits of fur clung to her fingers.

The coat had been slashed to ribbons.

At ten o'clock she went over to the office. Clyde was sitting at the large desk, the one Erich always used. "I always base here when Erich is going to be gone for a spell. Makes it easier." Clyde looked older. The heavy wrinkles around his eyes were more pronounced. She waited for him to explain why he'd been looking up at the house in the middle of the night. But he said nothing.

"How long is Erich planning to be gone?" she asked.

"He didn't say for sure, Miz Krueger."

"Clyde, why were you outside the house last night?"

"You saw me?"

"Yes, of course."

"Then you saw her too?"

"Her?"

Clyde burst out: "Miz Krueger, maybe Rooney ain't so crazy after all. You know she keeps saying she sees Caroline? Last night I couldn't sleep. Knowing they still don't want to let Rooney home more'n a few days at a time, wondering if I'm doing the right thing by her; anyhow I got up. And you know, Miz Krueger, how you can see a piece of the cemetery from our window? Well, I saw something moving there. And I went out."

Clyde's face became unnaturally pale. "Miz Krueger, I *saw Caroline.* Just like Rooney's been saying. She was walking from the cemetery to the house. I followed her. That hair, that cape she always wore. She went in the back door. I tried it after her but it was locked. I wasn't carrying my keys.

"I walked around and just waited. In a little while I saw the light go on in the master bedroom, then the light in Erich's old room. Then she came to the window and looked out and waved at me."

"Clyde, *I* was at the window. *I* waved at you."

"Oh, Jesus," Clyde whispered. "Rooney's been saying she sees Caroline. Tina talks about the lady in the painting. I think I'm following Caroline. Oh, Jesus"—he stared at her, horror in his face—"and all the time, just like Erich said, it's you we've been seeing."

"It wasn't me, Clyde," she protested. "I went upstairs because I heard someone walking around." She stopped, repelled by the disbelief in his face. She fled back to the house. Was Clyde right? Had she been walking near the graveyard? She'd been dreaming about the baby. And this morning she'd been thinking how much she hated the clothes Erich had bought her. Had she dreamed that too and then slashed the coat? Maybe she hadn't heard anyone after all. Maybe she'd just been sleepwalking and woke up when she was upstairs.

She was the lady Tina saw, the lady in the painting.

She made coffee, drank it scalding hot. She had not eaten since yesterday morning. She toasted an English muffin, forced herself to nibble on it.

Clyde would tell the doctors that he'd seen the women he thought was Caroline. He'd say that he followed her to the house and I admitted I waved to him.

Erich would come back and take care of her. She'd sign that statement and Erich would take care of her. For hours she sat at the kitchen table, then went to the desk and got the box of writing paper. Carefully she wrote, trying to remember Erich's exact words. She'd tell about last night too. She wrote:

And last night I must have been sleepwalking again. Clyde saw me. I walked in from the cemetery. I guess I went to the baby's grave. I woke up in the bedroom and saw Clyde from the window. I waved to him.

Clyde had been standing out there, standing in the ice-crusted snow. The snow.

She'd been in her stocking feet. If she'd been outside her feet would have been wet. The boots she'd been planning to wear on the trip were by the couch, still freshly polished. They hadn't been worn outside.

She might have imagined the draft of cold air, imagined the footsteps, forgotten about sleepwalking. But if she'd been out by the cemetery, her feet would have gotten wet, her stockings would have been stained.

Slowly she tore up the letter, tore it till it scattered in tiny pieces. Dispassionately she watched the pieces scatter around the kitchen. For the first time since Erich had gone, the sense of hopelessness began to lift.

She hadn't been outside. But Rooney had seen Caroline. Tina had seen her. Clyde had seen her. She, Jenny, had heard her upstairs last night. Caroline had slashed the mink coat. Maybe she was angry with Jenny for causing Erich so much trouble. Maybe she was still upstairs. *She had come back.*

Jenny got up. "Caroline," she called. "Caroline." She could hear her voice getting higher. Maybe Caroline couldn't hear her. Step by step she ascended the stairs. The master bedroom was empty. She detected the faint scent of pine that was always there. She reached into the crystal bowl, brought out three small cakes, left them on the pillow.

The attic. Perhaps she was in the attic. That's where she might have gone last night. "Caroline," Jenny called, trying to sound coaxing, "don't be afraid of me. Please come. You have to help me get the girls."

The attic was nearly dark. She walked up and down it. Caroline's vanity case with her ticket and appointment book. Where was the rest of her luggage? Why did Caroline keep coming back to the house? She had been so anxious to get away.

"Caroline," Jenny called softly, "please talk to me."

The bassinette was in the corner, covered now with a sheet. Jenny walked over to it, touched it tenderly, began to rock it. "My little love," she whispered. "Oh, little love."

Something was sliding across the sheet, something slipping toward her hand. A delicate gold chain, a heart-shaped pendant, the filigree workmanship like spun-gold thread, the center diamond that flashed in the dusk.

Jenny closed her hand over Nana's locket.

* * *

"*Nana.*" Saying the name aloud was like a drenching of cold water. What would Nana think of her, standing here, trying to talk to a dead woman?

The attic seemed intolerably confining. Clasping her hand over the locket she ran downstairs to the second floor, down to the main floor, into the kitchen. I am going mad, she thought. Aghast, she remembered calling Caroline's name.

Think about what Nana would tell her to do.

Everything looks better over a cup of tea, Jenny. Mechanically she put on the kettle.

What did you eat today, Jen? It's not good this business of skipping meals.

She went to the refrigerator, pulled out sandwich makings. A BLT down, she thought, and managed a smile.

As she ate, she tried to picture telling Nana about last night. "Clyde said he saw me but my feet weren't wet. Could it have been Caroline?"

She could just hear Nana's reaction. *There are no such things as ghosts, Jen. When you're dead, you're dead.*

Then how did the locket get upstairs?

Find out.

The telephone book was in the drawer under the wall phone. Holding the sandwich, Jenny went over and got it. She flipped the classified section to JEWELRY, BOUGHT AND SOLD. The jeweler to whom she'd sold the locket. She'd circled his ad with Magic Marker.

She dialed the number, asked to speak to the manager. Quickly she explained: "I'm Mrs. Krueger. I sold a locket to you last week. I think I'd like to buy it back."

"Mrs. Krueger, I wish you'd stop wasting my time. Your husband came in and told me you had no right to sell a family piece. I let him buy it for just what I paid you."

"*My husband!*"

"Yes, he came not twenty minutes after you sold it to me." The line went dead.

Jenny stared into the phone. Erich had suspected her. He had followed her that afternoon, probably in one of the farm vehicles. But how had the locket gotten to the attic?

She went to the desk, got out a pad of lined paper. One hour ago she'd planned to write the statement Erich had demanded. Now there was something else she needed to see in black and white.

She settled at the kitchen table. On the first line she wrote, *There are no ghosts.* On the second: *I could not have been outside last night.* One more, she thought. The next line she printed in caps: *I AM NOT A VIOLENT PERSON.*

Begin at the beginning, she thought. Write everything down. All the trouble began with that first phone call from Kevin. . . .

* * *

Clyde did not come near the house. The third day she went into the office. It was the tenth of February. Clyde was on the phone talking to a dealer. She sat watching him. When Erich was around, Clyde tended to fade into the background. With Erich gone, his voice took on a new note of authority. She listened as he arranged the sale of a two-year-old bull for over one hundred thousand dollars.

When he hung up, he looked at her warily. Obviously he was remembering their last conversation.

"Clyde, don't you have to consult with Erich when you sell a bull for that kind of money?"

"Miz Krueger, when Erich is here, he gets into the business as much as he wants. But the fact is he's never been much interested in running this farm or the limeworks."

"I see. Clyde, I've been doing a lot of thinking. Tell me. Where was Rooney Wednesday night when you thought you saw Caroline?"

"What do you mean, where was Rooney?"

"Just that. I called the hospital and spoke to Dr. Philstrom. He's the psychiatrist who came in to see me."

"I know who he is. He's Rooney's doctor."

"That's right. You didn't tell me Rooney had an overnight pass on Wednesday night."

"Wednesday night Rooney was in the hospital."

"No, she wasn't. She was staying with Maude Ekers. It was Maude's birthday. You were supposed to go to a cattle auction and you'd given permission for Maude to pick up Rooney. Rooney thought you were in St. Cloud."

"I was. I got back home round midnight. I'd forgotten Rooney was going to Maude's."

"Clyde, isn't it possible Rooney slipped out of Maude's house and was walking around on the farm?"

"No, it ain't."

"Clyde, she often walks around at night. You know that. Isn't it possible you saw her with a blanket wrapped around her, a blanket that might seem like a cape from a distance? Think of Rooney with her hair down."

"Rooney ain't worn her hair out of a bun for twenty years, 'cept of course . . ." He hesitated.

"Except when?"

" 'cept at night."

"Clyde, don't you see what I'm trying to tell you? Just one more question. Did Erich put a gold locket in the safe or give it to you to put there?"

"He put it in himself. He said you kept mislaying it and didn't want it lost."

"Did you tell Rooney that?"

''I might a mentioned it, just to talk, just to pass the time of day.''

''Clyde, Rooney knows the combination of this safe, doesn't she?''

He frowned, a worried frown. ''She might.''

''And she's home on passes more than you've admitted?''

''She's been home some.''

''And it's possible she was wandering around here Wednesday night. Clyde, open the safe. Show me my locket.''

Silently he obeyed. His finger fumbled as he worked the combination. The door swung open. He reached in, pulled out a small strongbox and opened it expectantly. Then he held it up as though hoping that a stronger light would reveal what he was seeking. Finally he said, his voice unnaturally soft, ''The locket ain't here.''

Two nights later, Erich phoned. ''Jenny!'' There was a singsong, teasing quality in his voice.

''*Erich! Erich!*''

''Where are you, Jen?''

''I'm downstairs, on the couch.'' She looked at the clock. It was after eleven. She had dozed off.

''Why?''

''It's lonesome upstairs, Erich.'' She wanted to tell him what she suspected about Rooney.

''Jenny.'' The anger in his voice bolted her awake. ''I want you where you belong in our room, in our bed. I want you to wear the special nightgown. Do you hear me?''

''Erich, please. Tina. Beth. How are they?''

''They're fine. Read the letter to me.''

''Erich, I found out something. Maybe you've been *wrong.*'' Too late she tried to call back the words. ''I mean, Erich, maybe we've both just not understood . . .''

''You haven't written the letter. . . .''

''I started to. But Erich what you think isn't true. I'm sure of that now.''

The connection broke.

Jenny rang the bell at Maude Ekers' kitchen door. How many months had it been since she'd been here? Since Maude told her to leave Joe alone?

Maude had been right to worry about Joe.

She was about to ring the bell again when the door opened. Joe was there, a much thinner Joe, the boyish face matured by tired lines around his eyes.

''Joe!''

He held his hands out. Impulsively she grasped them; with a rush of affection she kissed his cheek. ''Joe.''

"Jenny, I mean, Mrs. Krueger . . ." Awkwardly he stood aside to let her pass.

"Is your mother here?"

"She's working. I'm by myself."

"I'm just as glad. I have to talk to you. I've wanted to talk to you so much but you know . . ."

"I know, Jenny. I've caused you so much trouble. I'd like to go down on my knees for what I said the morning of the accident. I guess everyone thought I was saying that you . . . well, you'd hurt me. Like I told the sheriff I didn't mean that at all. I just meant, I thought I was dying and I was worried about telling you I'd seen you that night."

She took the seat across the kitchen table from him.

"Joe, so you mean you don't think you saw me that night?"

"Just like I tried to explain to the sheriff and like I told Mr. Krueger last week . . . there was something always bothering me about that night."

"Bothering you?"

"It's the way you move. You're so graceful, Jenny. You have such a quick, light step, like a deer. Whoever came down the porch that night walked *different.* It's hard to explain. And she was sort of leaning forward, so her hair was almost covering her face. You always stand so straight. . . ."

"Joe, do you think you might have seen Rooney wearing my coat that night?"

Joe looked puzzled. "How could that be? The reason I was standing there is because I saw Rooney on the path leading to the house and I didn't want to bump into her. Rooney was there all right but somebody else got in that car."

Jenny rubbed her hand over her forehead. These last few days she'd come to believe that Rooney was the key to everything that had happened. Rooney could let herself in and out of the house so silently. Rooney could even have overheard Erich and her talking about Kevin. Rooney could have made the phone call. Rooney knew about the panel between the bedrooms. Everything fit into place if Rooney, wearing her coat, had met Kevin that night.

Then who was wearing that coat? Who had arranged the meeting?

She didn't know.

But at least Joe had verified that he believed she, Jenny, was not that person.

She got up to go. There was no point in being here when Maude came home. Maude would be horrified. She tried to make herself smile. "Joe, I'm so glad to have seen you. We've missed you. It's good news that you'll be working for us again."

"I sure was glad when Mr. Krueger offered me the job. And like I say, I told him what I just told you."

"What did Erich say?"

''He told me I should keep my mouth shut, that I'd only start trouble raking up that story. And I swore I wouldn't mention it again to a soul. But of course he never meant I couldn't tell you.''

She made a business of pulling on her gloves. She mustn't let him see how shattered she was. *Erich had demanded that she sign that statement, saying she got in the car with Kevin, even after Joe told him he was sure someone else was wearing her coat.*

She had to think it through.

''Jenny, I guess I had an awful crush on you. I think I made it hard for you with Mr. Krueger.''

''Joe, it's all right.''

''But I have to tell you. Like I told Maw, it's just that you're the kind of person I want to find when I get serious about a girl. I explained that to Maw. She was so worried because she always said my uncle would have had such a different life if it wasn't for Caroline. But even that's working out. My uncle hasn't had a drop since my accident and they're getting together again.''

''Who's getting together again?''

''My uncle was keeping company at the time of the accident. When John Krueger told everybody Uncle Josh had been so careless 'cause he was mooning around Caroline, his girl got so upset she broke the engagement. And then my uncle began drinking. But now after all these years, they're starting to see each other.''

''Joe, who is your uncle seeing?''

''The girl he used to go around with. Woman, now, of course. You know, Jenny. Your housekeeper, Elsa.''

CHAPTER 34

Elsa had been engaged to Josh Brothers. She had never married. How much bitterness might have built up over the years against the Kruegers? Why had she taken the job at the farmhouse? The way Erich treated her was so belittling. Elsa could have taken the coat from the closet. Elsa could have overheard her and Erich talking. Elsa might have pumped the girls about Kevin.

But why?

She had to talk to someone; she had to trust someone.

Jenny stopped. The wind slapped at her forehead. There was one person she could trust, someone whose face now filled her vision.

She could trust Mark and he should be back from Florida now.

* * *

As soon as she reached the house, she looked up the number of Mark's clinic and phoned. Dr. Garrett was expected any minute; who was calling?

She did not want to leave her name. "What time would be good to reach him?"

"His clinic hours are between five and seven P.M."

She'd call him at home after that.

She walked over to the office. Clyde was just locking the desk. There was a wariness, a constraint between them now. "Clyde, how's Rooney?" she asked.

"I'm bringing her home for good tomorrow. But, Miz Krueger, one thing. I'd appreciate it if you stay away from Rooney. I mean don't ask her to your house; don't visit her." He looked unhappy. "Dr. Philstrom says Rooney getting into a stress situation could set her back."

"And I'm that stress situation?"

"All I know, Miz Krueger, is that Rooney ain't seen Caroline walking around the hospital."

"Clyde, before you lock up that desk, I wish you'd give me some money. Erich left so suddenly that I only have a few dollars and I need to get some odds and ends. Oh, yes, may I borrow your car to go into town?"

Clyde turned the key and dropped it in his pocket. "Erich was real plain about that, Miz Krueger. He don't want you borrowing cars and he told me anything you need till he gets back, you should just tell me and I'll see you get it. But he said real emphatic that he don't want no money given to you. He said it'll cost me my job if I give you a dime from the farm funds or lend my own money to you."

Something in her face made him adapt a friendlier tone. "Miz Krueger, you're not to want for anything. Just tell me what you need."

"I need . . ." Jenny bit her lip, turned and slammed out of the office. She ran along the path, tears of rage and humiliation blinding her.

The late-afternoon shadows were spreading like curtains on the pale brick of the farmhouse. At the edge of the woods the tall Norwegian pines were vividly lush against the stark nakedness of the maples and birches. The sun, hidden behind heavy charcoal clouds, was sending diffused rays over the horizon, streaking the sky with coldly beautiful shades of mauve and pink and cranberry.

A winter sky. A winter place. It had become her prison.

At eight minutes after seven, Jenny reached for the phone to call Mark. Her hand was touching the receiver when the phone rang. She grabbed it off the cradle. "Hello."

"Jenny, you must be sitting on top of the phone. Are you waiting for a call?" There was an edge to the teasing quality in Erich's tone.

Jenny felt her palms go damp. Instinctively she tightened her grasp on the receiver. "I've been hoping to hear from you." Did she sound natural? Did her nervousness show? "Erich, how are the girls?"

"They're fine, of course. What have you been doing today, Jenny?"

"Not much. Now that Elsa doesn't come in, I'm a bit busier in the house. I rather like that." Closing her eyes, trying to choose her words, she added lightly, "Oh, I saw Joe." She hurried on, not wanting to lie, not wanting to admit that she'd gone to the Ekers home. "He's so pleased that you rehired him, Erich."

"I suppose he told you the rest of the conversation I had with him?"

"What do you mean?"

"I mean that garbled story about seeing you get in the car and then deciding he hadn't seen you. You never admitted to me that Joe actually told you he'd seen you in the car that night. I always thought it was only Rooney who saw you."

"But Joe said . . . he told me that he told you . . . he's positive it was someone else wearing my coat."

"Jen, have you signed the statement?"

"Erich, don't you see we have a witness who swears . . ."

"What you mean is we have a witness who knows he saw you and who, to ingratiate himself with me, to get back his job, is now willing to change his story. Jenny, stop trying to avoid the truth. Either have that statement ready to read to me next time I call or forget about seeing the girls until they're adults."

Jenny's control snapped. "You can't do this. I'll swear out a warrant. They're my children. You can't run away with them."

"Jenny, they're just as much mine as yours. I've only taken them on a vacation. I've warned you there's no judge who would award them to you. I have a townful of witnesses who'll swear I'm a wonderful father. Jenny, I love you enough to give you a chance to live with them, to be cared for yourself. Don't push me too hard. Good-bye, Jenny. I'll call you soon."

Jenny stared at the dead receiver. All the tenuous confidence she had started to build vanished. Give up, something said to her. Write the confession. Read it to him. Be finished with it.

No. Biting her lips into a thin, firm line she dialed Mark's number.

He answered on the first ring. "Dr. Garrett."

"Mark." Why did that deep, warm voice bring quick tears to her eyes?

"Jenny. What's the matter? Where are you?"

"Mark, I . . . Could you . . . I *have* to talk to you." She paused, then went on: "But I wouldn't want anyone to see you here. If I cut through the west field, would you pick me up? Unless . . . I mean . . . If you have plans, don't bother. . . ."

"Wait near the millhouse. I'll be there in fifteen minutes."

Jenny went up to the master bedroom and turned on the reading light by the bed. She left a light on in the kitchen, a smaller one in the parlor. Clyde might investigate if the house was completely dark.

She'd have to take the chance that Erich wouldn't phone again in the next few hours.

She left the house and walked in the shadow of the stable and pole-barns. Behind the electric fences she could see the outlines of the cattle as they hunched near the barns. There was no grazing on the snow-covered ground and they tended to stay near the buildings where they were fed.

Less than ten minutes after she reached the mill, she heard the faint sound of a car approaching. Mark was driving with his parking lights on. She stood out in the clearing and waved. He stopped, leaned over and opened the door for her.

He seemed to understand that she wanted to get away quickly. It wasn't until they reached the county road that he spoke. "I understood you were in Houston with Erich, Jenny."

"We didn't go."

"Does Erich know you called me?"

"Erich's away. He took the children."

He whistled. "That's what Dad . . ." Then he stopped. She felt his glance, was acutely aware of his wind-tanned skin, his thick, sandy hair, the long capable fingers that gripped the steering wheel. Erich always made her uneasy; his very presence charged the atmosphere. Mark's presence had exactly the opposite effect.

It had been months since the one time she'd been in his home. At night it had the same welcoming atmosphere that she remembered. The wing chair, its velvet upholstery somewhat worn, was drawn up to the fireplace. An outsized oak coffee table in front of a Lawson couch held newspapers and magazines. The shelves on either side of the fireplace were crammed with books of every shape and size.

Mark took her coat. "Farm life certainly hasn't fattened you up," he observed. "Have you had dinner yet?"

"No."

"I thought not." He poured sherry for them. "My housekeeper was off today. I was just about to cook a hamburger when you phoned. I'll be right back."

Jenny sat on the couch, then instinctively reached down, pulled off her boots and curled up. She and Nana had had a Lawson sofa when she was growing up. She could remember wedging herself into a corner of it on rainy afternoons and happily reading the hours away.

In a few minutes Mark returned with a tray. "Minnesota plush," he smiled. "Hamburgers, French fries, lettuce and tomato."

The food smelled delicious. Jenny took a bite from hers and realized she'd been famished. She knew Mark was taking his cue from her, waiting for her to explain to him why she had called him. How much should she tell? Would Mark be horrified to know what Erich believed about her?

He was sitting in the wing chair, his long legs stretched toward her, his eyes concerned, his forehead creased in thought. She realized she didn't mind being studied by him. Oddly it was comforting, as though he would analyze what was wrong and make it right. His father had much that same look. Luke! She hadn't asked about him. "How is your father?"

"Coming along, but he gave me a real scare. He wasn't feeling well before he went back to Florida. Then he had the attack. But he's in his own place now and looks good. He really wanted you to come visit him, Jenny. He still does."

"I'm glad he's better."

Mark leaned forward. "Tell me about it, Jenny."

She told him everything, looking straight at him, watching his eyes darken, watching as tight lines formed around his eyes and mouth, watching as his expression softened when she talked about the baby and her voice broke.

"You see, I can understand why Erich believed I've done these terrible things. But now I don't believe I did them. So that means some woman is impersonating me. I was so sure it was Rooney but it can't be her. Now I wonder . . . Do you think Elsa? It seems so farfetched that she'd hold a grudge for twenty-five years. . . . Erich was only a child. . . ."

Mark did not reply. His face was troubled now, grave. "You don't think I could do those things?" Jenny burst out. "My God, are you like Erich? Do you think . . ."

The nerve under her left eye began to jump. She put her hand up to her face to stop it, then felt her knees start to tremble. Throwing her head down on her lap, she hugged her legs. Her whole body was shaking now, out of control.

"Jenny. Jenny." Mark's arms were around her, holding her. Her head was against his throat. His lips were on her hair.

"I couldn't hurt anyone. I can't sign and say that I could . . ."

His arms tightened. "Erich is in . . . insecure . . . . Oh, Jenny."

Long minutes passed before the trembling stopped. She made herself pull away. She felt his arms release her. Wordlessly they looked at each other, then Jenny turned away. There was an afghan draped over the back of the couch. He tucked it around her. "I think we could both use coffee."

While he was in the kitchen, she looked into the fireplace, watched as the log split and broke and caved into glowing embers. Suddenly she felt exhausted. But it was a different kind of fatigue, not tense and numbing but relaxing, the kind that came after a race had been run.

Unburdening herself to Mark, she felt as though she had rolled a stone off her shoulders. Listening to the clink of the cups and saucers in the kitchen, smelling the perking coffee, hearing his footsteps as he walked between stove and cabinet, remembering the feel of those arms . . .

When Mark brought in the coffee, she was able to make practical statements that helped dispel the emotionally charged atmosphere. "Erich knows I won't stay with him. The minute he brings the girls back I'll leave."

"You're sure you're going to leave him, Jenny?"

"As fast as I can. But first I want to force him to bring the girls back. They're my children."

"He's right that as their adoptive father, legally they're just as much his as yours. And, Jenny, Erich is capable of staying away indefinitely. Let me talk to a few people. I have a lawyer friend who's an expert in family law. But until then, when Erich phones, whatever you do, don't antagonize him; don't tell him you've been talking to me. Promise me that?"

"Of course."

He drove her home, stopping the car at the millhouse. But he insisted on walking with her through the quiet fields to the house. "I want to be sure you're in," he said. "Go right upstairs and if everything is all right, pull down the shades in your room."

"What do you mean, if everything is all right?"

"I mean that if by any chance Erich decided to come back tonight and realized that you were out, there might be trouble. I'll call you tomorrow after I speak to a few people."

"No, don't. Let me phone you. Clyde knows every call I get."

When they got to the dairy barn, he said, "I'll watch you from here. Try not to worry."

"I'll try. The one thing I don't worry about is that Erich does adore Tina and Beth. He'll be very good to them. That at least is a consolation."

Mark squeezed her hand but did not answer. Quickly she slipped along the side of the path through the west door into the kitchen and looked around. The cup and saucer she had left draining on the sink were still there. She smiled bitterly. She could be sure Erich hadn't come. That cup and saucer would have been put away.

Hurrying upstairs, she went into the master bedroom and began to pull down the shades. From one of the windows she watched as Mark's tall form disappeared into the darkness.

Fifteen minutes later she was in bed. This was the hardest time of all, when she couldn't walk across the hall and tuck Tina and Beth in. She tried to think of all the ways Erich would find to amuse them. They had loved going to the county fair with him last summer. Several times he'd spent a whole day with them in the amusement park. He was endlessly patient with the children.

But both girls had sounded so fretful when he let them speak to her that first night he'd taken them away.

Of course by now they'd be used to her absence, just the way they'd gotten used to her being in the hospital.

As she had told Mark, there was the one consolation that she wasn't worried about the girls.

Jenny remembered the way Mark had squeezed her hand when she said that.

Why?

All night she lay awake. If not Rooney . . . if not Elsa . . . then who?

At dawn she got up. She could not wait for Erich to come to her. She tried to close off the terrible nagging fears, the awful possibilities that had occurred to her during the night.

The cabin. She had to find it. Every instinct told her the place to begin was in the cabin.

CHAPTER 35

She began looking for the cabin at dawn. At four A.M. she'd turned on the radio and heard the weather report. The temperature was dropping sharply. It was now twelve degrees Fahrenheit. A strong cold wind from Canada was driving it down. A major snowstorm was predicted. It should hit the Granite Place area by tomorrow evening.

She made a thermos of coffee to take with her, put an extra sweater under her ski suit. Her breasts were so sore. Thinking of the baby so much during the night had been enough to start them throbbing. She could not let herself think about Tina and Beth now. She could only pray, numb, pleading words. . . . Take care of them, please. Let no harm come . . .

She knew the cabin must be about twenty minutes' walk from the edge of the woods. She'd start at the spot where Erich always disappeared into the trees and crisscross back and forth from that spot. It didn't matter how long it took.

At eleven she returned to the house, heated soup, changed her socks and mittens, found another scarf to tie around her face and set out again.

At five, just as the shadows were lengthening to near darkness, just as she was despairing that she would have to give up the search, she skied over a hilly mound and came on the small, bark-roofed cabin that had been the first Krueger home in Minnesota.

It had a closed-up, unused look, but what had she expected? That the chimney would be capped with smoke, lamps would be glowing, that . . . Yes. She dared to hope that Beth and Tina might be in here with Erich.

She kicked off her skies and with the hammer broke a window, then stepped over the low sill into the cabin. It was frigidly cold, with the deep chill of an unheated, sunless place. Blinking to adjust her eyes to the gloom, Jenny went to the other windows, pulled up the shades and looked around.

She saw a twenty-foot-square room, a Franklin stove, a faded Oriental rug, a couch . . . And paintings.

It seemed that every square inch of the walls was covered with Erich's art. Even the dim light could not hide the exquisite power and beauty of his work. As always the awareness of his genius calmed her. The fears she had harbored during the night suddenly became ludicrous.

The tranquillity of the subjects he had chosen: the polebarn in a winter storm, the doe, head poised about to flee into the woods, the calf reaching up to its mother. How could the person who could paint like this with so much sensitivity, so much authority, also be so hostile, so suspicious?

She was standing in front of a rack filled with canvases. Something about the top one caught her eye. Not understanding, she began to flip rapidly through the paintings in the rack. The signature in the right-hand corner. Not bold and scrawling like Erich's but delicately lettered with fine brushstrokes, a signature more in keeping with the peaceful themes in the paintings: *Caroline Bonardi.* Every one of them.

She began to study the paintings on the wall. Those that were framed were signed *Erich Krueger.* The unframed ones, *Caroline Bonardi.*

But Erich had said that Caroline had very little talent. . . .

Her eyes raced back and forth between a framed painting with Erich's signature, an unframed one signed by Caroline. The same use of diffused light, the same signature pine tree in the background, the same blending of color. Erich was copying Caroline's work.

No.

The framed canvases. Those were the ones he planned to exhibit next. Those were the ones he'd signed. He hadn't painted them. The same artist had done all of these. Erich was forging his name to Caroline's art. That was why he'd been so flustered when she pointed out that the elm in one of his supposedly new paintings had been cut down months before.

A charcoal sketch caught her eye. It was called *Self-Portrait.* It was a miniature of *Memory of Caroline,* probably the preliminary sketch Caroline had done before she started the painting that was her masterpiece.

Oh, God. Everything. Every emotion that she had attributed to Erich through his work was a lie.

Then why was he here so much? What did he do here? She saw the staircase, rushed up it. The loft sloped with the pitch of the roof and she had to bend forward at the top stair before she stepped into the room.

As she straightened up, a nightmarish blaze of color from the back wall assaulted her vision. Shocked, she stared at her own image. A mirror?

No. The painted face did not move as she approached it. The dusky light from the slitlike window played on the canvas, shading it in streaks, like a ghostly finger pointing.

A collage of scenes: violent scenes painted in violent colors. The center figure, herself, her mouth twisted in grief, staring down at puppetlike bodies. Beth and Tina slumped together on the floor, their blue jumpers tangled, their eyes bulging, their tongues protruding, blue corduroy belts wound around their throats. Far up on the wall behind her image, a window with a dark blue curtain. Peering through the opening in the curtain Erich's face, triumphant, sadistic. And all through the canvas in shades of green and black, a slithery figure, half-woman, half-snake, a woman with Caroline's face, the cape wrapped around her like the scaly skin of the snake. Caroline's figure bending over a surrealistic bassinette, a bassinette suspended from a hole in the sky, the woman's hands, grotesque, outsized like whale flippers covering the baby's face, the baby's hands thrust over his head, the fingers starlike, spread on the pillow.

The Caroline figure in the maroon coat, reflected in the windshield of a car; another face beside hers. Kevin's face, exaggerated, staring, grotesque, frightened, his bruised temple swelling into the windshield. The Caroline figure, her cape flung around her, holding the hooves of a wild horse, guiding them to descend on the sandy-haired figure on the ground. Joe. Joe cringing away from the hooves.

Jenny heard the sound from her throat, the keening wail, the screams of protest. It wasn't Caroline who was half-woman, half-snake. It was Erich's face peering out from the tangled dark hair, Erich's eyes wildly staring at her from the canvas.

No. No. No. These twisted, tortured revelations, this art—evil incarnate, brilliance beside which the pastel elegance of Caroline's talent faded into insignificance.

Erich had not painted the canvases he claimed as his own. But those he *had* painted were the genius of a twisted mind. They were shocking, awesome in their power, evil—and insane!

Jenny stared at her own image, at the faces of her children, their pleading eyes as the cord tightened around the small white throats.

At last she forced herself to wrench the canvas from the wall, her unwilling fingers grasping it as though they were closing around the fires of hell.

Somehow she managed to snap on her skis, start back through the woods. Night was descending, darkness spreading. The canvas caught the wind like a sail, whipped her from her own vague path, bruised her against trees. The wind mocked the constant screams for help that she heard screeching from her throat. Help me. Help me. Help me.

She lost the path, turned around in the darkness, saw again the outline of the cabin. No. No.

She would freeze out here, freeze and die out here, before she could find anyone to stop Erich if it weren't already too late. She lost track of time, not knowing how long she stumbled and fell and picked herself up and began again; how long she clutched the damning canvas to her, how long she screamed. She only knew that her voice was breaking into hoarse sobs when somehow she saw a glint through a clump of trees and realized she was at the edge of the woods.

The glint she had seen was the reflection of the moon on the granite stone of Caroline's grave.

With a last terrible effort she skied across the open fields. The house was totally dark; only the faint light of the crescent moon revealed its outlines. But the windows of the office were bright. She headed there, the canvas flapping more wildly without the trees to break the sharp wind.

She could no longer scream; there were no sounds left except the guttural moans she heard in her throat; her lips still formed the words help me, help me.

At the door of the office she tried to turn the handle with her frozen hands, tried to kick off her skis, but could not force her binders to release. Finally she banged at the door with her ski pole until it flung open, and she fell forward into Mark's arms.

''Jenny!'' His voice broke. ''Jenny!''

''Steady, Mrs. Krueger.'' Someone was pulling the skis off her feet. She knew that burly body, that thick, blunt profile. It was Sheriff Gunderson.

Mark was trying to pry her fingers loose from the canvas. ''Jenny, let me see that.'' And then his awed voice. ''Oh, my God.''

Her own voice was a witch's croak: ''Erich. Erich painted it. He killed my baby. He dresses like Caroline. Beth. Tina. . . . Maybe he's killed them too.''

''Erich painted this?'' This sheriff's voice, incredulous.

She whirled on him. ''Have you found my girls? Why are you here? Are my girls dead?''

''Jenny.'' Mark was holding her tightly, his hand stopping the flow of words from her mouth. ''Jenny, I called the sheriff because I couldn't reach you. Jenny, where did you find this?''

''In the cabin. . . . So many paintings. But not his. Caroline painted them.''

''Mrs. Krueger . . .''

On him she could vent her pain. She mimicked his heavy voice. ''Anything you want to tell me, Mrs. Krueger? Anything you suddenly remembered?'' She began to sob.

''Jenny,'' Mark implored, ''it's not the sheriff's fault. I should have realized. Dad had begun to suspect . . .''

The sheriff was studying the canvas, his face suddenly deflated, the skin folding into limp creases. His eyes were riveted on the upper-right-hand corner of the painting, with the bassinette suspended from a hole in the sky and the grotesque Caroline-like figure bending over it. ''Mrs. Krueger, Erich came to me. He said he understood that there'd been talk about the baby's death. He urged me to request an autopsy.''

The door swung open. Erich, Jenny thought. Oh, my God, Erich. But it was Clyde who rushed in, his expression frightened and disapproving. ''What in hell is going on around here?'' He looked at the canvas. Jenny watched as his leathery face drained to the color of white suede.

"Clyde, who's in there?" Rooney called. Her footsteps approached, crackling on the icy snow.

"Hide that thing," Clyde begged. "Don't let her see it. Here . . ." He thrust it into the supply closet.

Rooney appeared on the threshold of the office, her face filled out a little, her eyes wide and calm. Jenny felt the thin arms embracing her. "Jenny, I've missed you."

Through stiff lips she managed to say, "I've missed you too." She had begun to blame Rooney for everything that had happened. She had dismissed everything Rooney told her as the imagination of a sick mind.

"Jenny, where are the girls? Can I say hello to them?"

The question was a slap across the face. "Erich's away with the girls." She knew her voice was trembling, unnatural.

"Come on, Rooney. You can visit tomorrow. You better get home. The doctor wanted you to go straight to bed," Clyde urged.

He took her arm, propelled her forward, looked over his shoulder. "Be right back."

While they waited, she managed to tell them about her search for the cabin. "It was you, Mark. Last night. I said the children would be fine with Erich and you didn't say anything. Later on . . . in bed . . . I knew . . . you were worried about them. And I began to think—if not Rooney, if not Elsa, if not me . . . And my mind kept saying, Mark is afraid for the children. Then I thought. Erich. It has to be Erich.

"That first night . . . He made me wear Caroline's nightgown. . . . He wanted me to *be* Caroline. . . . He even went to sleep in his old bed. And the pine soap he put on the girls' pillows. I knew he'd done that. And Kevin. He must have written—or phoned—to say he was coming to Minnesota. . . . Erich was always toying with me. Erich must have known I met Kevin. He talked about the extra mileage in the car. He must have heard the gossip from the woman in church."

"Jenny."

"No, let me *tell* you. He took me back to that restaurant. When Kevin threatened to stop the adoption he told Kevin to come down. That's why the call was on our phone. Erich and I are the same height when I wear heels. With my coat . . . and the black wig—he could look enough like me until he got in the car. He must have hit Kevin. And Joe. He was jealous of Joe. He could have come home earlier that day; he knew about the rat poison. But my baby. He hated my baby. Maybe because of his red hair. Right from the beginning when he gave him Kevin's name, he must have been planning to kill him."

Were those dry, harsh sobs coming from her? She could not stop talking. She had to let it out.

"Those times I thought I felt someone leaning over me. He was opening the panel. He must have been wearing the wig. The night I went to have the baby. Woke him up. I touched Erich's eyelid. That's what scared me. That was what I'd feel when I reached up in the dark. . . . The soft eyelid and the thick lashes.''

Mark was rocking her in his arms.

''He has my children. He has my children.''

''Mrs. Krueger, can you find your way back to the cabin?'' Sheriff Gunderson's tone was urgent.

A chance to do something. ''Yes. If we start at the cemetery . . .''

''Jenny, you can't,'' Mark protested. ''We'll follow your tracks.''

But she would not let them go without her. Somehow she led them back, Mark and the sheriff and Clyde. They turned on the oil lamps, bathing the cabin in a mellow Victorian glow that only accentuated the gnawing cold. They stared at the delicate signature, *Caroline Bonardi,* then began to search the cupboards. But there were no personal papers; the cupboards were empty except for dishes and cutlery.

''He's got to keep his painting supplies somewhere,'' Mark snapped.

''But the loft is empty,'' Jenny said hopelessly. ''There was nothing in it except the canvas and the place is so small.''

''It can't be that small,'' Clyde objected. ''It's the size of the house. It might be partitioned off.''

There was a storage area that was half again the size of the loft room, accessible by a door in the right-hand corner, a door that Jenny hadn't noticed in the shadowy room. This area had stacks of file baskets; dozens more of Caroline's paintings in them; an easel, a cabinet with painting supplies; two suitcases. Jenny realized they matched the vanity case she'd found in the attic. A long green cape and dark wig were folded over one of the suitcases.

''Caroline's cape,'' Mark said quietly.

Jenny began rifling through the file cabinets. But they only held painting supplies: charcoals and umbras and turpentine and brushes and empty canvases. Nothing, nothing that might indicate where Erich had gone.

Clyde began searching through a bin of canvases near the door. ''Look.'' His cry was horror-filled. He had pulled out a canvas. This one in the murky green tones of stagnant water. A surrealistic collage of Erich as a child and Caroline. Scenes of crowding, overlapping. Erich with a hockey stick in his hand. Caroline bending over a calf; Erich pushing her; her body, sprawled in a tub, no that was the stock tank; her eyes staring up at him. The tip of the hockey stick flipping the overhead lamp into the tank. Erich's child-face demonic now, laughing into the agonized figure in the water.

''He killed Caroline,'' Clyde moaned. ''When he was ten years old, he killed his own mother.''

''What did you say?'' They all spun around. Rooney was in the doorway of the loft, Rooney with wide eyes no longer calm. ''Did you think I couldn't tell something was wrong?'' she asked. She was staring not at the canvas Clyde was holding, but beyond to the painting now revealed in the bin. Even with the distortions Jenny recognized Arden's face. Arden peering in the window of the cabin. A caped figure with dark hair and Erich's face behind her. Hands around Arden's throat, the fingers not attached to the hands. Arden lying in a grave on top of a casket, dirt being shoveled over her bright blue skirt, the name on the tombstone behind her head: CAROLINE BONARDI KRUEGER. And in the corner the slashing signature, *Erich Krueger.*

"Erich killed my little girl," Rooney moaned.

Somehow they made their way back to the house. Mark's hand held hers tightly, a silent Mark, not attempting to offer useless words of comfort.

In the house, Sheriff Gunderson got on the phone. "There's the chance that everything we believe he's done is the fantasy of a sick mind. There's one way we can be sure and we can't waste a minute finding out."

The cemetery was once again violated. Floodlights bathed the tombstones in unnatural night brilliance. Drills bore into the frozen ground of Caroline's grave. Rooney watched, surprisingly calm now.

As they looked down, they saw bits of blue wool mixed with the earth. A man's voice spoke from the grave: "She's here. For God's sake, get the mother away."

Clyde hugged Rooney, forcing her to retreat. "At least we know," he said.

Back at the house, the daylight was filtering in. Mark made coffee. When had Mark begun to suspect that the children were in danger with Erich? She asked him.

"Jenny, after I left you home last night, I called Dad. I knew he'd been terribly upset about what Tina said about how the lady in the painting had covered the baby. He admitted to me that he'd *known* Erich was psychotic as a child. Caroline had confided in him about Erich's obsession with her. She'd caught him watching her while she slept, keeping her nightgown under his pillow, wrapping himself in her cape. She took him to a doctor but John Krueger flatly refused to allow him to be treated. John said that no Krueger had emotional problems; it was just Caroline spoiling him; spending so much time with him, that was the problem.

"Caroline was on the verge of a breakdown by then. She did the only thing she could. She relinquished custody, with the understanding that John would send Erich to boarding school. She hoped a different atmosphere would help him. But after she died, John broke his promise. Erich never did get help.

"When Dad heard what Tina said about the lady in the painting, heard what Rooney said about seeing Caroline, he began to suspect what was happening. I think the realization brought on his heart attack. I only wish he'd confided in me. Of course he had absolutely no proof. But that was why he told me to urge Erich to allow you and the girls to visit him.''

''Mrs. Krueger.'' Sheriff Gunderson's voice was hesitant. Was he afraid she would keep blaming him? ''Dr. Philstrom from the hospital is here. We had him look at what's in the cabin. He has to talk to you.''

''Jenny, can you tell me exactly what Erich said the last time he phoned you?'' Dr. Philstrom asked.

''He was angry because I tried to tell him that maybe he was wrong about me.''

''Did he mention the girls?''

''He said they were fine.''

''How long since he put them on to talk to you?''

''Nine days.''

''I see. Jenny, I'll be honest. It doesn't look good but it would seem that Erich must have painted that last canvas before he disappeared with the girls. There's quite a lot of detail in it. Even if he's been in the cabin—and we know he has—there's a scissor there with bits of fur on it. Even so, it would seem that he painted that picture before he left with the children.''

A whisper of hope. ''You mean they may not be dead?''

''I don't want to encourage you unfairly. But think about it. Erich still fantasizes living with you, having you under his total power once he has that confession signed. He knows that without the children he can't hold you. So until he perceives a reunion with you as being hopeless, there's a chance, just a chance. . . .''

Jenny stood up. Tina. Beth. If you were dead I would know it. Just the way I knew Nana wouldn't live through that last night. Just the way I knew something was going to happen to the baby.

But Rooney hadn't known. For ten years now Rooney had waited for Arden to come home. And all the time Arden's body was buried within sight of Rooney's windows.

How often had she seen Rooney standing over Caroline's grave. Was it because something had compelled her to go there? Something deep in her subconscious that had told her she was visiting Arden's grave too?

She asked Dr. Philstrom about that, asked him gravely, heard her voice almost childlike. ''Is that *possible,* doctor?''

''I don't know, Jenny. I think Rooney instinctively suspected that Arden wouldn't deliberately run away. She knew her child.''

''I want my children,'' Jenny said. ''I want them now. How could Erich hate me so much, that he would hurt them?''

''You're talking about a totally irrational man,'' Dr. Philstrom said. ''A man who wanted you because you bear a startling resemblance to his mother, yet hated you for replacing her; who could not trust your love for him because he perceives himself as unlovable and who lived in mortal fear of losing you.''

''We're going to make up flyers, Mrs. Krueger,'' the sheriff said. ''We'll have their pictures in every hamlet in Minnesota and all the bordering states. We'll get television coverage. Somebody's got to have seen them. Clyde is going through all Erich's records of property holdings. We'll search out any property he owns. Don't forget. We know he was here at least once, and that was only five hours after he phoned you. We're concentrating on a radius of five hours' drive from here.''

The ringing of the telephone made them all jump. Sheriff Gunderson reached to pick it up. Some instinct made Jenny push his hand away.

''Hello.'' Her voice so unsteady. Would it be Erich? Oh, God, would it be Erich?

''Hello, Mommy.''

It was Beth.

CHAPTER 36

''Beth!'' She closed her eyes, jammed her knuckles against her mouth. Beth was still alive. Whatever he planned to do to them hadn't happened yet. The memory of the painting, Beth and Tina, stiff little puppets, the corduroy belts around their necks. She could not blot it out.

She felt Mark's hands, those strong hands on her shoulders, steadying her. She held out the receiver so he could try to listen too.

''Beth, hello, darling.'' She tried to sound carefree and pleased. It was so hard not to scream, *Beth, where are you?* ''Are you having a good time with Daddy?''

''Mommy, you're mean. You came into our room last night and you wouldn't talk to us. And you covered Tina too tight.''

Beth's plaintive voice was high-pitched enough for Mark to hear. She saw the agony in his eyes, knew it was reflected in her own. *Covered Tina too tight.* No. No. Please, God. No. The baby. Now Tina.

''Tina cried so hard.''

''Tina cried.'' Jenny tried to fight the waves of dizziness. She mustn't faint. ''Let me talk to her, Bethie. I love you, Mouse.''

Now Beth began to cry. ''I love you too, Mommy. Please come soon.''

''Mommy.'' Tina's helpless sobbing. ''You hurt me. The blanket was in my face.''

''Tina, I'm sorry, I'm sorry.'' Jenny tried not to let her voice break. ''I'm sorry, Tina.''

There was a clunk as the phone was moved, then Tina's wail.

''Jenny, why are you so upset? The girls were dreaming. It's just that they miss you as I do, darling.''

''*Erich.*'' Jenny knew she was shouting. ''Where are you, Erich?

Please, I promise you. I'll sign that confession. I'll sign anything. But please, I need my children.''

She felt Mark's grip on her shoulder, cautioning her. ''I mean I need my family, Erich.'' She forced her voice to calm, bit her lips over the urge to plead with him not to hurt them. ''Erich, we can be so happy. I don't know why I do such strange things when I'm asleep but you promised to take care of me. I'm sure I'll get better.''

''You were going to leave me, Jenny. You just pretended to love me.''

''Erich, come home and we'll talk. Or let me send the letter to you. Tell me where you are.''

''Have you talked to anyone about us?''

Jenny looked at Mark. He shook his head warningly. ''Why would I tell anyone about us?''

''I tried to phone you three times yesterday afternoon. You were out.''

''Erich, I hadn't heard from you for so long. I needed to get some fresh air. I skied for a while. I want to be able to ski with you again. We had such fun, remember?''

''I tried to phone Mark last evening. He wasn't home. Were you with him?''

''Erich, I was here. I'm always here waiting for you.'' Tina was screaming now. From the background she could hear road sounds again, like heavy trucks shifting gears on a grade. Could Erich have been at the farm last night? If so had he gone to the cabin? No, if he had been in the cabin and seen the broken window, realized that people had been there, he wouldn't be calling now.

''Jenny, I'll think about coming back. You just stay in the house. Don't go out. Don't go skiing. I want you right there. And someday I'll open the door and be there and we'll be a family again. Will you do that, Jenny?''

''Yes, Erich, yes. Yes. I promise.''

''Mommy, I want to talk to Mommy.'' Beth's pleading. ''Please, please. . . .''

There was a sharp, clicking sound and the dial tone began to hum in her ear.

Jenny listened while Mark repeated the conversation. She only interjected when the sheriff asked, ''But why would the kids have thought it was you?''

''Because he has my suitcases with him now,'' Jenny said. ''He probably put one of my robes on. . . . Maybe even that red one I've been missing. He must have a dark wig with him. When the children are very sleepy they see what they think they're seeing. Dr. Philstrom, what will he do now?''

''Jenny, anything is possible. I can't deny that. But I suspect that as long as he still holds the hope that you'll stay with him, the girls are fairly safe.''

''But Tina—last night. . . .''

"You have that answer. He tried to phone you in the afternoon and you were gone. He tried to phone Mark in the evening and couldn't reach him. It's uncanny how some psychotics develop almost a sixth sense. Some instinct told him you were together. In his frustration he came very near to harming Tina."

Jenny tried to swallow over the quiver in her voice. "He sounds so strange, almost rambling. Suppose he does come soon? He could conceivably decide to come back tonight. He knows every inch of this property. He could ski in. He could drive a car we wouldn't recognize. He could walk in from the riverbank. If he sees anyone around here who doesn't belong here, that will be the end. You've all got to go away. Suppose, oh, God, suppose he sees Caroline's grave has been disturbed? He'll know that Arden's body was found. Don't you see? You can't have any publicity. You can't send out flyers. You can't have strangers here. The cabin. If he goes to the cabin and sees the broken window . . . those bits of cloth tacked on the trees . . ."

Sheriff Gunderson looked from Mark to Dr. Philstrom. "Obviously you both agree. All right. Mark, will you ask Rooney and Clyde to come in here? I'll get the people from the coroner's office. They're still sifting the dirt in the cemetery."

Rooney was surprisingly composed. Jenny knew that Dr. Philstrom was studying her closely. But Rooney's concern seemed to be only for Jenny. She hugged her, laid her cheek on Jenny's. "I know. Oh, my dear, I know."

Clyde had aged ten years in the past hours. "I'm listing all the property Erich owns," he said. "I'll have that for you soon."

"The painting," Jenny said. "We've got to put that painting back. It was on the long wall in the loft."

"I left it in the supply closet in the office," Dr. Philstrom said. "But I think it might be better if Mrs. Toomis would agree to come back and stay in the hospital until this is over."

"I want to be with Clyde," Rooney said. "I want to be with Jenny. I'm all right. Don't you see. I *know*."

"Rooney stays with me," Clyde said flatly.

Sheriff Gunderson walked over to the window. "This place is a mess of footprints and tire tracks," he said. "What we need is a good snowstorm to cover them. Keep your fingers crossed. There's one due tonight."

The storm began in the early evening. Snowflakes fine and rapid bit at the house and barns and fields. The wind blew and scattered the flying flakes, eventually banking them in rapidly growing piles against the trees and buildings.

The next morning, in prayerful gratitude, Jenny observed the glaring whiteness outside. The violated grave would be quilted with snow, the tracks to the cabin obliterated. If Erich came he would not be suspicious; even Erich who could instantly sense a book out of place, a vase moved a quarter of an inch, would have nothing to trigger his awareness of their presence in the cabin.

During the night, pushing their way through the treacherous roads, Garrett and two deputies had come back. One had wired the phones to monitor incoming calls, had given Jenny a walkie-talkie and taught her how to use it. The other had made copies of the papers Clyde pulled from the files, the pages and pages of income tax forms showing the Krueger holdings: deeds, rental contracts, office buildings, warehouses. The originals were back in the files, the copies taken to be pored over by investigators who would then begin to search possible hiding places.

Jenny adamantly refused to allow a policeman to stay in the house. ''Erich could open the door and walk in. Suppose he realizes that someone else is here. And he *would.* You can count on it. I won't risk it.''

She began keeping track of days with the awareness of seconds turning into minutes, minutes crawling to the quarter hour, the half hour. She had found the cabin on the fifteenth. On the morning of the sixteenth, the grave had been opened and Erich had phoned. The snowstorm ended on the eighteenth. All through Minnesota the cleanup began. The phone lines were down all the seventeenth and most of the eighteenth. Suppose Erich tried to call? Would he realize that it wasn't her fault he couldn't get through. The entire area of Granite Place where the farm was located was harder hit than the rest of the county.

Don't let him get angry, she prayed. Don't let him take it out on the girls.

On the morning of the nineteenth she saw Clyde coming to the house. The upright set of his head and chest was gone. He bent forward as he walked the freshly plowed path, his face puckered not so much against the wind as under an invisible burden he seemed to be carrying.

He stepped into the kitchen foyer, stamping his feet to break the cold. ''He just called.''

''Erich! Clyde, why didn't you ring through? Why didn't you let me talk to him.''

''He didn't want to talk to you. He just wanted to know if the lines were down around here last night. He asked me whether or not you've been out. Miz Krueger, Jenny, he's uncanny. He told me I sounded funny. I said I didn't know about that; it's been pretty busy trying to feed all the cattle in this storm. That seemed to satisfy him. Then he said the other day . . . Remember when he called right after we found Arden?''

''Yes.''

''He said he'd been thinking about it. He said that I should have been in the office at that time, that the call should have been picked up there first. Jenny, it's like he's right here watching us. He seems to know every move we make.''

"What did you tell him?"

"I said that I'd gotten Rooney out of the hospital that morning and hadn't been to the office yet so that it was still on the night setting where it rings in the house. Then he asked me if Mark has been poking around here; that was the way he put it, 'poking around.' "

"What did you say?"

"I told him Dr. Ivanson had been checking the animals and should I have called Mark instead? He said no."

"Clyde, did he mention the children?"

"No, ma'am. Just said to tell you he'd be phoning and he wanted you in the house waiting for the call. Jenny, I tried to keep him on so they could maybe trace where he is but he talked so fast and got off so quick."

Mark phoned every day. "Jenny, I want to see you."

"Mark, Clyde's right. He is uncanny. He particularly asked about you. Please, stay away."

On the afternoon of the twenty-fifth Joe came to the house. "Mrs. Krueger, is Mr. Krueger all right?"

"What do you mean, Joe?"

"He phoned to see how I was feeling. Wanted to know if I've been seeing you. I said just the one time I bumped into you. I didn't say you'd come to our place. You know what I mean. He said he wanted me to come back to work when I'm ready but if I ever came near you or if he ever heard me call you Jenny, he'd shoot me with the same rifle he used to kill my dogs. He said my *dogs*. That means he did kill the other one too. He sounds crazy. I think it won't do no good for either you or me if I'm around here. You tell me what to do."

He sounds crazy. He was openly threatening Joe now. Despair anesthetized Jenny's terror. "Joe, did you tell anyone about this; did you tell your mother?"

"No, ma'am. I don't want to get her started."

"Joe, I beg you, don't tell anyone about that call. And if Erich phones back, just be very calm and easy with him. Tell him the doctor wants you to wait a few weeks more but don't tell him you refuse to work. And Joe, for God sake, don't tell him you've seen me again."

"Jenny, there's real bad trouble, isn't there?"

"Yes." It was useless to deny it.

"Where is he with your girls?"

"I don't know."

"I see. Jenny, I swear to God you can trust me."

"I know I can. And if he phones you again, let me know right away, please."

"I will."

"And, Joe . . . If—I mean he might come back here. If you happen to see him or the car. I need to know at once."

"You will. Elsa was over at our place for dinner with Uncle Josh. She was talking about you, saying what a lovely person you were."

"She never acted as though she liked me."

"She was scared of Mr. Krueger. He told her to know her place, to keep her mouth shut, to make sure nothing was ever out of place or changed in the house."

"I never could understand why she worked for us, the way Erich treated her."

"The kind of money he paid. Elsa said that she'd work for the devil for that big a salary." Joe put his hand on the doorknob. "Sounds like she *was* working for the devil, don't it, Jenny?"

February is not the shortest month of the year, Jenny thought. It seemed an eternity. Day after day. Minute after minute. The nighttime madness of lying in bed, watching the outline of the crystal bowl against the darkness. She wore Caroline's nightgown every night, kept a cake of pine soap under the pillow so the bed always held the faint scent of pine.

If Erich came in some night, quietly, stealthily, if he came into this room, this nightgown, this scent, might lull him into security.

When she did sleep she dreamt incessantly of the children. In sleep they were waiting for her. They would call "*Mommy, Mommy,*" and tumble into the bed, pressing small, wiggly bodies against her, and then as she tried to put her arms around them she awoke.

She never dreamt of the baby. It was as though the same total involvement she had given to preserving the small flicker of life in that tiny body now belonged to Tina and Beth.

She had the confession memorized; over and over it ran through her head: "I am not responsible . . ."

During the day she was never far from the phone. To pass the time she spent most mornings cleaning the house. She dusted and waxed and mopped, swept, polished silver. But she would not use the vacuum for fear of missing the first peal of the telephone.

Most afternoons Rooney came over, a quiet, different Rooney for whom the waiting was over. "I was thinking we might start quilts for the girls' beds," she suggested. "As long as Erich still thinks he can come here and find you and be a family with you and the girls, he won't hurt them. But in the meantime you gotta be busy at least with your hands. Otherwise you'll go crazy. So let's start quilts."

Rooney went up to the attic to get the bag with the leftover scraps of material. They began to sew. Jenny thought of the legend of the three sisters who spun, measured and cut the threads of time. But we're only two of the three, she thought. Erich is the third. It is he who can cut the strand of life.

Rooney sorted the pieces of material into neat piles on the kitchen table. "We'll want them bright and cheerful," she said, "so we won't use dark colors.'' She began whisking back into the bag the ones she was rejecting. ''This was from a tablecloth old Mrs. Krueger had. That's John's mother. Caroline and I used to laugh that anyone would want such a dismal-looking thing. And that sailcloth was from a bolt she bought to make a cover for the picnic table. That was the summer Erich was five. And, oh, I don't know why I don't just throw out the rest of this blue stuff. Remember I told you I made curtains for the big back room? When they were up you'd think you were in a cave. The whole room was so dark. Oh, well. . . .'' She pushed it into the sack. ''You never know when you might want to put your hand on it.''

They began to sew. It seemed to Jenny that the end of hope had robbed Rooney of intensity. Everything she said was expressed in the same middle key. ''Once Erich is found we're going to have a real funeral for Arden. The hardest for me now is to think back and remember how Erich encouraged me to think that Arden was still alive. Clyde said all along that she'd never run away. I shoulda known that. I guess I did know that. But every time I started to say that I guess my Arden is with God, why, then Erich would say, 'I don't believe that, Rooney.' He was so cruel getting up my hopes like that; kind of like never letting the wound heal. I tell you, Jenny, he don't deserve to live.''

''Rooney, please, don't talk like that.''

''I'm sorry, Jenny.''

Sheriff Gunderson phoned her every night. ''We've checked out the real estate. We've given pictures to all the police in those areas with the understanding there be no publicity and if they see him or the car they don't apprehend him. He's not at any of the places listed in his tax returns.''

He tried to offer cautious comfort. ''They say no news is good news, Mrs. Krueger. Right now the kids may be playing on a beach in Florida, getting a nice suntan.''

Pray God they were. She didn't believe it.

Mark phoned every night. They stayed on only a minute or two. ''Nothing, Jen.''

''Nothing.''

''All right, I won't tie up the line. Hang in there, Jenny.''

Hang in there. She tried to establish some sort of pattern to her days. The nights, either sleepless or wracked with torturing dreams, drove her from bed at dawn. For days she hadn't been outside the house. An early-morning television program featured a yoga exercise. Faithfully she sat in front of the set at six-thirty, mechanically following the prescribed routine of the day.

At seven o'clock *Good Morning America* came on. She forced herself to listen to the news, listen politely to the interviews. One day as she watched, pictures were flashed on the screen of children who had disappeared. Some of them had been missing for years. Amy . . . Roger . . .

Tommy . . . Linda . . . José . . . one after the other. Each representing heartbreak. Someday would they add Elizabeth and Christine . . . "nick-named Beth and Tina" to the list. "Their adoptive father left with them on February sixth, three years ago. If anyone has knowledge . . ."

The evenings had a ritual too. She sat in the family-room section of the kitchen and read or tried to watch television. Usually she would spin the dial and leave the set at where it stopped. Unseeingly she endured situation comedies, hockey games, old movies. She tried to read, but pages later she'd realize her mind hadn't taken in a thing.

The last night in February she was particularly restless.

It seemed as though there was a stillness in the house that was particularly jarring. The canned laughter during a program depicting a couple throwing bric-a-brac at each other made her snap off the set. She sat staring ahead, seeing nothing. The phone rang. By now without hope, she picked it up. "Hello."

"Jenny, this is Pastor Barstrom from Zion Lutheran. How have you been?"

"Very well, thank you."

"I hope Erich extended our sympathy at the loss of your baby. I wanted to visit you but he suggested I defer seeing you. Is Erich there?"

"No. He's away. I'm not sure when he'll be back."

"I see. Will you just remind him that our senior citizens center is almost complete? As the largest donor, I want to be sure he knows the dedication date is March tenth. He's a very generous man, Jenny."

"Yes. I'll tell him you called. Good night, Pastor."

The phone rang at quarter of two. She was lying in bed, a pile of books beside her, hoping that one of them would help her while away the night.

"Jenny."

"Yes." Was it Erich? He sounded different, high-pitched, tense.

"Jenny, who were you talking to on the phone? Around eight o'clock. You smiled while you were talking."

"Around eight?" She tried to sound thoughtful, tried not to scream out the words, *Where are Beth and Tina?* "Let's see," she made a point of the delay. Sheriff Gunderson? Mark? She didn't dare mention either. Pastor Barstrom. "Erich, Pastor Barstrom phoned. He wanted to talk to you, to invite you to the opening of the senior citizens' hall." Her hands clammy, her mouth trembling, she waited for his comment. Keep him on the phone. That way they might be able to trace the call.

"Are you sure it was Pastor Barstrom?"

"Erich, why would I say that?" She bit her lips. "How are the girls?"

"They're fine."

"Let me talk to them."

"They're very tired. I put them to bed. You looked nice tonight, Jenny."

"*I looked nice tonight.*" She felt herself begin to tremble.

"Yes, I was there. I was looking in the window. You should have guessed I was there. If you love me you would have guessed."

In the darkness Jenny watched the crystal bowl, eerie, green. "Why didn't you come in?"

"I didn't want to. I just wanted to make sure you were still there waiting for me."

"I am waiting for you, Erich, and I'm waiting for the girls. If you didn't want to be here, let me come and be with you."

"No . . . Not yet. Are you in bed now, Jenny?"

"Yes, of course."

"What nightgown have you got on?"

"The one you like. I wear it a lot."

"Maybe I should have stayed."

"Maybe you should. I wish you would."

There was a pause. In the background she could hear sounds of traffic. He must always call from the same phone. *He had been outside the window.*

"You didn't tell Pastor Barstrom that I'm mad at you."

"Of course not. He knows how much we love each other."

"Jenny, I tried to phone Mark but his line was busy. Were you talking to him?"

"No, I wasn't."

"You really were talking to Pastor Barstrom."

"Why don't you call and ask him?"

"No. I believe you. Jenny, I'll keep trying to get Mark. I just remembered. He has a book of mine. I want it back. It belongs on the third shelf of the library, the fourth from the right end." Erich's voice was changing, becoming whiny, fretful. There was something about it.

She was hearing it again. The high-pitched screaming that had nearly destroyed her with its accusations: "Is Mark your new boyfriend? Does he like to swim? Whore. Get out of Caroline's bed. Get out of it now."

There was a click. Then silence. Then the dial tone, a mild, impersonal buzz radiating from the receiver in her hand.

CHAPTER 37

Sheriff Gunderson phoned twenty minutes later. "Jenny, the phone company partially traced the call. We have the area he dialed from. It's around Duluth."

Duluth. The northern part of the state. Nearly six hours driving from here. That meant if he was staying in that area he had started down in the midafternoon in order to have been looking in the window at eight o'clock.

Who had been with the children all the hours he'd been gone? Or had he left them alone? Or weren't they alive anymore? She hadn't spoken to them since the sixteenth, almost two weeks ago.

''He's coming apart,'' she said tonelessly. Sheriff Gunderson did not try to offer empty cheer. ''Yes, I think he is.''

''What can you do?''

''Do you want us to go public? Release the facts to television stations, newspapers?''

''God, no. That would be signing the girls' death certificates.''

''Then we'll get a special squad combing the Duluth area. And we want to leave a detective in your house. Your own life may be in danger.''

''Absolutely not. He'd know.''

It was almost midnight. February 28 would become March 1. Jenny remembered the childhood superstition she had. If you fell asleep saying ''hare, hare'' on the last night of the month, and woke up in the morning the first day of the new month saying ''rabbit, rabbit,'' you would get your wish. Nana and she used to make a game of it.

''Hare, hare,'' Jenny said aloud into the quiet room. She raised her voice: ''Hare, hare.'' Shrieking, she screamed, ''Hare, hare, I want my children, I want my children!'' Sobbing, she collapsed back on the pillow. ''I want Beth, I want Tina.''

In the morning her eyes were so swollen she could barely see out of them. Somehow she got dressed, went downstairs, made coffee, rinsed off her cup and saucer. The thought of food sickened her and there was no use stacking the dishwasher with one lonely cup and saucer.

Slipping on her ski jacket she hurried outside and walked around to the window on the southern side of the house that looked into the family area of the kitchen. There were footsteps outlined in the snow below that window, footsteps that had come out of the woods, gone back to the woods. While she sat in that room, Erich had stood out here, his face pressed against the glass, watching her.

The sheriff phoned again at noon. ''Jenny, I played that tape for Dr. Philstrom. He thinks we'd better take the chance of going public in search for the children. But it's your decision.''

''Let me think on it.'' She wanted to ask Mark.

Rooney came over at two. ''Want to sew a little?''

''I suppose so.''

Placidly Rooney took a chair near the iron stove and got out the pieces she was working on.

''Well, we'll be seeing him soon,'' Rooney commented.

''Him?''

''Erich, of course. You know that promise Caroline made that she'd always be here on his birthday. Since she died twenty-six years ago, Erich has been on this place on his birthday. Pretty much like you saw him last year. Just kind of wandering around as though he's looking for something.''

''And you believe he'll be here this year?''

''He never missed yet.''

''Rooney, please help me, don't remind anyone.... Not Clyde or anyone about that.''

Seemingly pleased to be treated as a conspirator, Rooney nodded eagerly. ''We'll just wait for him, won't we, Jen?''

Jenny could not trust even Mark with the information. When he phoned to urge her to let the sheriff get help from the media, she declined. Finally she compromised. ''Give it one week more, please, Mark.''

The week would be up March 9. And Erich's birthday was March 8.

He would be here on the eighth. She was sure of it. If the sheriff and Mark suspected he was coming, the might insist on trying to hide some policemen around the farm. But Erich would know.

If the girls were still alive, this was her last chance to get them back. Erich was losing whatever grip he had on reality.

In the next week, Jenny moved in a near trance, her every thought a continuing prayer. *Oh, Lord in mercy, spare them.* She dug out the ivory case that held Nana's rosary beads. Jenny closed her hand around the rosary. She could not concentrate on formal prayer. ''Nana, come on, you say it for me.''

The second . . . the third . . . the fourth . . . the fifth . . . the sixth . . . Don't let it snow again. Don't let the roads be impassable. The seventh. On the morning of the seventh the phone rang. A person-to-person call from New York.

It was Mr. Hartley. ''Jenny, so long since I talked to you. How are you, the girls?''

''Fine, we're fine.''

''Jenny, I'm sorry, we've got a terrible problem. The Wellington Trust, remember they bought *Minnesota Harvest* and *Spring on the Farm?* Paid a lot of money, Jenny.''

''Yes.''

''They were having the paintings cleaned. And, Jenny, I'm sorry to tell you this but Erich forged his name to them. There's another signature under his, *Caroline Bonardi.* I'm afraid there's going to be a terrible scandal, Jenny. The Wellington people are having an emergency board meeting tomorrow afternoon. They've called a news conference about it. By tomorrow evening there will be a big news story.

''Stop them! You have to stop them!''

''Stop them? Jenny, how can I? Art forgery is serious business. When you pay six figures for a new artist . . . When that artist wins the most prestigious awards in the field . . . You can't keep quiet about a forger,

Jenny. I'm sorry. It's out of my hands. Right now they're investigating to find out who Caroline Bonardi is. In friendship I wanted you to know."

"I'll tell Erich. Thank you, Mr. Hartley." Long after she put the phone down, Jenny sat staring at the receiver. There was no way to stop the story. Reporters would be here looking to talk to Erich. It wouldn't take too much investigation to find that Caroline Bonardi was the daughter of the painter Everett Bonardi and the mother of Erich Krueger. Once they started examining the paintings carefully they'd be able to determine that all of them were over twenty-five years old.

She went to bed early in the hope that Erich might be more likely to come in if the house was dark. She bathed as she had that first night, only this time she used a handful of pine crystals in the tub. The fragrance of the pine filled the room. She let her hair trail in the water so that it too absorbed the scent. Each morning she rinsed out the aqua gown. Now she put it on, slipped a dry cake of soap under the pillow and looked around the bedroom. Nothing must be out of place, nothing must disturb Erich's sense of orderliness. The closet doors were closed. She moved the brush of the silver dressing set a half-inch nearer the nail buffer. The shades were drawn exactly even. She folded the cranberry brocade spread over the lace-edged sheet.

At last she got into bed. The walkie-talkie the sheriff had given her that she carried in the pocket of her jeans made an outline under her pillow. She slipped it in the night-table drawer.

Hour by hour she listened as the clock chimed the night away. Please, Erich, come, she thought. She willed him to come. Surely if he were in the house, if he crept down this hallway, the scent of pine would draw him in.

But when the first light of the sun began to filter through the drawn shades, there was still no sign of his presence. Jenny stayed in bed until eight o'clock. The coming of the day only increased her terror. She had been so sure that during the night she would hear faint footsteps, that the door would start to move, that Erich would be there looking for her, looking for Caroline.

Now she had only the hours until the evening news broadcast.

The day was overcast, but when she turned on the radio, there was no forecast of snow. She was not sure how to dress. Erich was so suspicious. If he came upon her in anything other than slacks and a sweater, he might accuse her of expecting another man.

She barely bothered to look in the mirror anymore. This morning she studied herself, saw with shock the prominent cheekbones, the haunted, staring look in her eyes, the way her hair had grown past her shoulders. With a clip, she caught it at the nape of her neck. She recalled the night she had looked in this mirror and, as she wiped away the steam, had seen Erich's face, Erich's outstretched arms holding the aqua gown. Her instincts had warned her about him that night but she hadn't listened.

Downstairs she scrutinized every detail of every room. She washed the surfaces of the kitchen counters and appliances. She'd barely used the kitchen for more than a can of soup these past weeks but Erich wanted everything mirror-bright. In the library, she ran a dustcloth over the bookshelves and noticed that the third shelf, fourth from the end, did have a vacancy, as Erich had said.

How odd that she had resisted truth so long, refused to face the obvious, lost the baby and maybe the girls because she didn't want to know what Erich was!

Clouds darkened the house at noon; a wind began to blow at three, sending a moaning sound through the chimneys but driving the clouds back so that the late-afternoon sun burst out, shining on the snow-crusted fields, making them glisten as though with warmth. Jenny walked from window to window, watching the woods, watching the road that led to the riverbank, straining her eyes to see if anyone was lurking under the protective overhang of the barn.

At four she watched the hired men begin to leave, men she'd never really gotten to know. Erich never let them near the house. She never went near them in the fields. The experience with Joe had been enough.

At five o'clock she turned on the radio for the news. The briskly crisp voice of the commentator reported on new budget cuts, another summit meeting in Geneva, the attempted assassination of the new president of Iran. "And now here's an item just in. . . . The Wellington Trust Fund has just announced a stunning art forgery. Prominent Minnesota artist Erich Krueger, who has been hailed as the most important American painter since Andrew Wyeth, has been forging his name to the work he has been representing as his own. The true artist is Caroline Bonardi. It has been determined that Caroline Bonardi was the daughter of the late, well-known portrait painter, Everett Bonardi, and the mother of Erich Krueger."

Jenny turned off the radio. Any minute the phone would start to ring. Within hours reporters would be swarming here. Erich would see them, would perhaps hear the broadcast, would know it was over. And he would take his final revenge on Jenny, if he hadn't already.

Blindly she stumbled out of the kitchen. What could she do? What could she do? Without knowing where she was going, she walked into the parlor. The evening sun was streaming into the room, illuminating Caroline's portrait. A bleak pity for the woman who had known this same bewildering helplessness made her study the painting: Caroline sitting on the porch, that dark green cape wrapped around her, the tiny tendrils of hair brushing her forehead. The sun setting, the small figure of the boy Erich running toward her.

The figure running toward her. . . .

The sun rays were diffused throughout the room. It would be a brilliant sunset, reds and oranges and purples and charcoal clouds streaked with diamond-tinted light.

The figure running toward her. . . .

Erich was out there somewhere in those woods. Jenny was sure of it. And there was only one way to force him to leave them.

The shawl Rooney had made for her. . . . No, it wasn't large enough, but if she wore something with it . . . The army blanket that had been Erich's father's in the cedar chest? That was almost the same color as Caroline's cape.

Racing up the two flights of stairs to the attic, she tore open the cedar chest, reached down into it, pushed aside the old World War Two uniforms. On the bottom was the army blanket, khaki-colored but not unlike the shade of the cape. A scissor? She had scissors in the sewing basket.

The sun was getting lower. In a few minutes it would begin to sink. . . .

Downstairs, with trembling hands she cut a hole in the middle of the blanket, a hole just large enough for her head, and drew it around her. Then she pulled the shawl over her shoulders. The blanket fell around her, draped capelike to the floor.

Her hair. It was longer than Caroline's now, but in the painting Caroline had it loosely drawn up into a Psyche knot. Jenny stood in front of the kitchen mirror, twisting her hair, curling small tendrils over her fingers, fastening it with the large barrette. Caroline inclined her head a little to one side; she held her hands in her lap, the right hand lying over the left. . . .

Jenny stood at the west door of the porch. I *am* Caroline, she thought. I will walk like Caroline, sit like her. I am going to watch the sunset as she always did. I am going to watch my little boy come running toward me.

She opened the door and unhurriedly stepped out into the sharp cold air. Closing the door she walked over to the swing, adjusted it so it directly faced the sunset and sat down.

She remembered to shake the shawl so that it folded over the left arm of the swing, as it had in the painting. She tilted her head so that it was at a slight angle to the right. She folded her hands in her lap until the right hand lay encased in the left palm. Then, slowly, very slowly, she began to rock the swing.

The sun slipped out from behind the last cloud. Now it was a fiery ball, low in the heavens, about to slip over the horizon, now it was going down, down, and the sky was diffused with color.

Jenny continued to rock.

Purples, and pinks and crimsons and oranges, and golds, and the occasional clouds billowing like gossamer, the wind just sharp enough to move the clouds, rustle the pines at the edge of the woods. . . .

Rock, back and forth. Study the sunset. All that matters is the sunset. The little boy will soon run out from the woods to join his mother. . . . Come, little boy. Come, Erich.

She heard a high wail, a wail that grew louder and shriller. "Aai . . . yee . . . devilll . . . devilll from the grave. . . . Go away. . . . Go away. . . ."

A figure was stumbling from the woods. A figure holding a rifle. A figure draped in a dark green cape, with long black hair that the wind blew in matted tangles, a figure with staring eyes and a face caught in a grimace of fear. . . .

Jenny stood up. The figure stopped, lifted the gun and aimed it.

''Erich, don't shoot!'' She stumbled to the door, turned the handle. The door was locked. It had snapped locked behind her. Lifting the army blanket, trying not to stumble over its trailing ends, she began to run, trying not to stumble over its trailing ends, she began to run, zigzagging down the porch steps, across the field, while she heard the sound of shots following her. A burning sensation bit into her shoulder . . . warmth flooded her arm. She staggered, but there was no place to run.

The strange screaming was behind her. ''Devilll, devilll . . .'' The dairy barn loomed to the right. Erich had never gone in there, not since Caroline died. Frantically she wrenched the door open, the door that led into the anteroom where the vats of milk were stored.

He was close behind her. She rushed into the inner area, the barn itself. The cows were in from the pastures, had already been milked. They stood in their stalls, watching with mild interest, grazing at the straw in the troughs before them. She could hear footsteps close behind her.

Blindly she ran to the end of the barn, as far as she could go. The stock tank was there, the pen for the new calves. The tank was dry. She turned to face Erich.

He was only ten feet away. He stopped and began to laugh. He lifted the gun to his shoulder and took aim with the same precision he had shown when he shot Joe's puppy. The stared at each other, mirror images with the dark green capes, the long dark hair. His hair too had been clumsily pinned up in a knot; his own blond curls escaping from under the wig gave the impression of tendrils on the forehead.

''Devilll . . . devilll. . . .''

She heard the gun going off, then a shriek that gurgled into a moan. But not from her lips. She opened her eyes. It was Erich who was sinking to the ground, Erich who was bleeding from the nose and mouth, Erich whose eyes were glazing, whose wig was matted with blood.

Behind him Rooney lowered a shotgun. ''That's for Arden,'' she said.

Jenny sank on her knees. ''Erich, the girls, are they alive?''

His eyes were dim but he nodded. ''Yes. . . .''

''Is someone with them?''

''No. . . . Alone. . . .''

''Erich, where *are* they?''

''His lips tried to form words. ''They're . . .'' He reached up for her hand, twisted his fingers around her thumb. . . . ''I'm sorry, Mommy. I'm sorry, Mommy . . . I didn't mean . . . to . . . hurt . . . you.''

His eyes closed. His body gave a last violent shudder and Jenny felt the pressure on her hand released.

CHAPTER 38

The house was crowded but she saw everyone as vague shadows on a screen. Sheriff Gunderson, the people from the coroner's office who chalked the outline of Erich's body and took it away, the reporters who swarmed in after the news of the art forgery and stayed for the far bigger story. They'd arrived in time to snap pictures of Erich, the cape draped around him, the wig matted with blood, the curiously peaceful face of death.

They'd been allowed to go to the cabin, to photograph and film Caroline's beautiful paintings, Erich's tortured canvases. "The greater the sense of urgency we give to the search, the more people will try to help," Wendell Gunderson said.

Mark was there. It was he who cut away the blanket and her blouse, bathed the wound, disinfected it, bandaged it. "That will hold it for the present. It's only a flesh wound, thank God."

She shivered at the touch of those long, gentle fingers through all the burning pain. If there was help possible it would come through Mark.

They found the car Erich had driven, found it hidden in one of the tractor paths on the farm. He'd rented the car in Duluth, six hours' drive away. He'd left the children at least thirteen hours ago. Left them where?

All through the evening the driveway was filled with cars. Maude and Joe Ekers came. Maude, her strong, capable bulk bending over Jenny. "I'm so sorry." A few minutes later Jenny heard her at the stove. And then the smell of perking coffee.

Pastor Barstrom came. "John Krueger worried so about Erich. But he never told me why. And then it seemed as though Erich was doing so well."

The weather report. "A storm is moving into Minnesota and the Dakotas." A storm. Oh, God, are the girls warm enough?

Clyde came to her. "Jenny, you gotta help me. They're talking about committing Rooney to the hospital again."

At last she was startled out of her lethargy. "She saved my life. If she hadn't shot Erich, he would have killed me."

"She told one of them reporters she did it for Arden," Clyde said. "Jenny, help me. If they lock her up, Rooney can't take it. She needs me. I need her."

Jenny got up from the couch, steadied herself against the wall, went looking for the sheriff. He was on the phone. "Get more flyers. Tack them up in every supermarket, every gas station. Go over the border into Canada."

When he hung up, she said, "Sheriff, why are you trying to put Rooney in the hospital?"

His voice was soothing. "Jenny, try to understand. Rooney intended to kill Erich. She was out there with a gun waiting for him."

"She was trying to protect me. She knew the danger I was in. She saved my life."

"All right, Jenny. Let me see what I can do."

Wordlessly, Jenny put her arms around Rooney. Rooney had loved Erich from the moment he'd been born. No matter what she said, she had not shot him because of Arden. She had shot him to save Jenny's life. I couldn't have killed him in cold blood, she thought. And neither could she.

The night wore on. All the properties were being searched again. Dozens of false reports were coming in. Snow was starting to fall, swift, biting flakes.

Maude made sandwiches. Jenny could not swallow. Finally she sipped consommé. At midnight Clyde took Rooney home. Maude and Joe left. The sheriff said, "I'll be at my desk all night. I'll call you if we hear anything." Only Mark remained.

"You must be tired. Go on home."

He didn't answer her. Instead he went and got blankets and pillows. He made her lie down on the couch by the stove; he poked a new log on the fire. He stretched out on the big chair.

In the dim light she stared at the cradle filled with wood, beside the chair. She had refused to pray after the baby died. She didn't realize how bitter she'd been. Now . . . I accept his loss. But please let me have my girls.

Could you strike a bargain with God?

Sometime during the night she began to doze. But the throbbing in her shoulder kept her on the edge of wakefulness. She felt herself stirring restlessly, making soft hurting sounds. And then it eased, the pain and the restless tossing. After a while when she opened her eyes, she found herself leaning against Mark, his arm around her, the quilt tucked over her.

Something was teasing her. Something in her subconscious that kept trying to surface, something desperately important that was eluding her. It was something to do with that last canvas and Erich watching her, his face peering through the window at her.

At seven o'clock Mark said, "I'll fix some toast and coffee." Jenny went upstairs and showered, wincing as the stream of water struck the adhesive on her shoulder.

Rooney and Clyde were in the house when she came back down. They sipped coffee together as they watched the national news. The girls' pictures would be shown on the *Today* show and on *Good Morning America.*

Rooney had brought the patches. "Do you want to sew, Jenny?"

"No, I can't."

"It helps me. We're making these for the girls' beds," she explained to Mark. "The girls are going to be found."

"Rooney, please!" Clyde tried to quiet her.

"But they are. You see how nice and bright the colors are. No dark stuff in my quilts. Oh, look, here's the story."

They watched as Jane Pauley began the report: "A forgery that rocked the art world yesterday turned out to be only a very small part of a far more dramatic tale.

"Erich Krueger . . ." They watched as Erich's face came on the screen. The picture was the same as the one on the brochure in the gallery: his bronze-gold, tightly curled hair, his dark blue eyes, the half-smile. They had films of the farm, a shot of the body being carried away.

Now Tina and Beth smiled from the screen. "And this morning those little girls are still missing," Jane Pauley said. "As he died, Erich Krueger told his wife that her children are still alive. But police are not certain he can be believed. The last canvas he painted seems to suggest Tina and Beth are dead."

The entire screen was filled with that last painting. Jenny looked at the limp puppet figures, her own tortured image staring, Erich looking in the window at them, laughing as he held back the curtain.

Mark jumped to turn off the set. "I told Gunderson not to let them take photographs in the cabin."

Rooney had jumped up too. "You should have showed me that painting!" she screamed. "You should have showed it to me. Don't you understand. The curtains . . . The blue curtains!"

The curtains! This was what had been gnawing at Jenny's memory. Rooney spilling the scraps onto the kitchen table, that dark blue material, the faint design visible in the painting.

"Rooney, where did he put them?" They were all shouting the same thing. *Where?*

Rooney, totally aware of the precious knowledge she held, tugged at Mark, excitedly crying, "Mark, *you* know. Your dad's fishing lodge. Erich always used to go up there with you. You didn't have curtains in the guest room. He said it was too bright. I gave him those eight years ago."

"Mark, could they be there?" Jenny cried.

"It's possible. Dad and I haven't been at the lodge in over a year. Erich has a key."

"Where is the lodge?"

"It's . . . in the Duluth area. On a small island. It makes sense. It's just . . ."

"Just what?" She could hear the sound of snow slapping against the windows.

"The lodge doesn't have central heating."

Clyde vocalized the fear that was now in all of them. "That place don't have central heating and you mean those kids may be alone in it now?"

Mark raced for the phone.

* * *

Thirty minutes later, the police chief from Hathaway Island returned their call.

"We've got 'em."

Agonized, Jenny listened to Mark's question. "Are they all right?" She grabbed the phone to hear the answer.

"Yep, but just barely. Krueger had threatened to punish them if they ever tried to set foot out of the house. But he'd been gone so long and the place was freezing so the older girl decided to take a chance. She managed to unlock the door. They'd just left the house to hunt for Mommy when we found them. They wouldn't a lasted half an hour in this storm. Wait a minute."

Jenny heard the phone being moved and then two small voices were saying, "Hello, Mommy." Mark's arms held her tightly as she sobbed, "Mouse. Tinker Bell. I love you. I love you."

CHAPTER 39

April broke over Minnesota like a godhead of plenty. The red haze haloed the trees as tiny buds began to form, waiting to burst into bloom. Deer ran from the woods; pheasants strutted on the roads; cattle wandered far into the pastures; the ground softened and snow melted down into the furrows, nourishing the spring crops as they pushed their way to the surface.

Beth and Tina began to ride again, Beth straight and careful, Tina always ready to give her pony a kick and send him racing. Jenny rode on Fire Maid beside Beth; Joe rode close to Tina.

Jenny could not get enough of being with the children: of being able to kiss the soft cheeks, hold the sturdy little hands, hear the prayers, answer the endless questions. Or listen to the frightened confidences. "Daddy scared me so much. He used to put his hands on my face like this. He looked so funny."

"Daddy didn't mean it. He didn't mean to hurt anyone. He couldn't help himself."

For so long she had wanted to go back to New York, to leave this place. Dr. Philstrom warned her against it. "Those ponies are the best therapy for the children."

"I cannot spend another night in this house."

Mark had provided the answer: the schoolhouse on the west end of his property that years before he'd converted for himself. "When Dad moved to Florida I took over the farmhouse and rented this place, but it's been empty for six months."

It was charming, with two bedrooms, a roomy kitchen, a quaint parlor, small enough that when Tina cried out in terror-filled dreams, Jenny could be at her side instantly. "I'm here, Tinker Bell. Go back to sleep."

She told Luke of her plans to turn over Krueger Farm to the Historical Society.

"Be sure, Jenny," he told her. "It's worth a fortune and God knows you earned the right to have it."

"There's plenty for me without it. And I could never live there again." She closed her eyes against the memory of the bassinette in the attic, the panel behind the headboard, the owl sculpture, the portrait of Caroline.

Rooney visited frequently, proudly driving the car Clyde had bought her, a contented Rooney who no longer needed to wait home in case Arden chose to return. "You can accept anything, Jenny, if you have to. Not knowing is the worst torture."

The people of Granite Place came calling. "It's about time we welcomed you here, Jenny." Most of them added: "We're so sorry, Jenny." They brought cuttings and seeds for her.

Her fingers in the soft, moist earth as she planted her garden.

The sound of the comfortably shabby station wagon in the driveway. The girls running to meet Uncle Mark. The joyful awareness that like the earth she too was ready for a new season, a new beginning.

About the Author

MARY HIGGINS CLARK, America's bestselling suspense writer, is the author of nine novels which together have sold more that 15 million copies in the United States. She began writing for a living after her husband died and left her a widow with five children. After many rejections, Clark published her first suspense novel *Where Are The Children?* in 1975; it was an immediate bestseller!

In 1979 Mary Higgins Clark graduated from Fordham University at Lincoln Center with a B.A. in philosophy; nine years later she received an honorary Ph.D. from her alma mater. In 1980, she was awarded the Grand Prix de Literature of France, and was the 1987 president of the Mystery Writers of America.